A MESS OF EVERYTHING

FANTAGRAPHICS BOOKS | 7563 LAKE CITY WAY NE | SEATTLE, WASHINGTON 98115

Design by **ADAM GRANO** | Promotion by **ERIC REYNOLDS**
Published by **GARY GROTH AND KIM THOMPSON**

ISBN: 978-1-56097-956-2
First printing, March 2009. Printed in China.

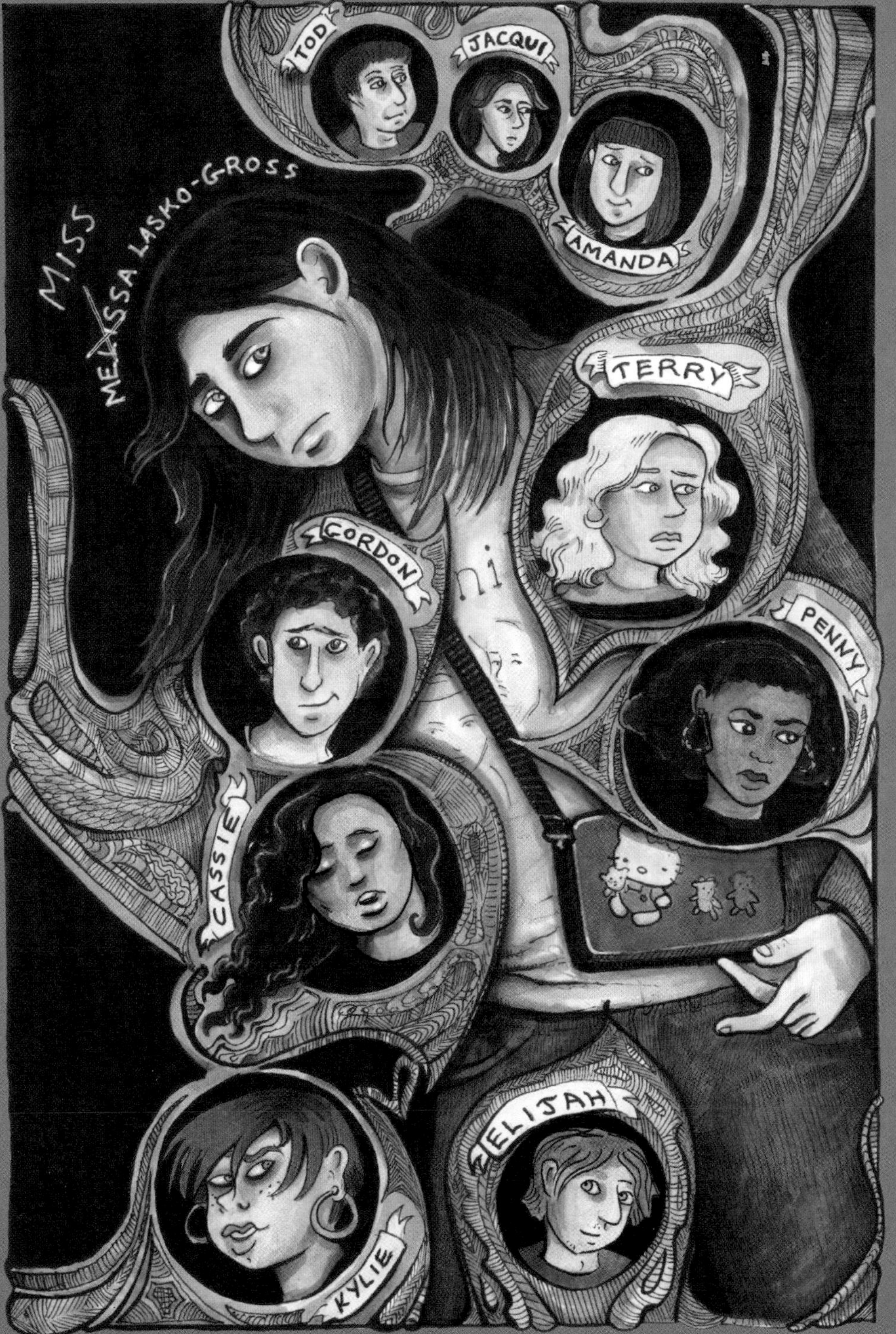
MISS
ME~~LI~~SSA LASKO-GROSS
TOD
JACQUI
AMANDA
TERRY
GORDON
PENNY
CASSIE
ELIJAH
KYLIE

A MESS OF EVERY

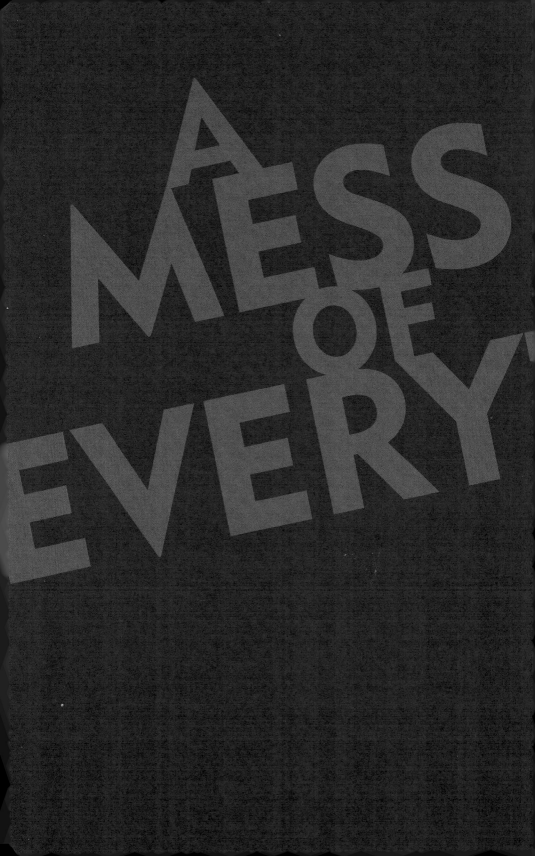

THING

Graphic
Novel
Lasko-
Gross

MISS LASKO-GROSS
FANTAGRAPHICS BOOKS

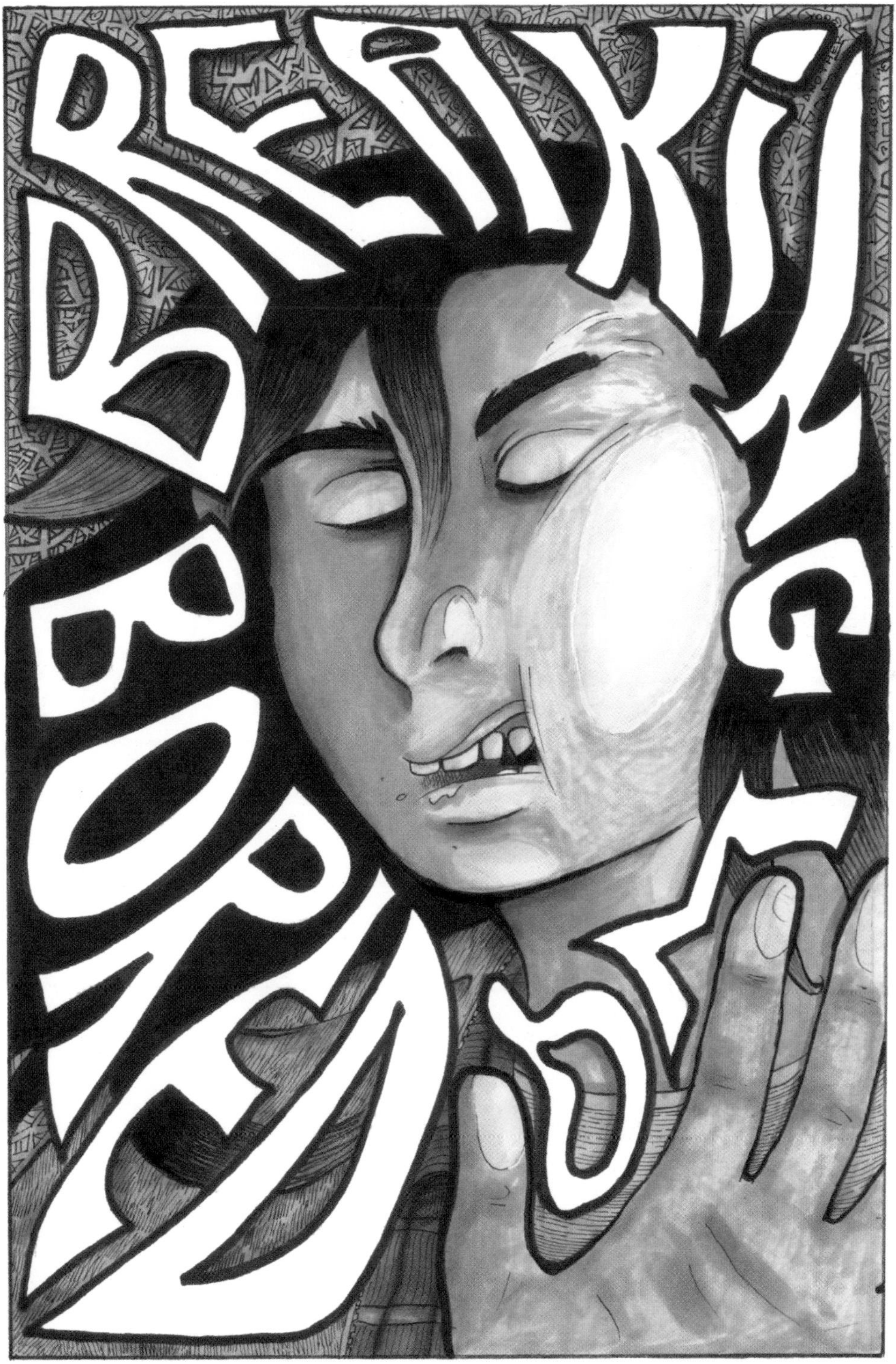

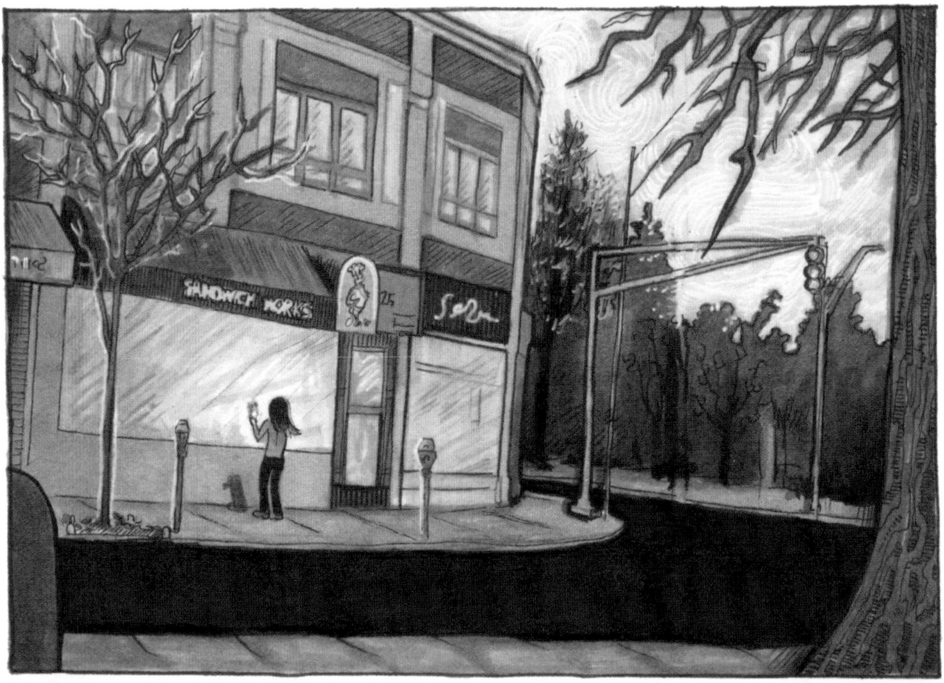
SANDWICH WORKS

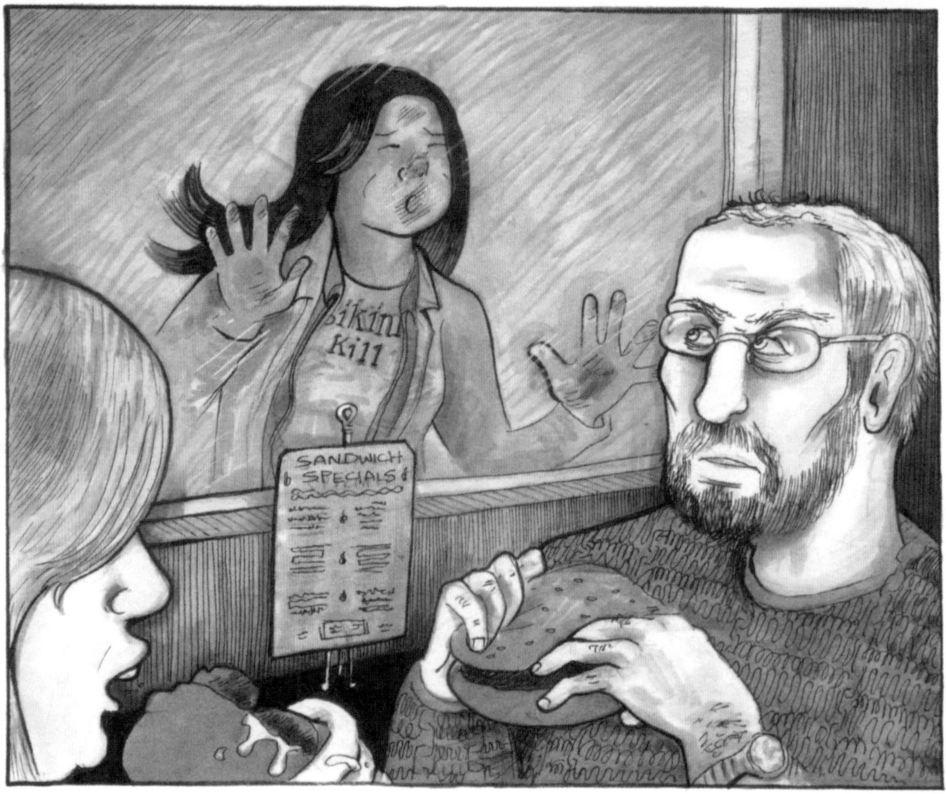
Bikini Kill
SANDWICH SPECIALS

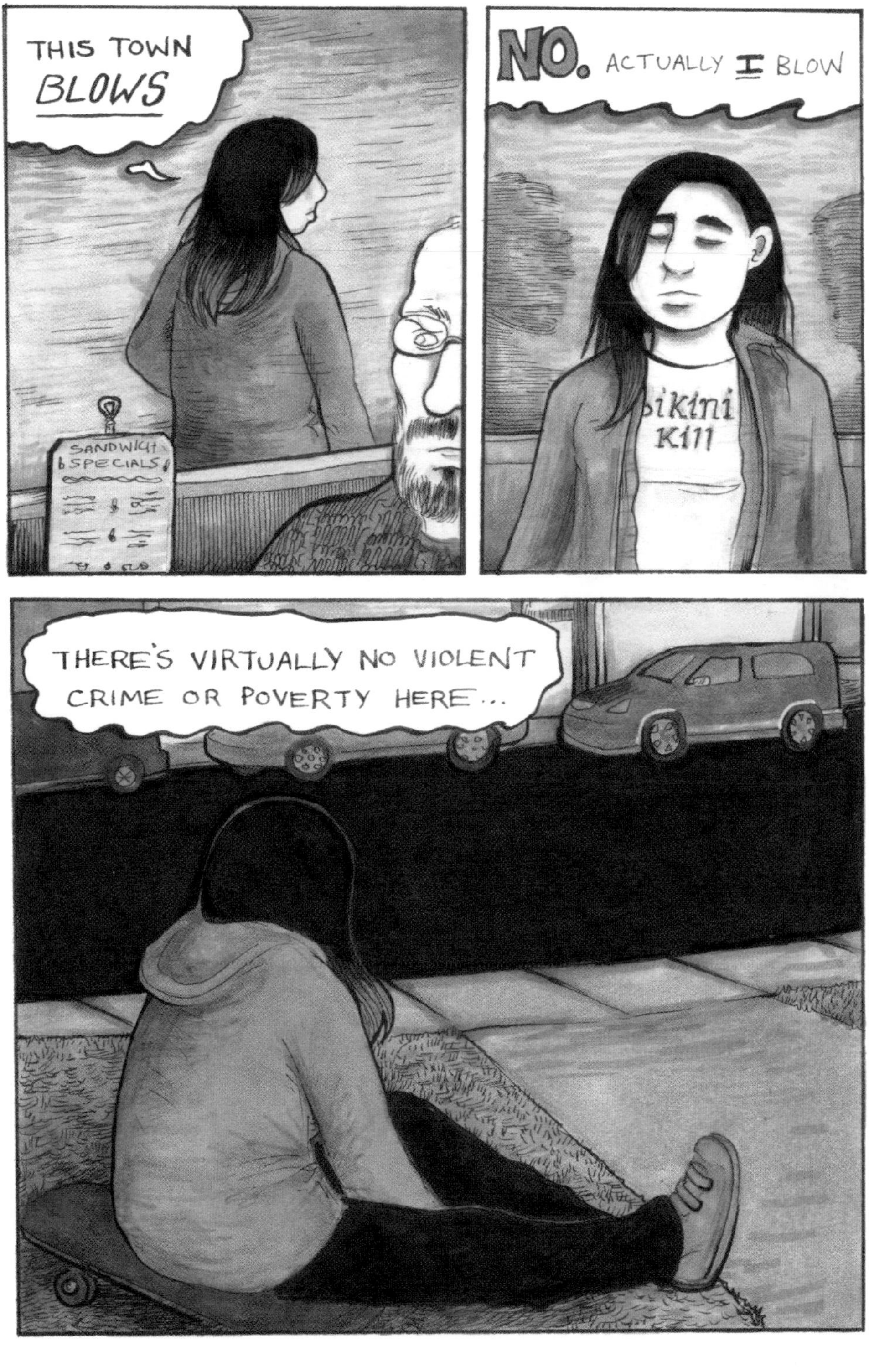
THIS TOWN BLOWS
SANDWICH SPECIALS
NO. ACTUALLY I BLOW
Bikini Kill
THERE'S VIRTUALLY NO VIOLENT CRIME OR POVERTY HERE...

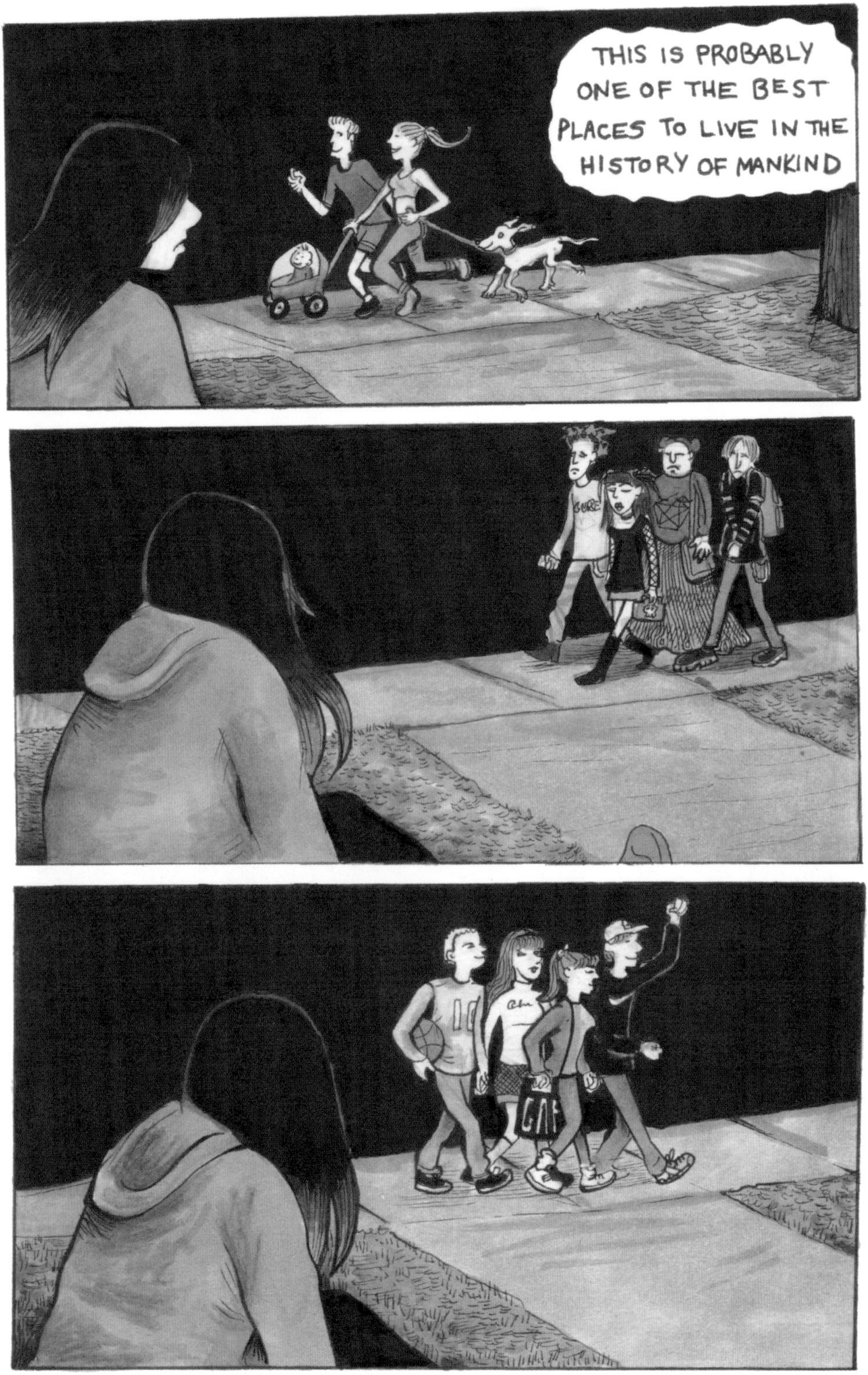
THIS IS PROBABLY ONE OF THE BEST PLACES TO LIVE IN THE HISTORY OF MANKIND

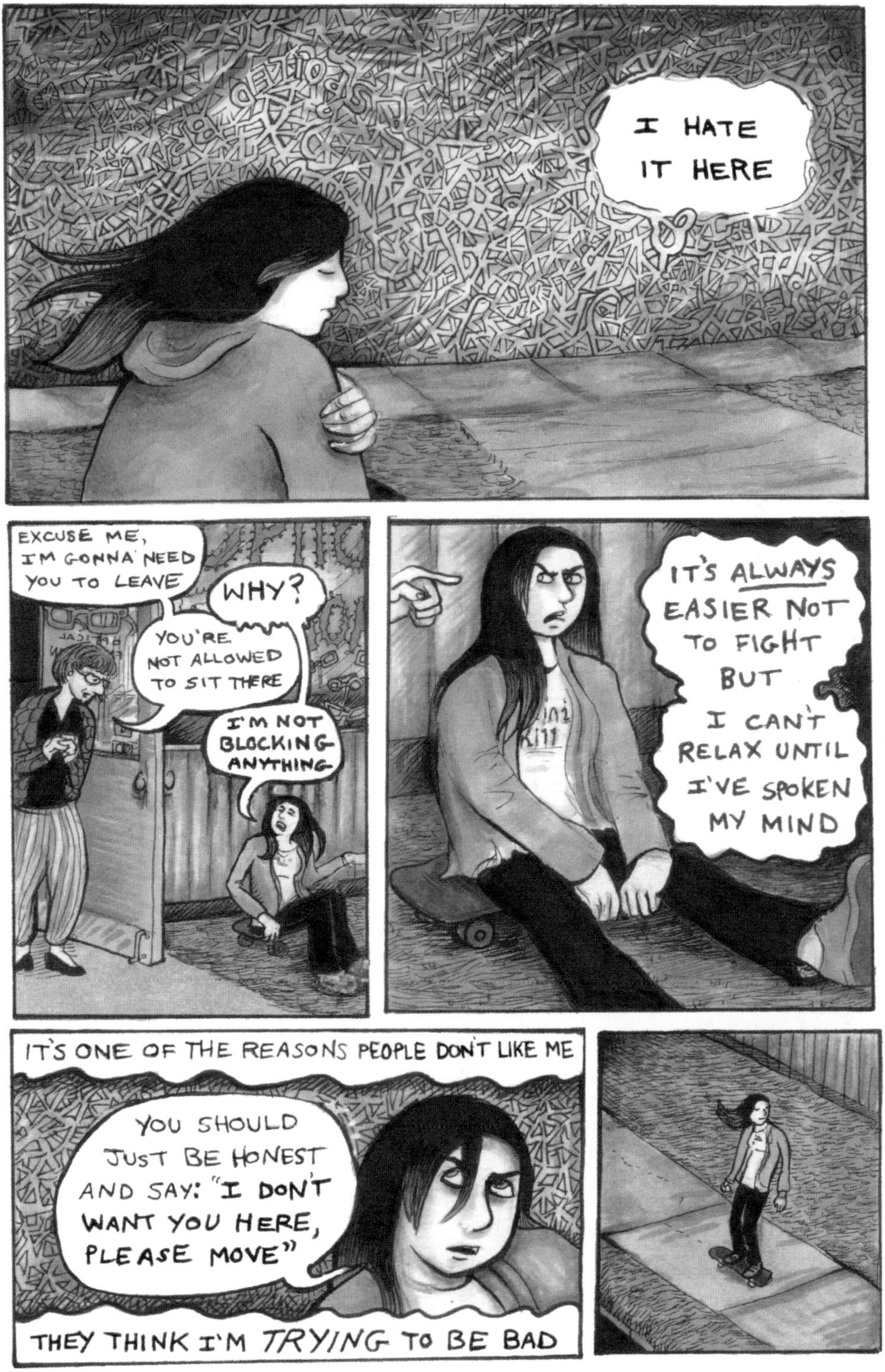
I HATE IT HERE
EXCUSE ME, I'M GONNA NEED YOU TO LEAVE
WHY?
YOU'RE NOT ALLOWED TO SIT THERE
I'M NOT BLOCKING ANYTHING
IT'S ALWAYS EASIER NOT TO FIGHT BUT I CAN'T RELAX UNTIL I'VE SPOKEN MY MIND
IT'S ONE OF THE REASONS PEOPLE DON'T LIKE ME
YOU SHOULD JUST BE HONEST AND SAY: "I DON'T WANT YOU HERE, PLEASE MOVE"
THEY THINK I'M TRYING TO BE BAD

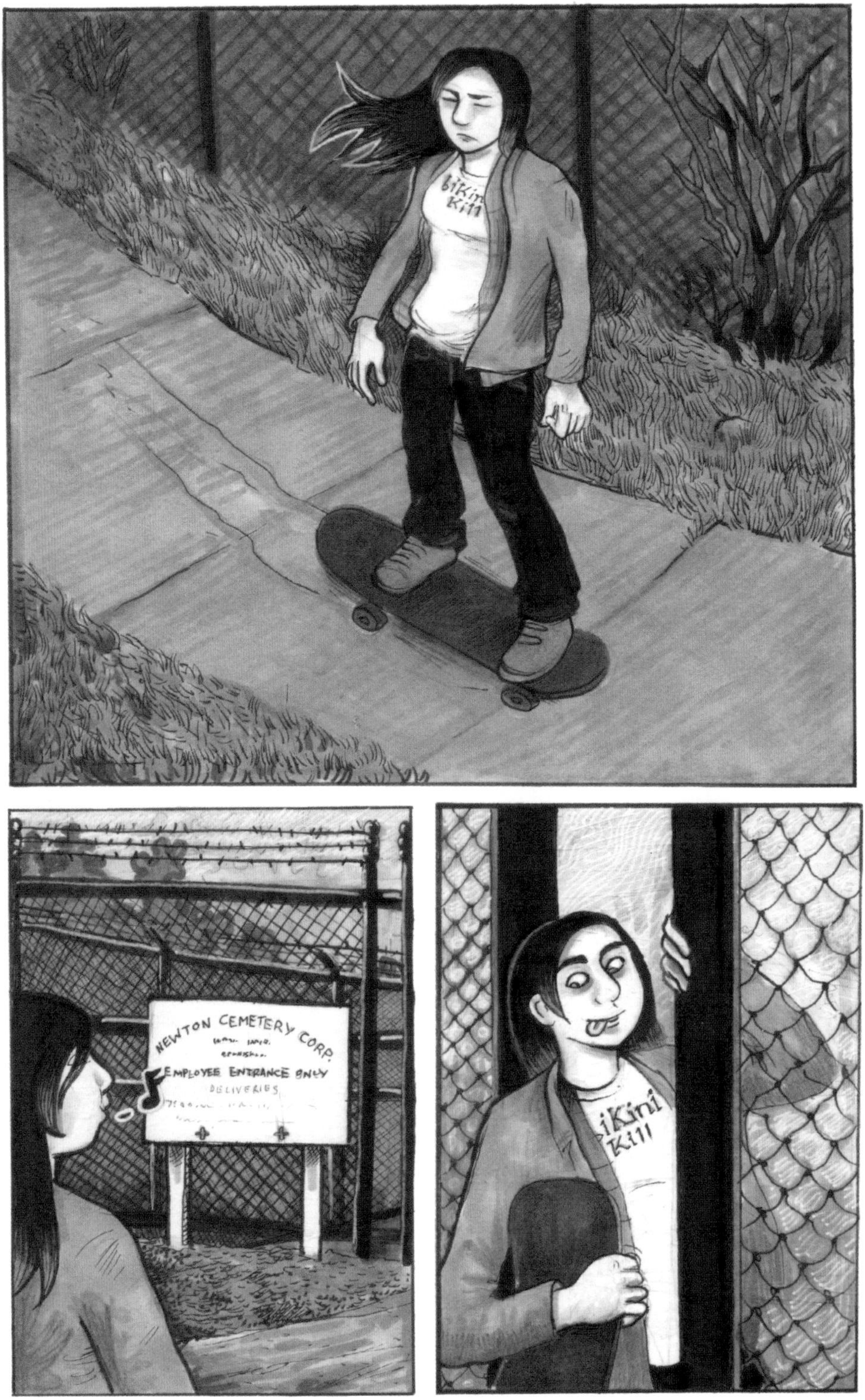
biKini Kill
NEWTON CEMETERY CORP.
EMPLOYEE ENTRANCE ONLY
DELIVERIES
iKini Kill

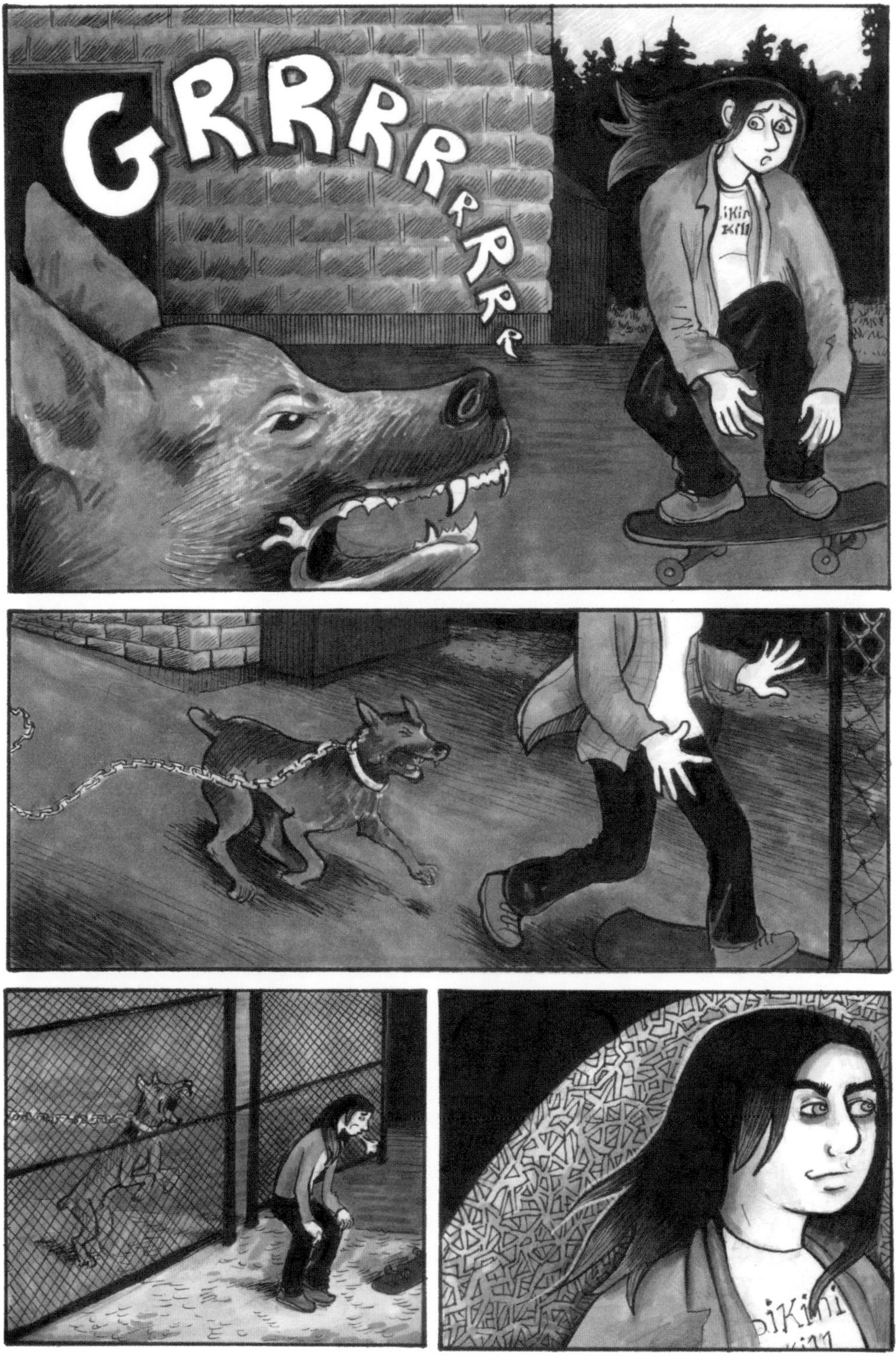
GRRRRRRRR

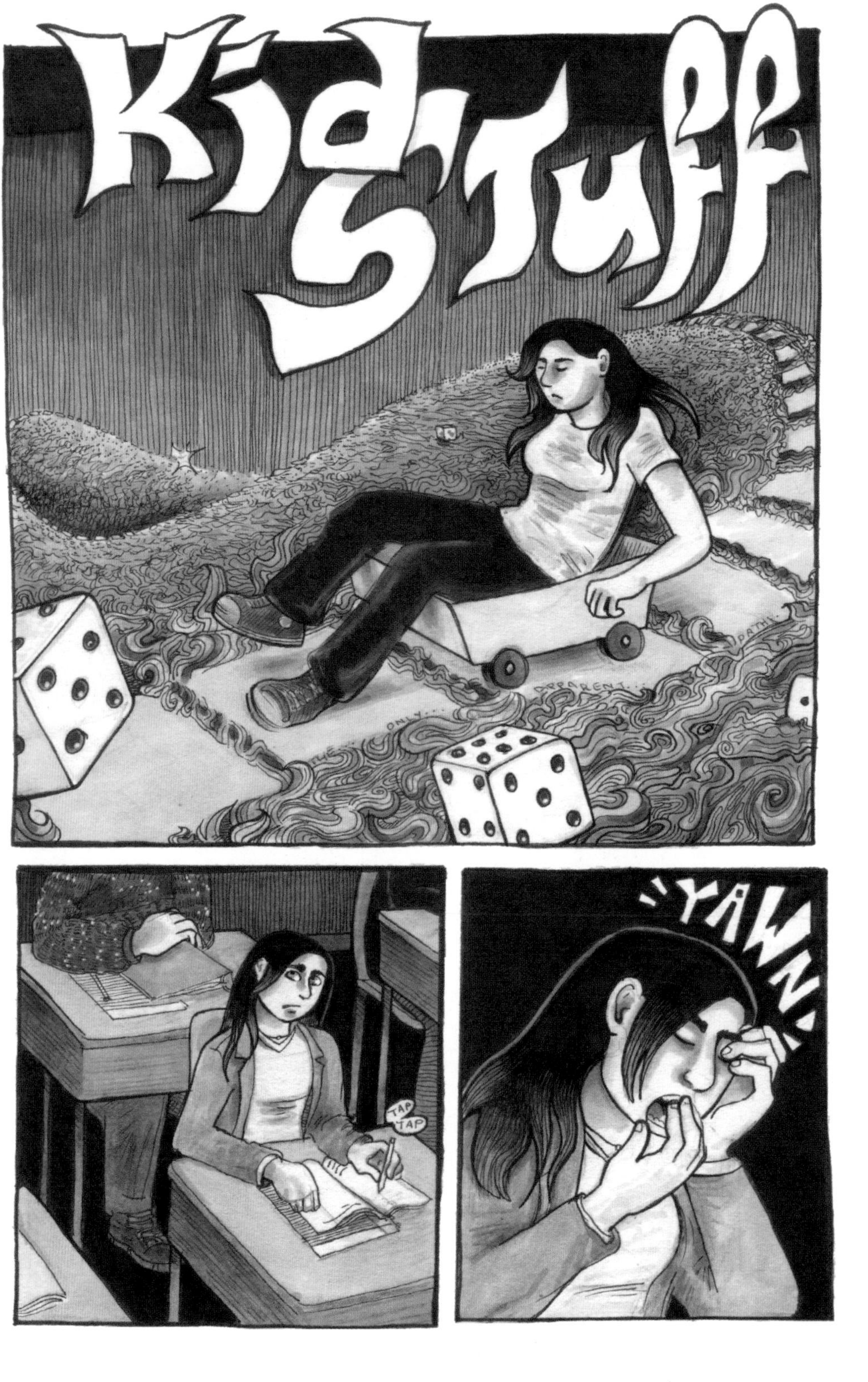
Kid Stuff
THE... ONLY... APPARENT... PATH!
TAP TAP
"YAWN"

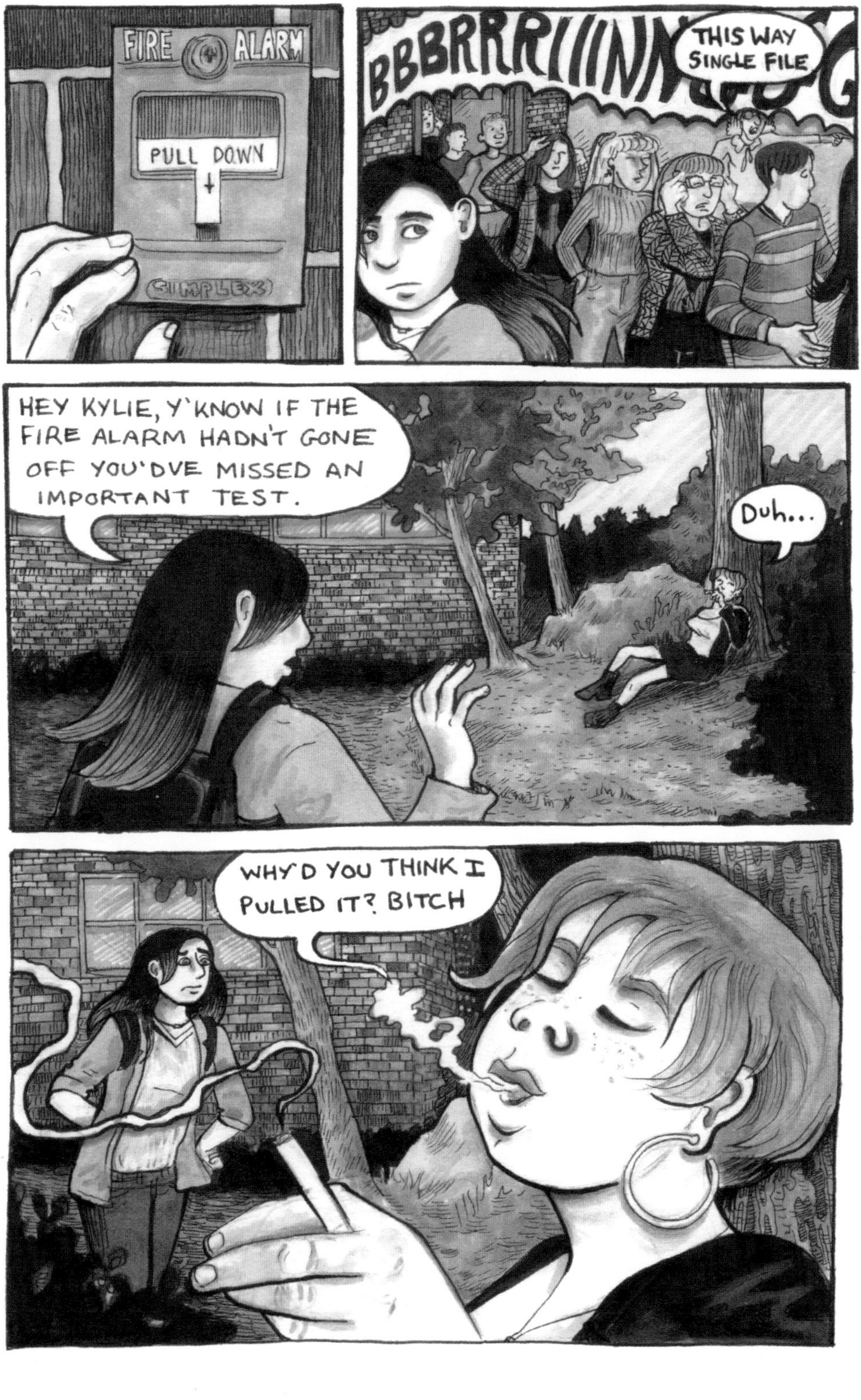
FIRE ALARM
PULL DOWN
SIMPLEX
BBBRRRRIIINNNGGG
THIS WAY SINGLE FILE
HEY KYLIE, Y'KNOW IF THE FIRE ALARM HADN'T GONE OFF YOU'DVE MISSED AN IMPORTANT TEST.
Duh...
WHY'D YOU THINK I PULLED IT? BITCH

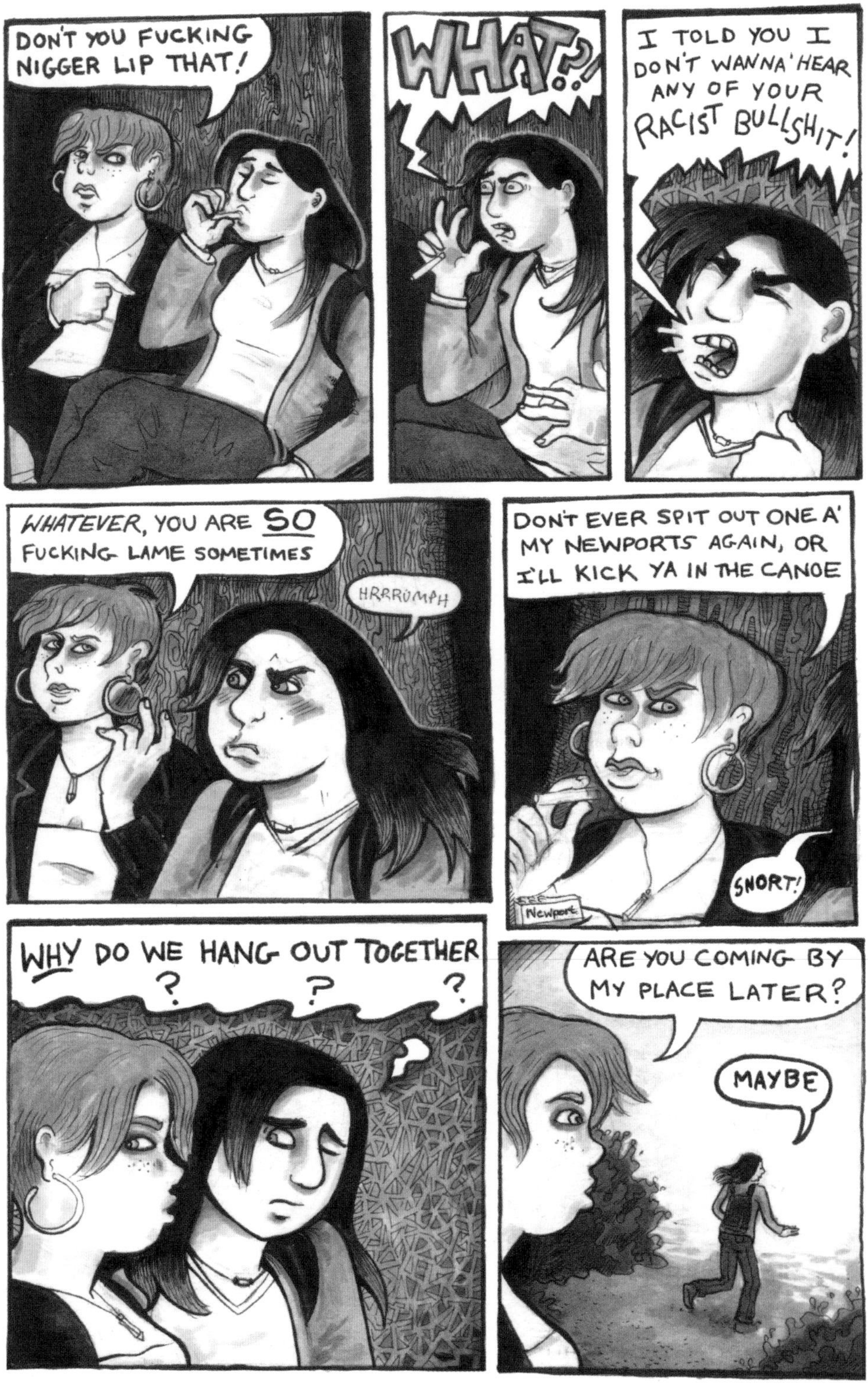
DON'T YOU FUCKING NIGGER LIP THAT!
WHAT?!
I TOLD YOU I DON'T WANNA' HEAR ANY OF YOUR RACIST BULLSHIT!
WHATEVER, YOU ARE SO FUCKING LAME SOMETIMES
HRRRUMPH
DON'T EVER SPIT OUT ONE A' MY NEWPORTS AGAIN, OR I'LL KICK YA IN THE CANOE
SNORT!
Newport
WHY DO WE HANG OUT TOGETHER ? ? ?
ARE YOU COMING BY MY PLACE LATER?
MAYBE

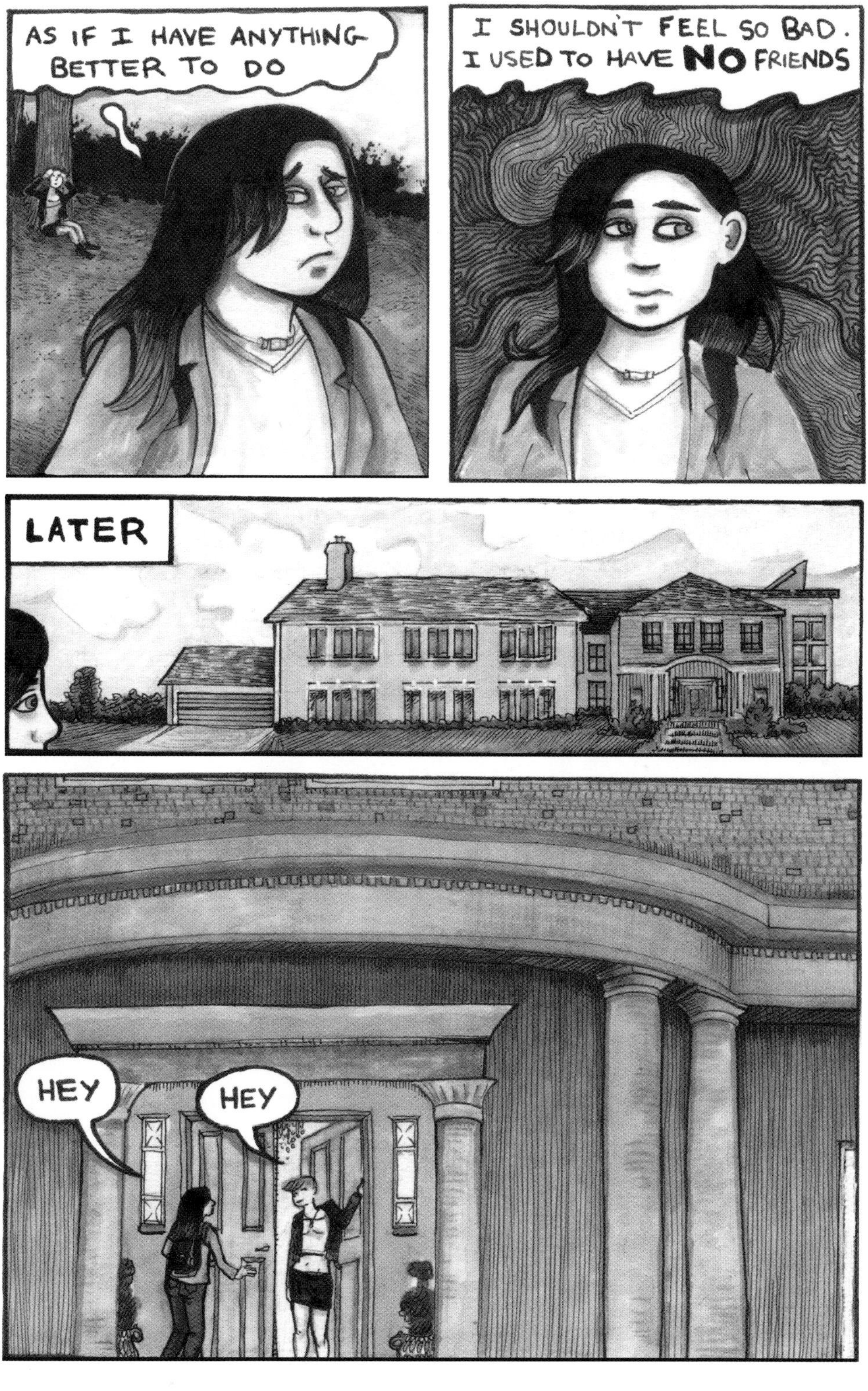
AS IF I HAVE ANYTHING BETTER TO DO
I SHOULDN'T FEEL SO BAD. I USED TO HAVE NO FRIENDS
LATER
HEY
HEY

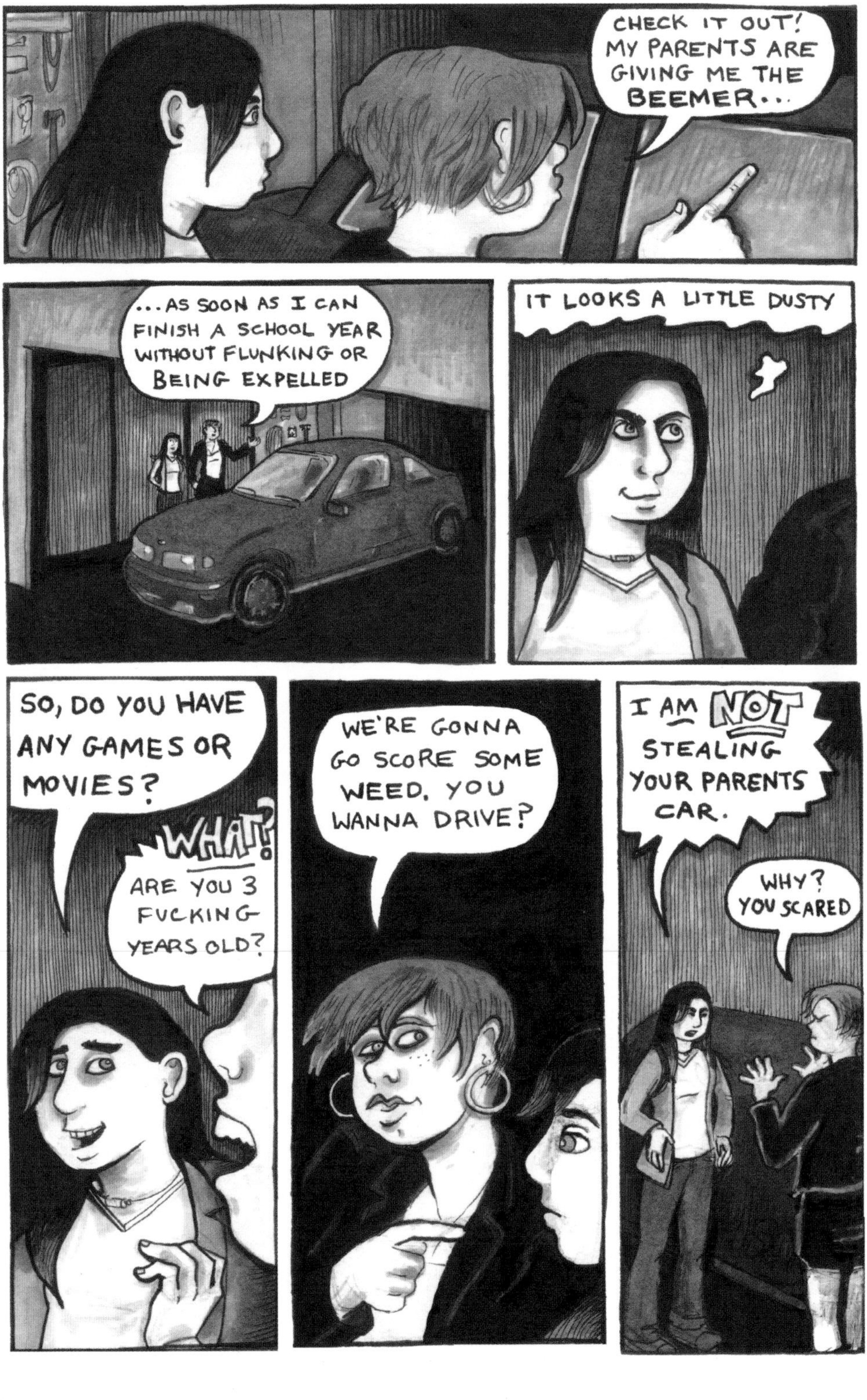
CHECK IT OUT! MY PARENTS ARE GIVING ME THE BEEMER...
...AS SOON AS I CAN FINISH A SCHOOL YEAR WITHOUT FLUNKING OR BEING EXPELLED
IT LOOKS A LITTLE DUSTY
SO, DO YOU HAVE ANY GAMES OR MOVIES?
WHAT? ARE YOU 3 FUCKING YEARS OLD?
WE'RE GONNA GO SCORE SOME WEED. YOU WANNA DRIVE?
I AM NOT STEALING YOUR PARENTS CAR.
WHY? YOU SCARED

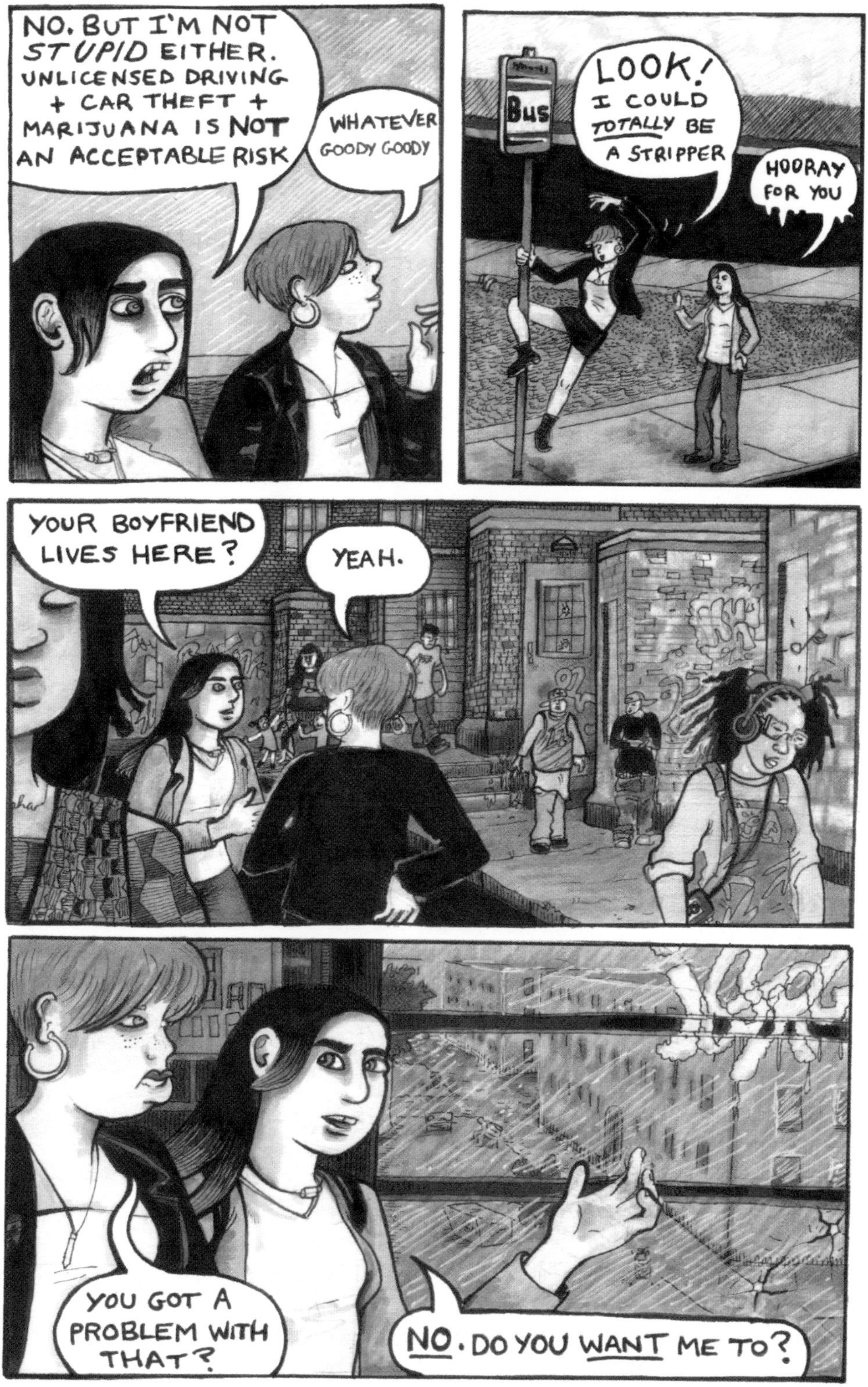
NO. BUT I'M NOT STUPID EITHER. UNLICENSED DRIVING + CAR THEFT + MARIJUANA IS NOT AN ACCEPTABLE RISK
WHATEVER GOODY GOODY
LOOK! I COULD TOTALLY BE A STRIPPER
HOORAY FOR YOU
BUS
YOUR BOYFRIEND LIVES HERE?
YEAH.
YOU GOT A PROBLEM WITH THAT?
NO. DO YOU WANT ME TO?

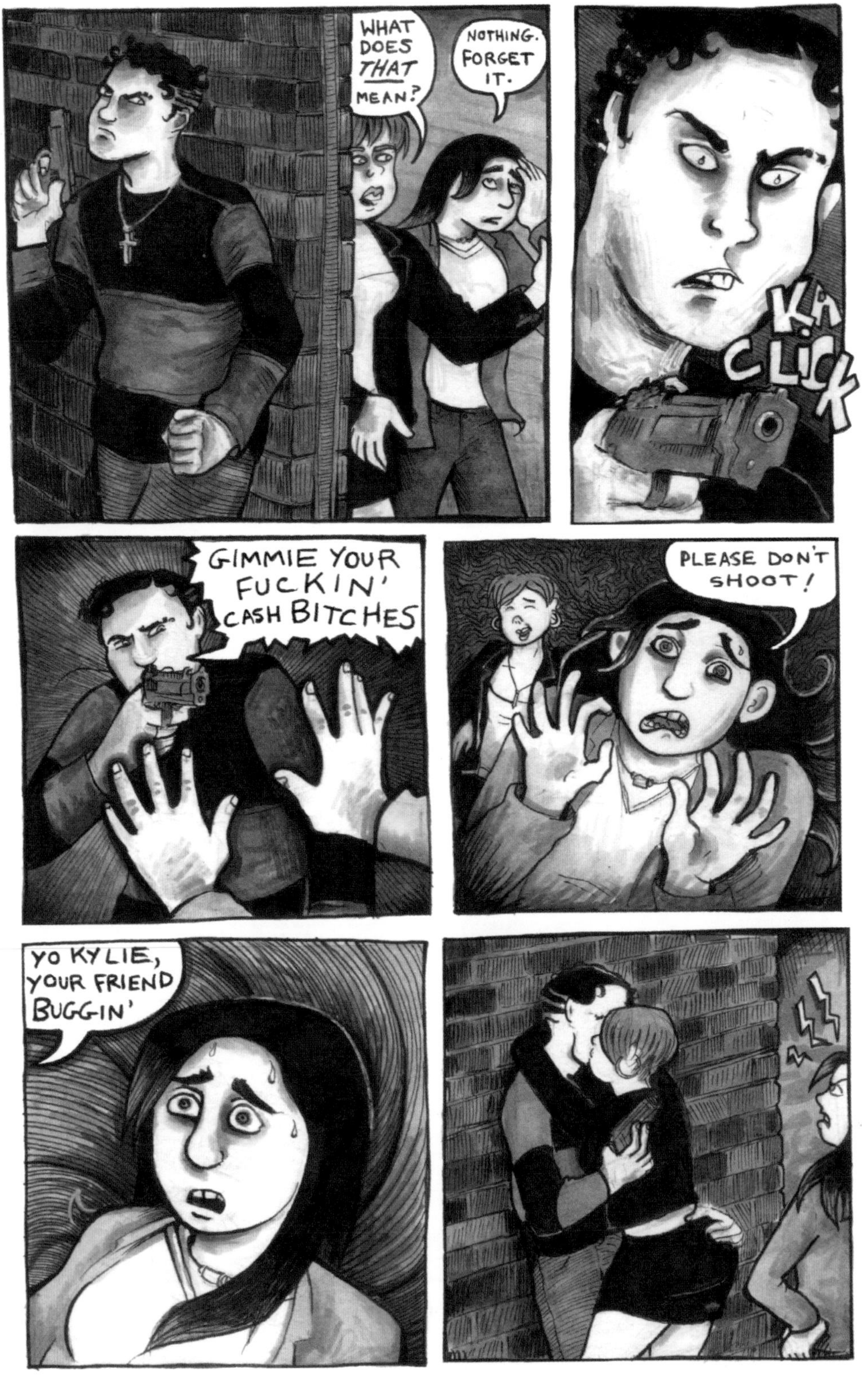
WHAT DOES THAT MEAN?
NOTHING. FORGET IT.
KA CLICK
GIMMIE YOUR FUCKIN' CASH BITCHES
PLEASE DON'T SHOOT!
YO KYLIE, YOUR FRIEND BUGGIN'

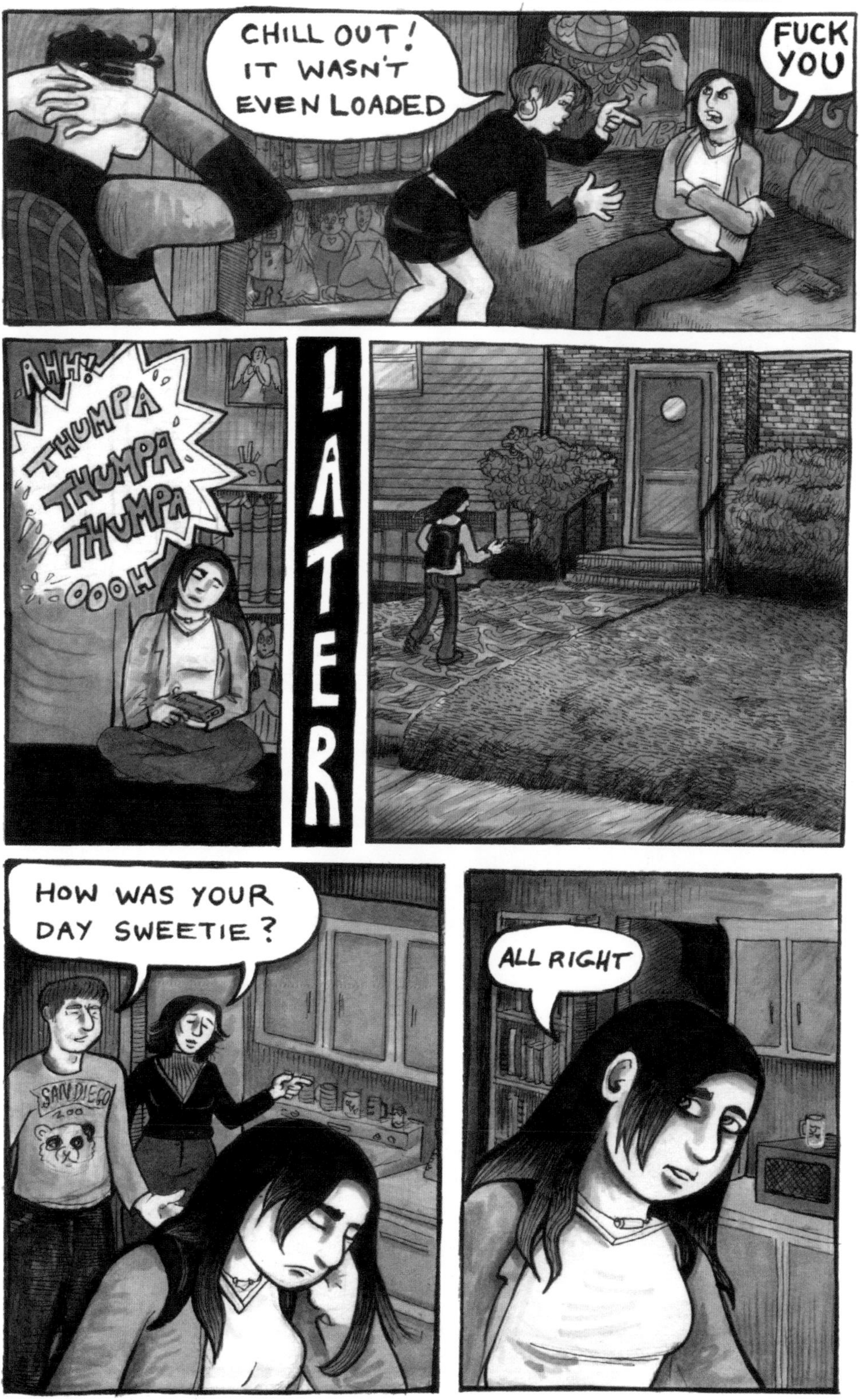
CHILL OUT! IT WASN'T EVEN LOADED
FUCK YOU
AHH!
THUMPA THUMPA THUMPA
OOOH
LATER
HOW WAS YOUR DAY SWEETIE?
SAN DIEGO ZOO
ALL RIGHT

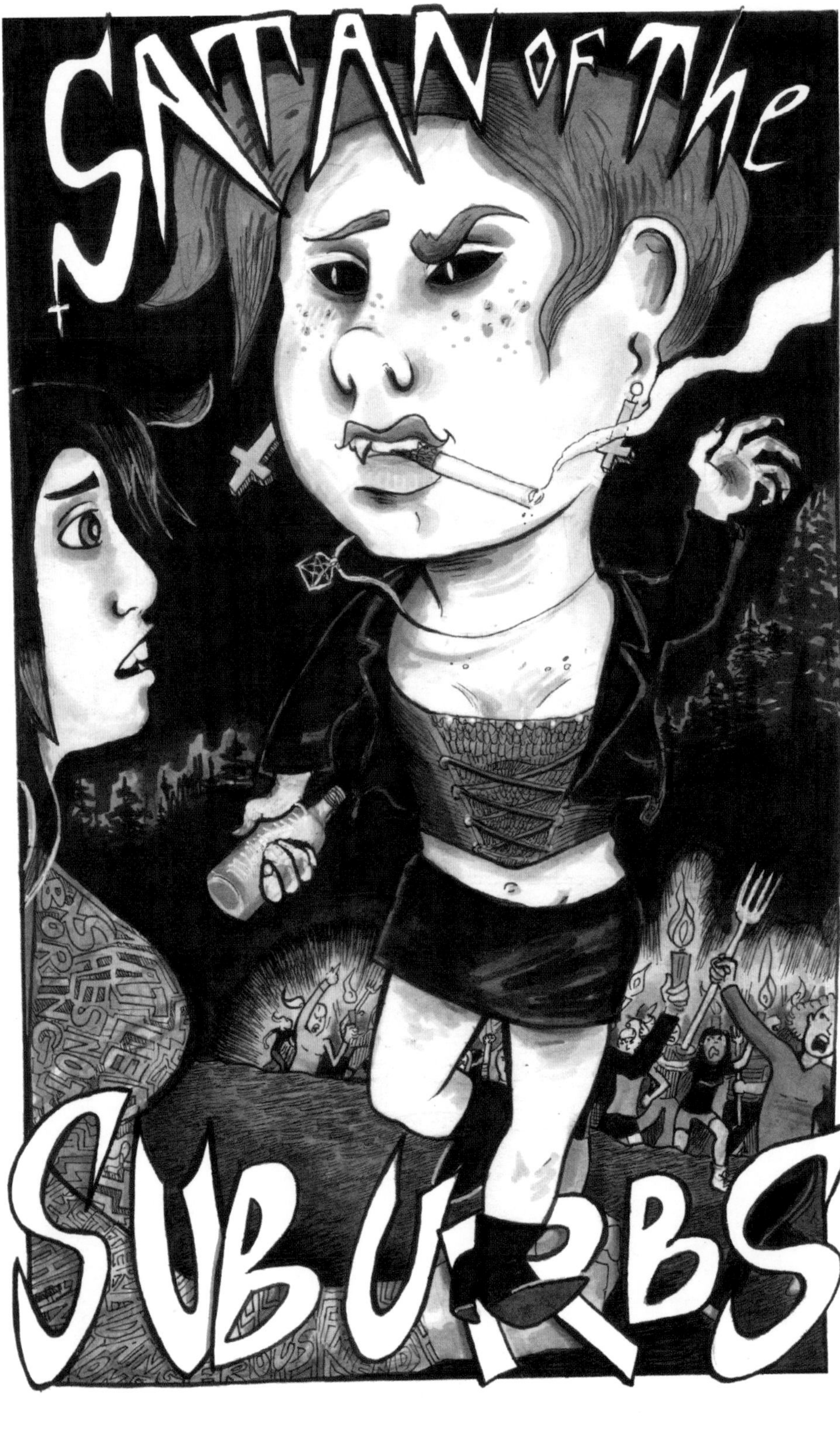
SATAN of The
SUBURBS

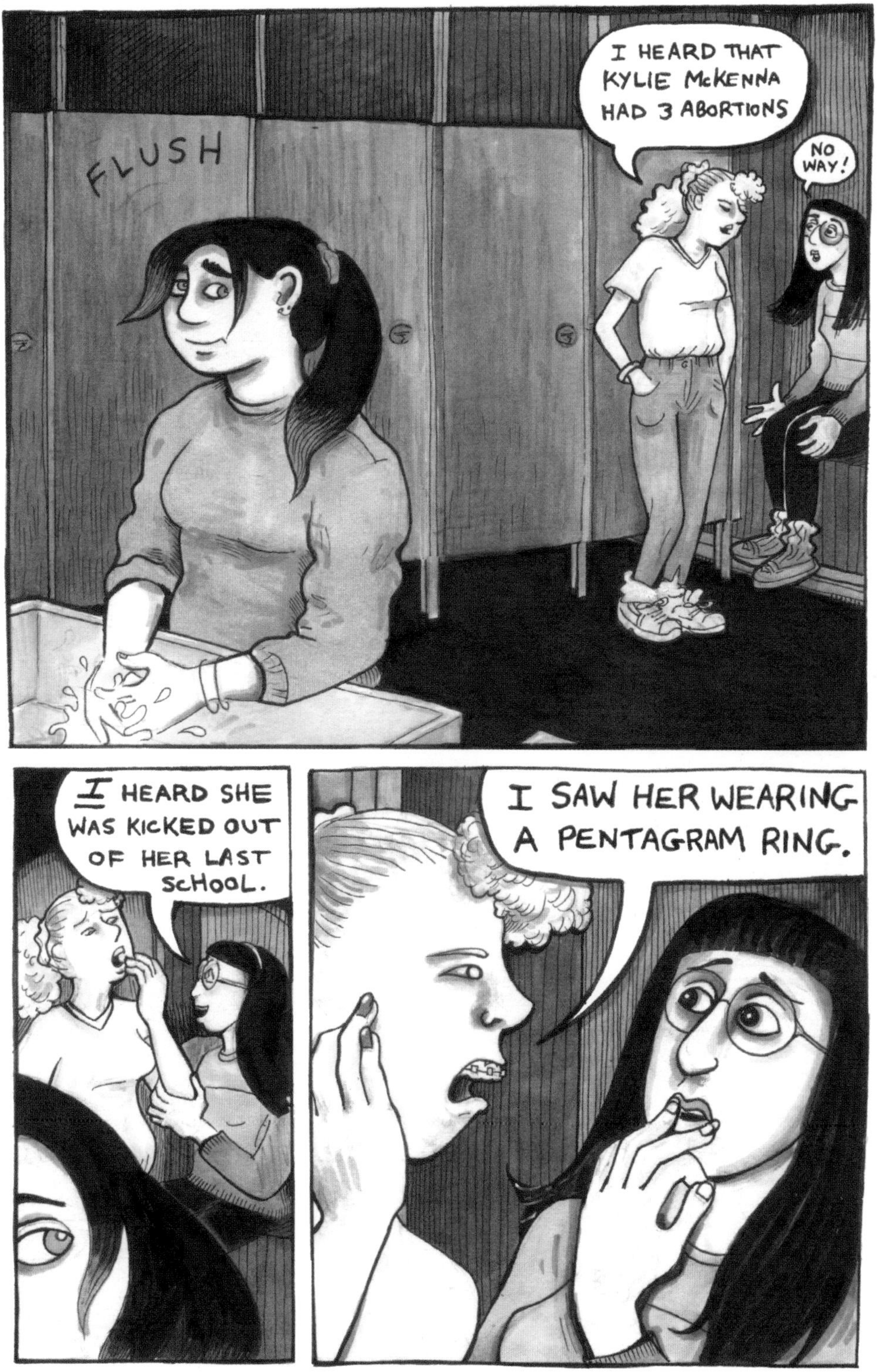
FLUSH
I HEARD THAT KYLIE McKENNA HAD 3 ABORTIONS
NO WAY!
I HEARD SHE WAS KICKED OUT OF HER LAST SCHOOL.
I SAW HER WEARING A PENTAGRAM RING.

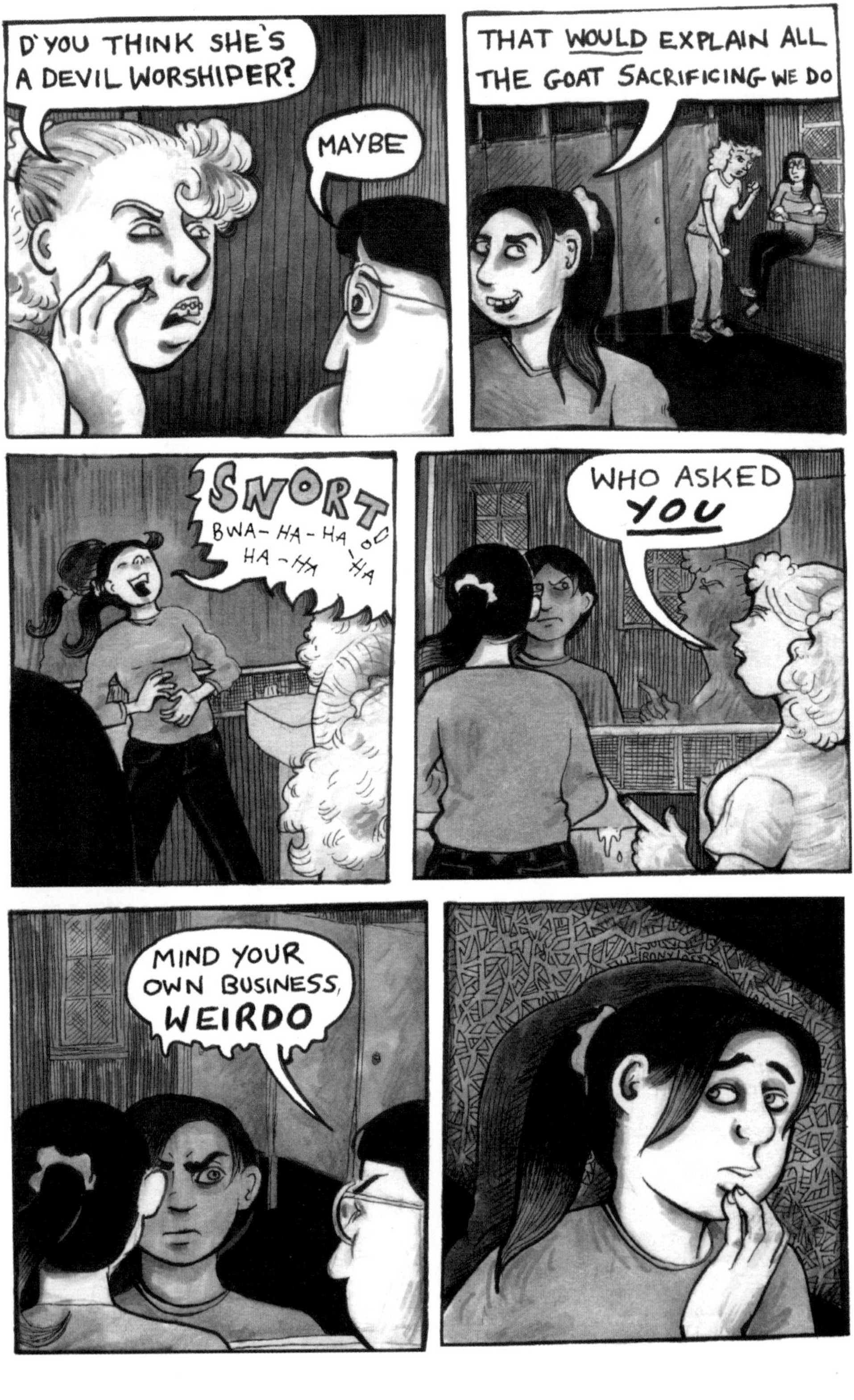
D'YOU THINK SHE'S A DEVIL WORSHIPER?
MAYBE
THAT WOULD EXPLAIN ALL THE GOAT SACRIFICING WE DO
SNORT
BWA-HA-HA-HA-HA-HA-HA
WHO ASKED YOU
MIND YOUR OWN BUSINESS, WEIRDO

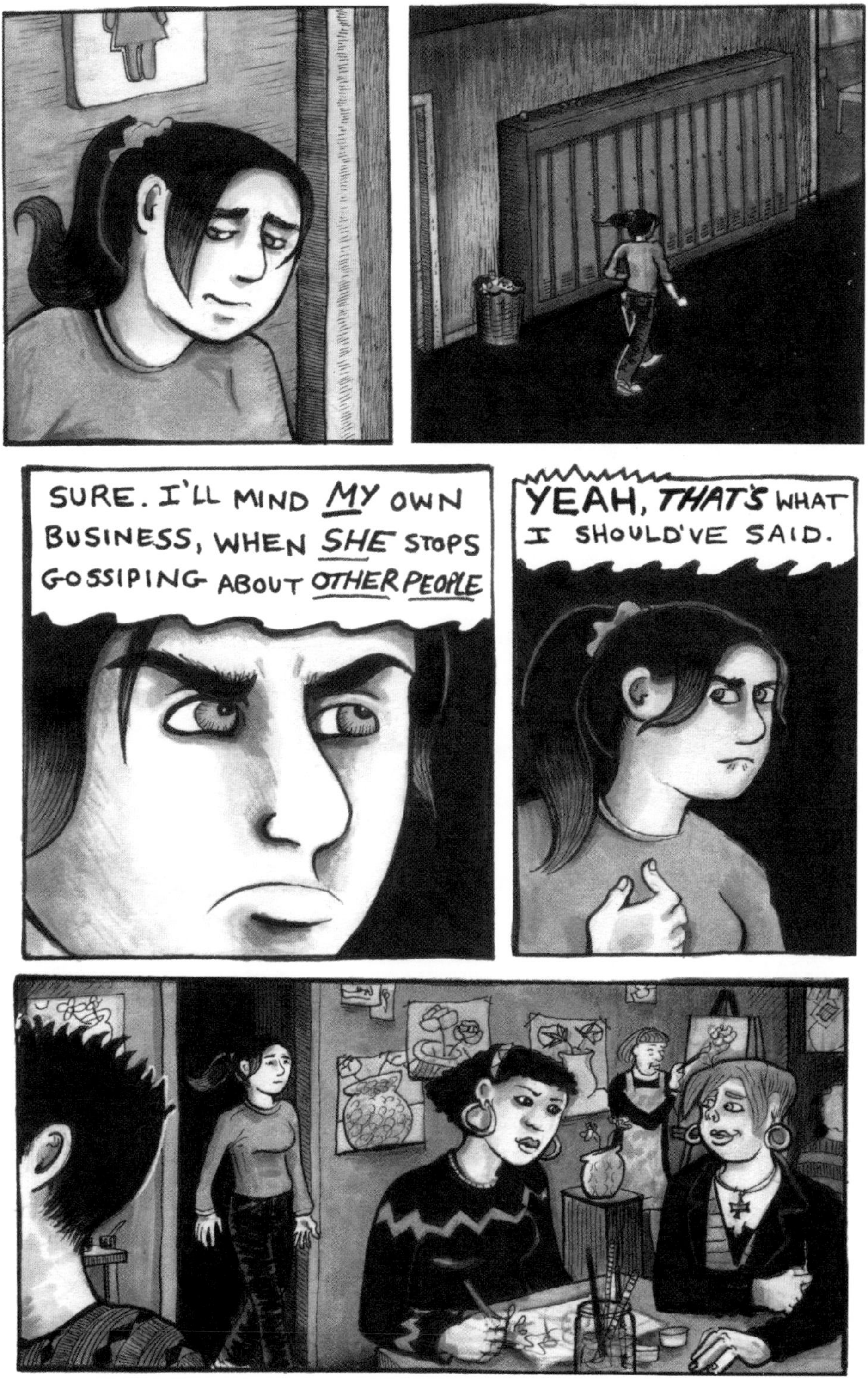
SURE. I'LL MIND MY OWN BUSINESS, WHEN SHE STOPS GOSSIPING ABOUT OTHER PEOPLE
YEAH, THAT'S WHAT I SHOULD'VE SAID.

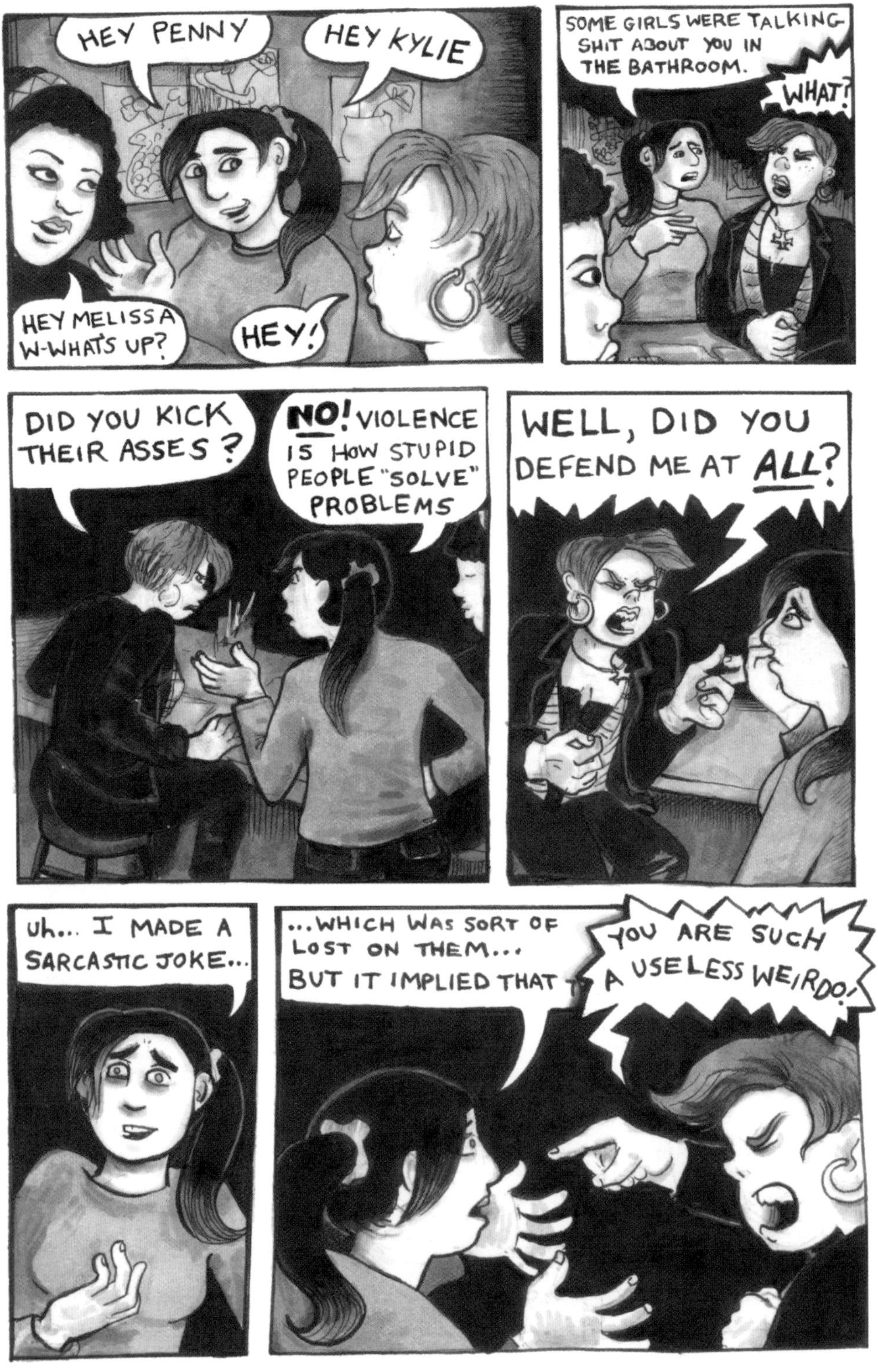
HEY PENNY
HEY KYLIE
HEY MELISSA W-WHAT'S UP?
HEY!
SOME GIRLS WERE TALKING SHIT ABOUT YOU IN THE BATHROOM.
WHAT?
DID YOU KICK THEIR ASSES?
NO! VIOLENCE IS HOW STUPID PEOPLE "SOLVE" PROBLEMS
WELL, DID YOU DEFEND ME AT ALL?
uh... I MADE A SARCASTIC JOKE...
...WHICH WAS SORT OF LOST ON THEM... BUT IT IMPLIED THAT
YOU ARE SUCH A USELESS WEIRDO!

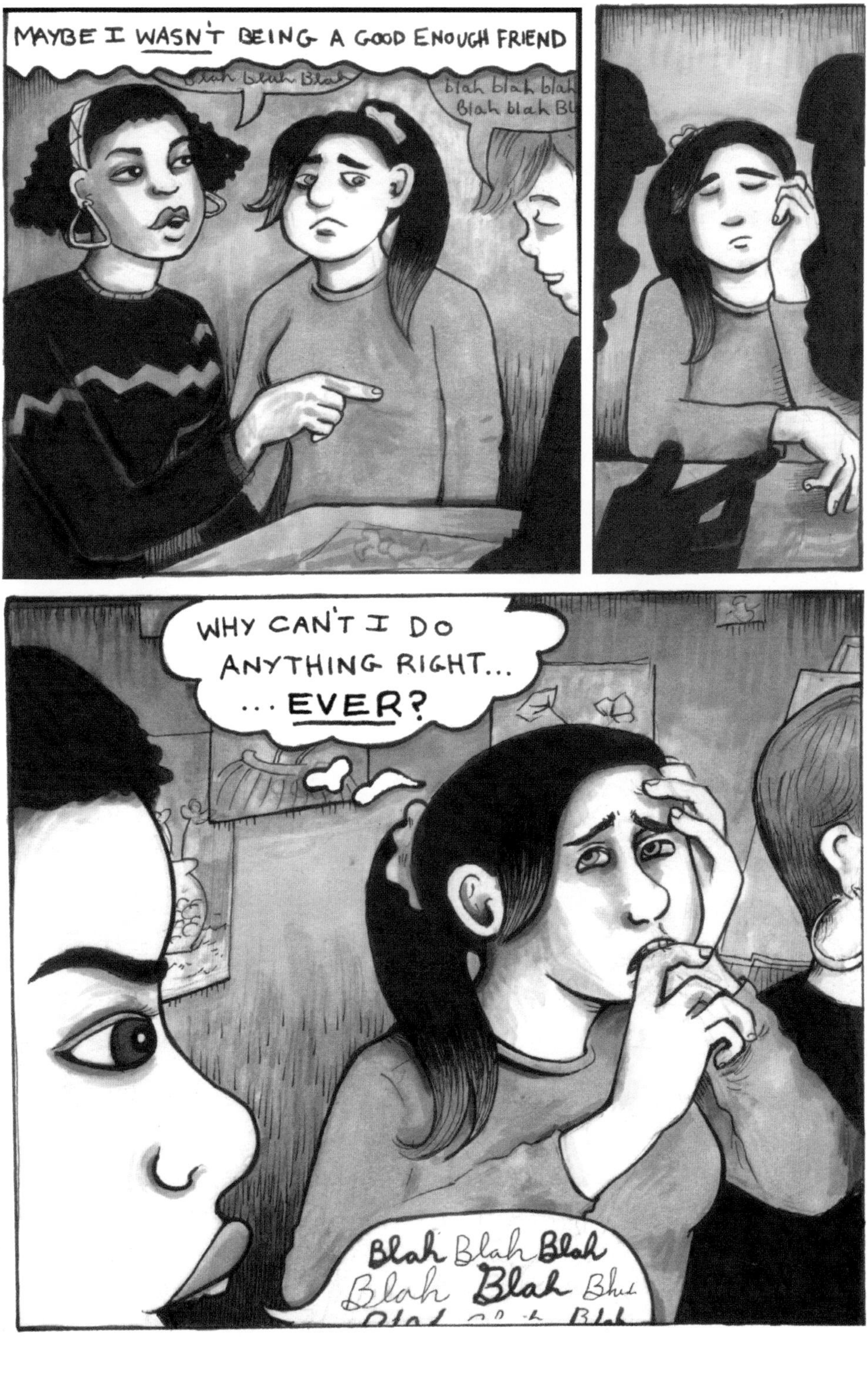
MAYBE I WASN'T BEING A GOOD ENOUGH FRIEND
Blah blah Blah
blah blah blah Blah blah
WHY CAN'T I DO ANYTHING RIGHT... ...EVER?
Blah Blah Blah Blah Blah

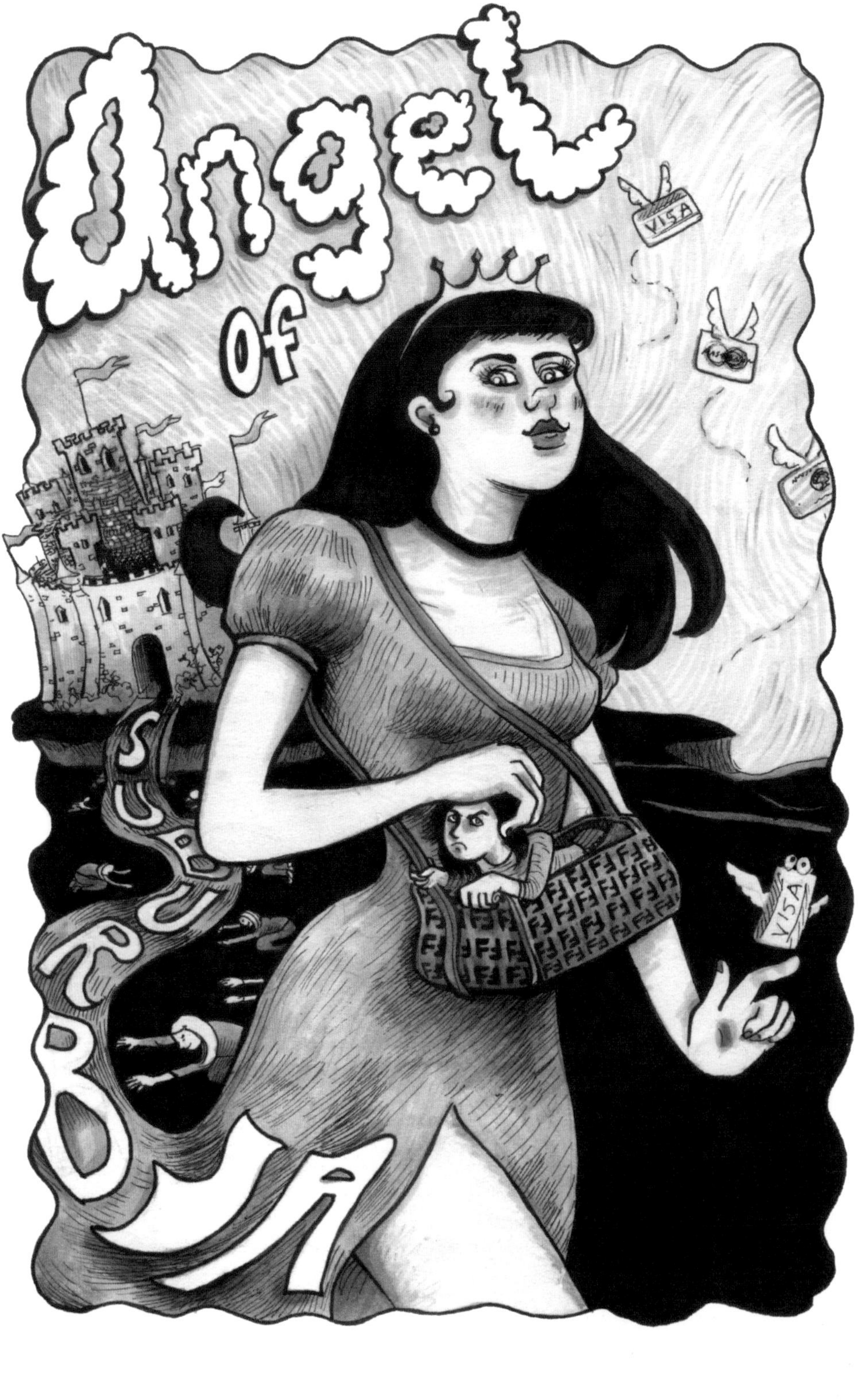
Angel
of
VISA
VISA
VISA

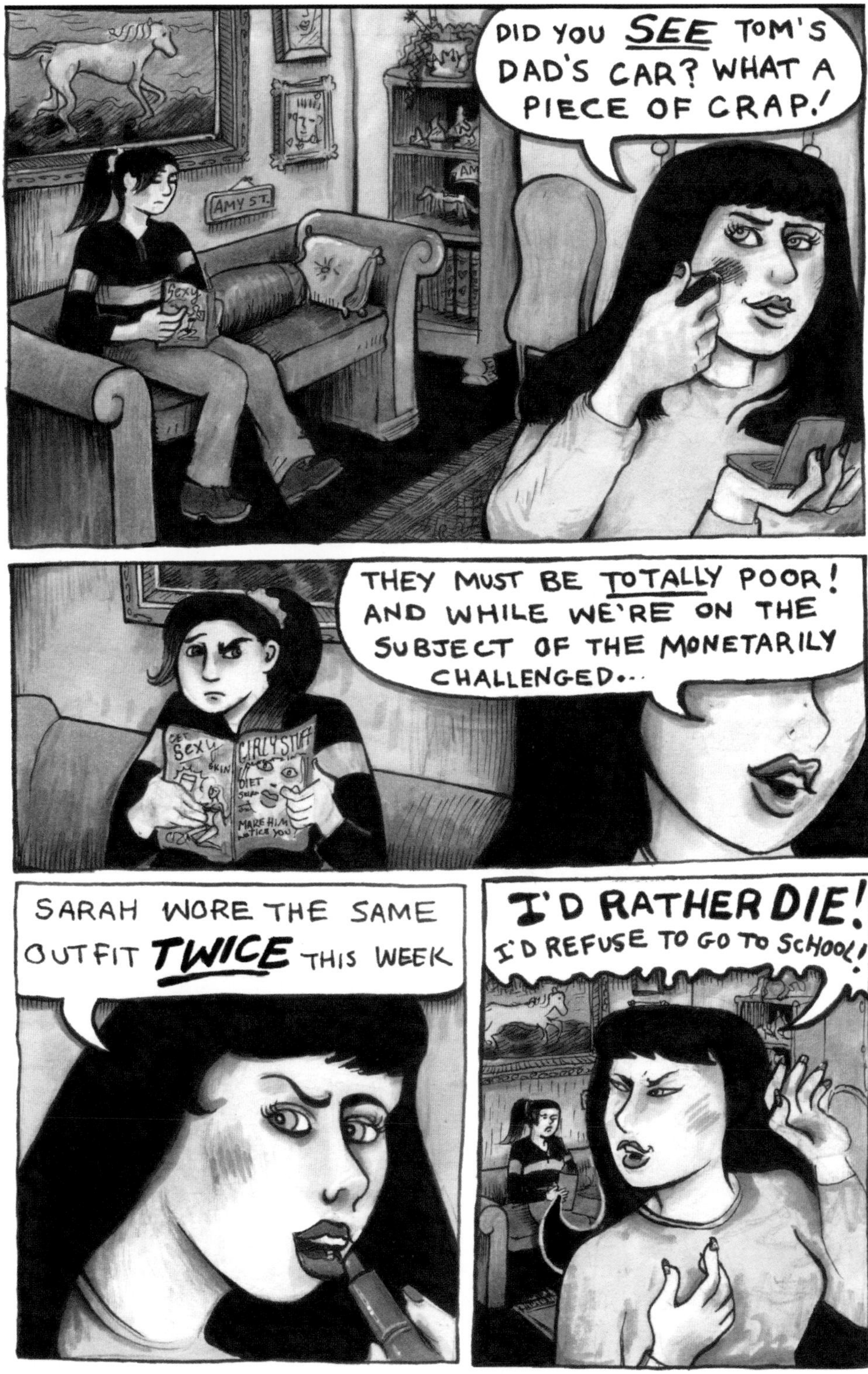
DID YOU SEE TOM'S DAD'S CAR? WHAT A PIECE OF CRAP!
THEY MUST BE TOTALLY POOR! AND WHILE WE'RE ON THE SUBJECT OF THE MONETARILY CHALLENGED...
SARAH WORE THE SAME OUTFIT TWICE THIS WEEK
I'D RATHER DIE! I'D REFUSE TO GO TO SCHOOL!

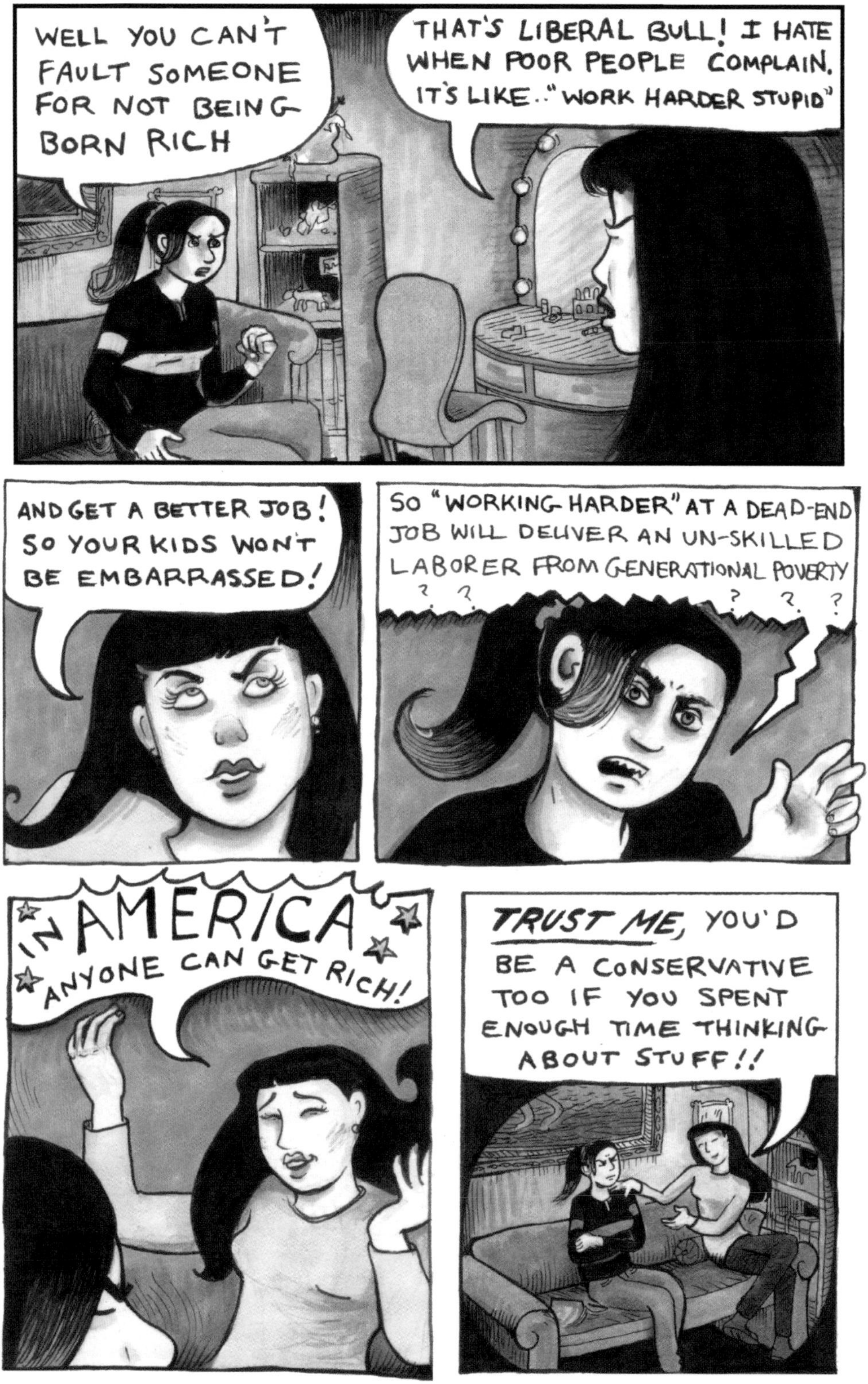
WELL YOU CAN'T FAULT SOMEONE FOR NOT BEING BORN RICH
THAT'S LIBERAL BULL! I HATE WHEN POOR PEOPLE COMPLAIN. IT'S LIKE.."WORK HARDER STUPID"
AND GET A BETTER JOB! SO YOUR KIDS WON'T BE EMBARRASSED!
SO "WORKING HARDER" AT A DEAD-END JOB WILL DELIVER AN UN-SKILLED LABORER FROM GENERATIONAL POVERTY ? ? ? ? ?
IN AMERICA ANYONE CAN GET RICH!
TRUST ME, YOU'D BE A CONSERVATIVE TOO IF YOU SPENT ENOUGH TIME THINKING ABOUT STUFF!!

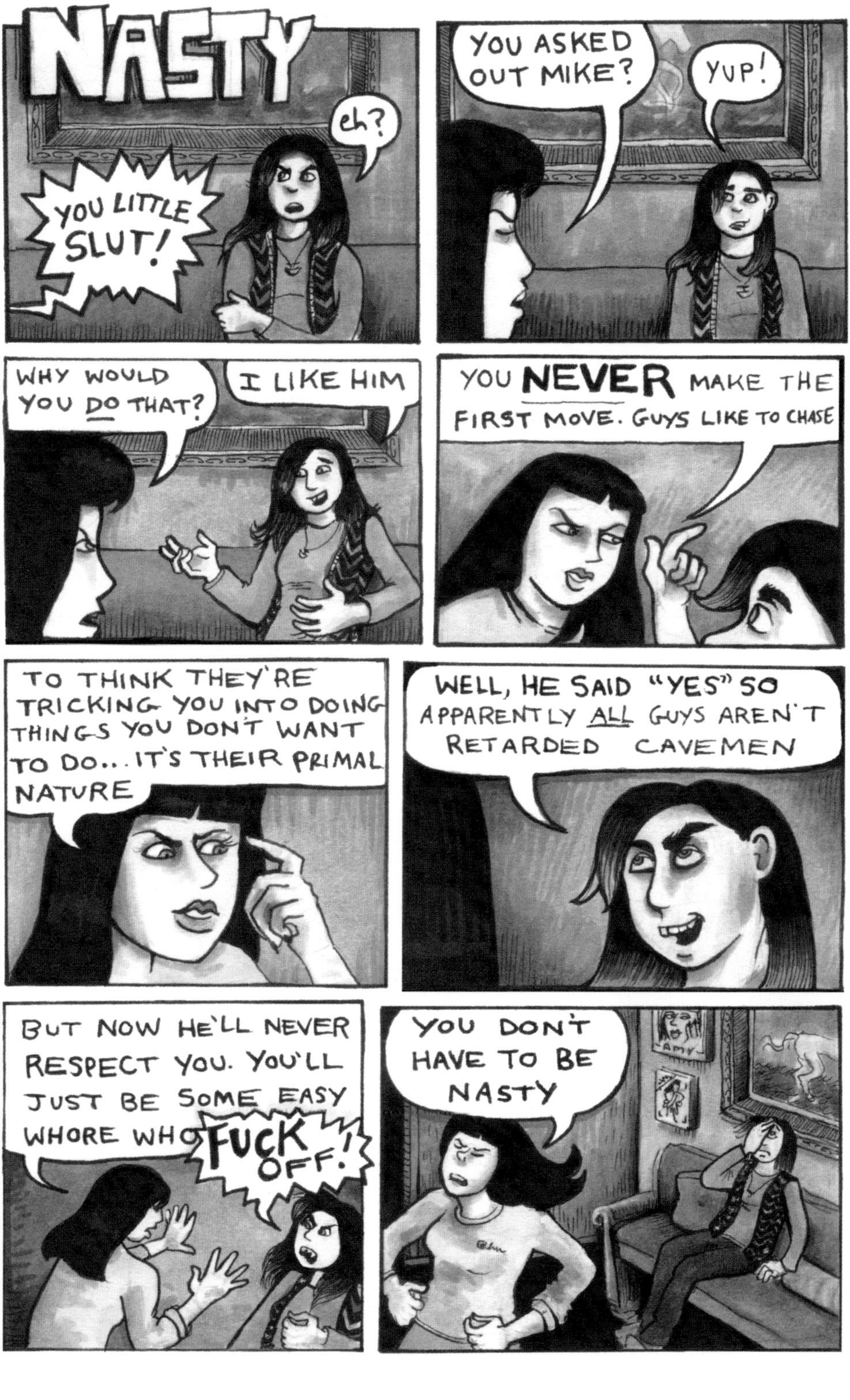
NASTY
YOU LITTLE SLUT!
eh?
YOU ASKED OUT MIKE?
YUP!
WHY WOULD YOU DO THAT?
I LIKE HIM
YOU NEVER MAKE THE FIRST MOVE. GUYS LIKE TO CHASE
TO THINK THEY'RE TRICKING YOU INTO DOING THINGS YOU DON'T WANT TO DO... IT'S THEIR PRIMAL NATURE
WELL, HE SAID "YES" SO APPARENTLY ALL GUYS AREN'T RETARDED CAVEMEN
BUT NOW HE'LL NEVER RESPECT YOU. YOU'LL JUST BE SOME EASY WHORE WHO
FUCK OFF!
YOU DON'T HAVE TO BE NASTY
AMY

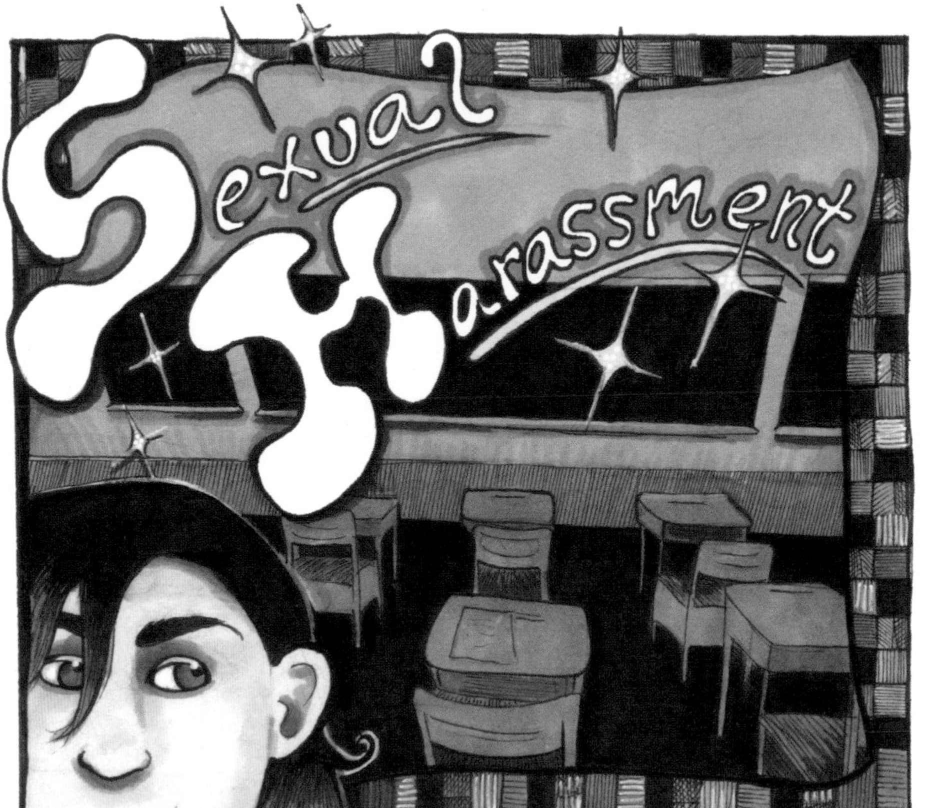
Sexual Harassment

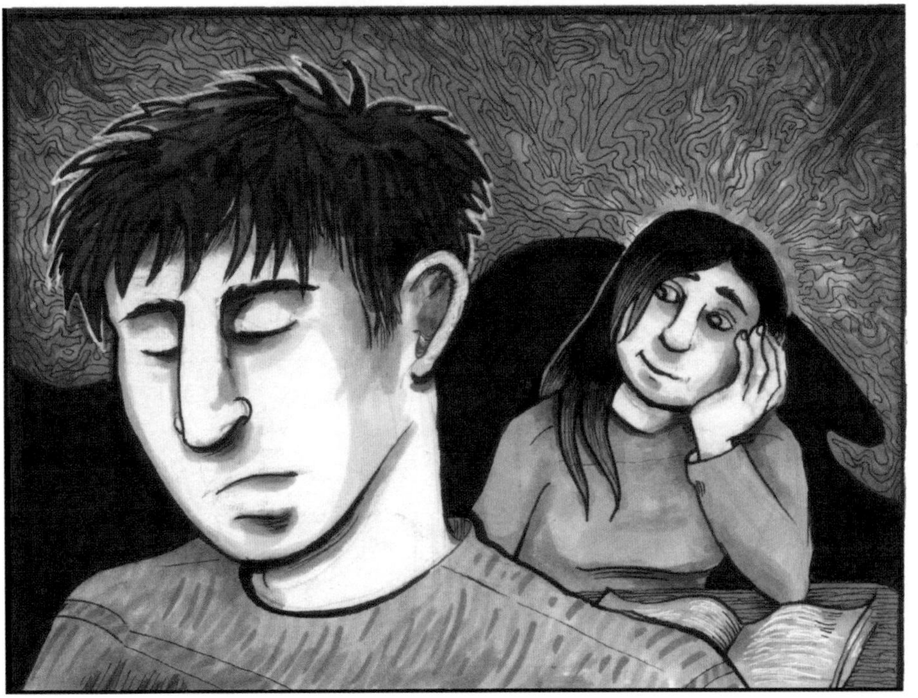

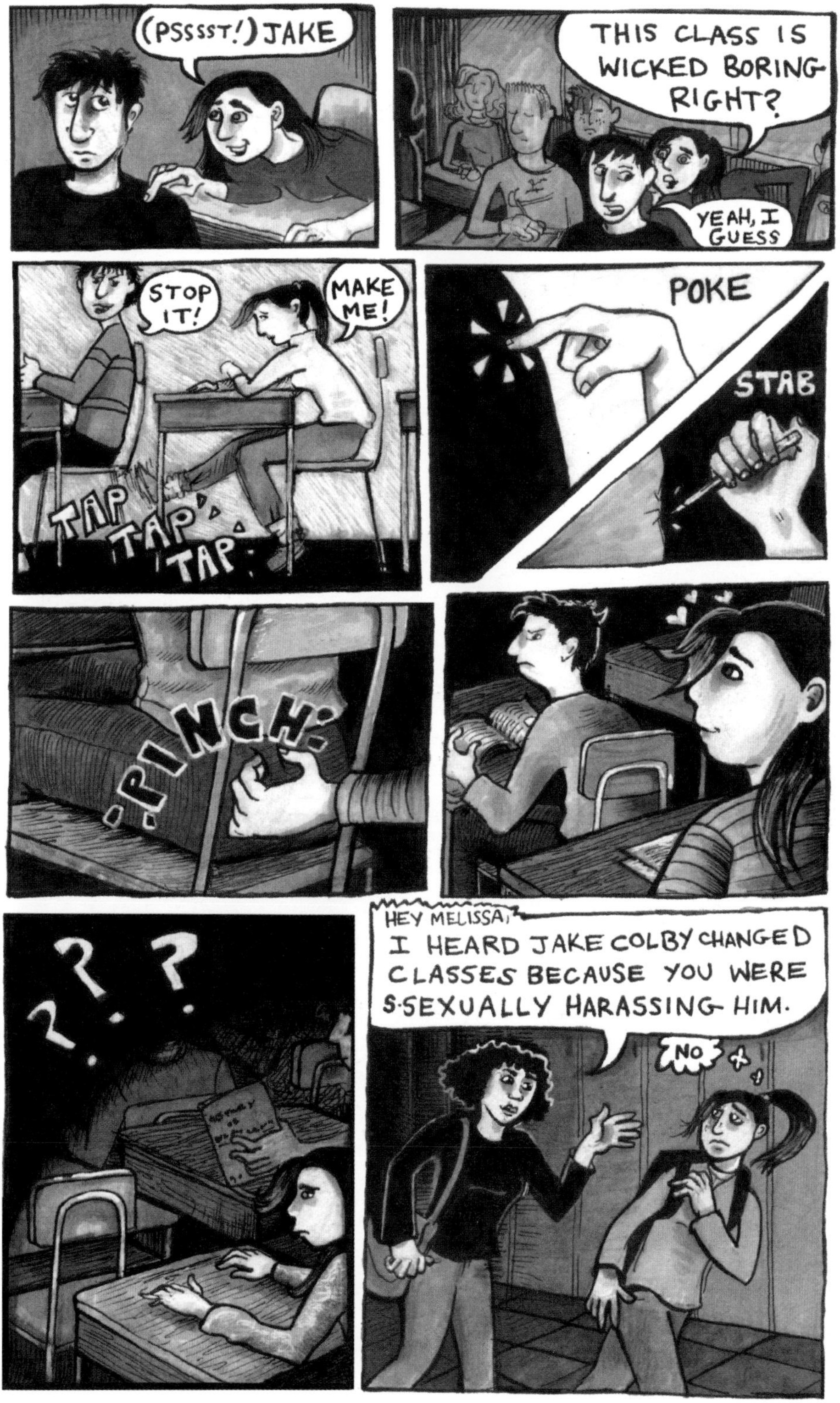
(PSSSST!) JAKE
THIS CLASS IS WICKED BORING RIGHT?
YEAH, I GUESS
STOP IT!
MAKE ME!
TAP TAP TAP
POKE
STAB
PINCH!
? ? ?
HEY MELISSA,
I HEARD JAKE COLBY CHANGED CLASSES BECAUSE YOU WERE S-SEXUALLY HARASSING HIM.
NO

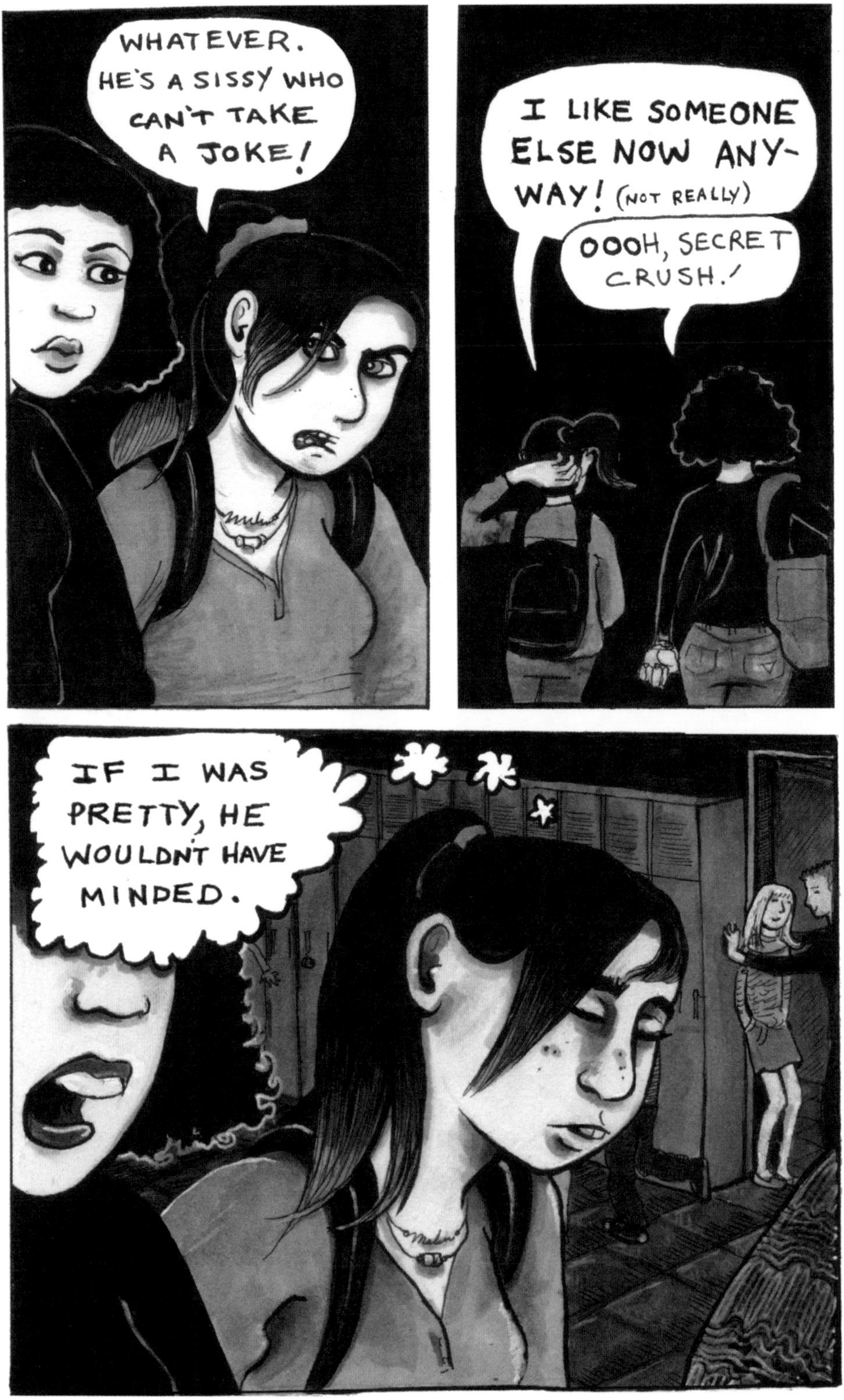
WHATEVER. HE'S A SISSY WHO CAN'T TAKE A JOKE!
I LIKE SOMEONE ELSE NOW ANY-WAY! (NOT REALLY)
OOOH, SECRET CRUSH!
IF I WAS PRETTY, HE WOULDN'T HAVE MINDED.

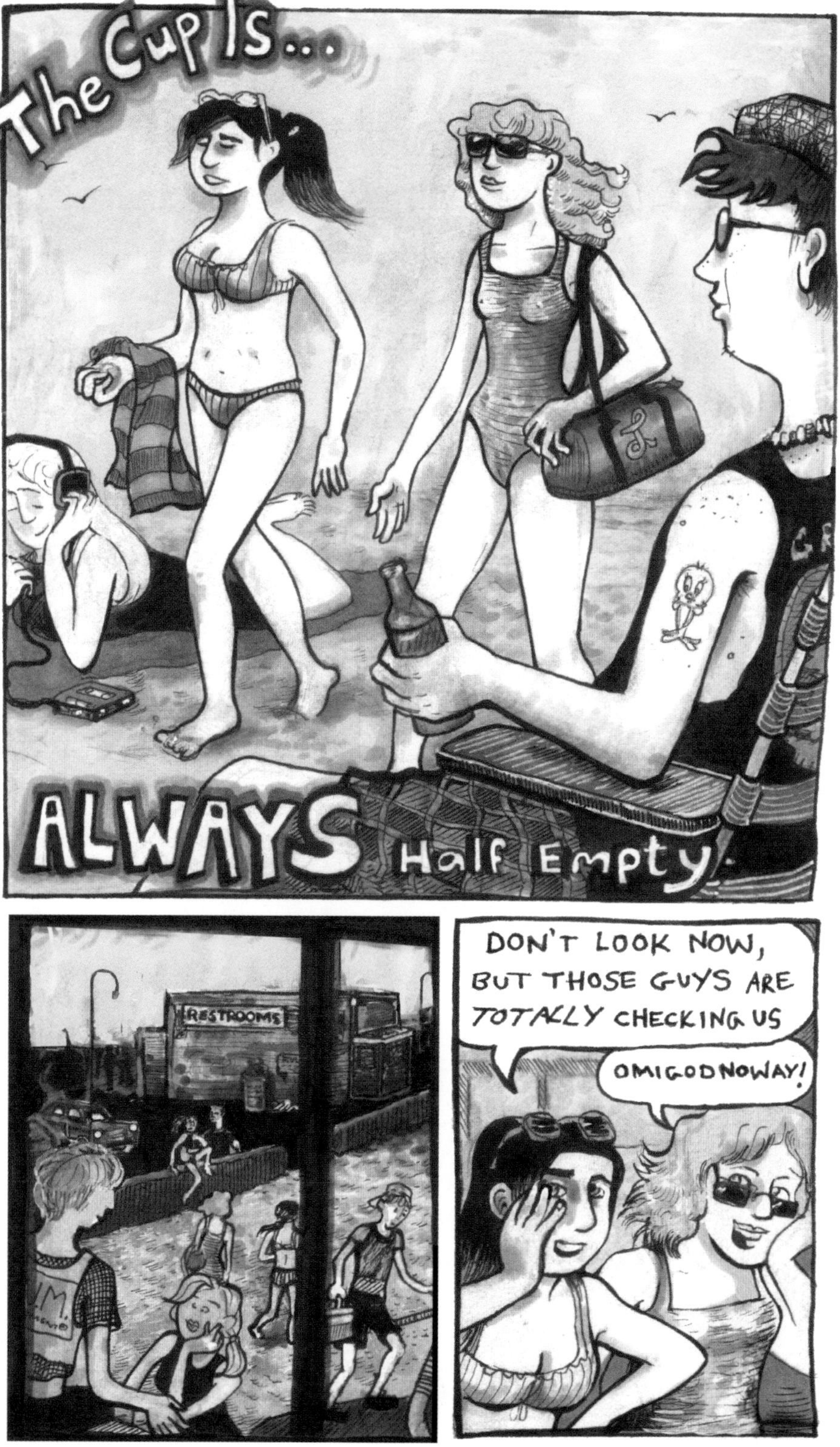
The Cup Is...
ALWAYS Half Empty
RESTROOMS
DON'T LOOK NOW, BUT THOSE GUYS ARE TOTALLY CHECKING US
OMIGODNOWAY!

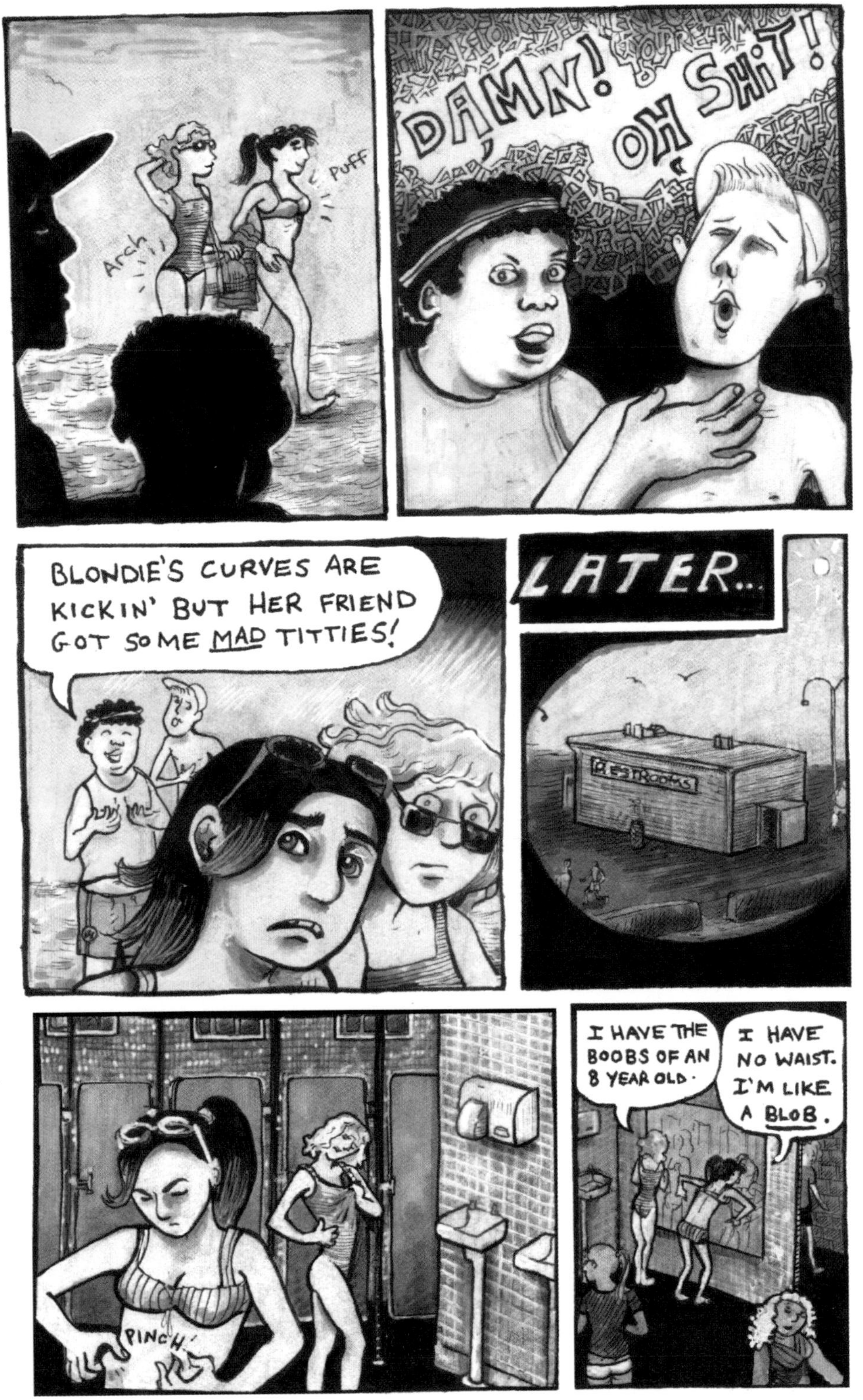
Arch
Puff
DAMN!
OH SHIT!
BLONDIE'S CURVES ARE KICKIN' BUT HER FRIEND GOT SOME MAD TITTIES!
LATER...
RESTROOMS
PINCH!
I HAVE THE BOOBS OF AN 8 YEAR OLD.
I HAVE NO WAIST. I'M LIKE A BLOB.

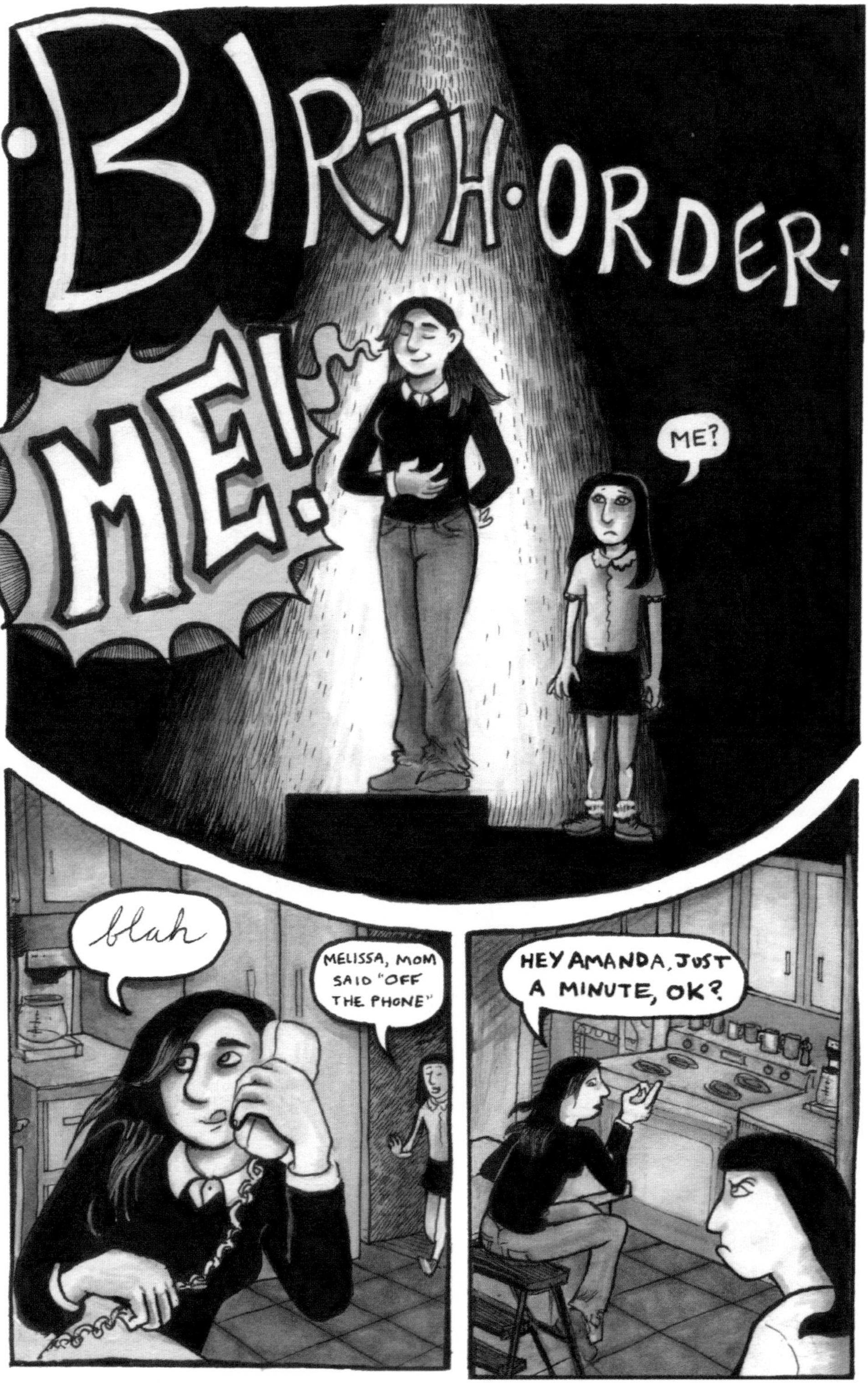
·BIRTH·ORDER·
ME!
ME?
blah
MELISSA, MOM SAID "OFF THE PHONE"
HEY AMANDA, JUST A MINUTE, OK?

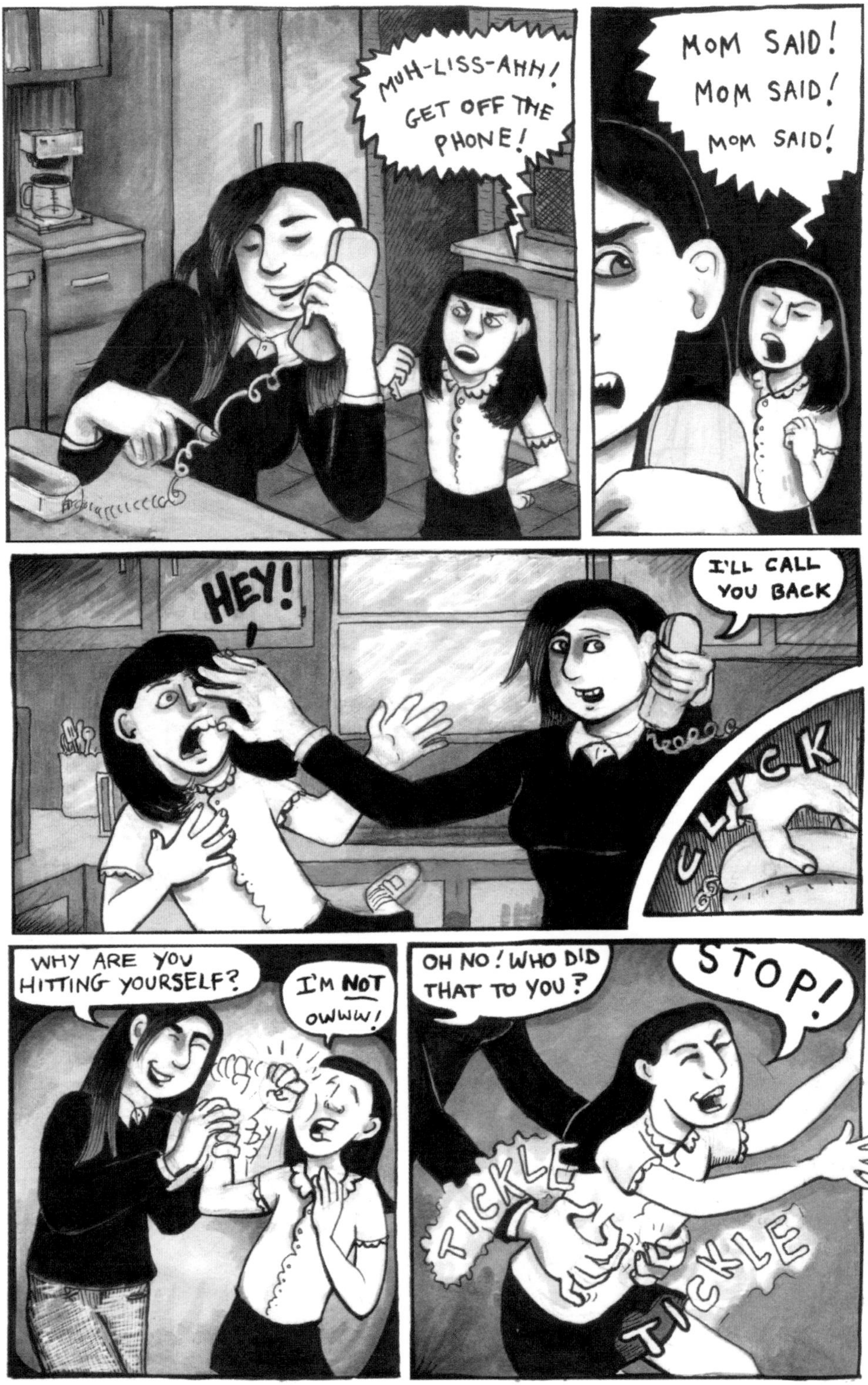
MUH-LISS-AHH! GET OFF THE PHONE!
MOM SAID! MOM SAID! MOM SAID!
HEY!
I'LL CALL YOU BACK
CLICK
WHY ARE YOU HITTING YOURSELF?
I'M NOT OWWW!
OH NO! WHO DID THAT TO YOU?
STOP!
TICKLE
TICKLE
TICKLE

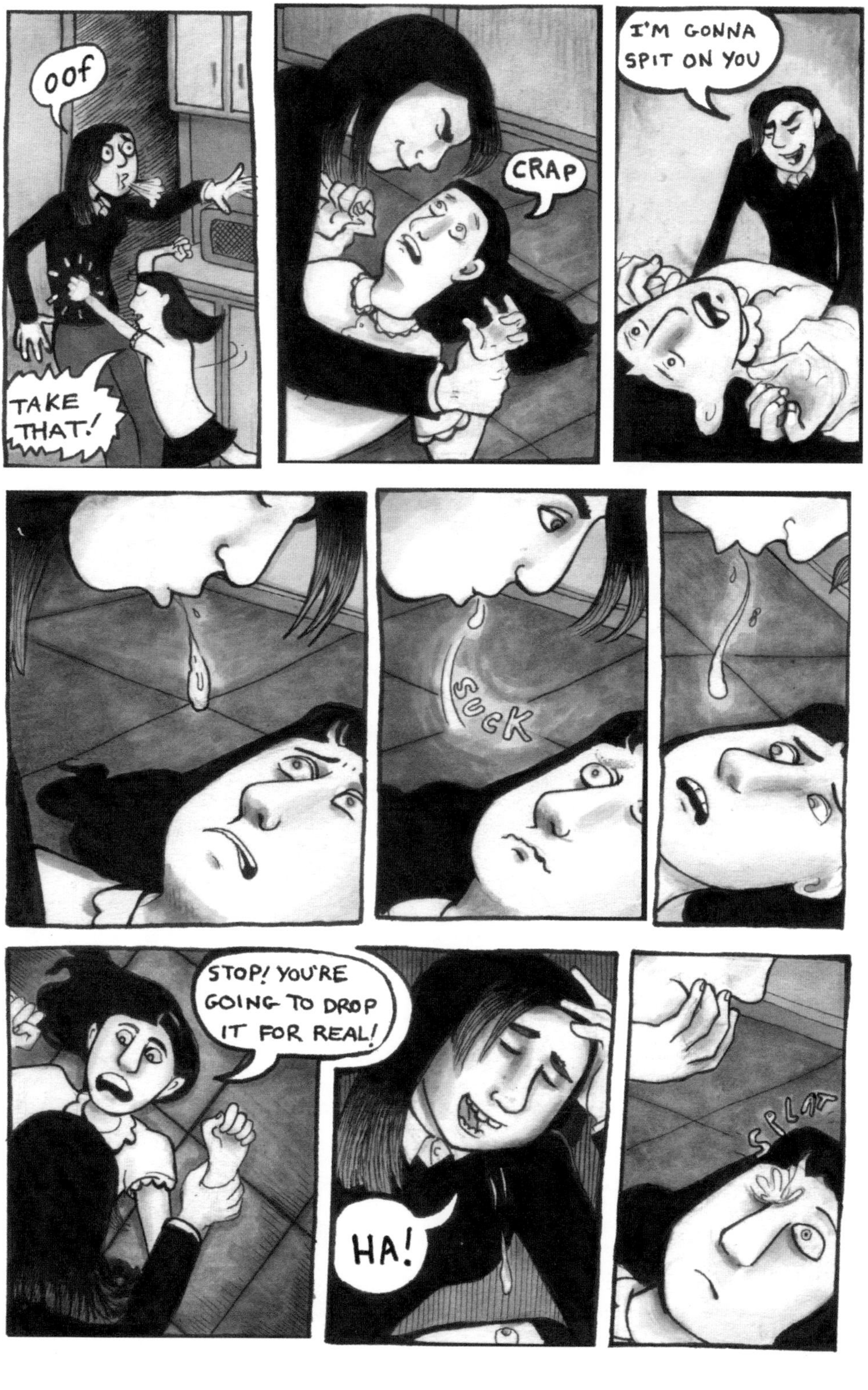
oof
TAKE THAT!
CRAP
I'M GONNA SPIT ON YOU
SUCK
STOP! YOU'RE GOING TO DROP IT FOR REAL!
HA!
SPLAT

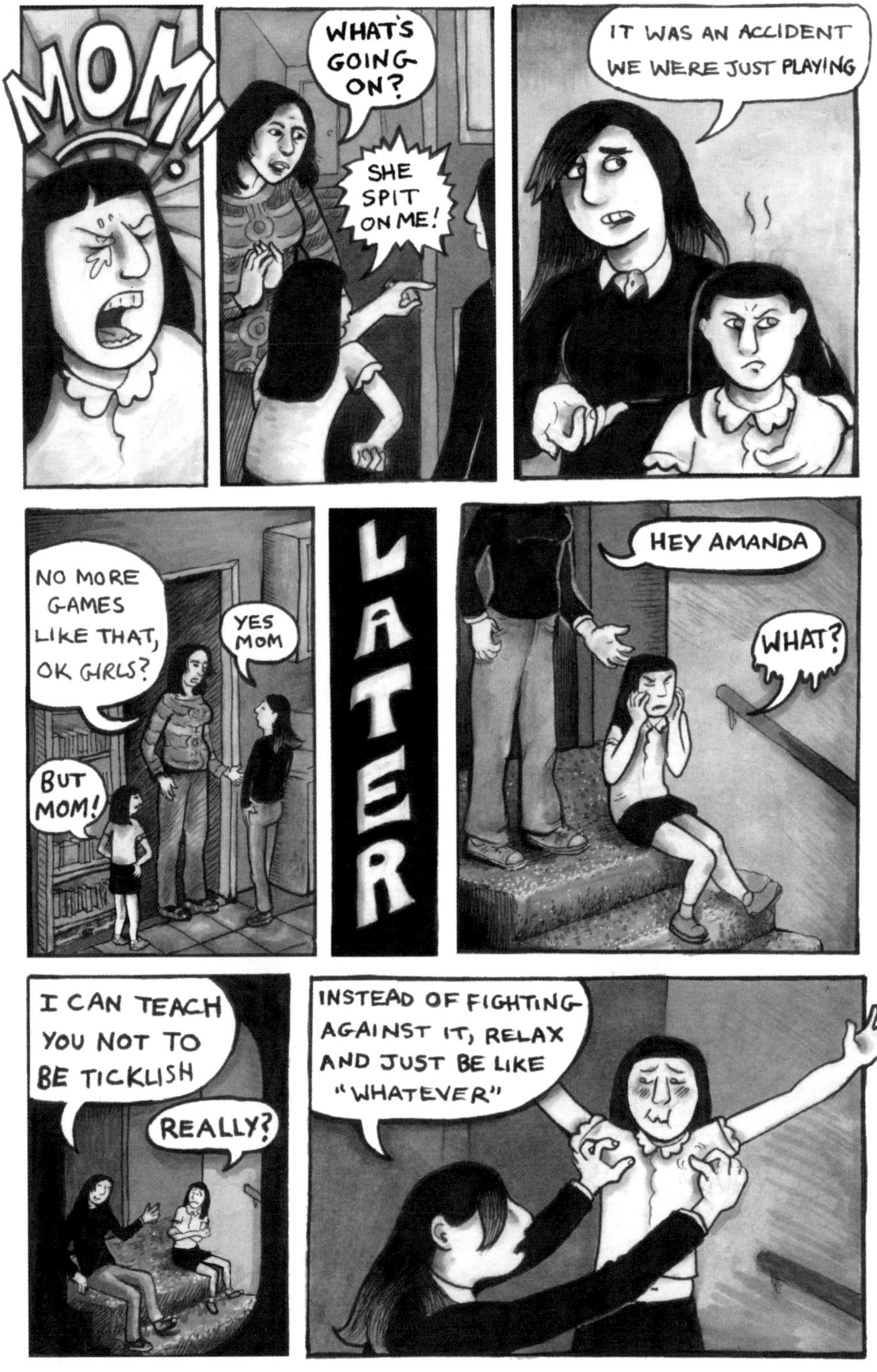
MOM!
WHAT'S GOING ON?
SHE SPIT ON ME!
IT WAS AN ACCIDENT WE WERE JUST PLAYING
NO MORE GAMES LIKE THAT, OK GIRLS?
YES MOM
BUT MOM!
LATER
HEY AMANDA
WHAT?
I CAN TEACH YOU NOT TO BE TICKLISH
REALLY?
INSTEAD OF FIGHTING AGAINST IT, RELAX AND JUST BE LIKE "WHATEVER"

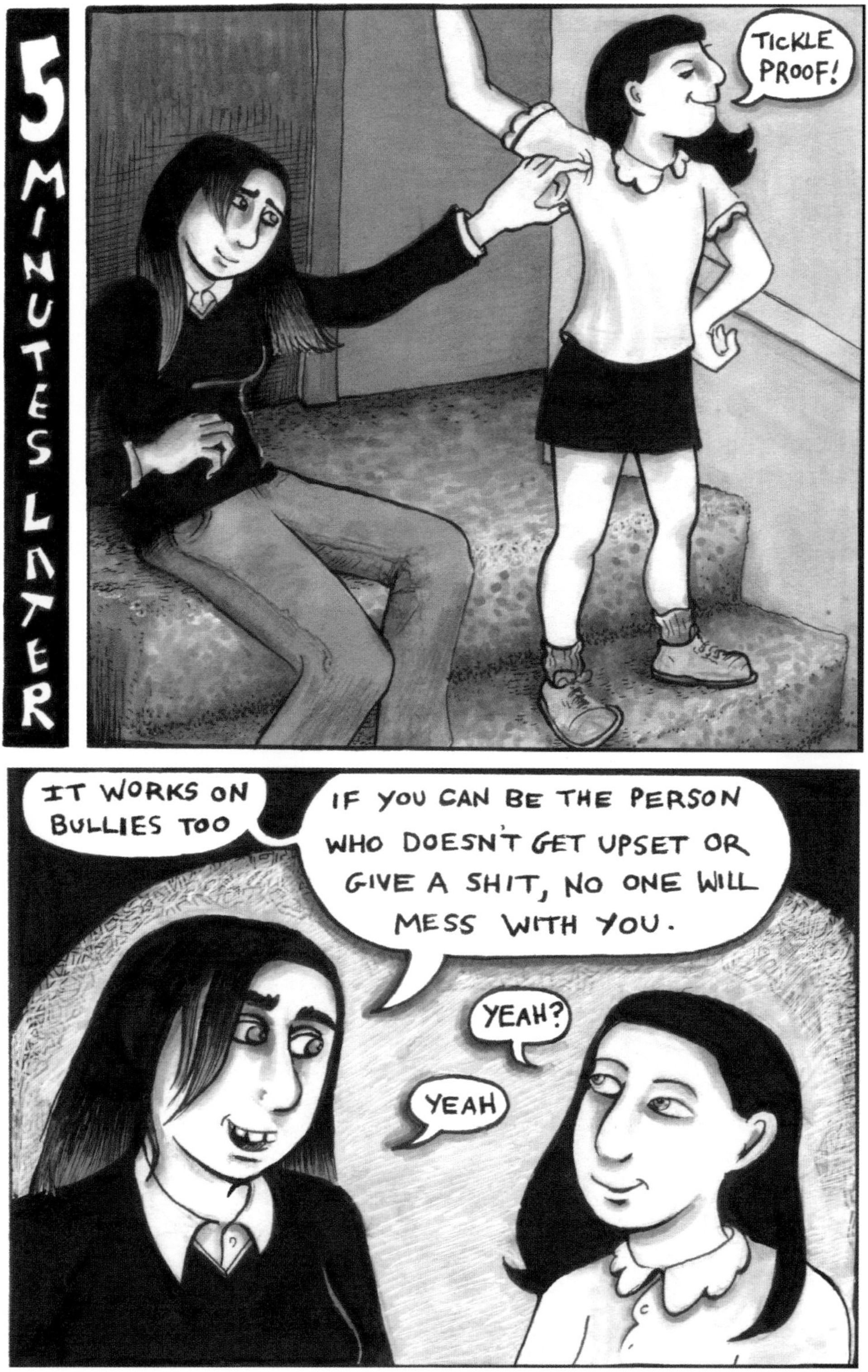
5 MINUTES LATER
TICKLE PROOF!
IT WORKS ON BULLIES TOO
IF YOU CAN BE THE PERSON WHO DOESN'T GET UPSET OR GIVE A SHIT, NO ONE WILL MESS WITH YOU.
YEAH?
YEAH

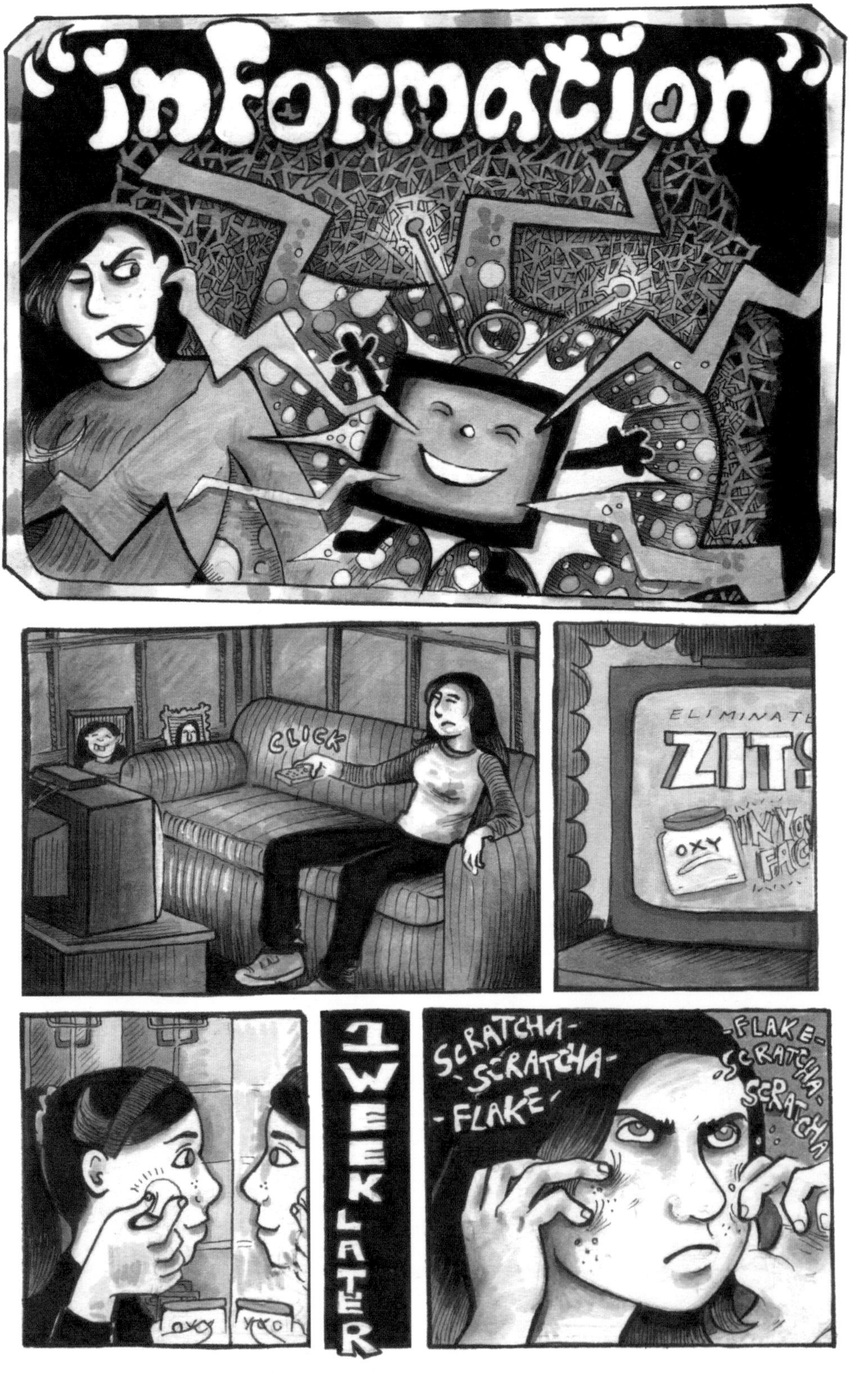
"information"
CLICK
ELIMINATE
ZITS
OXY
OXY
OXY
1 WEEK LATER
SCRATCHA-
-SCRATCHA-
-FLAKE-
-FLAKE-
SCRATCHA-
SCRATCHA

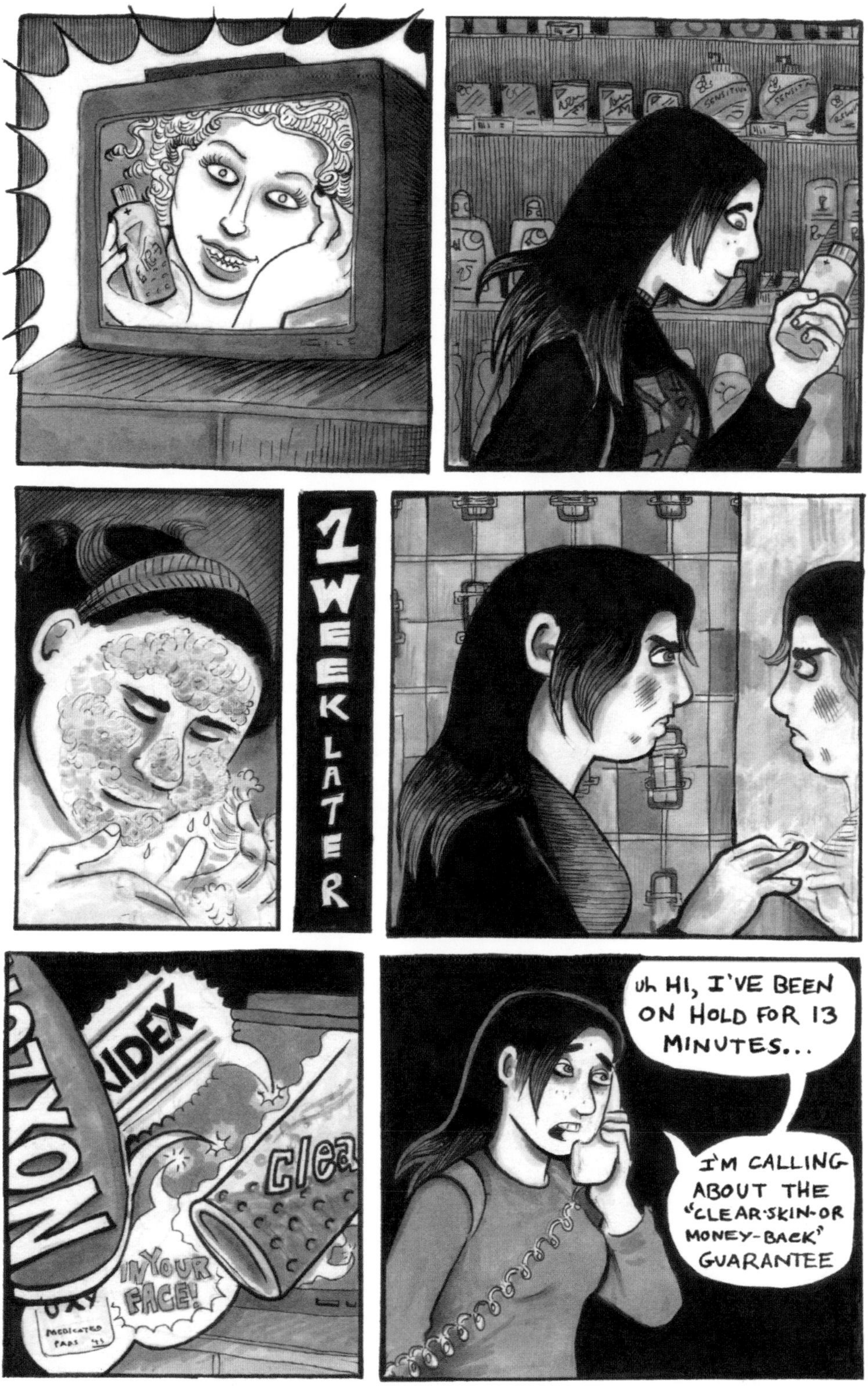
1 WEEK LATER
NOXZEMA
STRIDEX
clea
IN YOUR FACE!
OXY
MEDICATED PADS
uh HI, I'VE BEEN ON HOLD FOR 13 MINUTES...
I'M CALLING ABOUT THE "CLEAR-SKIN-OR MONEY-BACK" GUARANTEE

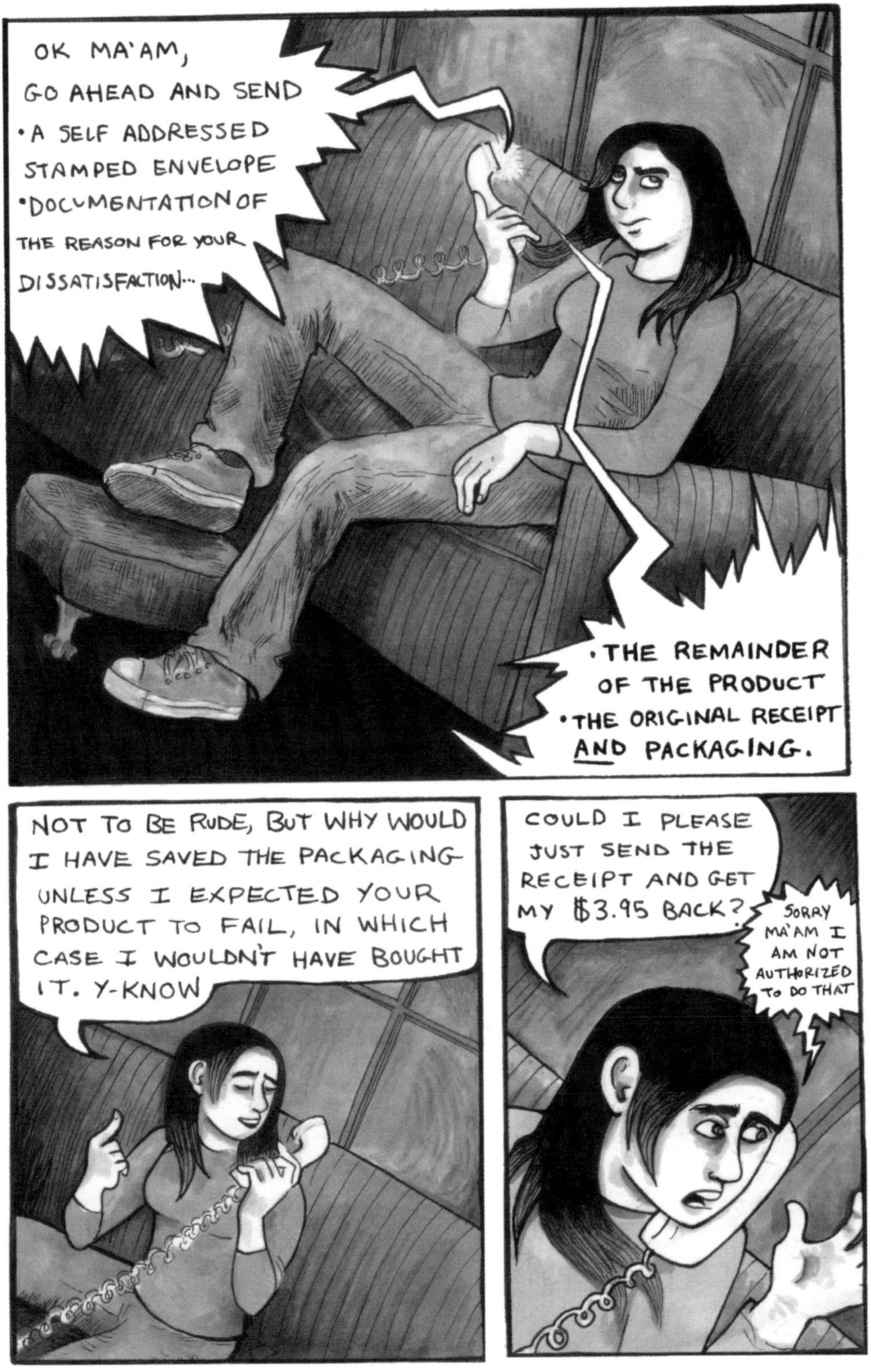

OK MA'AM, GO AHEAD AND SEND
• A SELF ADDRESSED STAMPED ENVELOPE
• DOCUMENTATION OF THE REASON FOR YOUR DISSATISFACTION...
• THE REMAINDER OF THE PRODUCT
• THE ORIGINAL RECEIPT AND PACKAGING.
NOT TO BE RUDE, BUT WHY WOULD I HAVE SAVED THE PACKAGING UNLESS I EXPECTED YOUR PRODUCT TO FAIL, IN WHICH CASE I WOULDN'T HAVE BOUGHT IT. Y-KNOW
COULD I PLEASE JUST SEND THE RECEIPT AND GET MY $3.95 BACK?
SORRY MA'AM I AM NOT AUTHORIZED TO DO THAT

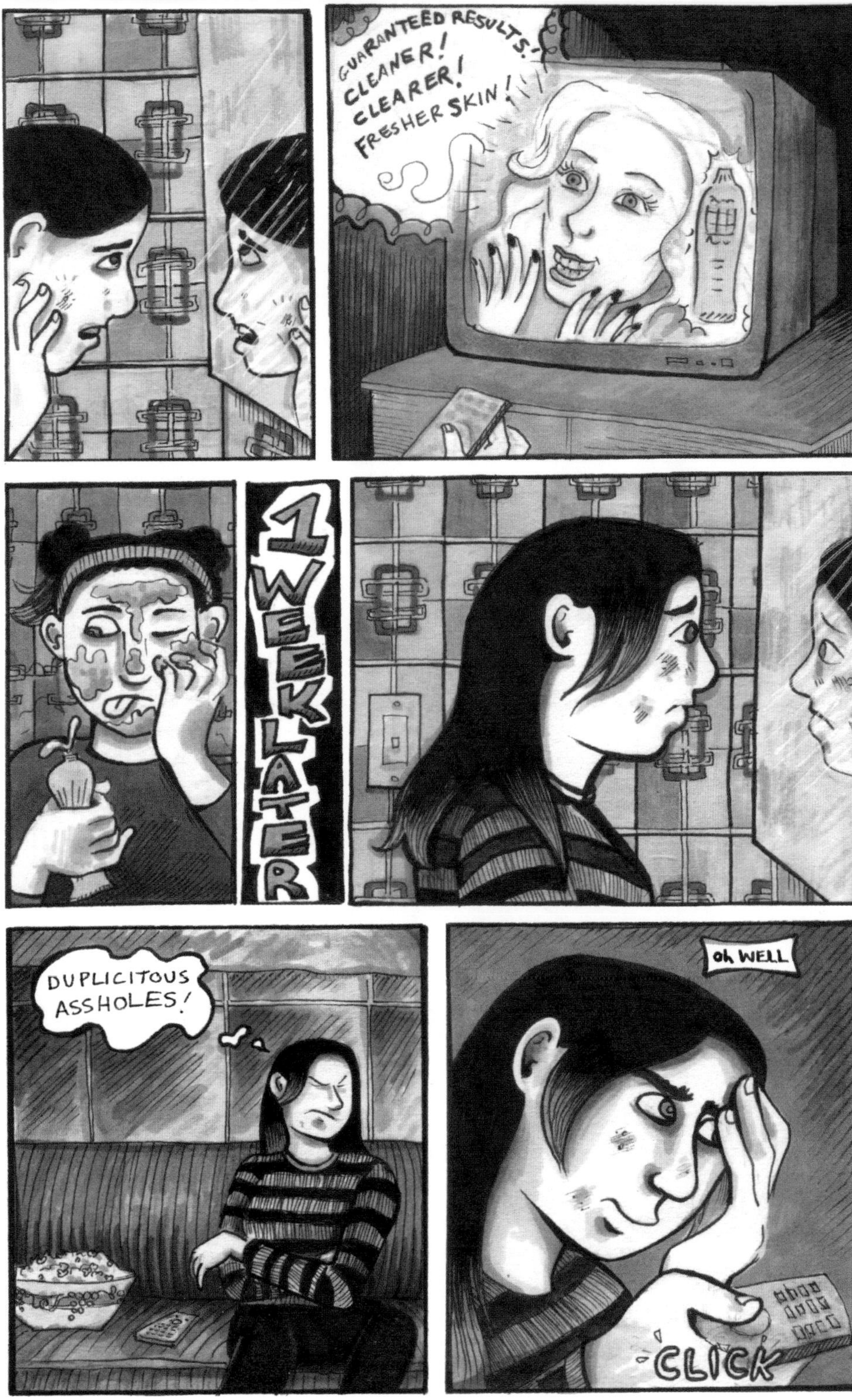
GUARANTEED RESULTS!
CLEANER!
CLEARER!
FRESHER SKIN!
1 WEEK LATER
DUPLICITOUS ASSHOLES!
oh WELL
CLICK

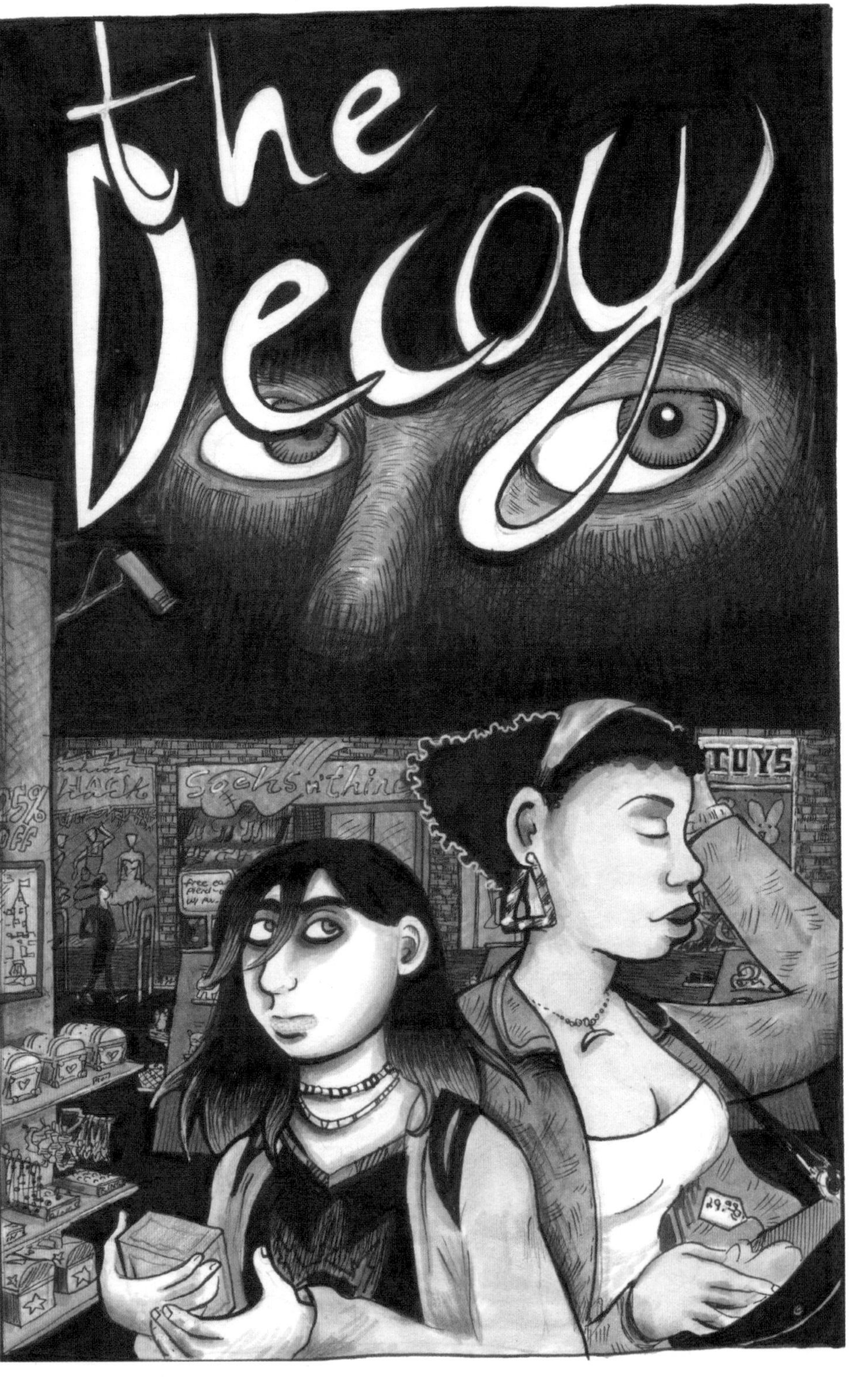
the Decoy
25% OFF
TOYS
19.99

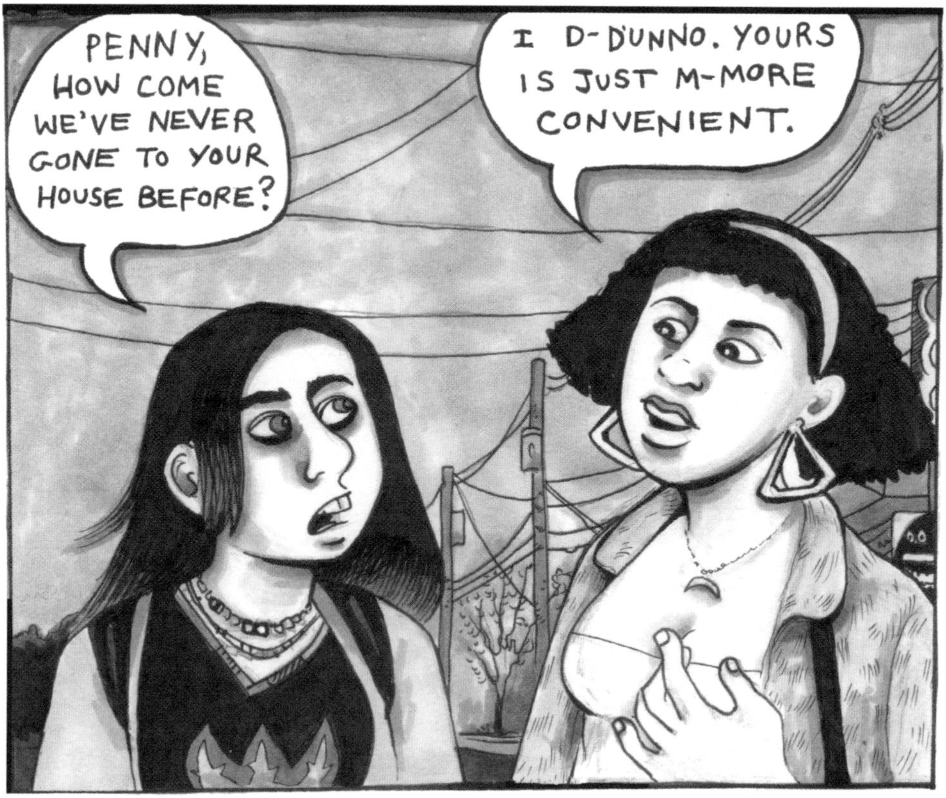
PENNY, HOW COME WE'VE NEVER GONE TO YOUR HOUSE BEFORE?
I D-D'UNNO. YOURS IS JUST M-MORE CONVENIENT.

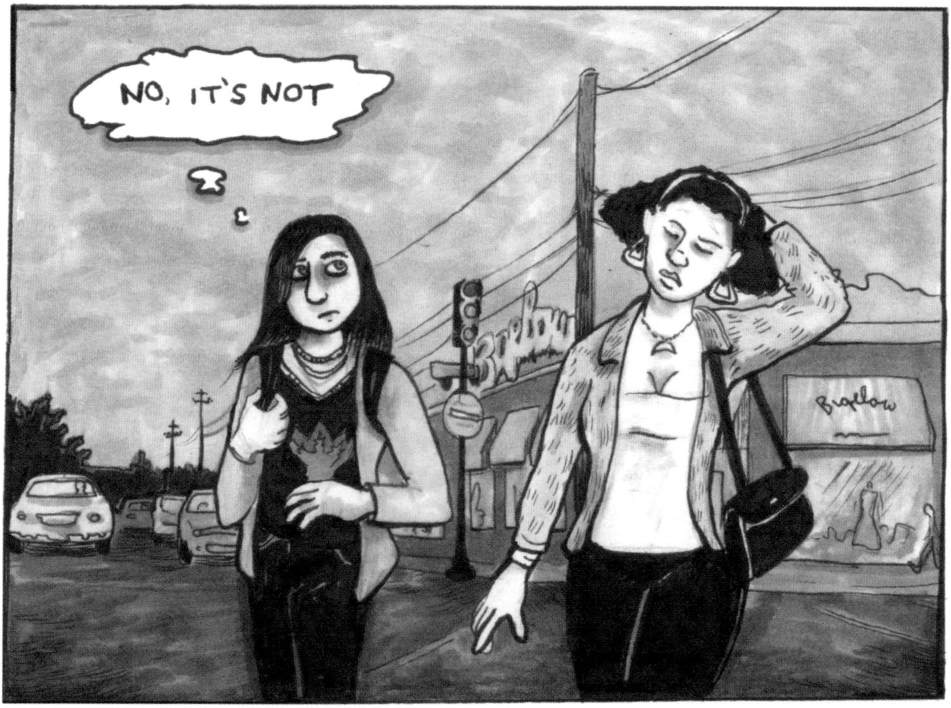
NO, IT'S NOT

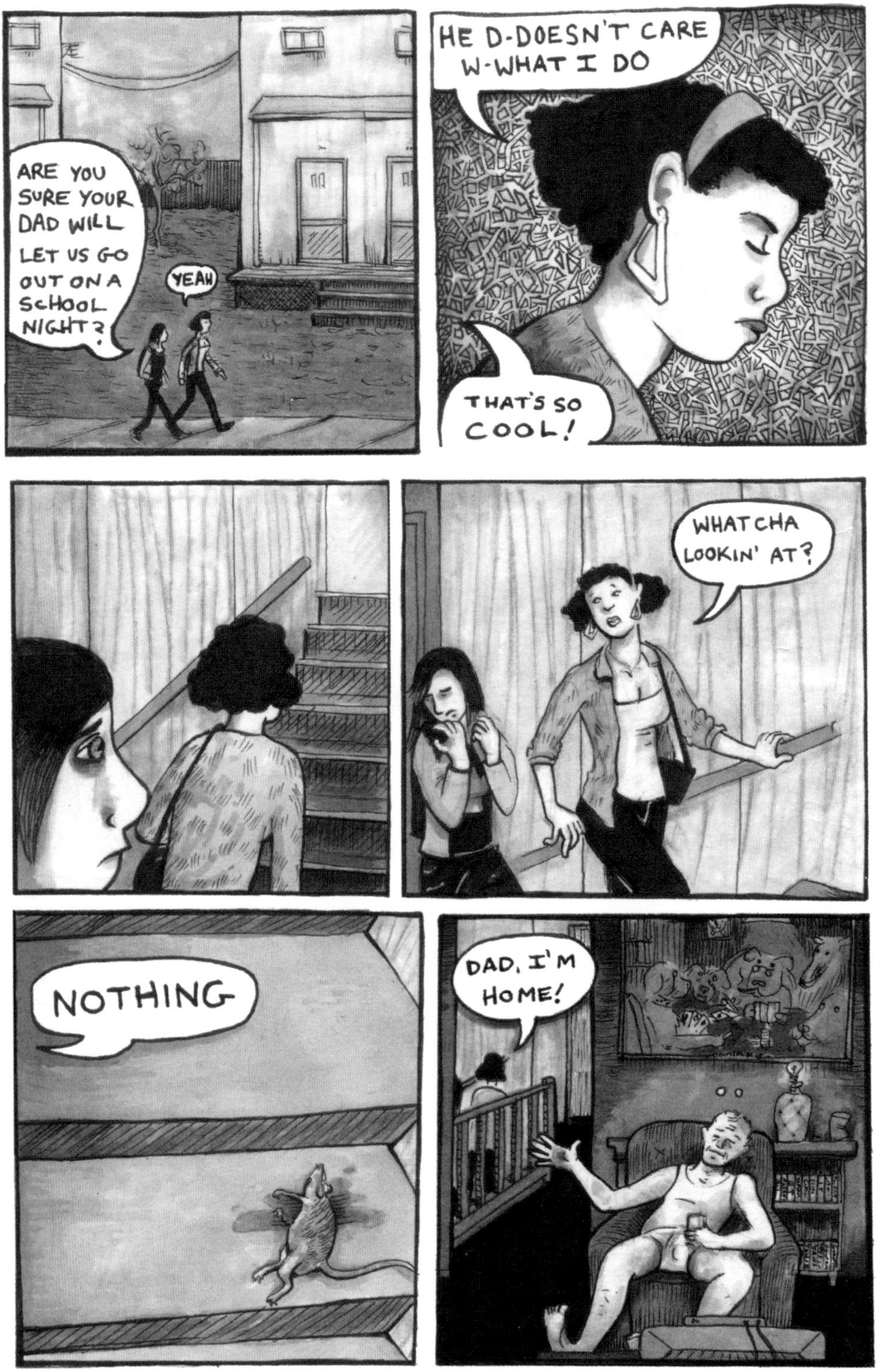
ARE YOU SURE YOUR DAD WILL LET US GO OUT ON A SCHOOL NIGHT?
YEAH
HE D-DOESN'T CARE W-WHAT I DO
THAT'S SO COOL!
WHATCHA LOOKIN' AT?
NOTHING
DAD, I'M HOME!

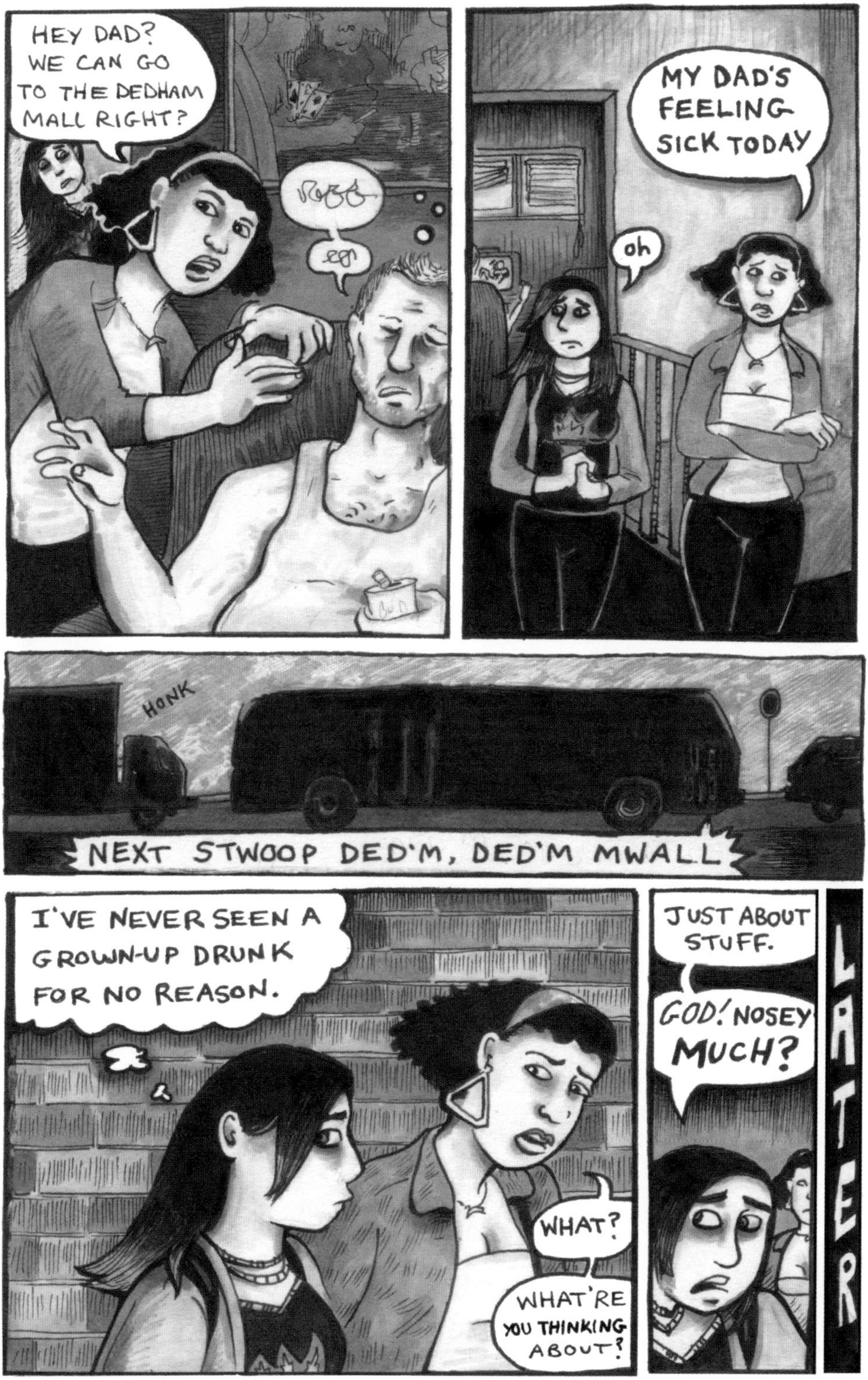
HEY DAD? WE CAN GO TO THE DEDHAM MALL RIGHT?
MY DAD'S FEELING SICK TODAY
oh
HONK
NEXT STWOOP DED'M, DED'M MWALL
I'VE NEVER SEEN A GROWN-UP DRUNK FOR NO REASON.
WHAT?
WHAT'RE YOU THINKING ABOUT?
JUST ABOUT STUFF.
GOD! NOSEY MUCH?
LATER

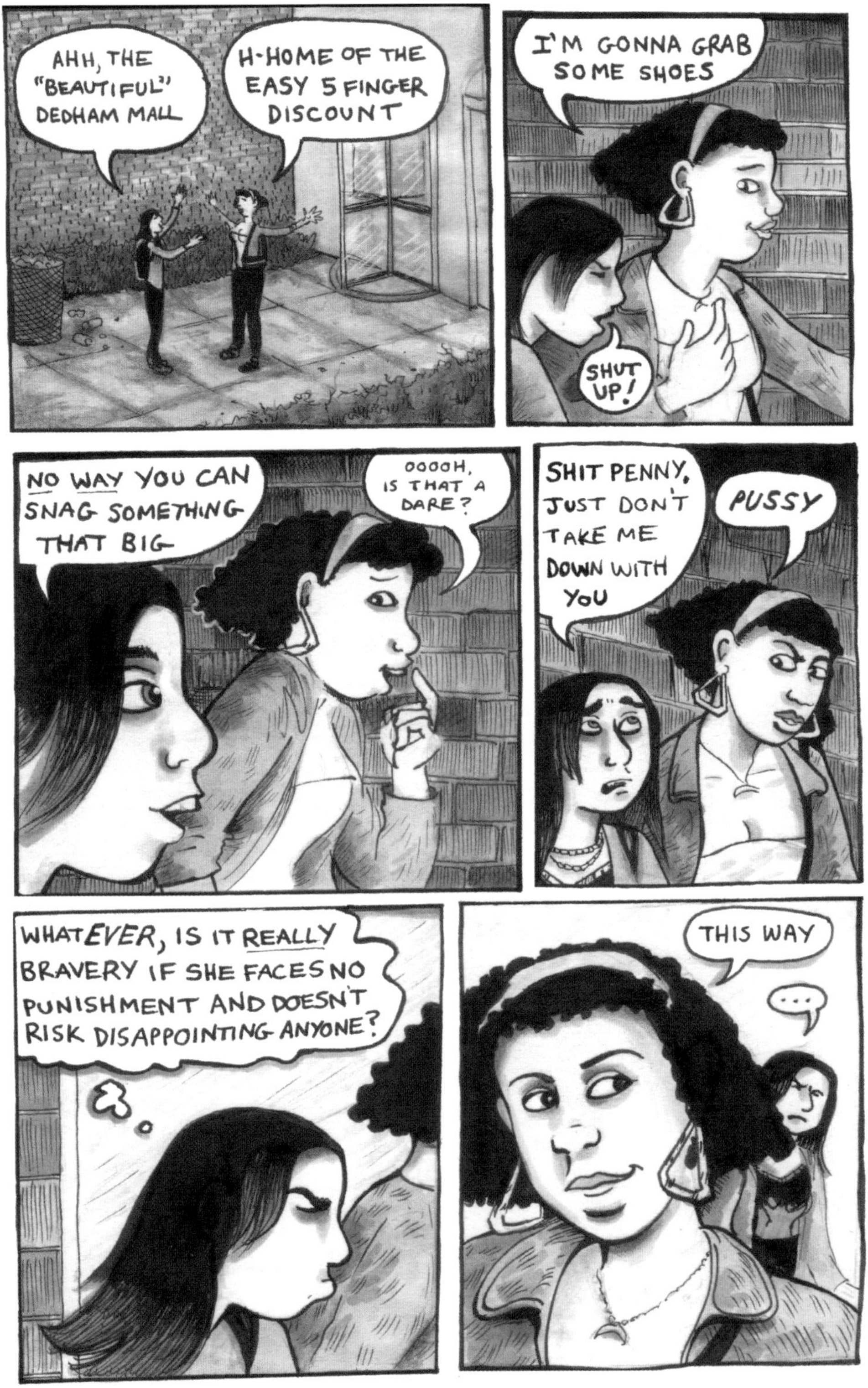
AHH, THE "BEAUTIFUL" DEDHAM MALL
H-HOME OF THE EASY 5 FINGER DISCOUNT
I'M GONNA GRAB SOME SHOES
SHUT UP!
NO WAY YOU CAN SNAG SOMETHING THAT BIG
OOOOH, IS THAT A DARE?
SHIT PENNY, JUST DON'T TAKE ME DOWN WITH YOU
PUSSY
WHATEVER, IS IT REALLY BRAVERY IF SHE FACES NO PUNISHMENT AND DOESN'T RISK DISAPPOINTING ANYONE?
THIS WAY
...

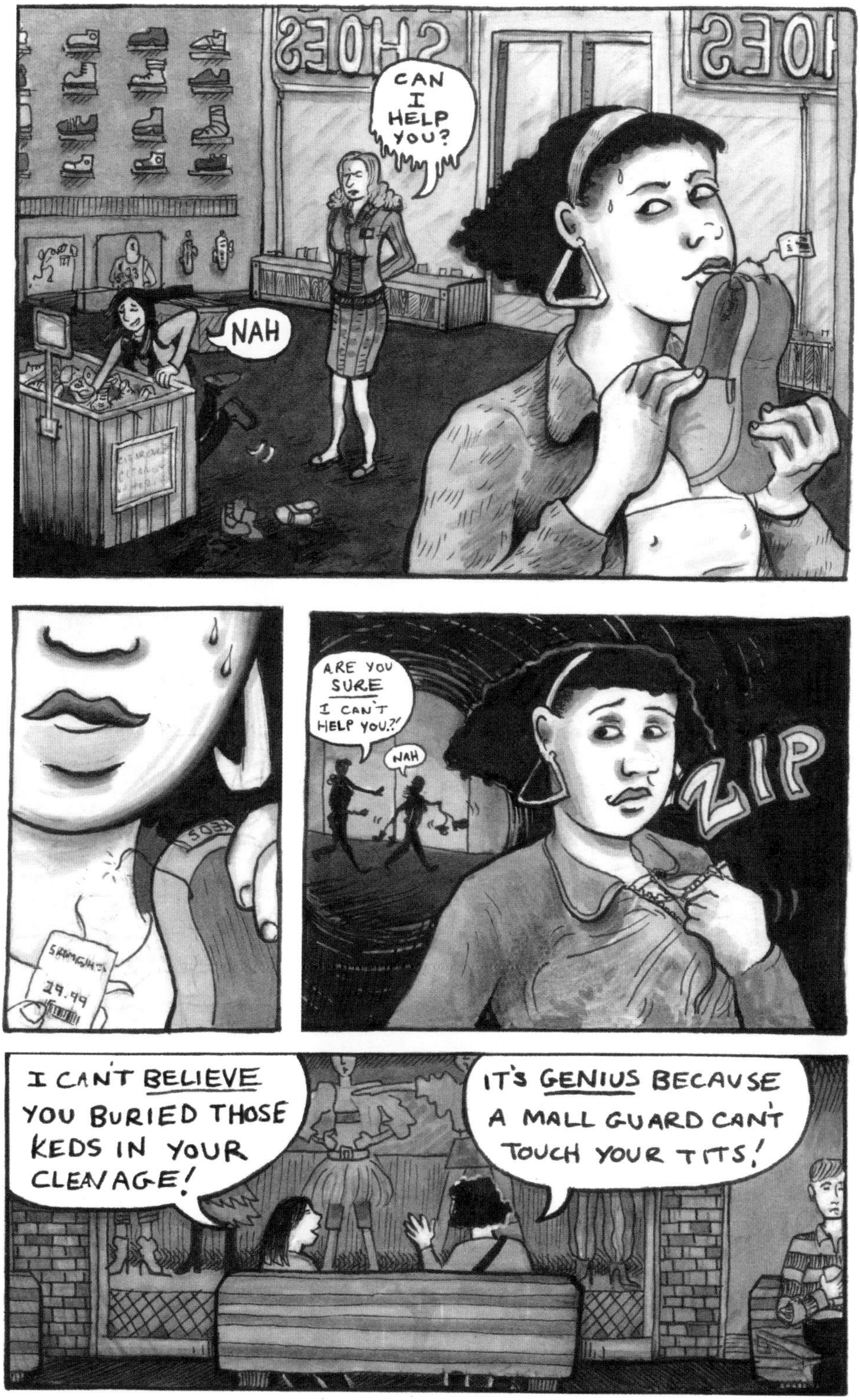
CAN I HELP YOU?
NAH
ARE YOU SURE I CAN'T HELP YOU?
NAH
ZIP
I CAN'T BELIEVE YOU BURIED THOSE KEDS IN YOUR CLEAVAGE!
IT'S GENIUS BECAUSE A MALL GUARD CAN'T TOUCH YOUR TITS!

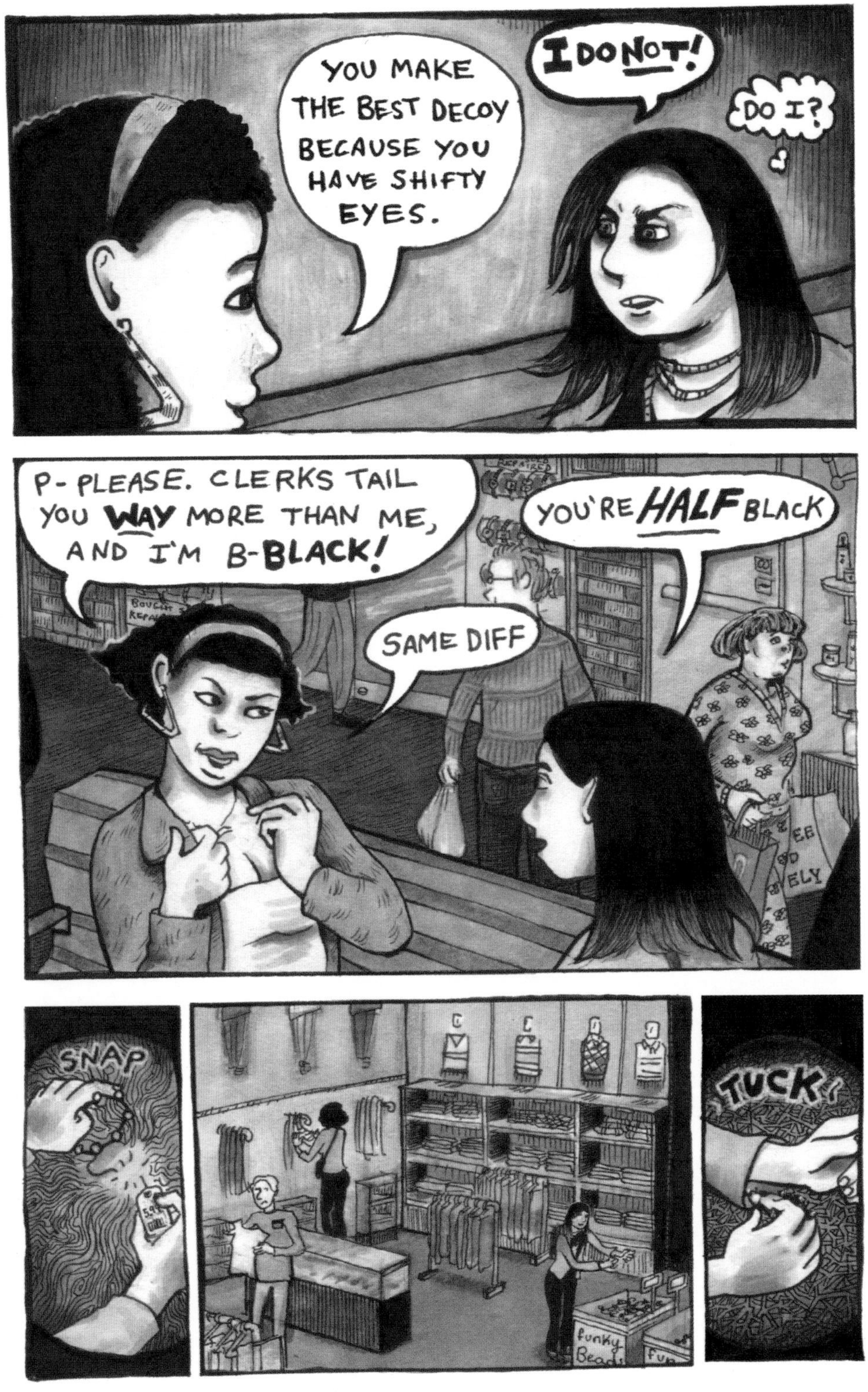
YOU MAKE THE BEST DECOY BECAUSE YOU HAVE SHIFTY EYES.
I DO NOT!
DO I?
P-PLEASE. CLERKS TAIL YOU WAY MORE THAN ME, AND I'M B-BLACK!
YOU'RE HALF BLACK
SAME DIFF
SNAP
Funky Beads
TUCK!

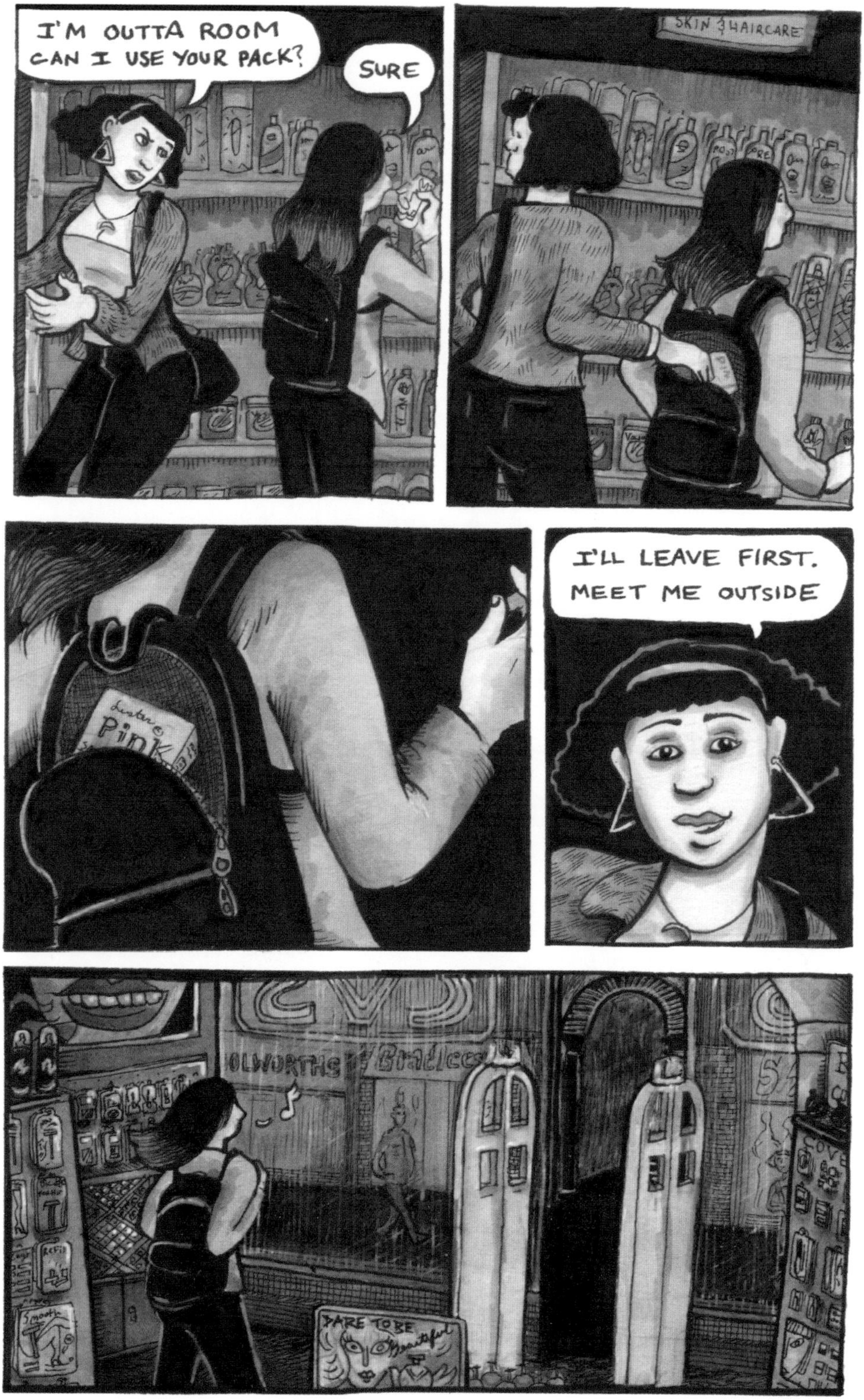
I'M OUTTA ROOM CAN I USE YOUR PACK?
SURE
SKIN & HAIRCARE
Lustre Pink
I'LL LEAVE FIRST. MEET ME OUTSIDE
OLWORTHS
DARE TO BE beautiful

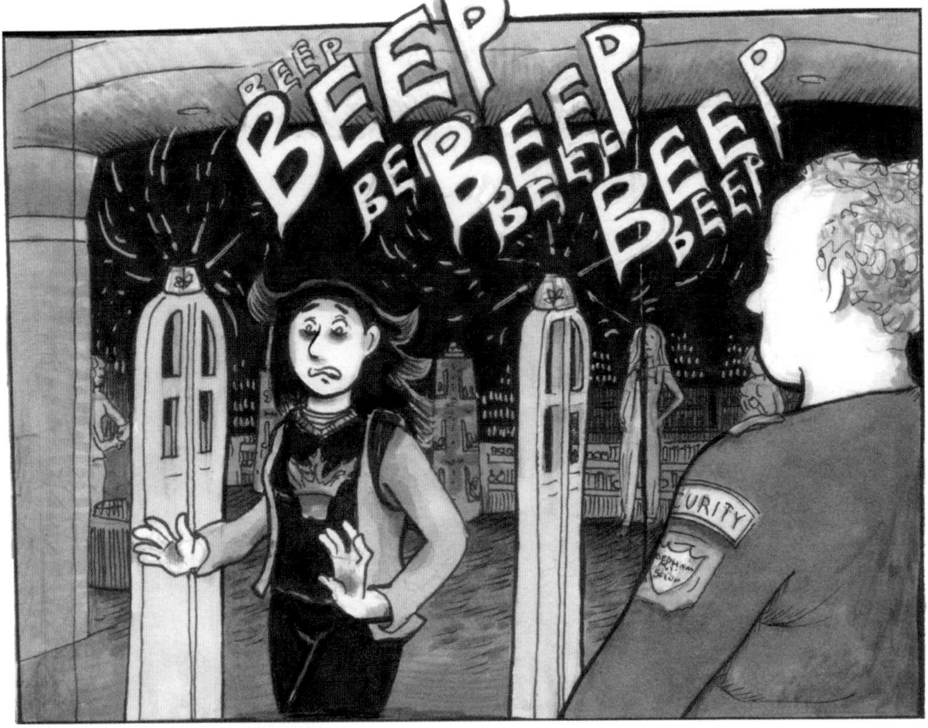
BEEP
BEEP
BEEP
BEEP
BEEP
BEEP
BEEP
BEEP
CURITY

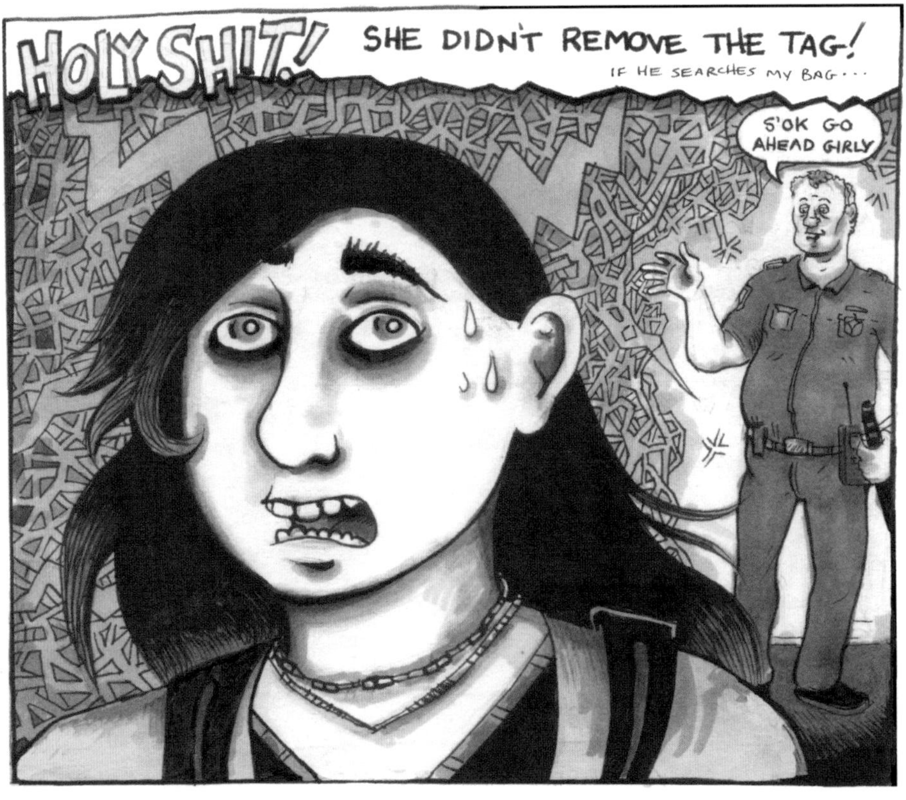
HOLY SHIT!
SHE DIDN'T REMOVE THE TAG!
IF HE SEARCHES MY BAG...
S'OK GO AHEAD GIRLY

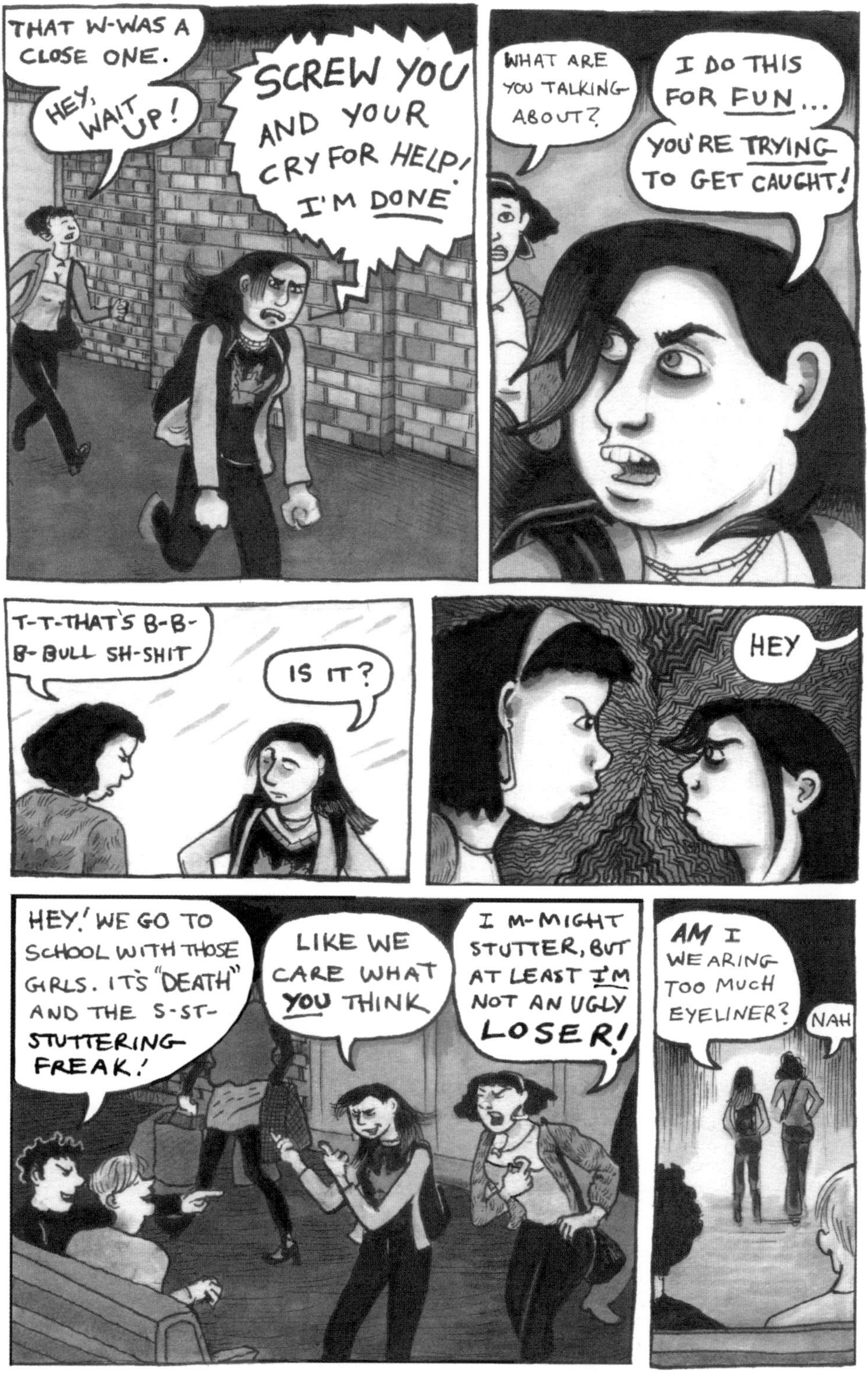
THAT W-WAS A CLOSE ONE.
HEY, WAIT UP!
SCREW YOU AND YOUR CRY FOR HELP! I'M DONE
WHAT ARE YOU TALKING ABOUT?
I DO THIS FOR FUN...
YOU'RE TRYING TO GET CAUGHT!
T-T-THAT'S B-B-B-BULL SH-SHIT
IS IT?
HEY
HEY! WE GO TO SCHOOL WITH THOSE GIRLS. IT'S "DEATH" AND THE S-ST-STUTTERING FREAK!
LIKE WE CARE WHAT YOU THINK
I M-MIGHT STUTTER, BUT AT LEAST I'M NOT AN UGLY LOSER!
AM I WEARING TOO MUCH EYELINER?
NAH

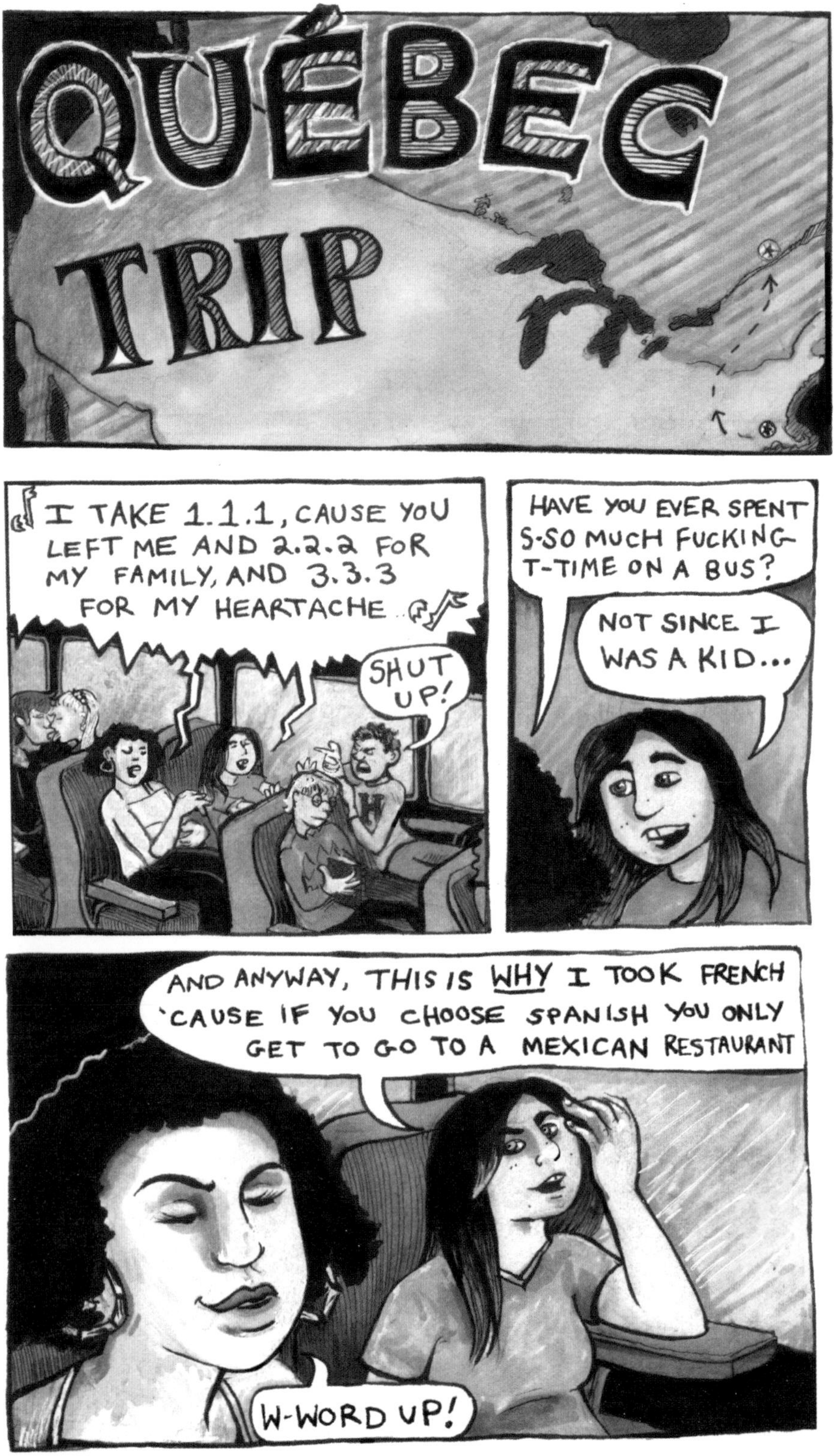
QUÉBEC TRIP
I TAKE 1.1.1, CAUSE YOU LEFT ME AND 2.2.2 FOR MY FAMILY, AND 3.3.3 FOR MY HEARTACHE
SHUT UP!
HAVE YOU EVER SPENT S-SO MUCH FUCKING T-TIME ON A BUS?
NOT SINCE I WAS A KID...
AND ANYWAY, THIS IS WHY I TOOK FRENCH 'CAUSE IF YOU CHOOSE SPANISH YOU ONLY GET TO GO TO A MEXICAN RESTAURANT
W-WORD UP!

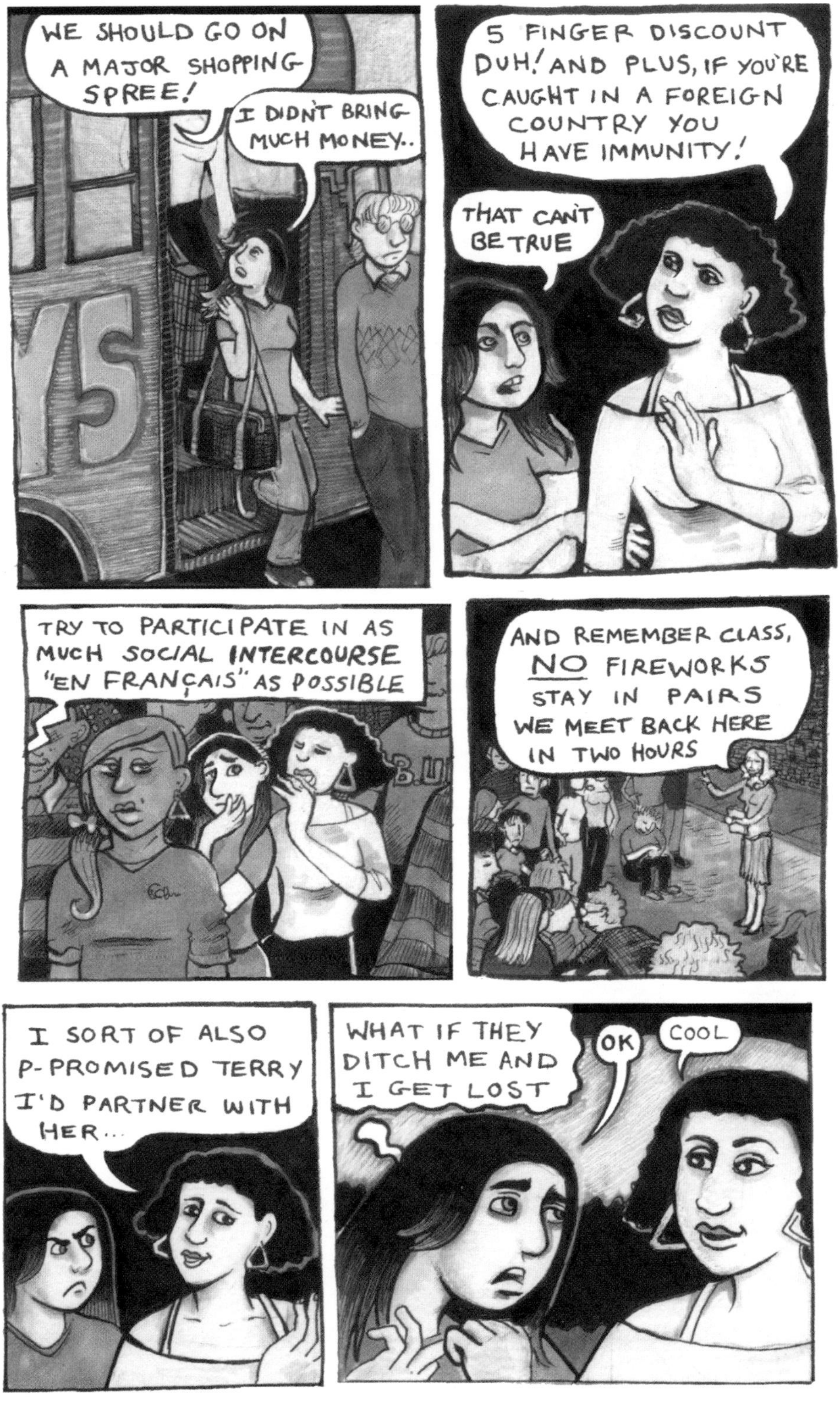
WE SHOULD GO ON A MAJOR SHOPPING SPREE!
I DIDN'T BRING MUCH MONEY..
5 FINGER DISCOUNT DUH! AND PLUS, IF YOU'RE CAUGHT IN A FOREIGN COUNTRY YOU HAVE IMMUNITY!
THAT CAN'T BE TRUE
TRY TO PARTICIPATE IN AS MUCH SOCIAL INTERCOURSE "EN FRANÇAIS" AS POSSIBLE
AND REMEMBER CLASS, NO FIREWORKS STAY IN PAIRS WE MEET BACK HERE IN TWO HOURS
I SORT OF ALSO P-PROMISED TERRY I'D PARTNER WITH HER...
WHAT IF THEY DITCH ME AND I GET LOST
OK
COOL

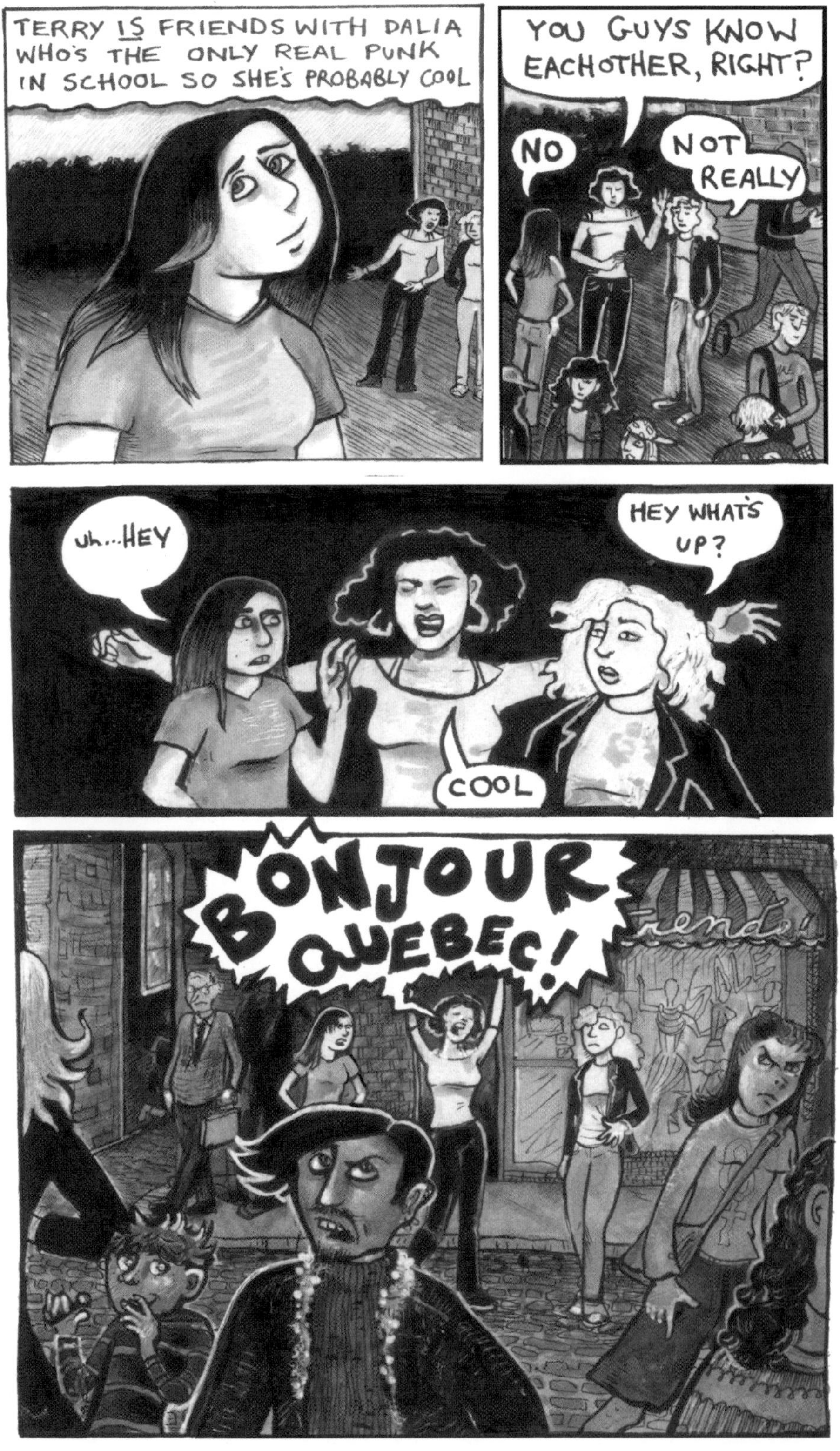
TERRY IS FRIENDS WITH DALIA WHO'S THE ONLY REAL PUNK IN SCHOOL SO SHE'S PROBABLY COOL
YOU GUYS KNOW EACHOTHER, RIGHT?
NO
NOT REALLY
uh...HEY
HEY WHAT'S UP?
COOL
BONJOUR QUEBEC!

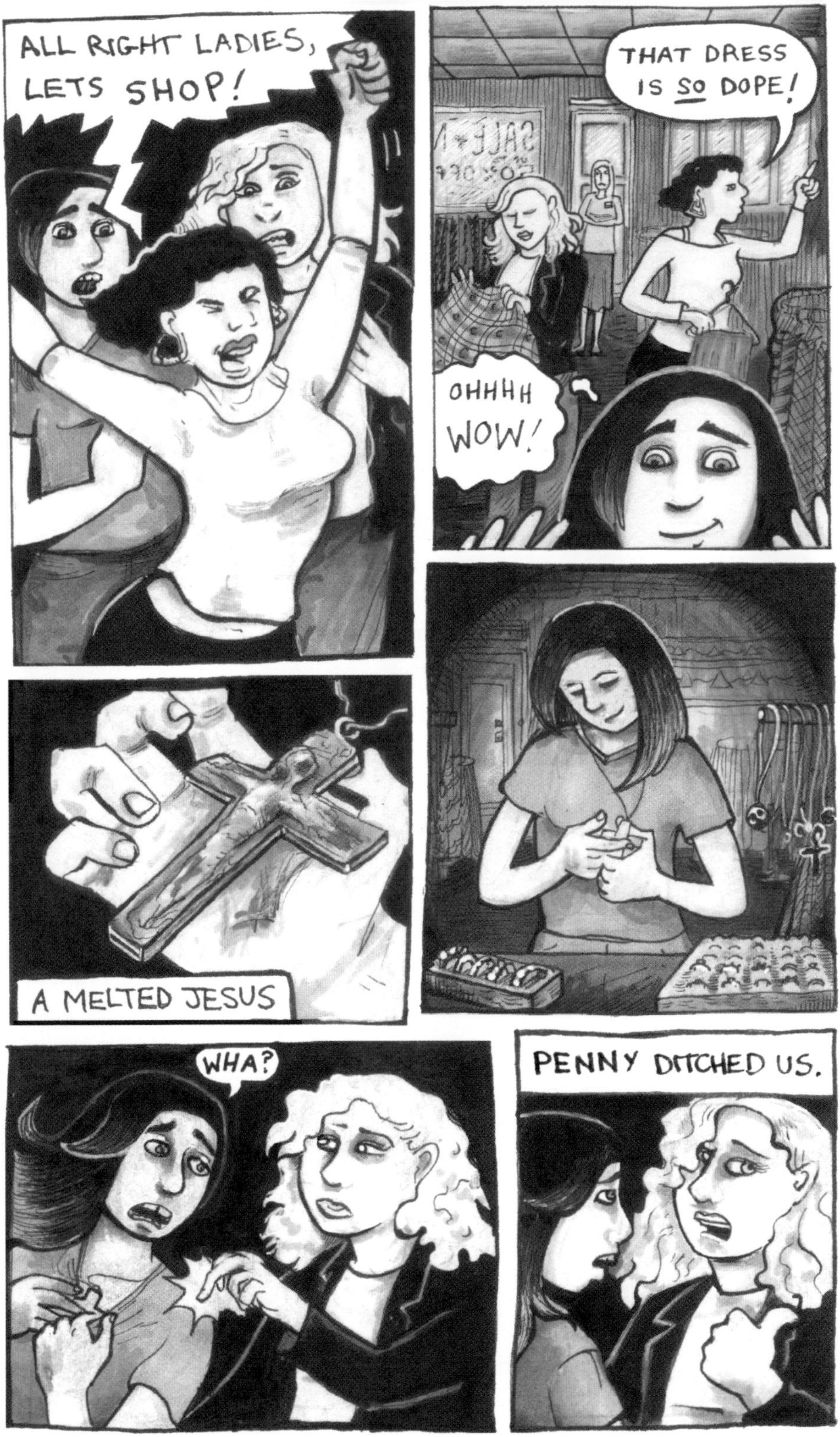
ALL RIGHT LADIES, LETS SHOP!
THAT DRESS IS SO DOPE!
OHHHH WOW!
A MELTED JESUS
WHA?
PENNY DITCHED US.

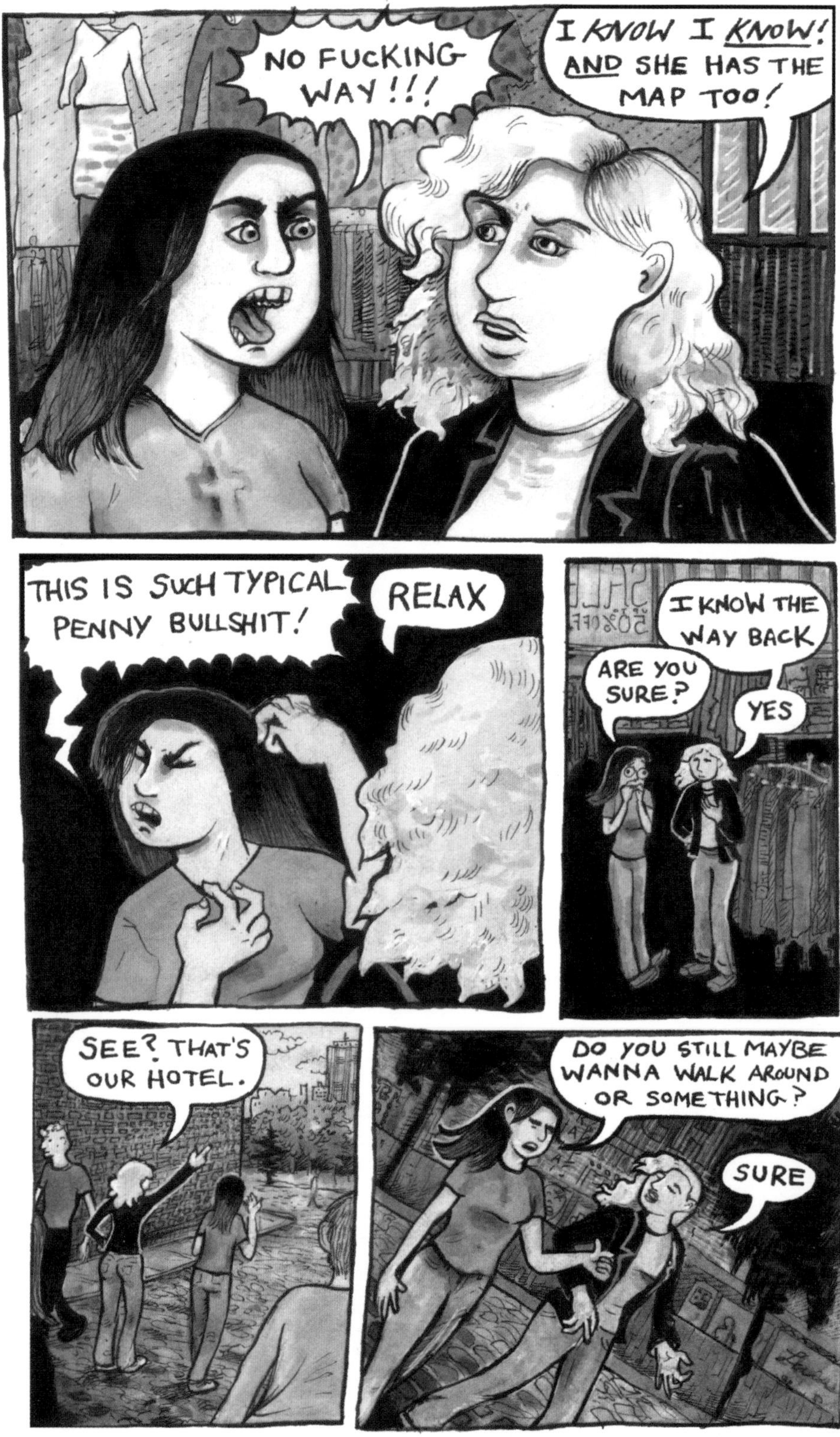
NO FUCKING WAY!!!
I KNOW I KNOW! AND SHE HAS THE MAP TOO!
THIS IS SUCH TYPICAL PENNY BULLSHIT!
RELAX
I KNOW THE WAY BACK
ARE YOU SURE?
YES
SEE? THAT'S OUR HOTEL.
DO YOU STILL MAYBE WANNA WALK AROUND OR SOMETHING?
SURE

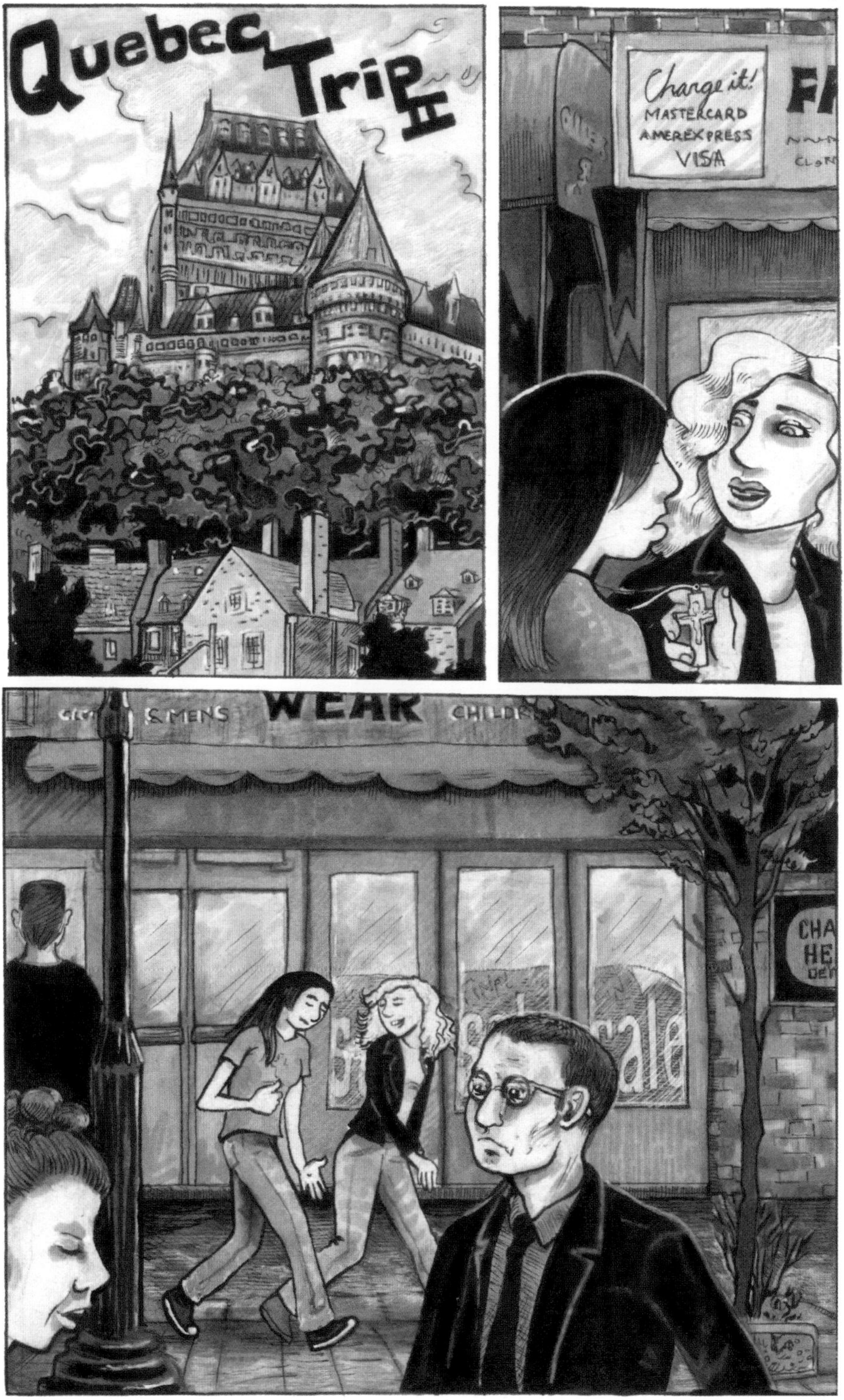
Quebec Trip II
Charge it!
MASTERCARD
AMEREXPRESS
VISA
WEAR

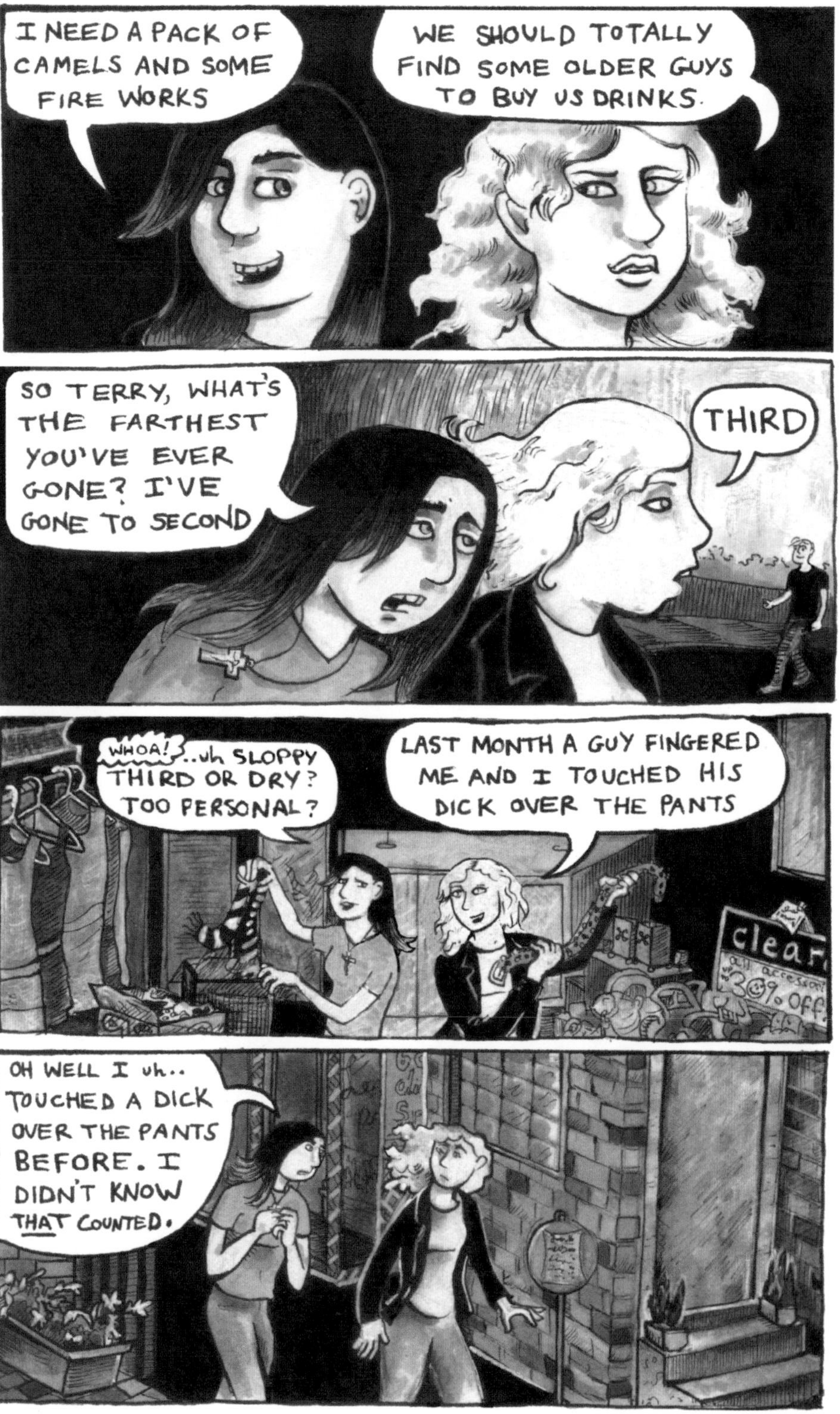
I NEED A PACK OF CAMELS AND SOME FIRE WORKS
WE SHOULD TOTALLY FIND SOME OLDER GUYS TO BUY US DRINKS.
SO TERRY, WHAT'S THE FARTHEST YOU'VE EVER GONE? I'VE GONE TO SECOND
THIRD
WHOA! ..uh SLOPPY THIRD OR DRY? TOO PERSONAL?
LAST MONTH A GUY FINGERED ME AND I TOUCHED HIS DICK OVER THE PANTS
clear
all accessory 30% off
OH WELL I uh.. TOUCHED A DICK OVER THE PANTS BEFORE. I DIDN'T KNOW THAT COUNTED.

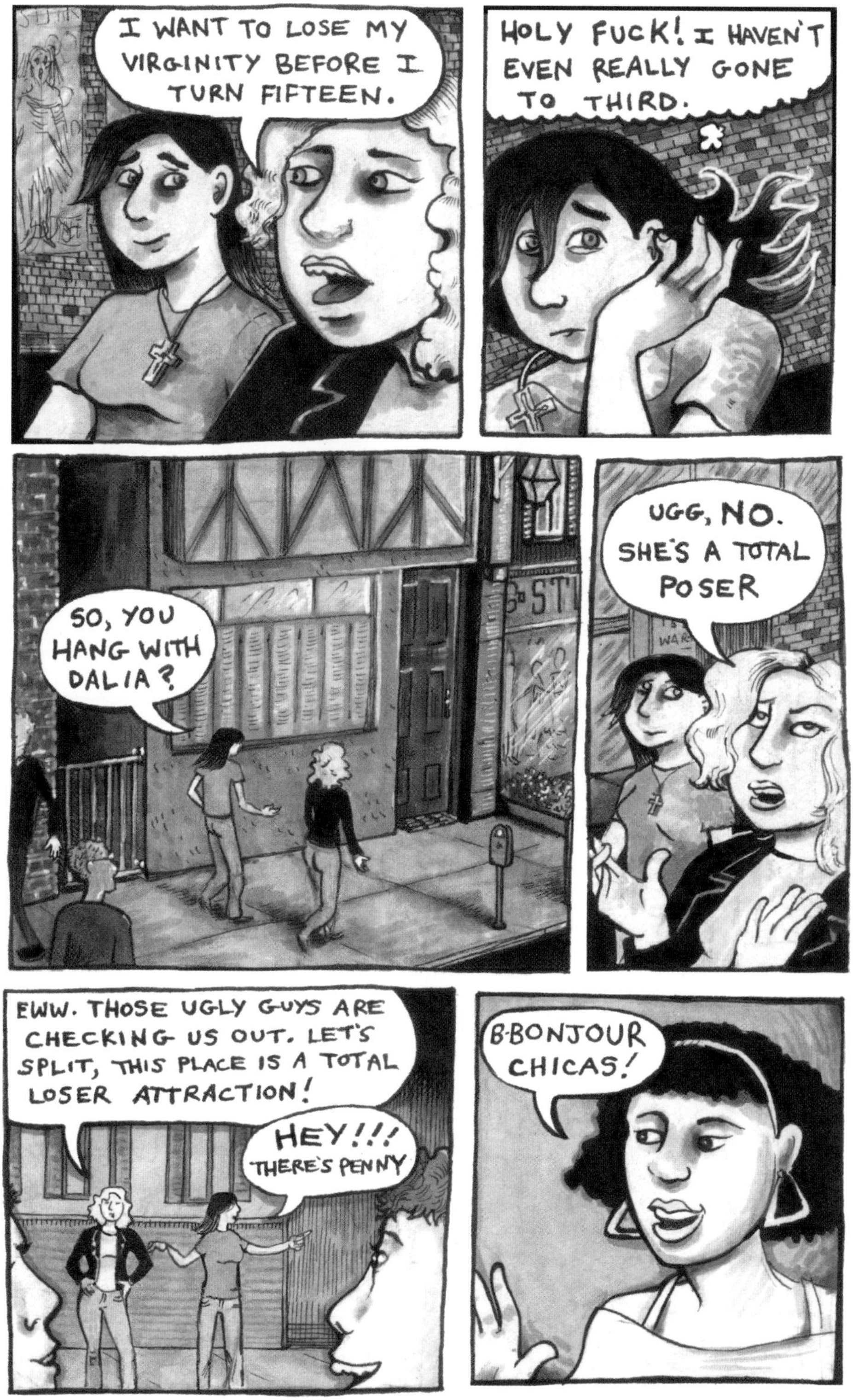
I WANT TO LOSE MY VIRGINITY BEFORE I TURN FIFTEEN.
HOLY FUCK! I HAVEN'T EVEN REALLY GONE TO THIRD.
SO, YOU HANG WITH DALIA?
UGG, NO. SHE'S A TOTAL POSER
EWW. THOSE UGLY GUYS ARE CHECKING US OUT. LET'S SPLIT, THIS PLACE IS A TOTAL LOSER ATTRACTION!
HEY!!! THERE'S PENNY
B-BONJOUR CHICAS!

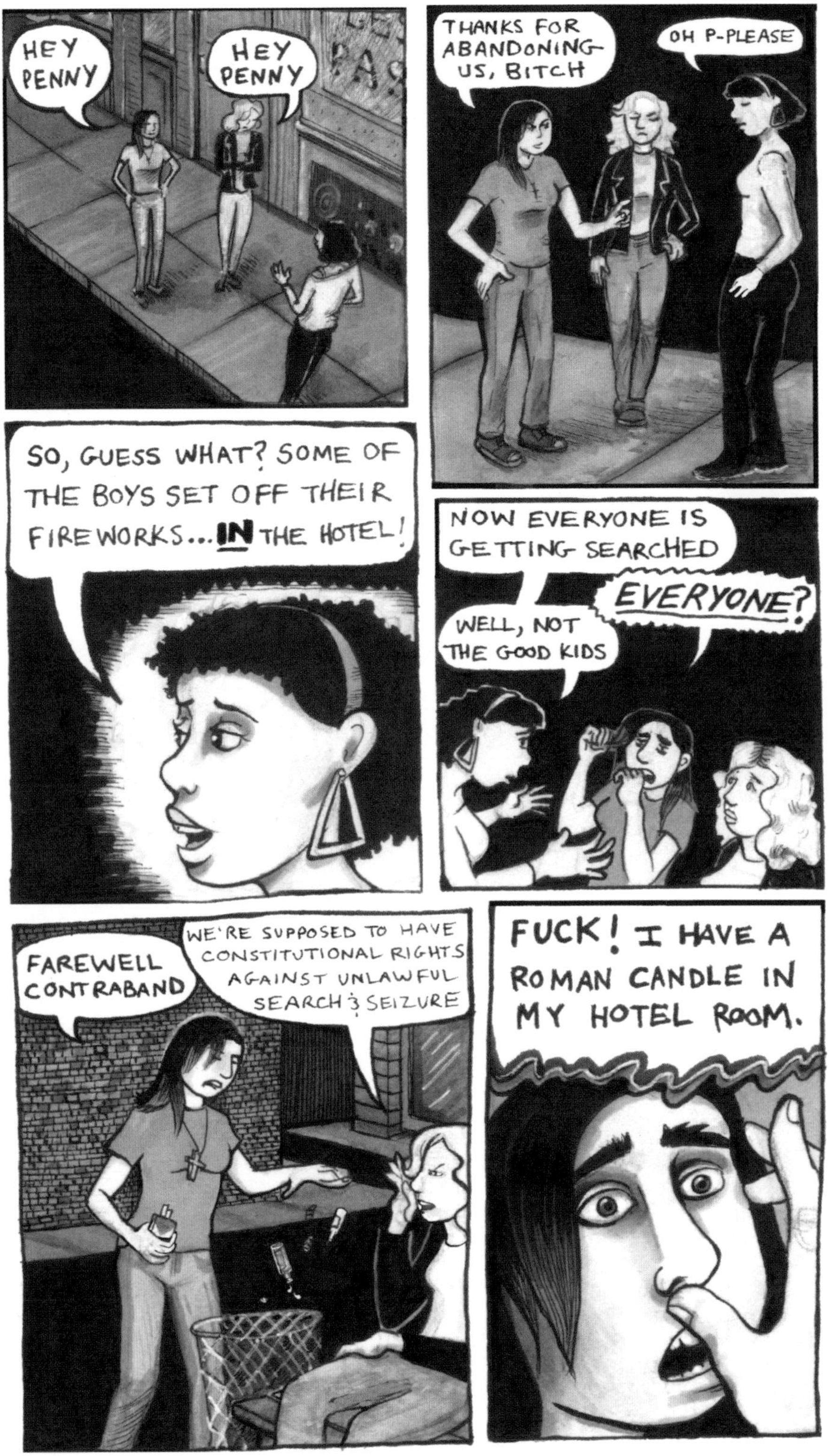
HEY PENNY
HEY PENNY
THANKS FOR ABANDONING US, BITCH
OH P-PLEASE
SO, GUESS WHAT? SOME OF THE BOYS SET OFF THEIR FIREWORKS... IN THE HOTEL!
NOW EVERYONE IS GETTING SEARCHED
EVERYONE?
WELL, NOT THE GOOD KIDS
FAREWELL CONTRABAND
WE'RE SUPPOSED TO HAVE CONSTITUTIONAL RIGHTS AGAINST UNLAWFUL SEARCH & SEIZURE
FUCK! I HAVE A ROMAN CANDLE IN MY HOTEL ROOM.

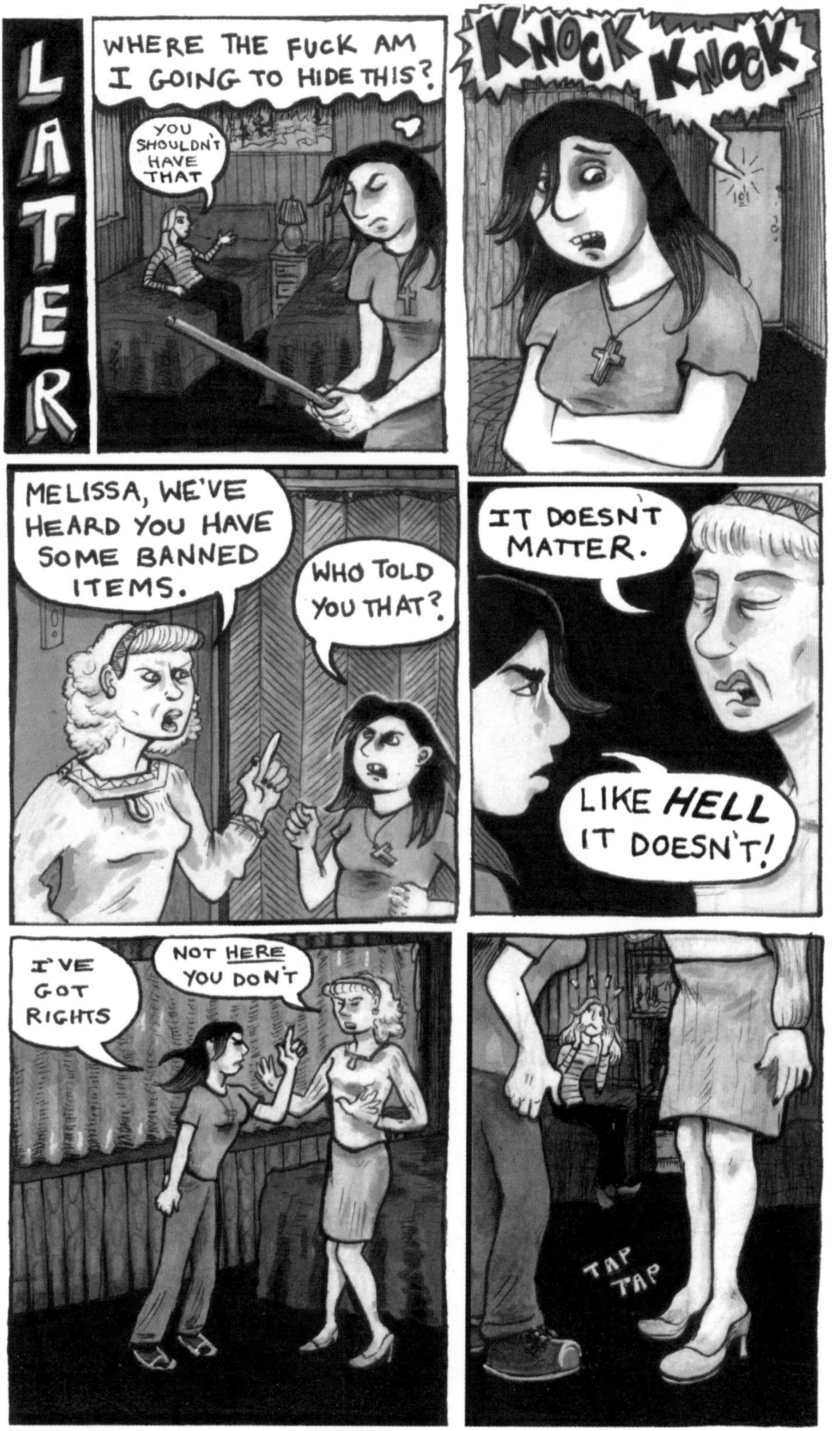
LATER
WHERE THE FUCK AM I GOING TO HIDE THIS?
YOU SHOULDN'T HAVE THAT
KNOCK KNOCK
MELISSA, WE'VE HEARD YOU HAVE SOME BANNED ITEMS.
WHO TOLD YOU THAT?
IT DOESN'T MATTER.
LIKE HELL IT DOESN'T!
I'VE GOT RIGHTS
NOT HERE YOU DON'T
TAP TAP

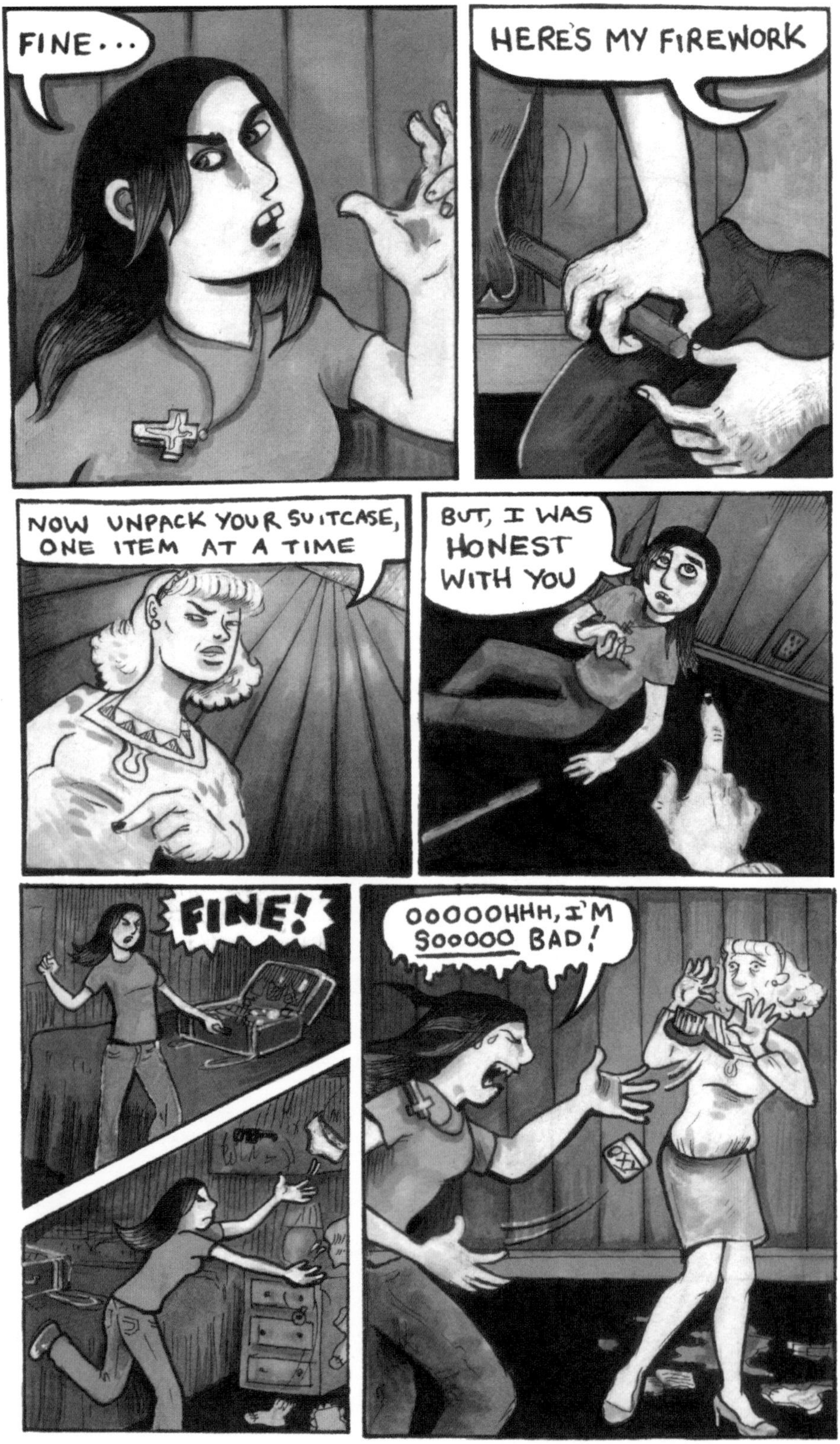
FINE...
HERE'S MY FIREWORK
NOW UNPACK YOUR SUITCASE, ONE ITEM AT A TIME
BUT, I WAS HONEST WITH YOU
FINE!
OOOOOHHH, I'M SOOOOO BAD!

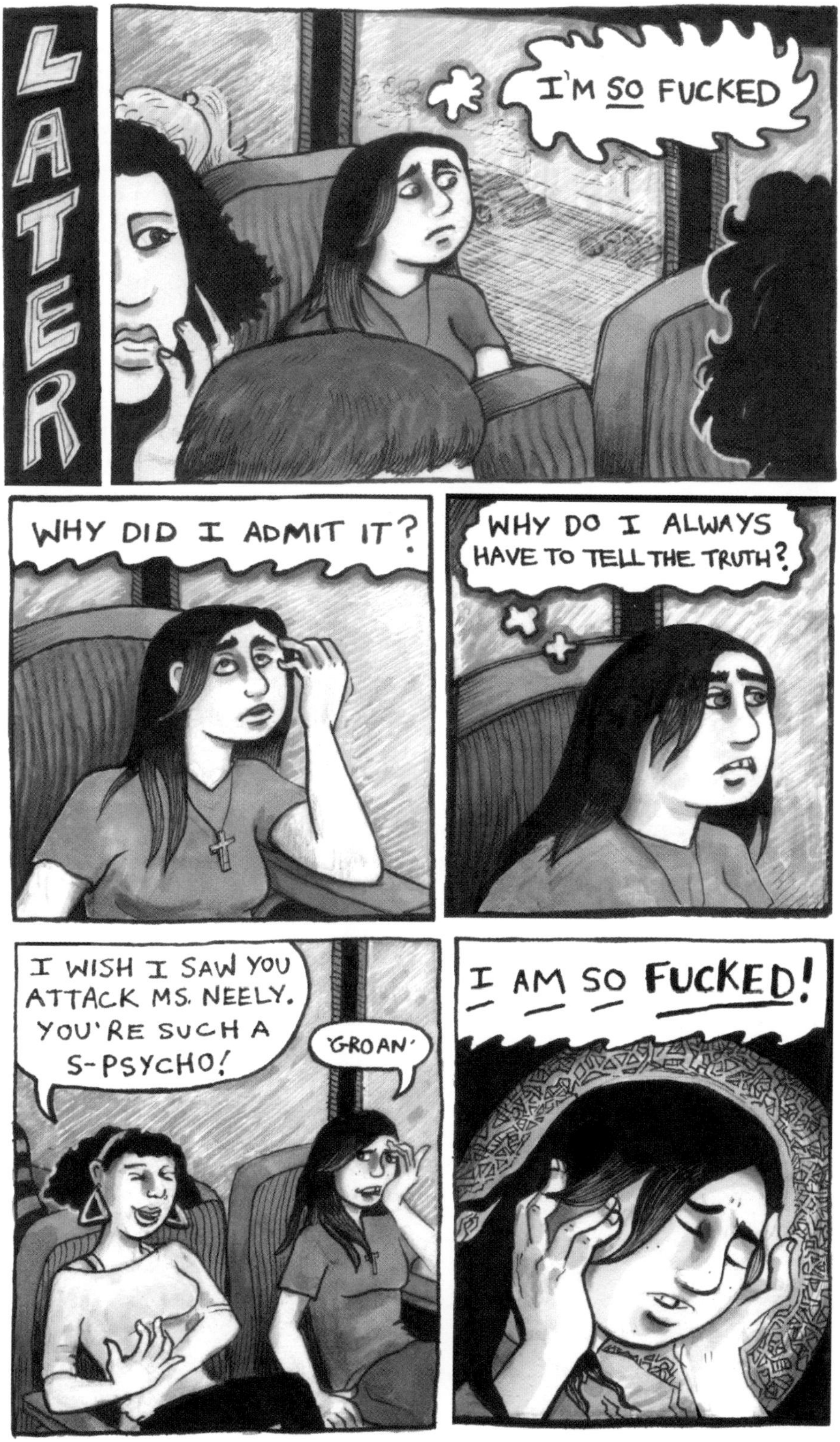
LATER
I'M SO FUCKED
WHY DID I ADMIT IT?
WHY DO I ALWAYS HAVE TO TELL THE TRUTH?
I WISH I SAW YOU ATTACK MS. NEELY. YOU'RE SUCH A S-PSYCHO!
'GROAN'
I AM SO FUCKED!

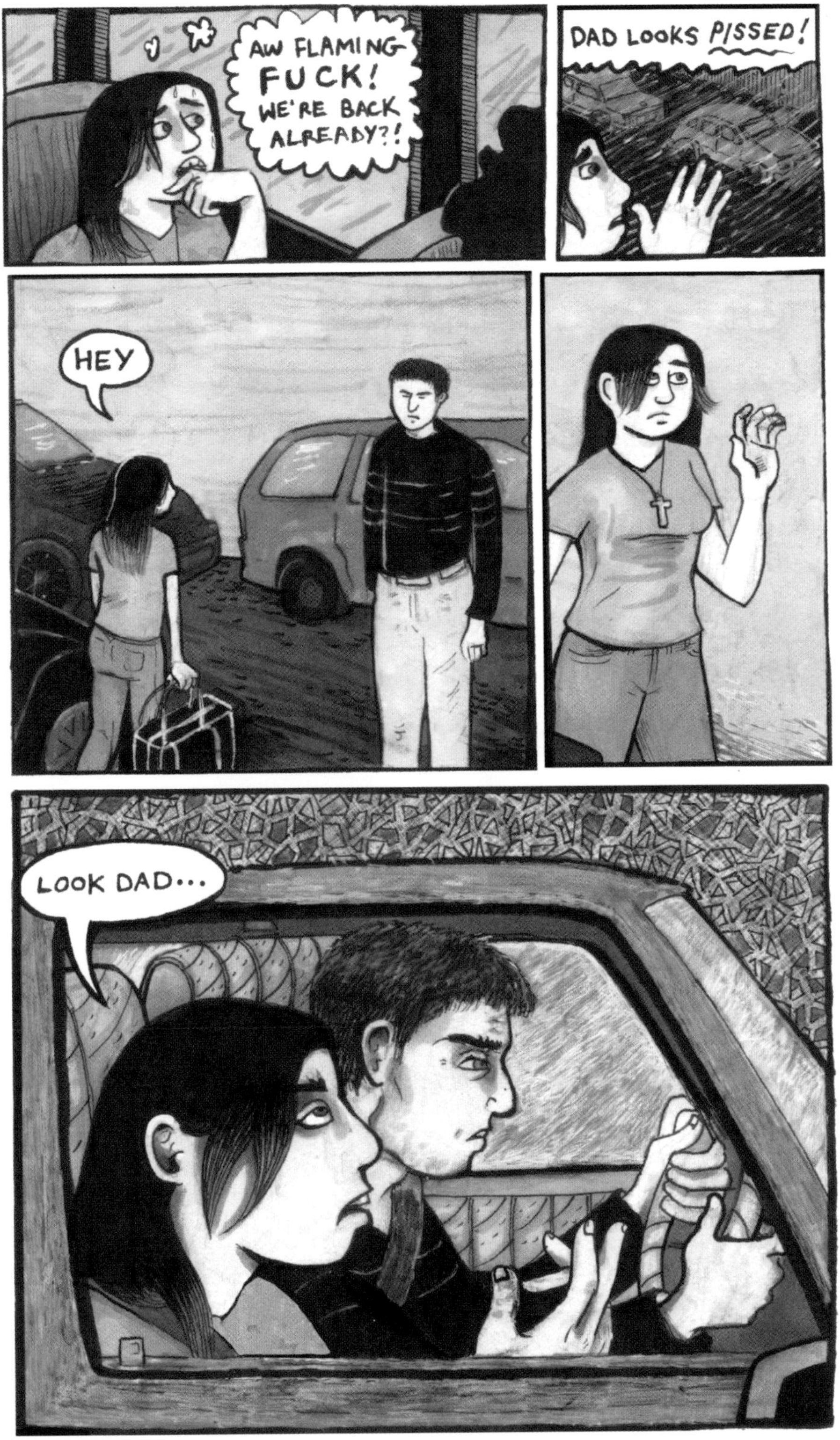
AW FLAMING FUCK! WE'RE BACK ALREADY?!
DAD LOOKS PISSED!
HEY
LOOK DAD...

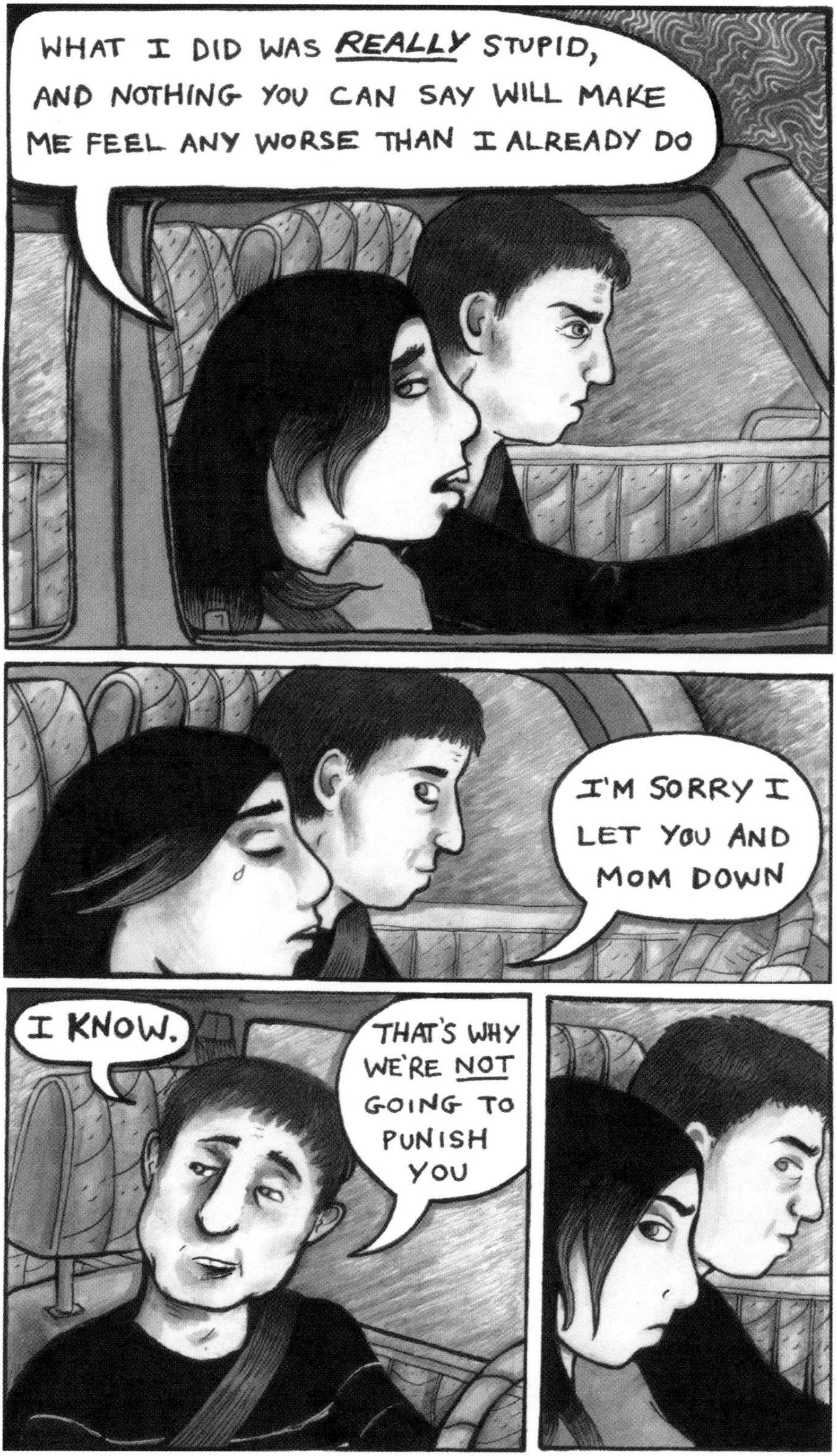
WHAT I DID WAS REALLY STUPID, AND NOTHING YOU CAN SAY WILL MAKE ME FEEL ANY WORSE THAN I ALREADY DO
I'M SORRY I LET YOU AND MOM DOWN
I KNOW.
THAT'S WHY WE'RE NOT GOING TO PUNISH YOU

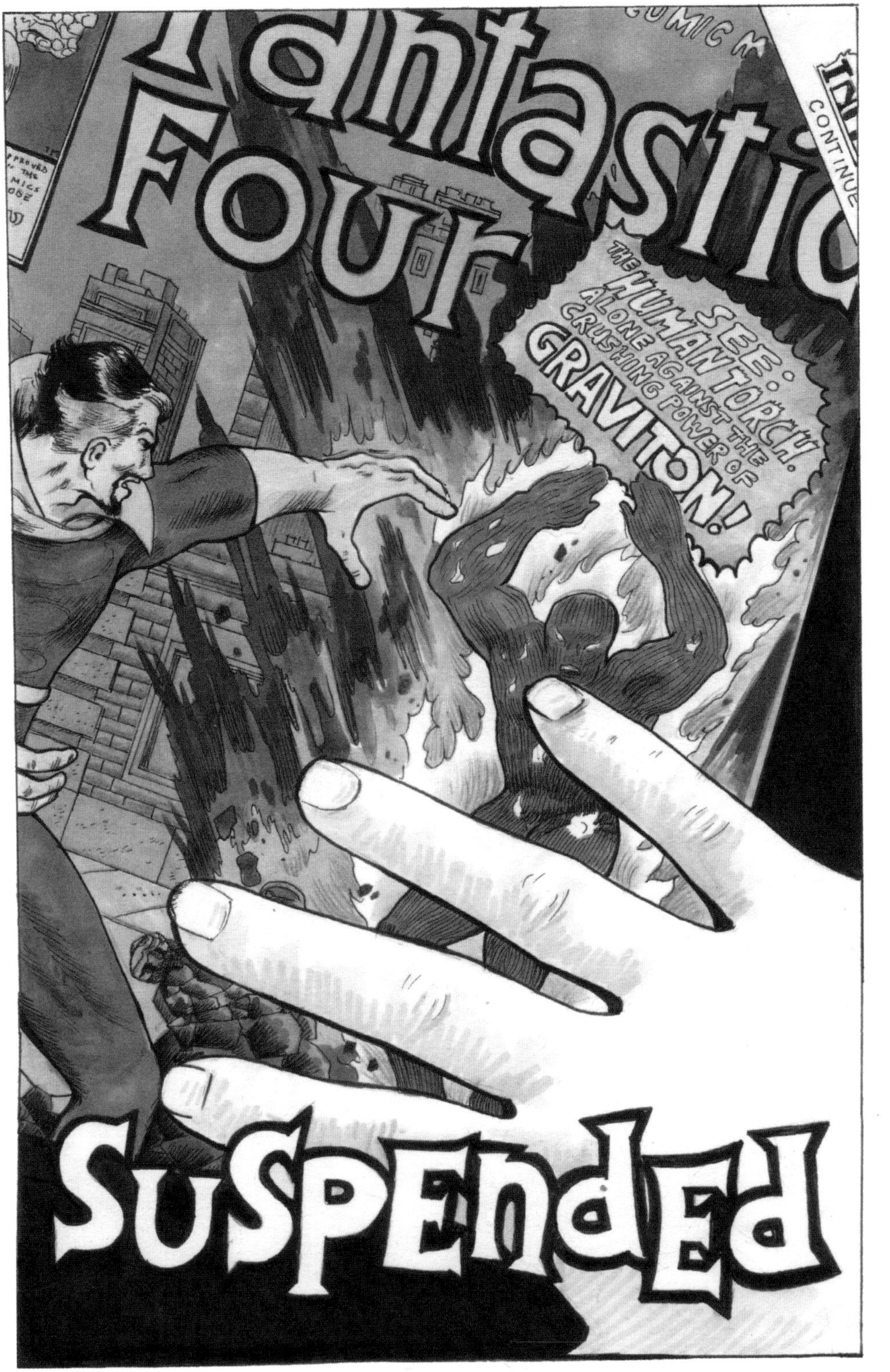
Four
SEE: THE HUMAN TORCH! ALONE AGAINST THE CRUSHING POWER OF GRAVITON!
CONTINUE
SUSPENDED

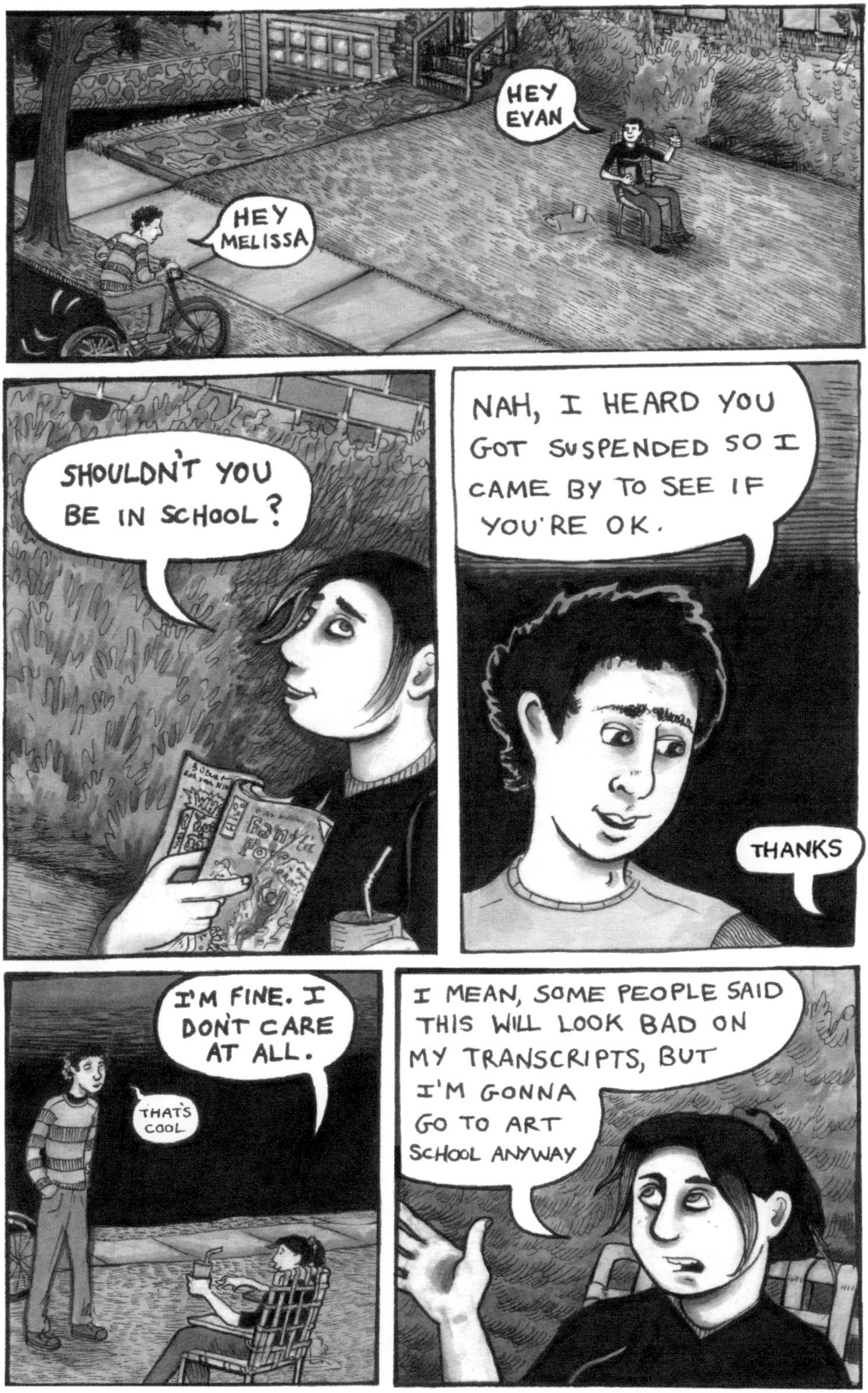
HEY EVAN
HEY MELISSA
SHOULDN'T YOU BE IN SCHOOL?
NAH, I HEARD YOU GOT SUSPENDED SO I CAME BY TO SEE IF YOU'RE OK.
THANKS
I'M FINE. I DON'T CARE AT ALL.
THAT'S COOL
I MEAN, SOME PEOPLE SAID THIS WILL LOOK BAD ON MY TRANSCRIPTS, BUT I'M GONNA GO TO ART SCHOOL ANYWAY

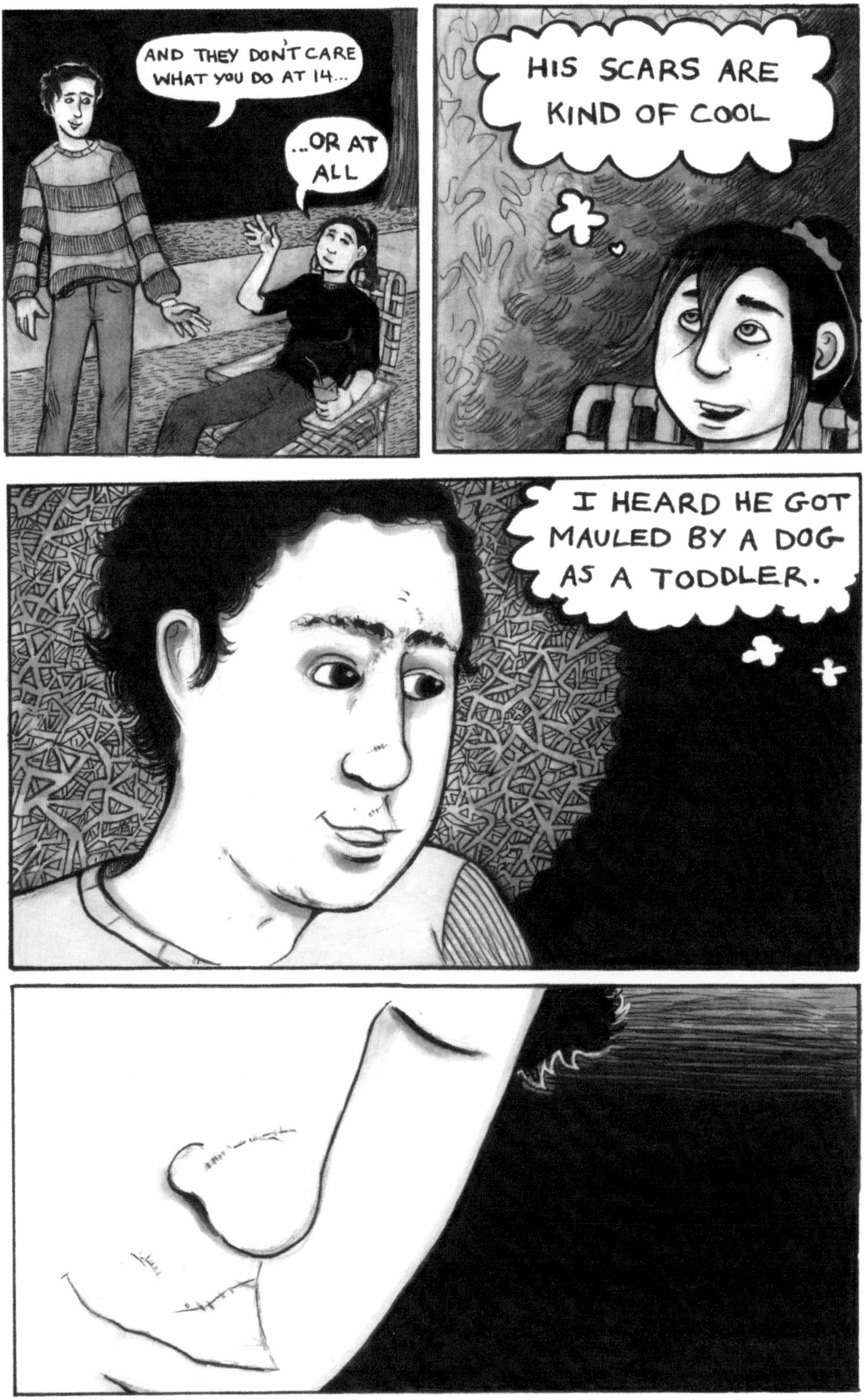
AND THEY DON'T CARE WHAT YOU DO AT 14...
...OR AT ALL
HIS SCARS ARE KIND OF COOL
I HEARD HE GOT MAULED BY A DOG AS A TODDLER.

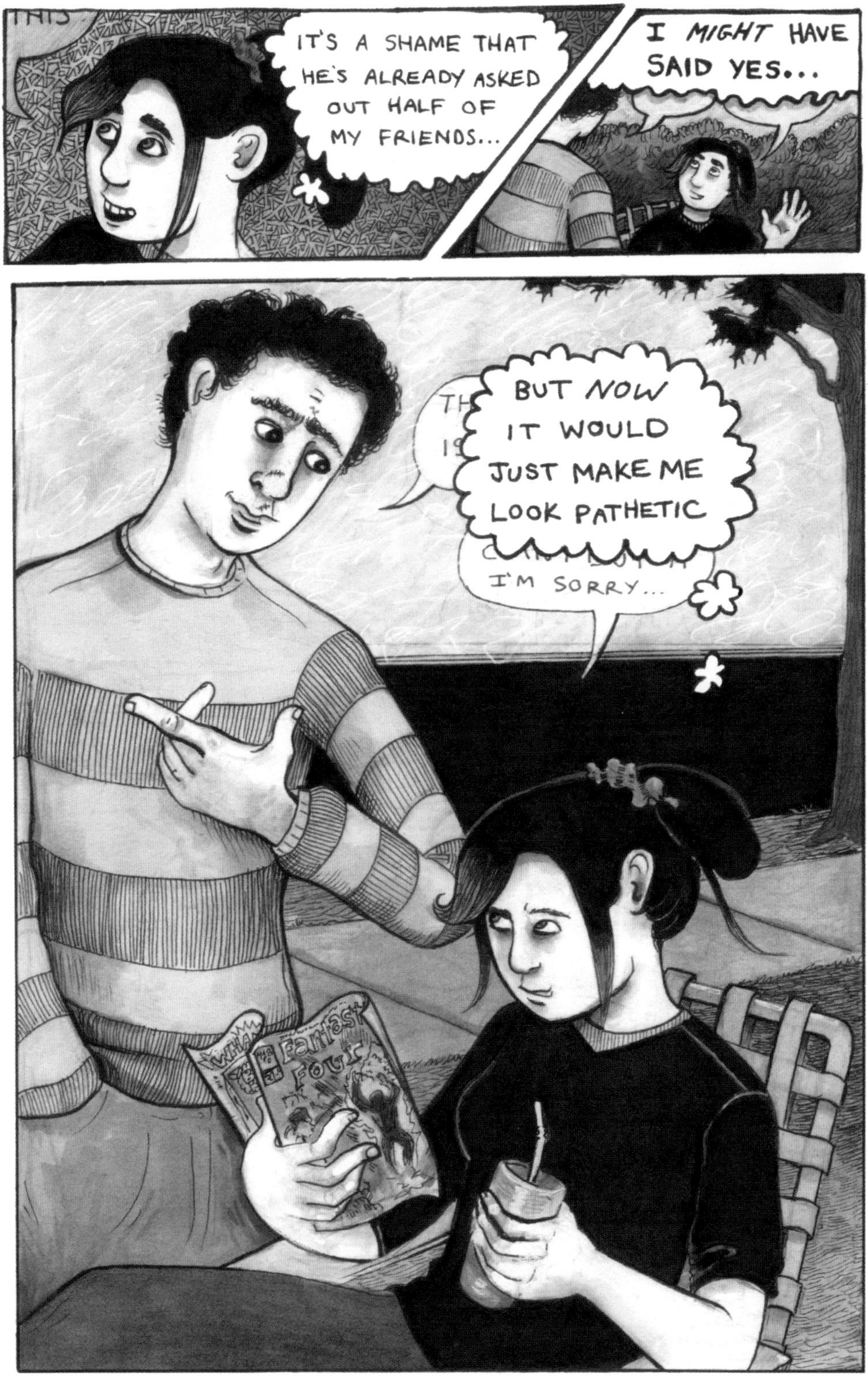
IT'S A SHAME THAT HE'S ALREADY ASKED OUT HALF OF MY FRIENDS...
I *MIGHT* HAVE SAID YES...
BUT *NOW* IT WOULD JUST MAKE ME LOOK PATHETIC
I'M SORRY...

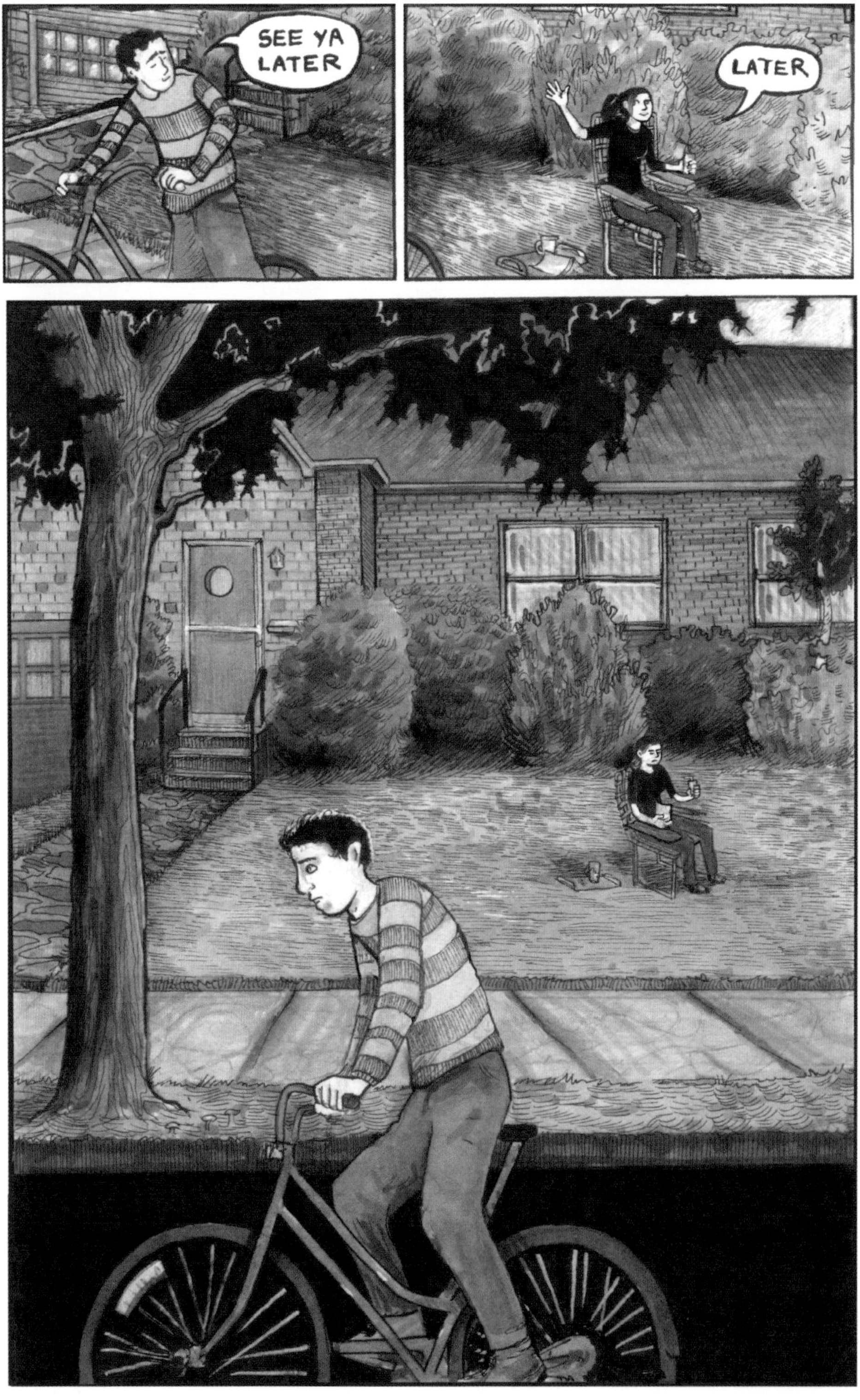
SEE YA LATER
LATER

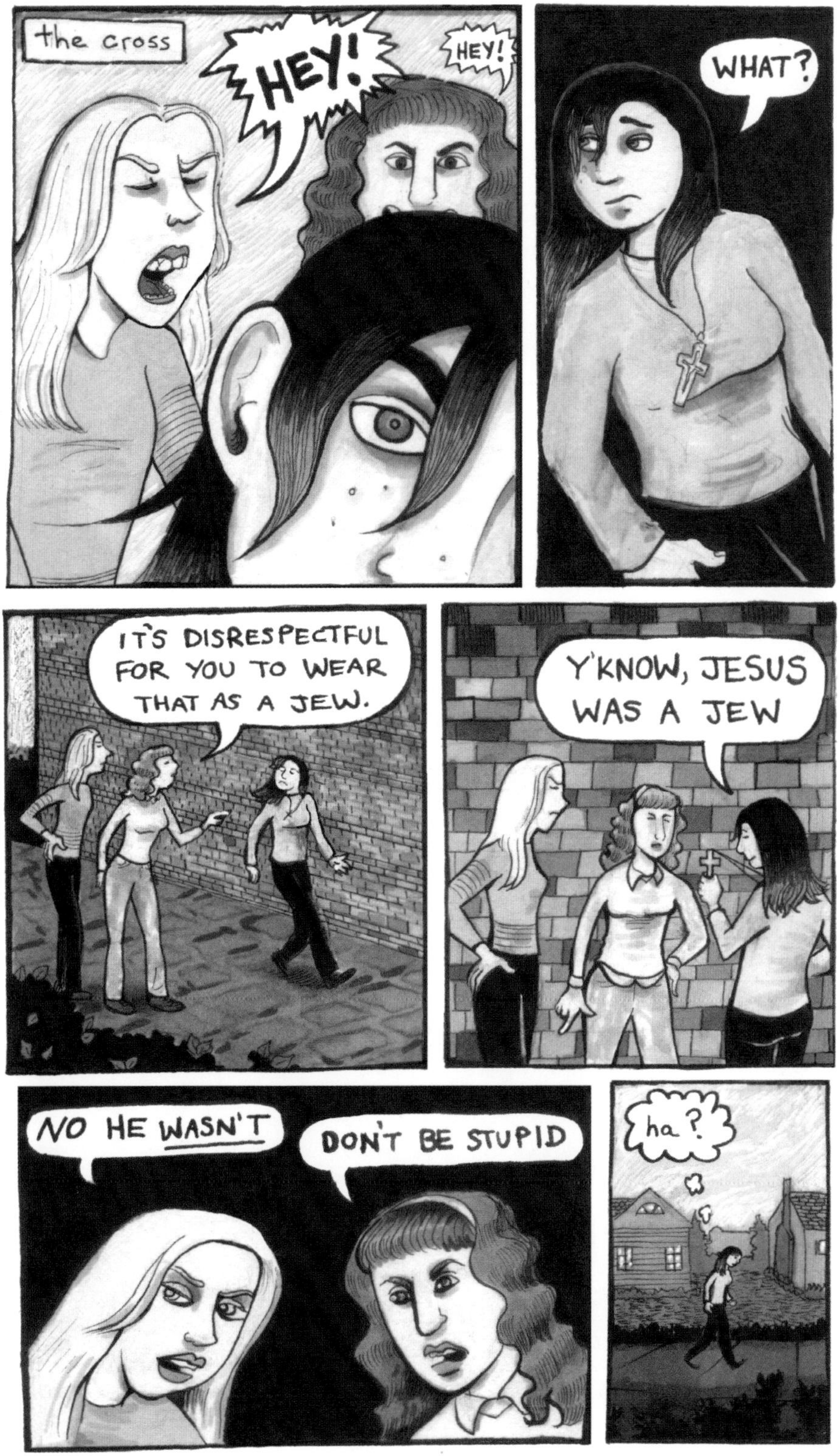
the cross
HEY!
HEY!
WHAT?
IT'S DISRESPECTFUL FOR YOU TO WEAR THAT AS A JEW.
Y'KNOW, JESUS WAS A JEW
NO HE WASN'T
DON'T BE STUPID
ha?

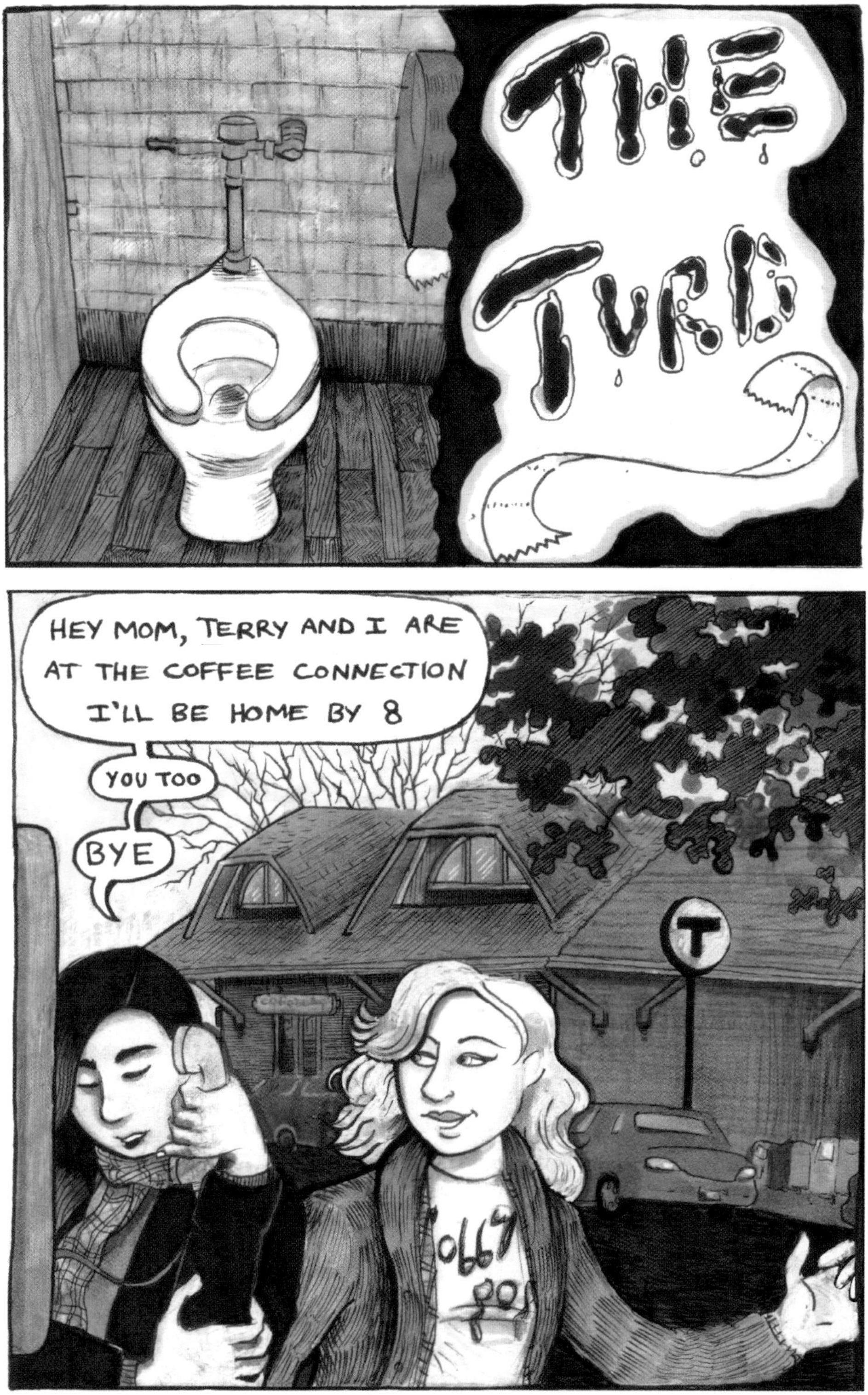
THE TURD
HEY MOM, TERRY AND I ARE AT THE COFFEE CONNECTION I'LL BE HOME BY 8
YOU TOO
BYE

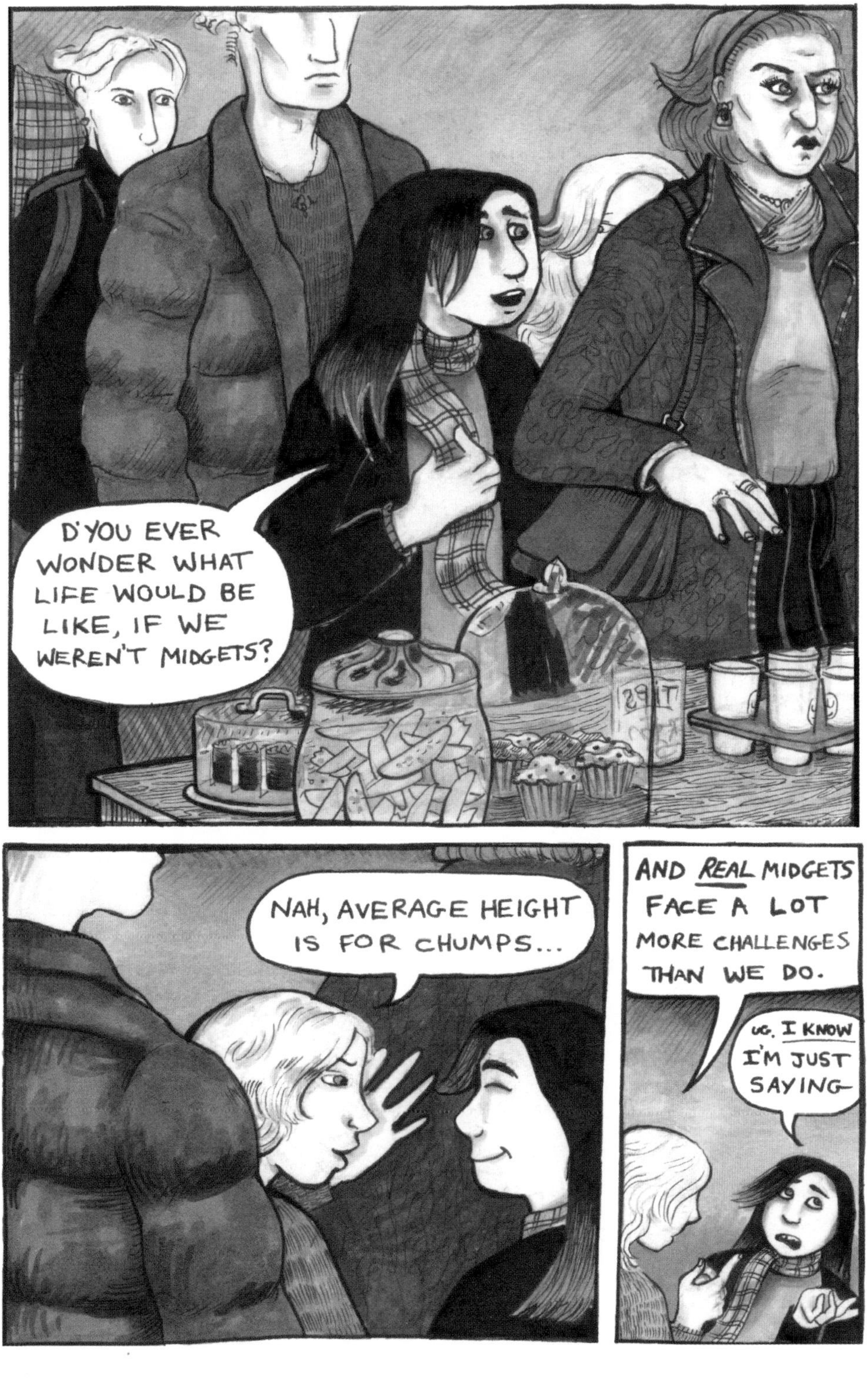
D'YOU EVER WONDER WHAT LIFE WOULD BE LIKE, IF WE WEREN'T MIDGETS?
TIPS
NAH, AVERAGE HEIGHT IS FOR CHUMPS...
AND REAL MIDGETS FACE A LOT MORE CHALLENGES THAN WE DO.
UG. I KNOW I'M JUST SAYING—

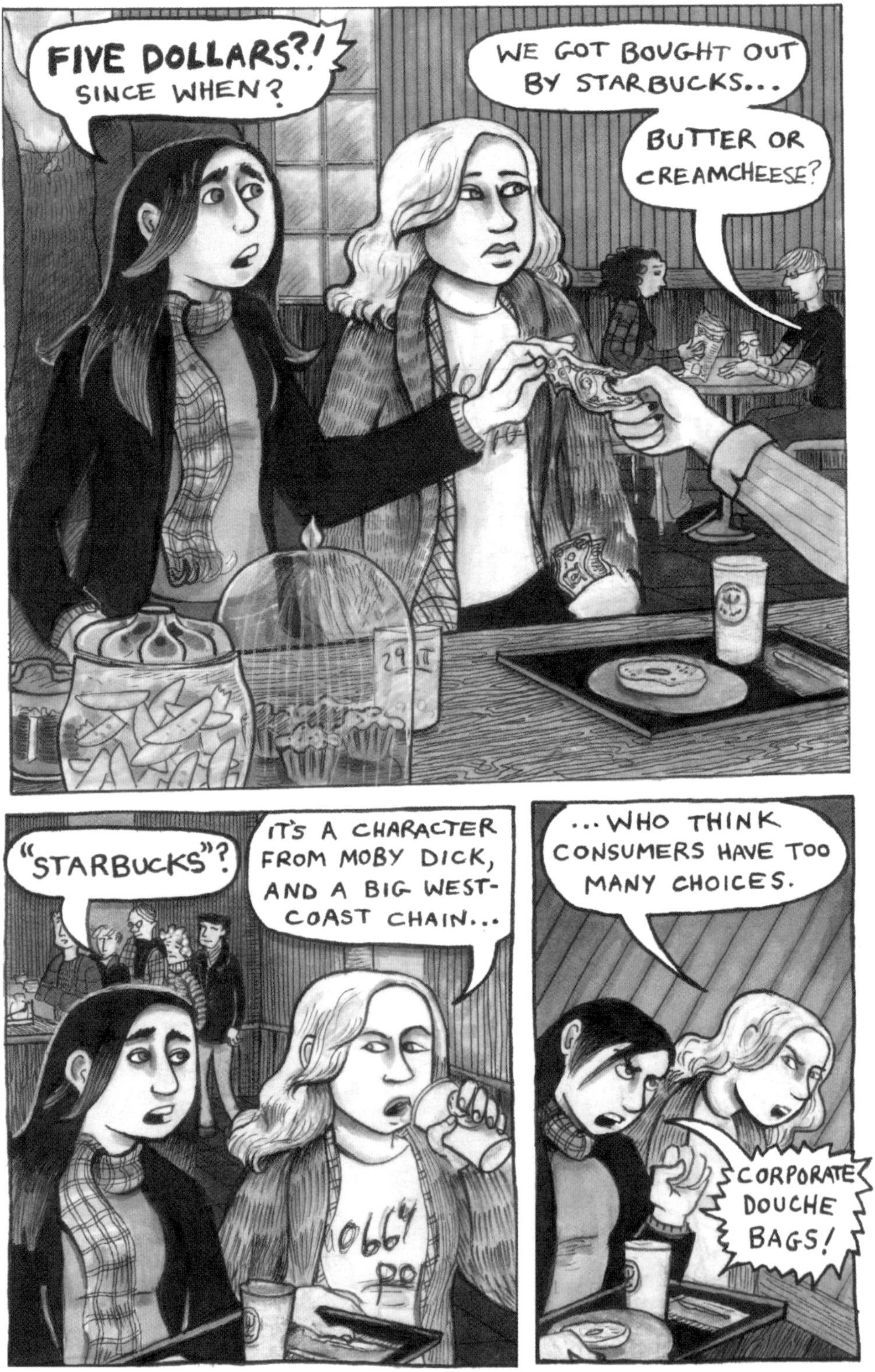
FIVE DOLLARS?! SINCE WHEN?
WE GOT BOUGHT OUT BY STARBUCKS...
BUTTER OR CREAMCHEESE?
"STARBUCKS"?
IT'S A CHARACTER FROM MOBY DICK, AND A BIG WEST-COAST CHAIN...
...WHO THINK CONSUMERS HAVE TOO MANY CHOICES.
CORPORATE DOUCHE BAGS!

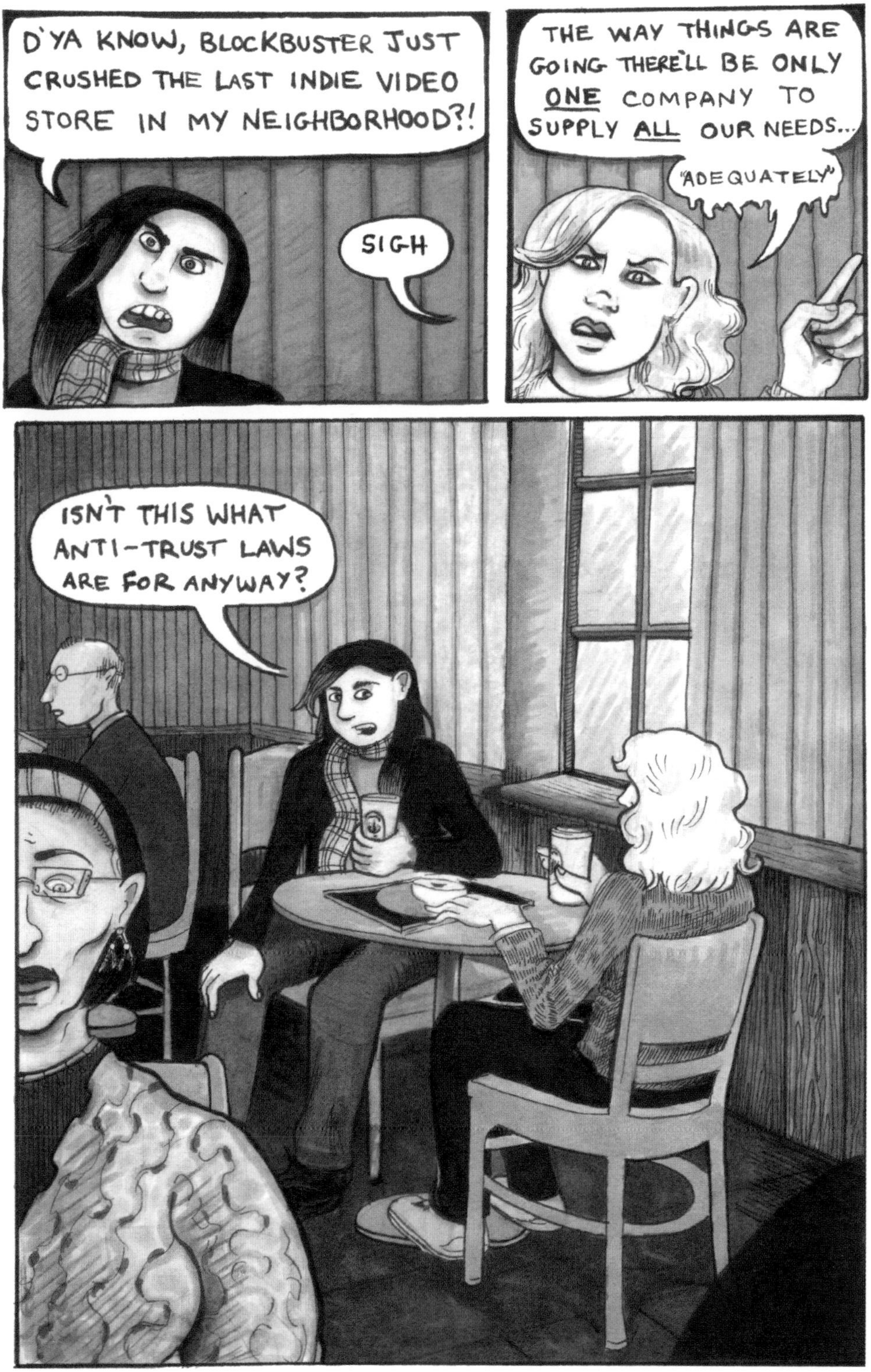
D'YA KNOW, BLOCKBUSTER JUST CRUSHED THE LAST INDIE VIDEO STORE IN MY NEIGHBORHOOD?!
SIGH
THE WAY THINGS ARE GOING THERE'LL BE ONLY ONE COMPANY TO SUPPLY ALL OUR NEEDS...
"ADEQUATELY"
ISN'T THIS WHAT ANTI-TRUST LAWS ARE FOR ANYWAY?

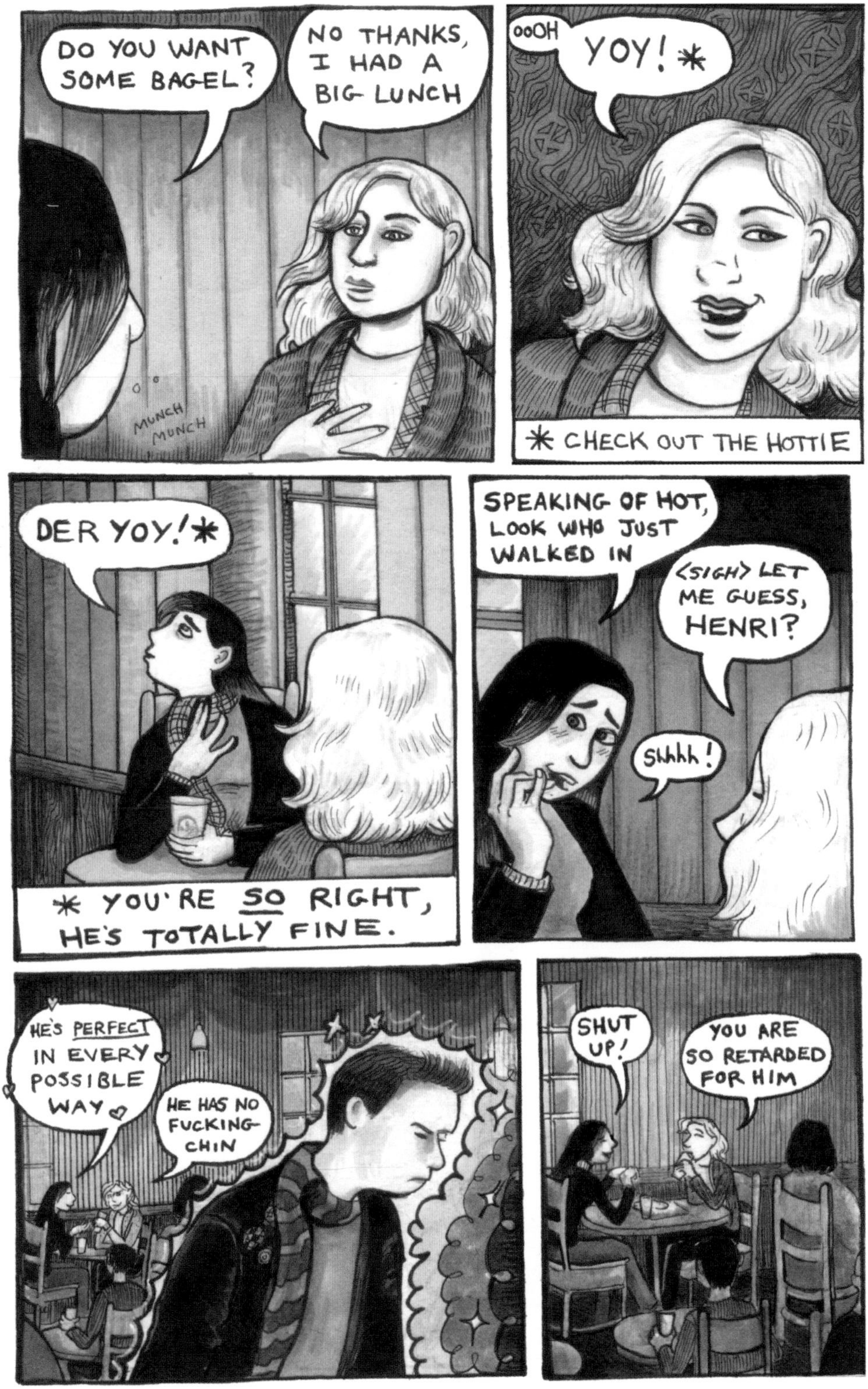
DO YOU WANT SOME BAGEL?
NO THANKS, I HAD A BIG LUNCH
MUNCH MUNCH
OOOH
YOY! *
* CHECK OUT THE HOTTIE
DER YOY! *
* YOU'RE SO RIGHT, HE'S TOTALLY FINE.
SPEAKING OF HOT, LOOK WHO JUST WALKED IN
<SIGH> LET ME GUESS, HENRI?
Shhhh!
HE'S PERFECT IN EVERY POSSIBLE WAY
HE HAS NO FUCKING CHIN
SHUT UP!
YOU ARE SO RETARDED FOR HIM

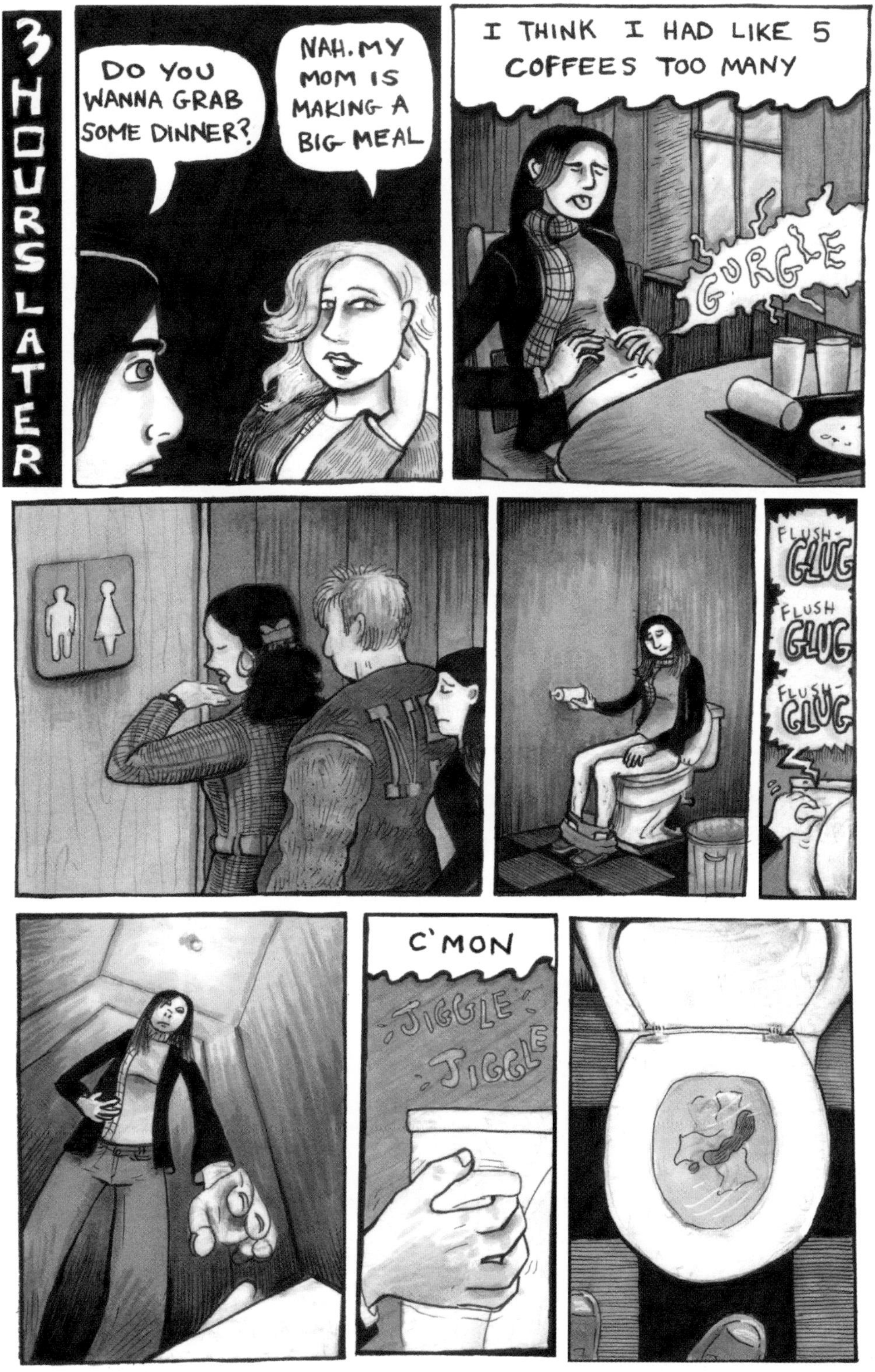
3 HOURS LATER
DO YOU WANNA GRAB SOME DINNER?
NAH. MY MOM IS MAKING A BIG MEAL
I THINK I HAD LIKE 5 COFFEES TOO MANY
GURGLE
FLUSH-GLUG
FLUSH GLUG
FLUSH-GLUG
C'MON
JIGGLE
JIGGLE

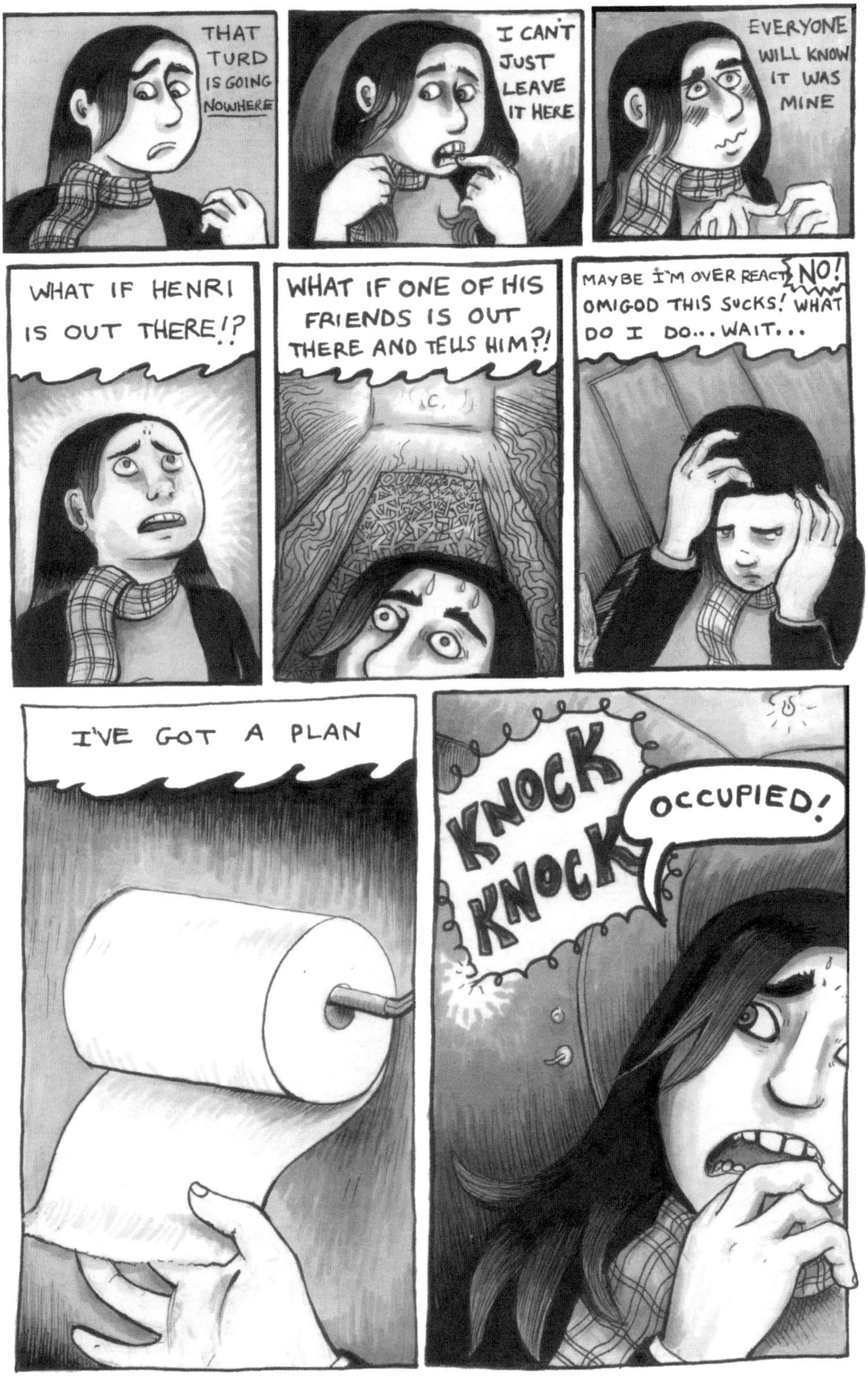
THAT TURD IS GOING NOWHERE
I CAN'T JUST LEAVE IT HERE
EVERYONE WILL KNOW IT WAS MINE
WHAT IF HENRI IS OUT THERE!?
WHAT IF ONE OF HIS FRIENDS IS OUT THERE AND TELLS HIM?!
MAYBE I'M OVER REACT NO! OMIGOD THIS SUCKS! WHAT DO I DO... WAIT...
I'VE GOT A PLAN
KNOCK KNOCK
OCCUPIED!

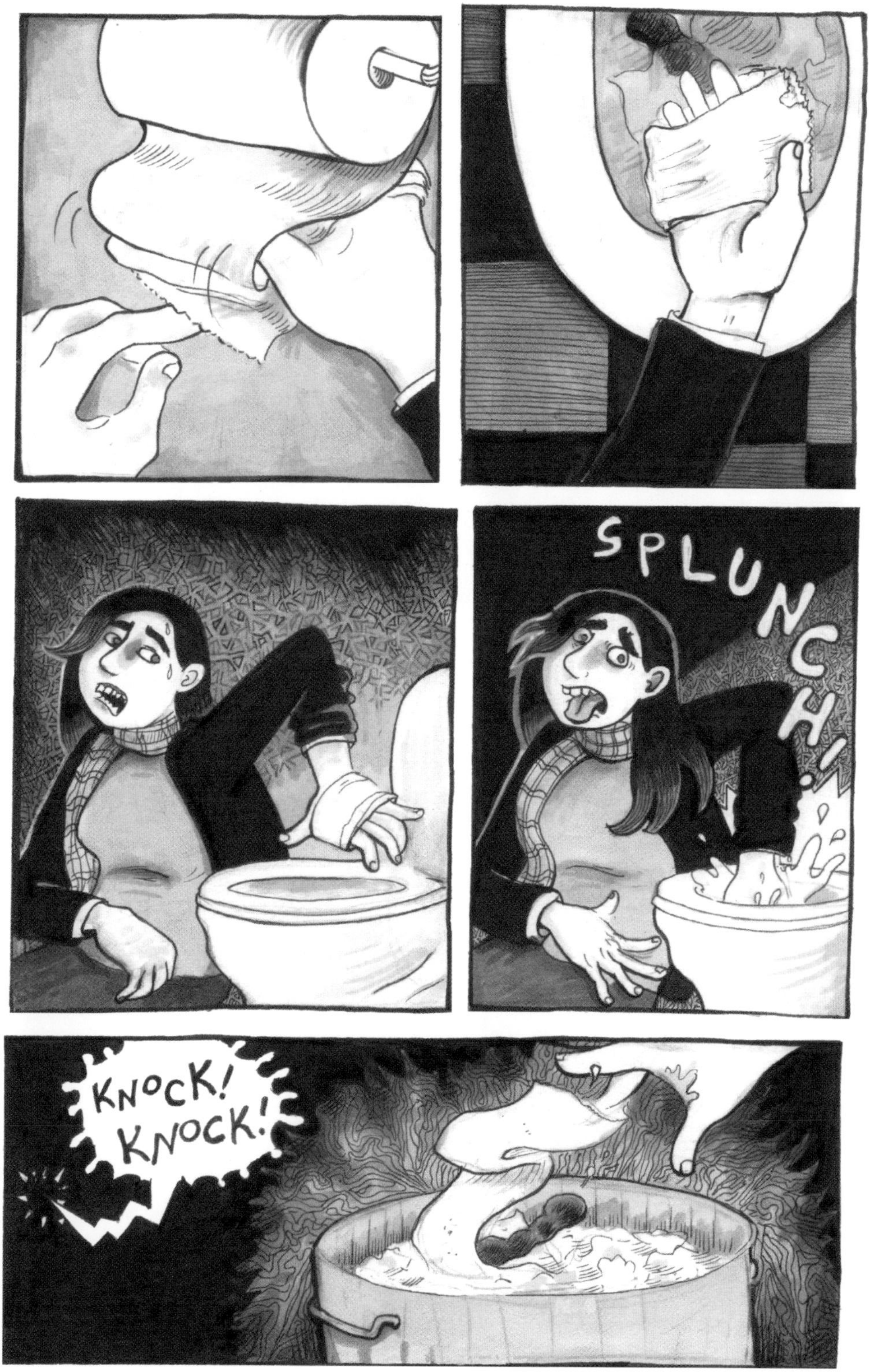
SPLUNCH!
KNOCK! KNOCK!

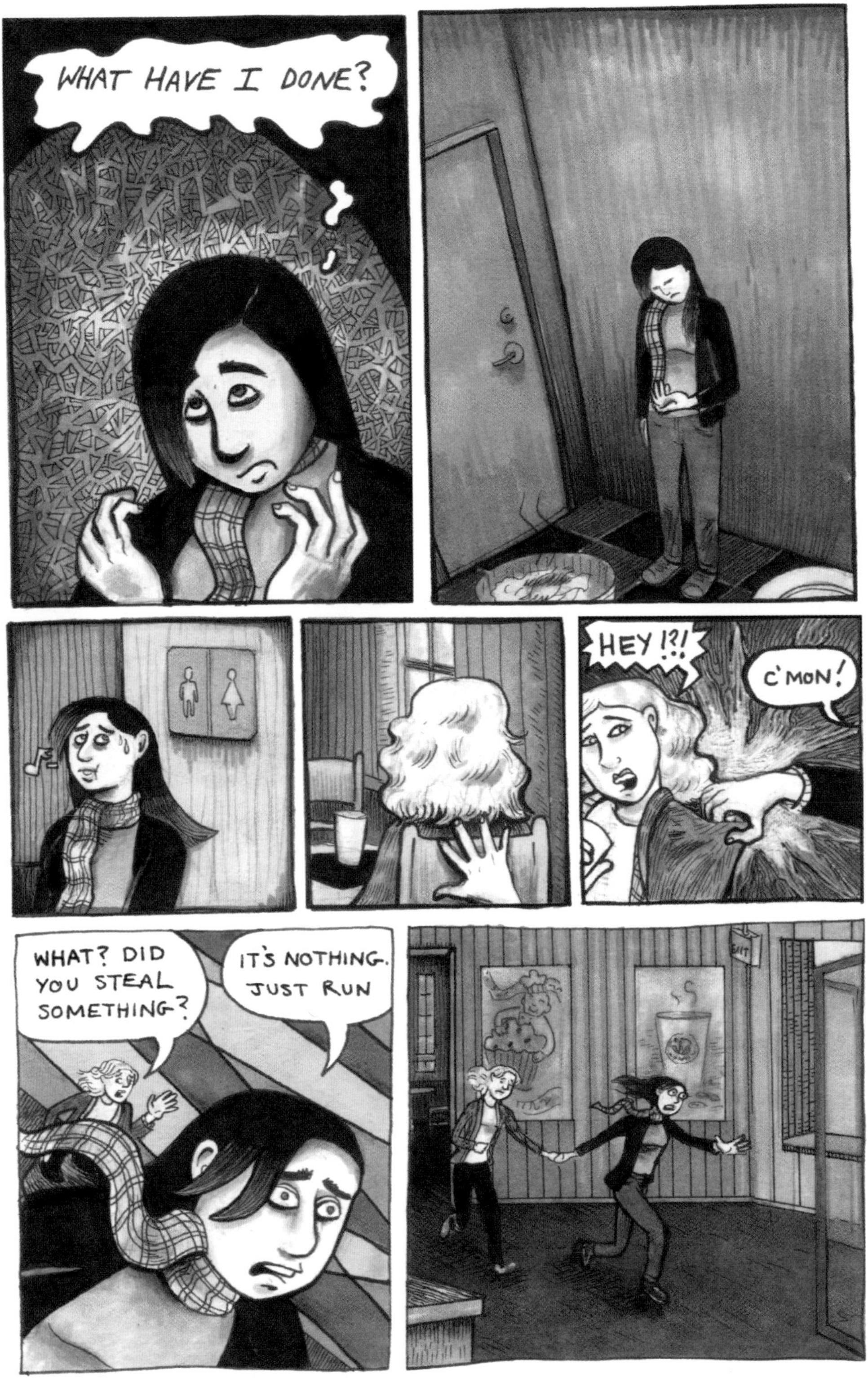
WHAT HAVE I DONE?
HEY !?!
C'MON!
WHAT? DID YOU STEAL SOMETHING?
IT'S NOTHING. JUST RUN

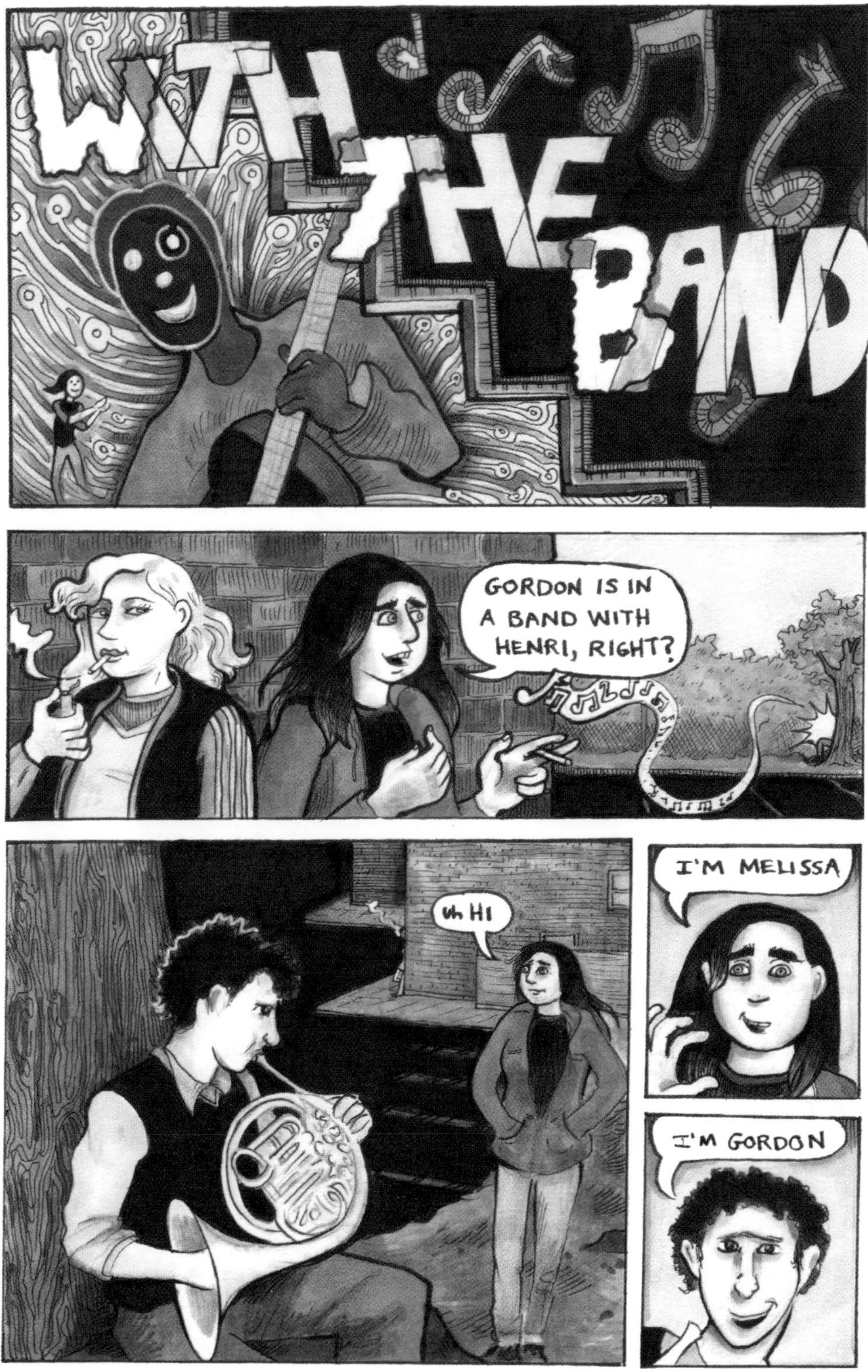
WITH THE BAND
GORDON IS IN A BAND WITH HENRI, RIGHT?
uh HI
I'M MELISSA
I'M GORDON

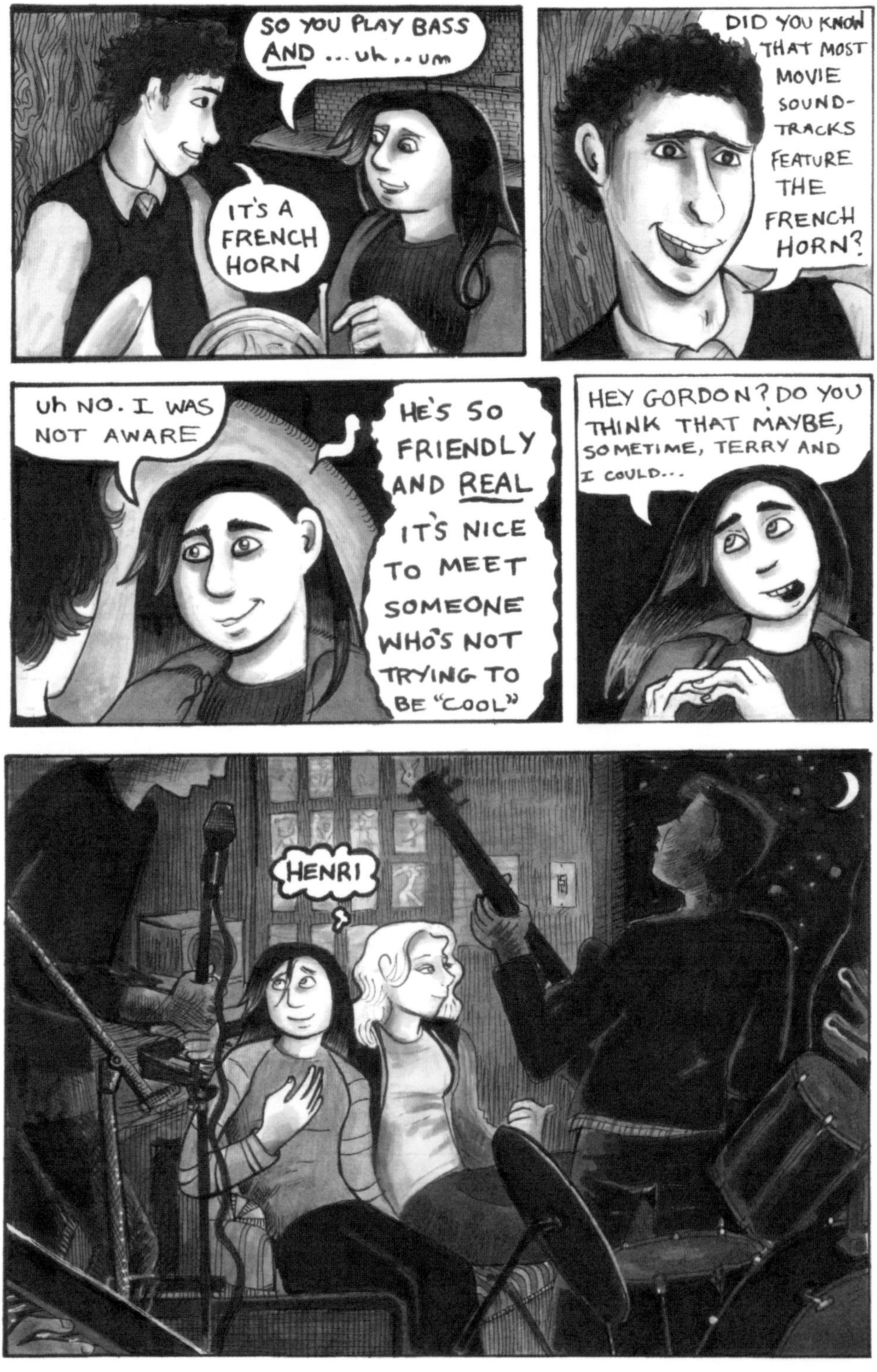
SO YOU PLAY BASS AND ...uh..um
IT'S A FRENCH HORN
DID YOU KNOW THAT MOST MOVIE SOUND-TRACKS FEATURE THE FRENCH HORN?
uh NO. I WAS NOT AWARE
HE'S SO FRIENDLY AND REAL
IT'S NICE TO MEET SOMEONE WHO'S NOT TRYING TO BE "COOL"
HEY GORDON? DO YOU THINK THAT MAYBE, SOMETIME, TERRY AND I COULD...
HENRI

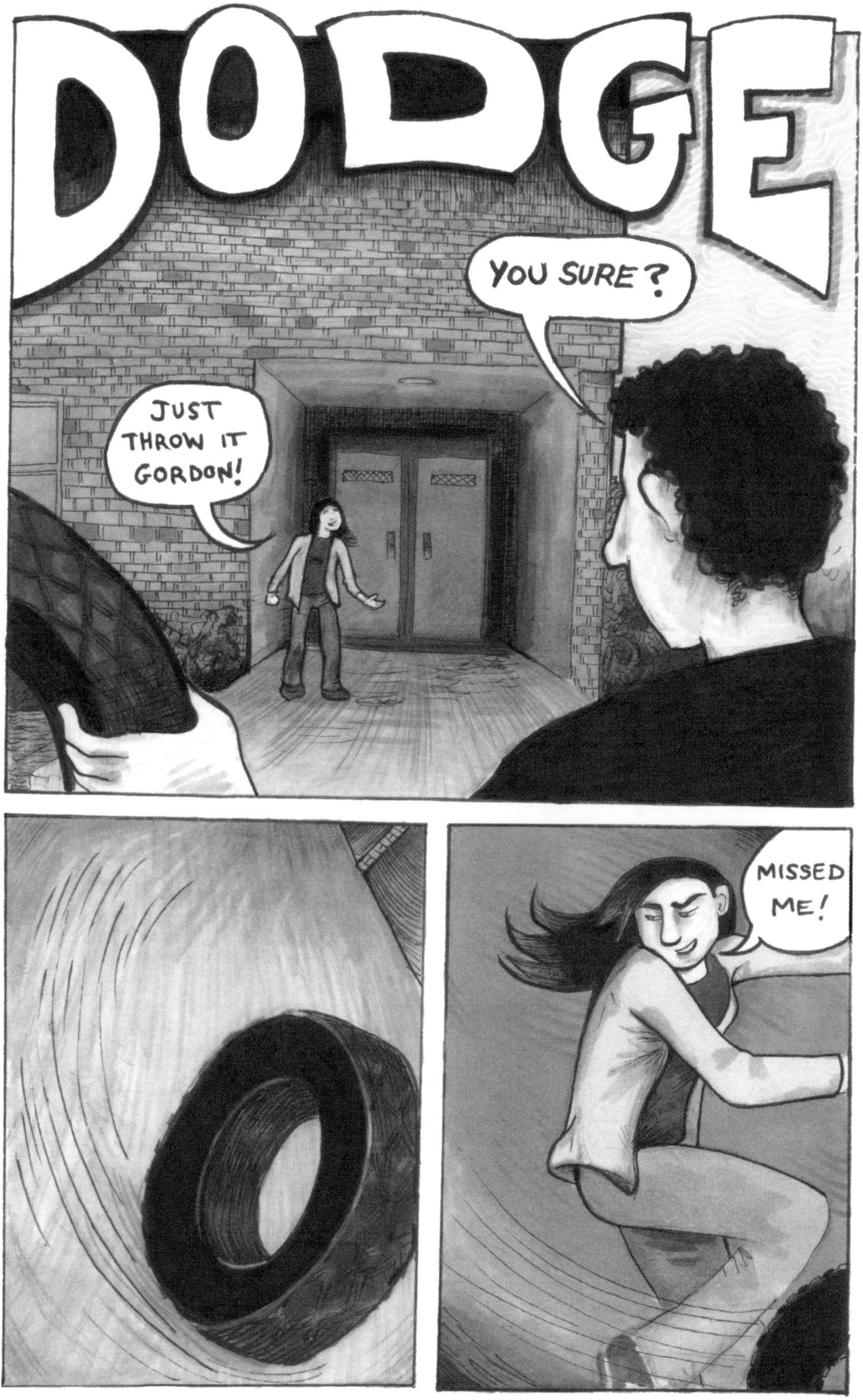
DODGE
YOU SURE?
JUST THROW IT GORDON!
MISSED ME!

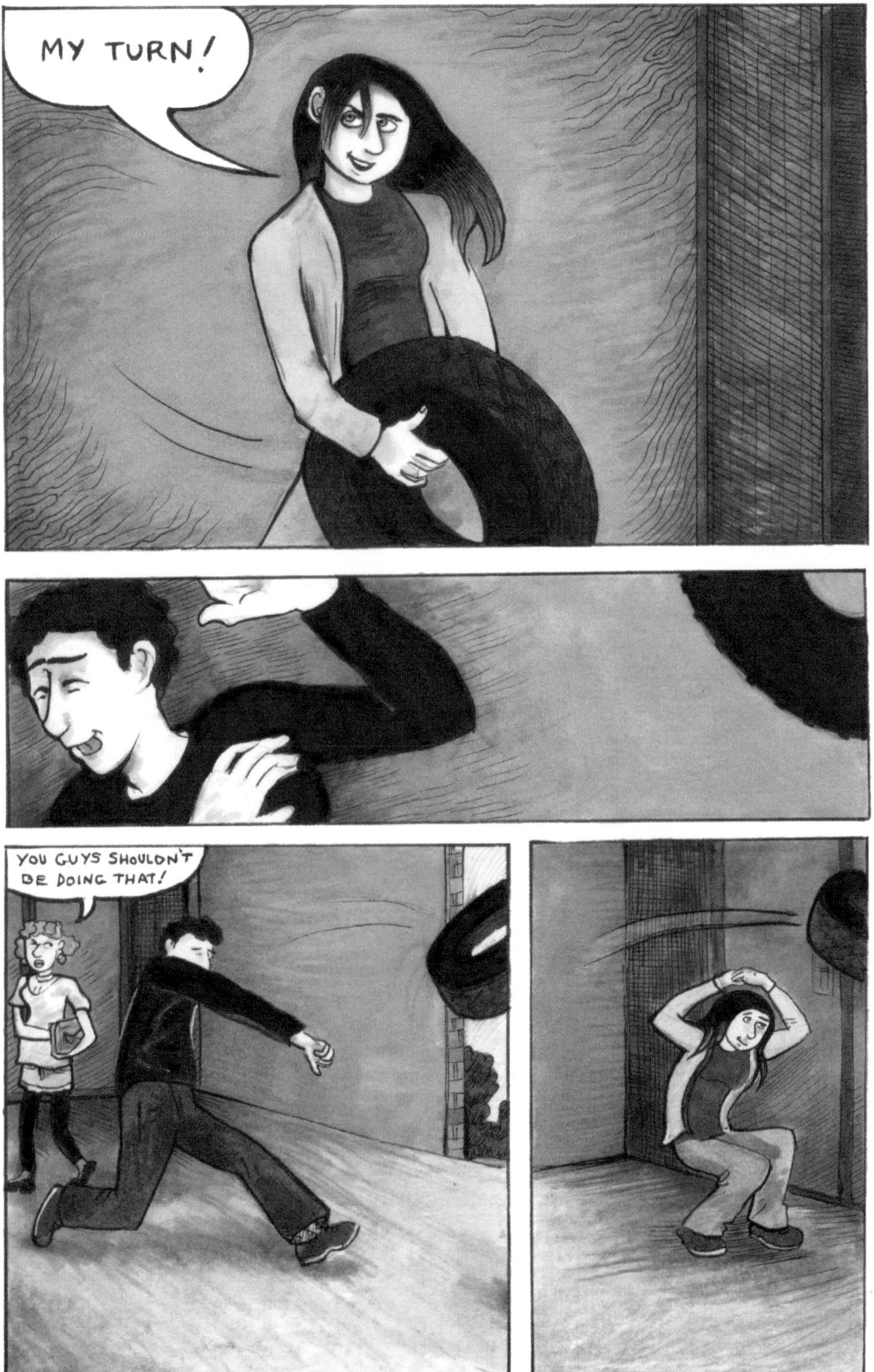
MY TURN!
YOU GUYS SHOULDN'T BE DOING THAT!

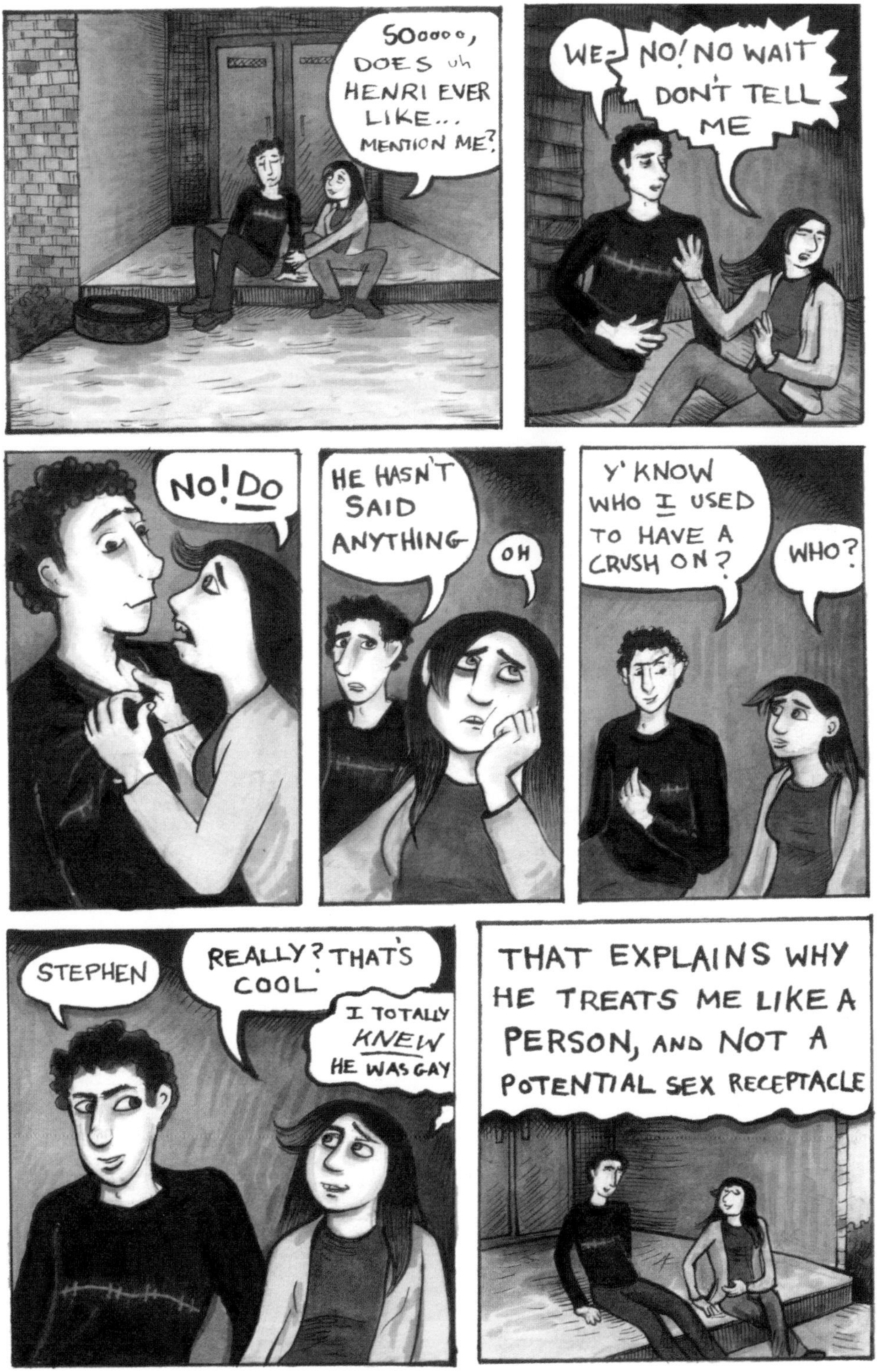
SOooooo, DOES uh HENRI EVER LIKE... MENTION ME?
WE-
NO! NO WAIT DON'T TELL ME
NO! DO
HE HASN'T SAID ANYTHING
OH
Y' KNOW WHO I USED TO HAVE A CRUSH ON?
WHO?
STEPHEN
REALLY? THAT'S COOL
I TOTALLY KNEW HE WAS GAY
THAT EXPLAINS WHY HE TREATS ME LIKE A PERSON, AND NOT A POTENTIAL SEX RECEPTACLE

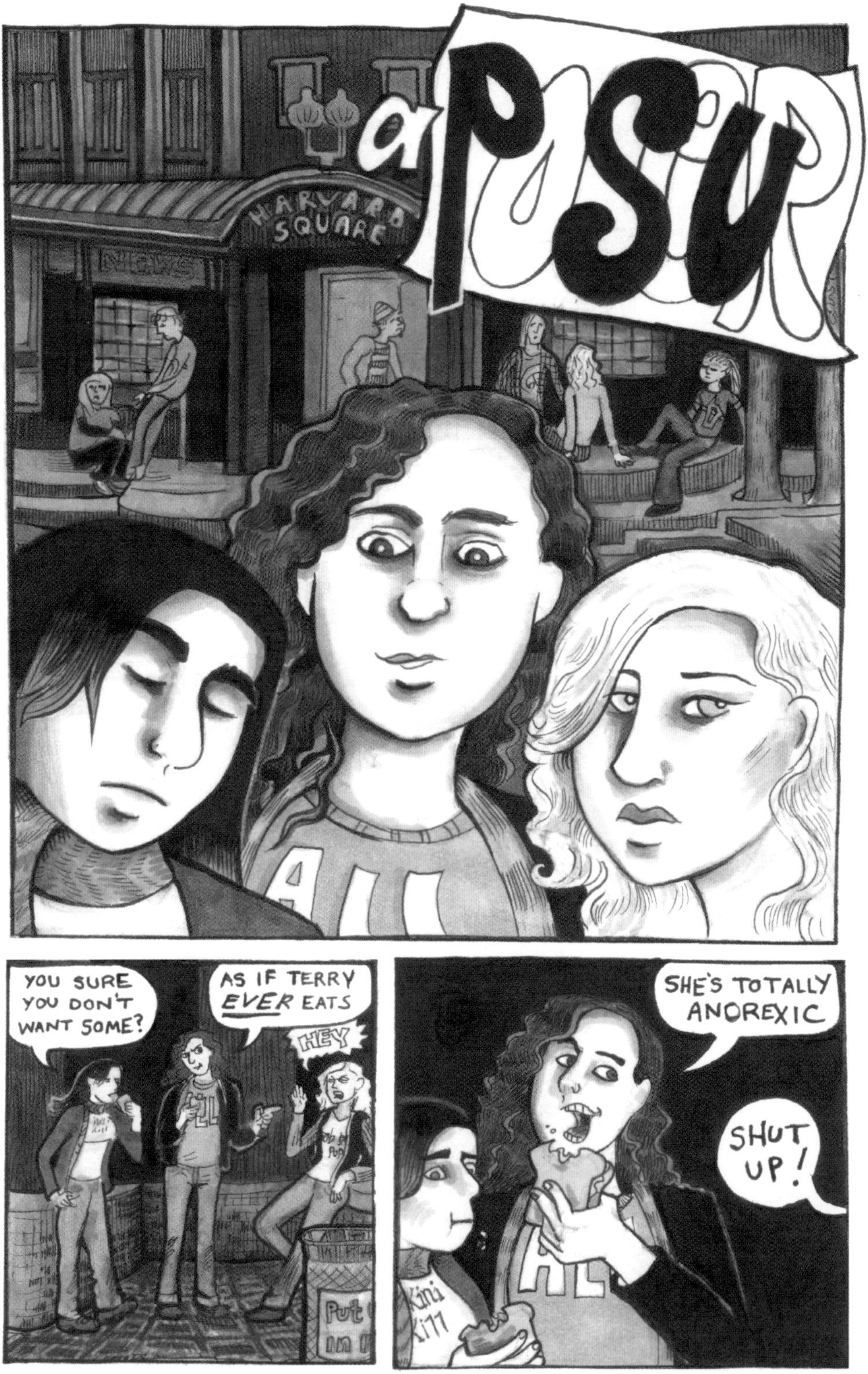
a POSEUR
HARVARD SQUARE
NEWS
YOU SURE YOU DON'T WANT SOME?
AS IF TERRY *EVER* EATS
HEY
SHE'S TOTALLY ANOREXIC
SHUT UP!

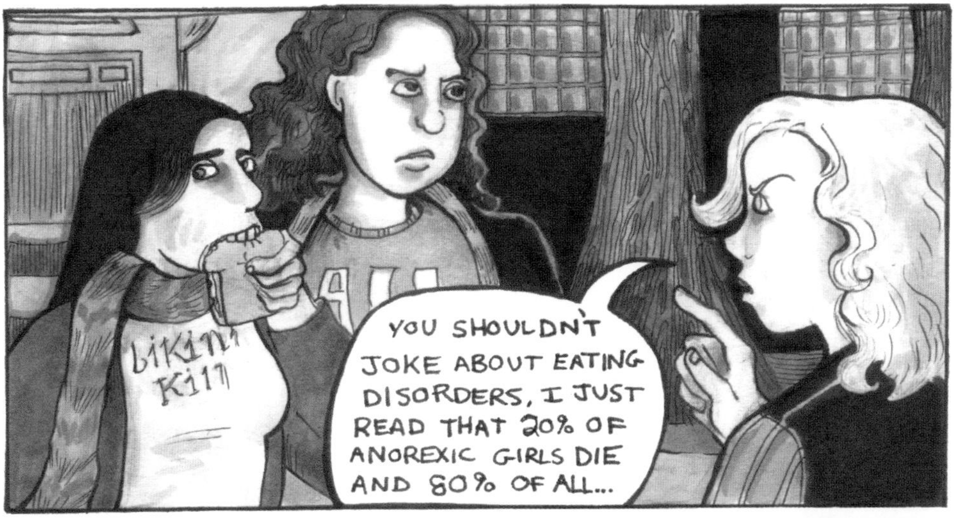
bikini Kill
YOU SHOULDN'T JOKE ABOUT EATING DISORDERS, I JUST READ THAT 20% OF ANOREXIC GIRLS DIE AND 80% OF ALL...

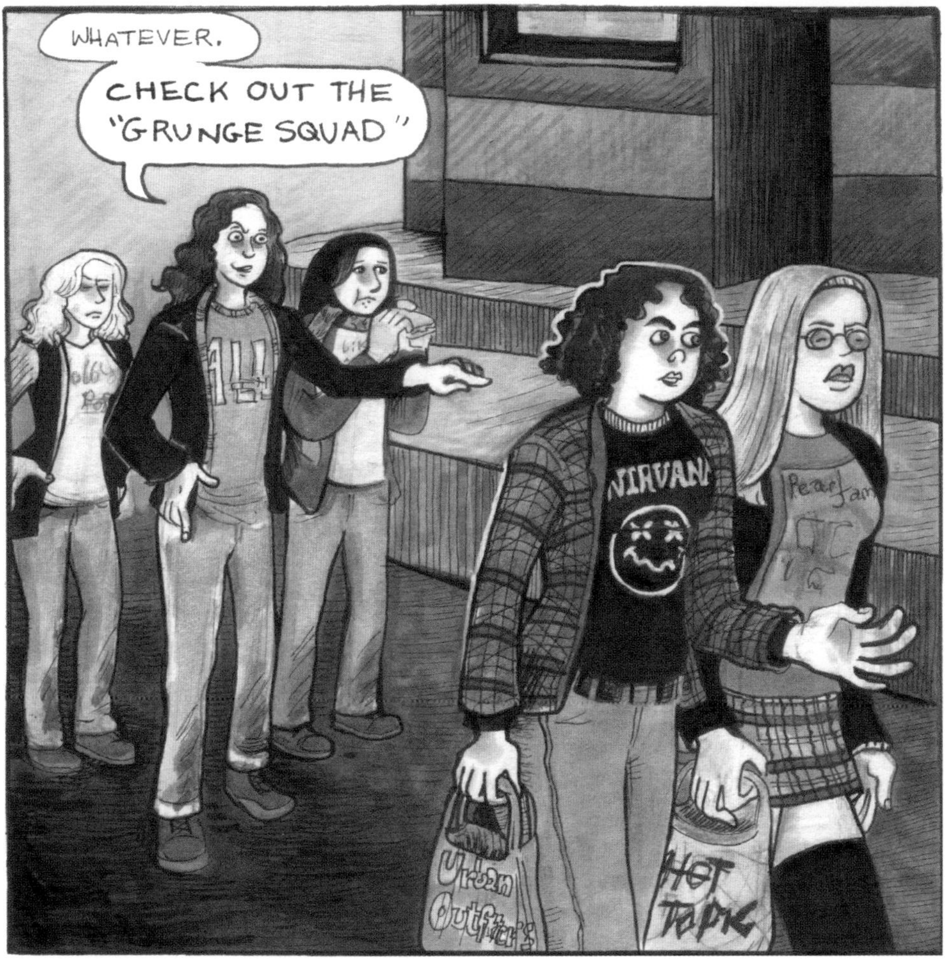
WHATEVER.
CHECK OUT THE "GRUNGE SQUAD"

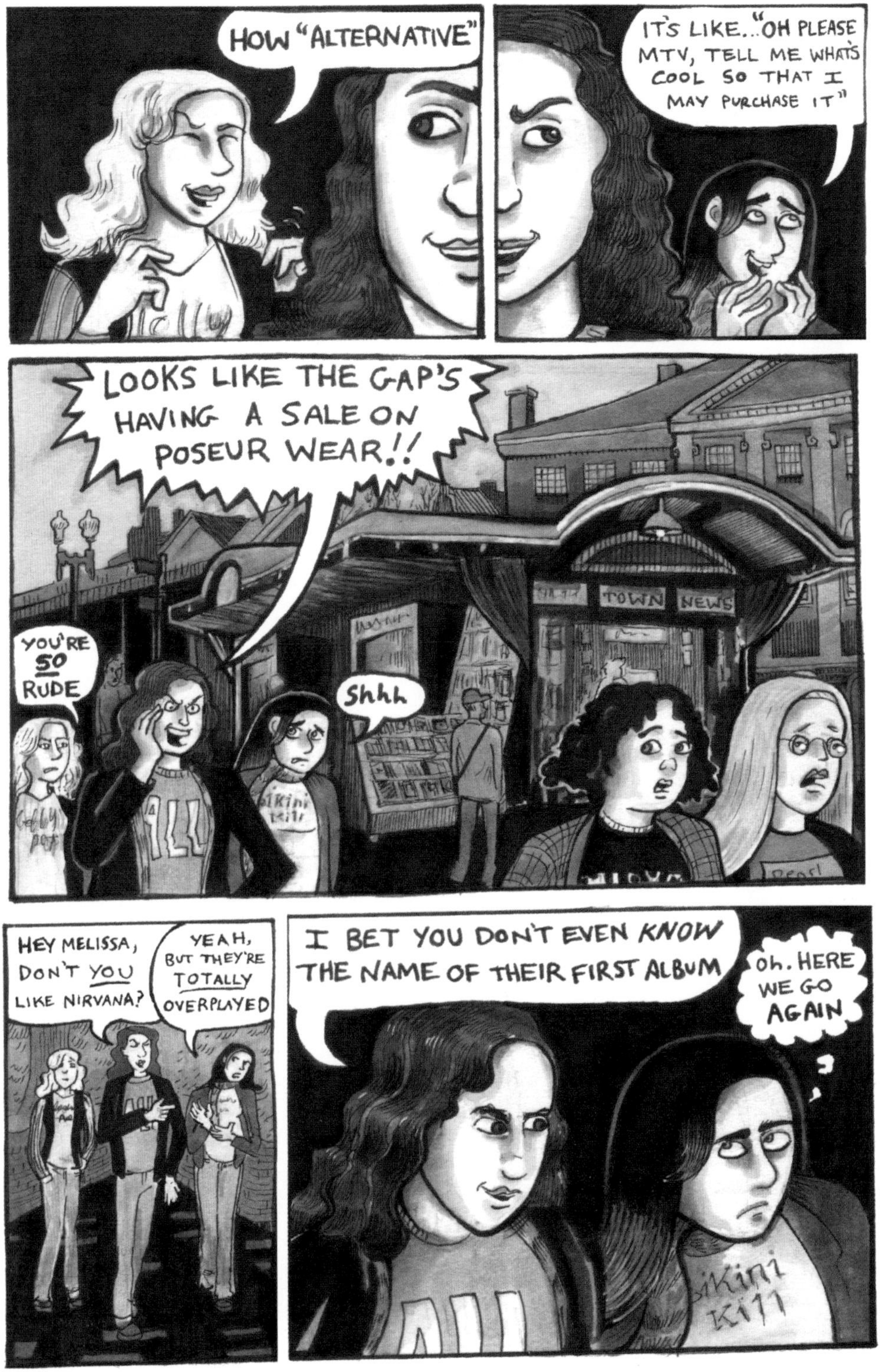
HOW "ALTERNATIVE"
IT'S LIKE..."OH PLEASE MTV, TELL ME WHAT'S COOL SO THAT I MAY PURCHASE IT"
LOOKS LIKE THE GAP'S HAVING A SALE ON POSEUR WEAR!!
YOU'RE SO RUDE
Shhh
TOWN NEWS
HEY MELISSA, DON'T YOU LIKE NIRVANA?
YEAH, BUT THEY'RE TOTALLY OVERPLAYED
I BET YOU DON'T EVEN KNOW THE NAME OF THEIR FIRST ALBUM
Oh. HERE WE GO AGAIN

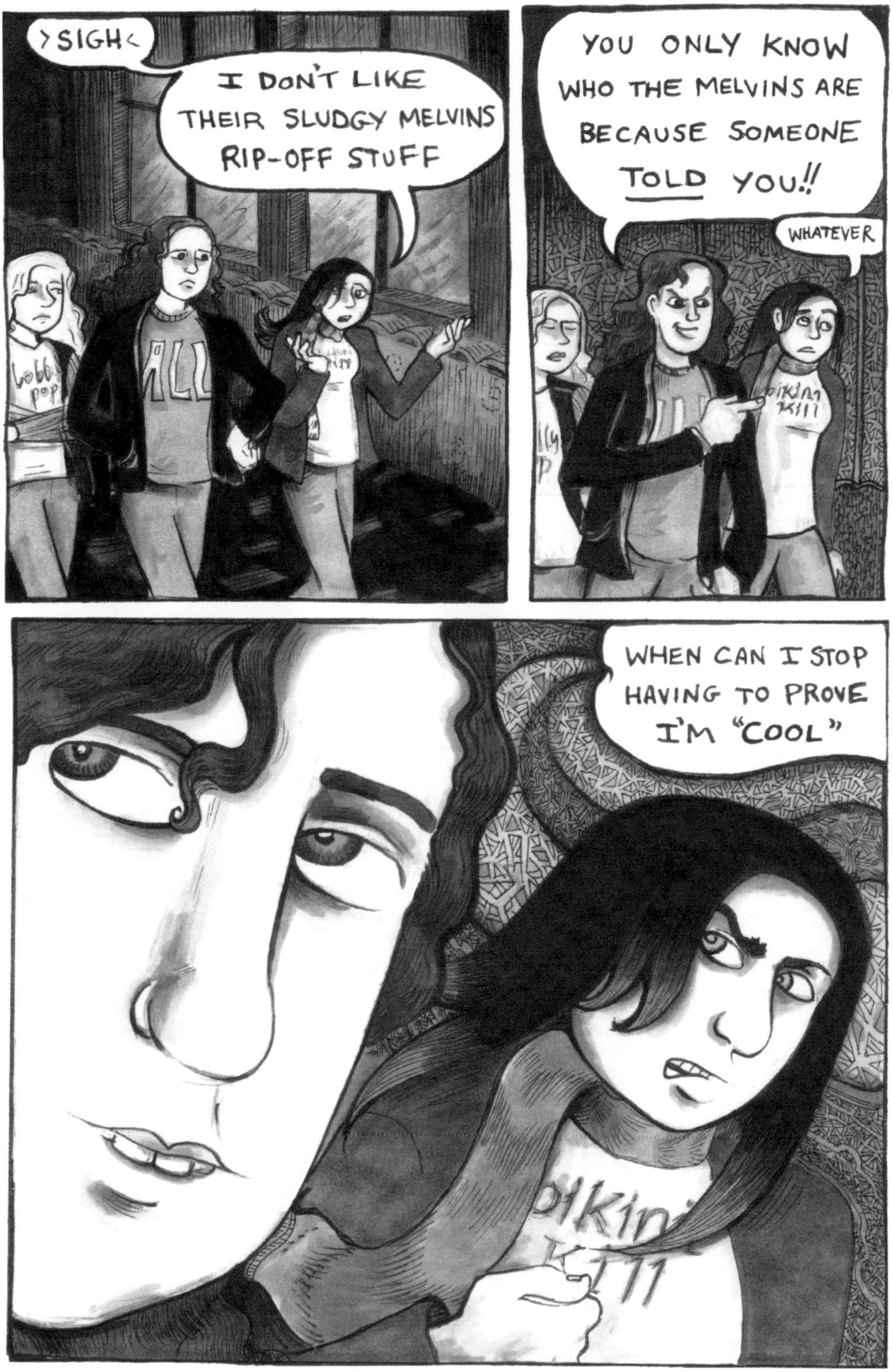
>SIGH<
I DON'T LIKE THEIR SLUDGY MELVINS RIP-OFF STUFF
YOU ONLY KNOW WHO THE MELVINS ARE BECAUSE SOMEONE TOLD YOU!!
WHATEVER
WHEN CAN I STOP HAVING TO PROVE I'M "COOL"

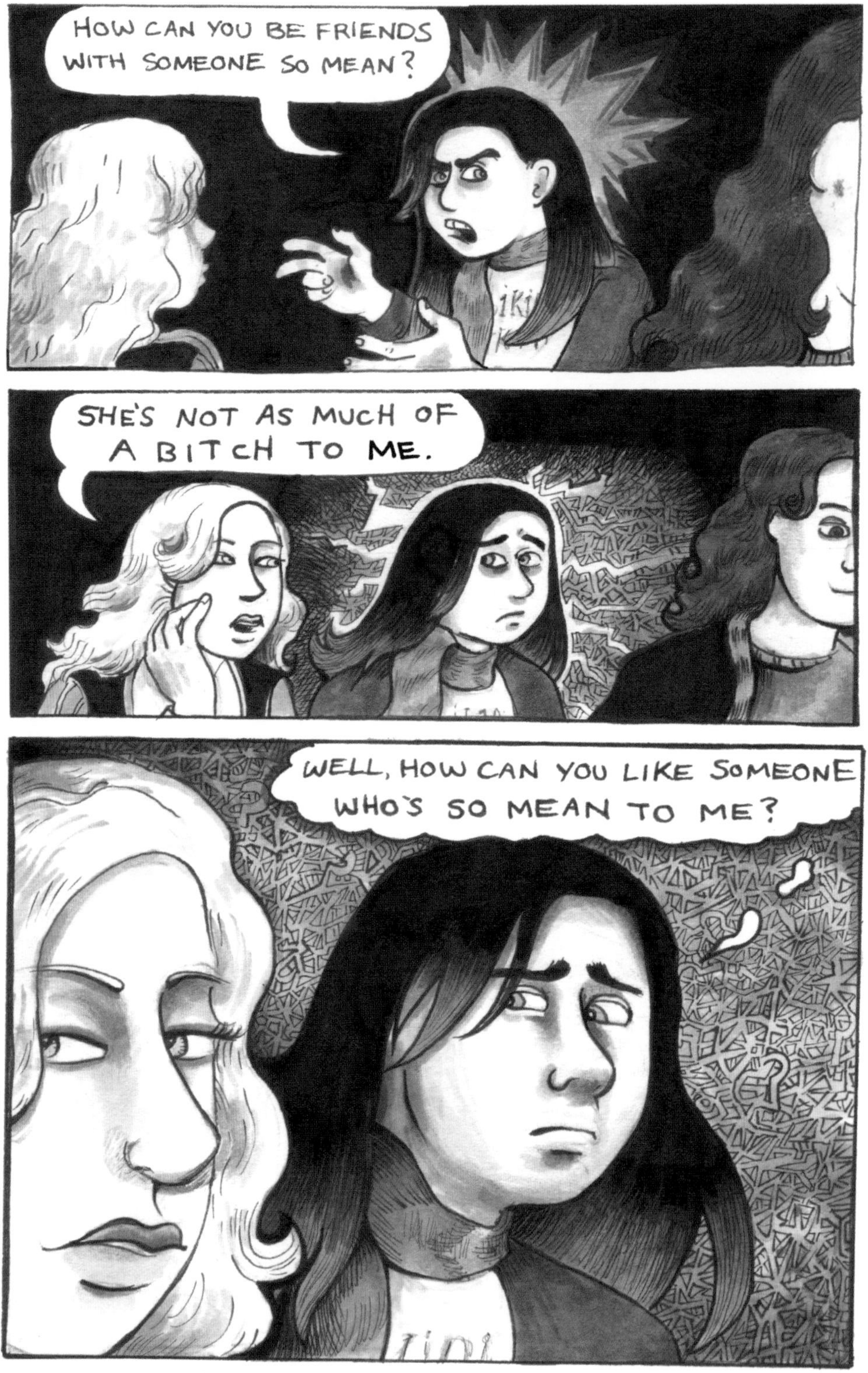
HOW CAN YOU BE FRIENDS WITH SOMEONE SO MEAN?
SHE'S NOT AS MUCH OF A BITCH TO ME.
WELL, HOW CAN YOU LIKE SOMEONE WHO'S SO MEAN TO ME?

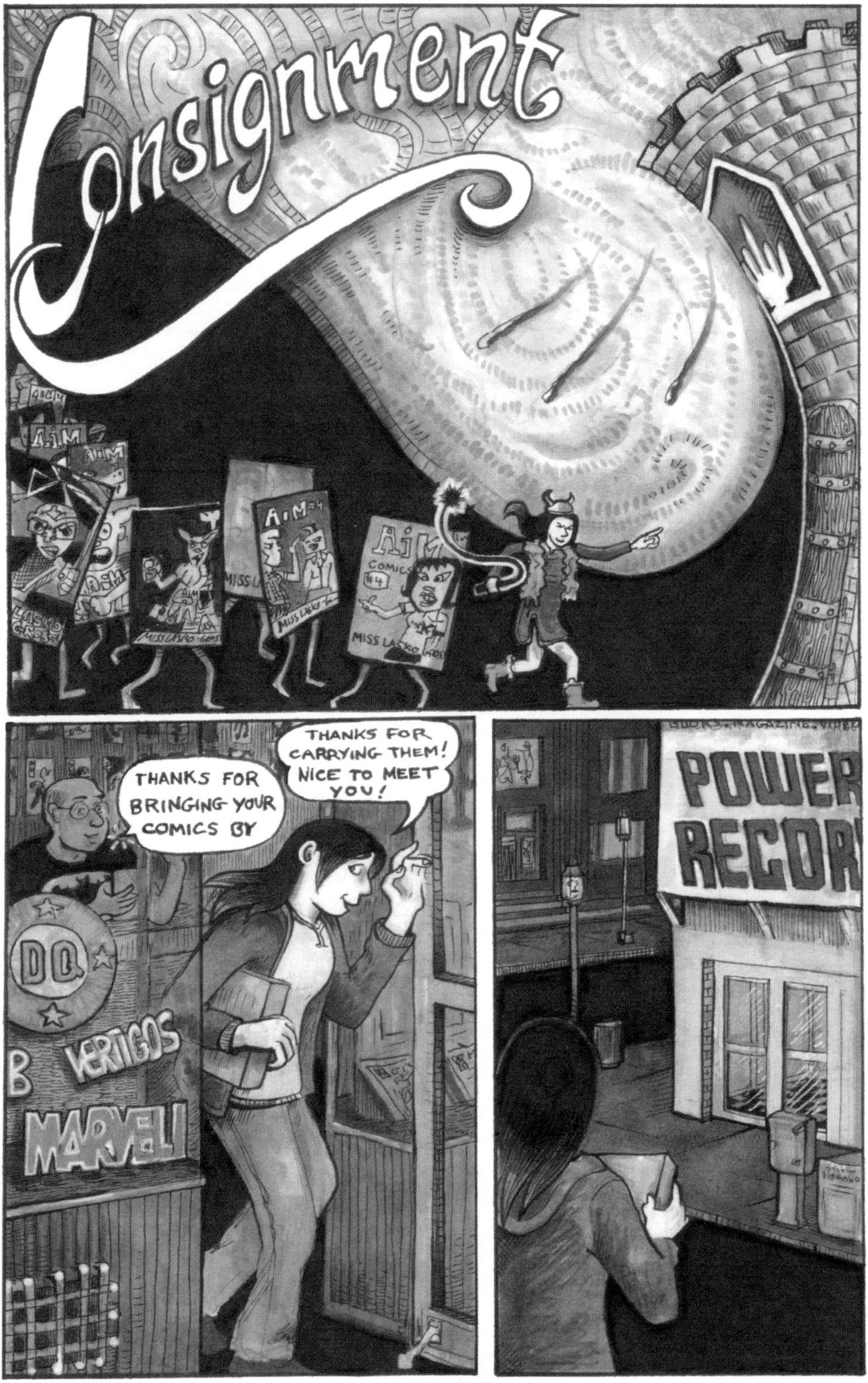
Consignment
THANKS FOR BRINGING YOUR COMICS BY
THANKS FOR CARRYING THEM! NICE TO MEET YOU!
DQ
B
VERTIGOS
MARVEL
POWER
RECOR

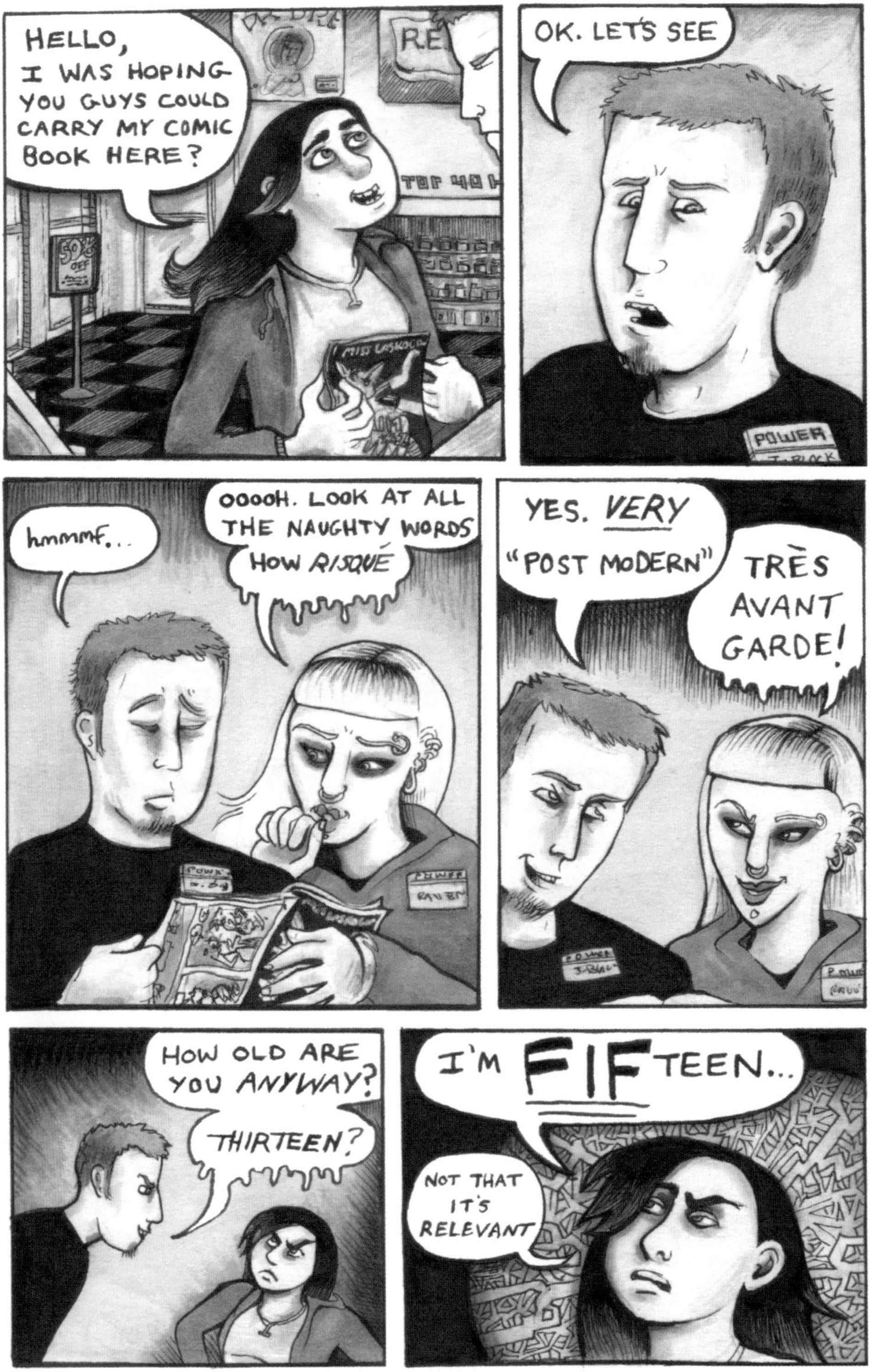
HELLO, I WAS HOPING YOU GUYS COULD CARRY MY COMIC BOOK HERE?
OK. LET'S SEE
hmmmf...
OOOOH. LOOK AT ALL THE NAUGHTY WORDS HOW RISQUÉ
YES. VERY "POST MODERN"
TRÈS AVANT GARDE!
HOW OLD ARE YOU ANYWAY?
THIRTEEN?
I'M FIFTEEN...
NOT THAT IT'S RELEVANT

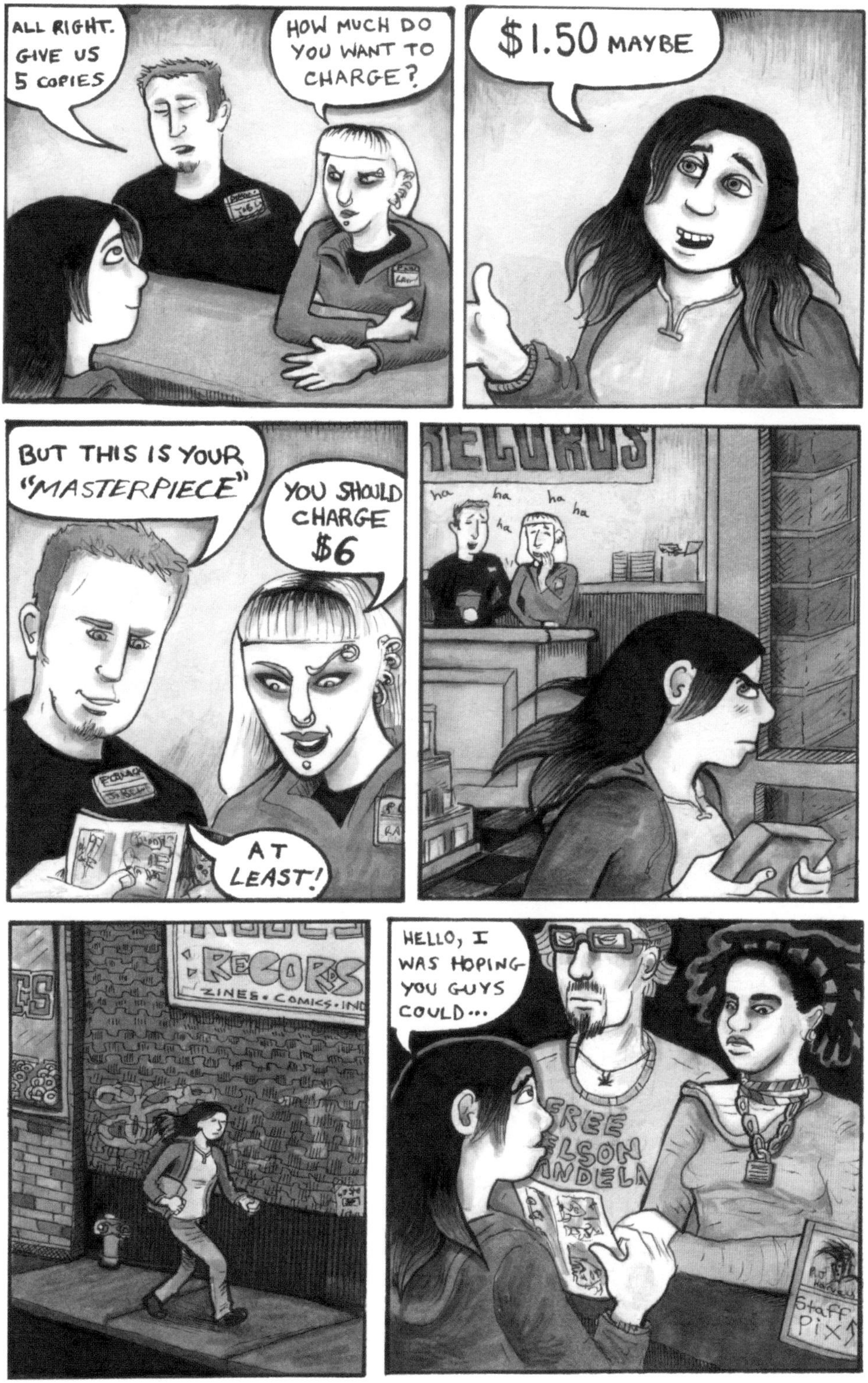
ALL RIGHT. GIVE US 5 COPIES
HOW MUCH DO YOU WANT TO CHARGE?
$1.50 MAYBE
BUT THIS IS YOUR "MASTERPIECE"
YOU SHOULD CHARGE $6
AT LEAST!
ha ha ha ha ha
ZINES • COMICS • IN
HELLO, I WAS HOPING YOU GUYS COULD...
Staff PIX

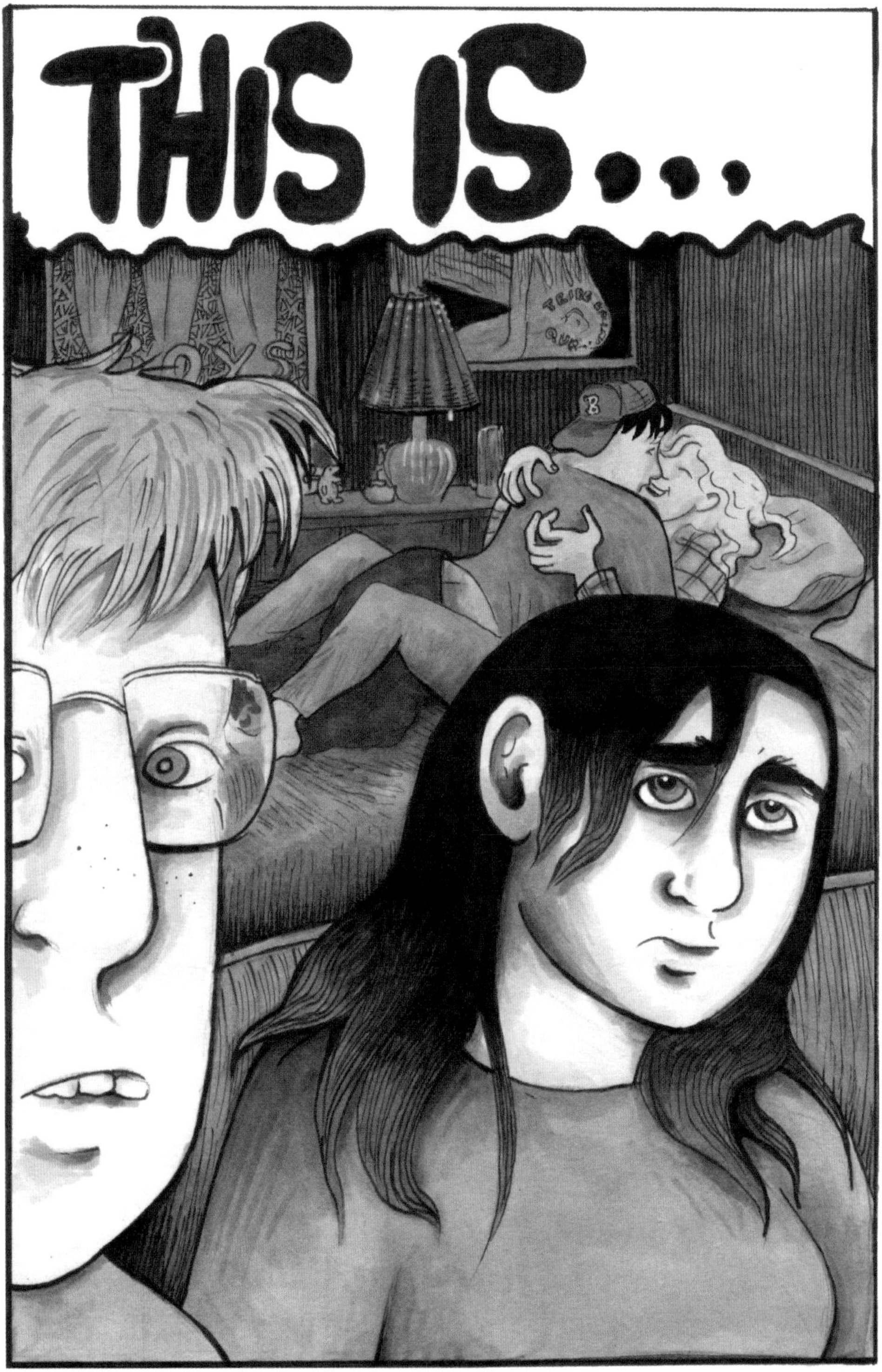
THIS IS...

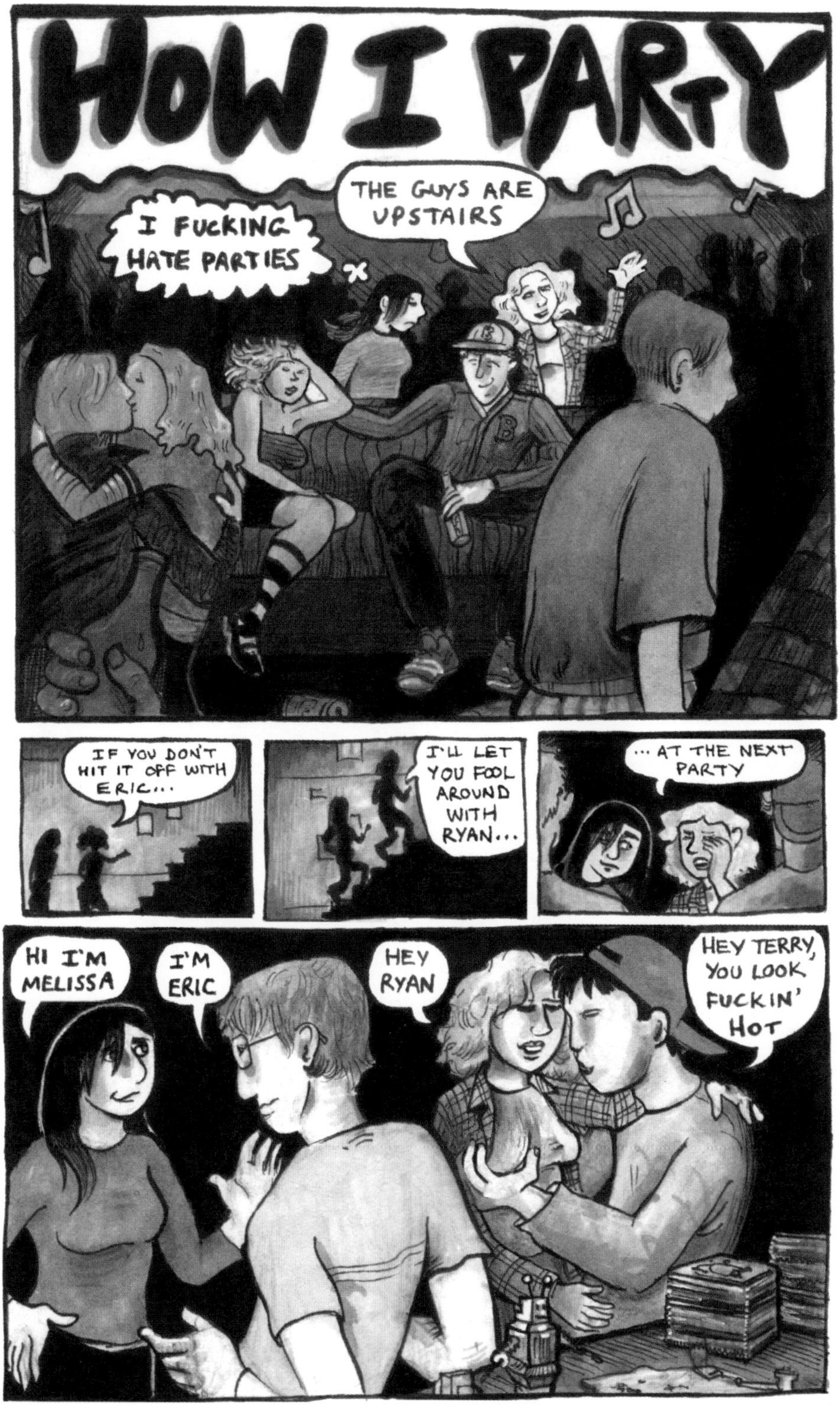
HOW I PARTY
I FUCKING HATE PARTIES
THE GUYS ARE UPSTAIRS
IF YOU DON'T HIT IT OFF WITH ERIC...
I'LL LET YOU FOOL AROUND WITH RYAN...
...AT THE NEXT PARTY
HI I'M MELISSA
I'M ERIC
HEY RYAN
HEY TERRY, YOU LOOK FUCKIN' HOT

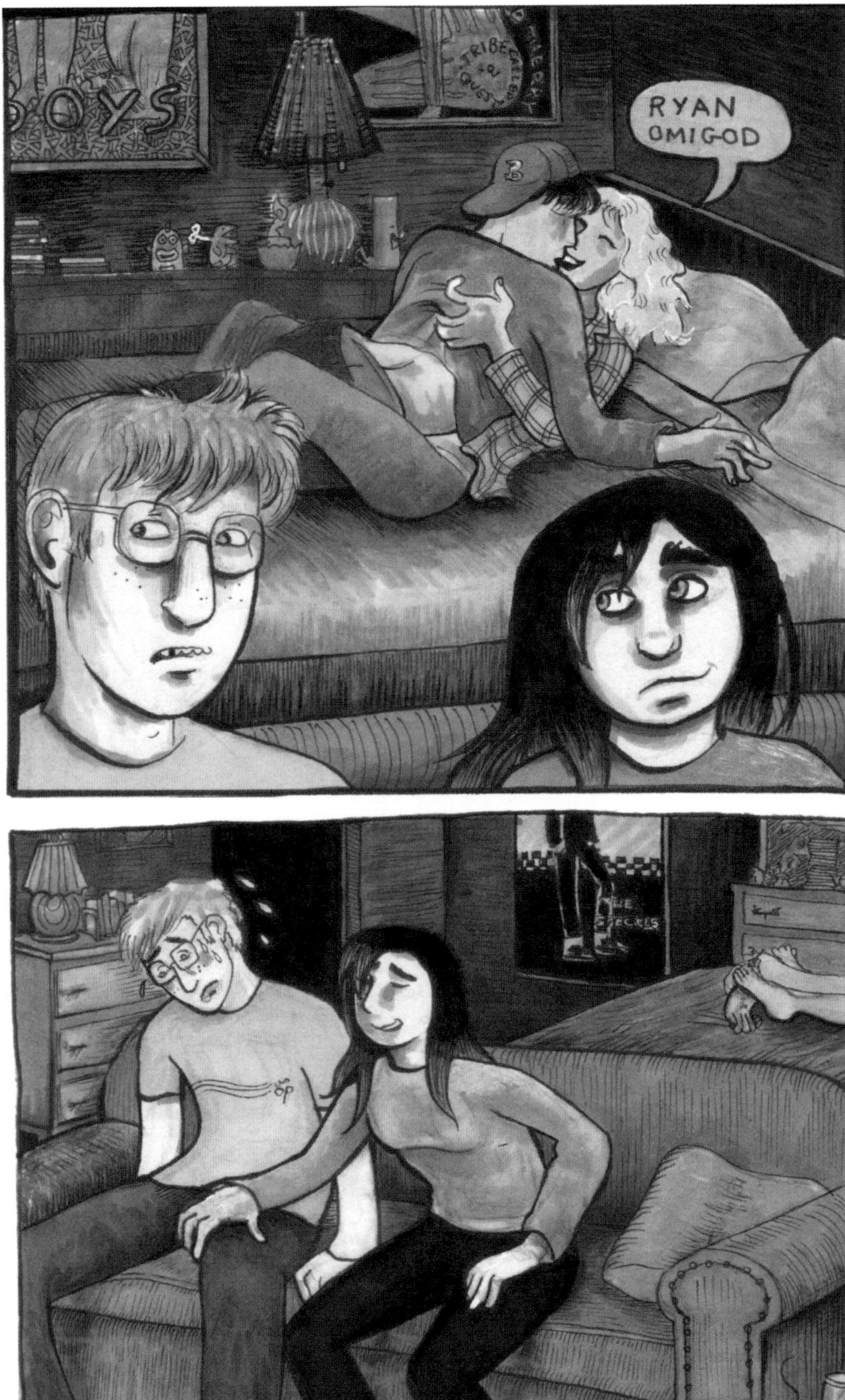
RYAN
OMIGOD

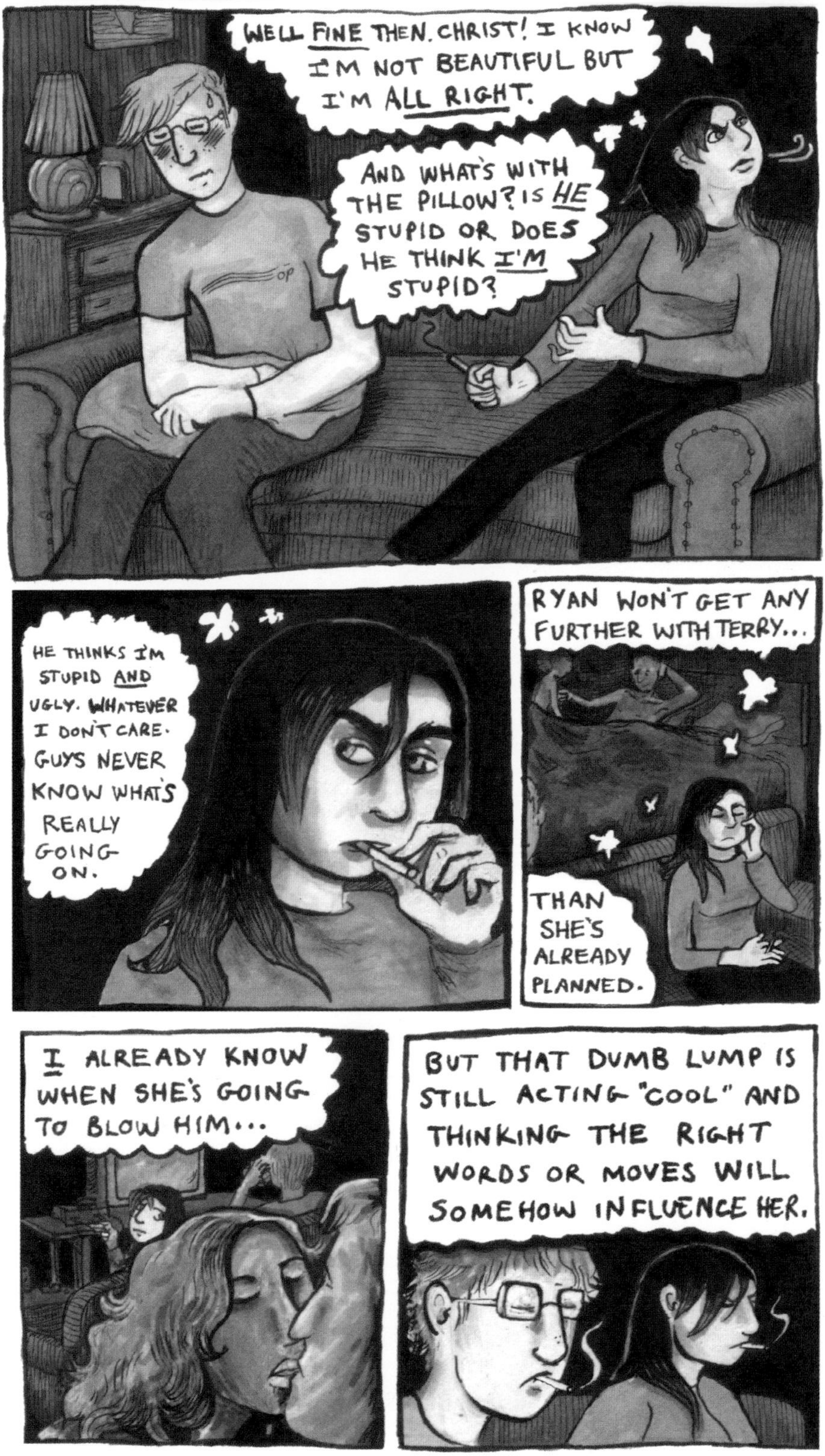
WELL FINE THEN. CHRIST! I KNOW I'M NOT BEAUTIFUL BUT I'M ALL RIGHT.
AND WHAT'S WITH THE PILLOW? IS HE STUPID OR DOES HE THINK I'M STUPID?
HE THINKS I'M STUPID AND UGLY. WHATEVER I DON'T CARE. GUYS NEVER KNOW WHAT'S REALLY GOING ON.
RYAN WON'T GET ANY FURTHER WITH TERRY...
THAN SHE'S ALREADY PLANNED.
I ALREADY KNOW WHEN SHE'S GOING TO BLOW HIM...
BUT THAT DUMB LUMP IS STILL ACTING "COOL" AND THINKING THE RIGHT WORDS OR MOVES WILL SOMEHOW INFLUENCE HER.

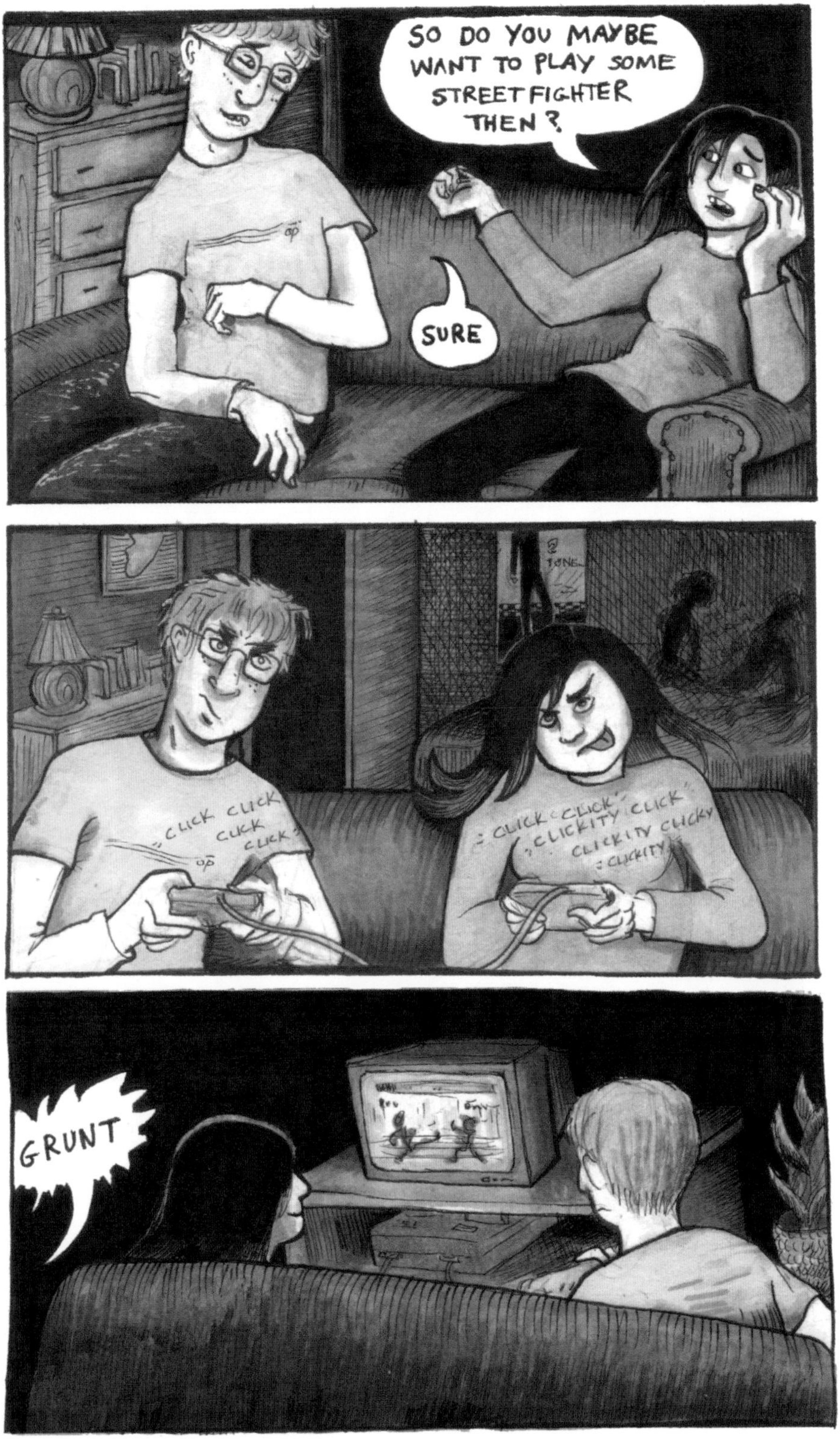
SO DO YOU MAYBE WANT TO PLAY SOME STREETFIGHTER THEN?
SURE
CLICK CLICK CLICK CLICK
CLICK CLICK CLICKITY CLICK CLICKITY CLICKITY CLICKY CLICKITY
GRUNT

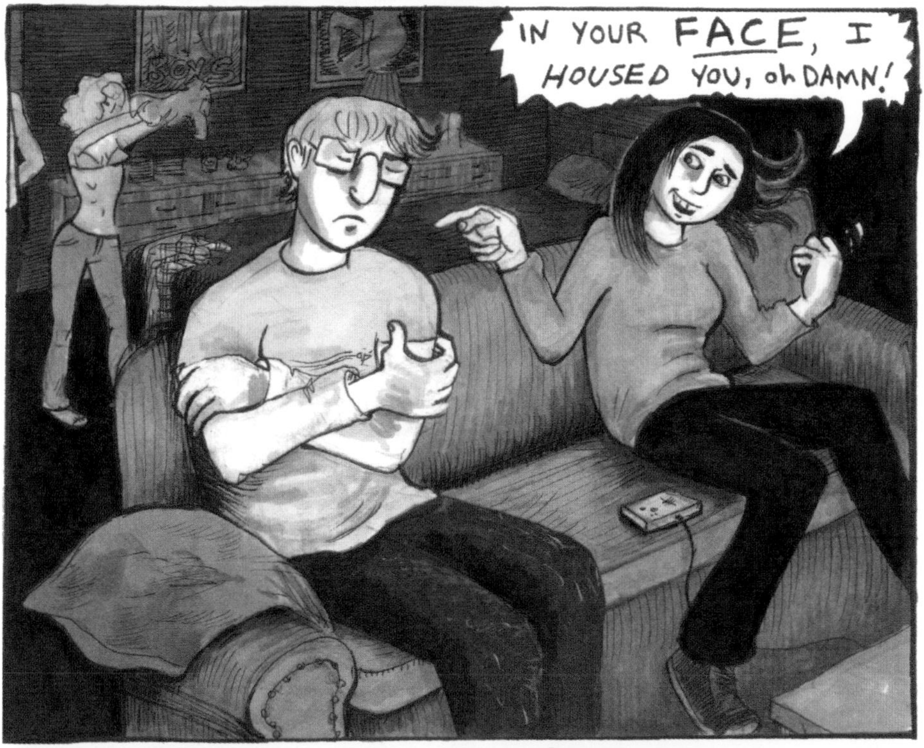
IN YOUR FACE, I HOUSED YOU, oh DAMN!

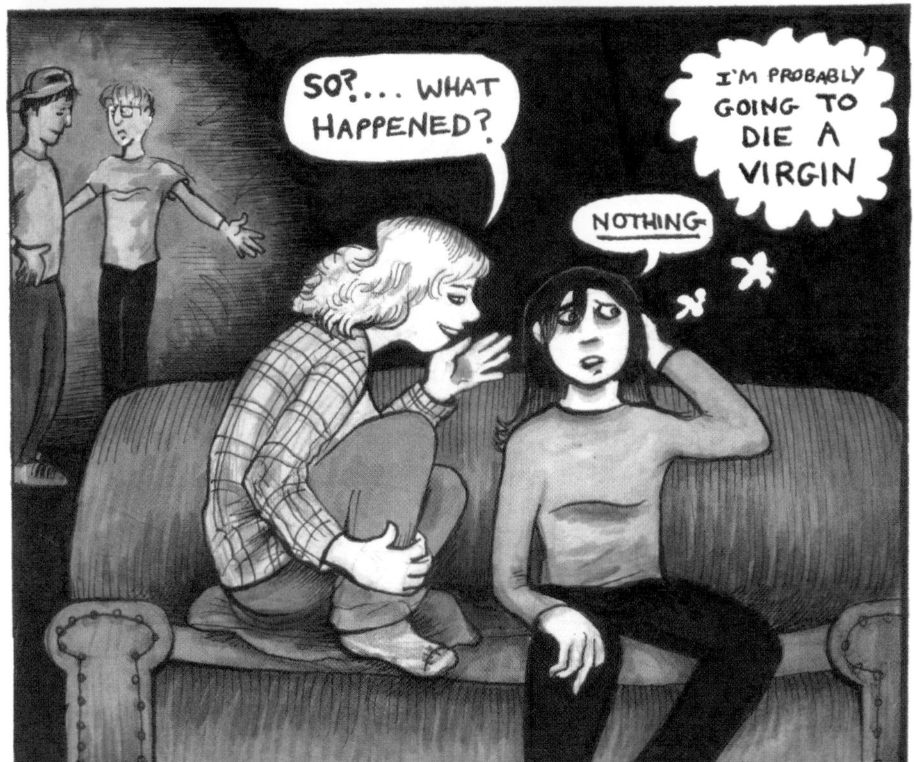
SO?... WHAT HAPPENED?
I'M PROBABLY GOING TO DIE A VIRGIN
NOTHING

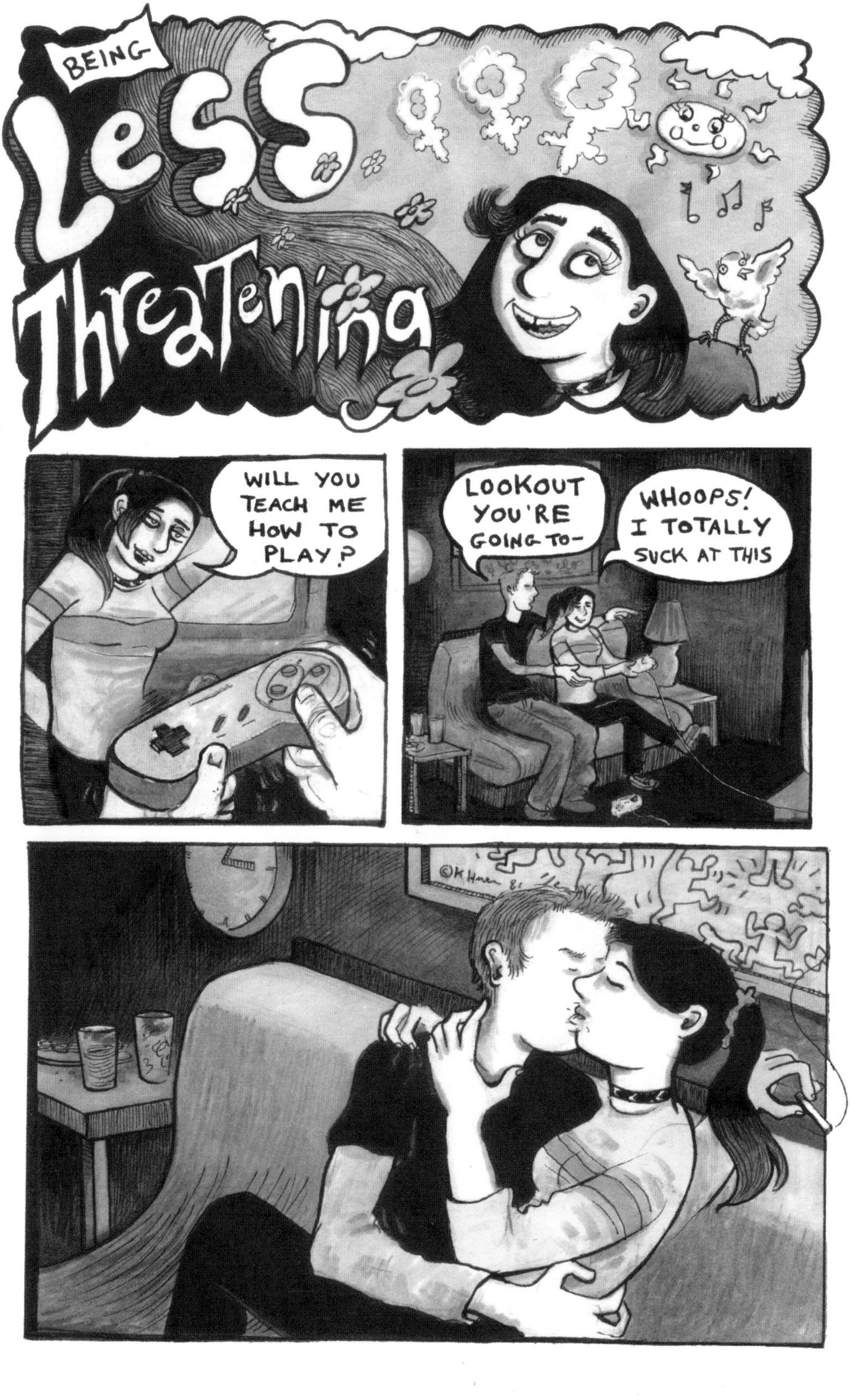
BEING
LESS THREATENING
WILL YOU TEACH ME HOW TO PLAY?
LOOKOUT YOU'RE GOING TO-
WHOOPS! I TOTALLY SUCK AT THIS

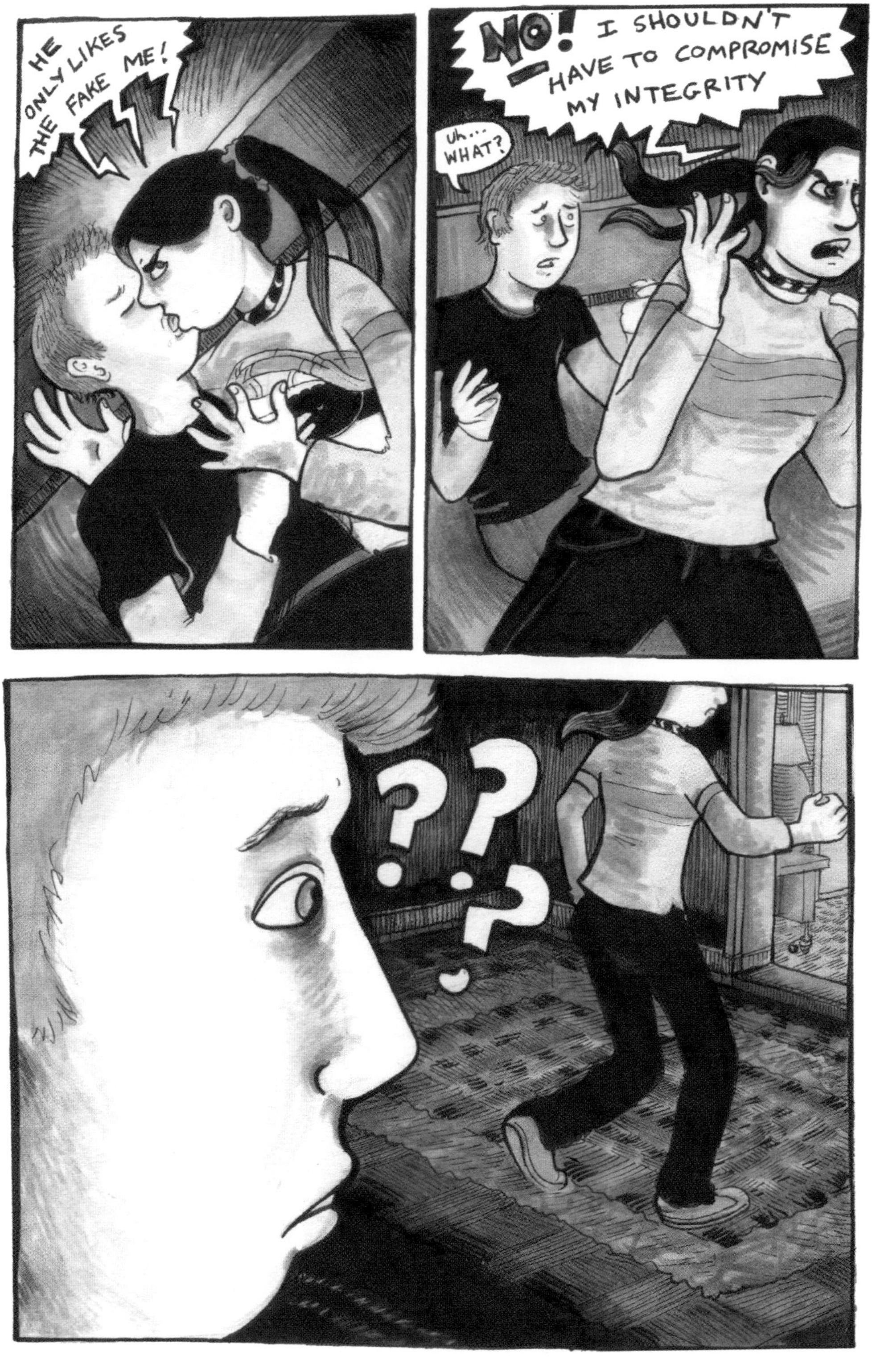
HE ONLY LIKES THE FAKE ME!
NO! I SHOULDN'T HAVE TO COMPROMISE MY INTEGRITY
Uh... WHAT?
???

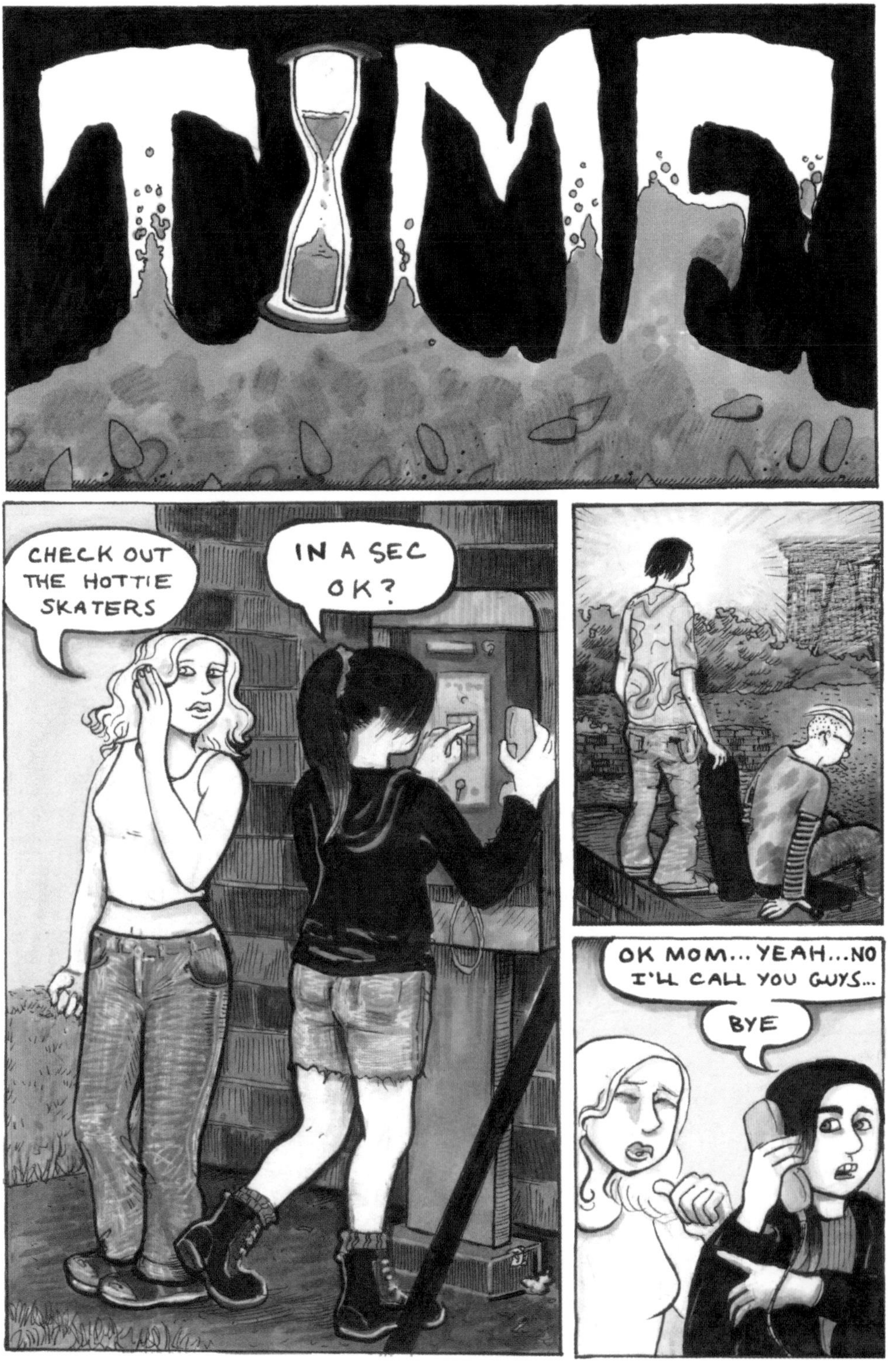
TIME
CHECK OUT THE HOTTIE SKATERS
IN A SEC OK?
OK MOM... YEAH... NO I'LL CALL YOU GUYS...
BYE

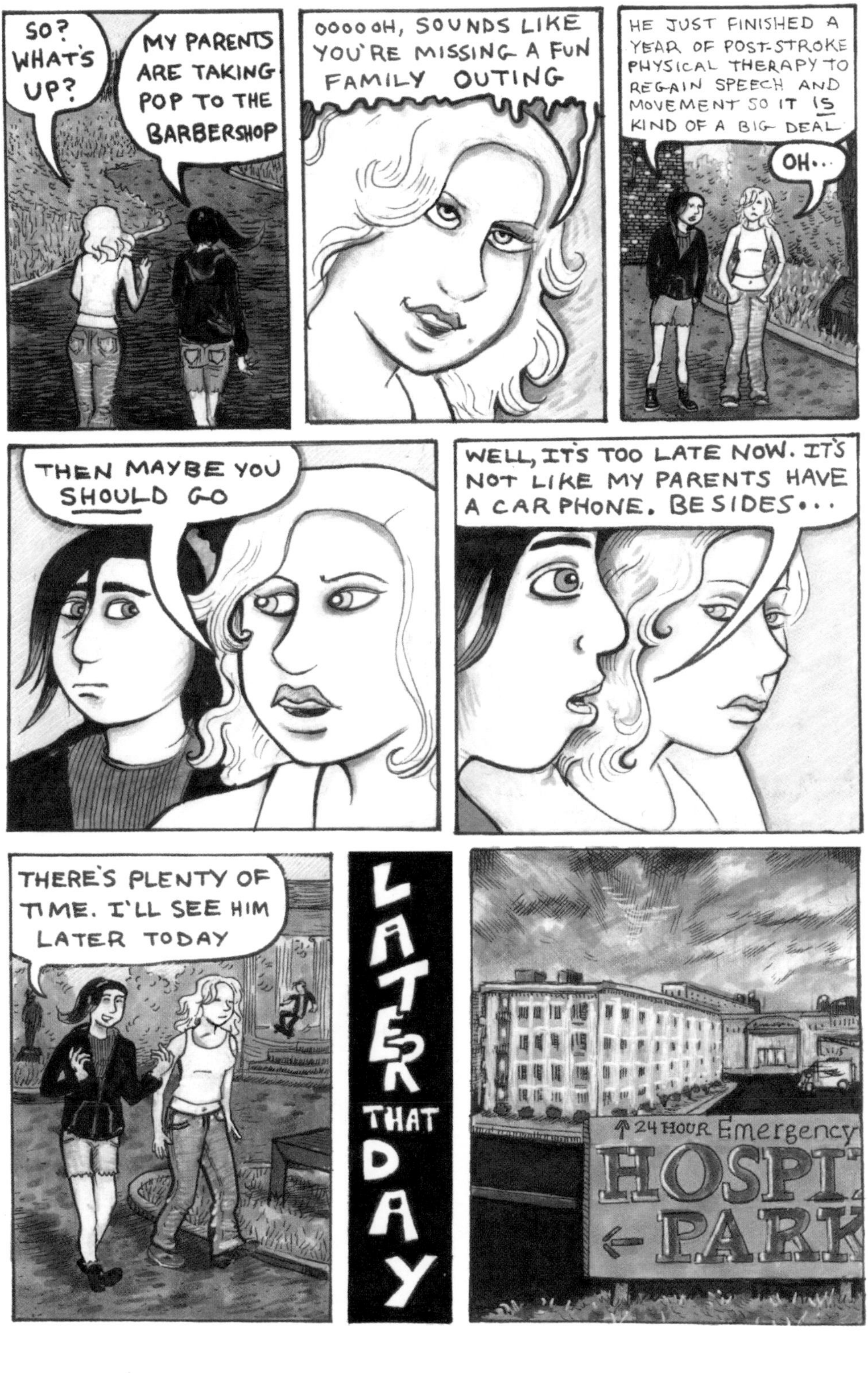
SO? WHAT'S UP?
MY PARENTS ARE TAKING POP TO THE BARBERSHOP
OOOOOH, SOUNDS LIKE YOU'RE MISSING A FUN FAMILY OUTING
HE JUST FINISHED A YEAR OF POST-STROKE PHYSICAL THERAPY TO REGAIN SPEECH AND MOVEMENT SO IT IS KIND OF A BIG DEAL
OH...
THEN MAYBE YOU SHOULD GO
WELL, IT'S TOO LATE NOW. IT'S NOT LIKE MY PARENTS HAVE A CAR PHONE. BESIDES...
THERE'S PLENTY OF TIME. I'LL SEE HIM LATER TODAY
LATER THAT DAY
24 HOUR Emergency
HOSPI
PARK

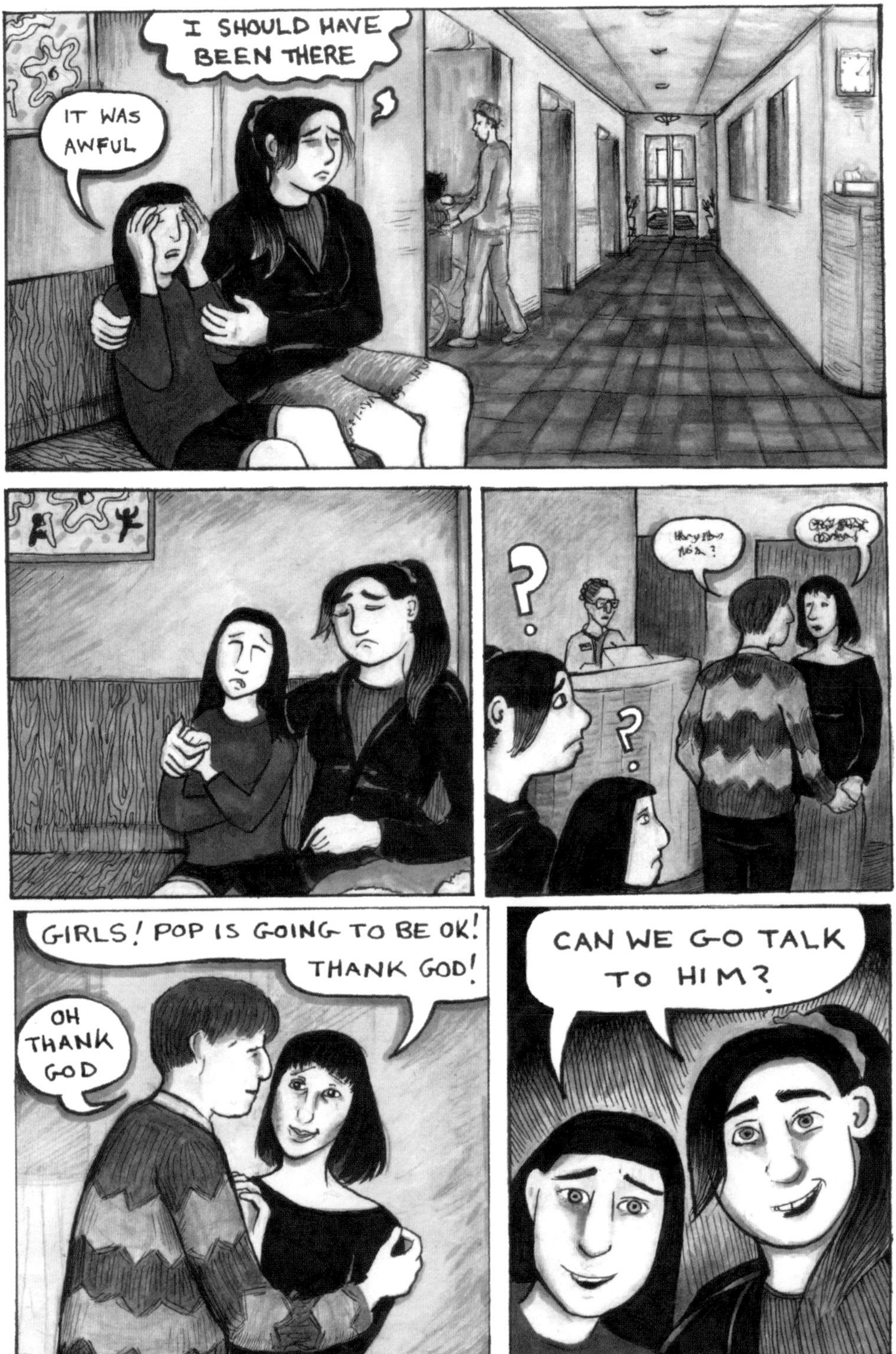
I SHOULD HAVE BEEN THERE
IT WAS AWFUL
GIRLS! POP IS GOING TO BE OK! THANK GOD!
OH THANK GOD
CAN WE GO TALK TO HIM?

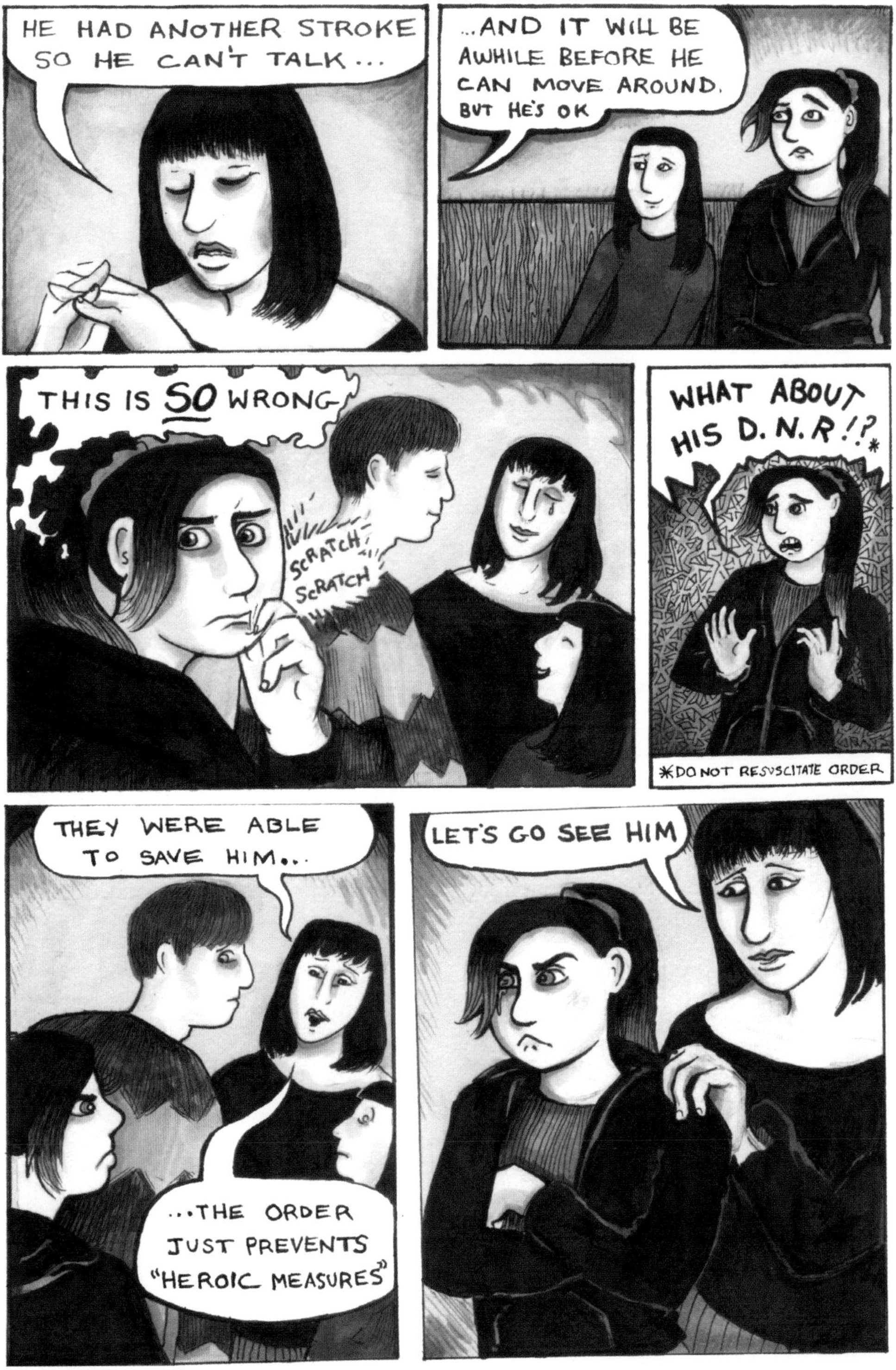
HE HAD ANOTHER STROKE SO HE CAN'T TALK...
...AND IT WILL BE AWHILE BEFORE HE CAN MOVE AROUND. BUT HE'S OK
THIS IS SO WRONG
SCRATCH SCRATCH
WHAT ABOUT HIS D.N.R!?*
*DO NOT RESUSCITATE ORDER
THEY WERE ABLE TO SAVE HIM...
...THE ORDER JUST PREVENTS "HEROIC MEASURES"
LET'S GO SEE HIM

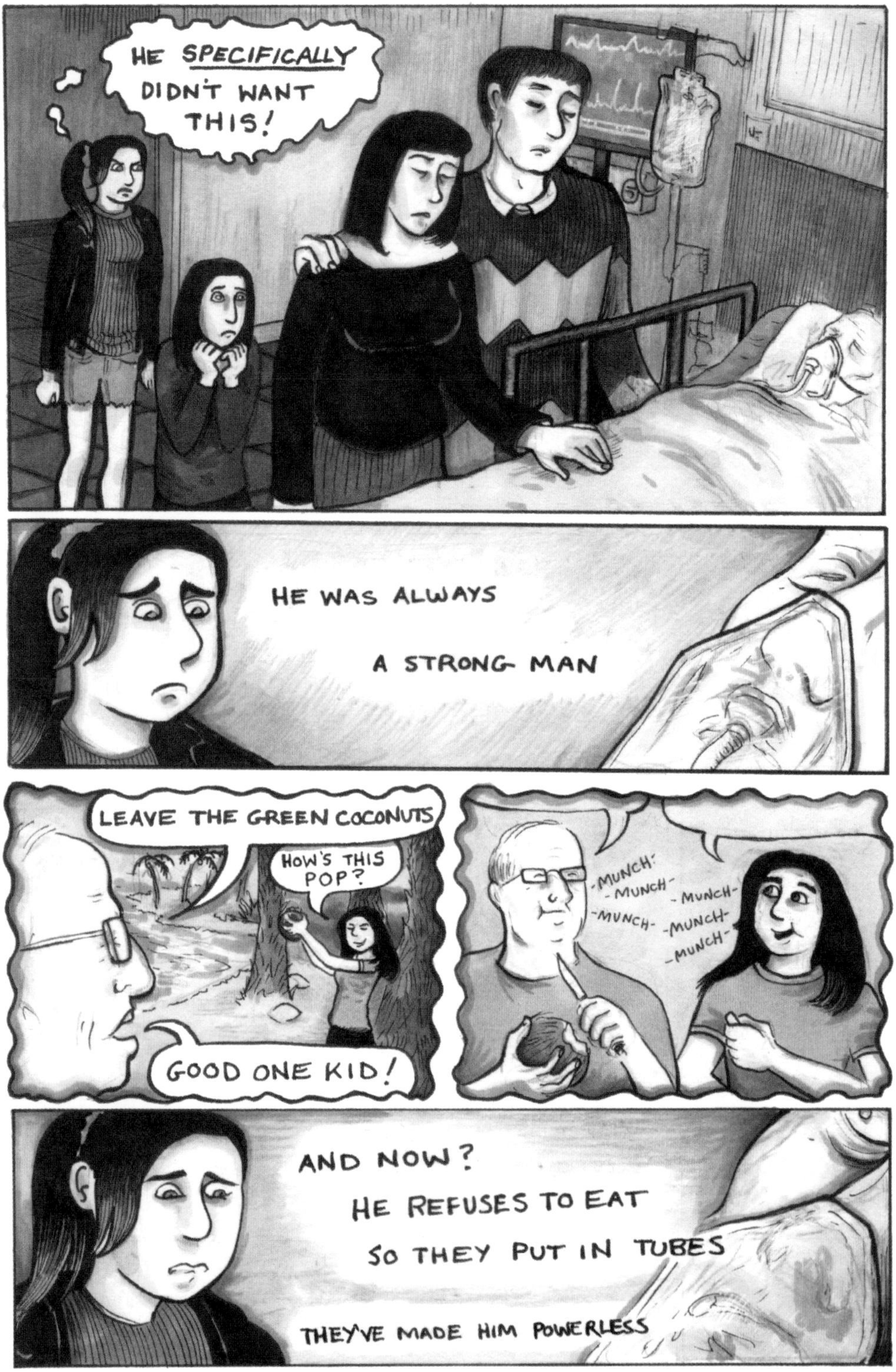
HE SPECIFICALLY DIDN'T WANT THIS!
HE WAS ALWAYS
A STRONG MAN
LEAVE THE GREEN COCONUTS
HOW'S THIS POP?
GOOD ONE KID!
-MUNCH-
-MUNCH-
-MUNCH-
-MUNCH-
-MUNCH-
-MUNCH-
AND NOW?
HE REFUSES TO EAT
SO THEY PUT IN TUBES
THEY'VE MADE HIM POWERLESS

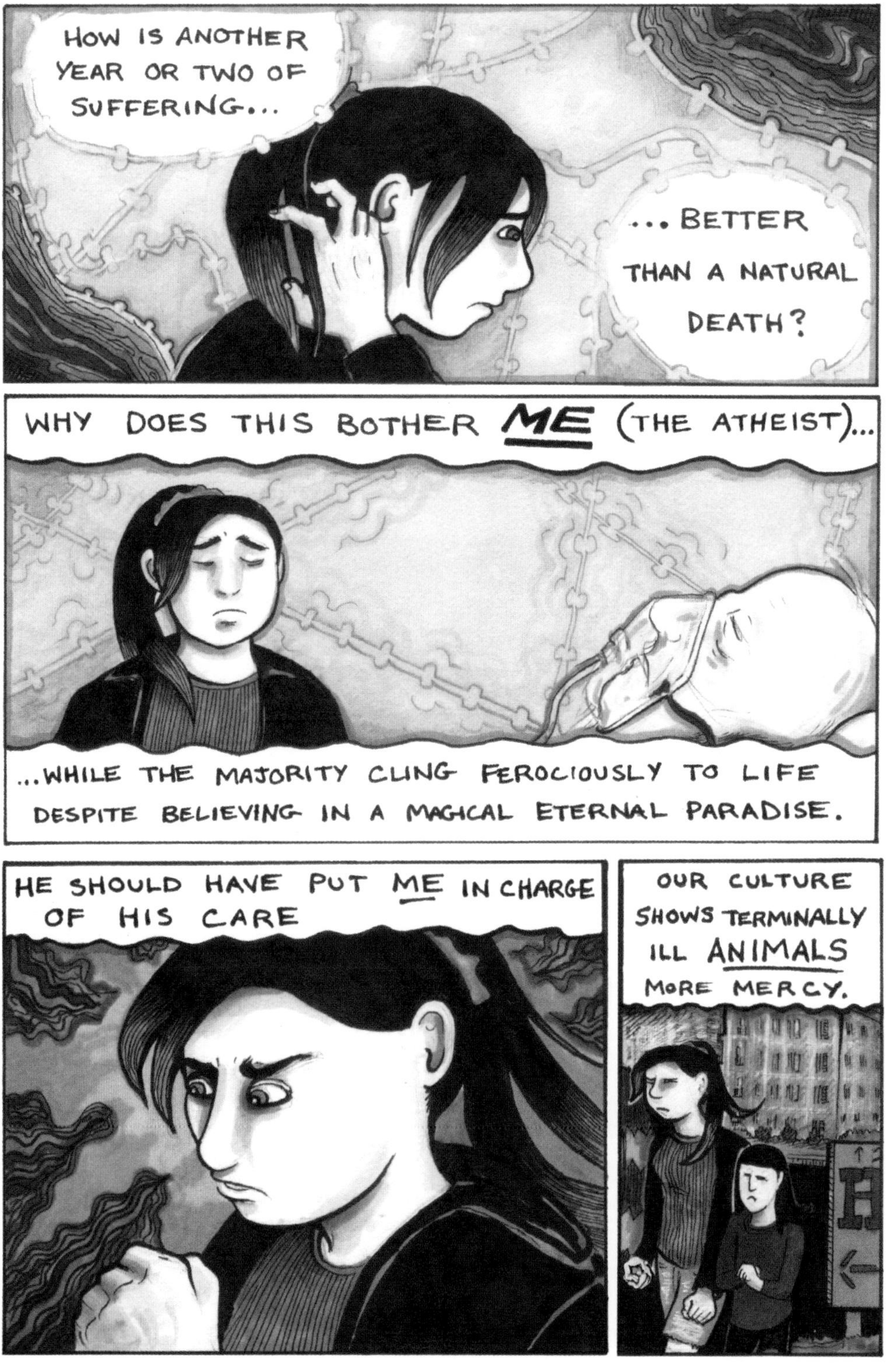
HOW IS ANOTHER YEAR OR TWO OF SUFFERING...
...BETTER THAN A NATURAL DEATH?
WHY DOES THIS BOTHER ME (THE ATHEIST)...
...WHILE THE MAJORITY CLING FEROCIOUSLY TO LIFE DESPITE BELIEVING IN A MAGICAL ETERNAL PARADISE.
HE SHOULD HAVE PUT ME IN CHARGE OF HIS CARE
OUR CULTURE SHOWS TERMINALLY ILL ANIMALS MORE MERCY.

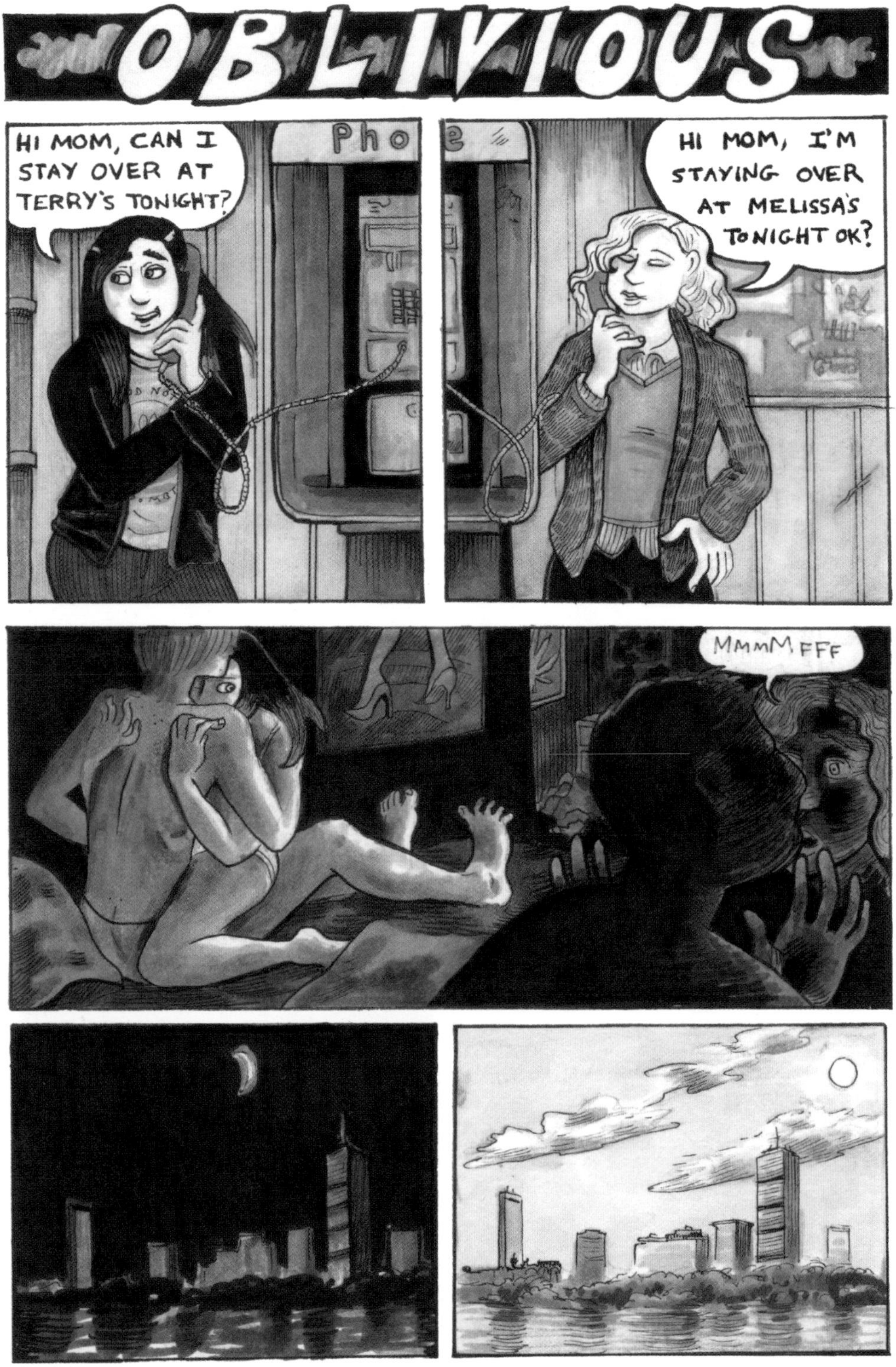
OBLIVIOUS
HI MOM, CAN I STAY OVER AT TERRY'S TONIGHT?
Phone
HI MOM, I'M STAYING OVER AT MELISSA'S TONIGHT OK?
MMMMFFF

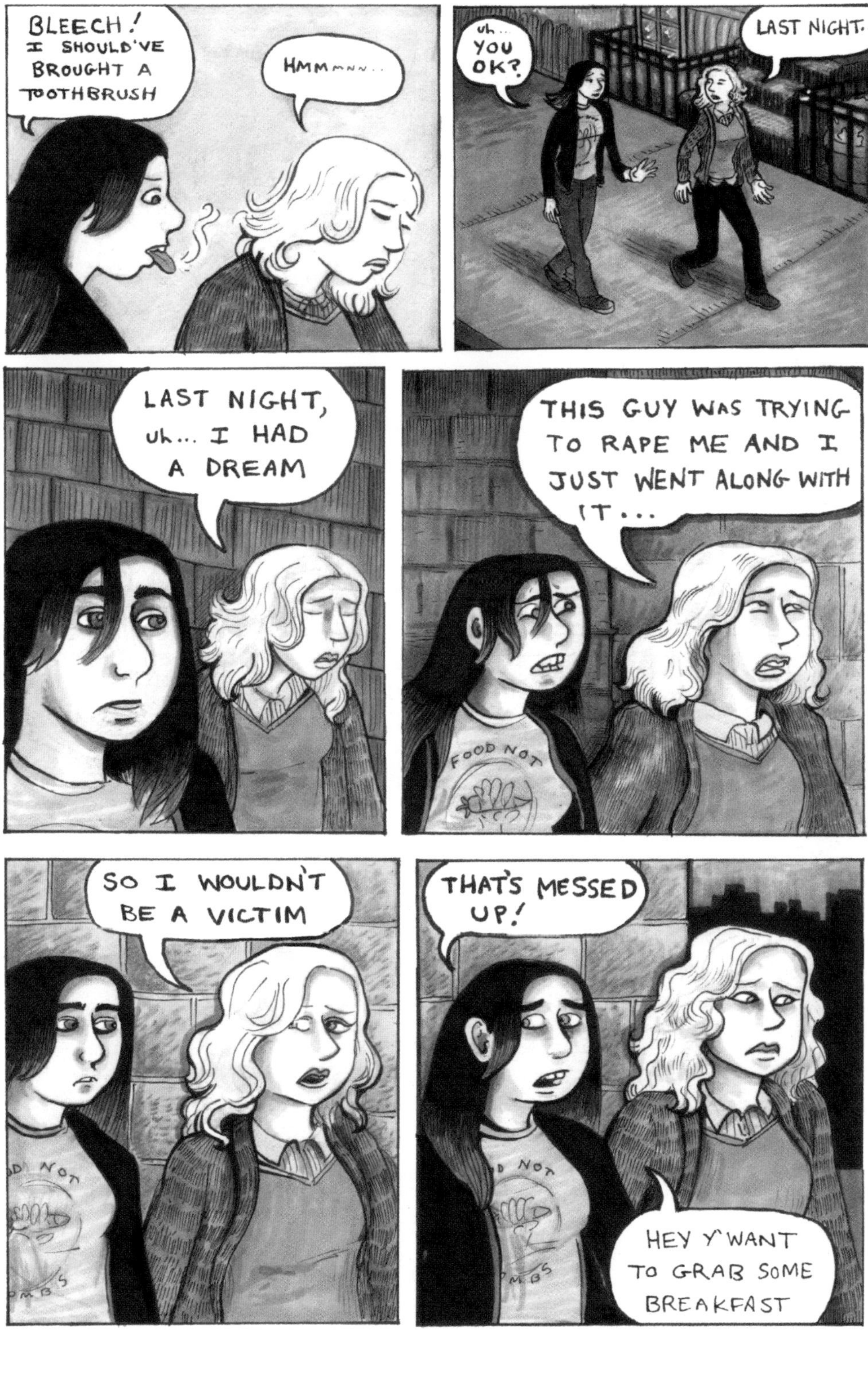
BLEECH! I SHOULD'VE BROUGHT A TOOTHBRUSH
HMMmnn..
uh... YOU OK?
LAST NIGHT..
LAST NIGHT, uh... I HAD A DREAM
THIS GUY WAS TRYING TO RAPE ME AND I JUST WENT ALONG WITH IT...
FOOD NOT
SO I WOULDN'T BE A VICTIM
THAT'S MESSED UP!
HEY Y'WANT TO GRAB SOME BREAKFAST

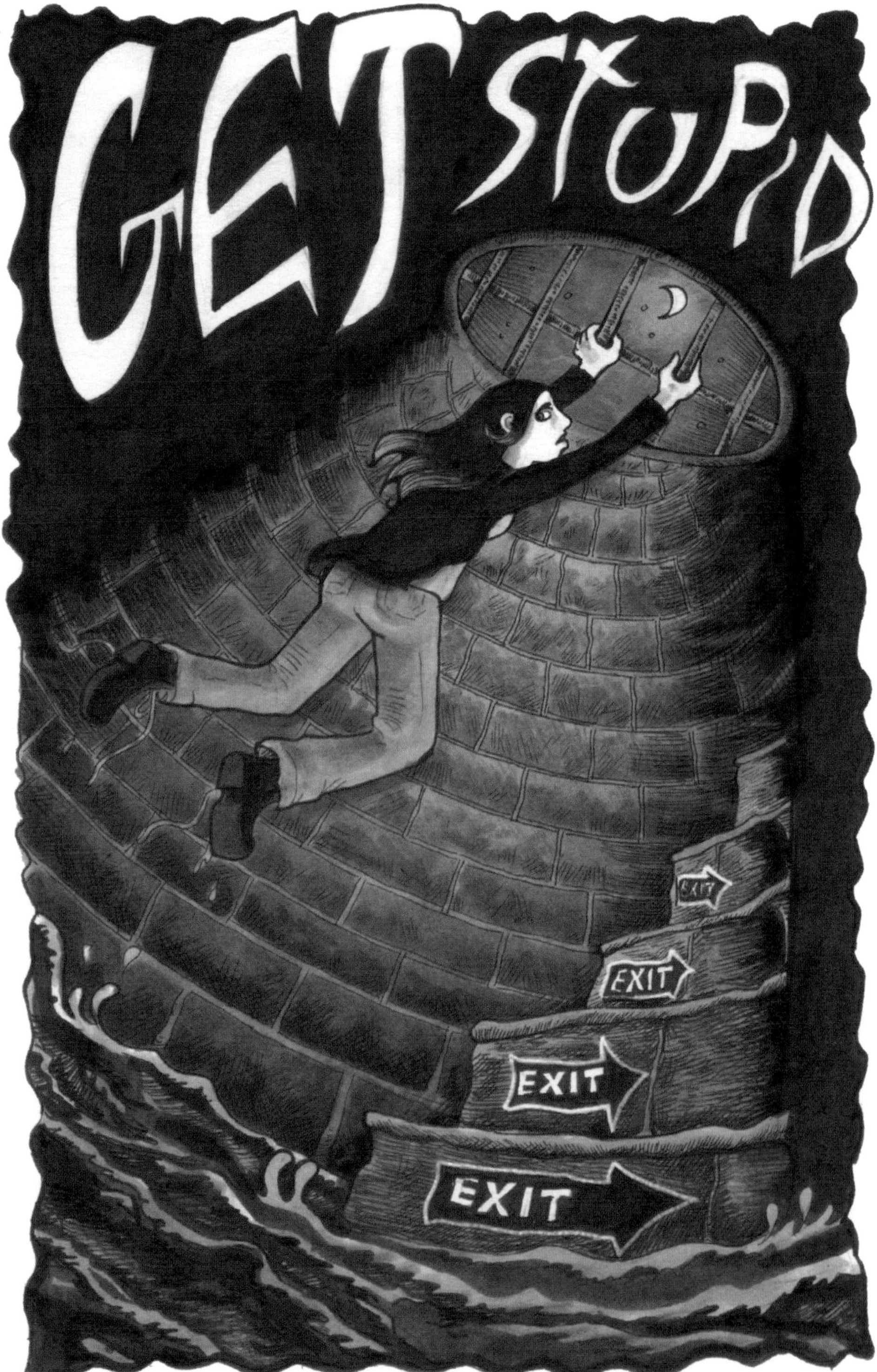
GET STUPID
EXIT
EXIT
EXIT
EXIT

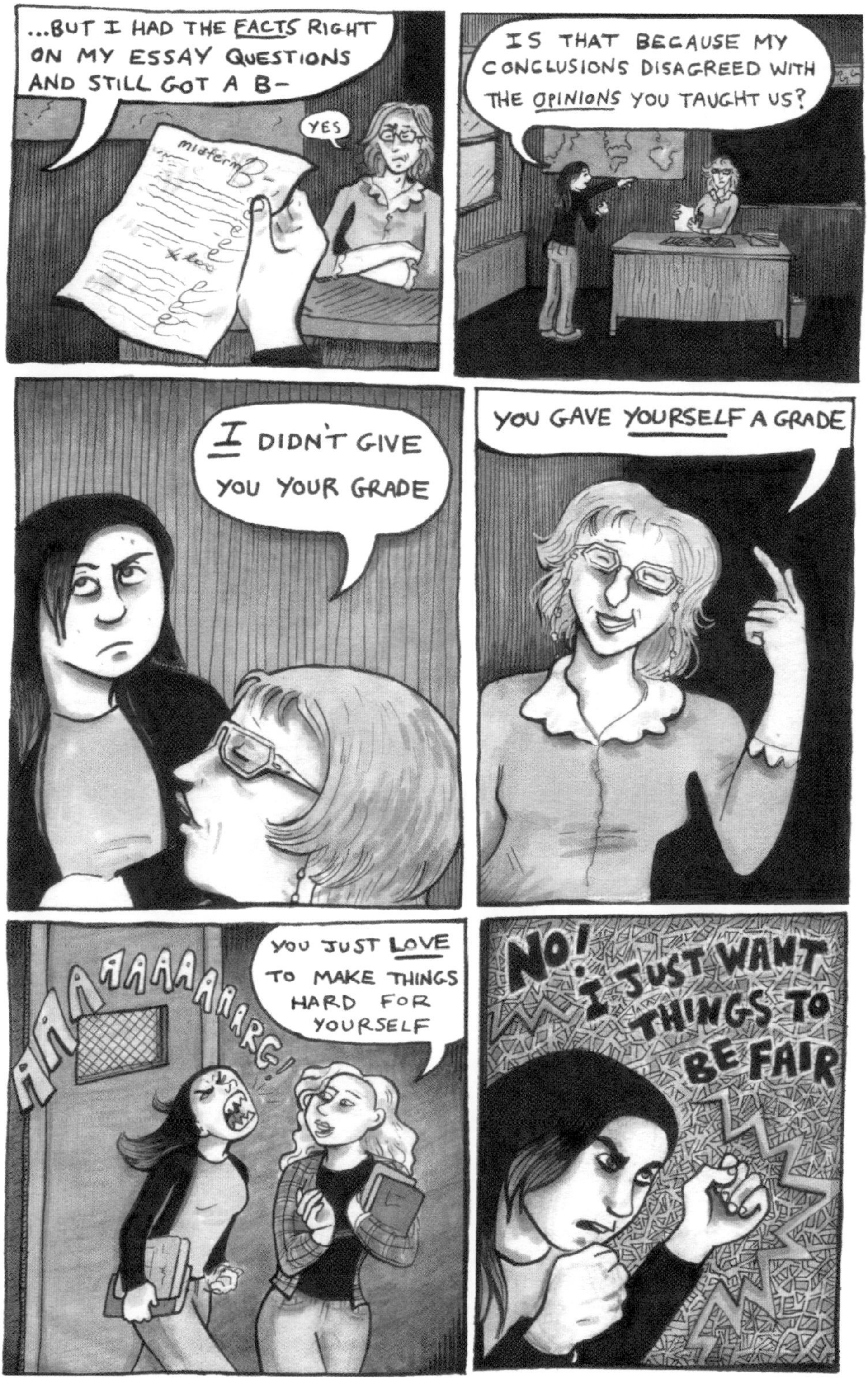
...BUT I HAD THE FACTS RIGHT ON MY ESSAY QUESTIONS AND STILL GOT A B-
YES
midterm B-
IS THAT BECAUSE MY CONCLUSIONS DISAGREED WITH THE OPINIONS YOU TAUGHT US?
I DIDN'T GIVE YOU YOUR GRADE
YOU GAVE YOURSELF A GRADE
AAAAAAAAAAARG!
YOU JUST LOVE TO MAKE THINGS HARD FOR YOURSELF
NO! I JUST WANT THINGS TO BE FAIR

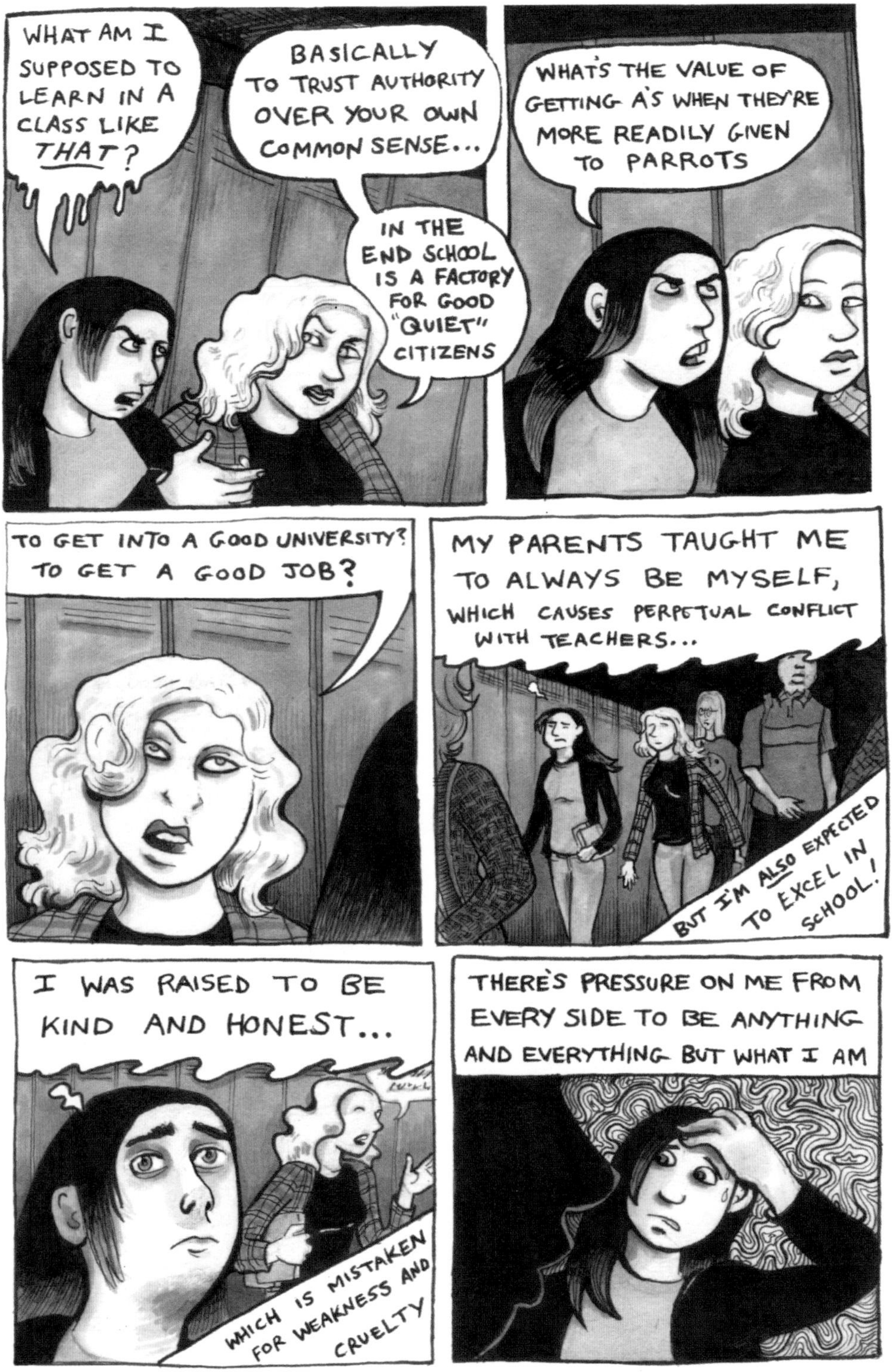
WHAT AM I SUPPOSED TO LEARN IN A CLASS LIKE THAT?
BASICALLY TO TRUST AUTHORITY OVER YOUR OWN COMMON SENSE...
IN THE END SCHOOL IS A FACTORY FOR GOOD "QUIET" CITIZENS
WHAT'S THE VALUE OF GETTING A'S WHEN THEY'RE MORE READILY GIVEN TO PARROTS
TO GET INTO A GOOD UNIVERSITY? TO GET A GOOD JOB?
MY PARENTS TAUGHT ME TO ALWAYS BE MYSELF,
WHICH CAUSES PERPETUAL CONFLICT WITH TEACHERS...
BUT I'M ALSO EXPECTED TO EXCEL IN SCHOOL!
I WAS RAISED TO BE KIND AND HONEST...
WHICH IS MISTAKEN FOR WEAKNESS AND CRUELTY
THERE'S PRESSURE ON ME FROM EVERY SIDE TO BE ANYTHING AND EVERYTHING BUT WHAT I AM

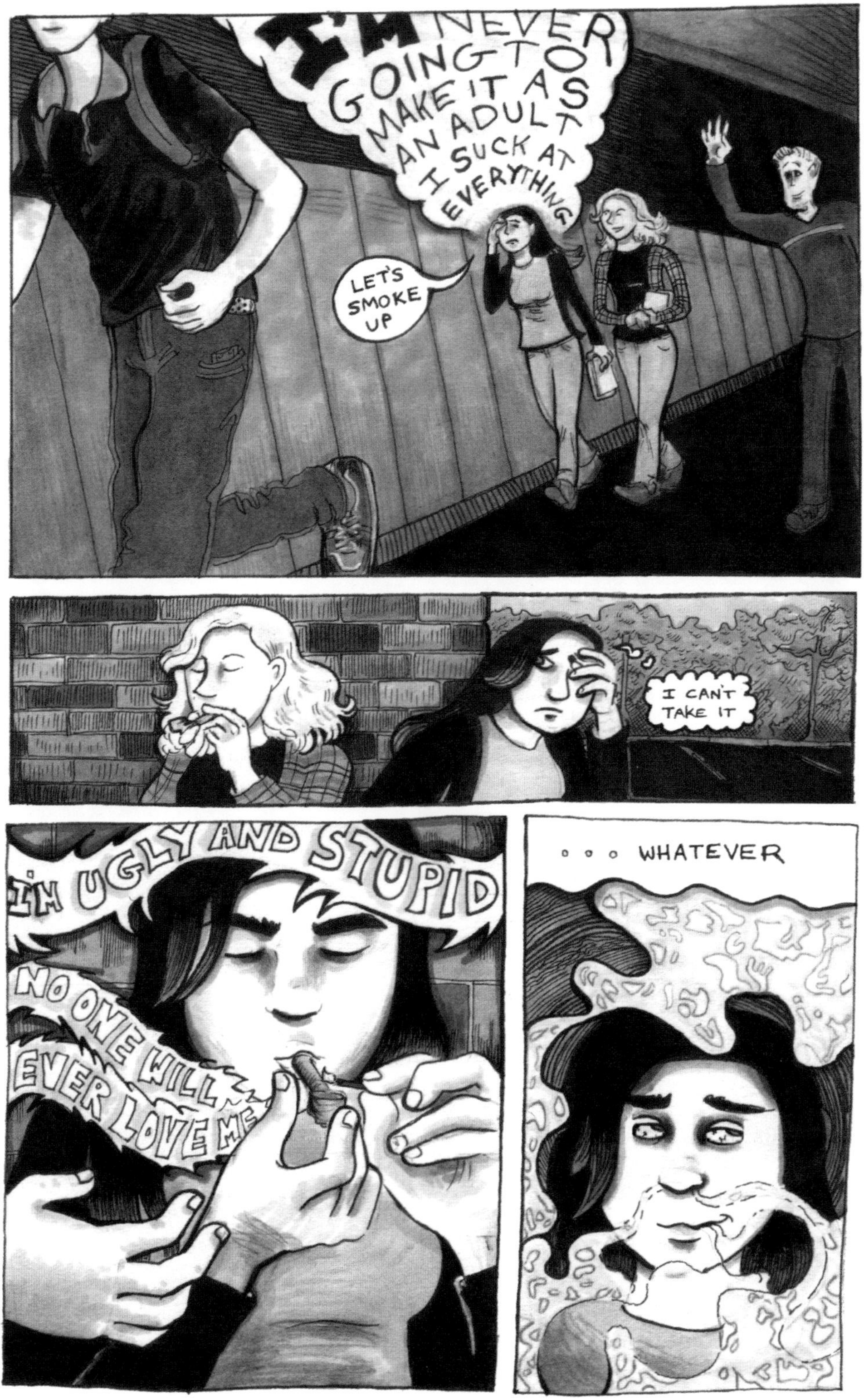
I'M NEVER GOING TO MAKE IT AS AN ADULT
I SUCK AT EVERYTHING
LET'S SMOKE UP
I CAN'T TAKE IT
I'M UGLY AND STUPID
NO ONE WILL EVER LOVE ME
. . . WHATEVER

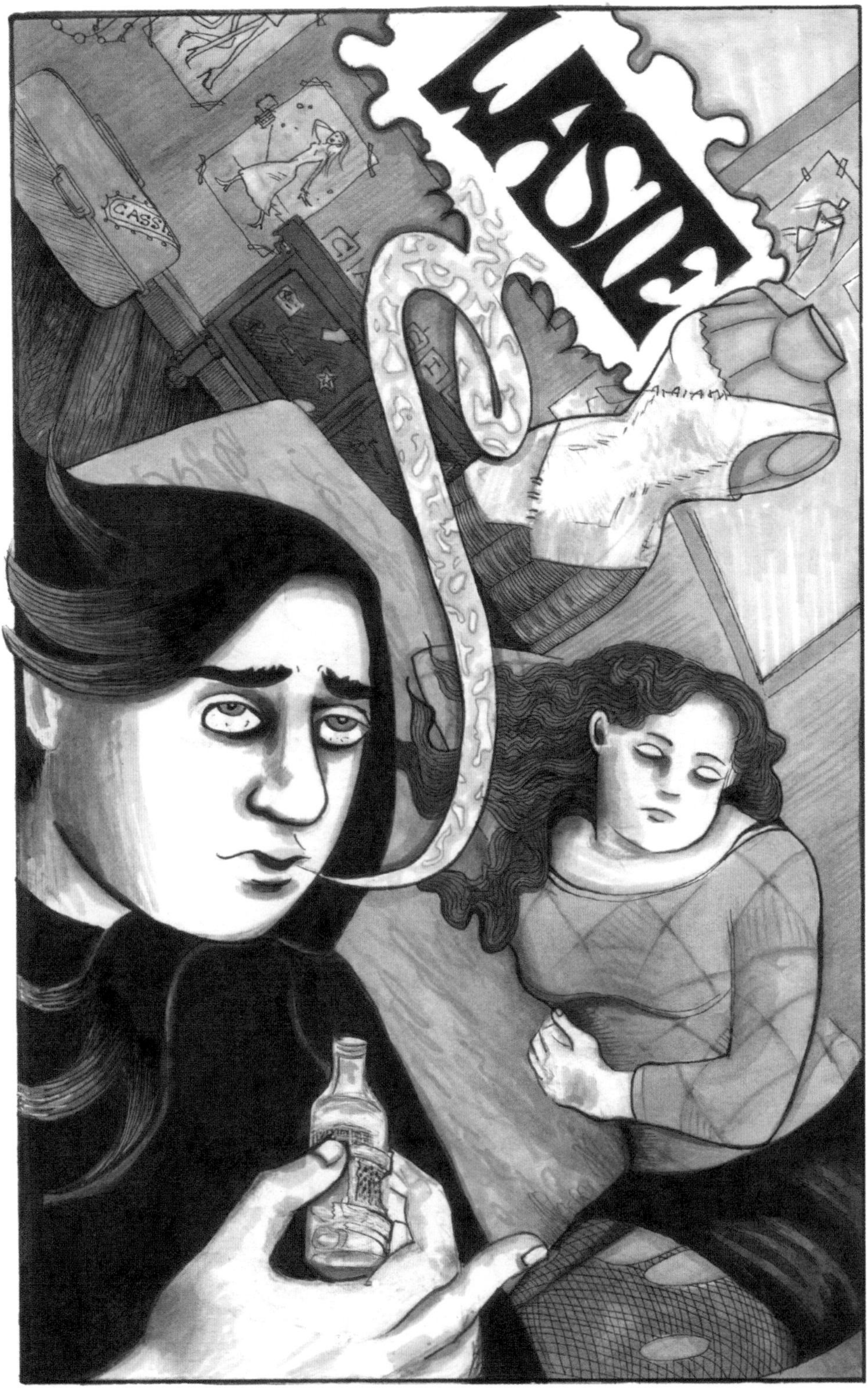

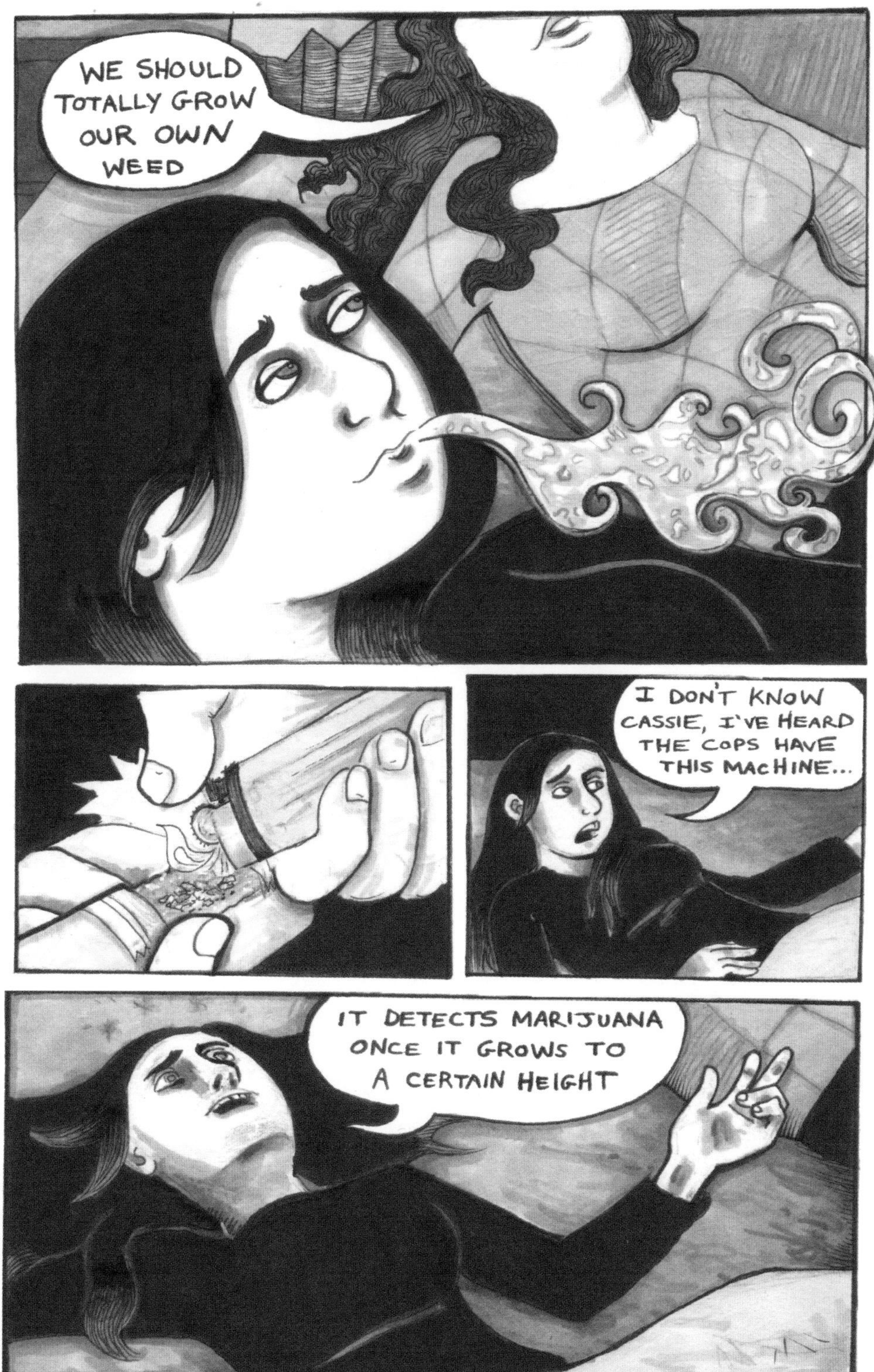
WE SHOULD TOTALLY GROW OUR OWN WEED
I DON'T KNOW CASSIE, I'VE HEARD THE COPS HAVE THIS MACHINE...
IT DETECTS MARIJUANA ONCE IT GROWS TO A CERTAIN HEIGHT

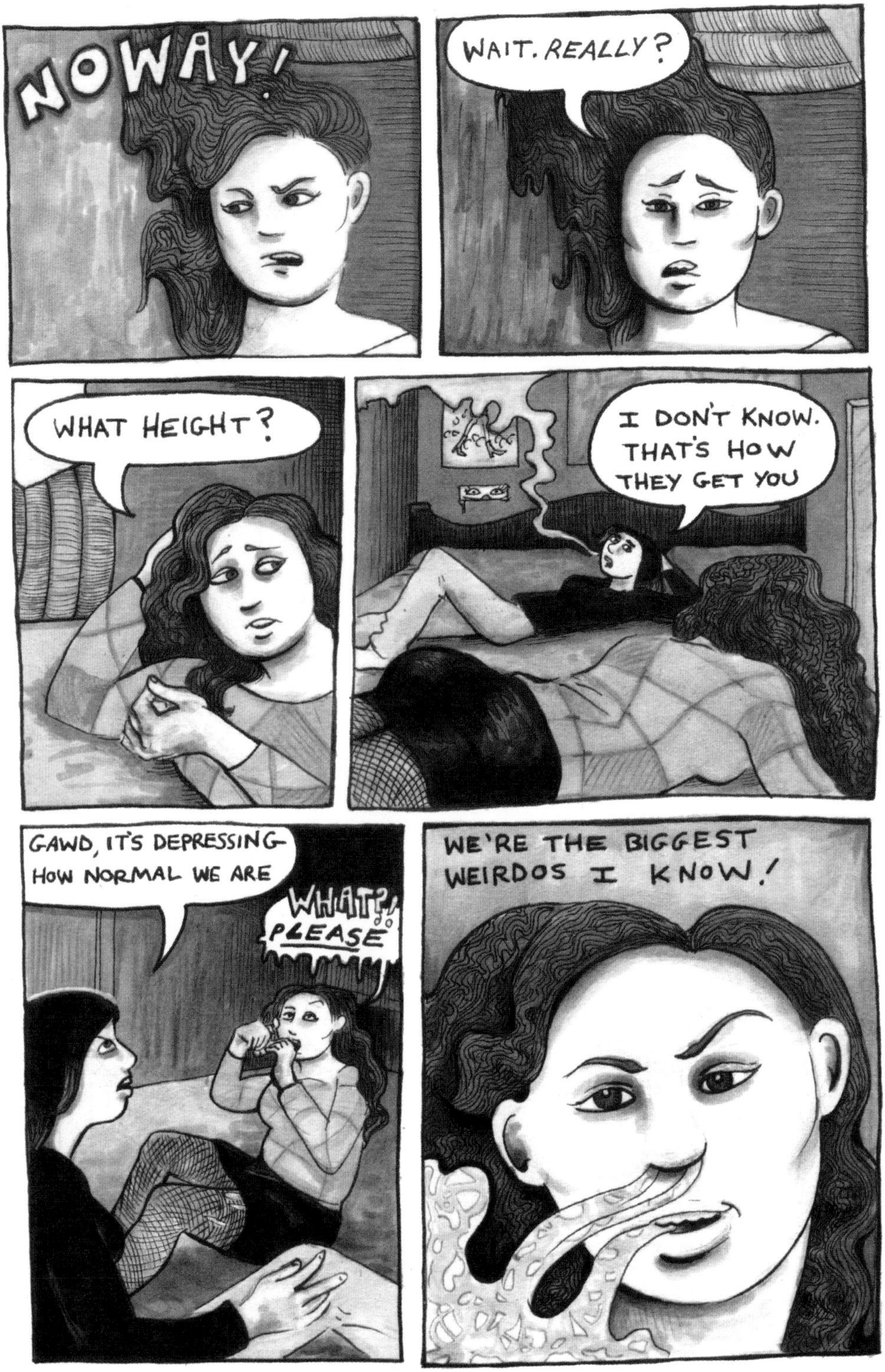
NOWAY!
WAIT. REALLY?
WHAT HEIGHT?
I DON'T KNOW. THAT'S HOW THEY GET YOU
GAWD, IT'S DEPRESSING HOW NORMAL WE ARE
WHAT?! PLEASE
WE'RE THE BIGGEST WEIRDOS I KNOW!

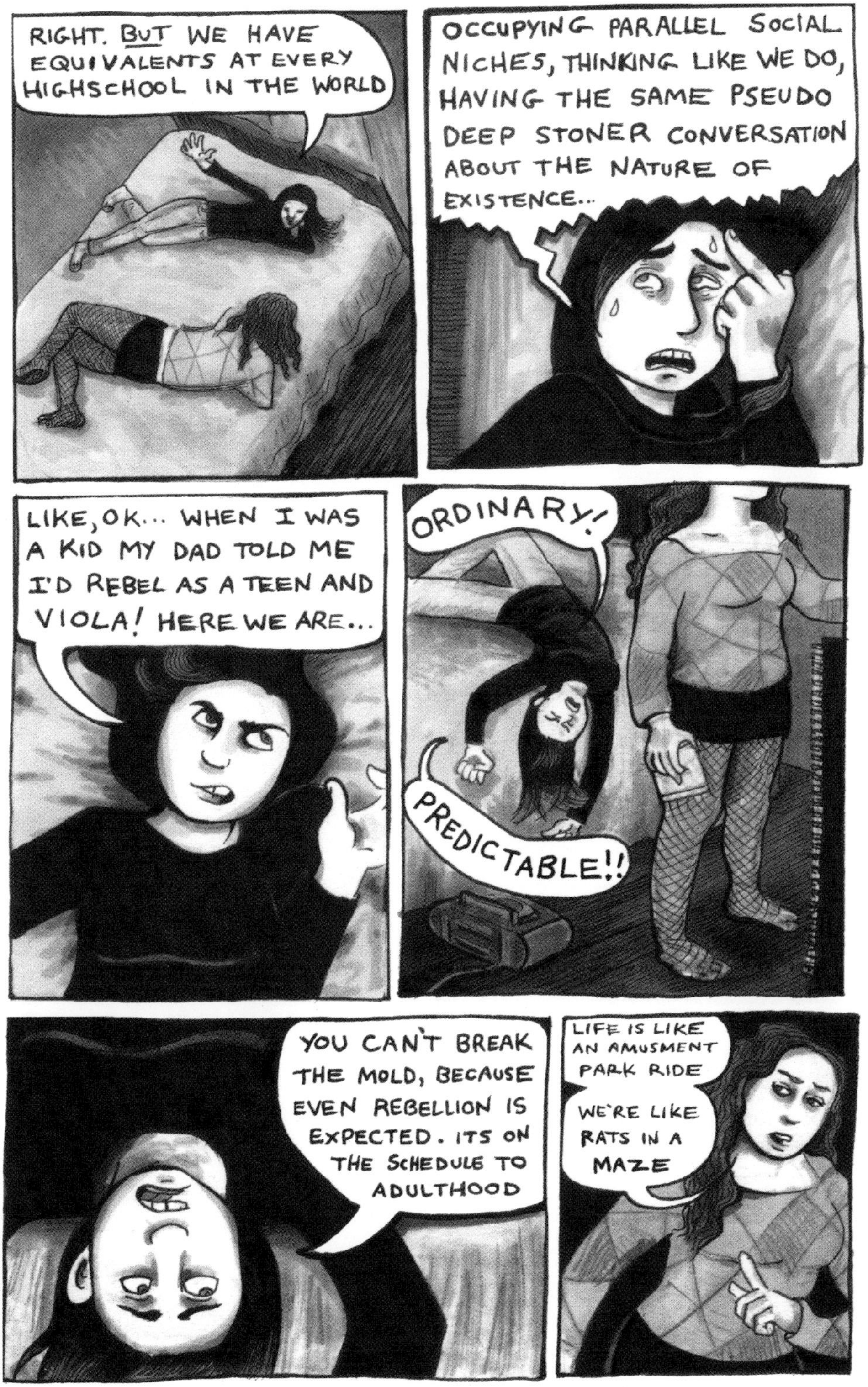
RIGHT. BUT WE HAVE EQUIVALENTS AT EVERY HIGHSCHOOL IN THE WORLD
OCCUPYING PARALLEL SOCIAL NICHES, THINKING LIKE WE DO, HAVING THE SAME PSEUDO DEEP STONER CONVERSATION ABOUT THE NATURE OF EXISTENCE...
LIKE, OK... WHEN I WAS A KID MY DAD TOLD ME I'D REBEL AS A TEEN AND VIOLA! HERE WE ARE...
ORDINARY!
PREDICTABLE!!
YOU CAN'T BREAK THE MOLD, BECAUSE EVEN REBELLION IS EXPECTED. ITS ON THE SCHEDULE TO ADULTHOOD
LIFE IS LIKE AN AMUSMENT PARK RIDE
WE'RE LIKE RATS IN A MAZE

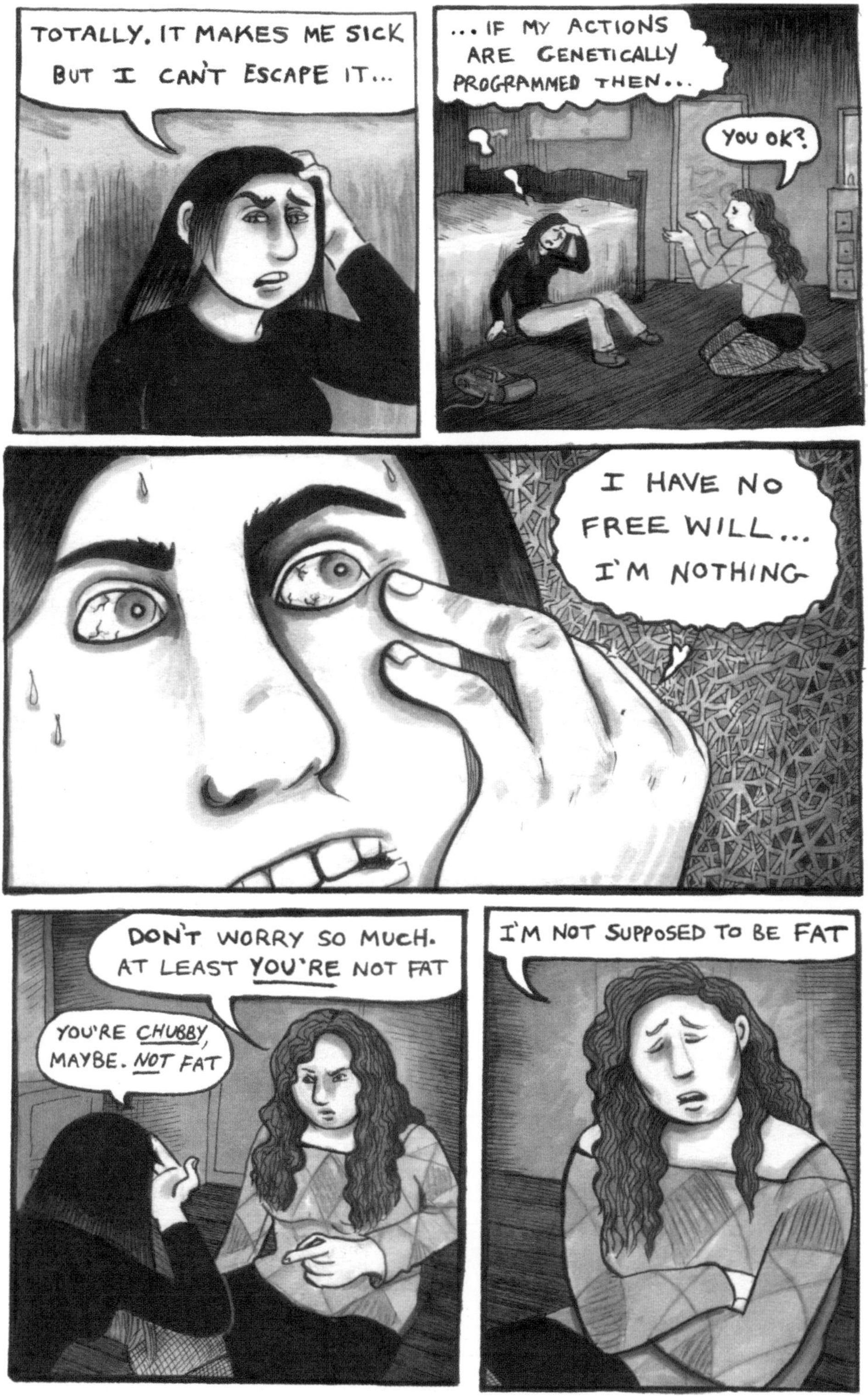
TOTALLY. IT MAKES ME SICK BUT I CAN'T ESCAPE IT...
...IF MY ACTIONS ARE GENETICALLY PROGRAMMED THEN...
YOU OK?
I HAVE NO FREE WILL... I'M NOTHING
DON'T WORRY SO MUCH. AT LEAST YOU'RE NOT FAT
YOU'RE CHUBBY, MAYBE. NOT FAT
I'M NOT SUPPOSED TO BE FAT

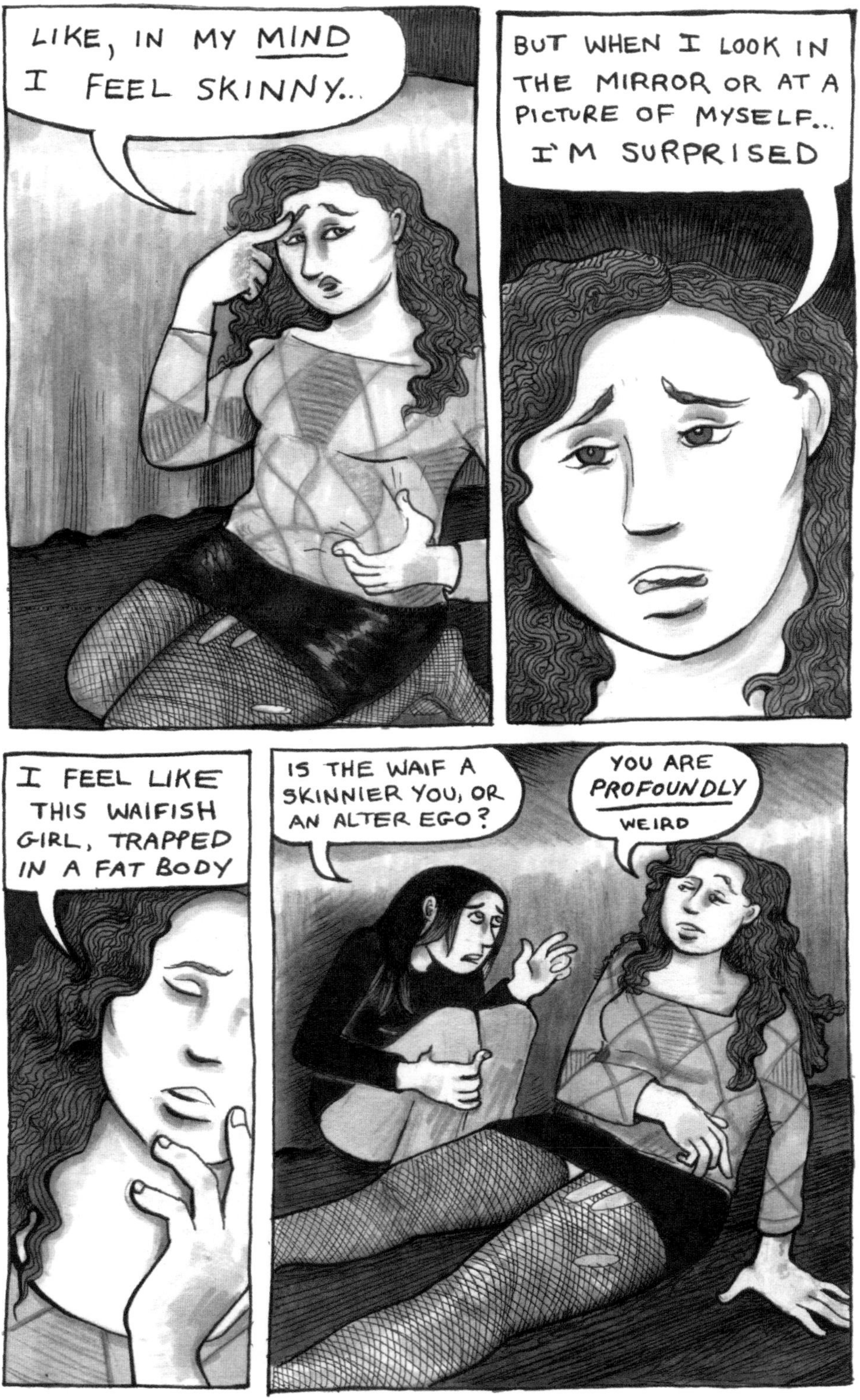
LIKE, IN MY MIND I FEEL SKINNY...
BUT WHEN I LOOK IN THE MIRROR OR AT A PICTURE OF MYSELF... I'M SURPRISED
I FEEL LIKE THIS WAIFISH GIRL, TRAPPED IN A FAT BODY
IS THE WAIF A SKINNIER YOU, OR AN ALTER EGO?
YOU ARE PROFOUNDLY WEIRD

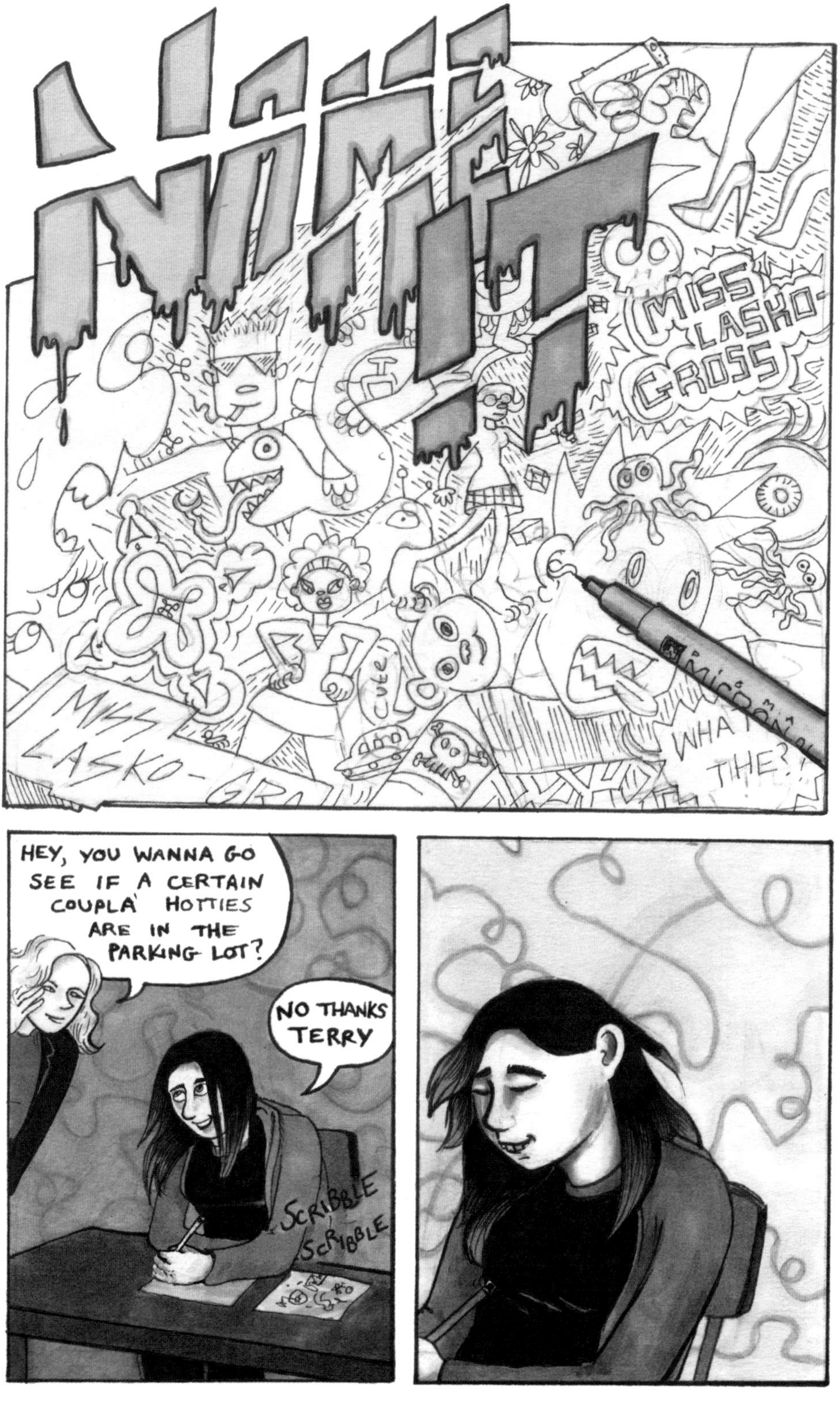
MISS LASKO-GROSS
CUTE
WHAT THE?!
HEY, YOU WANNA GO SEE IF A CERTAIN COUPLA' HOTTIES ARE IN THE PARKING LOT?
NO THANKS TERRY
SCRIBBLE SCRIBBLE

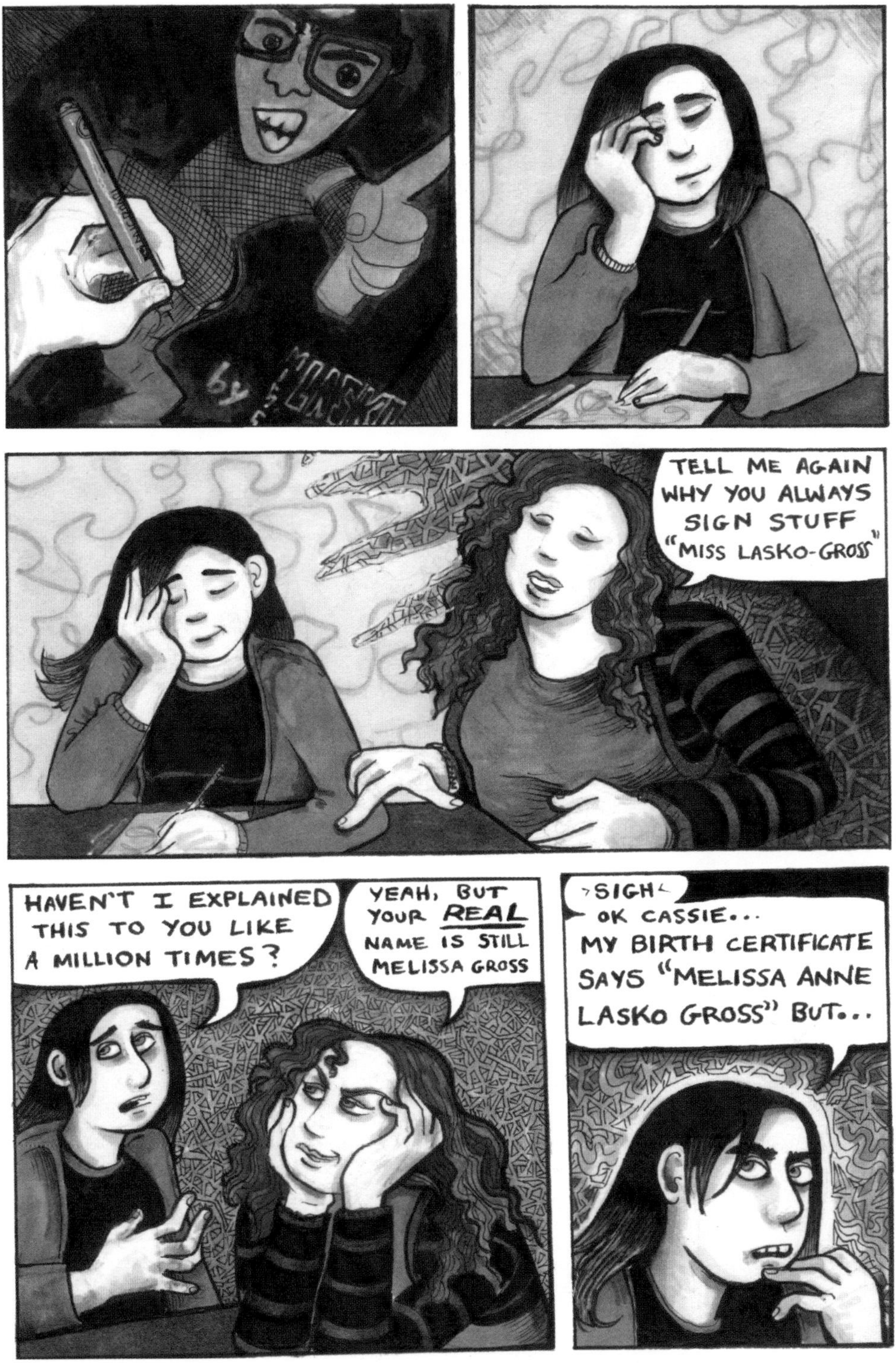
TELL ME AGAIN WHY YOU ALWAYS SIGN STUFF "MISS LASKO-GROSS"
HAVEN'T I EXPLAINED THIS TO YOU LIKE A MILLION TIMES?
YEAH, BUT YOUR REAL NAME IS STILL MELISSA GROSS
>SIGH<
OK CASSIE...
MY BIRTH CERTIFICATE SAYS "MELISSA ANNE LASKO GROSS" BUT...

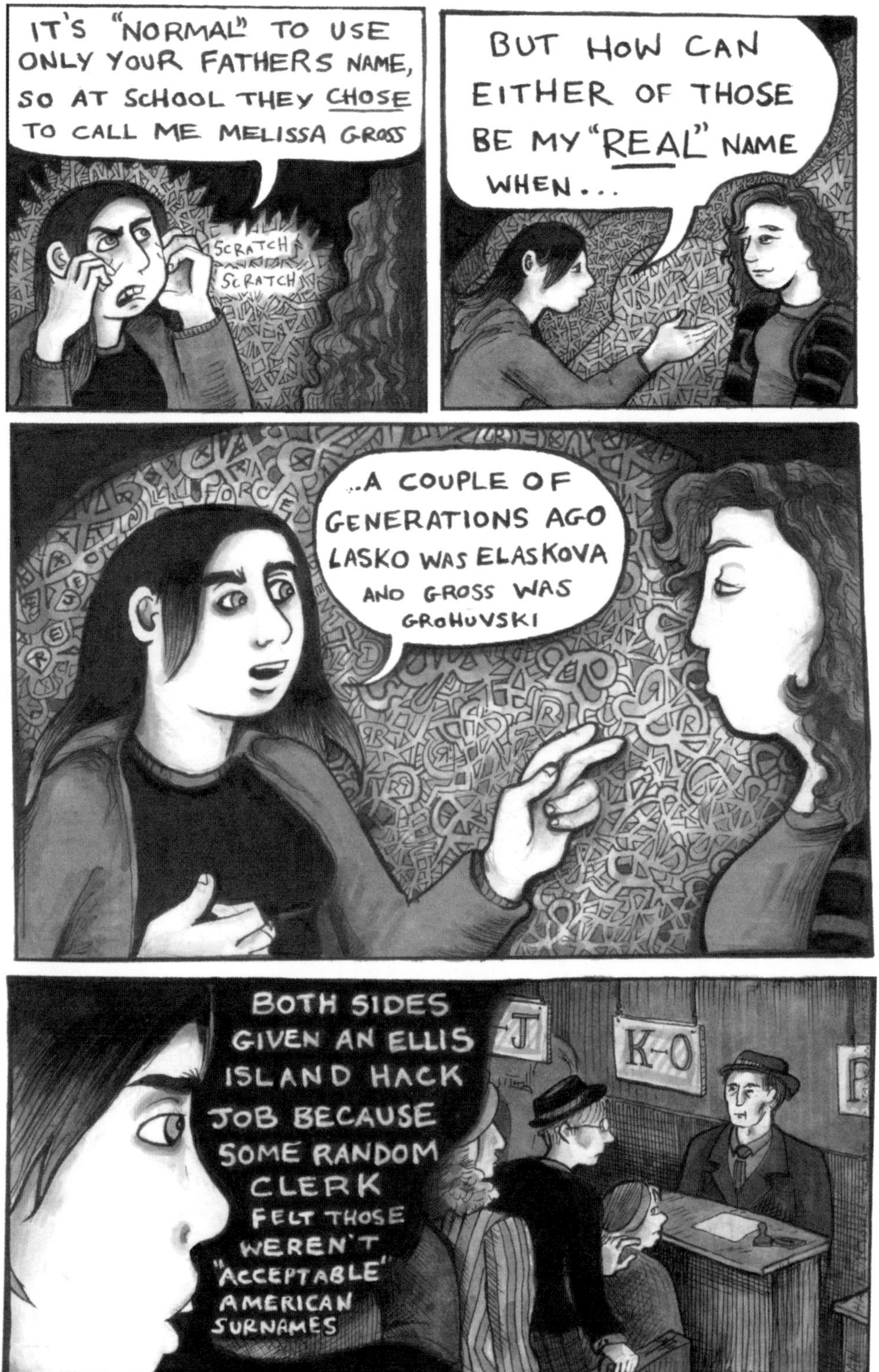
IT'S "NORMAL" TO USE ONLY YOUR FATHERS NAME, SO AT SCHOOL THEY CHOSE TO CALL ME MELISSA GROSS
SCRATCH
SCRATCH
BUT HOW CAN EITHER OF THOSE BE MY "REAL" NAME WHEN...
...A COUPLE OF GENERATIONS AGO LASKO WAS ELASKOVA AND GROSS WAS GROHUVSKI
BOTH SIDES GIVEN AN ELLIS ISLAND HACK JOB BECAUSE SOME RANDOM CLERK FELT THOSE WEREN'T "ACCEPTABLE" AMERICAN SURNAMES
J
K-O
P

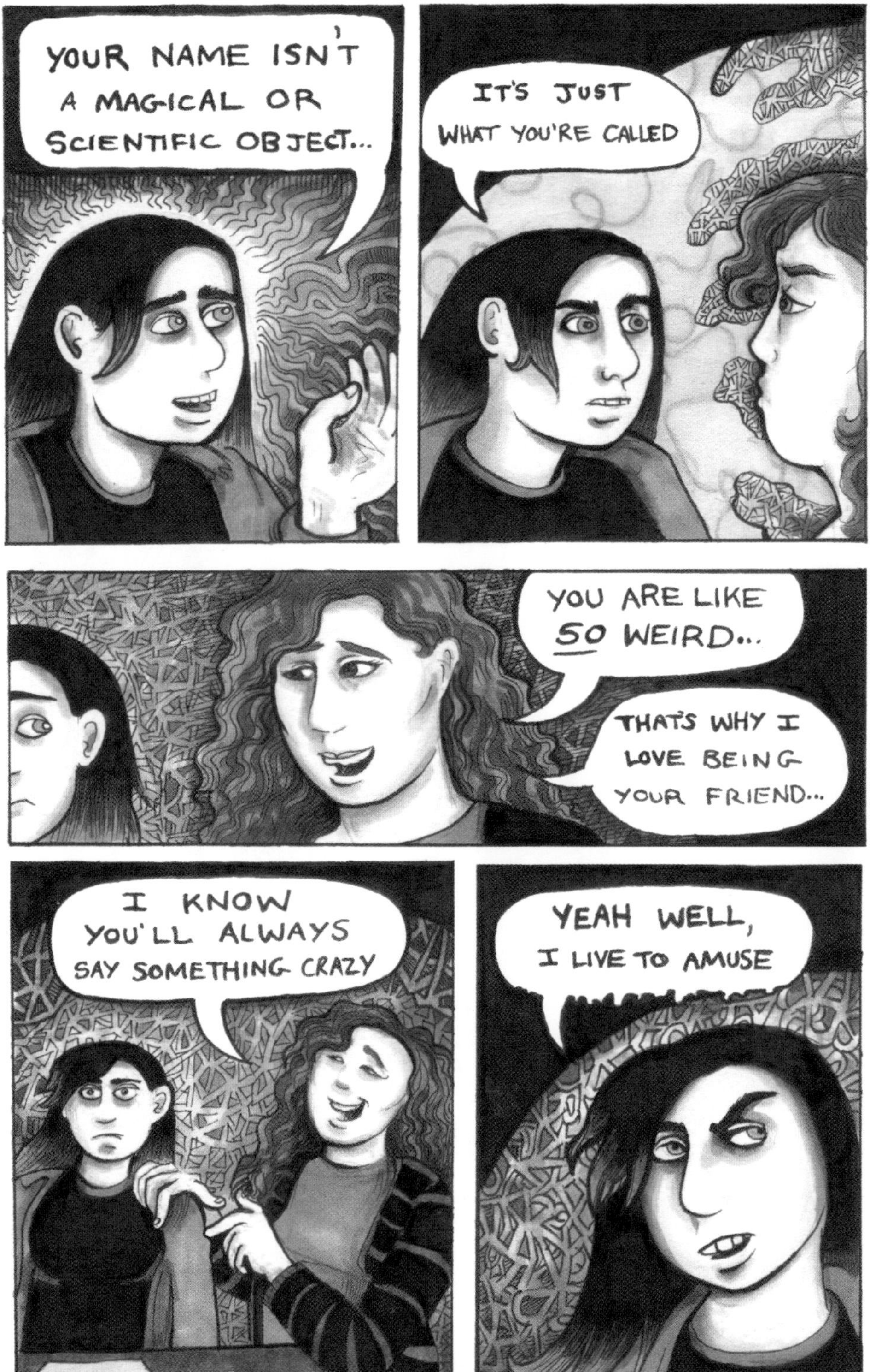
YOUR NAME ISN'T A MAGICAL OR SCIENTIFIC OBJECT...
IT'S JUST WHAT YOU'RE CALLED
YOU ARE LIKE SO WEIRD...
THAT'S WHY I LOVE BEING YOUR FRIEND...
I KNOW YOU'LL ALWAYS SAY SOMETHING CRAZY
YEAH WELL, I LIVE TO AMUSE

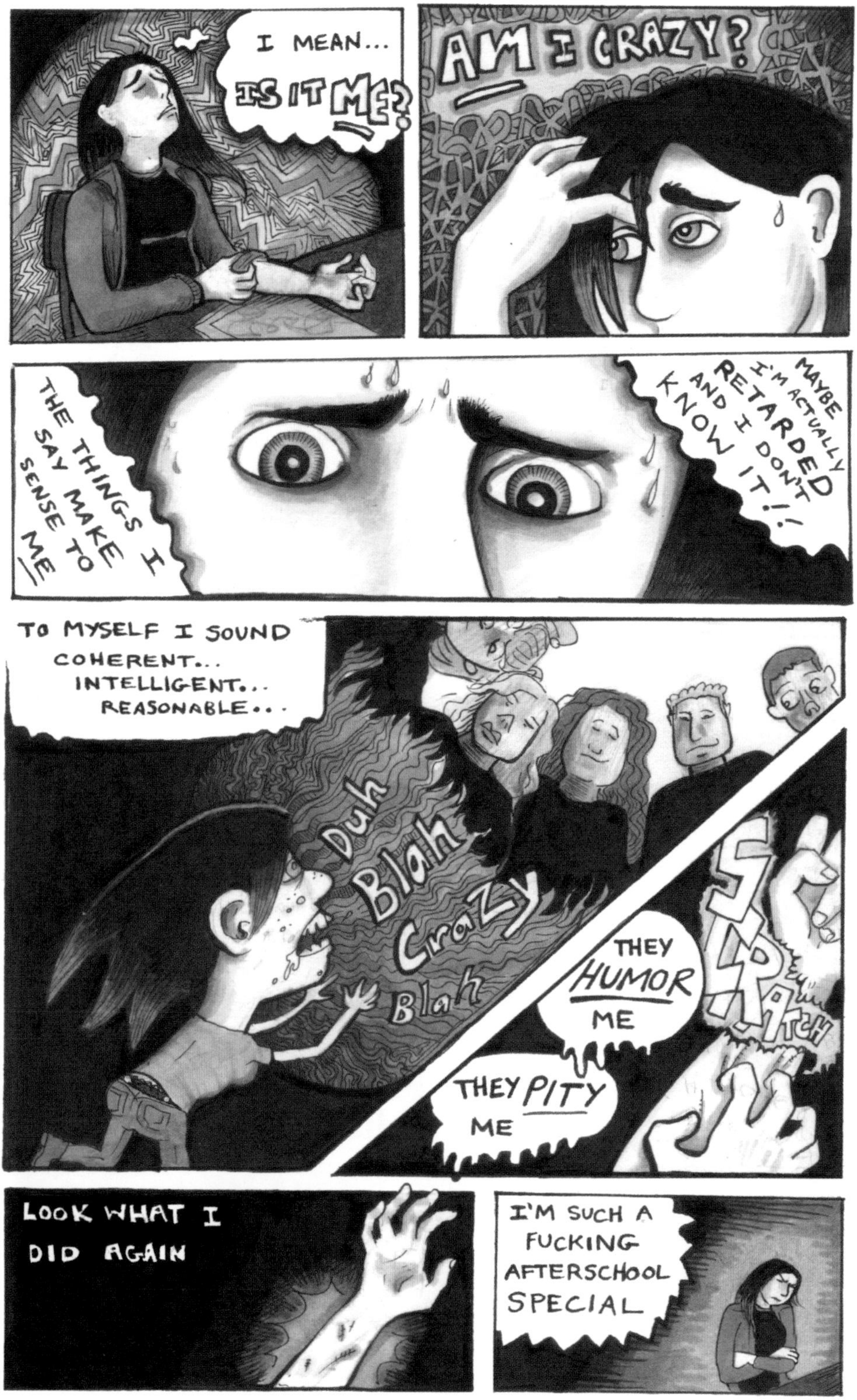
I MEAN...
IS IT ME?
AM I CRAZY?
THE THINGS I SAY MAKE SENSE TO ME
MAYBE I'M ACTUALLY RETARDED AND I DON'T KNOW IT!!
TO MYSELF I SOUND COHERENT... INTELLIGENT... REASONABLE...
Duh
Blah
Crazy
Blah
THEY HUMOR ME
THEY PITY ME
SCRATCH
LOOK WHAT I DID AGAIN
I'M SUCH A FUCKING AFTERSCHOOL SPECIAL

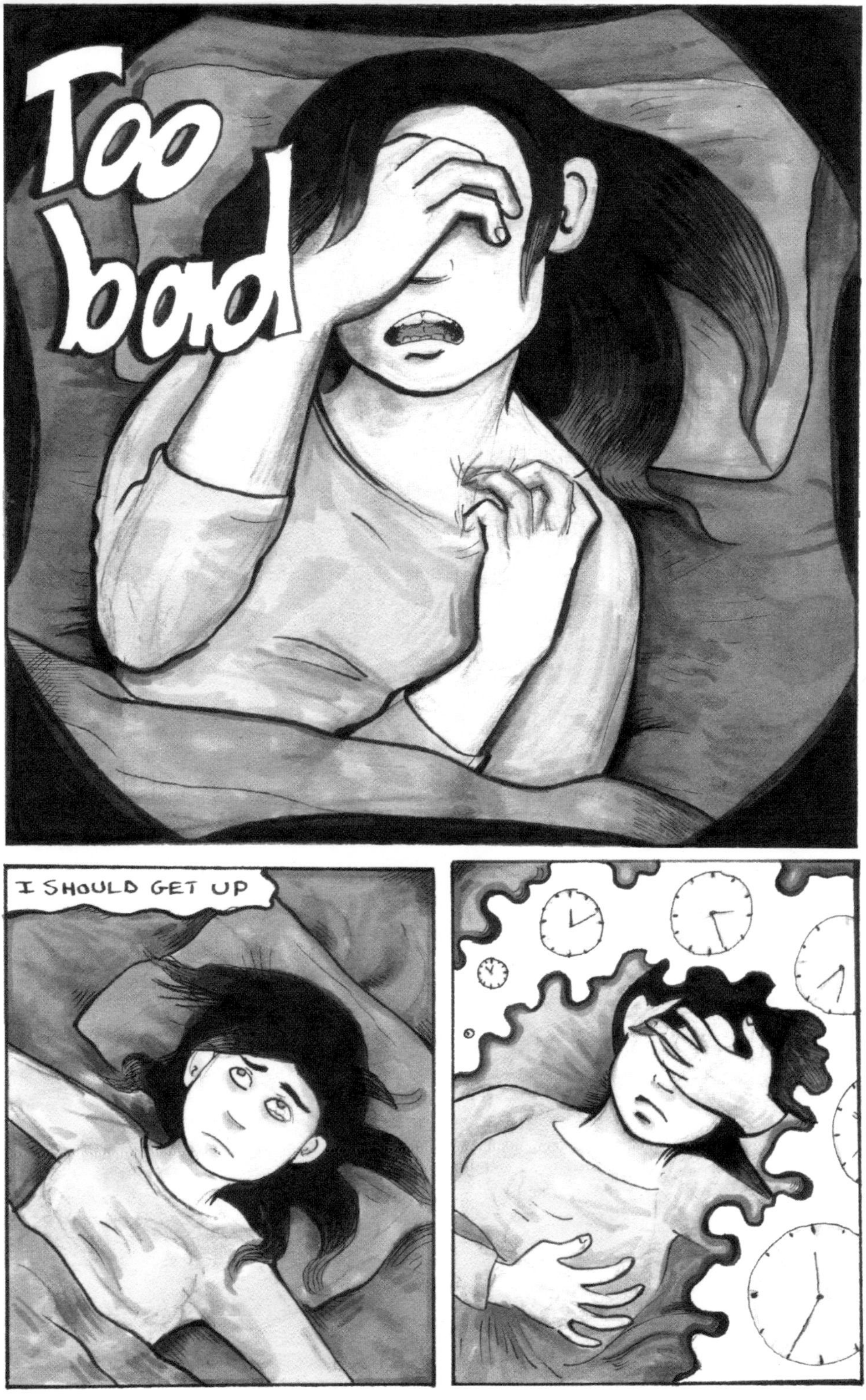
Too bad
I SHOULD GET UP

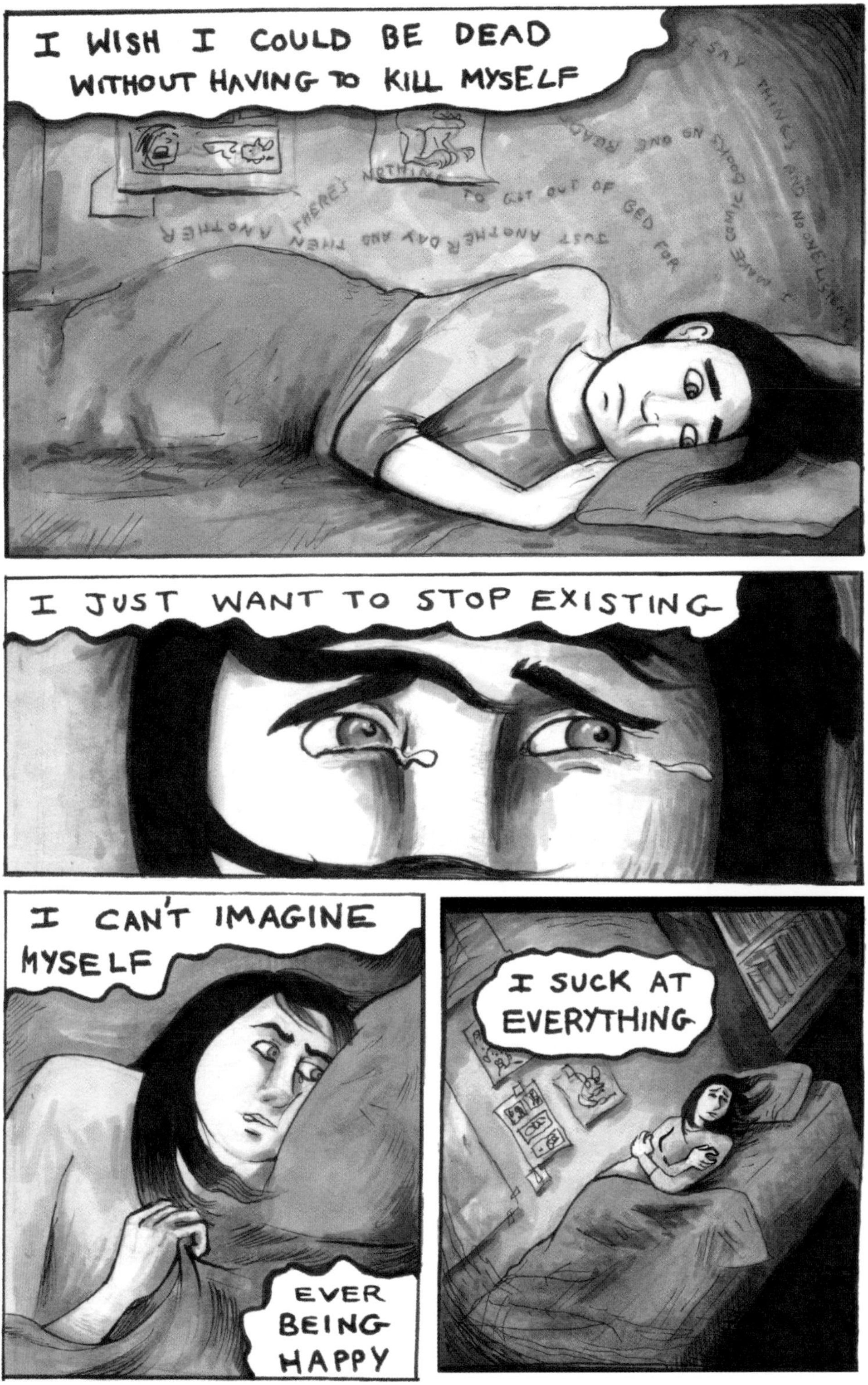
I WISH I COULD BE DEAD WITHOUT HAVING TO KILL MYSELF
I SAY THINGS AND NO ONE LISTENS
I MAKE COMIC BOOKS NO ONE READS
THERE'S NOTHING TO GET OUT OF BED FOR
JUST ANOTHER DAY AND THEN ANOTHER
I JUST WANT TO STOP EXISTING
I CAN'T IMAGINE MYSELF
EVER BEING HAPPY
I SUCK AT EVERYTHING

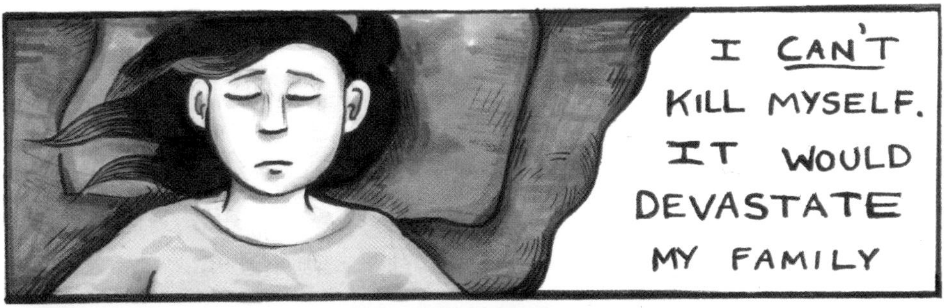
I CAN'T KILL MYSELF. IT WOULD DEVASTATE MY FAMILY

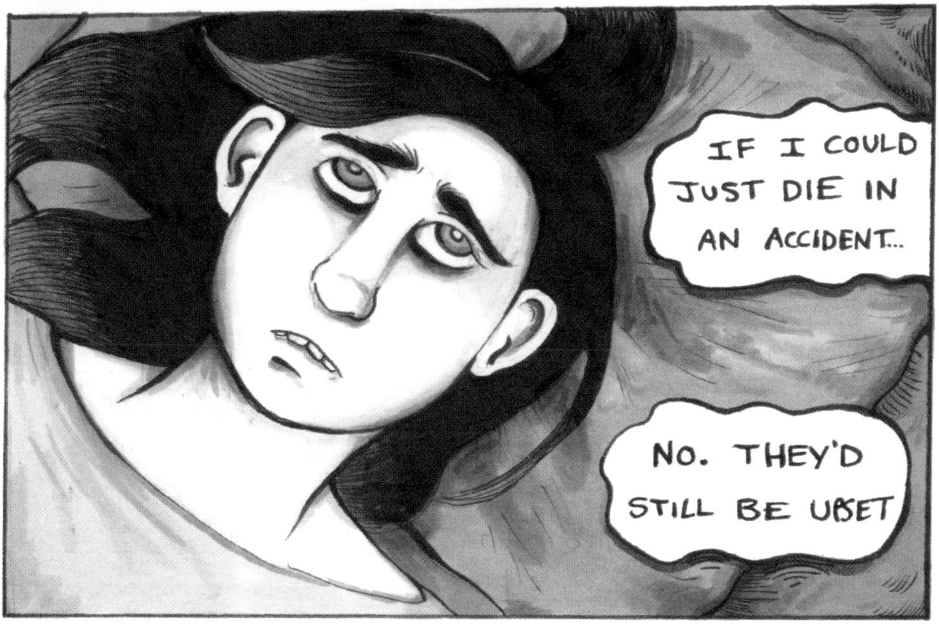
IF I COULD JUST DIE IN AN ACCIDENT...
NO. THEY'D STILL BE UPSET

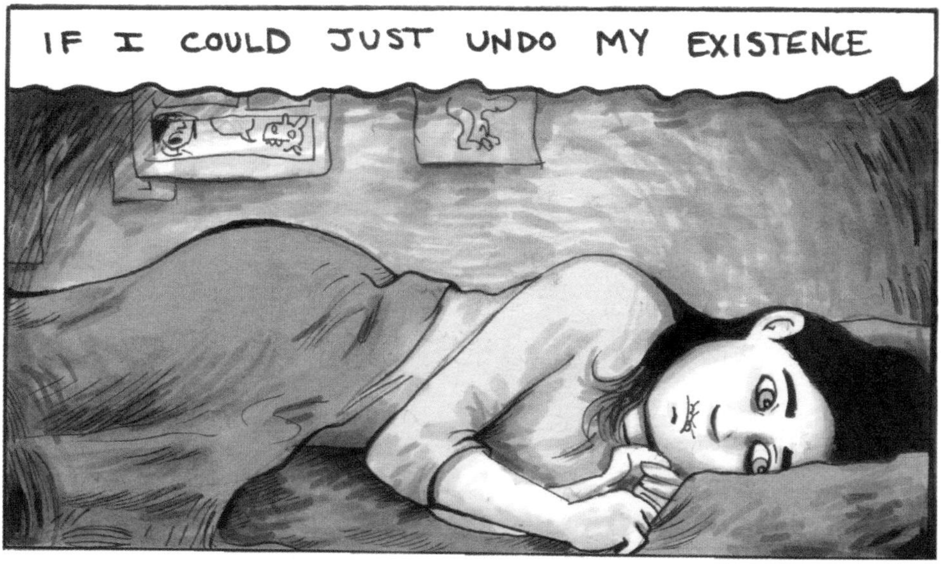
IF I COULD JUST UNDO MY EXISTENCE

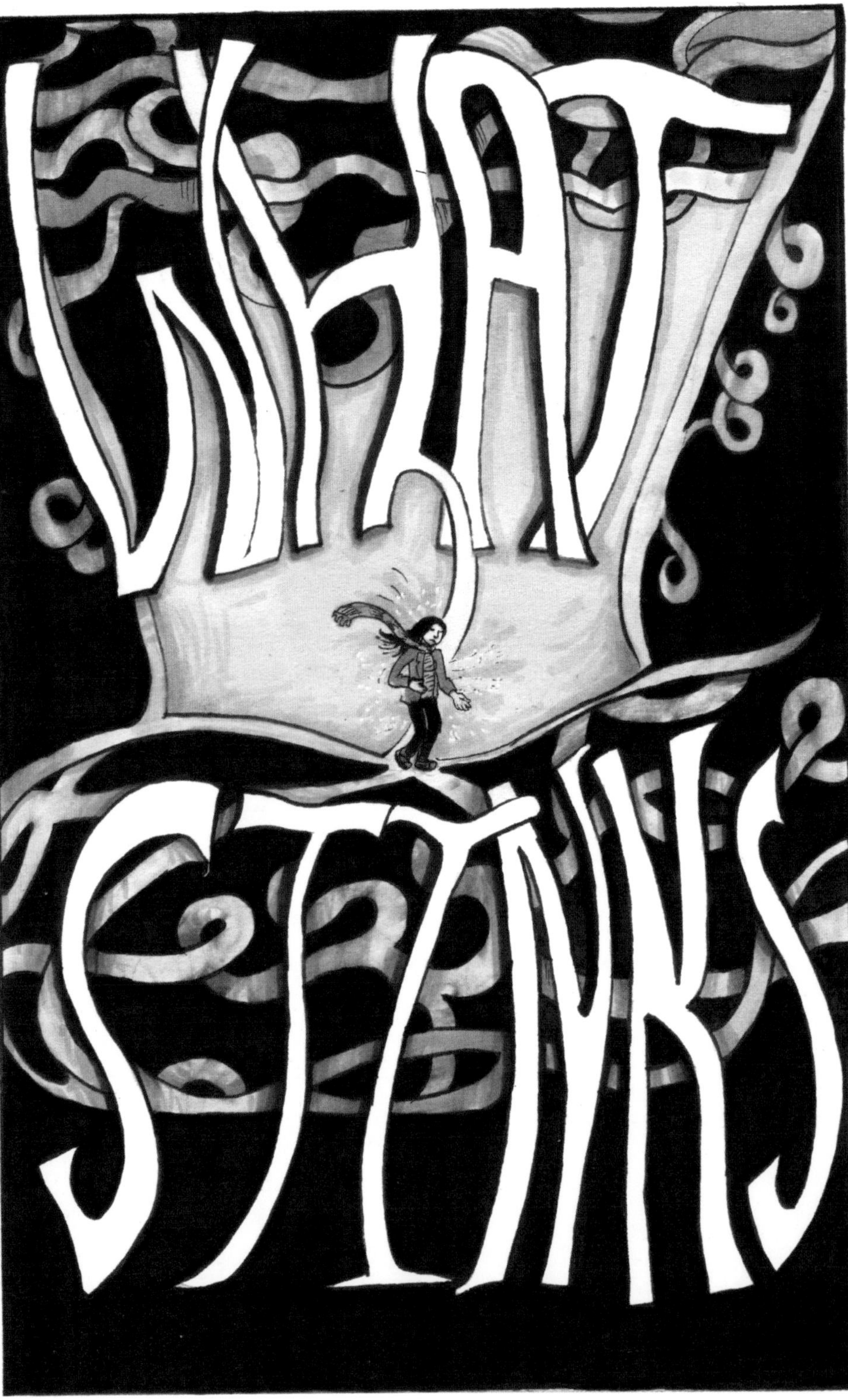
WHAT
STINKS

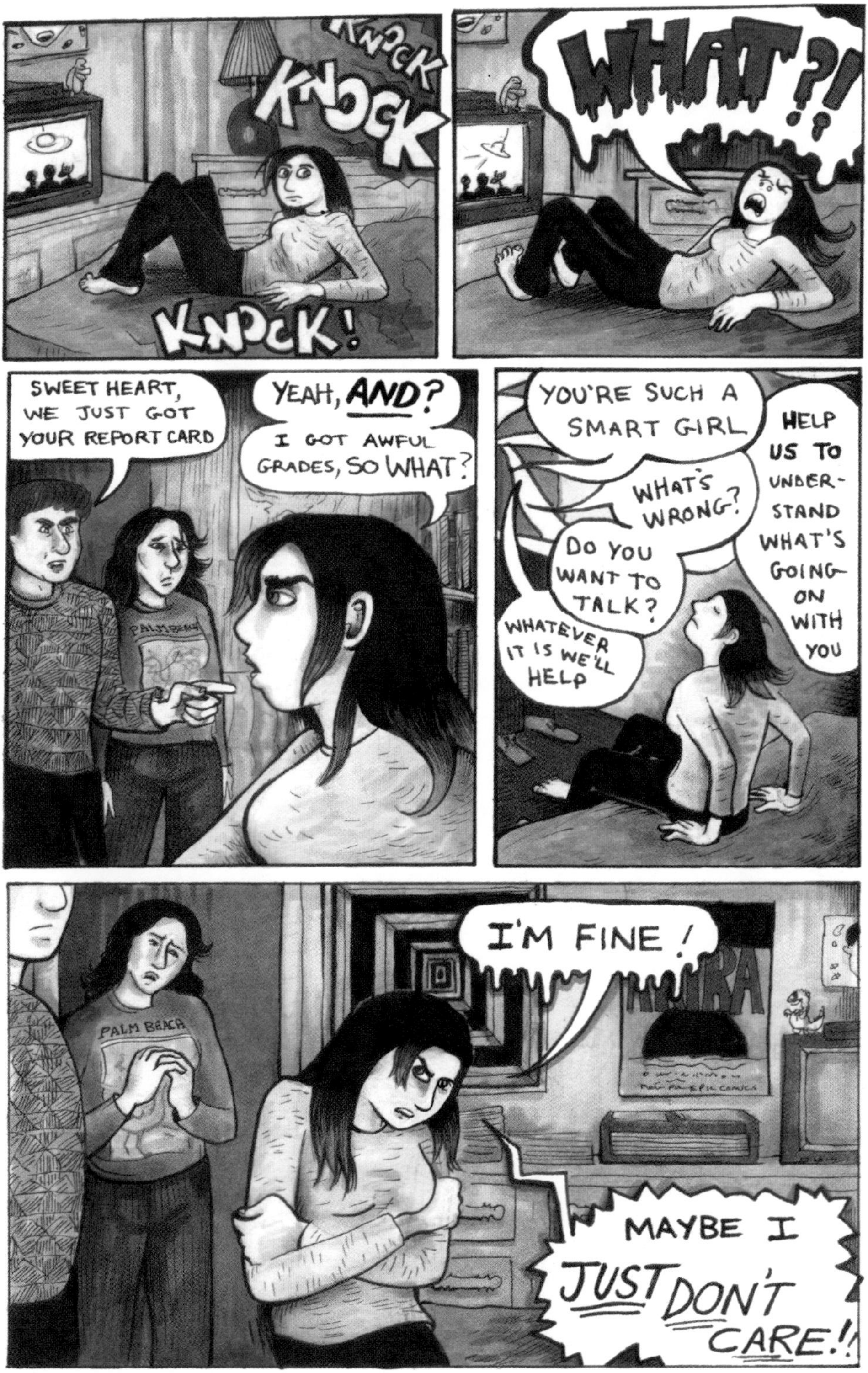
KNOCK
KNOCK
KNOCK!
WHAT?!
SWEET HEART, WE JUST GOT YOUR REPORT CARD
YEAH, AND?
I GOT AWFUL GRADES, SO WHAT?
YOU'RE SUCH A SMART GIRL
WHAT'S WRONG?
DO YOU WANT TO TALK?
WHATEVER IT IS WE'LL HELP
HELP US TO UNDER-STAND WHAT'S GOING ON WITH YOU
I'M FINE!
MAYBE I JUST DON'T CARE!!

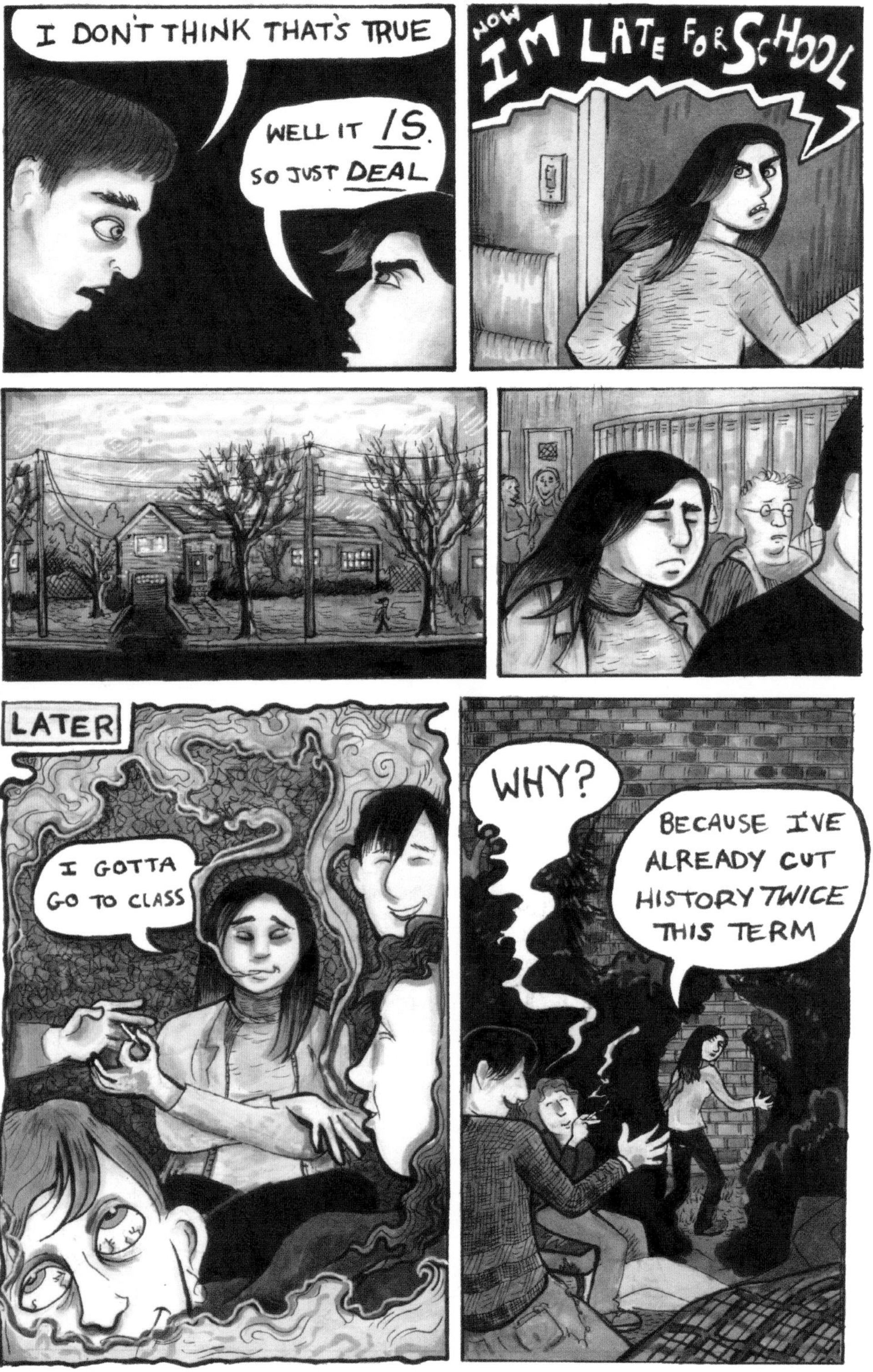
I DON'T THINK THAT'S TRUE
WELL IT IS. SO JUST DEAL
NOW I'M LATE FOR SCHOOL
LATER
I GOTTA GO TO CLASS
WHY?
BECAUSE I'VE ALREADY CUT HISTORY TWICE THIS TERM

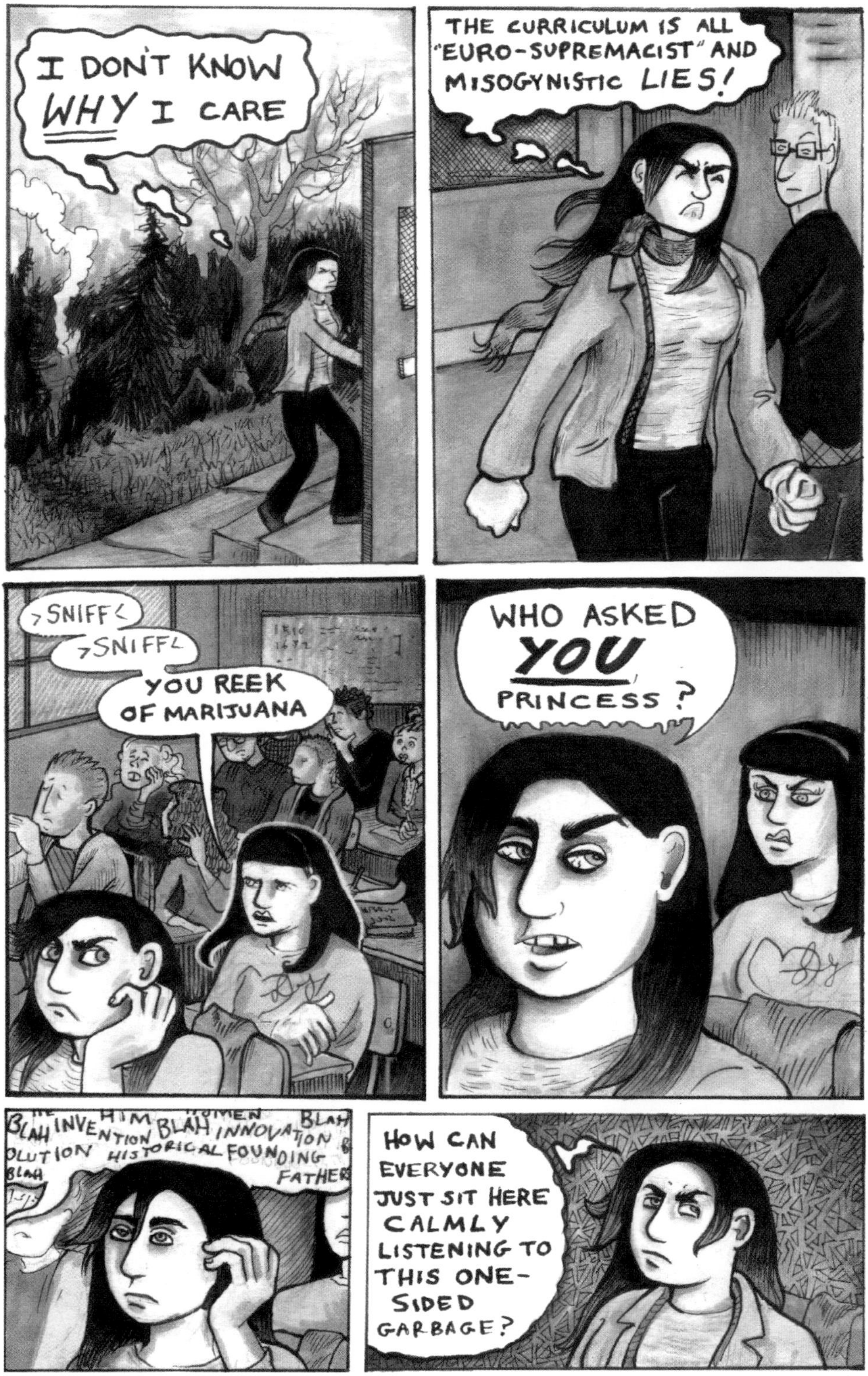
I DON'T KNOW WHY I CARE
THE CURRICULUM IS ALL "EURO-SUPREMACIST" AND MISOGYNISTIC LIES!
>SNIFF<
>SNIFF<
YOU REEK OF MARIJUANA
WHO ASKED YOU, PRINCESS?
HIM WOMEN
BLAH INVENTION BLAH INNOVATION BLAH
OLUTION HISTORICAL FOUNDING
BLAH FATHER
HOW CAN EVERYONE JUST SIT HERE CALMLY LISTENING TO THIS ONE-SIDED GARBAGE?

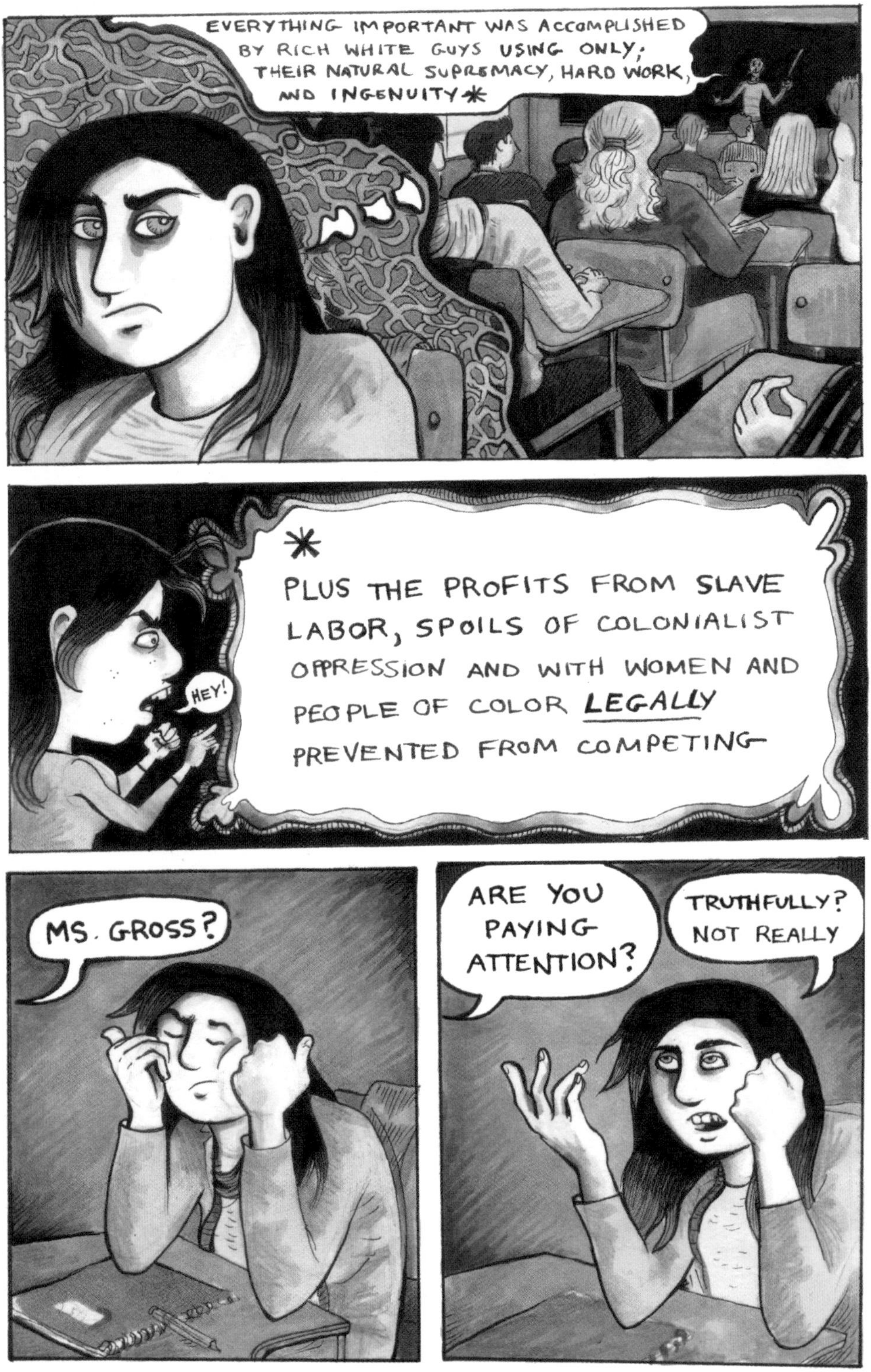
EVERYTHING IMPORTANT WAS ACCOMPLISHED BY RICH WHITE GUYS USING ONLY; THEIR NATURAL SUPREMACY, HARD WORK, AND INGENUITY*
* PLUS THE PROFITS FROM SLAVE LABOR, SPOILS OF COLONIALIST OPPRESSION AND WITH WOMEN AND PEOPLE OF COLOR LEGALLY PREVENTED FROM COMPETING
HEY!
MS. GROSS?
ARE YOU PAYING ATTENTION?
TRUTHFULLY? NOT REALLY

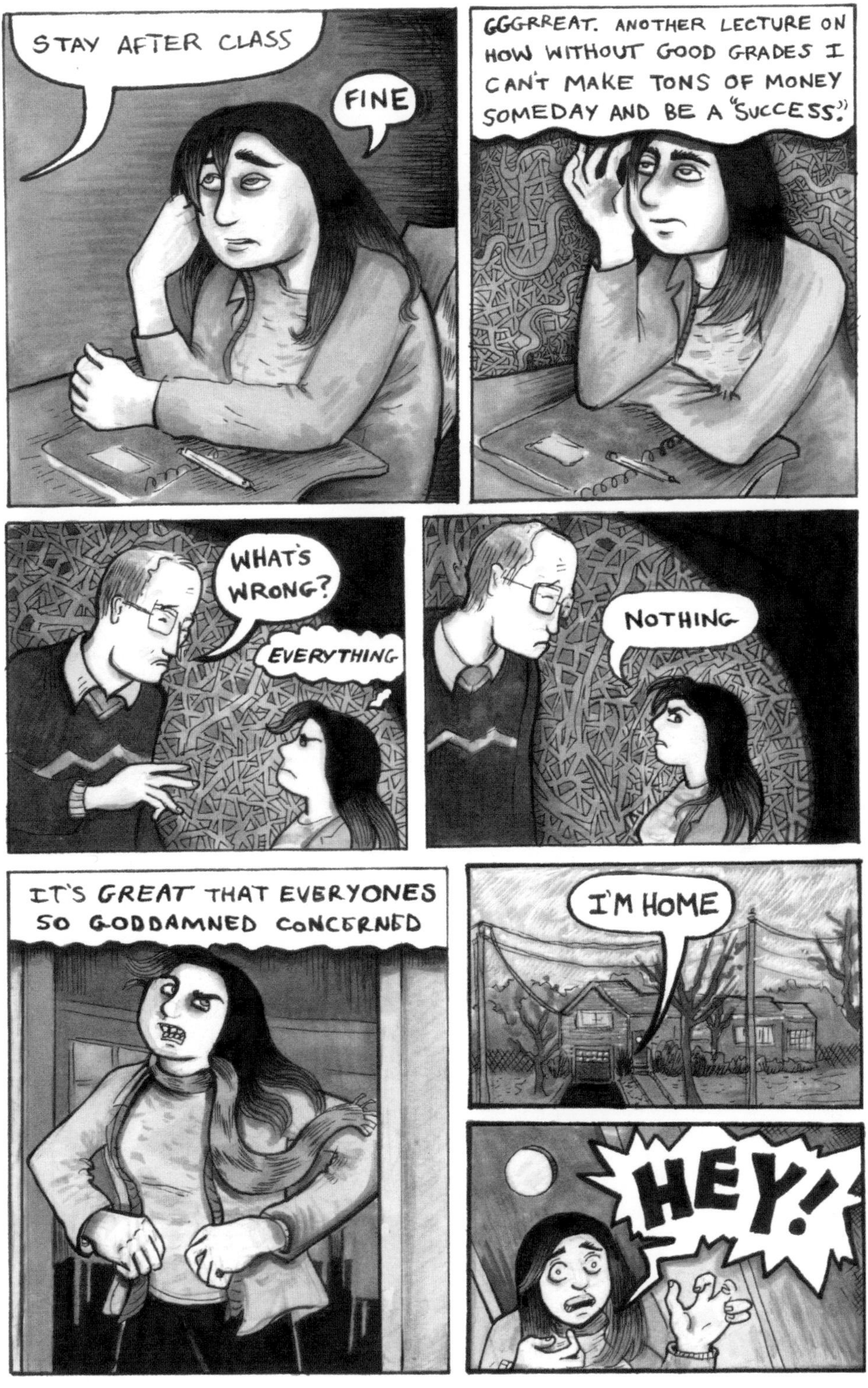
STAY AFTER CLASS
FINE
GGGRREAT. ANOTHER LECTURE ON HOW WITHOUT GOOD GRADES I CAN'T MAKE TONS OF MONEY SOMEDAY AND BE A "SUCCESS."
WHAT'S WRONG?
EVERYTHING
NOTHING
IT'S GREAT THAT EVERYONES SO GODDAMNED CONCERNED
I'M HOME
HEY!

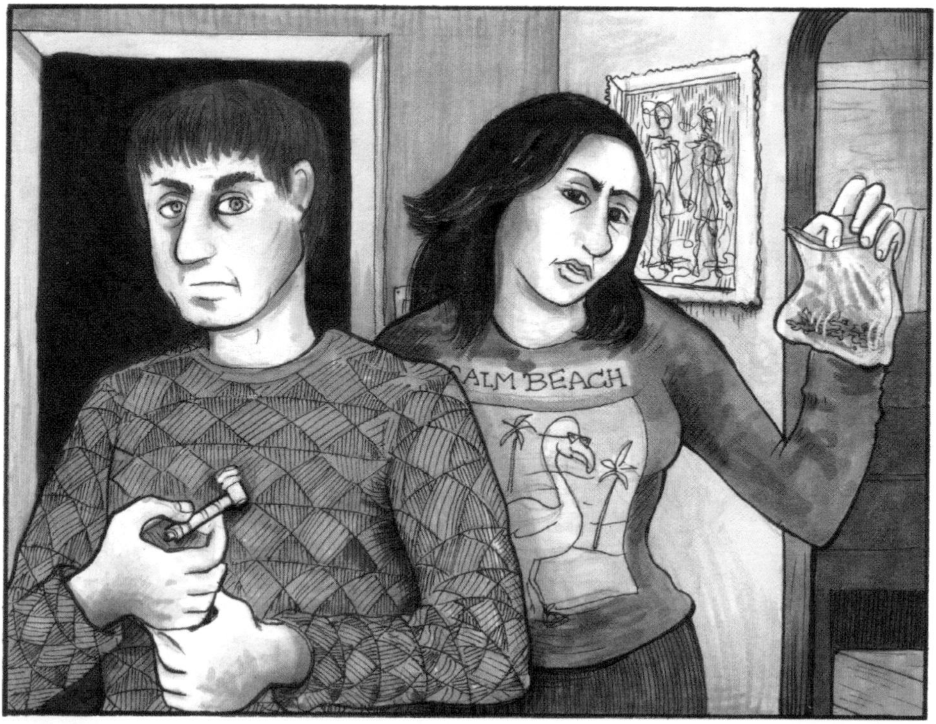
PALM BEACH

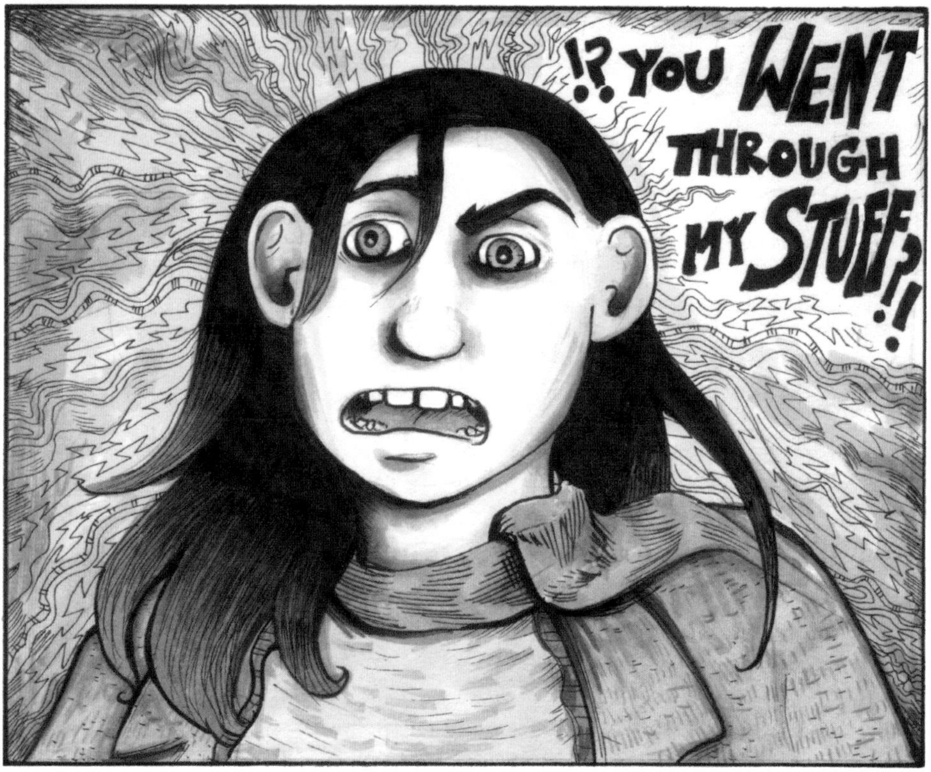
!? YOU WENT THROUGH MY STUFF?!!

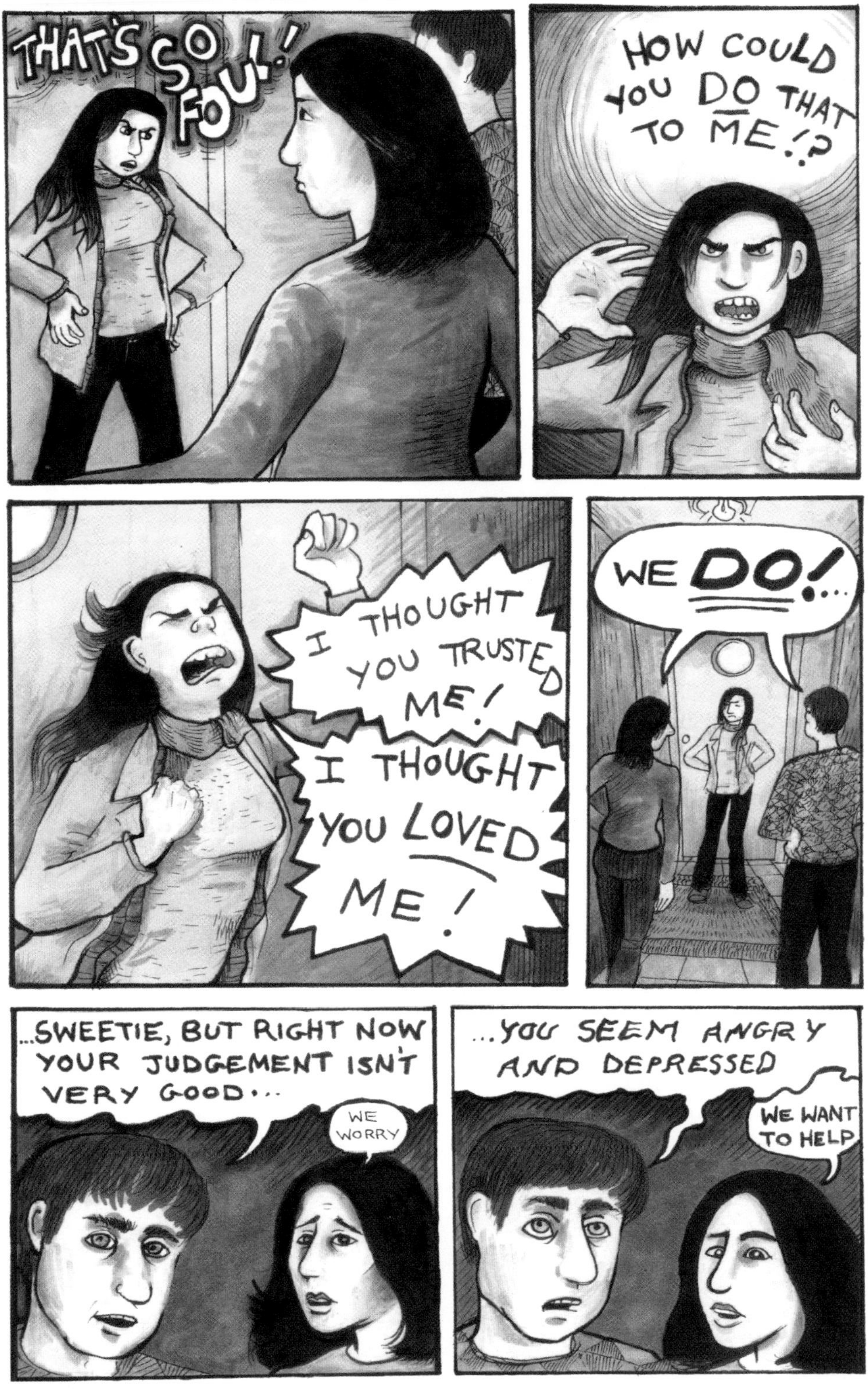
THAT'S SO FOUL!
HOW COULD YOU DO THAT TO ME!?
I THOUGHT YOU TRUSTED ME!
I THOUGHT YOU LOVED ME!
WE DO!...
...SWEETIE, BUT RIGHT NOW YOUR JUDGEMENT ISN'T VERY GOOD...
WE WORRY
...YOU SEEM ANGRY AND DEPRESSED
WE WANT TO HELP

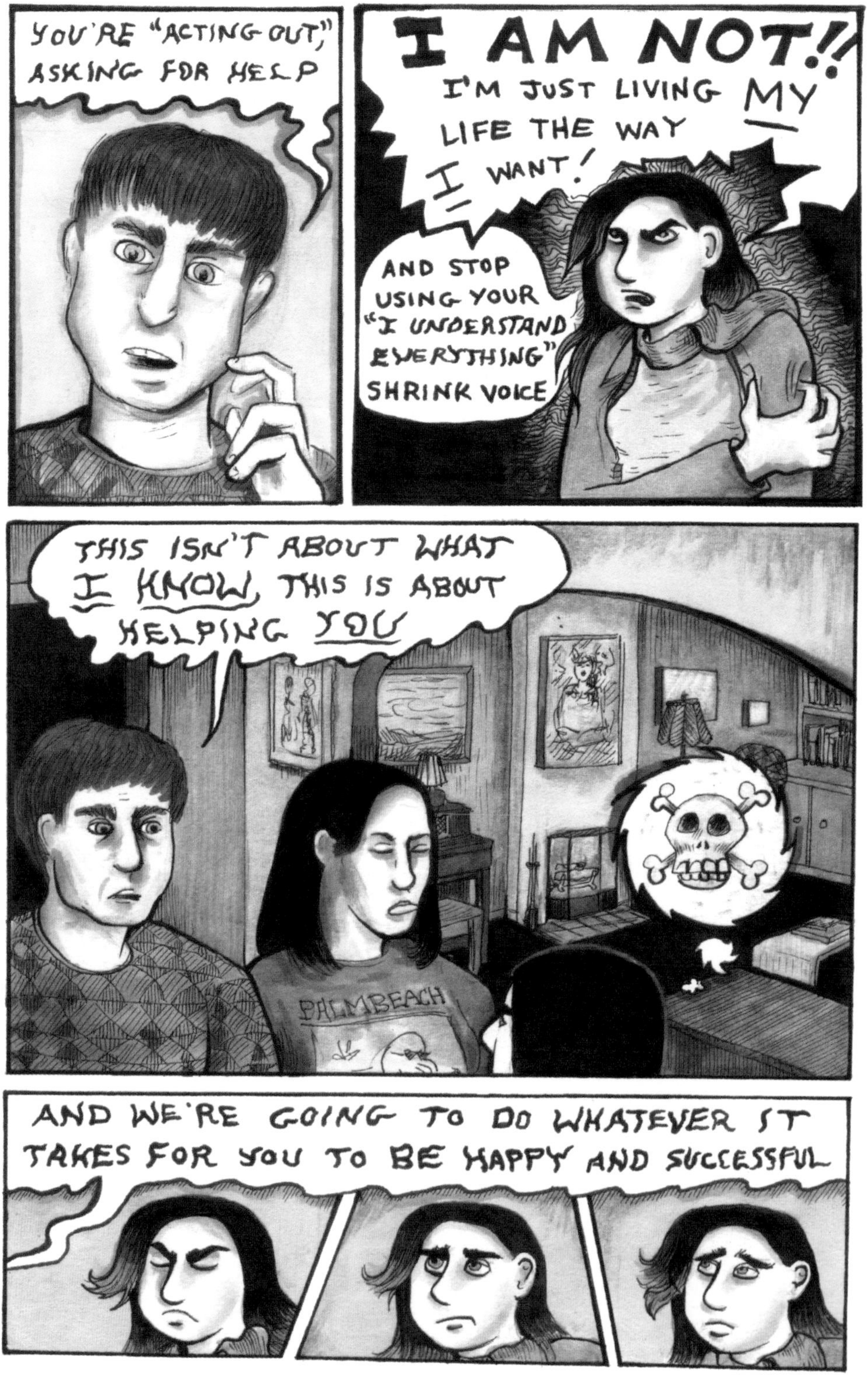
YOU'RE "ACTING OUT," ASKING FOR HELP
I AM NOT!!
I'M JUST LIVING MY LIFE THE WAY I WANT!
AND STOP USING YOUR "I UNDERSTAND EVERYTHING" SHRINK VOICE
THIS ISN'T ABOUT WHAT I KNOW, THIS IS ABOUT HELPING YOU
PALMBEACH
AND WE'RE GOING TO DO WHATEVER IT TAKES FOR YOU TO BE HAPPY AND SUCCESSFUL

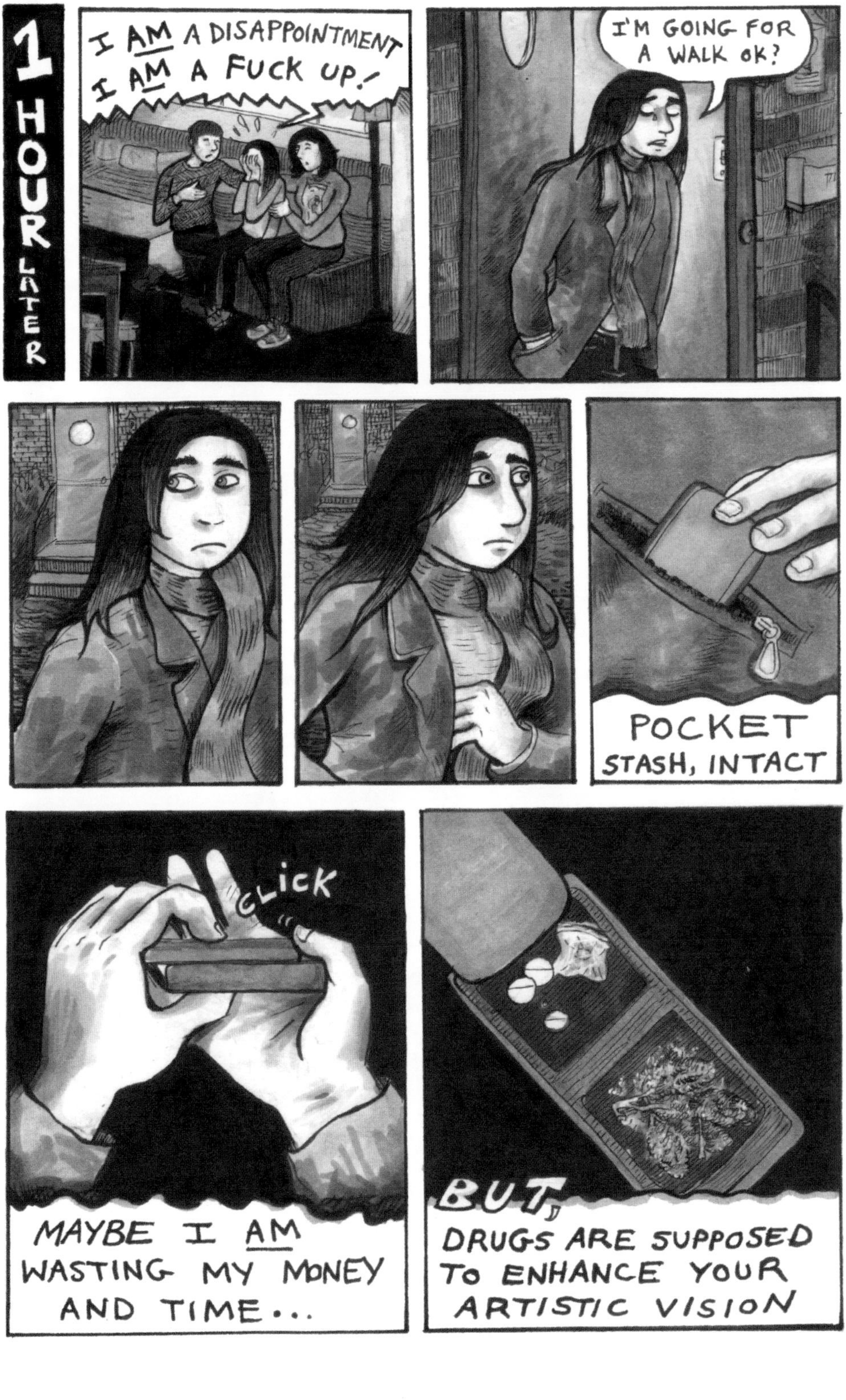
1 HOUR LATER
I AM A DISAPPOINTMENT
I AM A FUCK UP!
I'M GOING FOR A WALK OK?
POCKET STASH, INTACT
CLICK
MAYBE I AM WASTING MY MONEY AND TIME...
BUT,
DRUGS ARE SUPPOSED TO ENHANCE YOUR ARTISTIC VISION

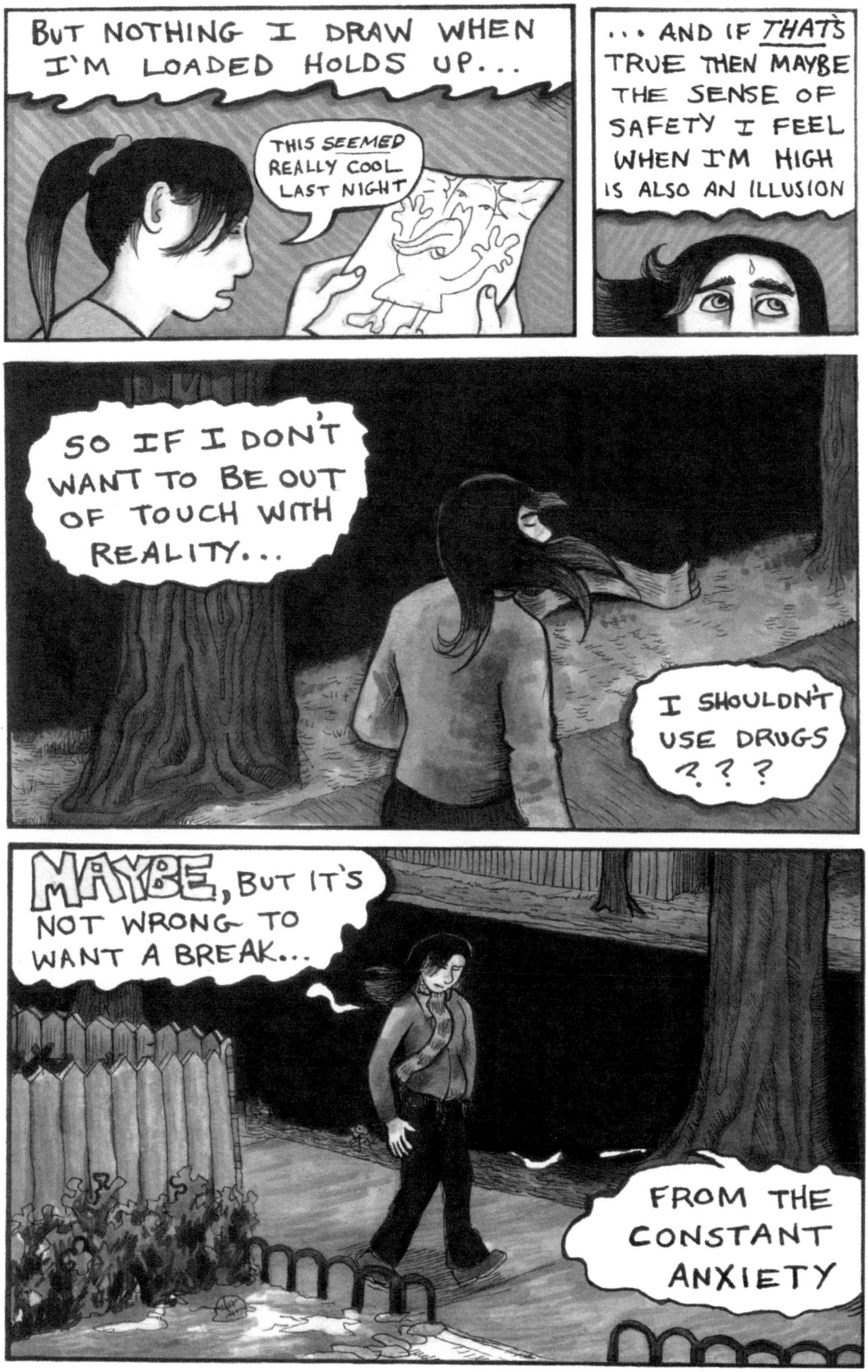
BUT NOTHING I DRAW WHEN I'M LOADED HOLDS UP...
THIS SEEMED REALLY COOL LAST NIGHT
... AND IF THAT'S TRUE THEN MAYBE THE SENSE OF SAFETY I FEEL WHEN I'M HIGH IS ALSO AN ILLUSION
SO IF I DON'T WANT TO BE OUT OF TOUCH WITH REALITY...
I SHOULDN'T USE DRUGS ???
MAYBE, BUT IT'S NOT WRONG TO WANT A BREAK...
FROM THE CONSTANT ANXIETY

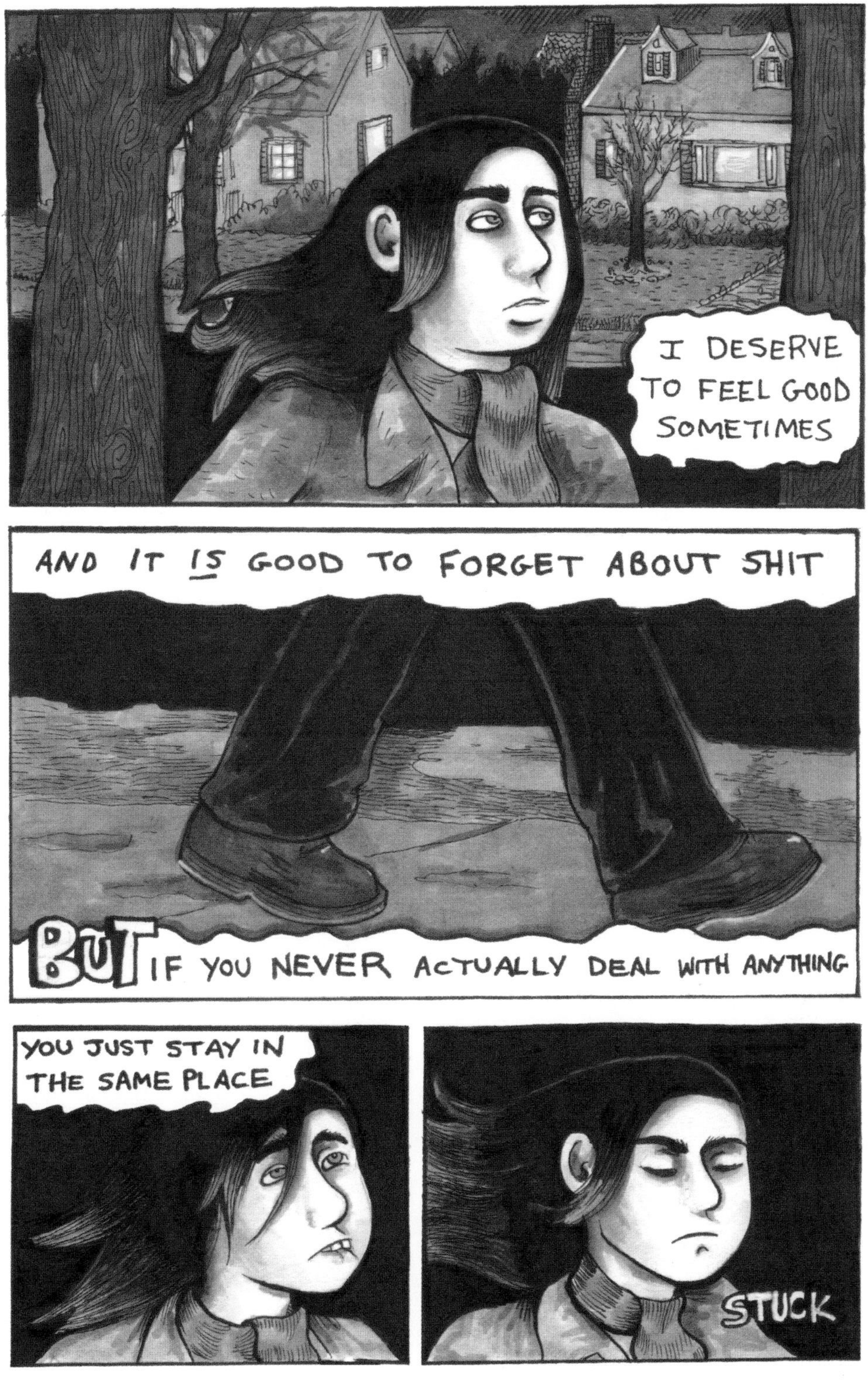
I DESERVE TO FEEL GOOD SOMETIMES
AND IT IS GOOD TO FORGET ABOUT SHIT
BUT IF YOU NEVER ACTUALLY DEAL WITH ANYTHING
YOU JUST STAY IN THE SAME PLACE
STUCK

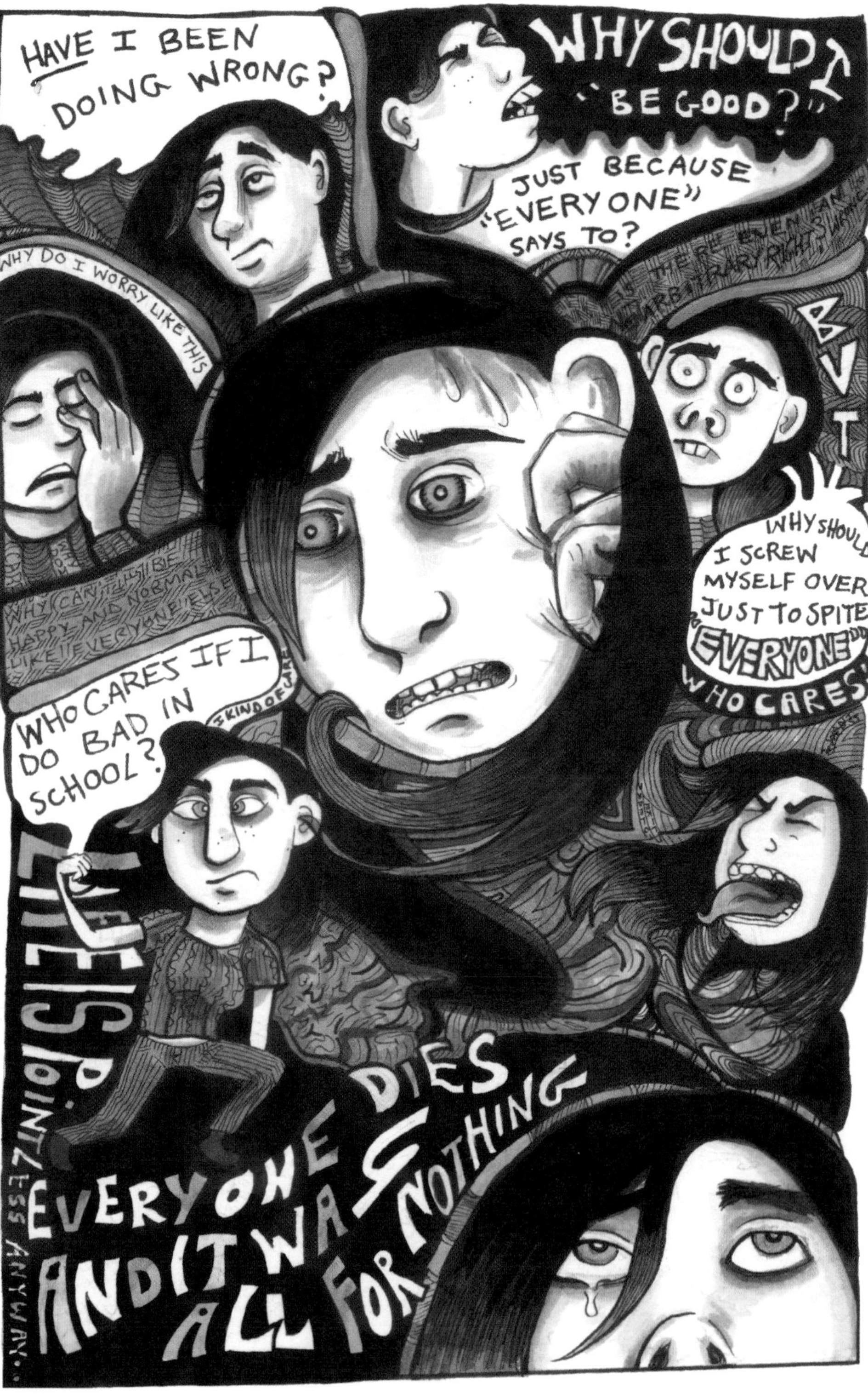
HAVE I BEEN DOING WRONG?
WHY SHOULD I "BE GOOD?"
JUST BECAUSE "EVERYONE" SAYS TO?
WHY DO I WORRY LIKE THIS
IS THERE EVEN AN ARBITRARY RIGHT & WRONG
BUT
WHY CAN'T I BE HAPPY AND NORMAL LIKE EVERYONE ELSE
WHY SHOULD I SCREW MYSELF OVER JUST TO SPITE "EVERYONE"
WHO CARES!
WHO CARES IF I DO BAD IN SCHOOL?
I KIND OF CARE
LIFE IS POINTLESS ANYWAY..
EVERYONE DIES
AND IT WAS ALL FOR NOTHING

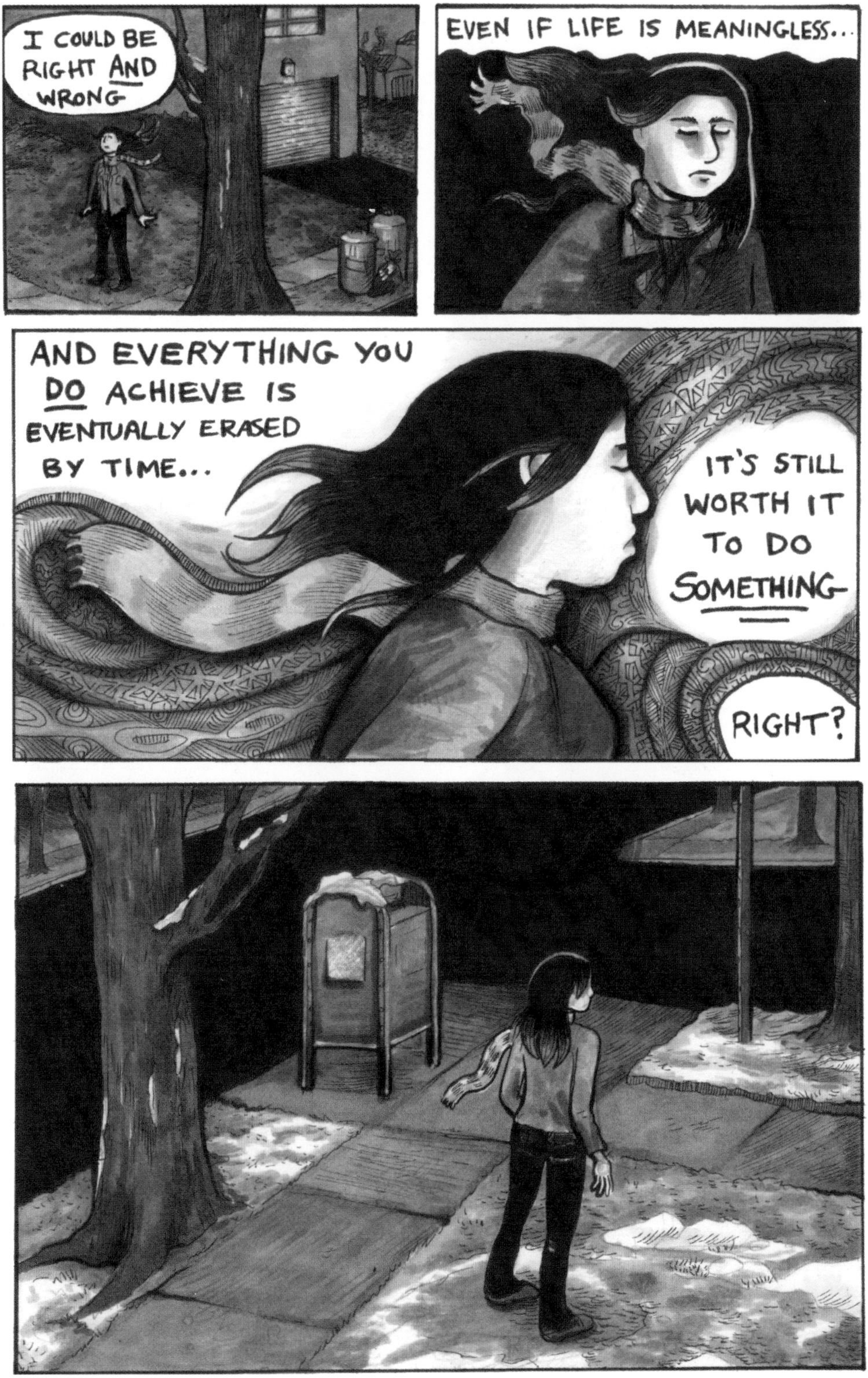
I COULD BE RIGHT AND WRONG
EVEN IF LIFE IS MEANINGLESS...
AND EVERYTHING YOU DO ACHIEVE IS EVENTUALLY ERASED BY TIME...
IT'S STILL WORTH IT TO DO SOMETHING
RIGHT?

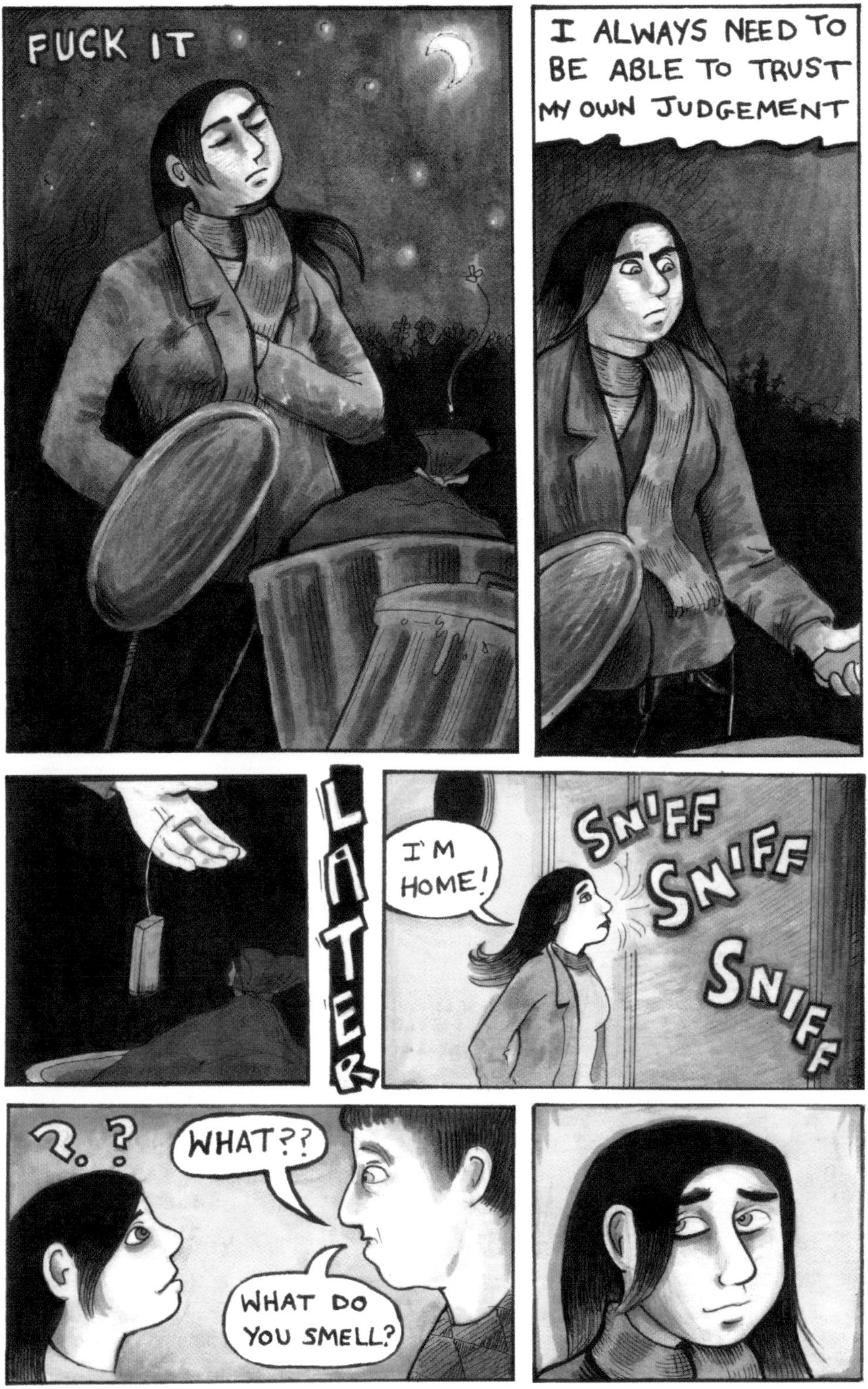
FUCK IT
I ALWAYS NEED TO BE ABLE TO TRUST MY OWN JUDGEMENT
LATER
I'M HOME!
SNIFF SNIFF SNIFF
?. ?
WHAT??
WHAT DO YOU SMELL?

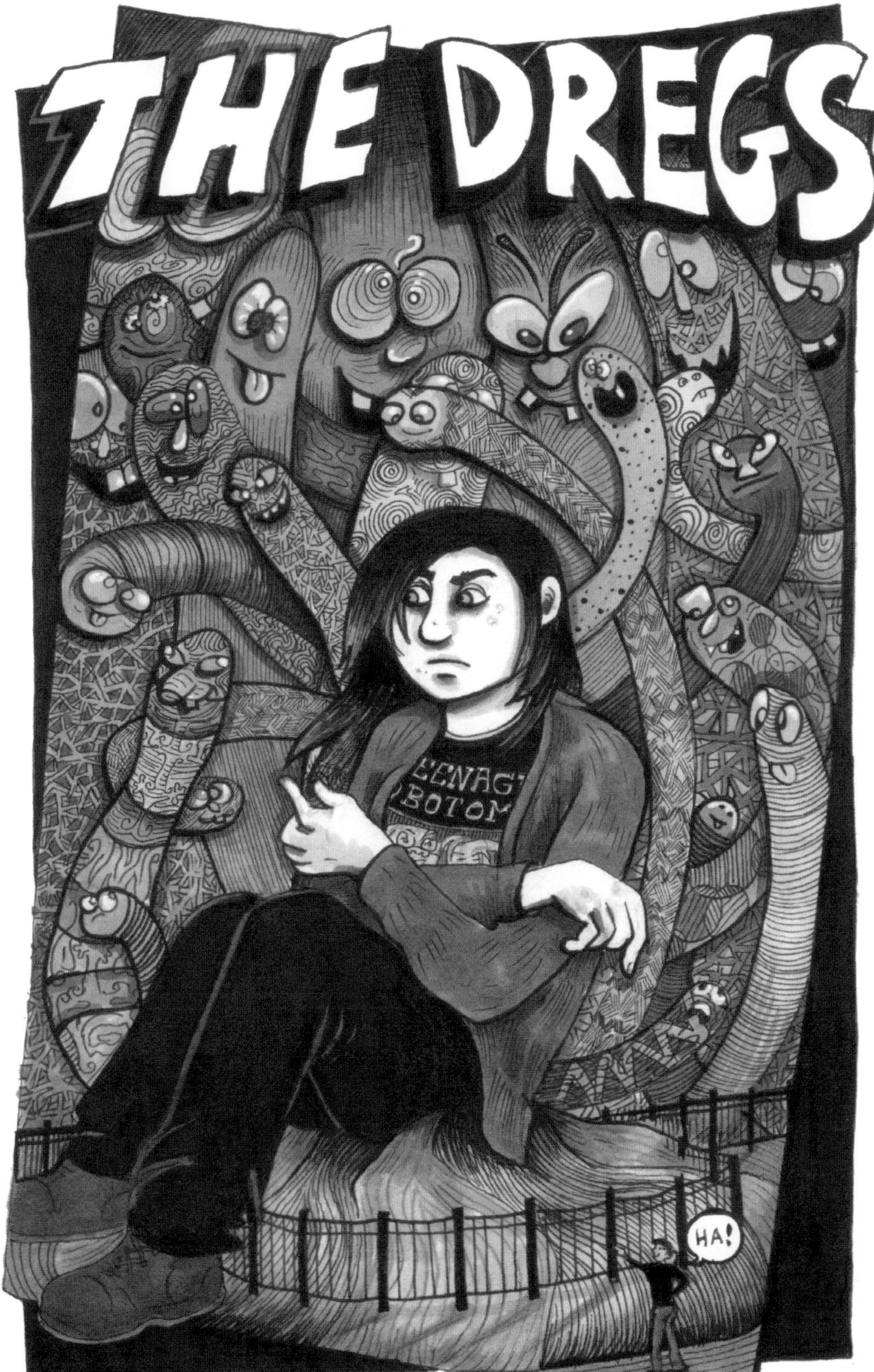
THE DREGS
HA!

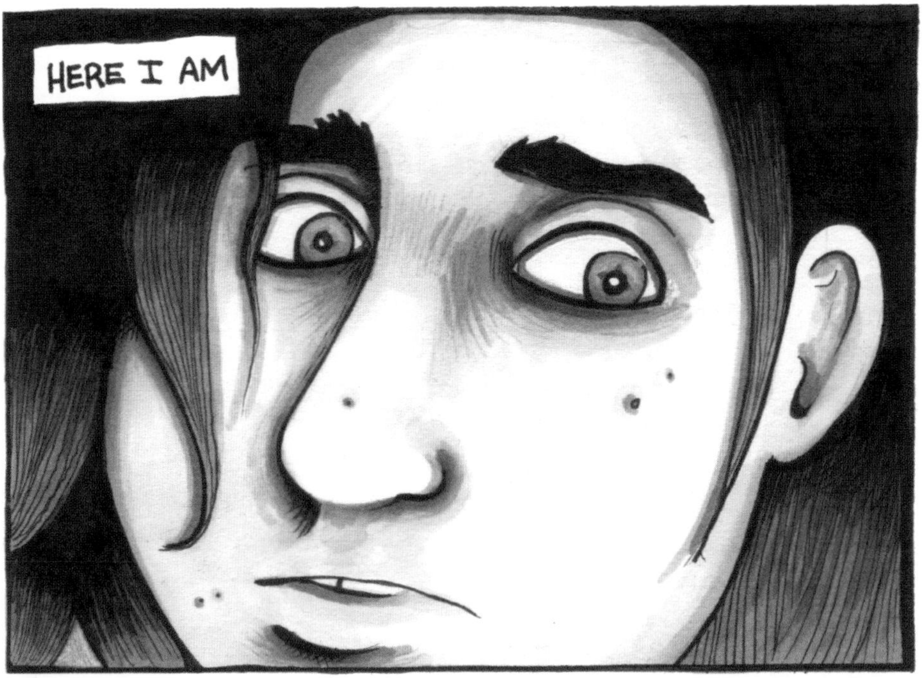
HERE I AM

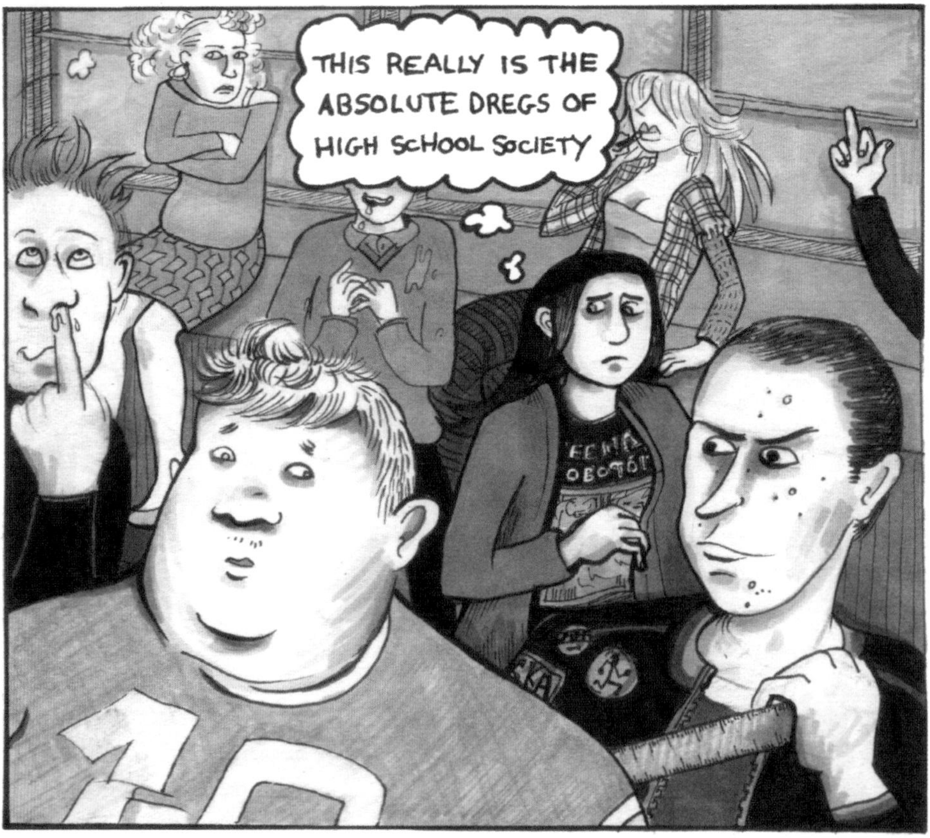
THIS REALLY IS THE ABSOLUTE DREGS OF HIGH SCHOOL SOCIETY

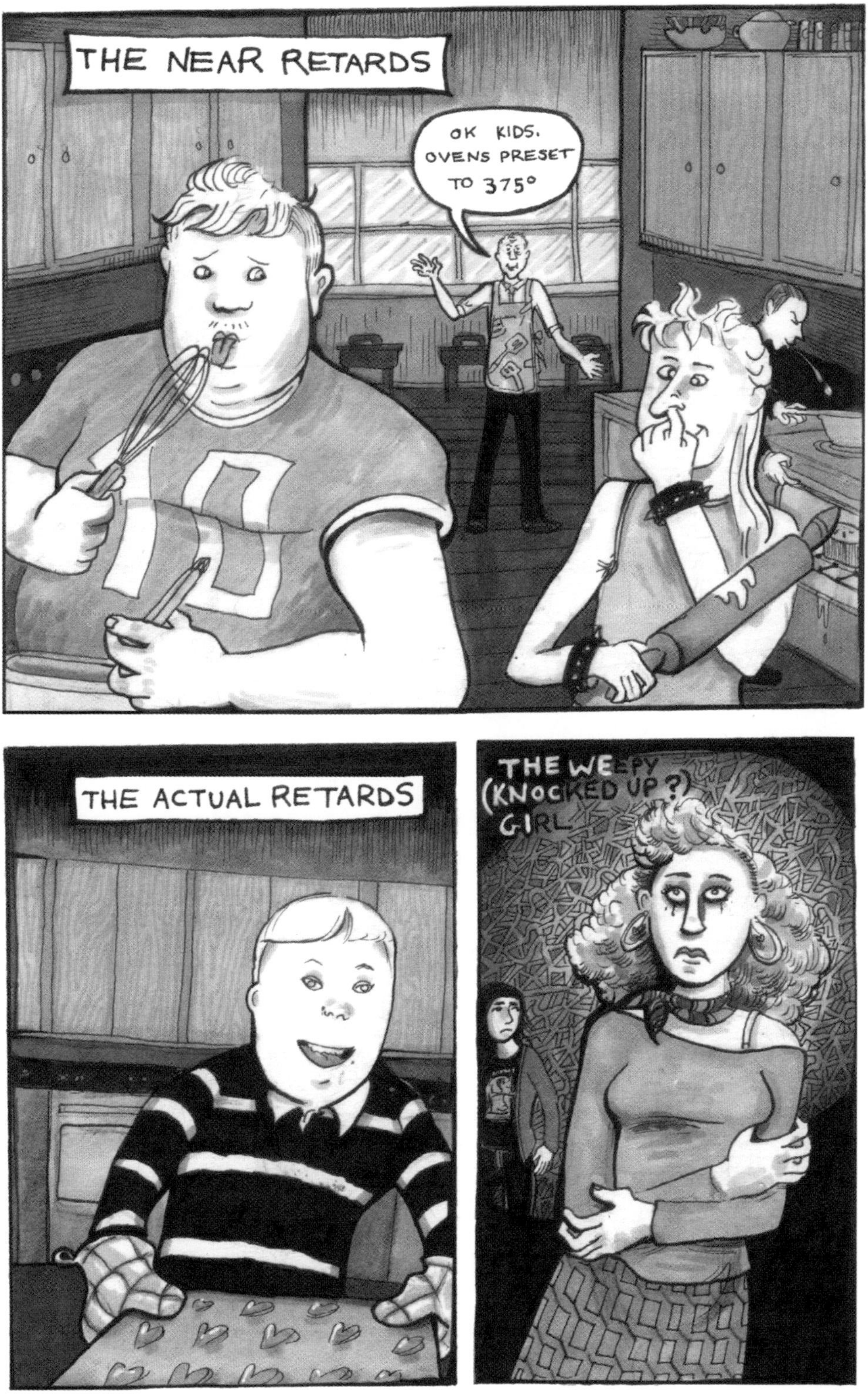
THE NEAR RETARDS
OK KIDS. OVENS PRESET TO 375°
THE ACTUAL RETARDS
THE WEEPY (KNOCKED UP?) GIRL

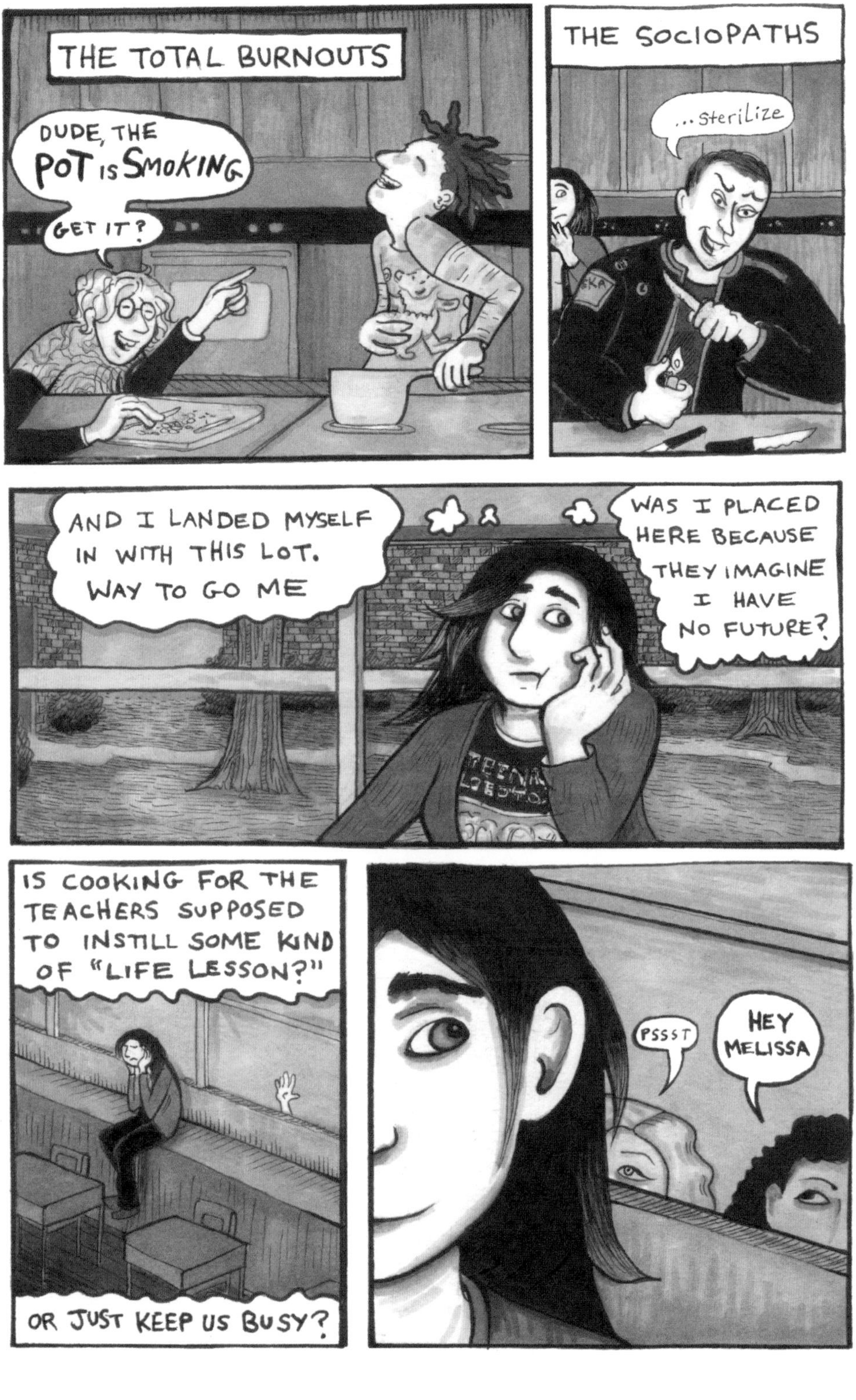
THE TOTAL BURNOUTS
DUDE, THE POT IS SMOKING
GET IT?
THE SOCIOPATHS
...sterilize
AND I LANDED MYSELF IN WITH THIS LOT. WAY TO GO ME
WAS I PLACED HERE BECAUSE THEY IMAGINE I HAVE NO FUTURE?
IS COOKING FOR THE TEACHERS SUPPOSED TO INSTILL SOME KIND OF "LIFE LESSON?"
OR JUST KEEP US BUSY?
PSSST
HEY MELISSA

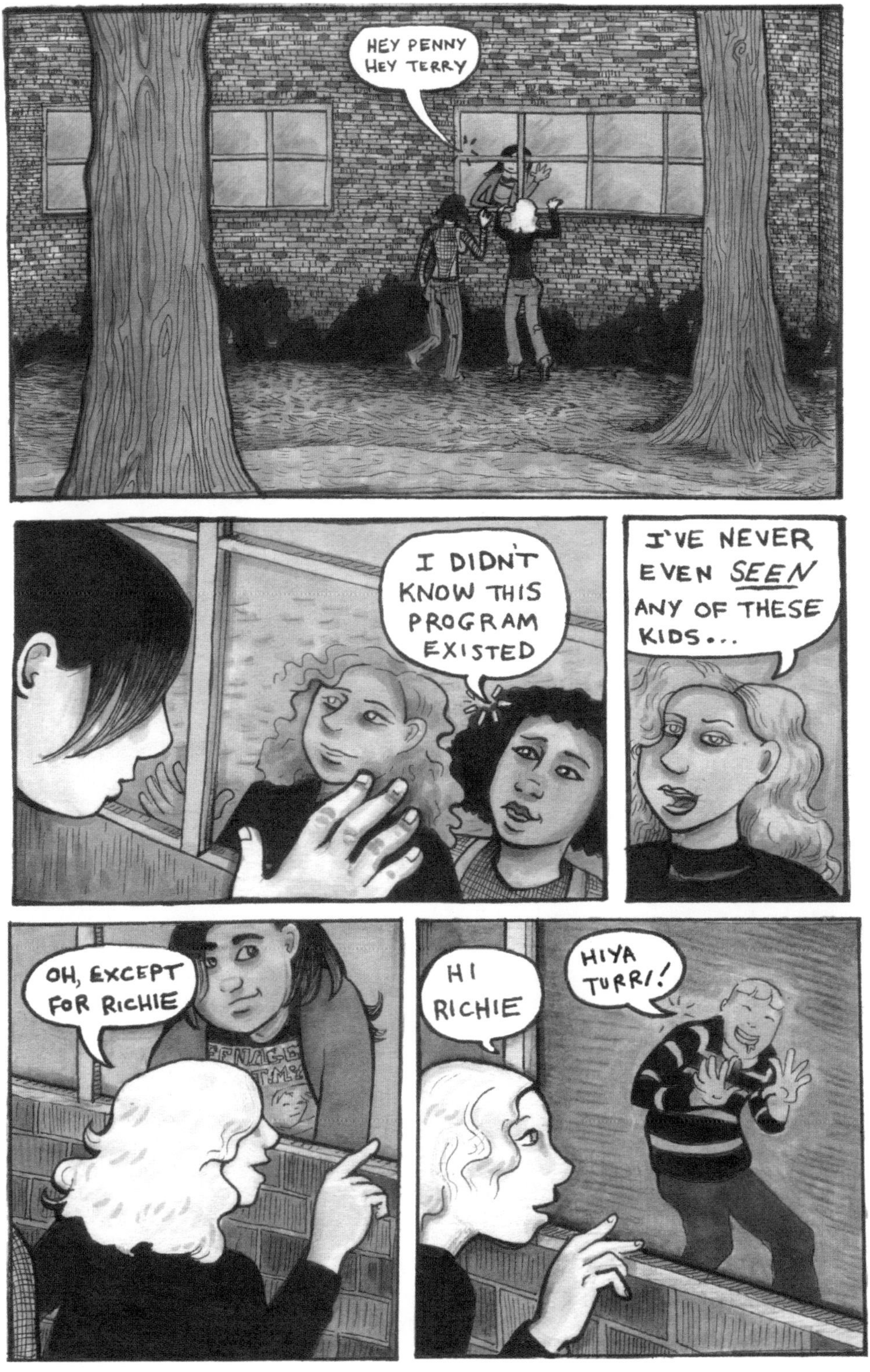
HEY PENNY
HEY TERRY
I DIDN'T KNOW THIS PROGRAM EXISTED
I'VE NEVER EVEN SEEN ANY OF THESE KIDS...
OH, EXCEPT FOR RICHIE
HI RICHIE
HIYA TURRI!

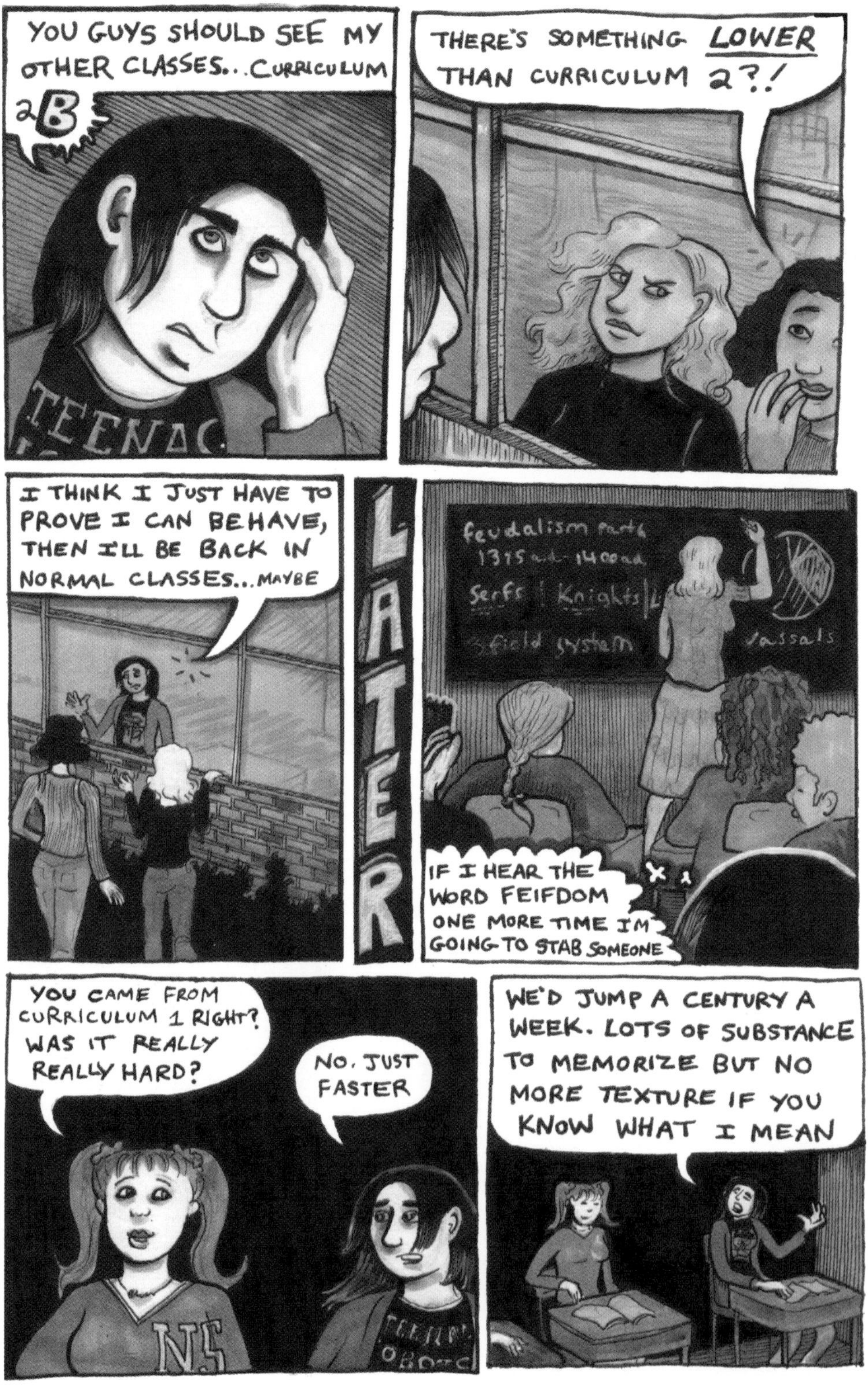
YOU GUYS SHOULD SEE MY OTHER CLASSES...CURRICULUM 2B
TEENAG
THERE'S SOMETHING LOWER THAN CURRICULUM 2?!
I THINK I JUST HAVE TO PROVE I CAN BEHAVE, THEN I'LL BE BACK IN NORMAL CLASSES...MAYBE
LATER
feudalism part 6
1315 a.d.-1400 a.d.
Serfs
Knights
3 field system
vassals
IF I HEAR THE WORD FEIFDOM ONE MORE TIME I'M GOING TO STAB SOMEONE
YOU CAME FROM CURRICULUM 1 RIGHT? WAS IT REALLY REALLY HARD?
NO. JUST FASTER
NS
WE'D JUMP A CENTURY A WEEK. LOTS OF SUBSTANCE TO MEMORIZE BUT NO MORE TEXTURE IF YOU KNOW WHAT I MEAN

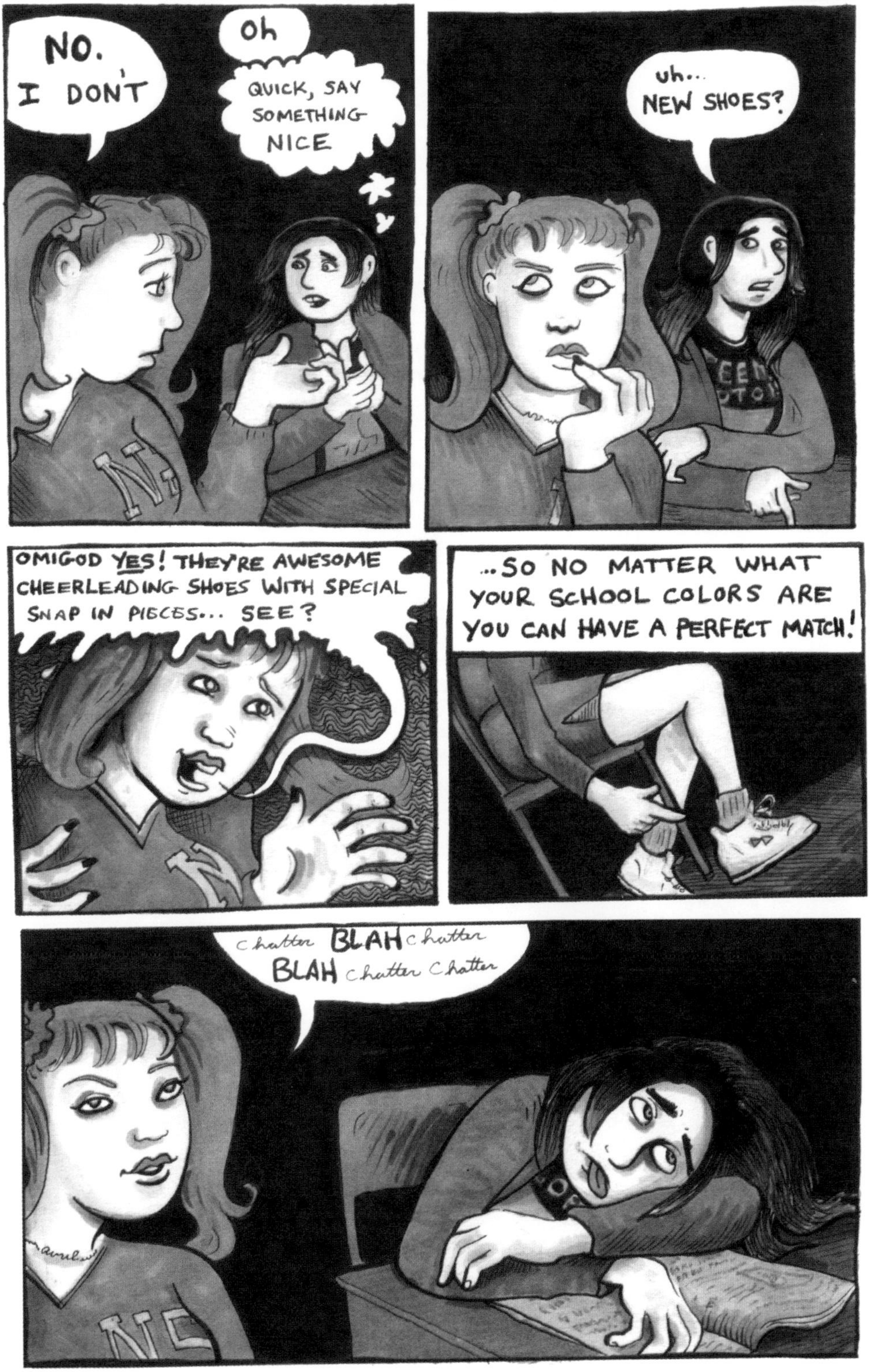
NO. I DON'T
Oh
QUICK, SAY SOMETHING NICE
uh... NEW SHOES?
OMIGOD YES! THEY'RE AWESOME CHEERLEADING SHOES WITH SPECIAL SNAP IN PIECES... SEE?
...SO NO MATTER WHAT YOUR SCHOOL COLORS ARE YOU CAN HAVE A PERFECT MATCH!
Chatter BLAH chatter BLAH Chatter Chatter

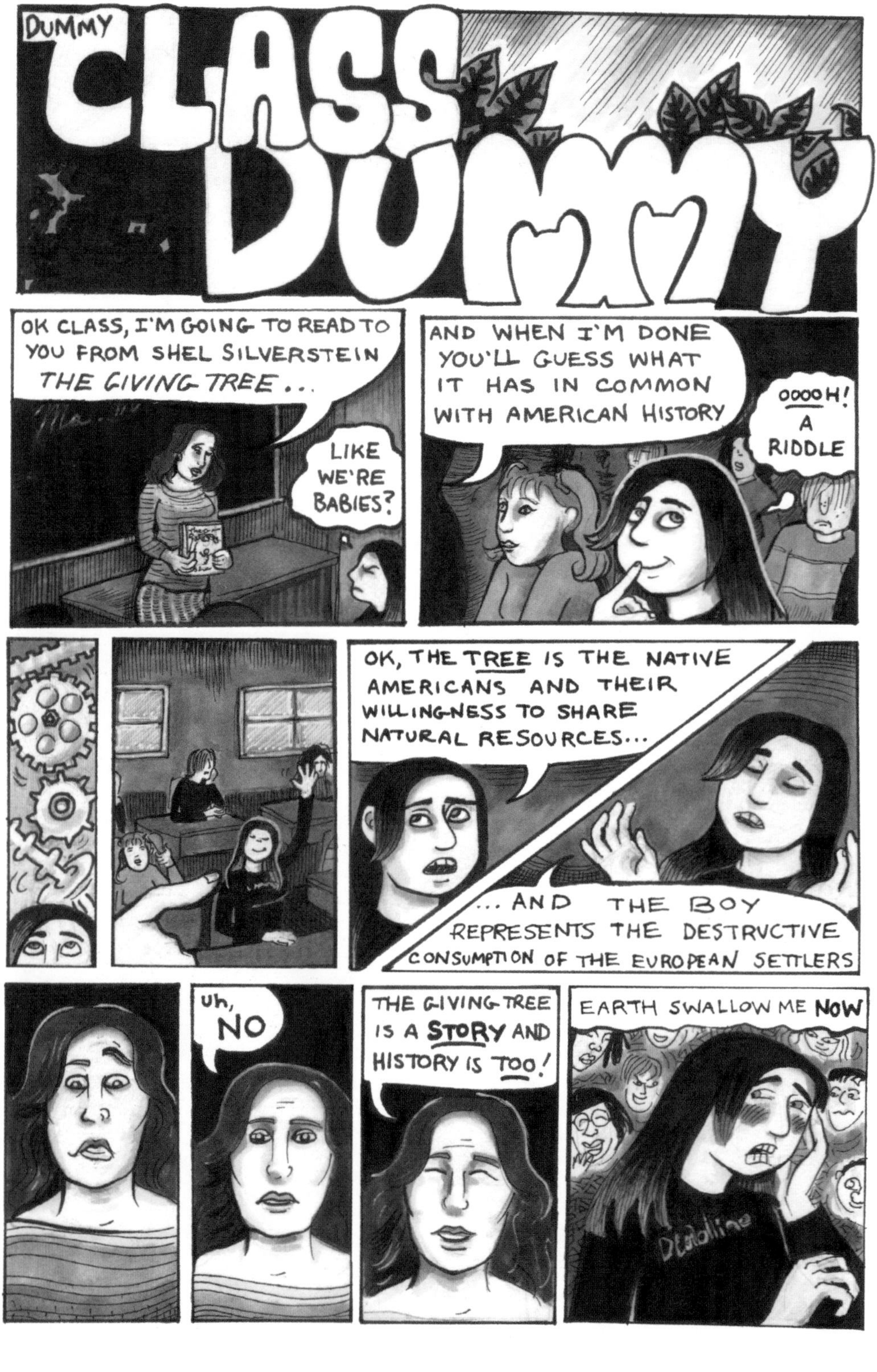
DUMMY
CLASS DUMMY
OK CLASS, I'M GOING TO READ TO YOU FROM SHEL SILVERSTEIN THE GIVING TREE...
LIKE WE'RE BABIES?
AND WHEN I'M DONE YOU'LL GUESS WHAT IT HAS IN COMMON WITH AMERICAN HISTORY
OOOOH! A RIDDLE
OK, THE TREE IS THE NATIVE AMERICANS AND THEIR WILLINGNESS TO SHARE NATURAL RESOURCES...
...AND THE BOY REPRESENTS THE DESTRUCTIVE CONSUMPTION OF THE EUROPEAN SETTLERS
Uh, NO
THE GIVING TREE IS A STORY AND HISTORY IS TOO!
EARTH SWALLOW ME NOW

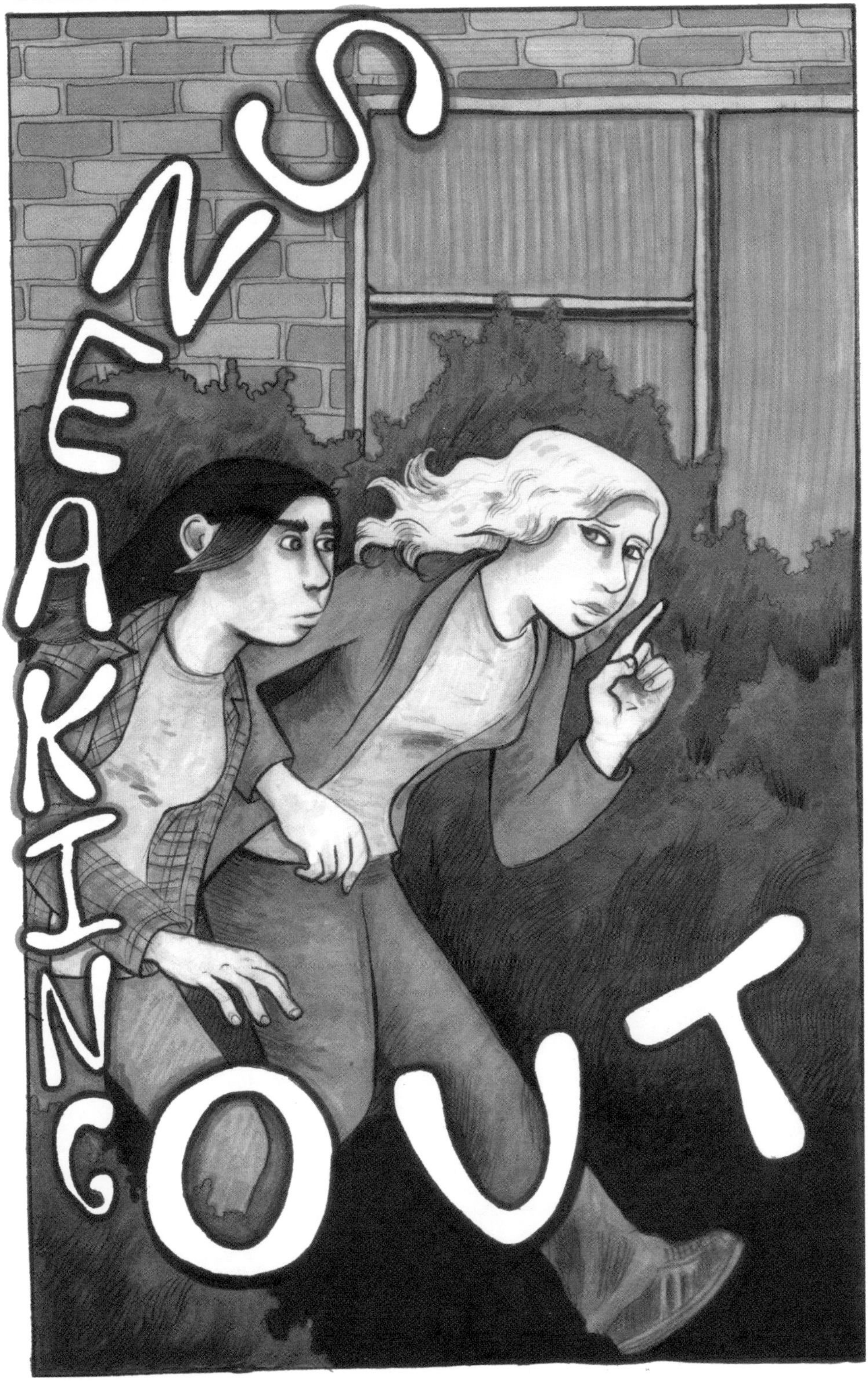
SNEAKING
OUT

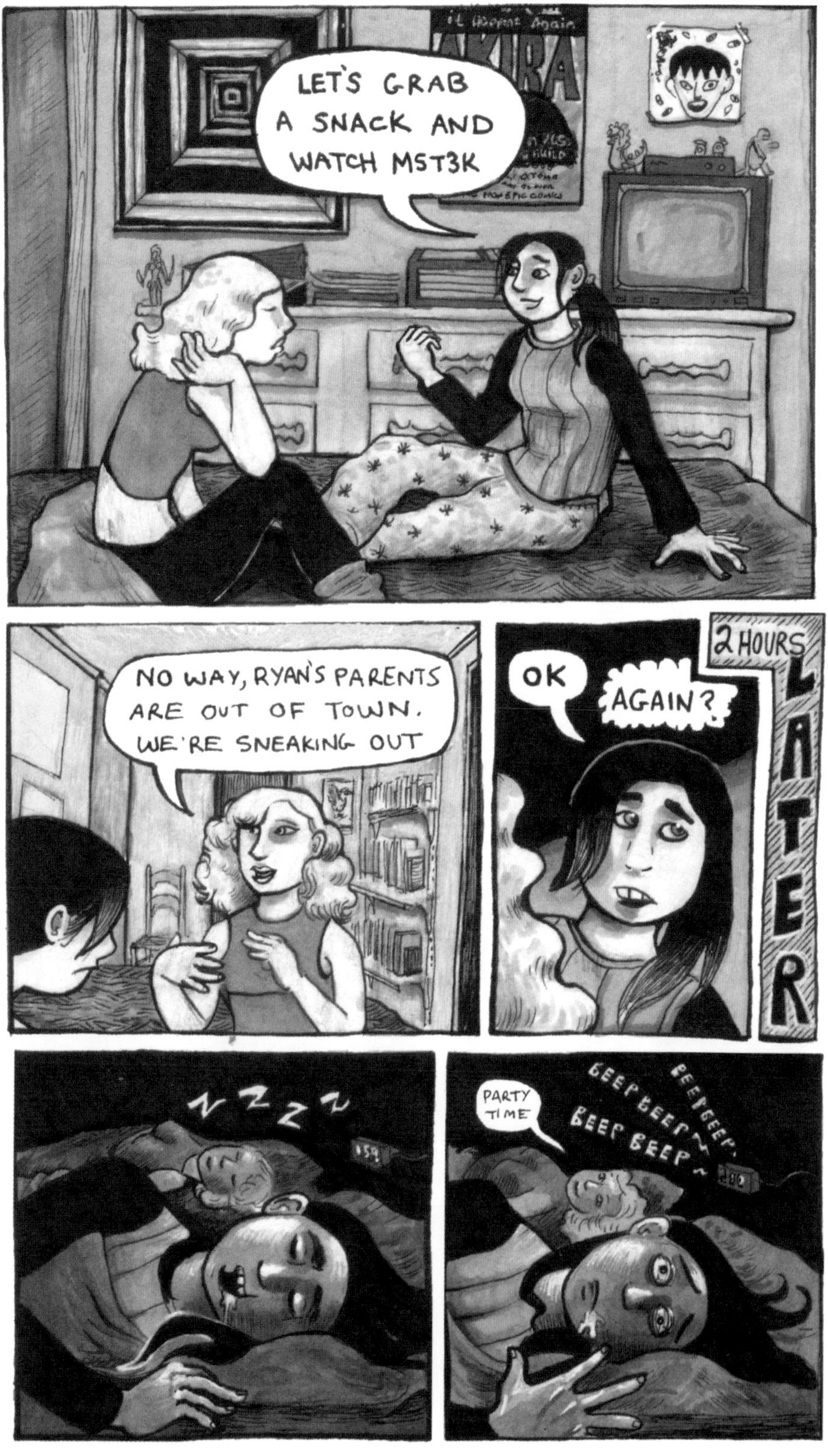
AKIRA
LET'S GRAB A SNACK AND WATCH MST3K
NO WAY, RYAN'S PARENTS ARE OUT OF TOWN. WE'RE SNEAKING OUT
OK
AGAIN?
2 HOURS LATER
ZZZZ
PARTY TIME
BEEP BEEP BEEP BEEP
BEEP BEEP

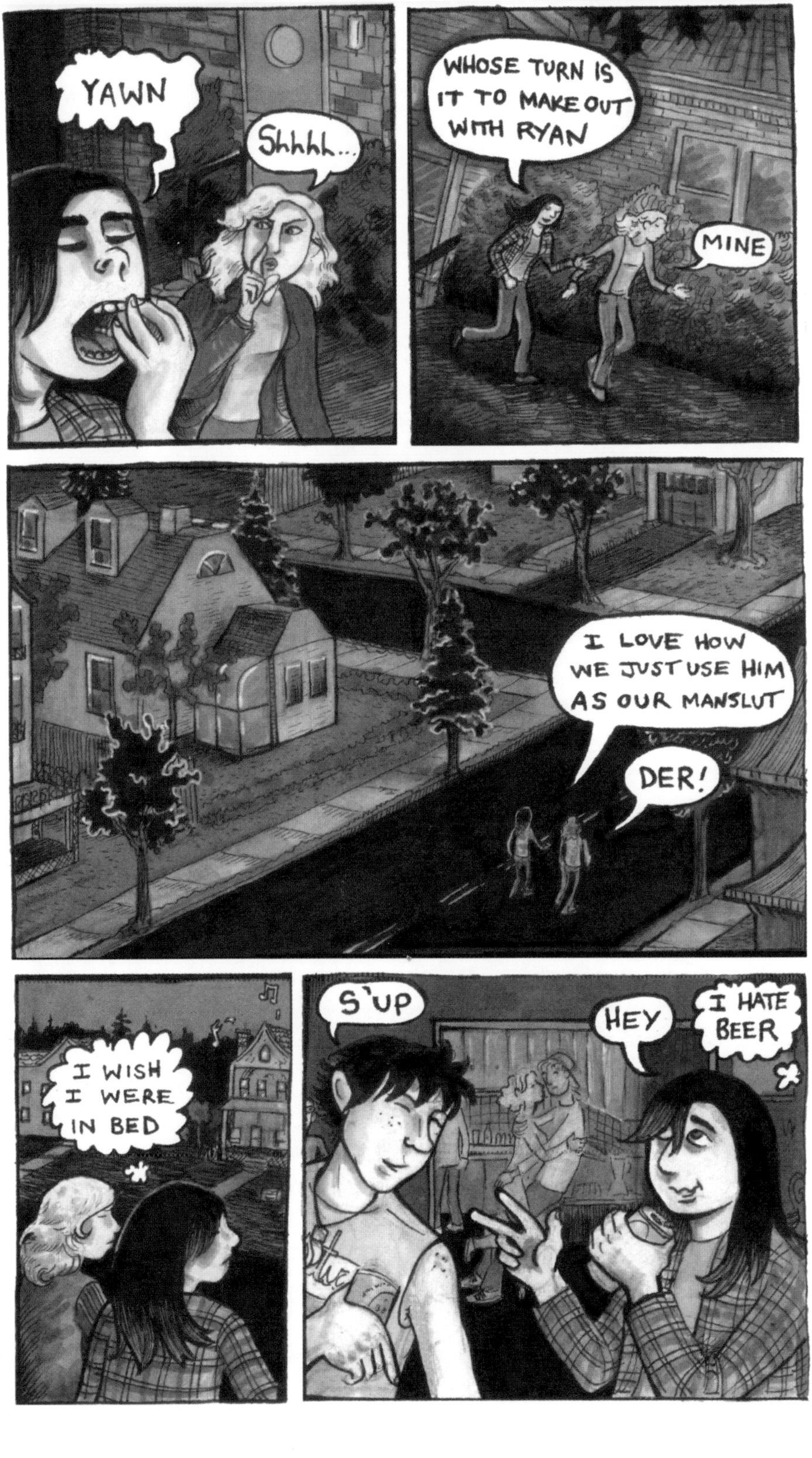
YAWN
Shhhh...
WHOSE TURN IS IT TO MAKE OUT WITH RYAN
MINE
I LOVE HOW WE JUST USE HIM AS OUR MANSLUT
DER!
I WISH I WERE IN BED
S'UP
HEY
I HATE BEER

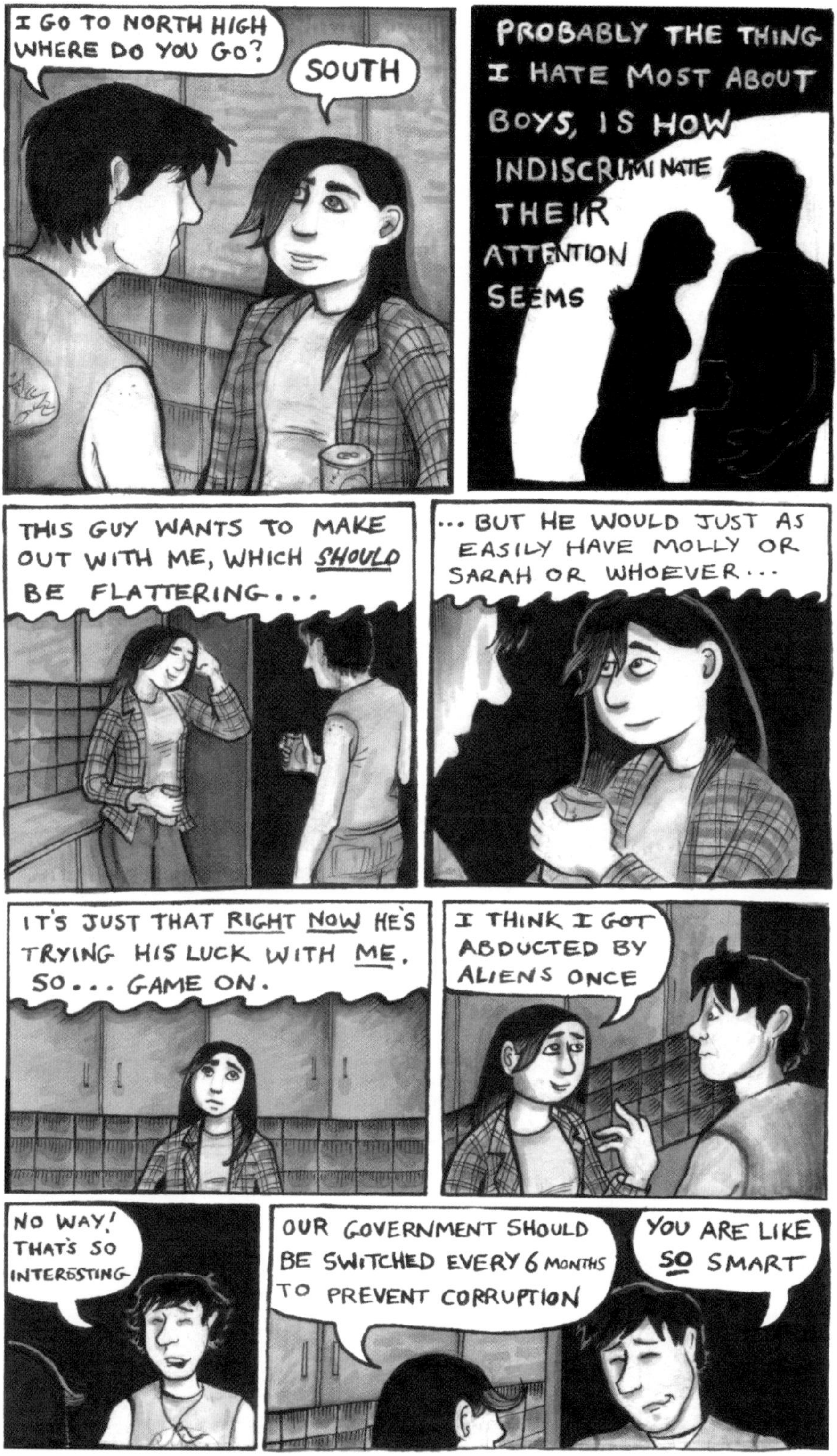
I GO TO NORTH HIGH
WHERE DO YOU GO?
SOUTH
PROBABLY THE THING I HATE MOST ABOUT BOYS, IS HOW INDISCRIMINATE THEIR ATTENTION SEEMS
THIS GUY WANTS TO MAKE OUT WITH ME, WHICH SHOULD BE FLATTERING...
...BUT HE WOULD JUST AS EASILY HAVE MOLLY OR SARAH OR WHOEVER...
IT'S JUST THAT RIGHT NOW HE'S TRYING HIS LUCK WITH ME. SO... GAME ON.
I THINK I GOT ABDUCTED BY ALIENS ONCE
NO WAY! THAT'S SO INTERESTING
OUR GOVERNMENT SHOULD BE SWITCHED EVERY 6 MONTHS TO PREVENT CORRUPTION
YOU ARE LIKE SO SMART

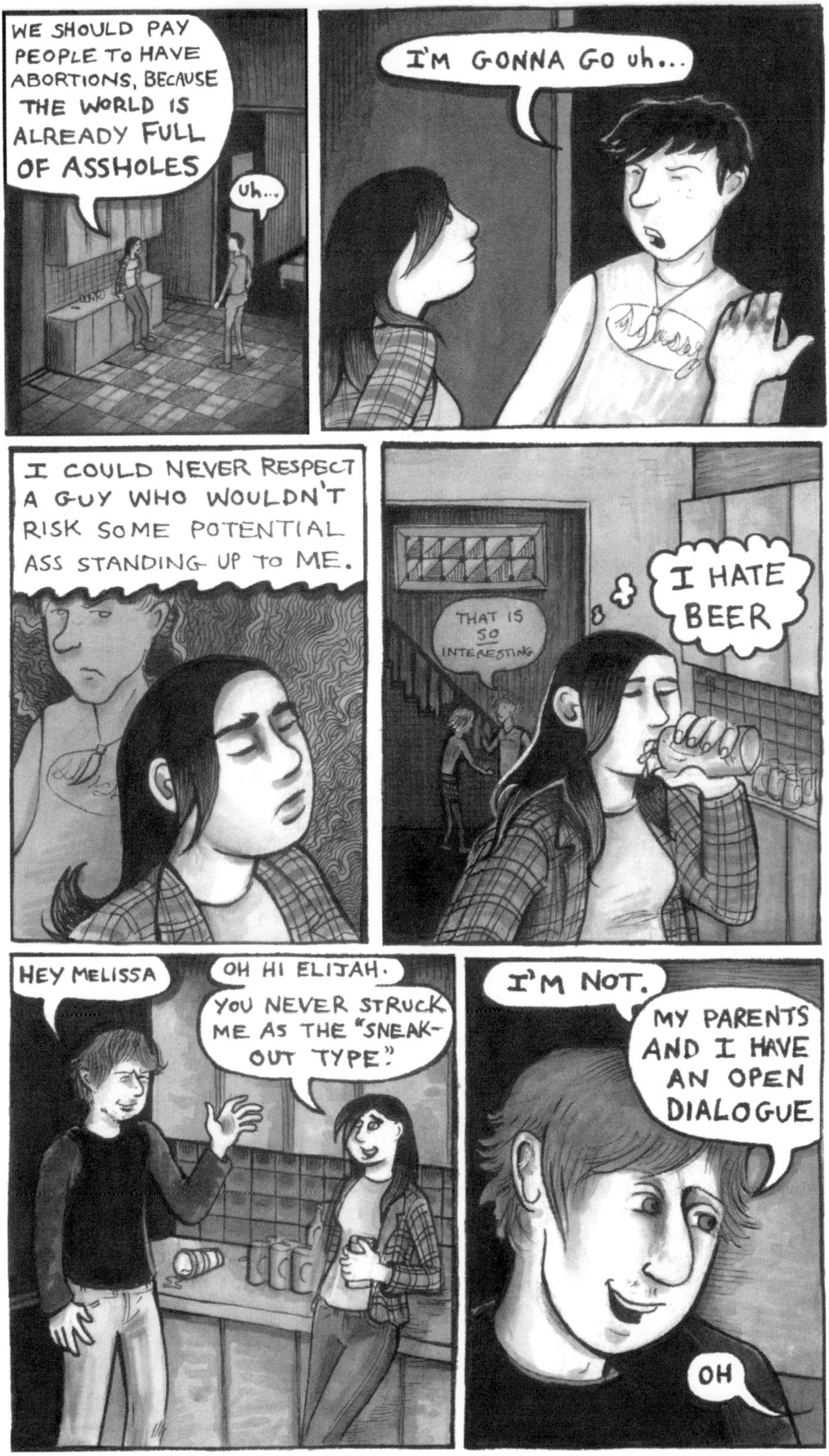
WE SHOULD PAY PEOPLE TO HAVE ABORTIONS, BECAUSE THE WORLD IS ALREADY FULL OF ASSHOLES
Uh...
I'M GONNA GO uh...
I COULD NEVER RESPECT A GUY WHO WOULDN'T RISK SOME POTENTIAL ASS STANDING UP TO ME.
THAT IS SO INTERESTING
I HATE BEER
HEY MELISSA
OH HI ELIJAH.
YOU NEVER STRUCK ME AS THE "SNEAK-OUT TYPE."
I'M NOT.
MY PARENTS AND I HAVE AN OPEN DIALOGUE
OH

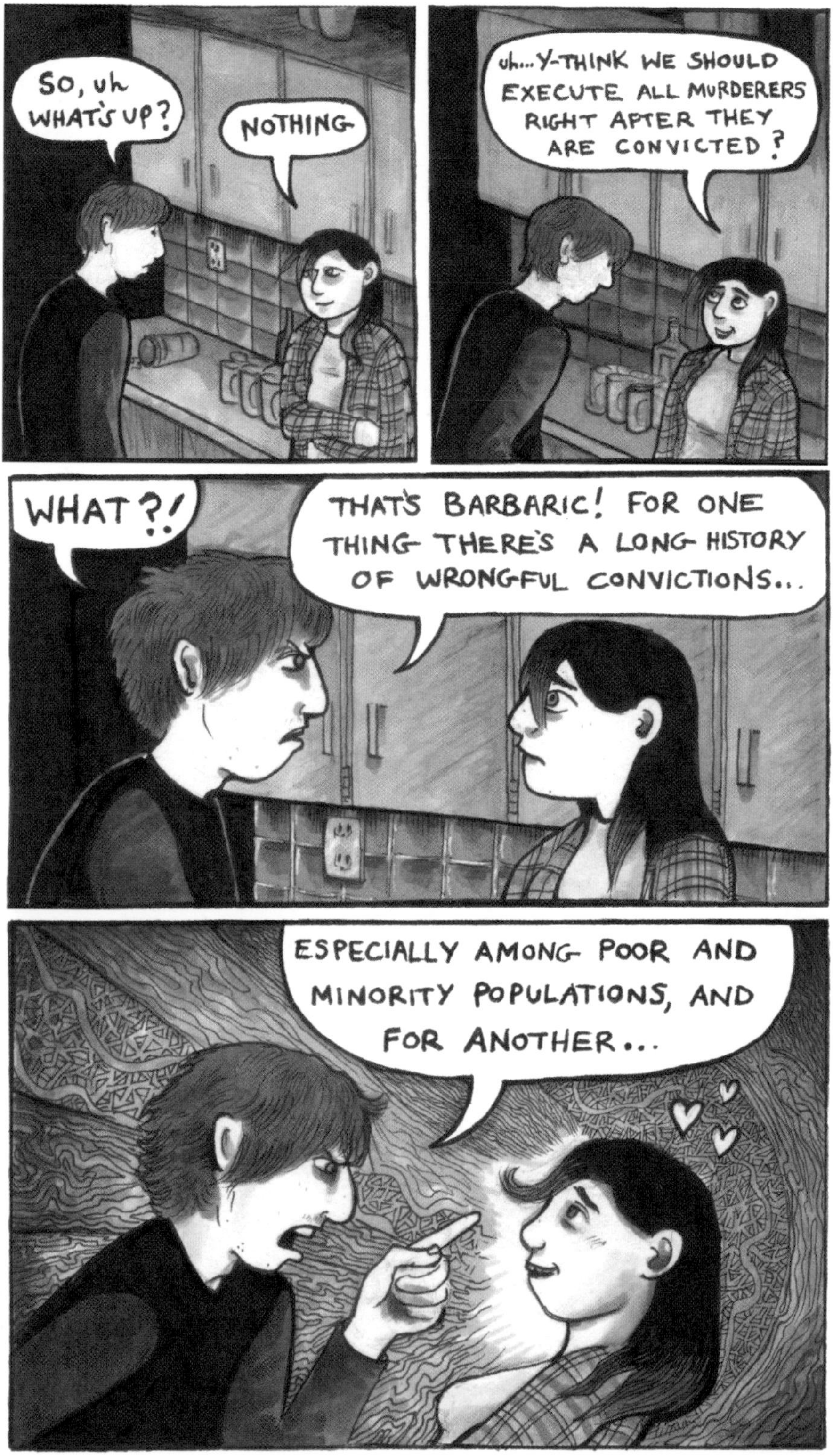
So, uh WHAT'S UP?
NOTHING
uh... Y-THINK WE SHOULD EXECUTE ALL MURDERERS RIGHT AFTER THEY ARE CONVICTED?
WHAT?!
THAT'S BARBARIC! FOR ONE THING THERE'S A LONG HISTORY OF WRONGFUL CONVICTIONS...
ESPECIALLY AMONG POOR AND MINORITY POPULATIONS, AND FOR ANOTHER...

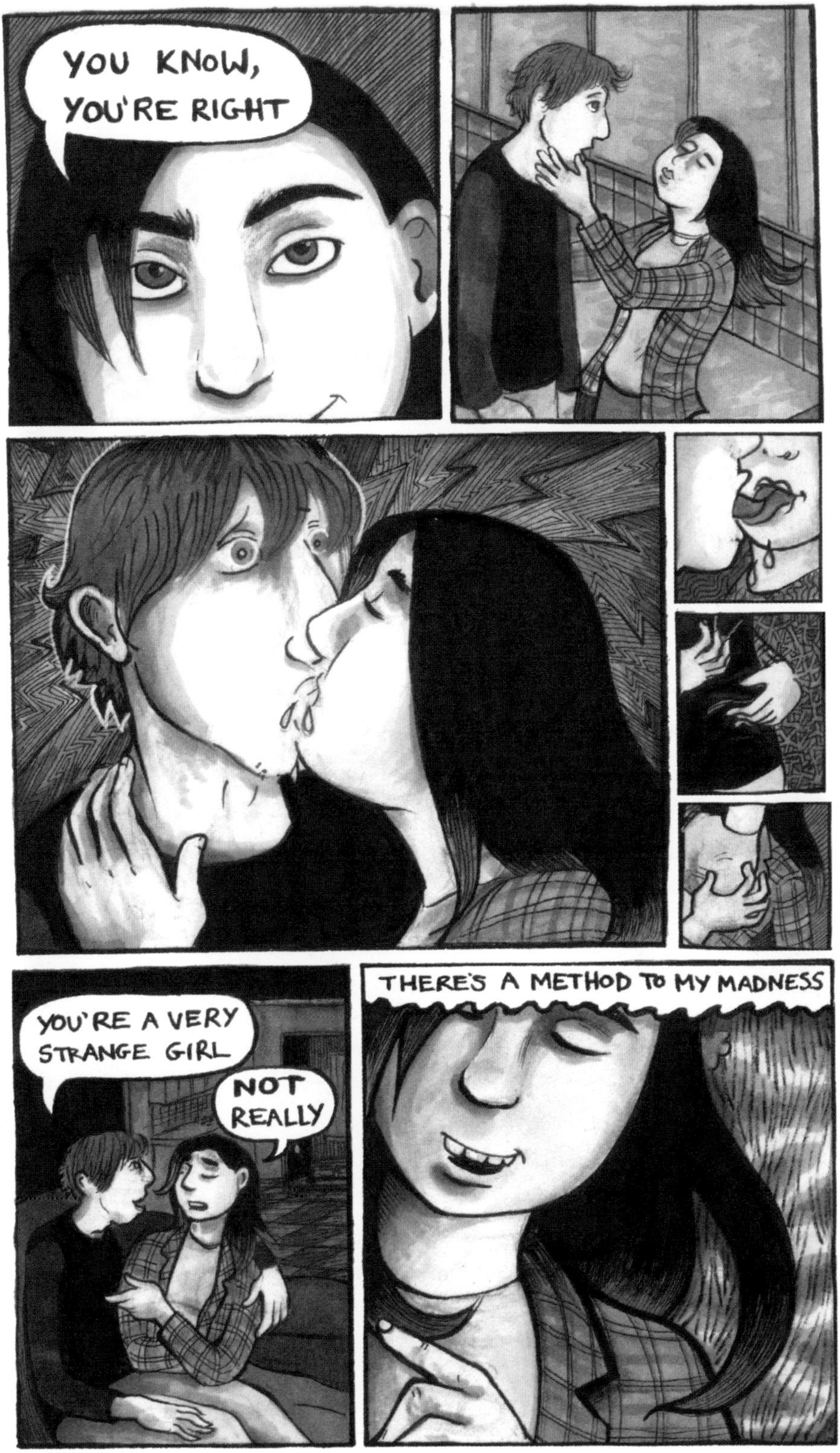
YOU KNOW, YOU'RE RIGHT
YOU'RE A VERY STRANGE GIRL
NOT REALLY
THERE'S A METHOD TO MY MADNESS

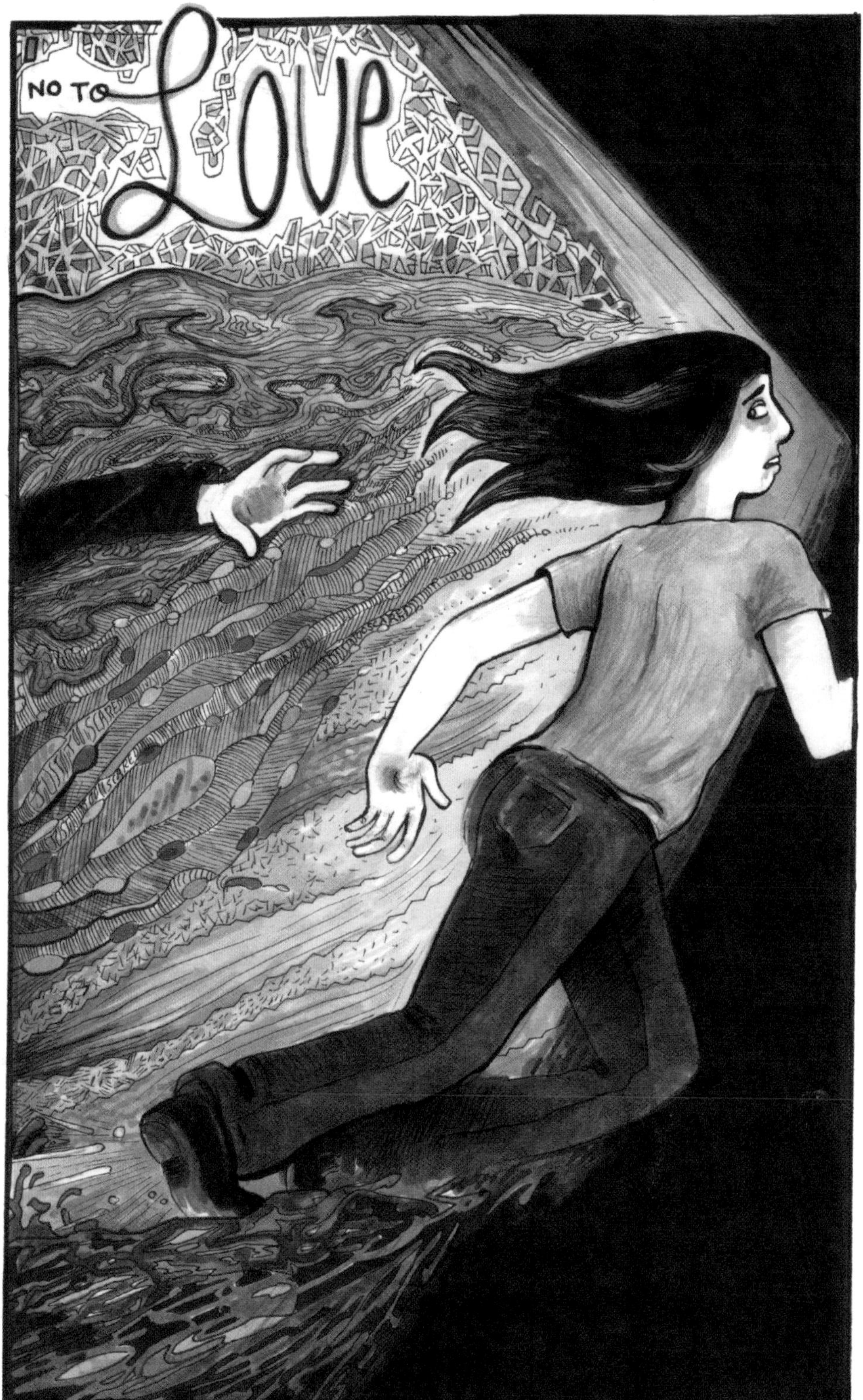
NO TO
Love

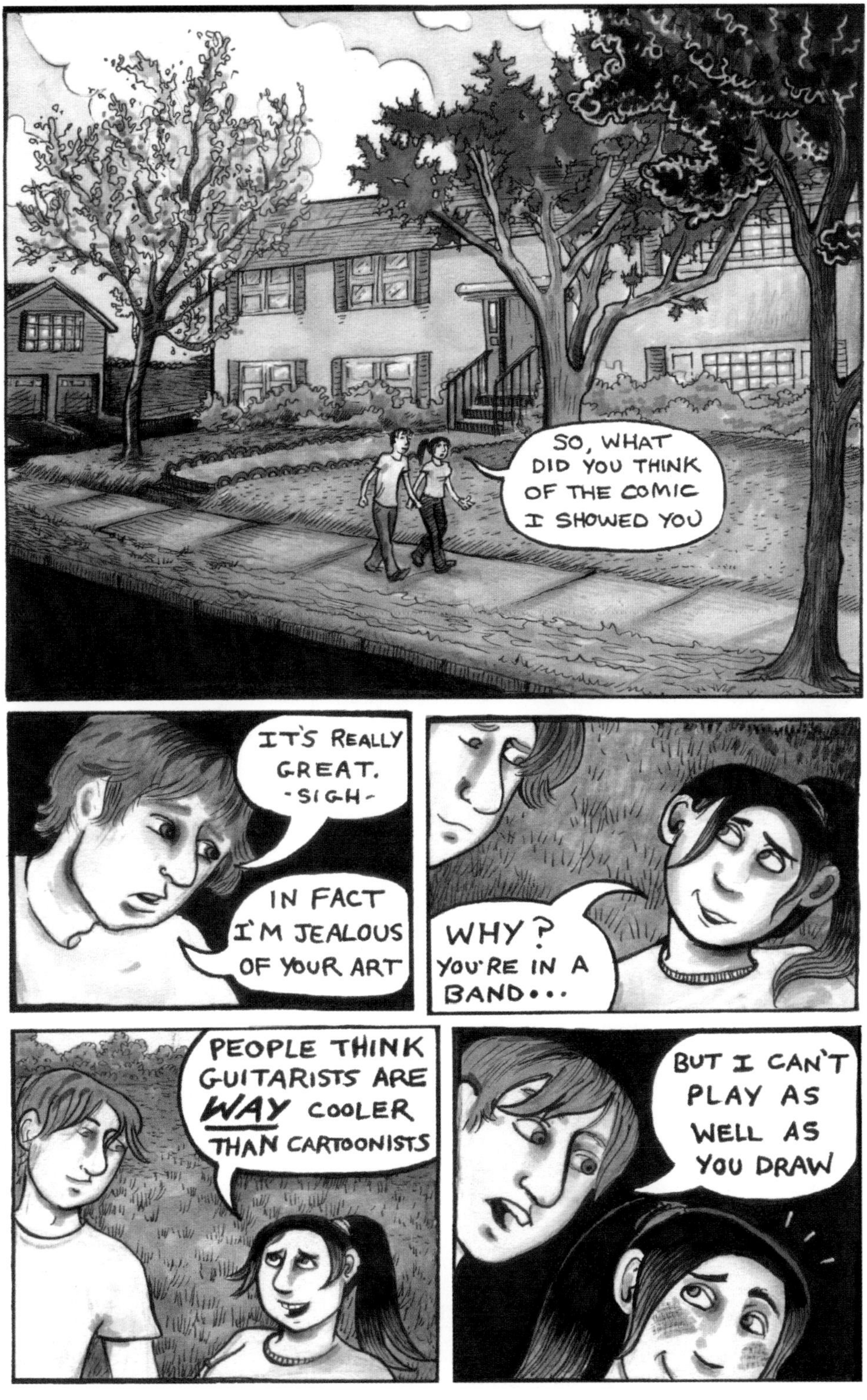
SO, WHAT DID YOU THINK OF THE COMIC I SHOWED YOU
IT'S REALLY GREAT. -SIGH-
IN FACT I'M JEALOUS OF YOUR ART
WHY? YOU'RE IN A BAND...
PEOPLE THINK GUITARISTS ARE WAY COOLER THAN CARTOONISTS
BUT I CAN'T PLAY AS WELL AS YOU DRAW

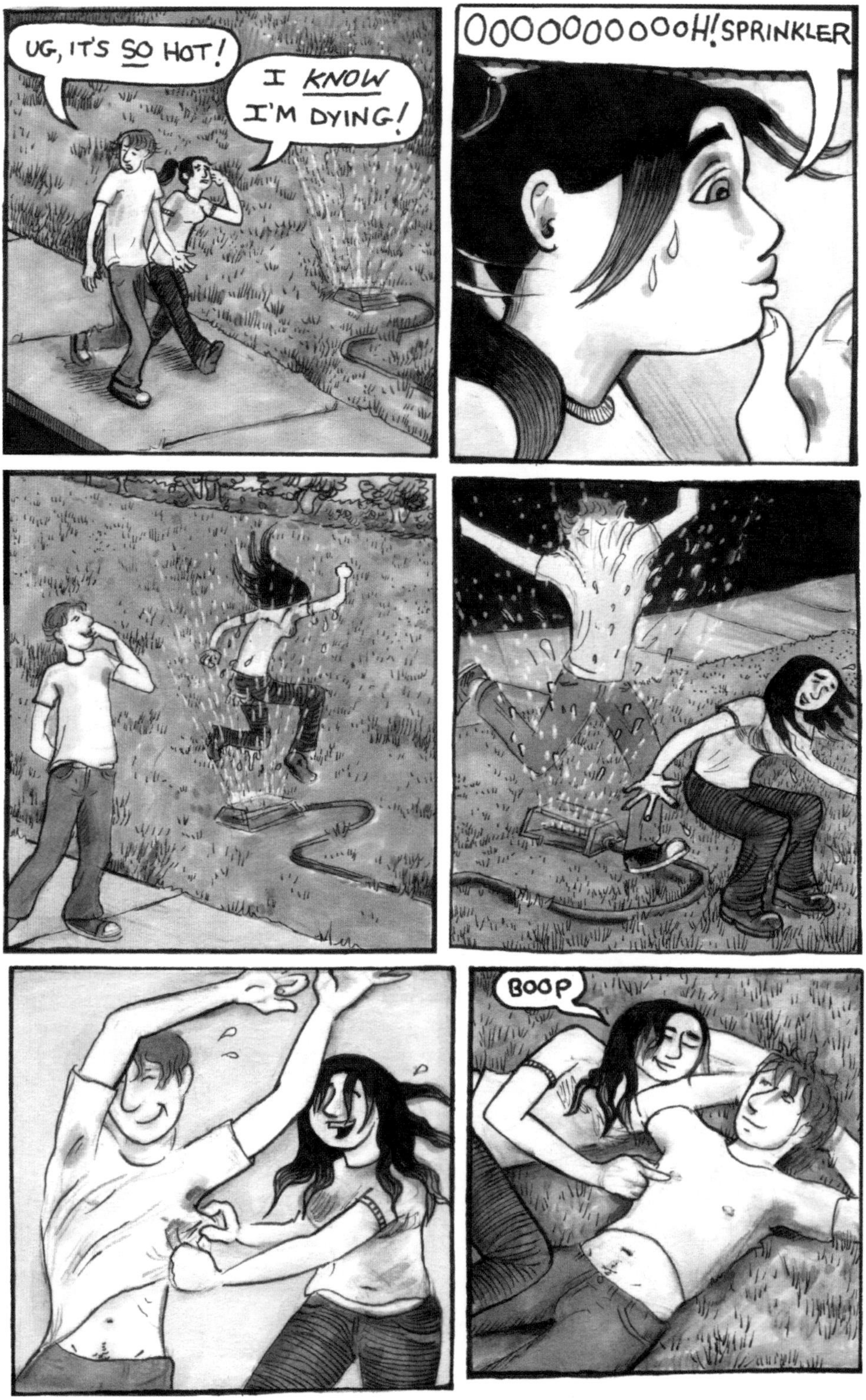
UG, IT'S SO HOT!
I KNOW I'M DYING!
OOOOOOOOOOOH! SPRINKLER
BOOP

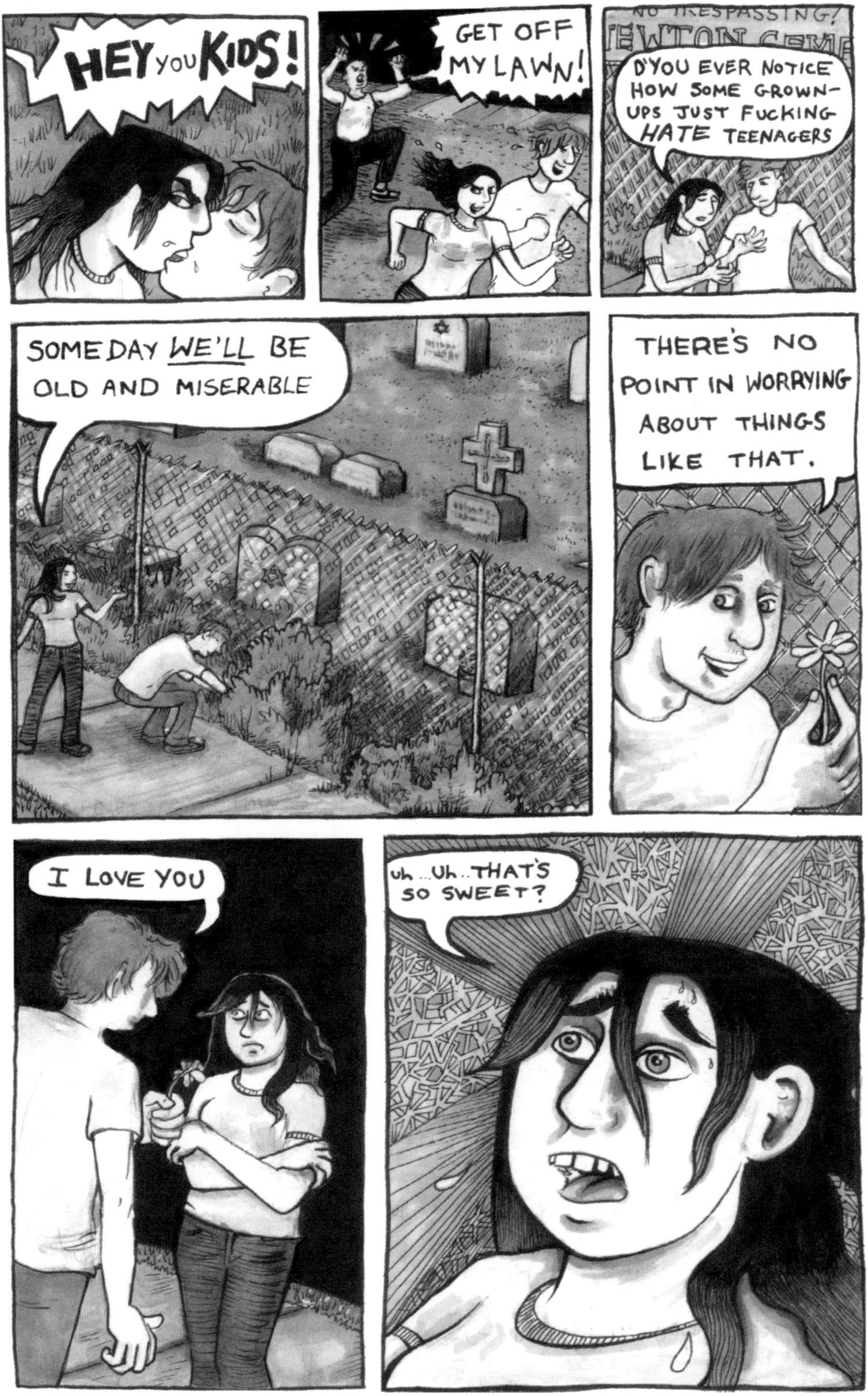
HEY you KIDS!
GET OFF MY LAWN!
NO TRESPASSING!
D'YOU EVER NOTICE HOW SOME GROWN-UPS JUST FUCKING HATE TEENAGERS
SOMEDAY WE'LL BE OLD AND MISERABLE
THERE'S NO POINT IN WORRYING ABOUT THINGS LIKE THAT.
I LOVE YOU
uh...Uh..THAT'S SO SWEET?

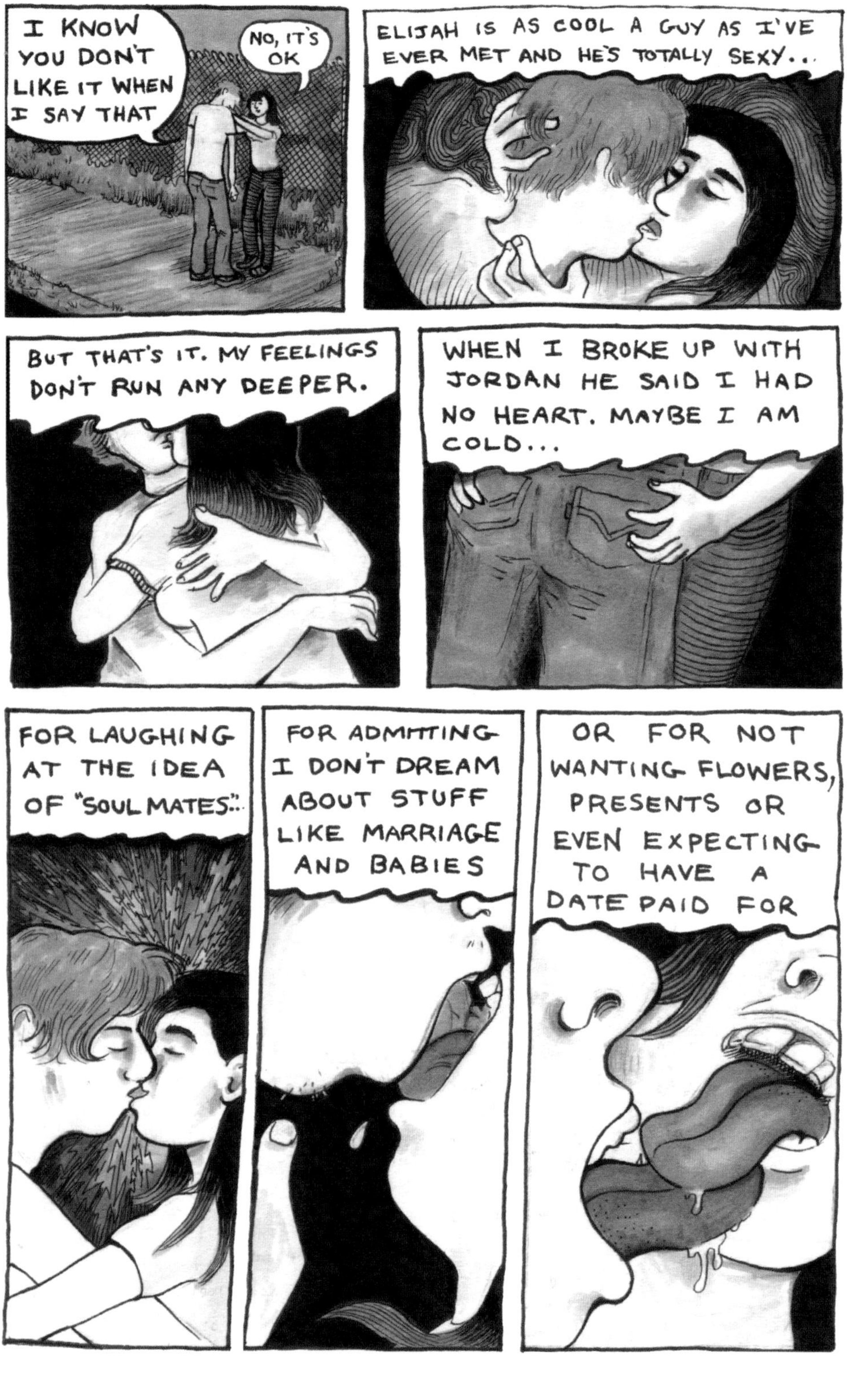
I KNOW YOU DON'T LIKE IT WHEN I SAY THAT
NO, IT'S OK
ELIJAH IS AS COOL A GUY AS I'VE EVER MET AND HE'S TOTALLY SEXY...
BUT THAT'S IT. MY FEELINGS DON'T RUN ANY DEEPER.
WHEN I BROKE UP WITH JORDAN HE SAID I HAD NO HEART. MAYBE I AM COLD...
FOR LAUGHING AT THE IDEA OF "SOUL MATES"...
FOR ADMITTING I DON'T DREAM ABOUT STUFF LIKE MARRIAGE AND BABIES
OR FOR NOT WANTING FLOWERS, PRESENTS OR EVEN EXPECTING TO HAVE A DATE PAID FOR

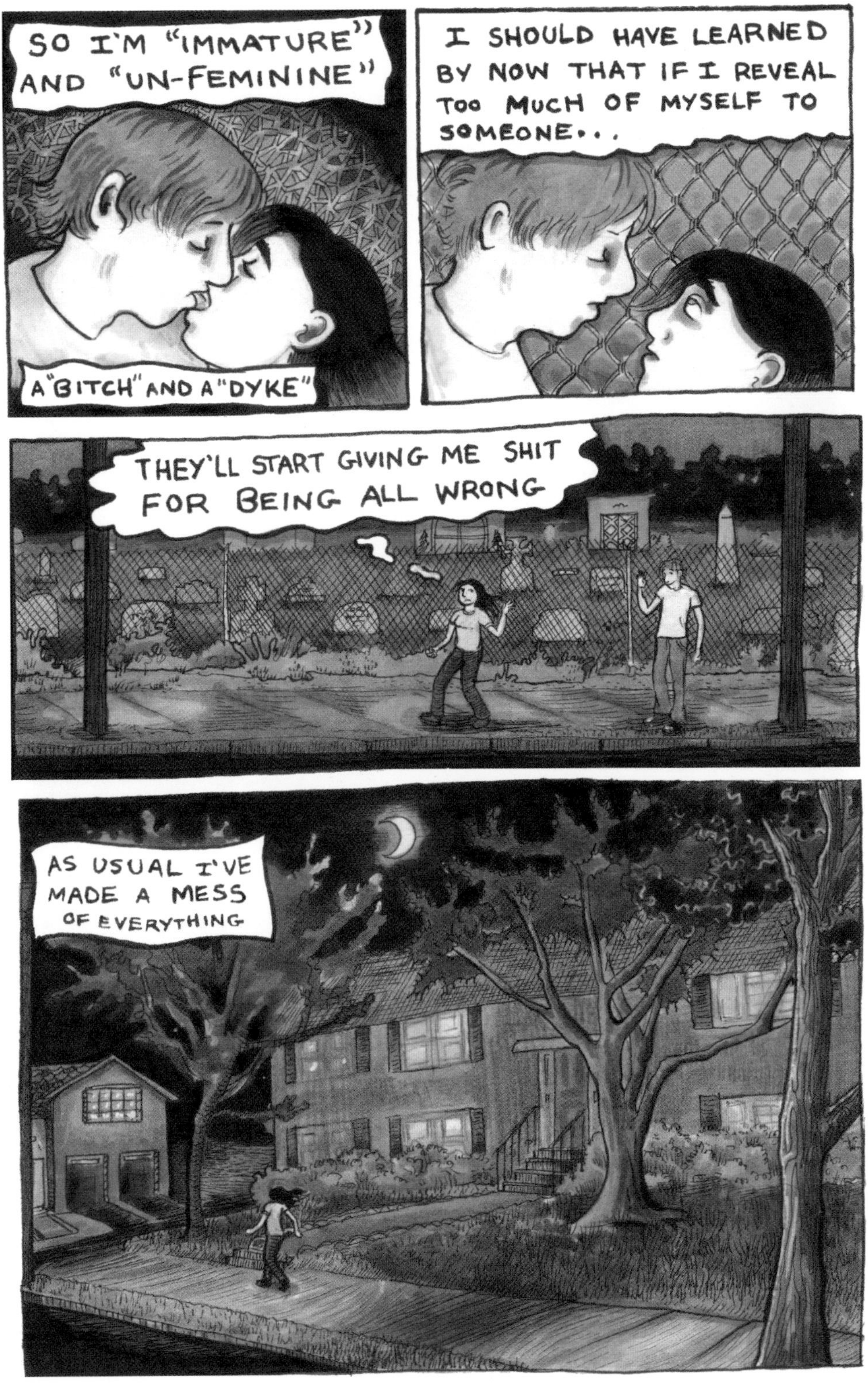
SO I'M "IMMATURE" AND "UN-FEMININE"
A "BITCH" AND A "DYKE"
I SHOULD HAVE LEARNED BY NOW THAT IF I REVEAL TOO MUCH OF MYSELF TO SOMEONE...
THEY'LL START GIVING ME SHIT FOR BEING ALL WRONG
AS USUAL I'VE MADE A MESS OF EVERYTHING

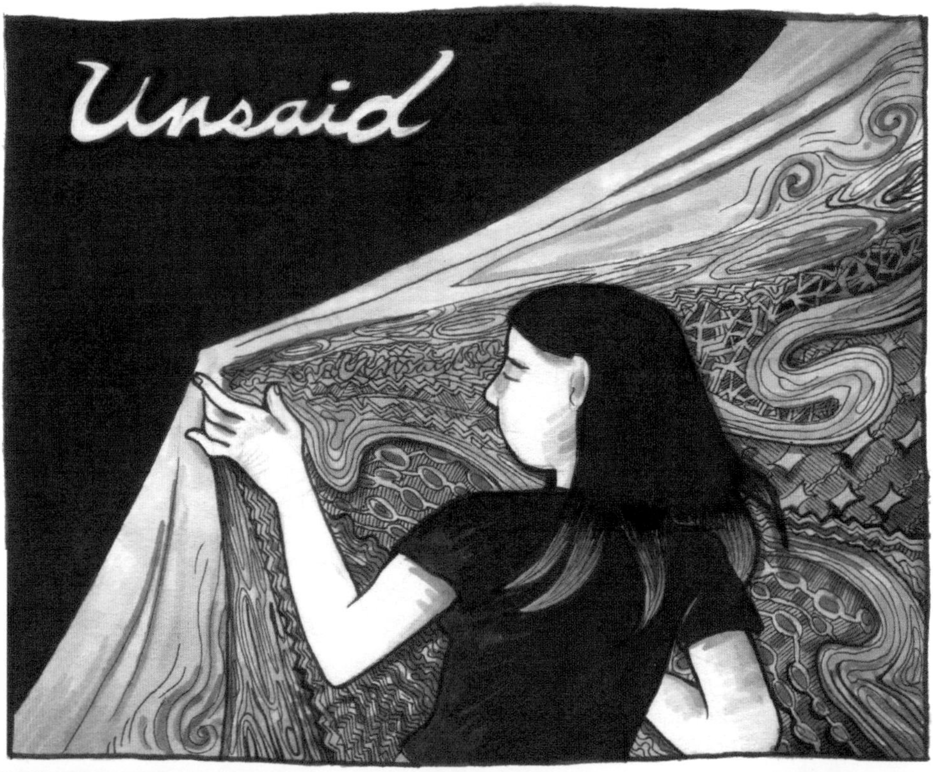
Unsaid

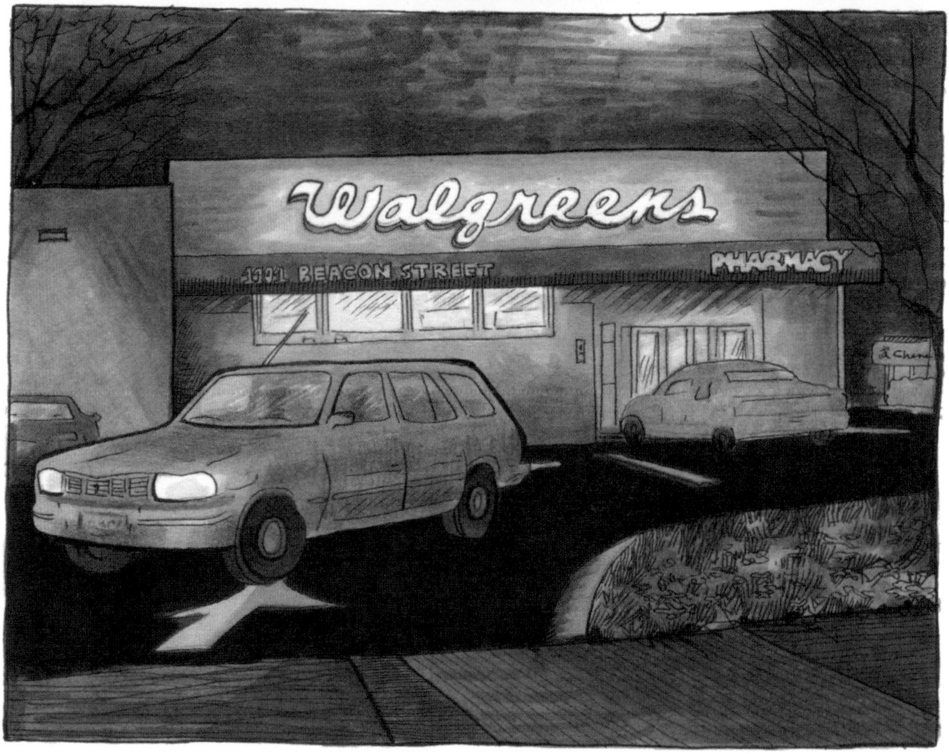
Walgreens
BEACON STREET
PHARMACY

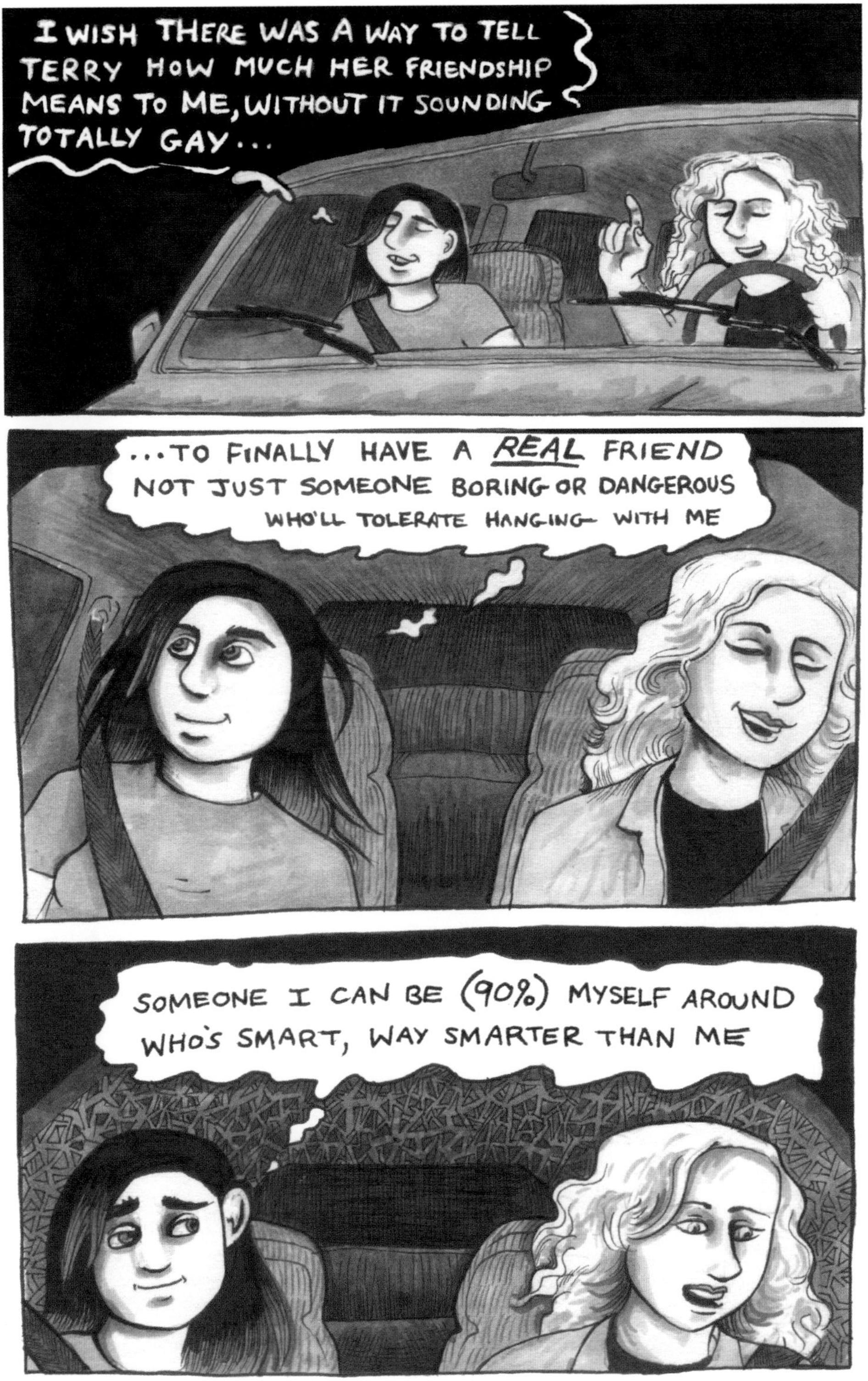
I WISH THERE WAS A WAY TO TELL TERRY HOW MUCH HER FRIENDSHIP MEANS TO ME, WITHOUT IT SOUNDING TOTALLY GAY...
...TO FINALLY HAVE A REAL FRIEND NOT JUST SOMEONE BORING OR DANGEROUS WHO'LL TOLERATE HANGING WITH ME
SOMEONE I CAN BE (90%) MYSELF AROUND WHO'S SMART, WAY SMARTER THAN ME

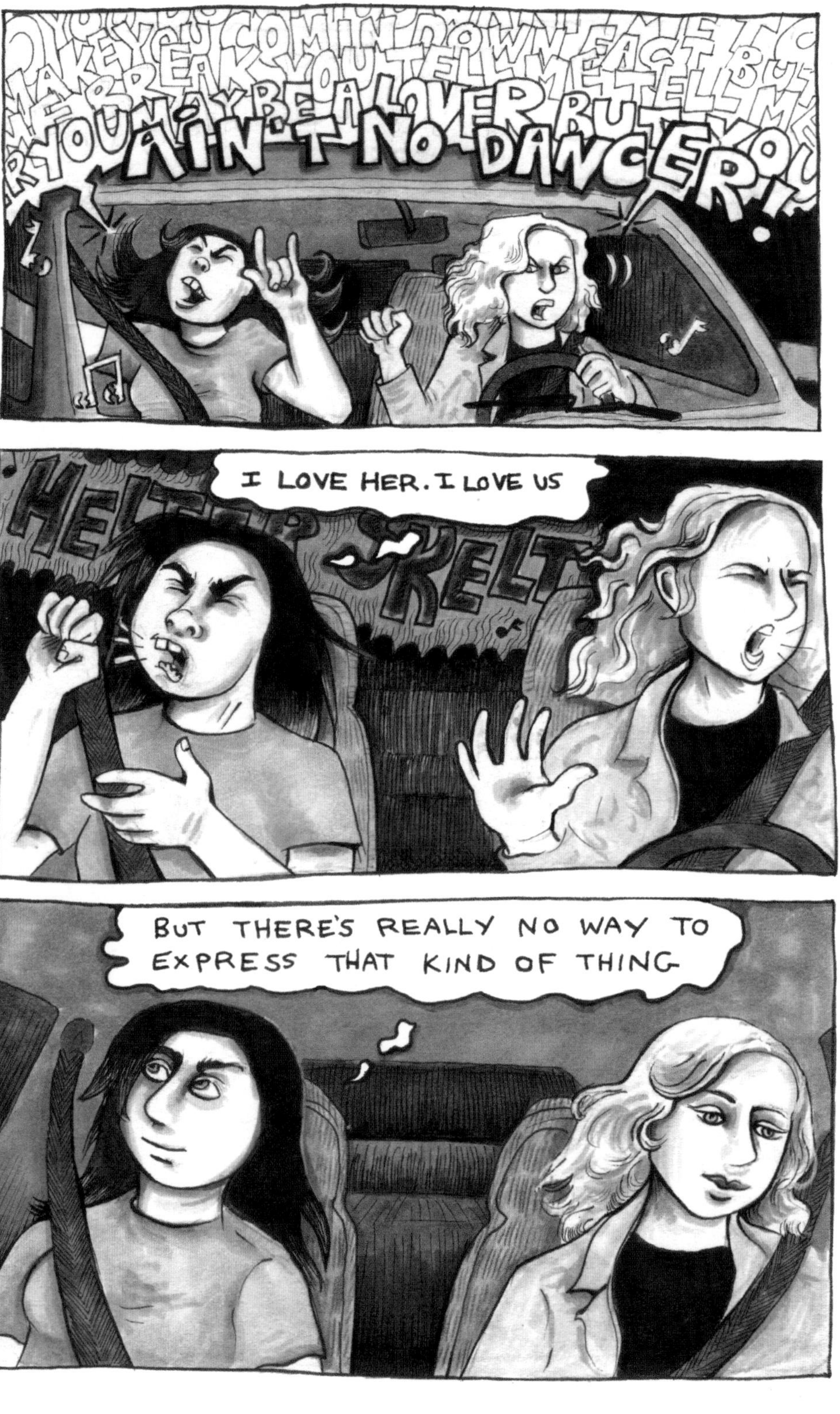
YOU MAY BE A LOVER BUT YOU
AIN'T NO DANCER!
I LOVE HER. I LOVE US
BUT THERE'S REALLY NO WAY TO EXPRESS THAT KIND OF THING

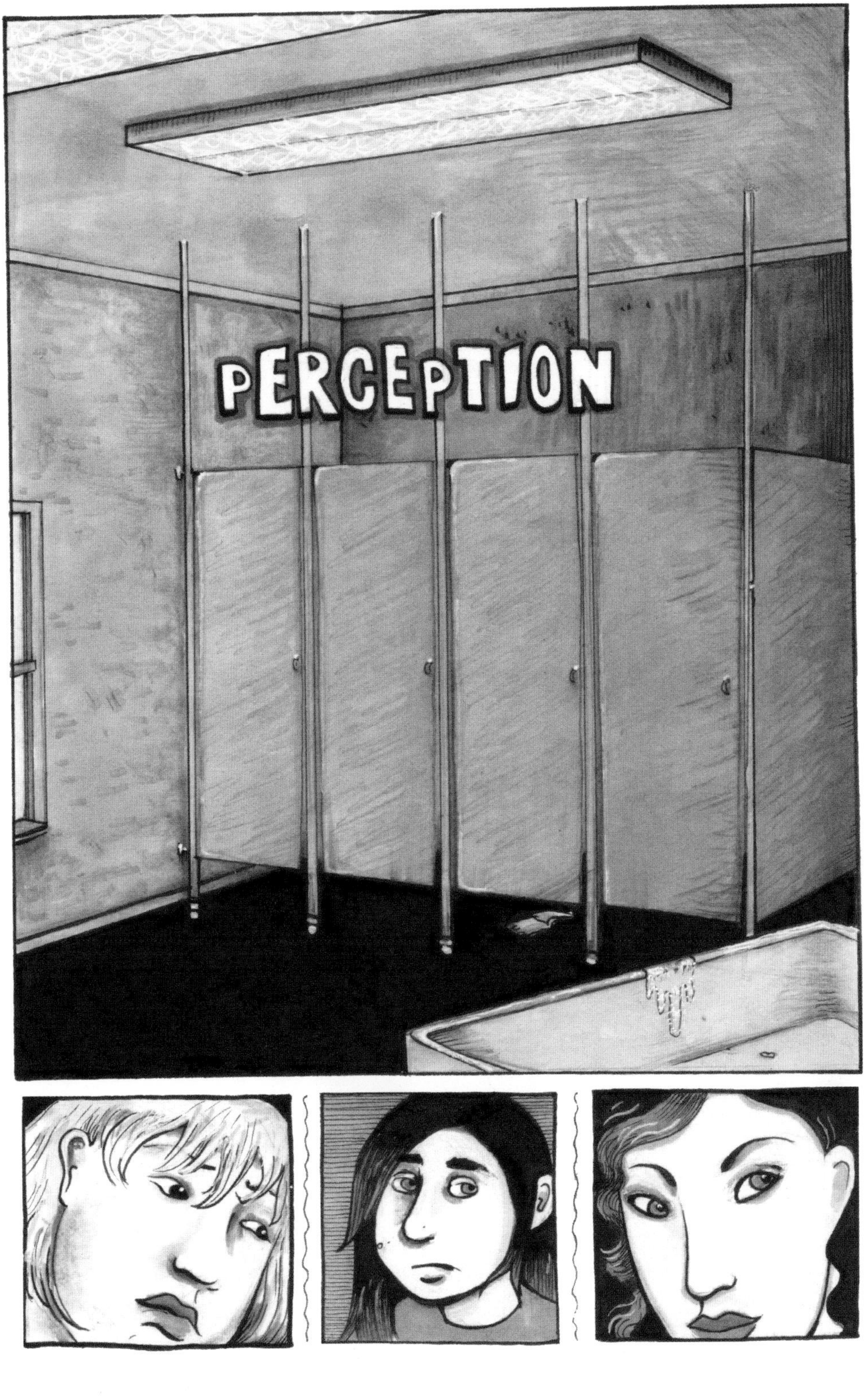
PERCEPTION

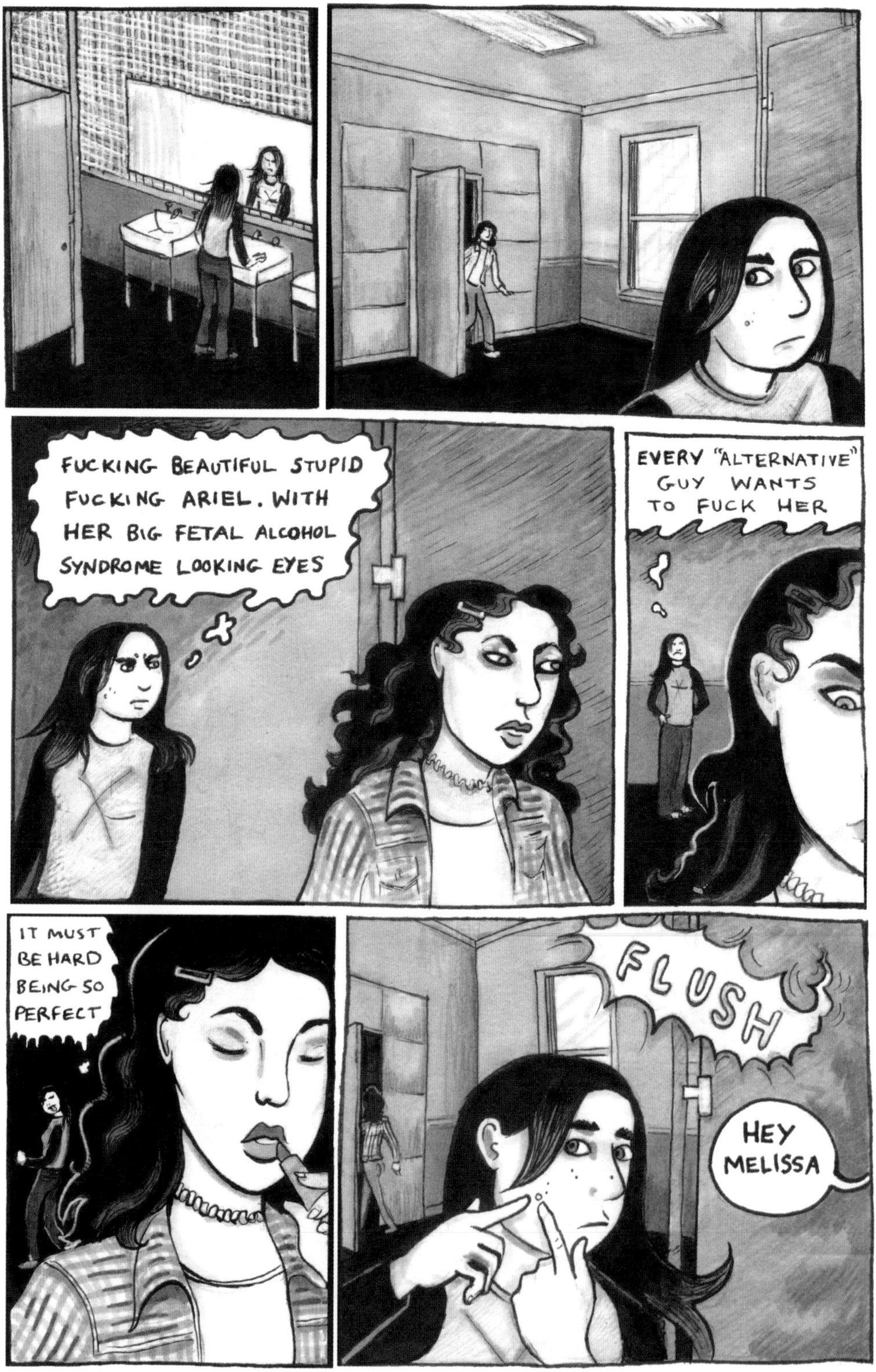
FUCKING BEAUTIFUL STUPID FUCKING ARIEL. WITH HER BIG FETAL ALCOHOL SYNDROME LOOKING EYES
EVERY "ALTERNATIVE" GUY WANTS TO FUCK HER
IT MUST BE HARD BEING SO PERFECT
FLUSH
HEY MELISSA

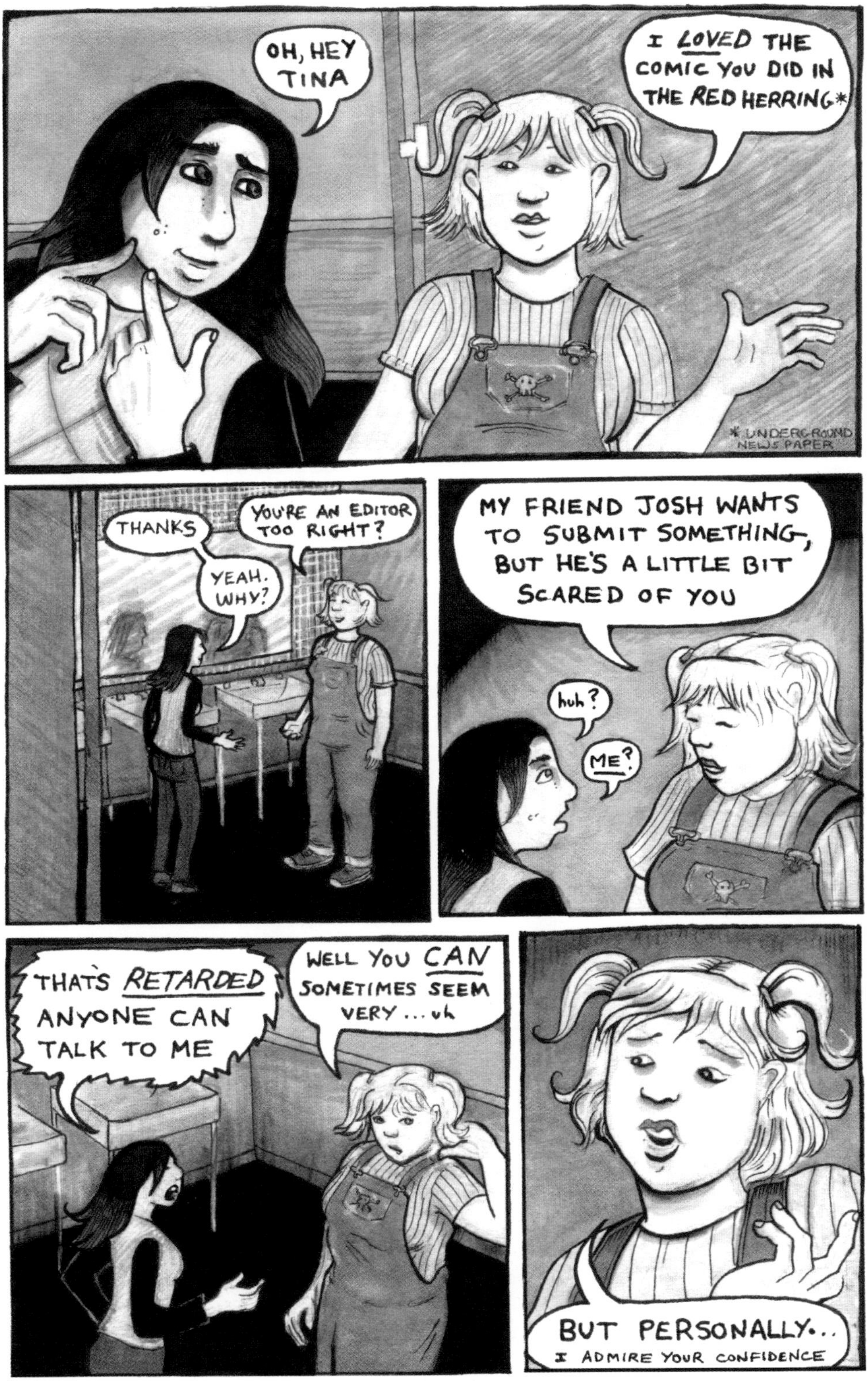
OH, HEY TINA
I LOVED THE COMIC YOU DID IN THE RED HERRING*
* UNDERGROUND NEWS PAPER
THANKS
YOU'RE AN EDITOR TOO RIGHT?
YEAH. WHY?
MY FRIEND JOSH WANTS TO SUBMIT SOMETHING, BUT HE'S A LITTLE BIT SCARED OF YOU
huh?
ME?
THAT'S RETARDED ANYONE CAN TALK TO ME
WELL YOU CAN SOMETIMES SEEM VERY ... uh
BUT PERSONALLY...
I ADMIRE YOUR CONFIDENCE

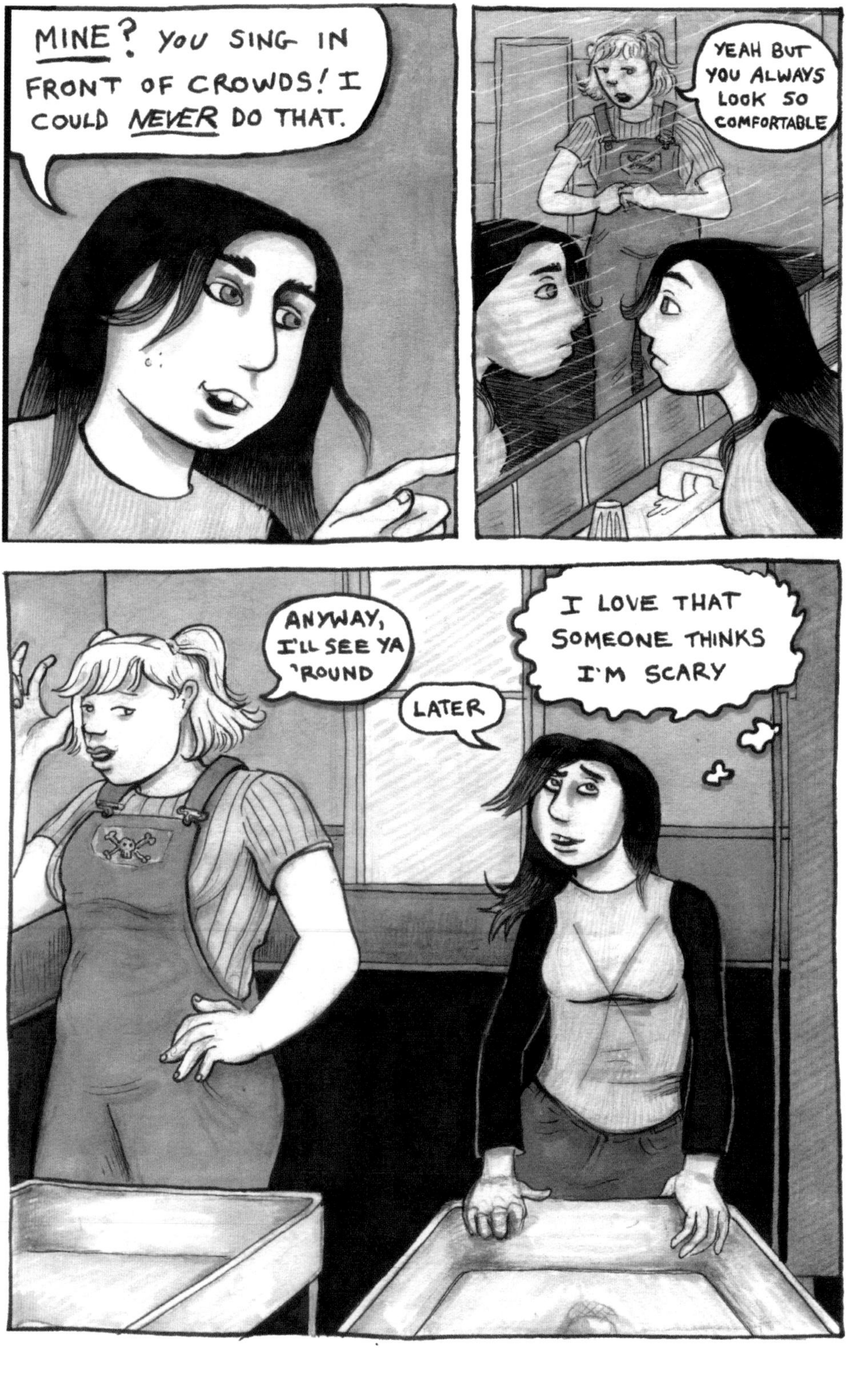
MINE? YOU SING IN FRONT OF CROWDS! I COULD NEVER DO THAT.
YEAH BUT YOU ALWAYS LOOK SO COMFORTABLE
ANYWAY, I'LL SEE YA 'ROUND
LATER
I LOVE THAT SOMEONE THINKS I'M SCARY

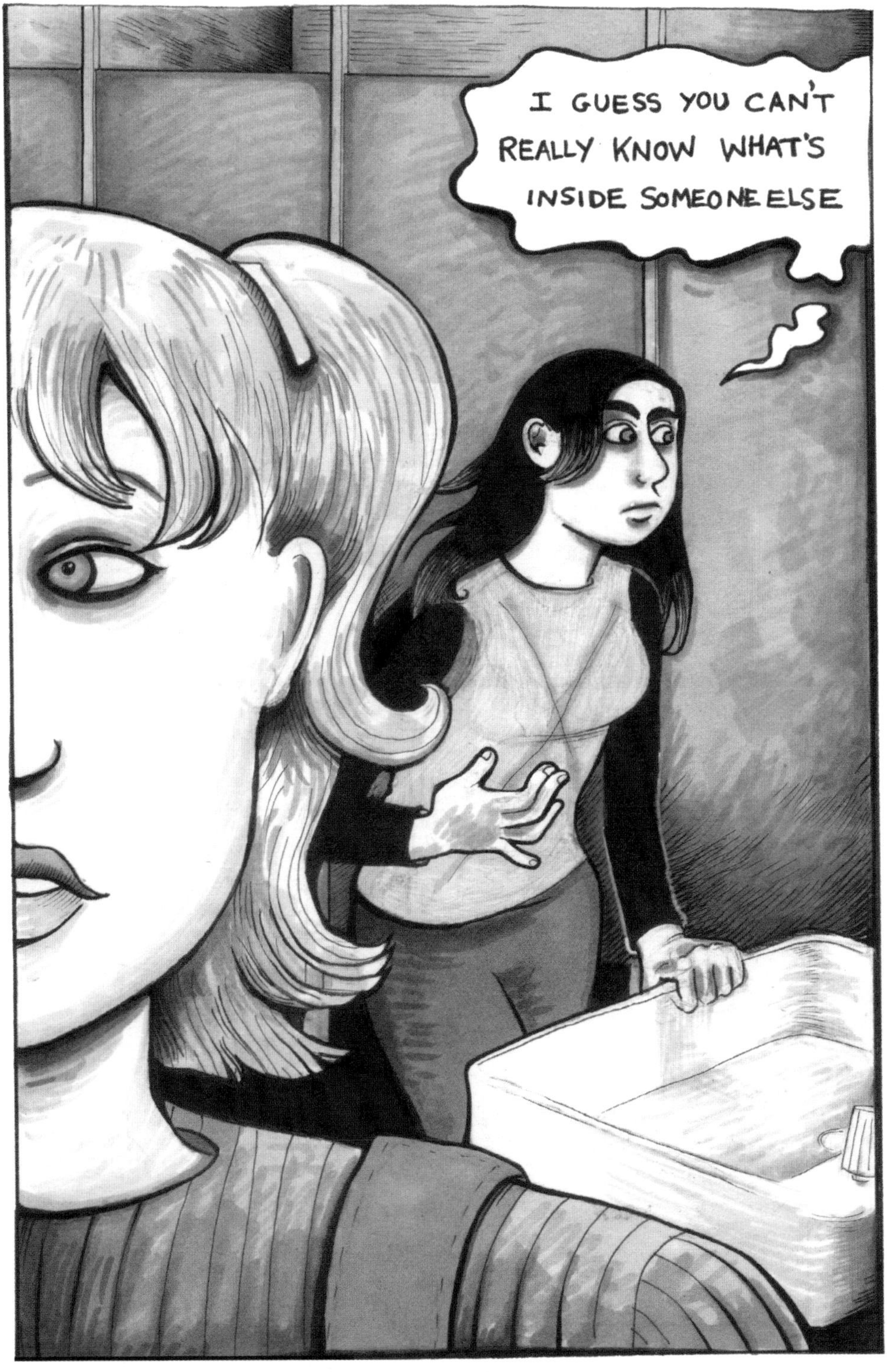
I GUESS YOU CAN'T REALLY KNOW WHAT'S INSIDE SOMEONE ELSE

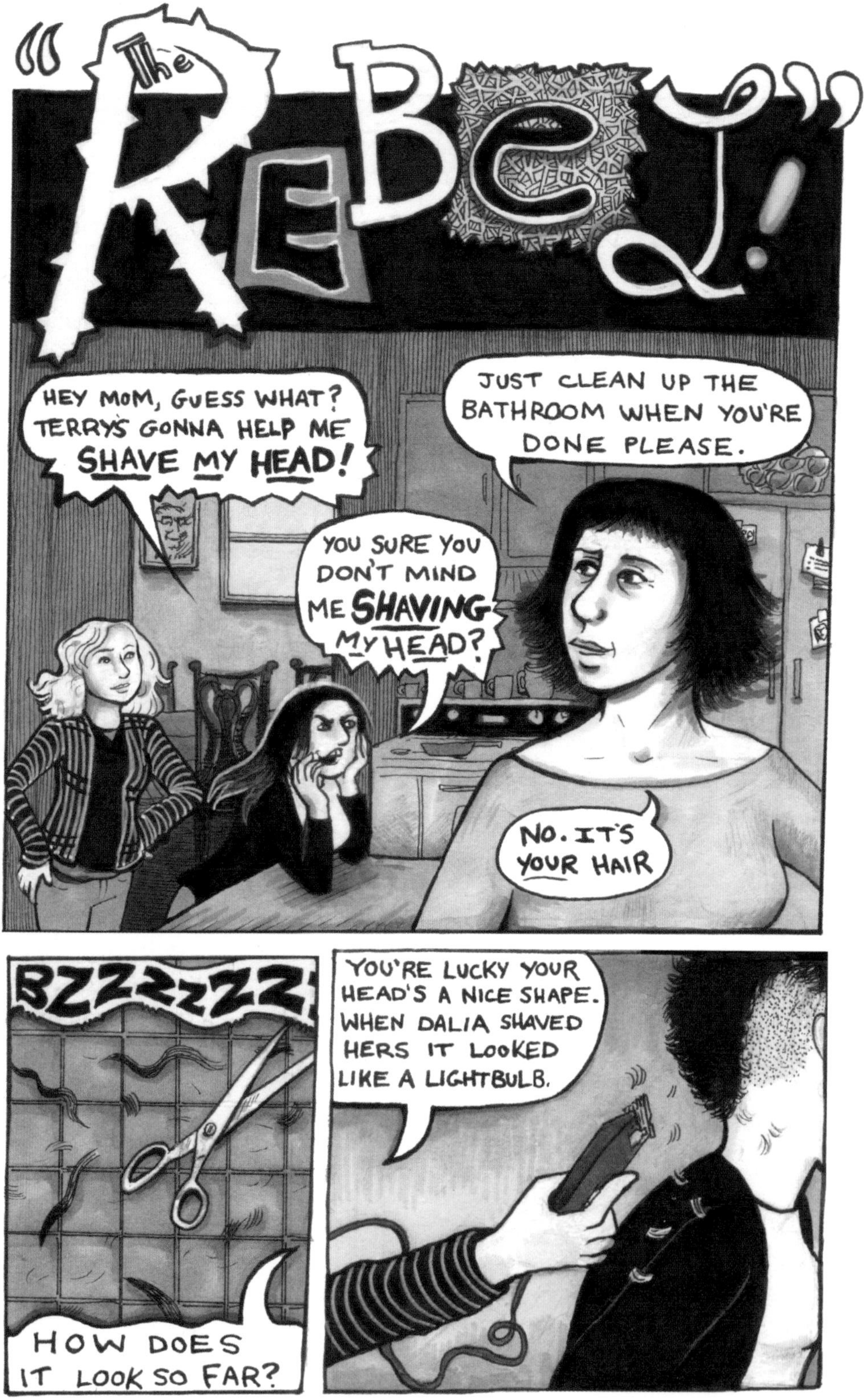
"The REBEL!"
HEY MOM, GUESS WHAT? TERRY'S GONNA HELP ME SHAVE MY HEAD!
JUST CLEAN UP THE BATHROOM WHEN YOU'RE DONE PLEASE.
YOU SURE YOU DON'T MIND ME SHAVING MY HEAD?
NO. IT'S YOUR HAIR
BZZZzzZZ!
HOW DOES IT LOOK SO FAR?
YOU'RE LUCKY YOUR HEAD'S A NICE SHAPE. WHEN DALIA SHAVED HERS IT LOOKED LIKE A LIGHTBULB.

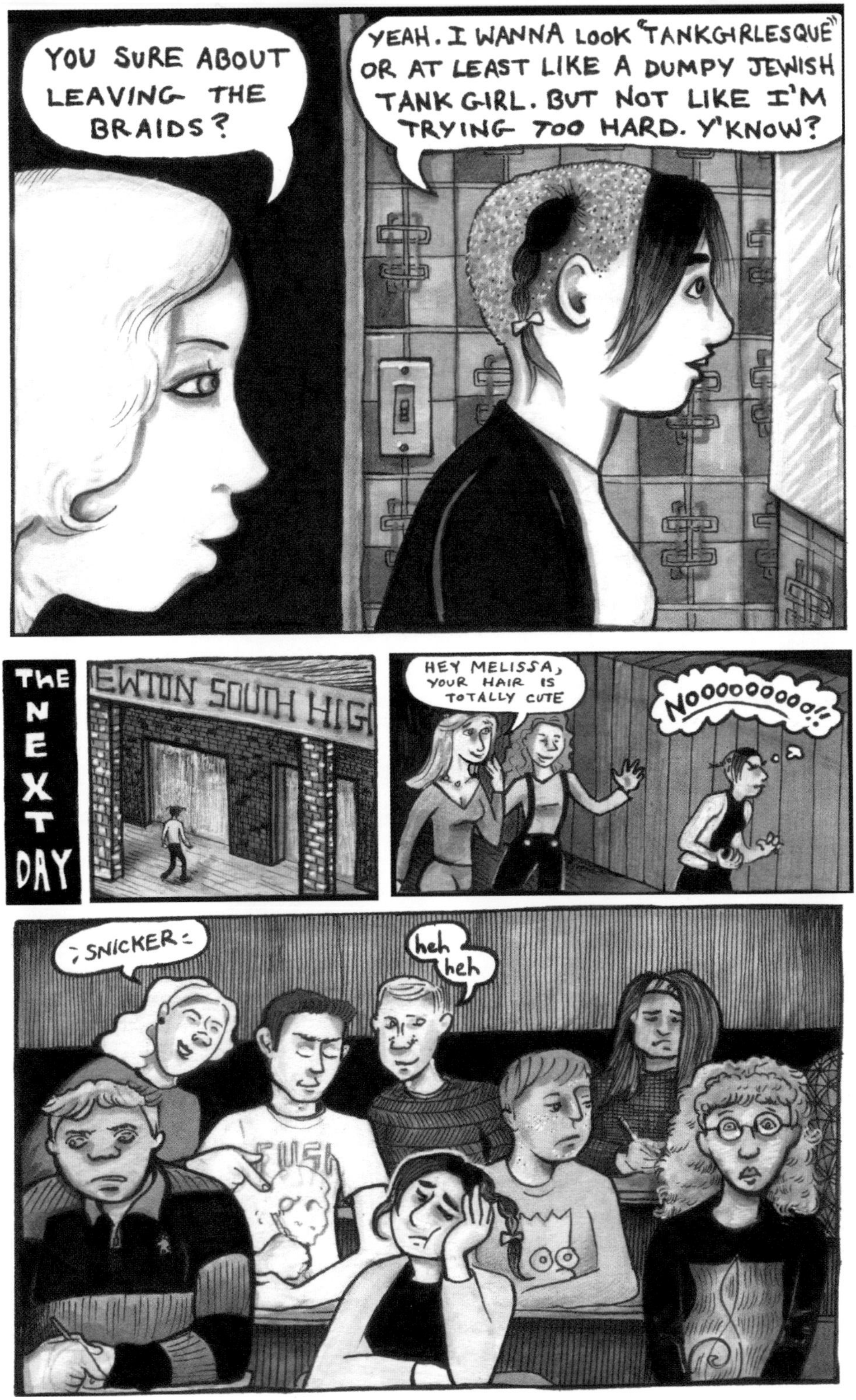
YOU SURE ABOUT LEAVING THE BRAIDS?
YEAH. I WANNA LOOK "TANKGIRLESQUE" OR AT LEAST LIKE A DUMPY JEWISH TANK GIRL. BUT NOT LIKE I'M TRYING TOO HARD. Y'KNOW?
THE NEXT DAY
EWTON SOUTH HIG
HEY MELISSA, YOUR HAIR IS TOTALLY CUTE
NOOOOOOOOO!!
SNICKER
heh heh

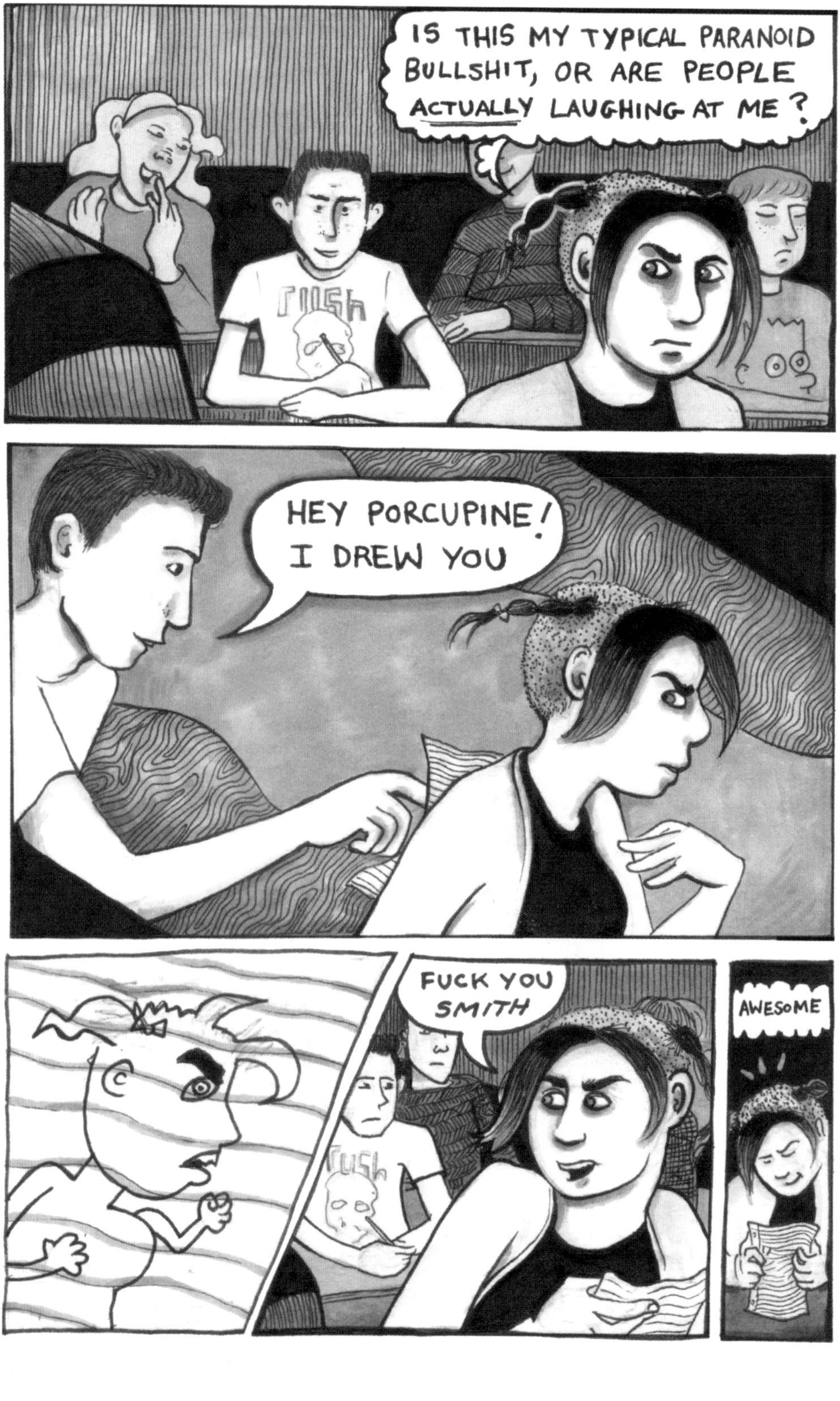
IS THIS MY TYPICAL PARANOID BULLSHIT, OR ARE PEOPLE ACTUALLY LAUGHING AT ME?
RUSH
HEY PORCUPINE! I DREW YOU
FUCK YOU SMITH
RUSH
AWESOME

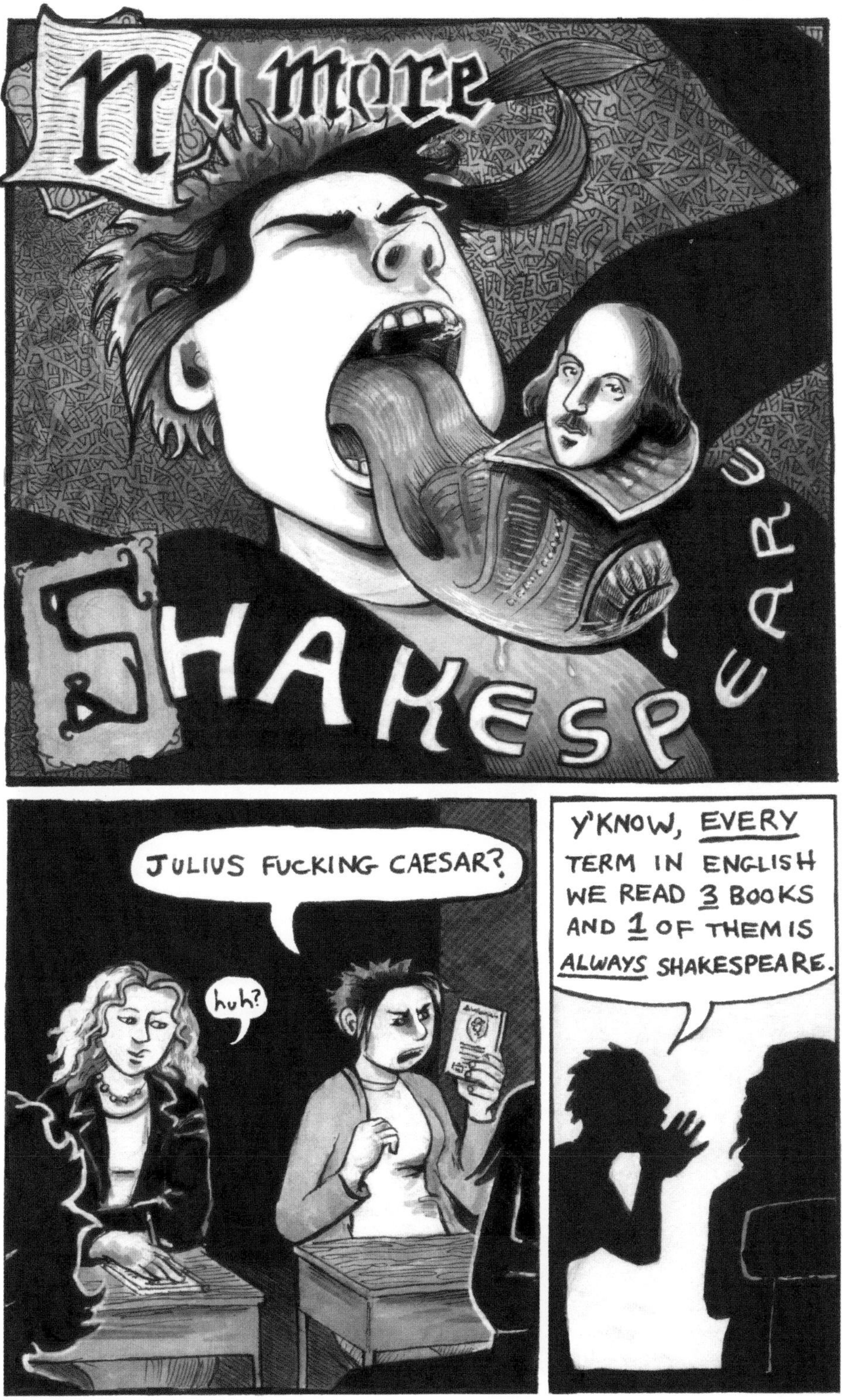

No more
SHAKESPEARE
JULIUS FUCKING CAESAR?
huh?
Y'KNOW, EVERY TERM IN ENGLISH WE READ 3 BOOKS AND 1 OF THEM IS ALWAYS SHAKESPEARE.

THOU PROTESTETH THE BARD?

I JUST-

GIRLS. DO YOU HAVE SOMETHING TO SHARE WITH THE CLASS

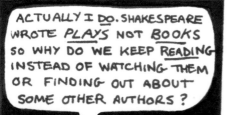

ACTUALLY I DO. SHAKESPEARE WROTE *PLAYS* NOT *BOOKS* SO WHY DO WE KEEP READING INSTEAD OF WATCHING THEM OR FINDING OUT ABOUT SOME OTHER AUTHORS?

WE SPEND MORE TIME DECODING STAGE DIRECTION AND ELIZABETHAN CULTURAL REFERENCES THAN WE DO ENJOYING THE STORIES

OK.

DOES ANYONE ELSE FIND SHAKESPEARE TOO DIFFICULT?

NO! THAT'S NOT WHAT I MEANT!

'TIS A COMMENT SPOKEN BY AN IDIOT FULL OF SOUND AND FURY S

SHUT UP

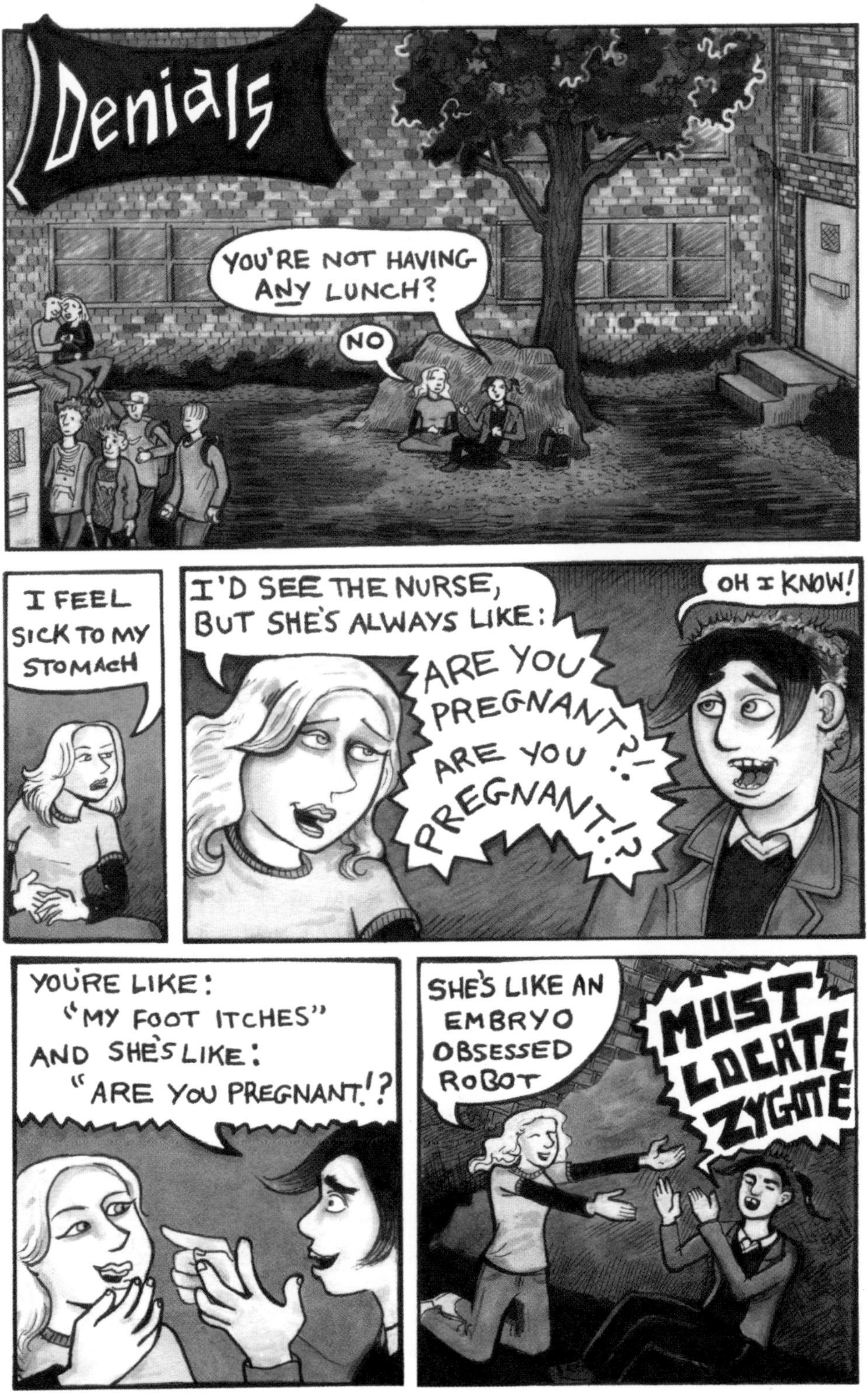
Denials
YOU'RE NOT HAVING ANY LUNCH?
NO
I FEEL SICK TO MY STOMACH
I'D SEE THE NURSE, BUT SHE'S ALWAYS LIKE:
ARE YOU PREGNANT?!! ARE YOU PREGNANT!?
OH I KNOW!
YOU'RE LIKE: "MY FOOT ITCHES" AND SHE'S LIKE: "ARE YOU PREGNANT!?
SHE'S LIKE AN EMBRYO OBSESSED ROBOT
MUST LOCATE ZYGOTE

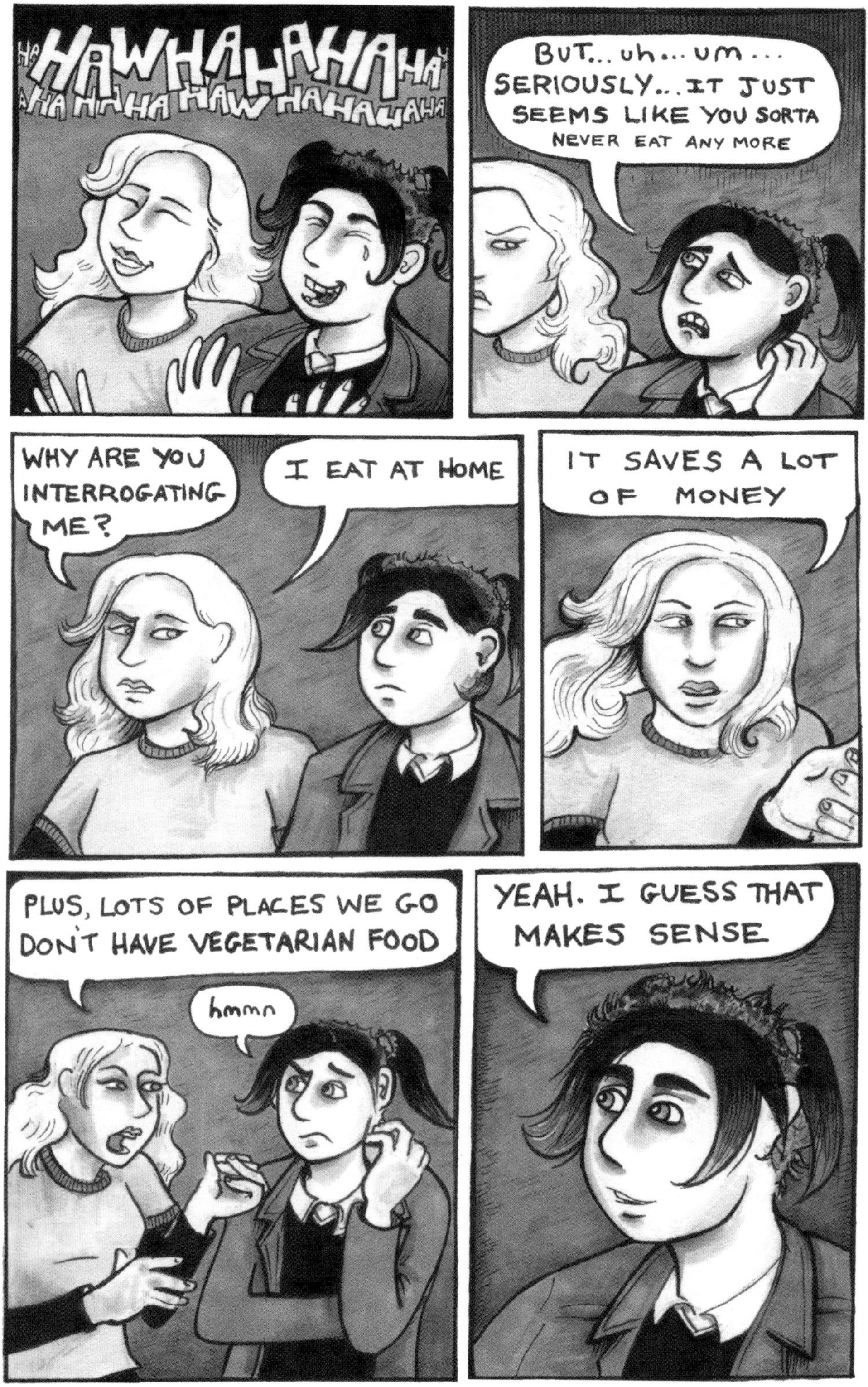
HA HAWHAHAHAHAHA
AHA HAHAHA HAW HAHAHAHAHA
BUT... uh... um...
SERIOUSLY... IT JUST SEEMS LIKE YOU SORTA NEVER EAT ANY MORE
WHY ARE YOU INTERROGATING ME?
I EAT AT HOME
IT SAVES A LOT OF MONEY
PLUS, LOTS OF PLACES WE GO DON'T HAVE VEGETARIAN FOOD
hmmn
YEAH. I GUESS THAT MAKES SENSE

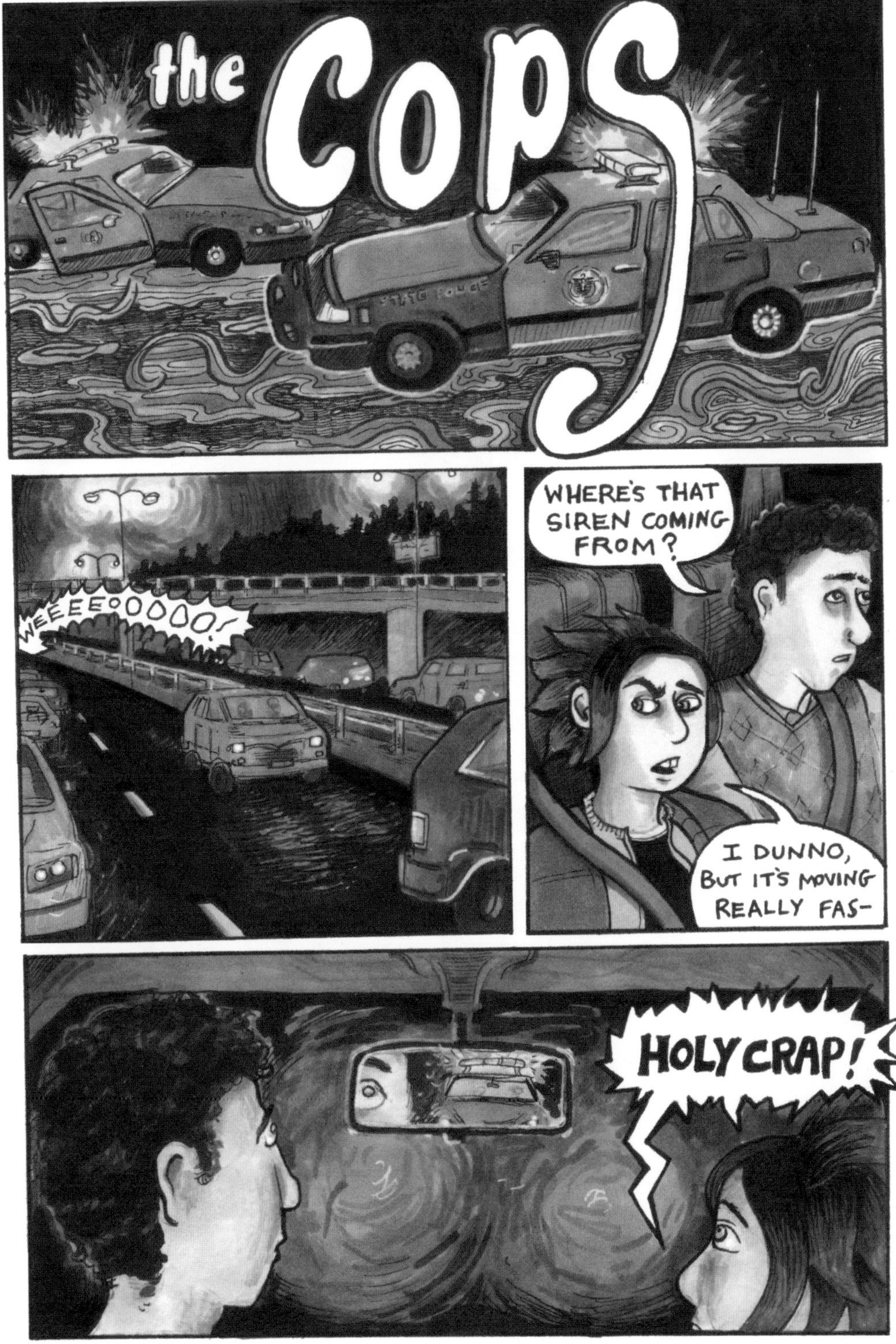
the COPS
STATE POLICE
WEEEEOOOOO!
WHERE'S THAT SIREN COMING FROM?
I DUNNO, BUT IT'S MOVING REALLY FAS-
HOLY CRAP!

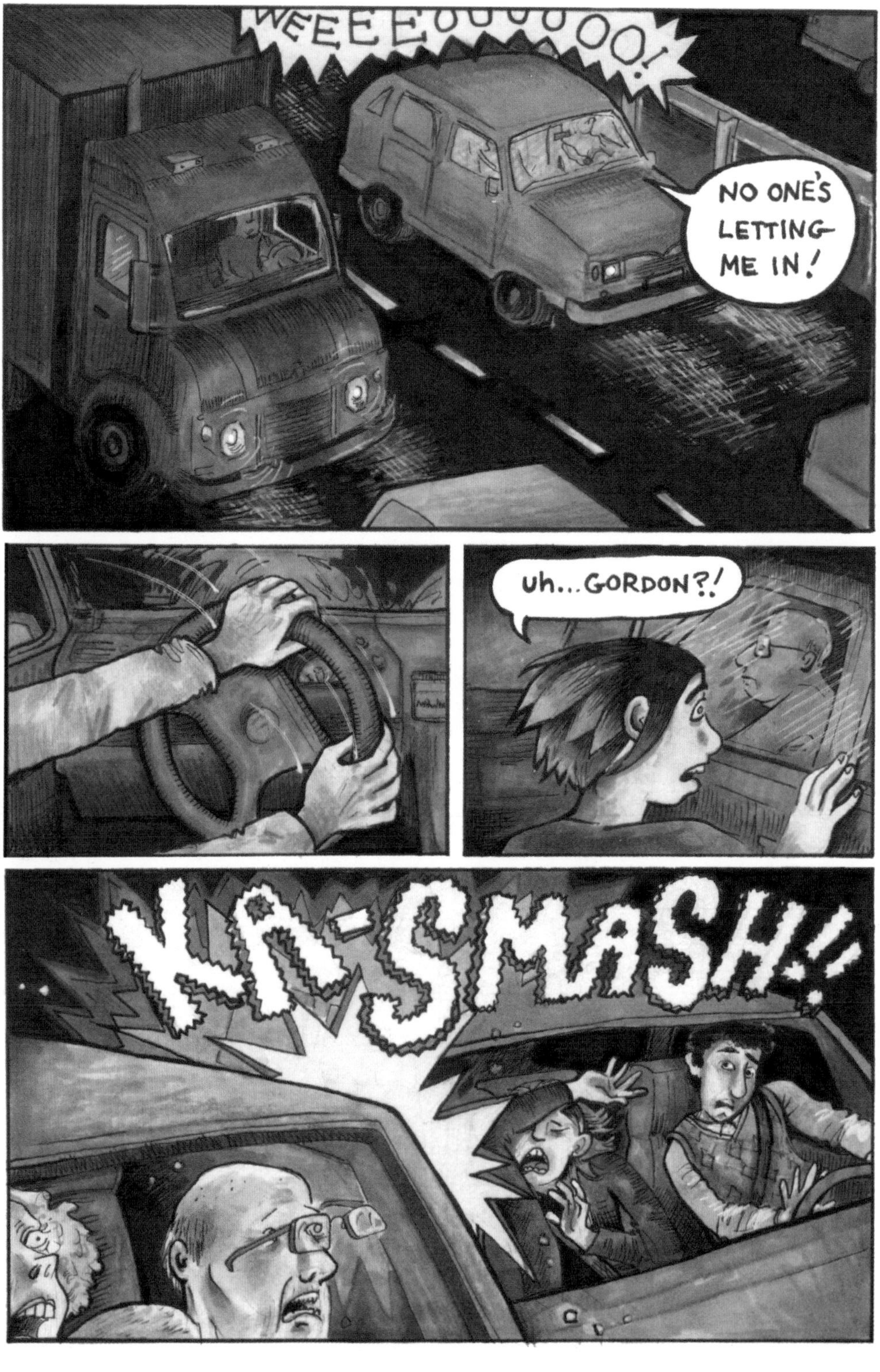
WEEEEOOOOOOO!
NO ONE'S LETTING ME IN!
uh... GORDON?!
KA-SMASH!!

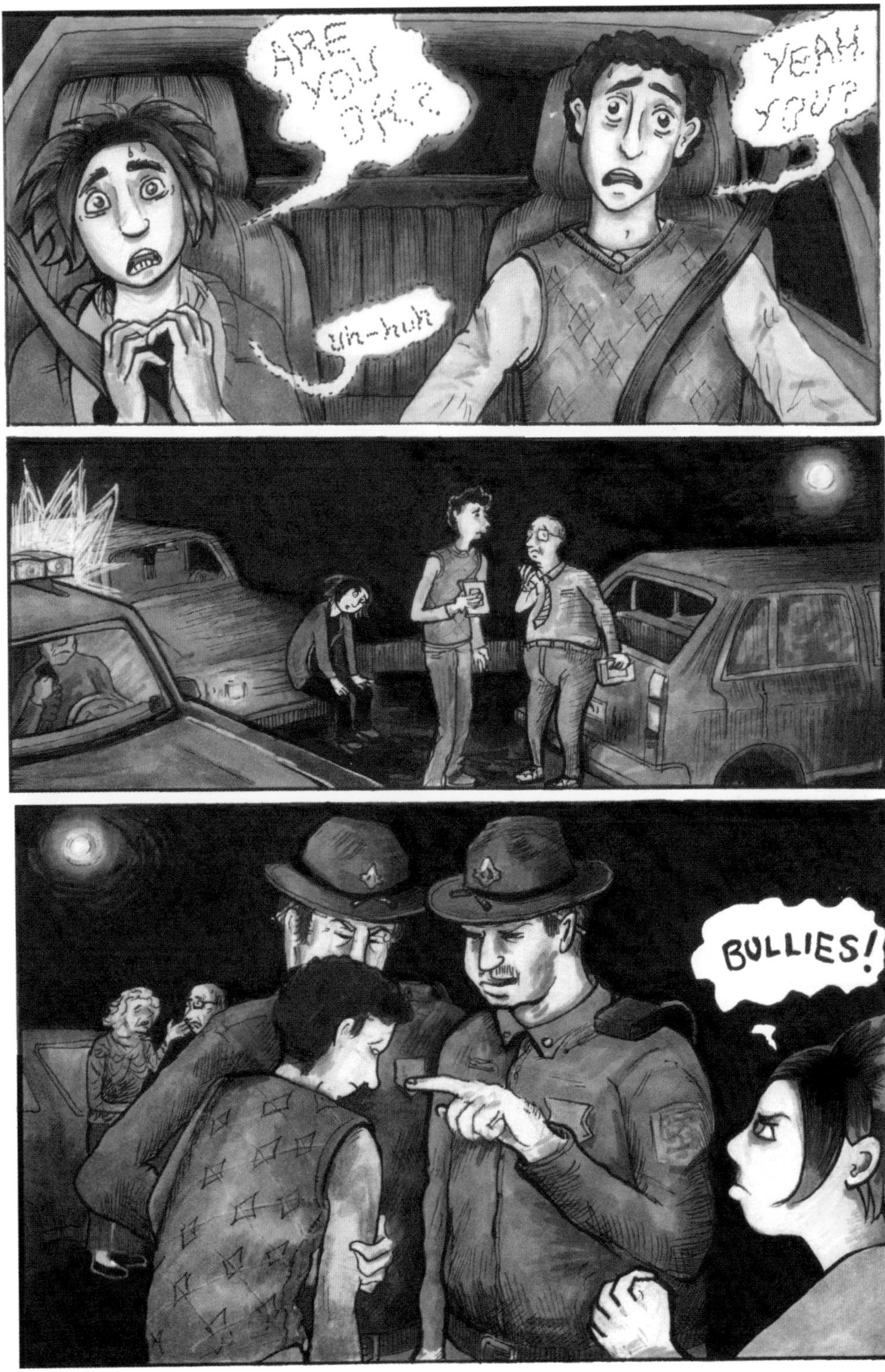
ARE YOU OK?
YEAH. YOU?
uh-huh
BULLIES!

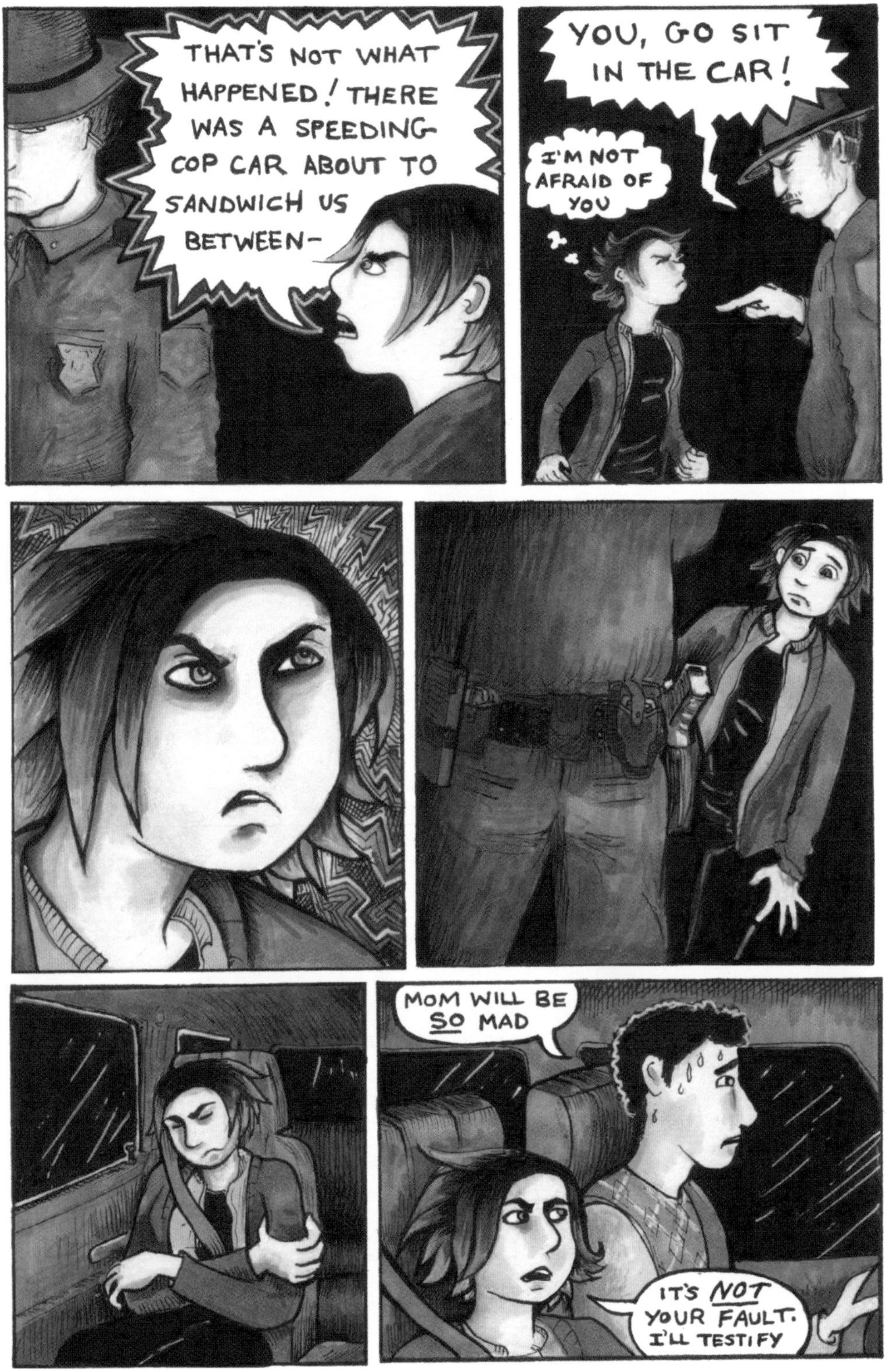
THAT'S NOT WHAT HAPPENED! THERE WAS A SPEEDING COP CAR ABOUT TO SANDWICH US BETWEEN-
YOU, GO SIT IN THE CAR!
I'M NOT AFRAID OF YOU
MOM WILL BE SO MAD
IT'S NOT YOUR FAULT. I'LL TESTIFY

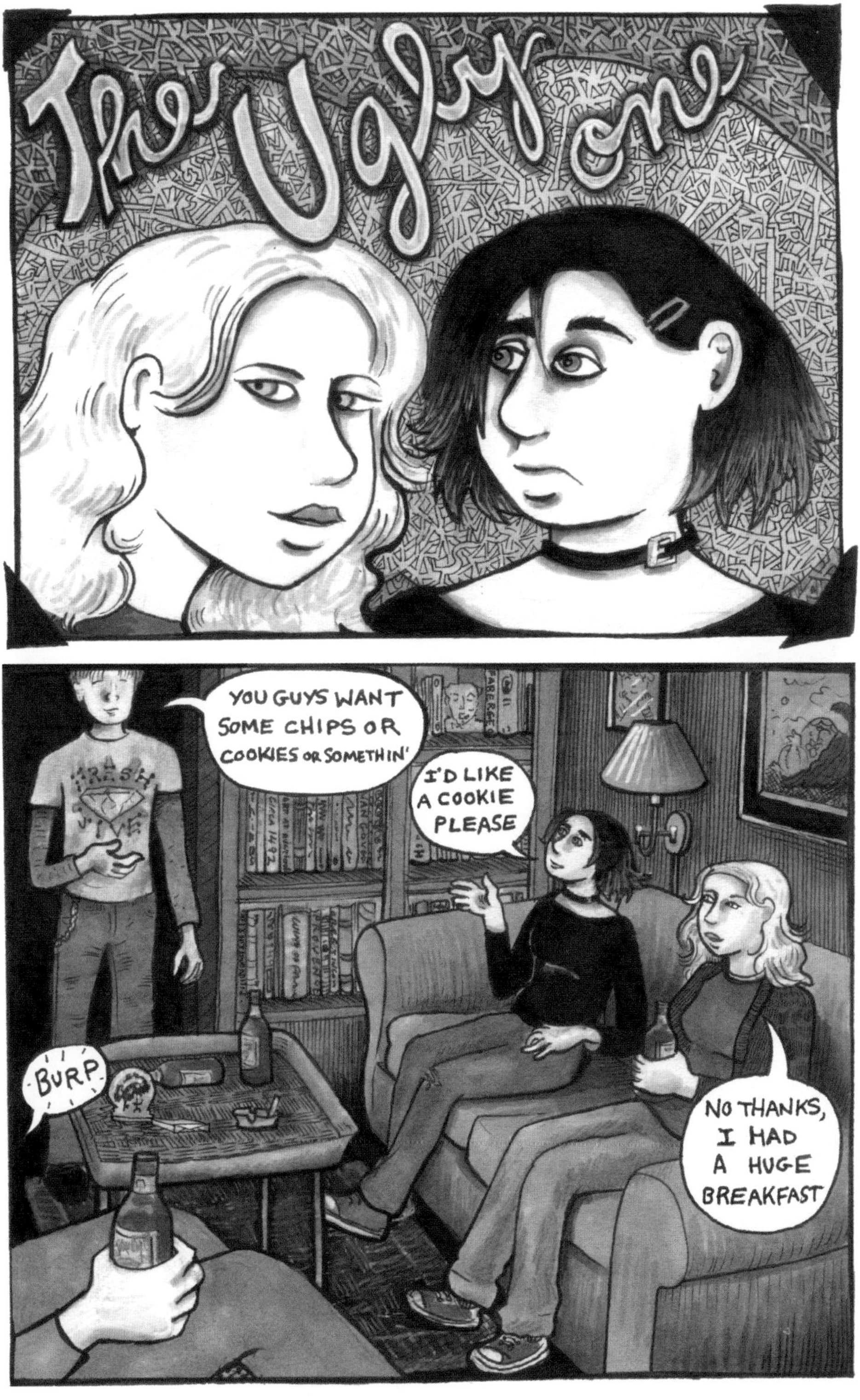
The Ugly One
YOU GUYS WANT SOME CHIPS OR COOKIES OR SOMETHIN'
I'D LIKE A COOKIE PLEASE
NO THANKS, I HAD A HUGE BREAKFAST
BURP

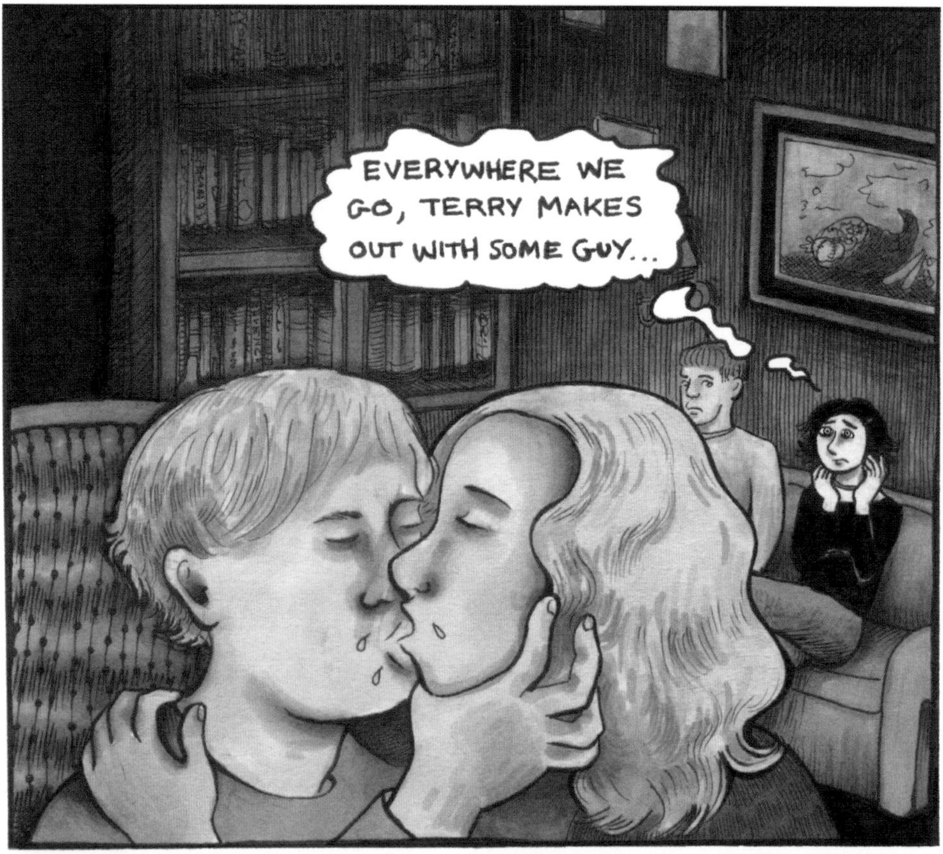
EVERYWHERE WE GO, TERRY MAKES OUT WITH SOME GUY...

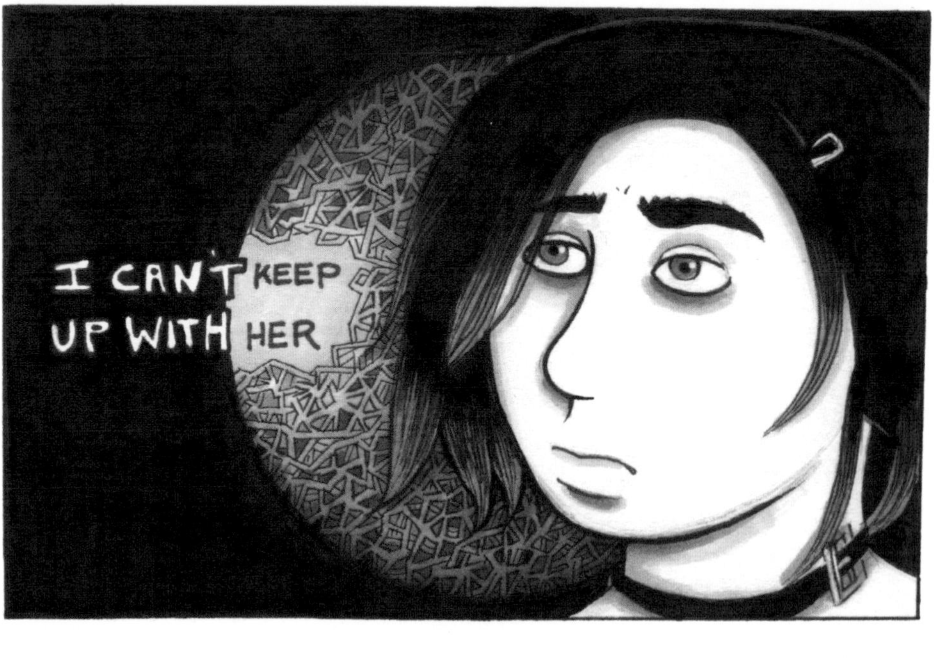
I CAN'T KEEP UP WITH HER

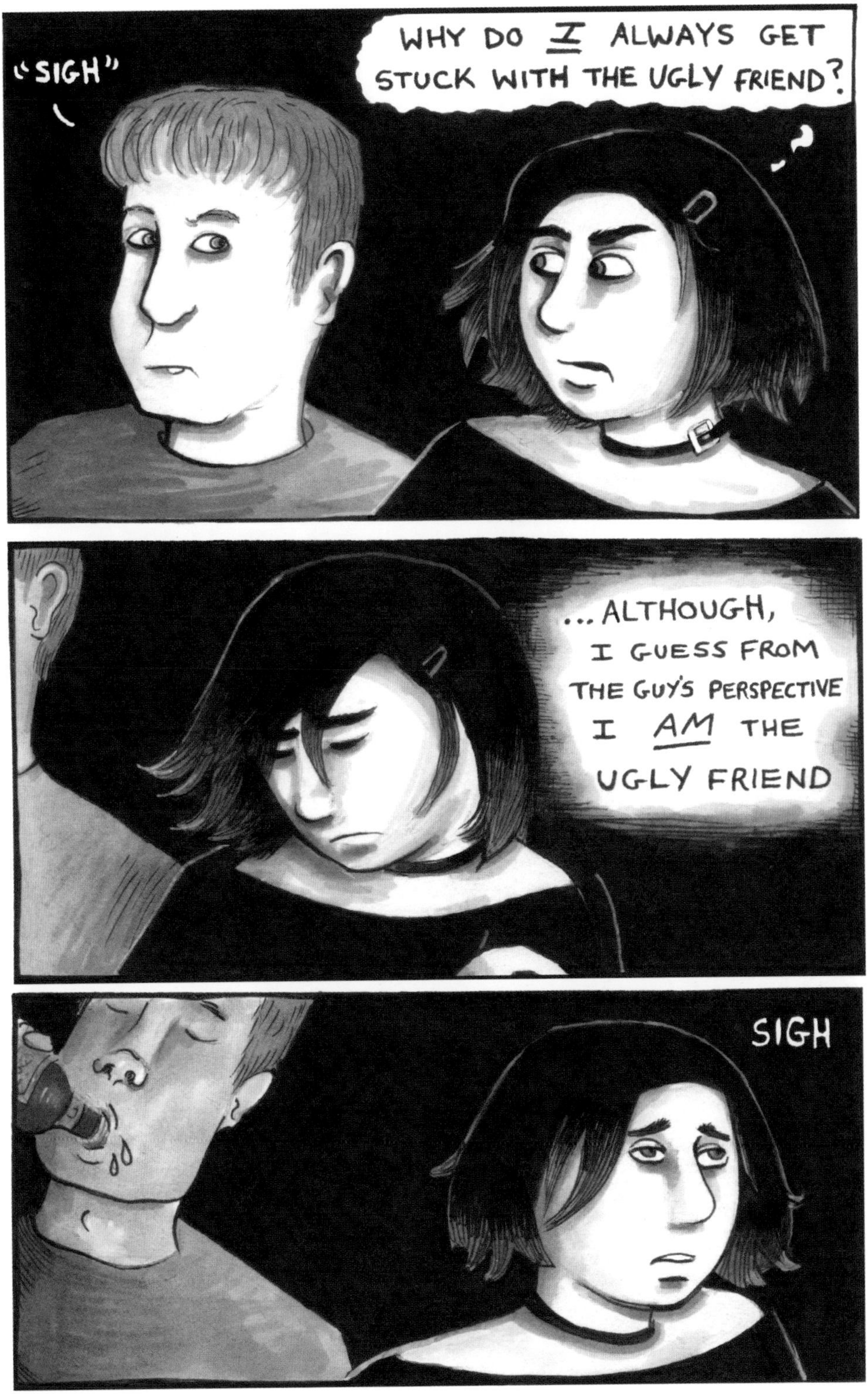
"SIGH"
WHY DO I ALWAYS GET STUCK WITH THE UGLY FRIEND?
...ALTHOUGH, I GUESS FROM THE GUY'S PERSPECTIVE I AM THE UGLY FRIEND
SIGH

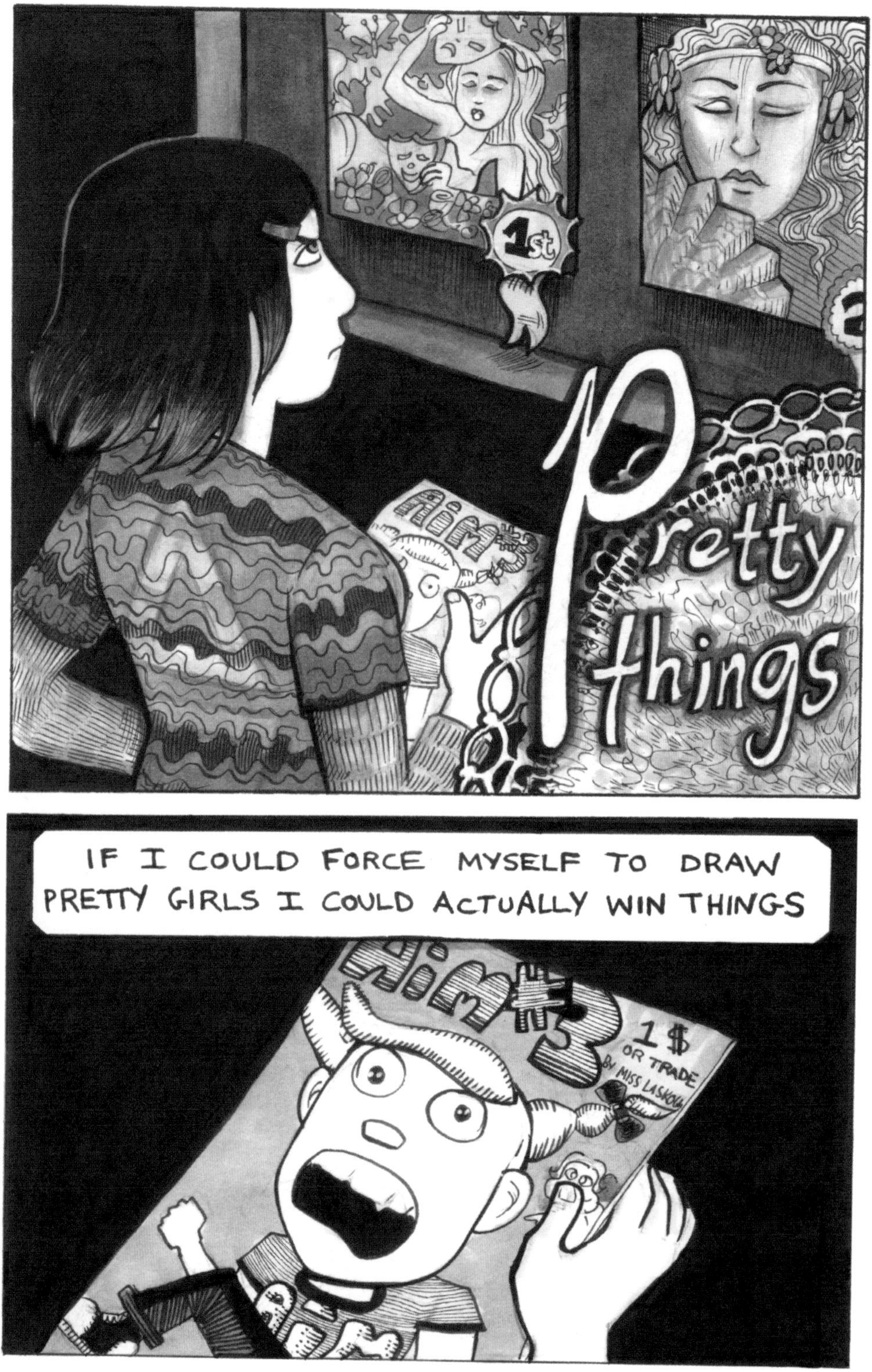
1st
Pretty things
Him#3
IF I COULD FORCE MYSELF TO DRAW PRETTY GIRLS I COULD ACTUALLY WIN THINGS
Him#3
1$
OR TRADE
BY MISS LASKOW

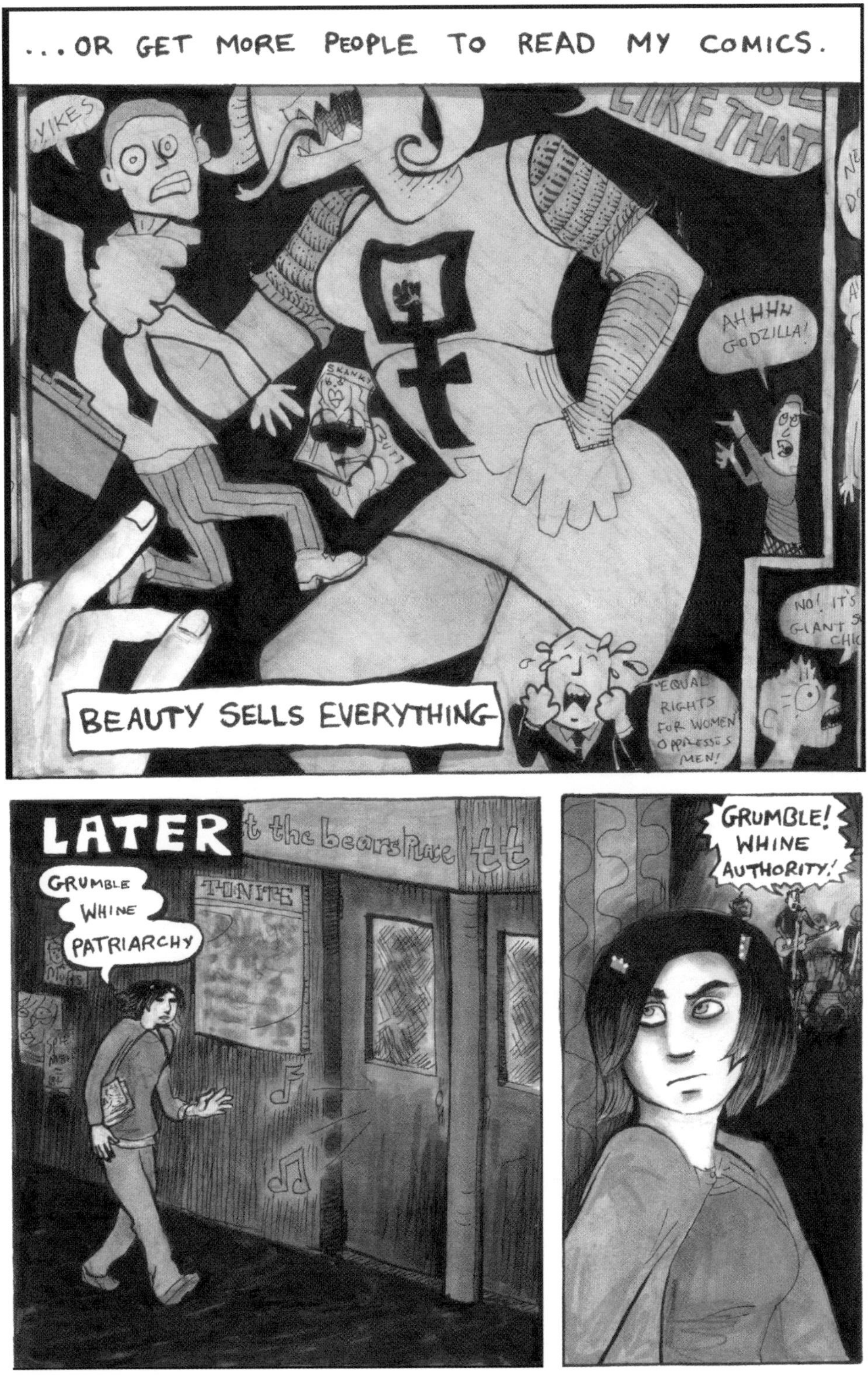
...OR GET MORE PEOPLE TO READ MY COMICS.
YIKES
LIKE THAT
SKANKY
BUTT
AHHHH GODZILLA!
NO! IT'S
GIANT
BEAUTY SELLS EVERYTHING
EQUAL RIGHTS FOR WOMEN OPPRESSES MEN!
LATER
the bears Place
TONITE
GRUMBLE WHINE PATRIARCHY
GRUMBLE! WHINE AUTHORITY!

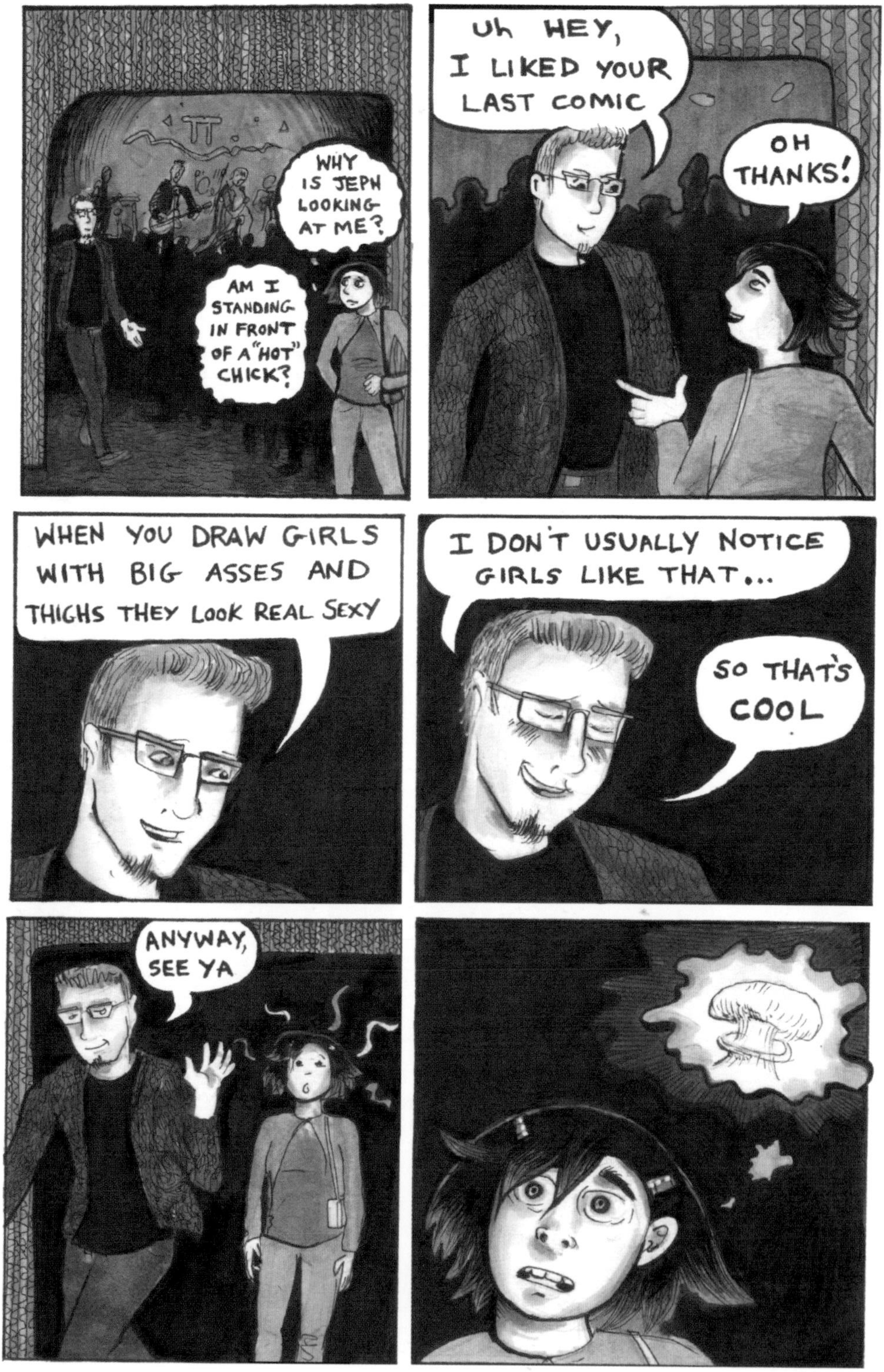
WHY IS JEPH LOOKING AT ME?
AM I STANDING IN FRONT OF A "HOT" CHICK?
Uh HEY, I LIKED YOUR LAST COMIC
OH THANKS!
WHEN YOU DRAW GIRLS WITH BIG ASSES AND THIGHS THEY LOOK REAL SEXY
I DON'T USUALLY NOTICE GIRLS LIKE THAT...
SO THAT'S COOL
ANYWAY, SEE YA

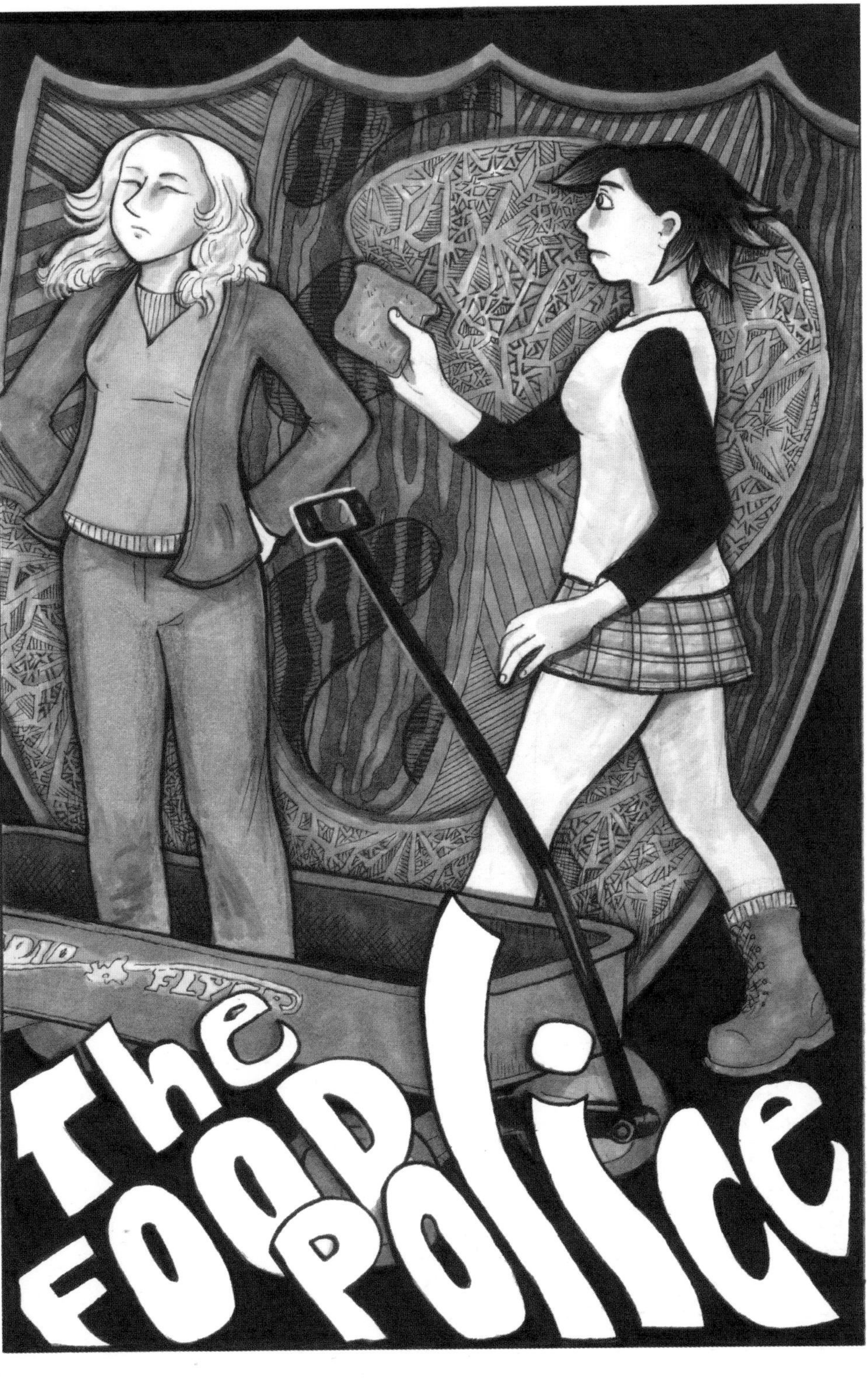
FLYER
The Food Police

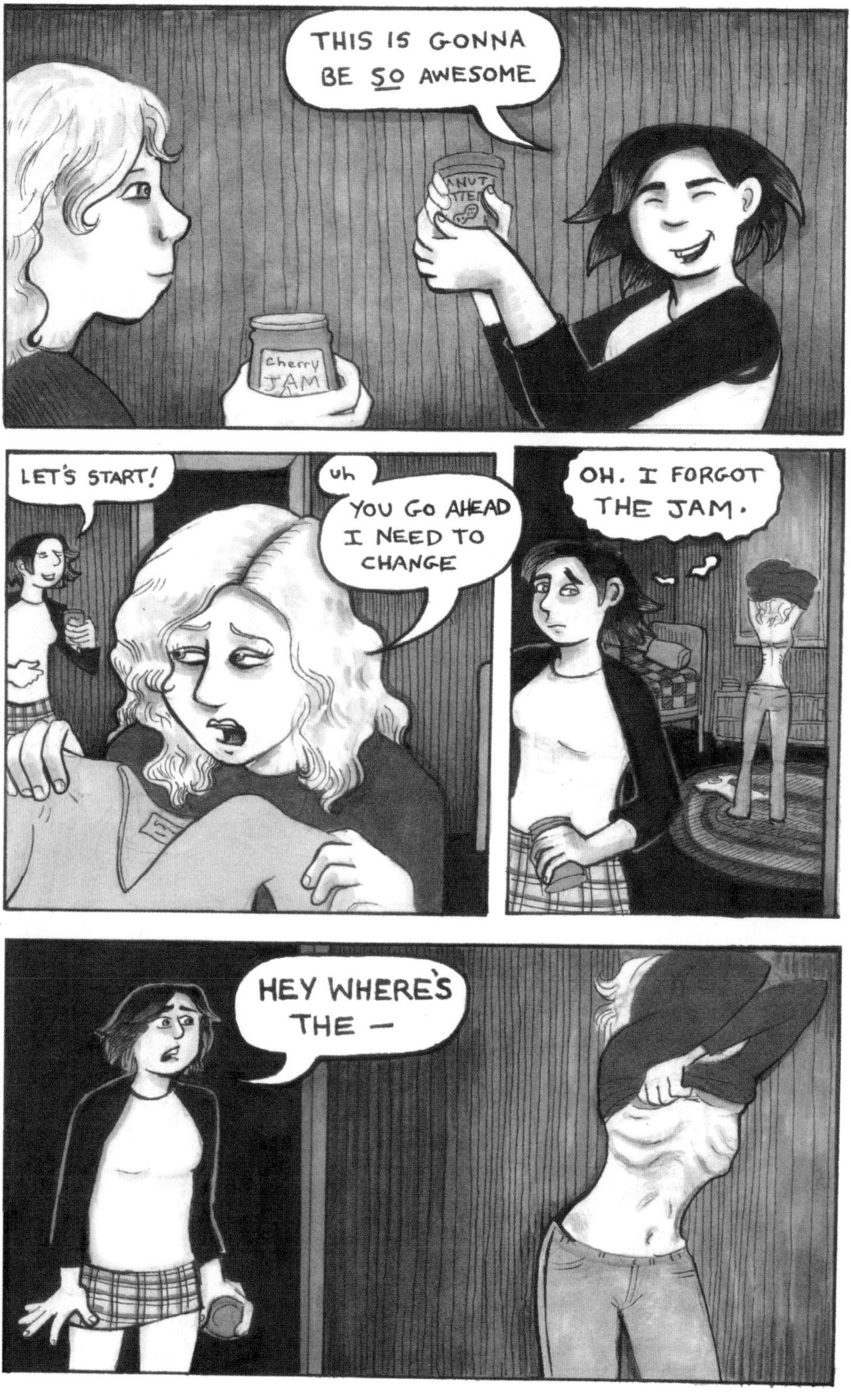
THIS IS GONNA BE SO AWESOME
Cherry JAM
LET'S START!
uh
YOU GO AHEAD I NEED TO CHANGE
OH. I FORGOT THE JAM.
HEY WHERE'S THE —

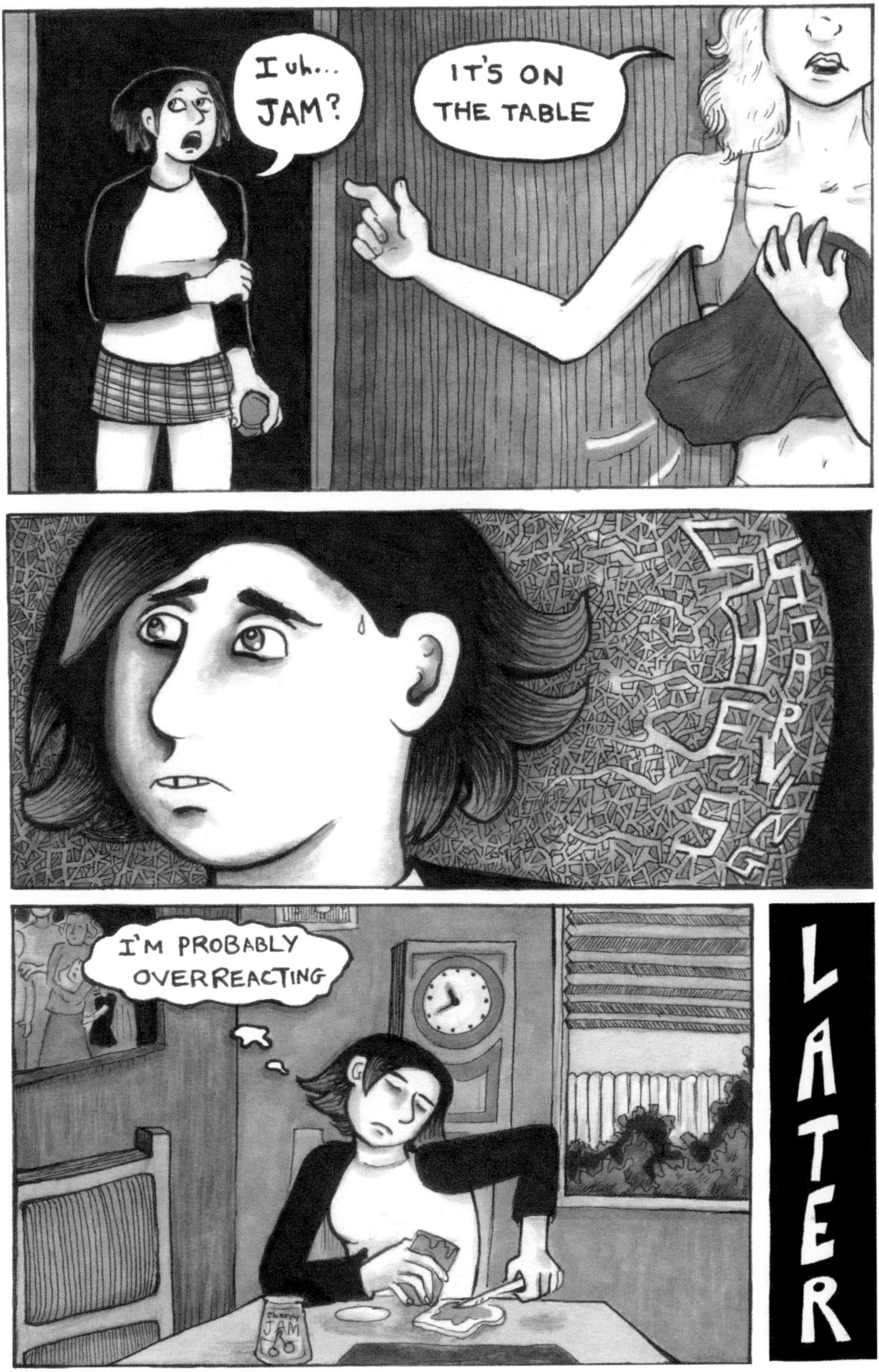
I uh... JAM?
IT'S ON THE TABLE
I'M PROBABLY OVERREACTING
LATER

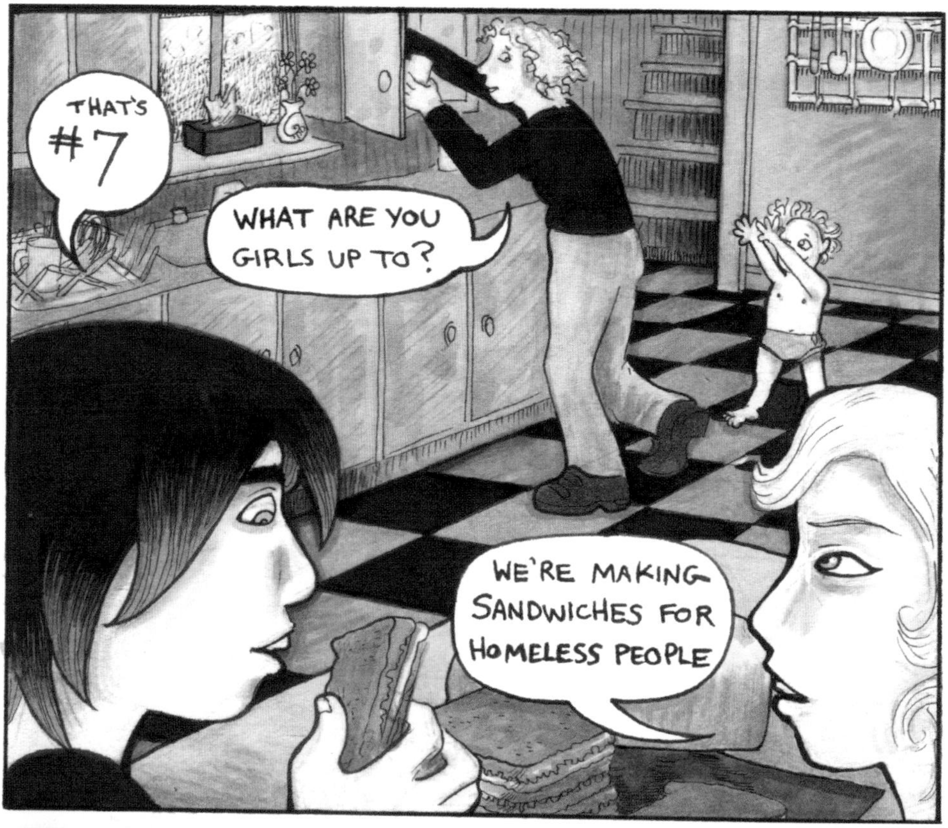
THAT'S #7
WHAT ARE YOU GIRLS UP TO?
WE'RE MAKING SANDWICHES FOR HOMELESS PEOPLE

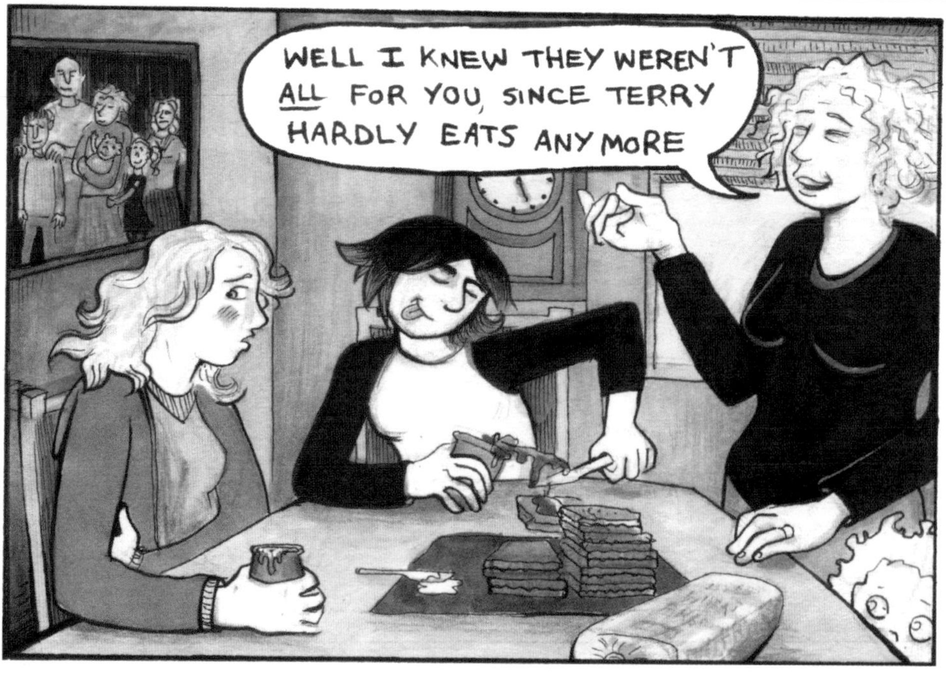
WELL I KNEW THEY WEREN'T ALL FOR YOU, SINCE TERRY HARDLY EATS ANYMORE

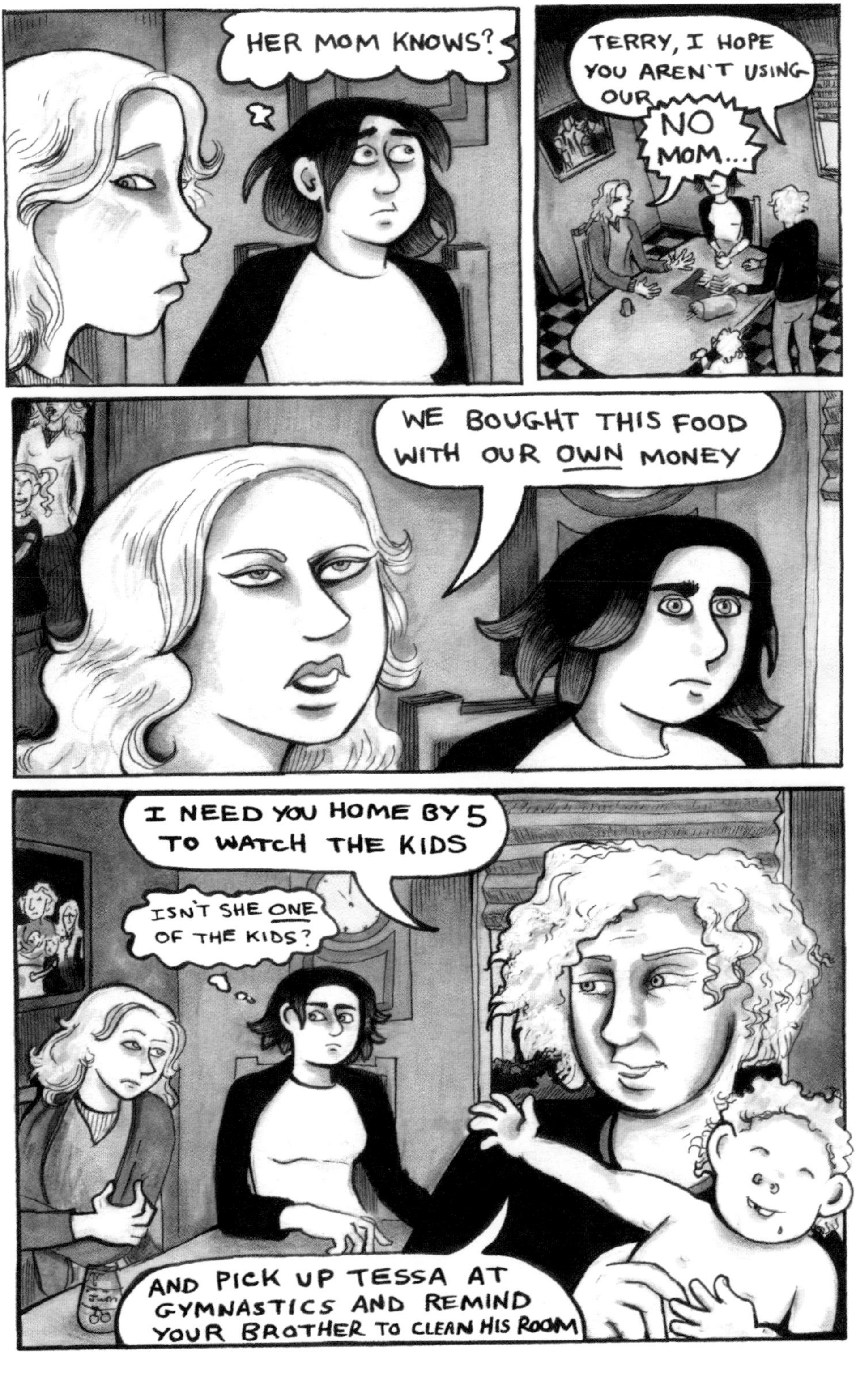
HER MOM KNOWS?
TERRY, I HOPE YOU AREN'T USING OUR
NO MOM...
WE BOUGHT THIS FOOD WITH OUR OWN MONEY
I NEED YOU HOME BY 5 TO WATCH THE KIDS
ISN'T SHE ONE OF THE KIDS?
AND PICK UP TESSA AT GYMNASTICS AND REMIND YOUR BROTHER TO CLEAN HIS ROOM

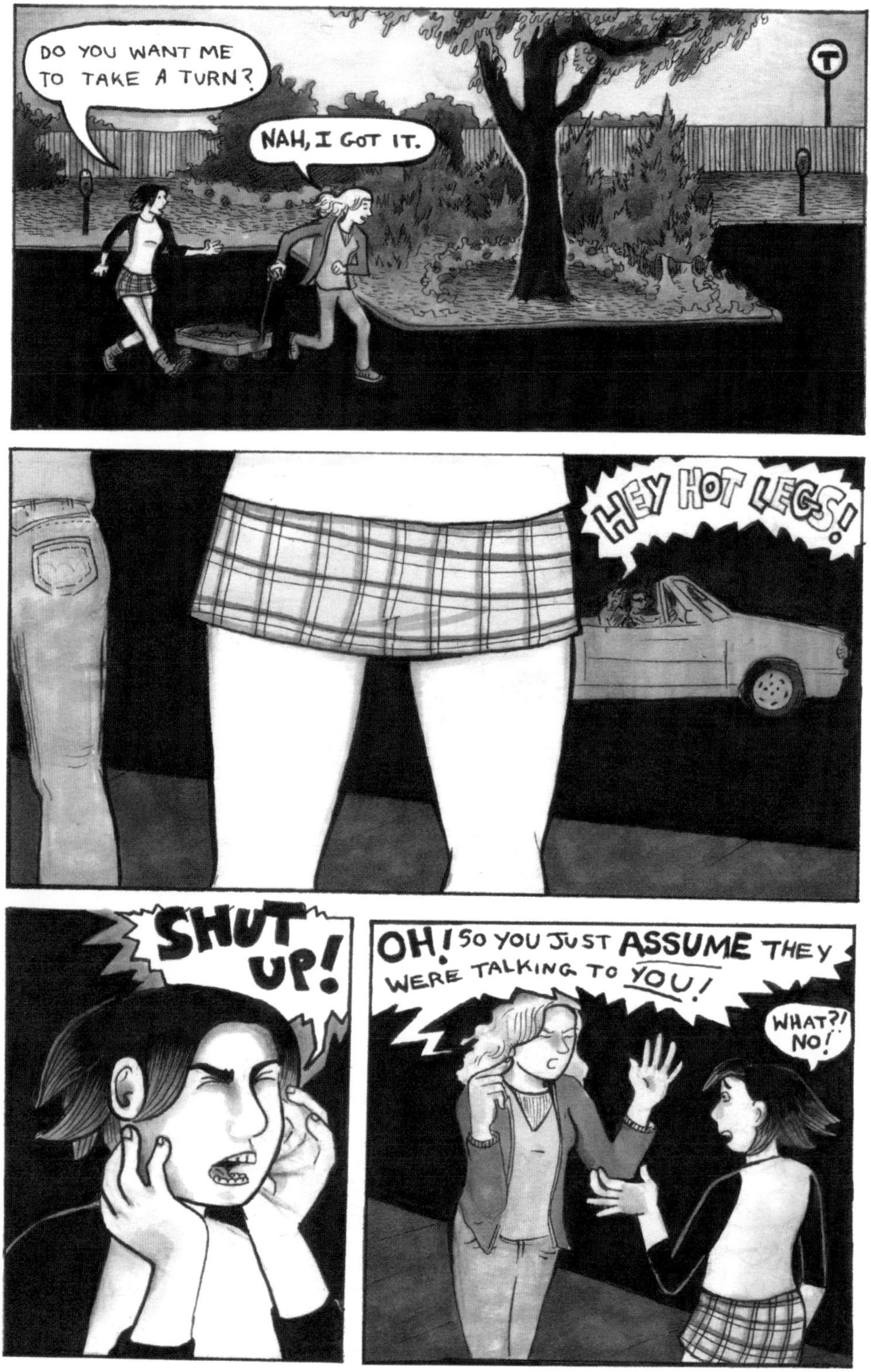
DO YOU WANT ME TO TAKE A TURN?
NAH, I GOT IT.
HEY HOT LEGS!
SHUT UP!
OH! SO YOU JUST ASSUME THEY WERE TALKING TO YOU!
WHAT?! NO!

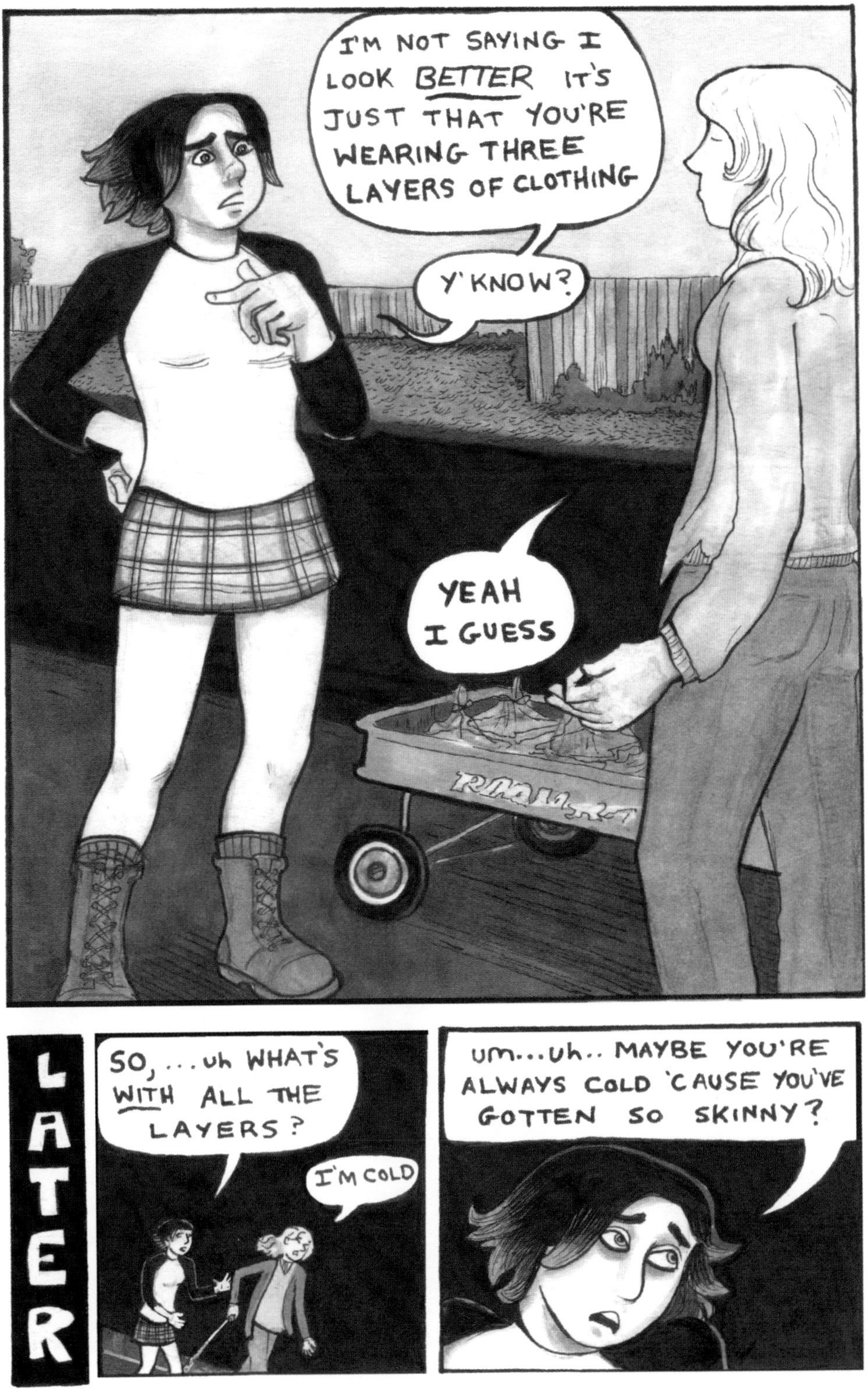
I'M NOT SAYING I LOOK BETTER IT'S JUST THAT YOU'RE WEARING THREE LAYERS OF CLOTHING
Y' KNOW?
YEAH I GUESS
LATER
SO, ... uh WHAT'S WITH ALL THE LAYERS?
I'M COLD
um...uh.. MAYBE YOU'RE ALWAYS COLD 'CAUSE YOU'VE GOTTEN SO SKINNY?

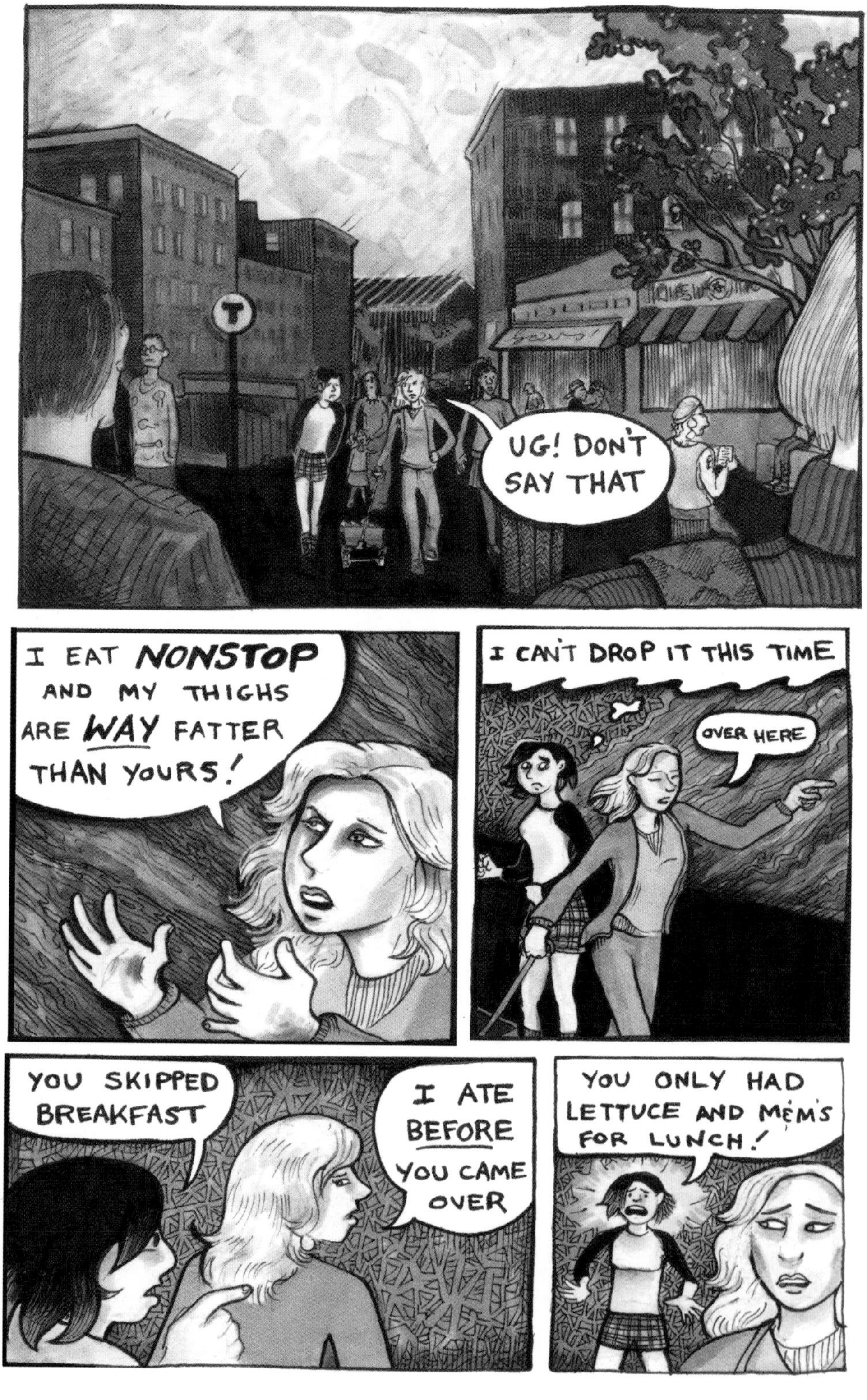
UG! DON'T SAY THAT
I EAT NONSTOP AND MY THIGHS ARE WAY FATTER THAN YOURS!
I CAN'T DROP IT THIS TIME
OVER HERE
YOU SKIPPED BREAKFAST
I ATE BEFORE YOU CAME OVER
YOU ONLY HAD LETTUCE AND M&M'S FOR LUNCH!

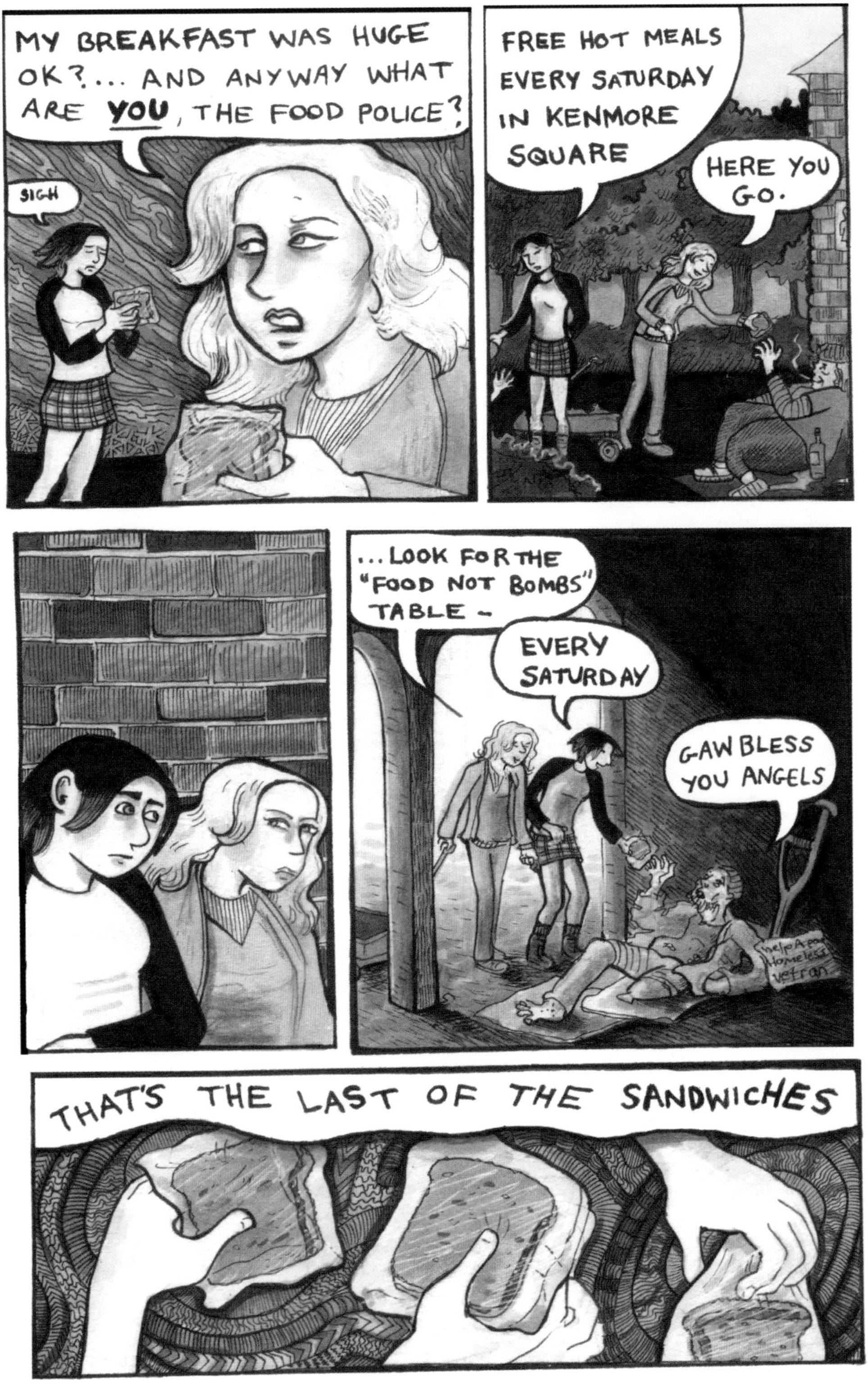
MY BREAKFAST WAS HUGE OK?... AND ANYWAY WHAT ARE YOU, THE FOOD POLICE?
SIGH
FREE HOT MEALS EVERY SATURDAY IN KENMORE SQUARE
HERE YOU GO.
...LOOK FOR THE "FOOD NOT BOMBS" TABLE -
EVERY SATURDAY
GAW BLESS YOU ANGELS
THAT'S THE LAST OF THE SANDWICHES

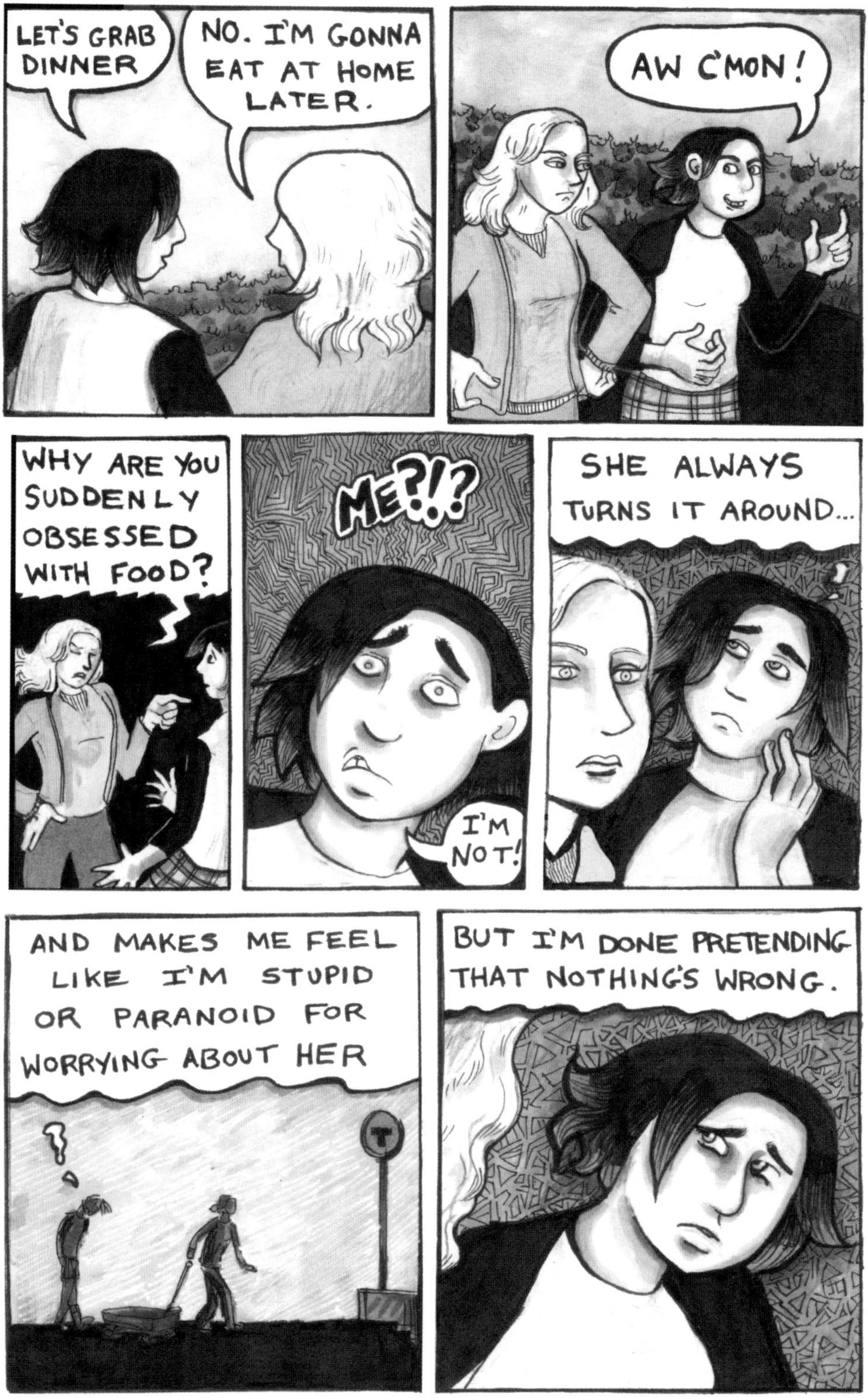
LET'S GRAB DINNER
NO. I'M GONNA EAT AT HOME LATER.
AW C'MON!
WHY ARE YOU SUDDENLY OBSESSED WITH FOOD?
ME?!?
I'M NOT!
SHE ALWAYS TURNS IT AROUND...
AND MAKES ME FEEL LIKE I'M STUPID OR PARANOID FOR WORRYING ABOUT HER
BUT I'M DONE PRETENDING THAT NOTHING'S WRONG.

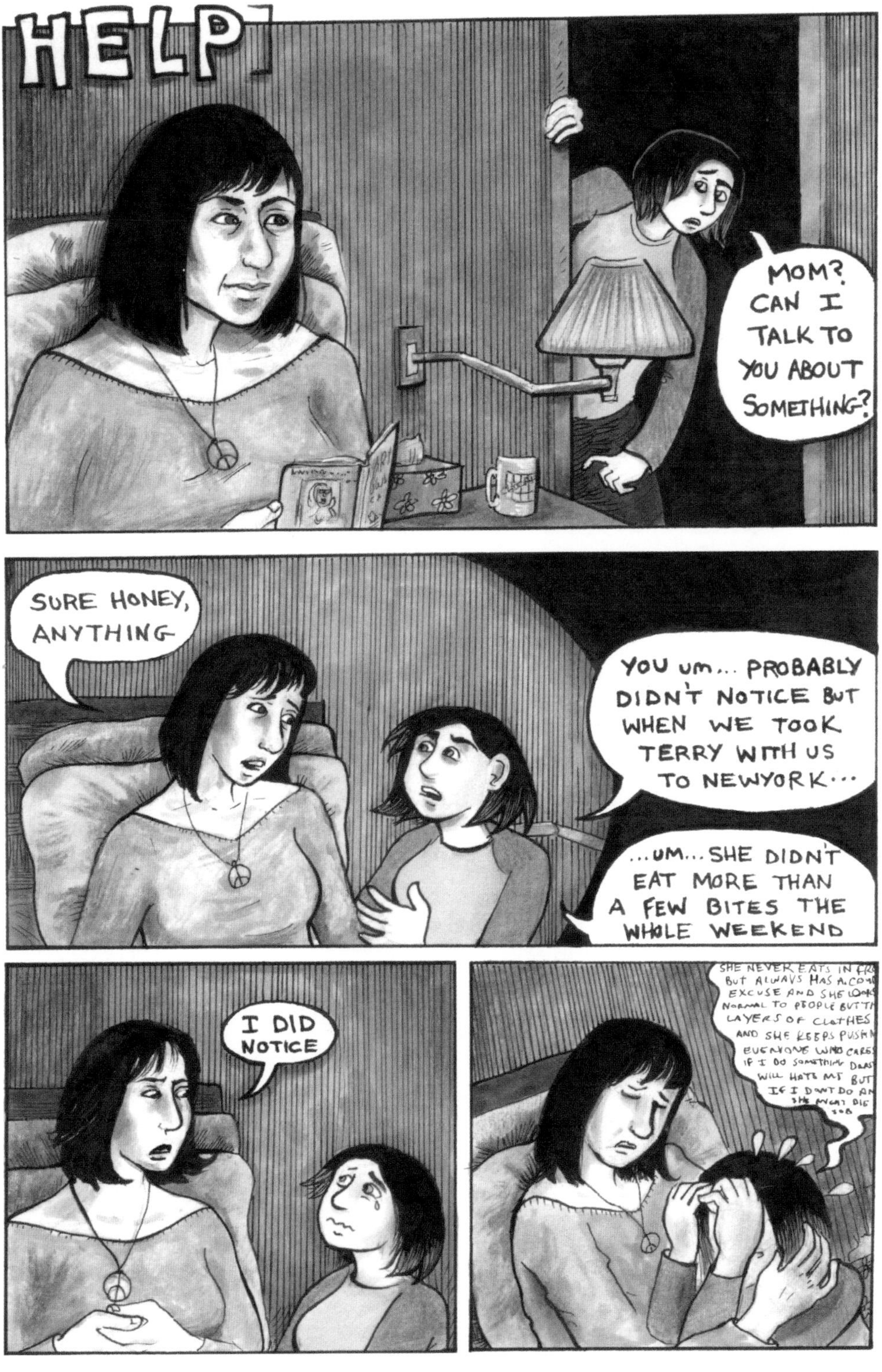
HELP
MOM? CAN I TALK TO YOU ABOUT SOMETHING?
SURE HONEY, ANYTHING
YOU um... PROBABLY DIDN'T NOTICE BUT WHEN WE TOOK TERRY WITH US TO NEWYORK...
...UM... SHE DIDN'T EAT MORE THAN A FEW BITES THE WHOLE WEEKEND
I DID NOTICE
SHE NEVER EATS IN
BUT ALWAYS HAS A
EXCUSE AND SHE
NORMAL TO PEOPLE BUT
LAYERS OF CLOTHES
AND SHE KEEPS
EVERYONE WHO CARES
IF I DO SOMETHING
WILL HATE ME BUT
IF I DON'T DO
SHE MIGHT DIE

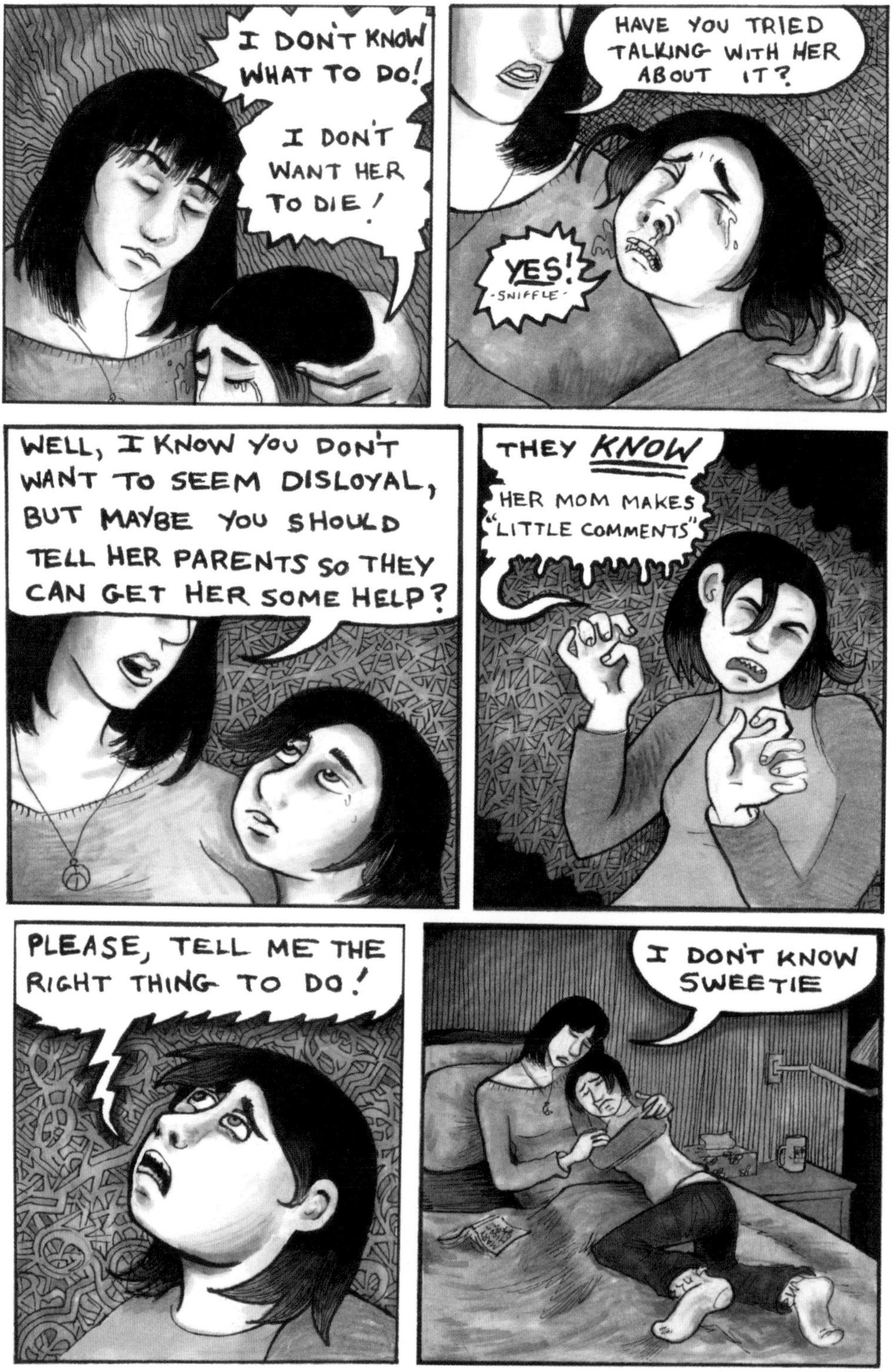
I DON'T KNOW WHAT TO DO!
I DON'T WANT HER TO DIE!
HAVE YOU TRIED TALKING WITH HER ABOUT IT?
YES!
-SNIFFLE-
WELL, I KNOW YOU DON'T WANT TO SEEM DISLOYAL, BUT MAYBE YOU SHOULD TELL HER PARENTS SO THEY CAN GET HER SOME HELP?
THEY KNOW
HER MOM MAKES "LITTLE COMMENTS"
PLEASE, TELL ME THE RIGHT THING TO DO!
I DON'T KNOW SWEETIE

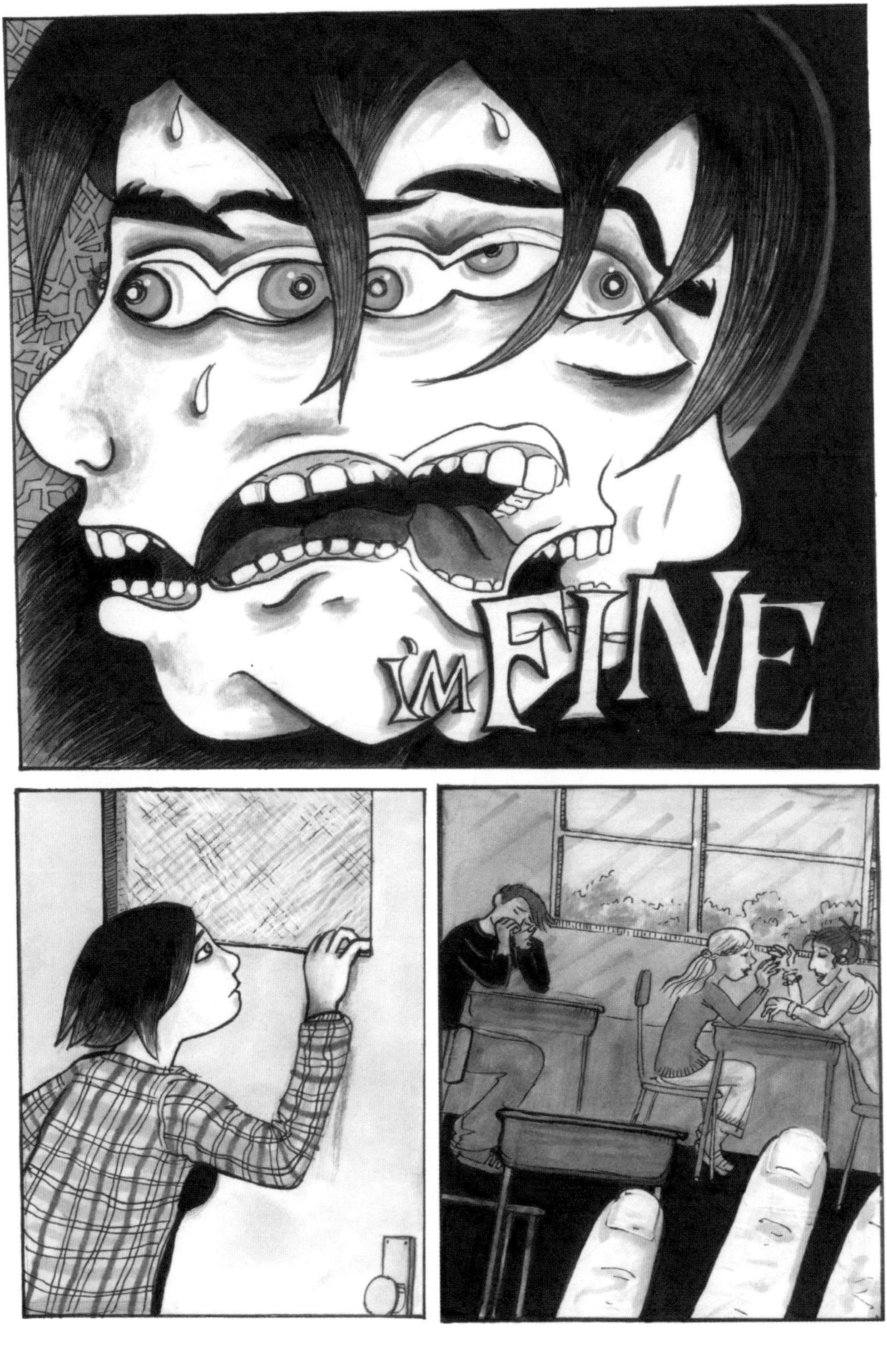
I'M FINE

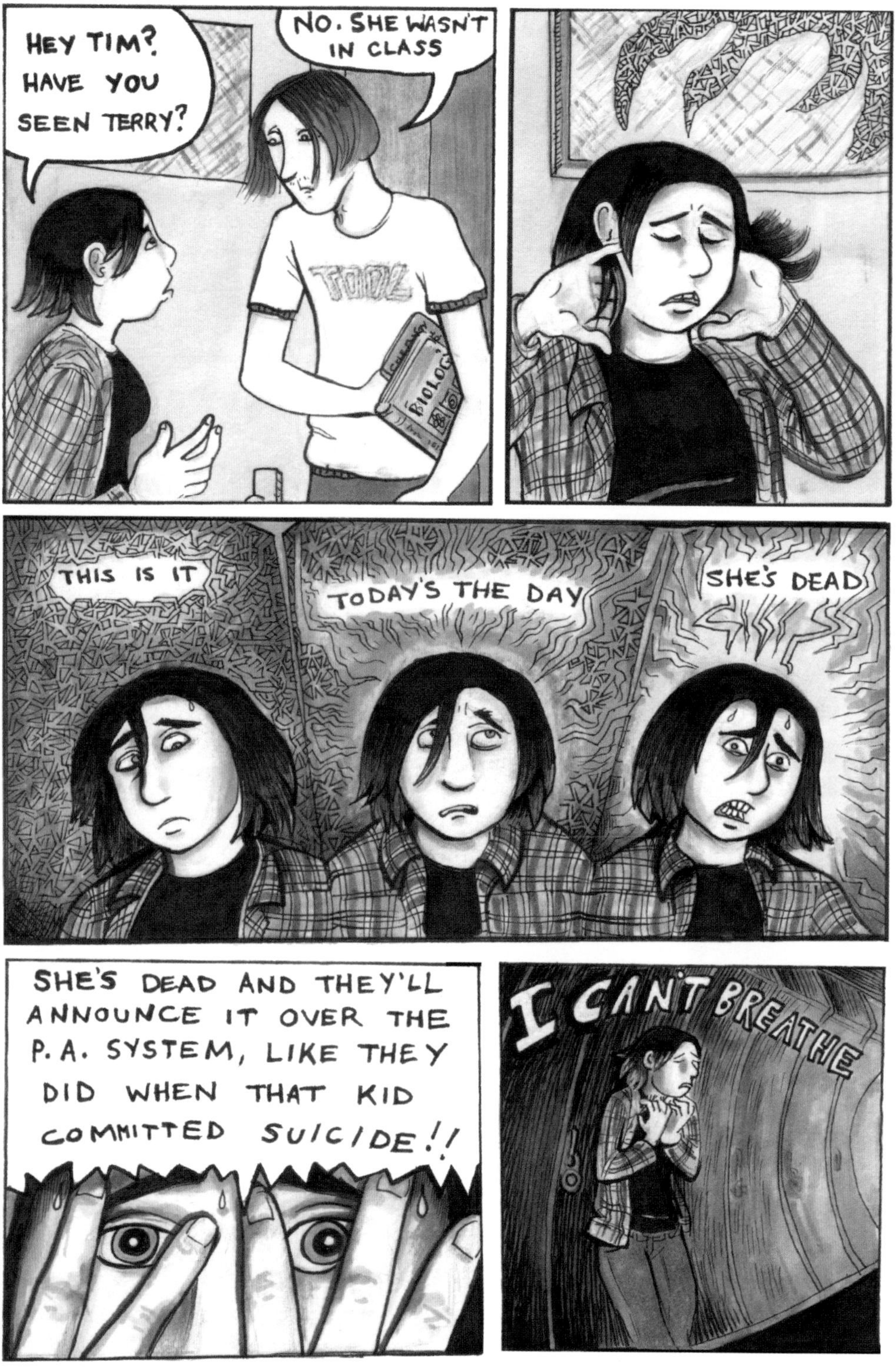
HEY TIM? HAVE YOU SEEN TERRY?
NO. SHE WASN'T IN CLASS
THIS IS IT
TODAY'S THE DAY
SHE'S DEAD
SHE'S DEAD AND THEY'LL ANNOUNCE IT OVER THE P. A. SYSTEM, LIKE THEY DID WHEN THAT KID COMMITTED SUICIDE!!
I CAN'T BREATHE

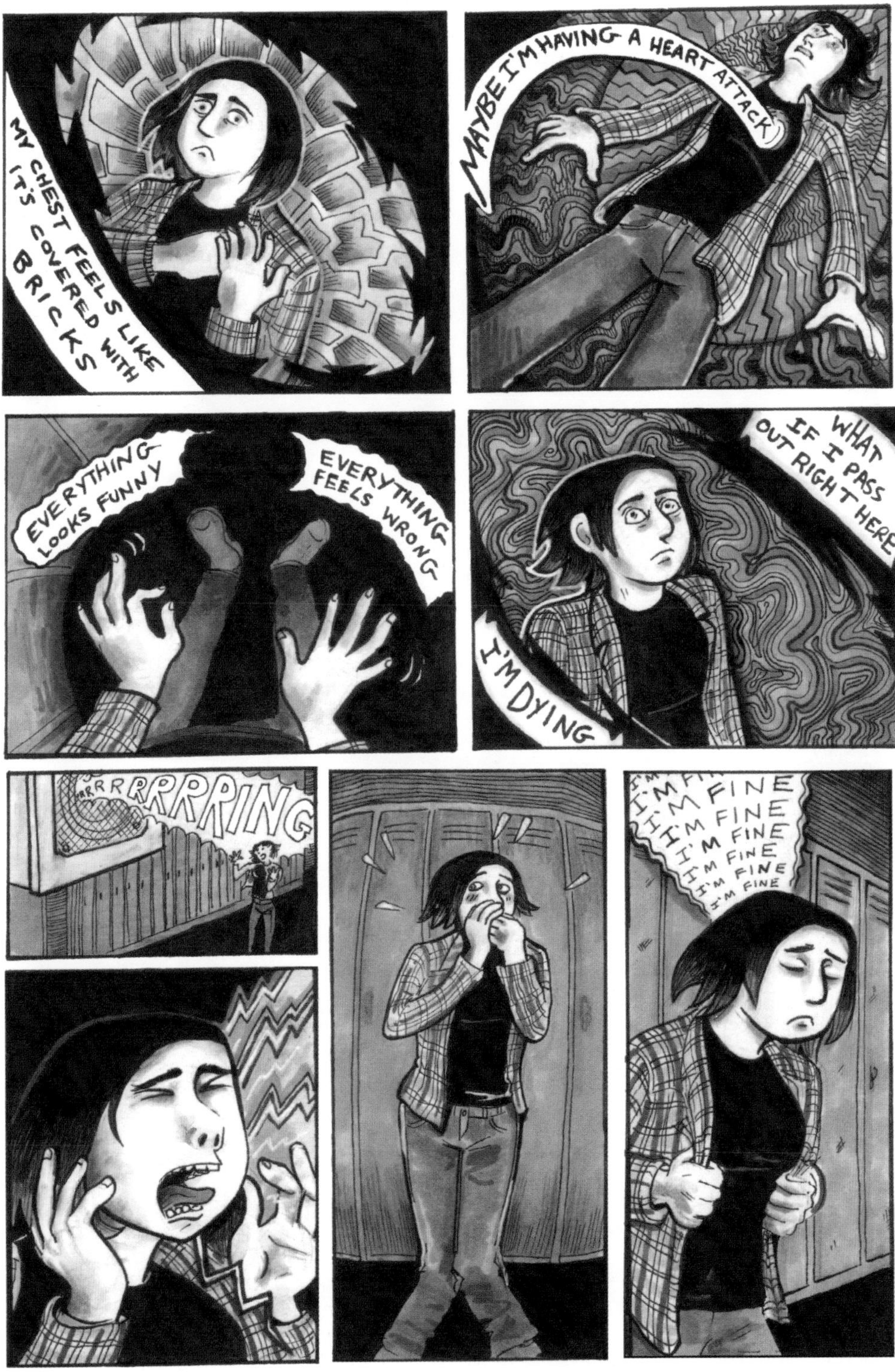
MY CHEST FEELS LIKE IT'S COVERED WITH BRICKS
MAYBE I'M HAVING A HEART ATTACK
EVERYTHING LOOKS FUNNY
EVERYTHING FEELS WRONG
WHAT IF I PASS OUT RIGHT HERE
I'M DYING
rrrRRRRRRING
I'M FINE
I'M FINE
I'M FINE
I'M FINE
I'M FINE
I'M FINE

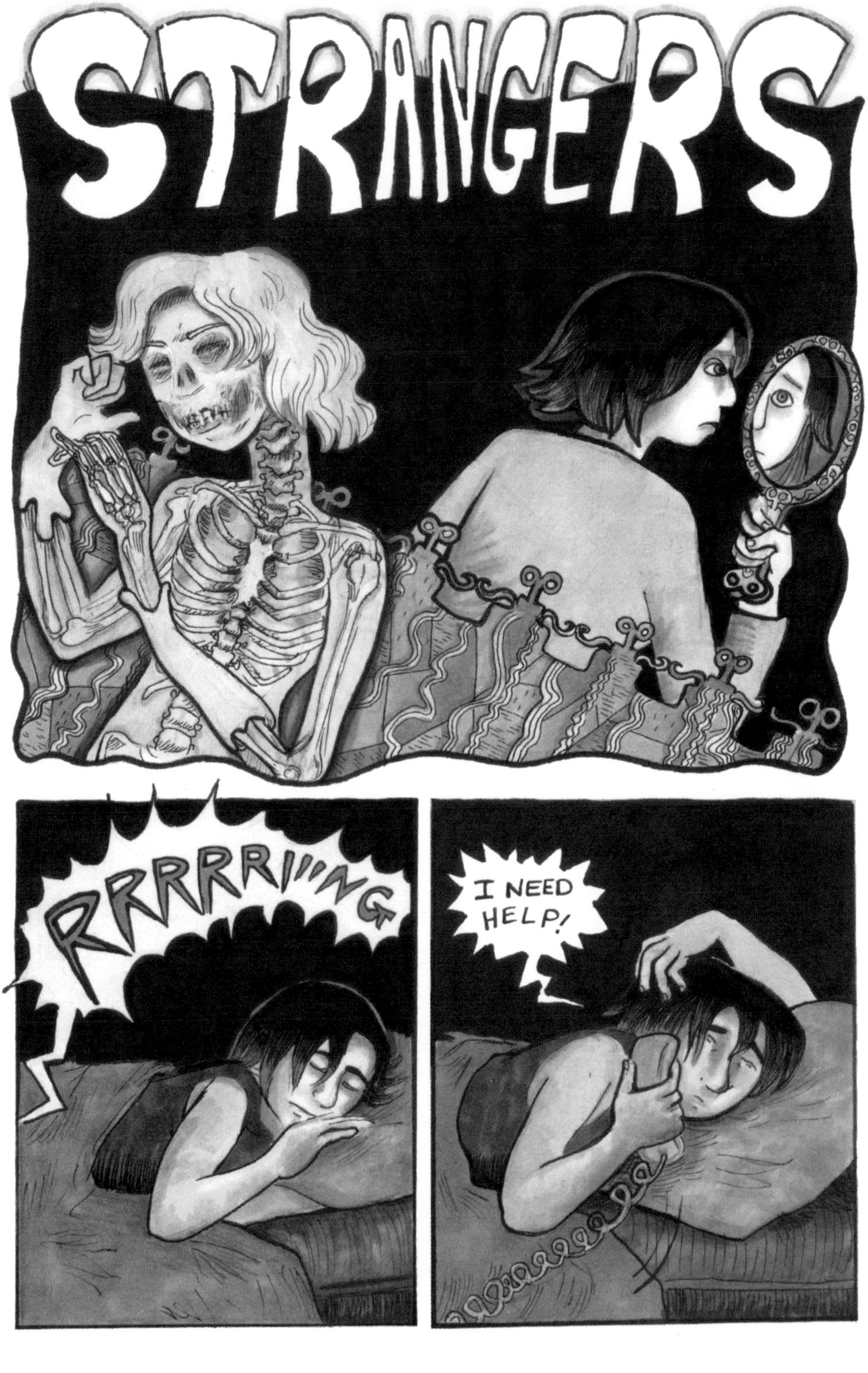
STRANGERS
RRRRRI''NG
I NEED HELP!

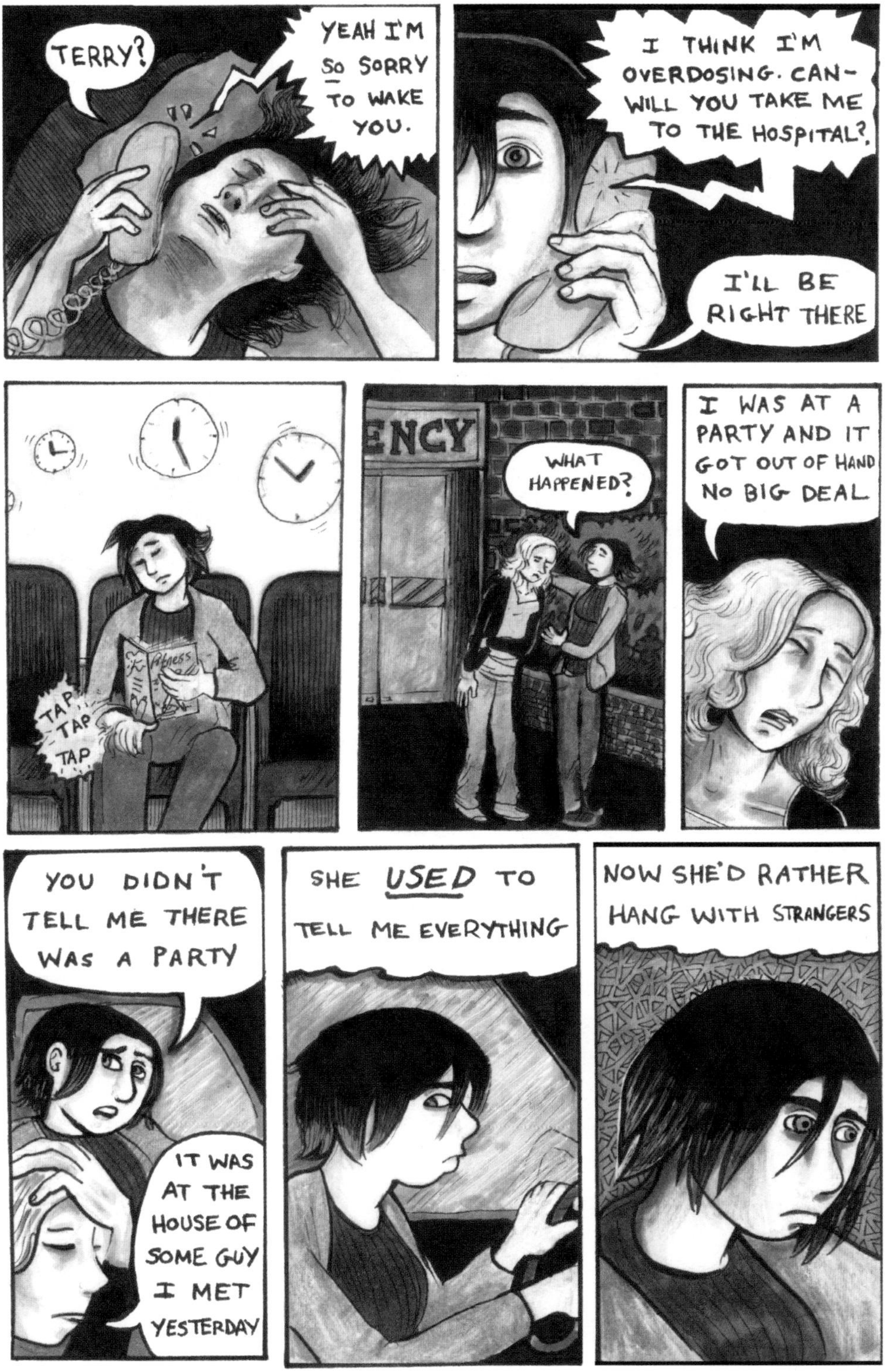
TERRY?
YEAH I'M SO SORRY TO WAKE YOU.
I THINK I'M OVERDOSING. CAN- WILL YOU TAKE ME TO THE HOSPITAL?
I'LL BE RIGHT THERE
TAP TAP TAP
ENCY
WHAT HAPPENED?
I WAS AT A PARTY AND IT GOT OUT OF HAND NO BIG DEAL
YOU DIDN'T TELL ME THERE WAS A PARTY
IT WAS AT THE HOUSE OF SOME GUY I MET YESTERDAY
SHE USED TO TELL ME EVERYTHING
NOW SHE'D RATHER HANG WITH STRANGERS

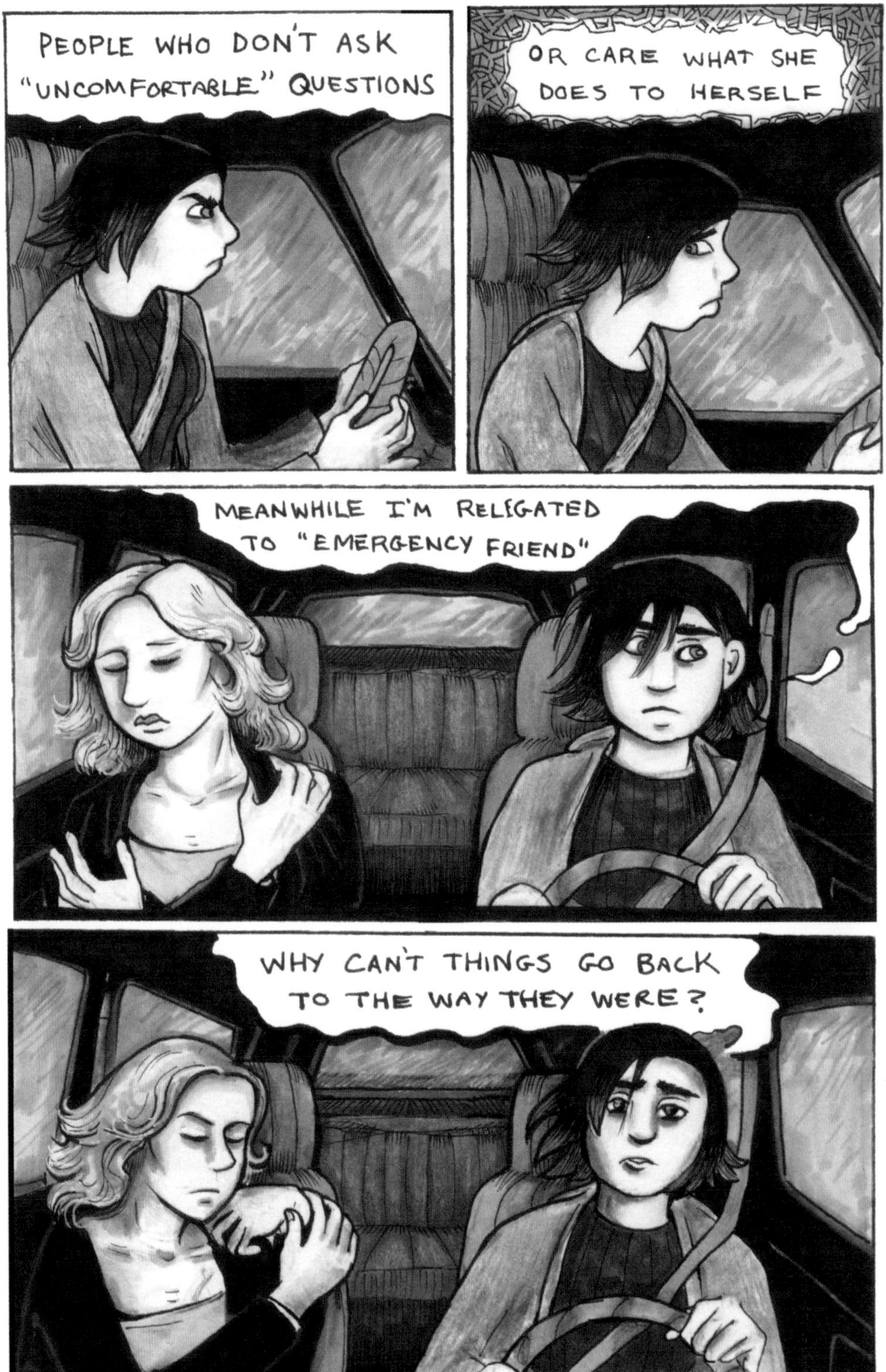
PEOPLE WHO DON'T ASK "UNCOMFORTABLE" QUESTIONS
OR CARE WHAT SHE DOES TO HERSELF
MEANWHILE I'M RELEGATED TO "EMERGENCY FRIEND"
WHY CAN'T THINGS GO BACK TO THE WAY THEY WERE?

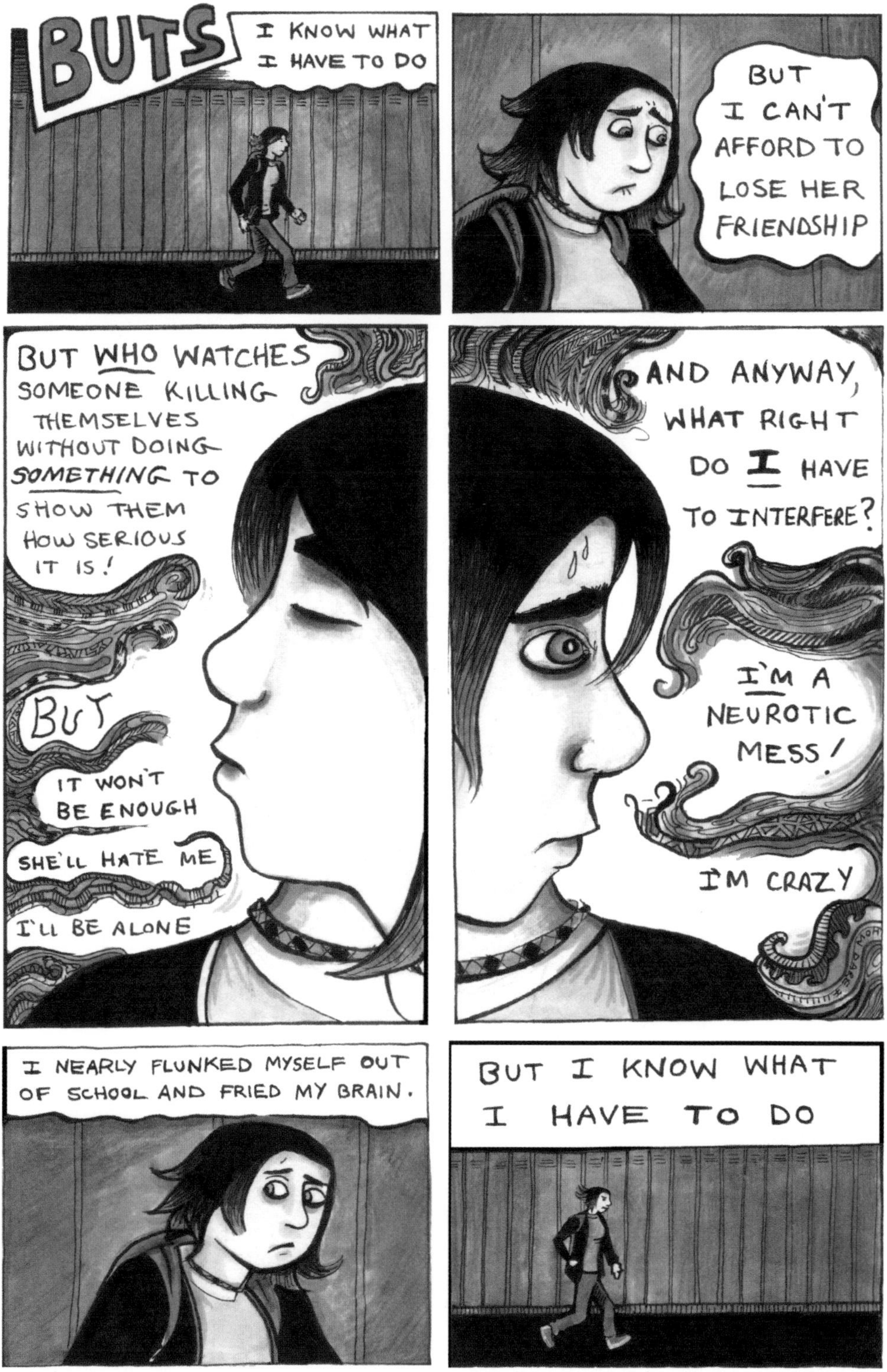
BUTS
I KNOW WHAT I HAVE TO DO
BUT I CAN'T AFFORD TO LOSE HER FRIENDSHIP
BUT WHO WATCHES SOMEONE KILLING THEMSELVES WITHOUT DOING SOMETHING TO SHOW THEM HOW SERIOUS IT IS!
BUT
IT WON'T BE ENOUGH
SHE'LL HATE ME
I'LL BE ALONE
AND ANYWAY, WHAT RIGHT DO I HAVE TO INTERFERE?
I'M A NEUROTIC MESS!
I'M CRAZY
I NEARLY FLUNKED MYSELF OUT OF SCHOOL AND FRIED MY BRAIN.
BUT I KNOW WHAT I HAVE TO DO

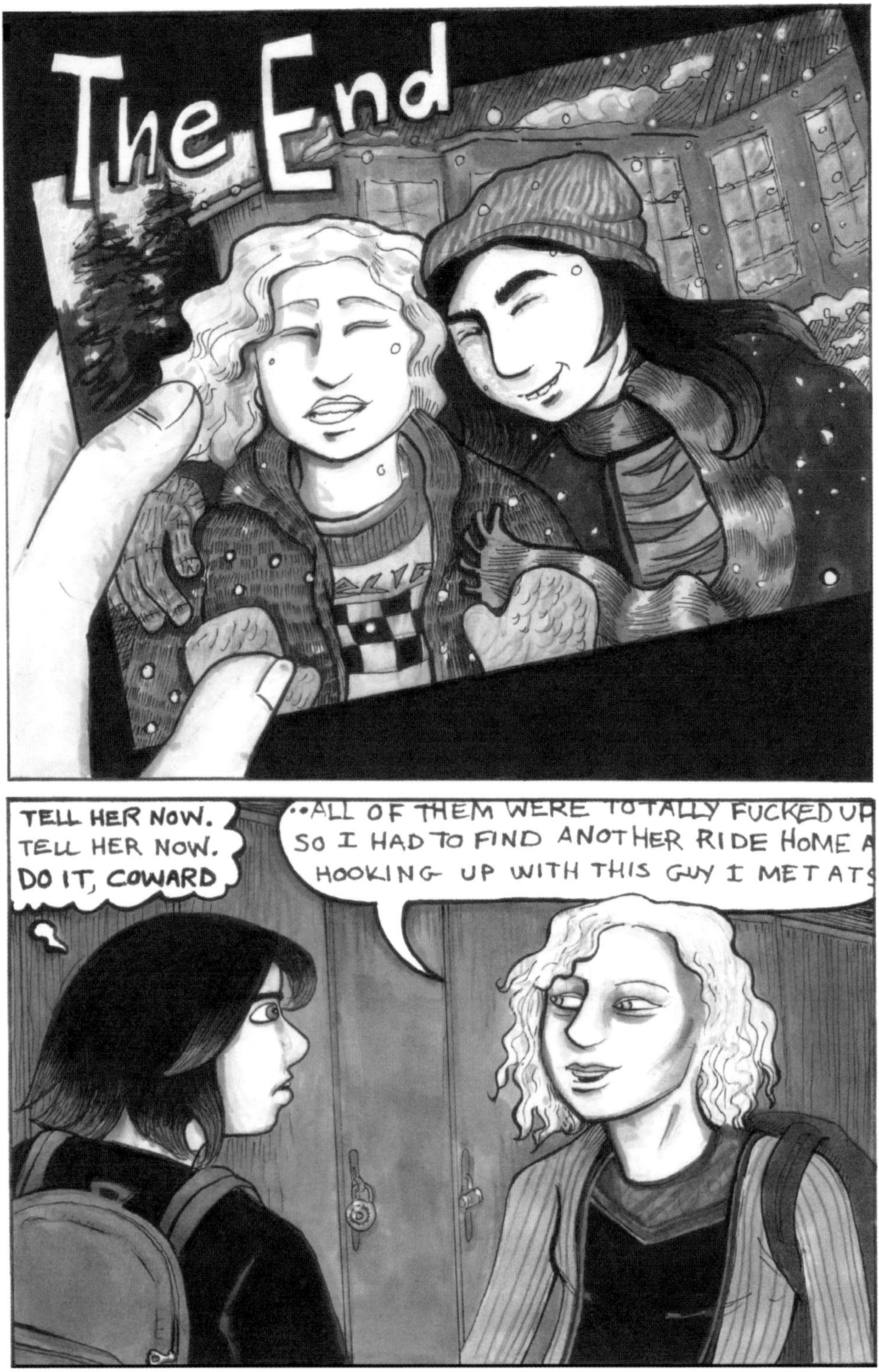
The End
TELL HER NOW. TELL HER NOW. DO IT, COWARD
..ALL OF THEM WERE TOTALLY FUCKED UP SO I HAD TO FIND ANOTHER RIDE HOME A HOOKING UP WITH THIS GUY I MET AT S

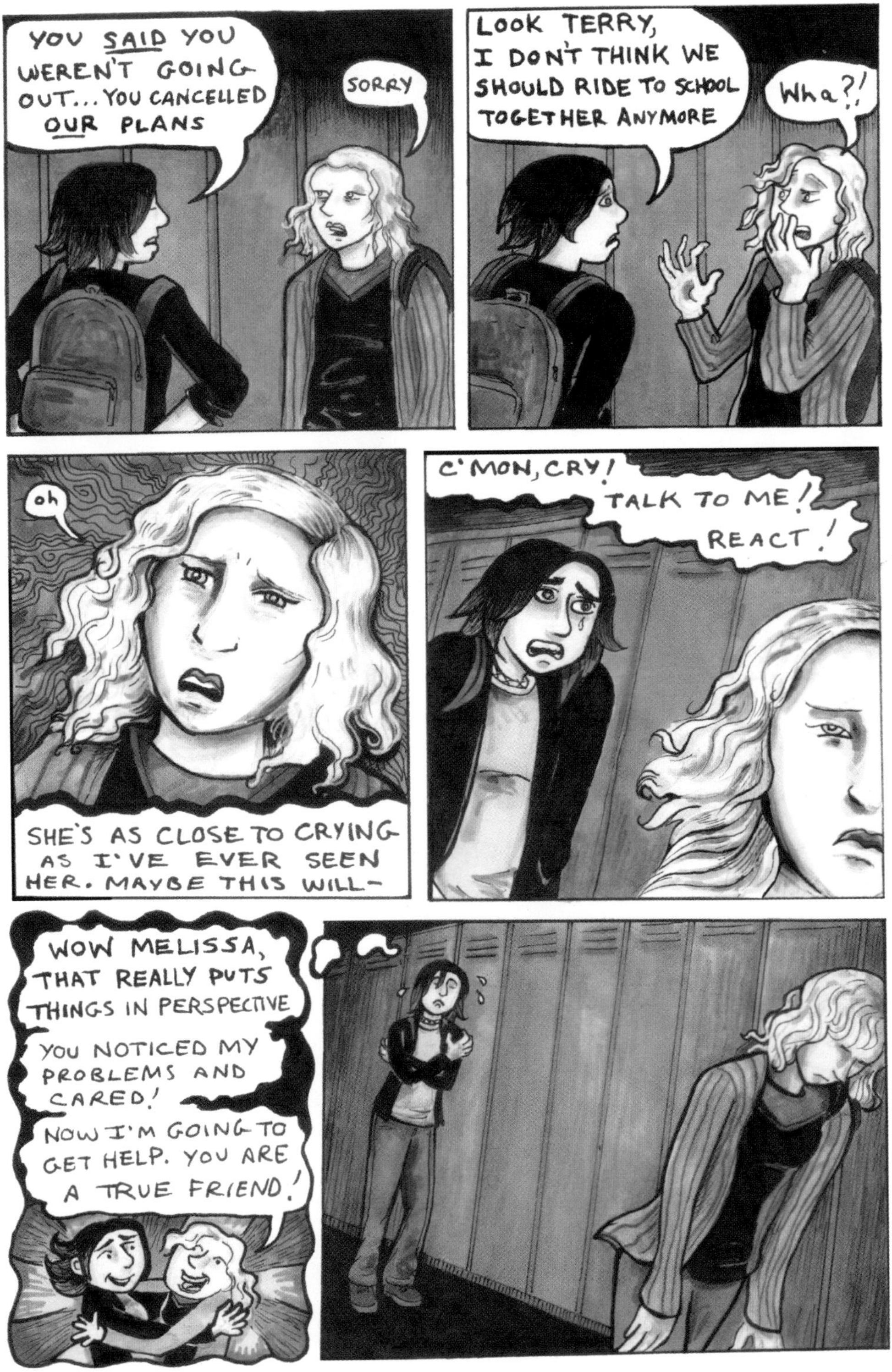
YOU SAID YOU WEREN'T GOING OUT... YOU CANCELLED OUR PLANS
SORRY
LOOK TERRY, I DON'T THINK WE SHOULD RIDE TO SCHOOL TOGETHER ANYMORE
Wha?!
oh
SHE'S AS CLOSE TO CRYING AS I'VE EVER SEEN HER. MAYBE THIS WILL-
C'MON, CRY!
TALK TO ME!
REACT!
WOW MELISSA, THAT REALLY PUTS THINGS IN PERSPECTIVE
YOU NOTICED MY PROBLEMS AND CARED!
NOW I'M GOING TO GET HELP. YOU ARE A TRUE FRIEND!

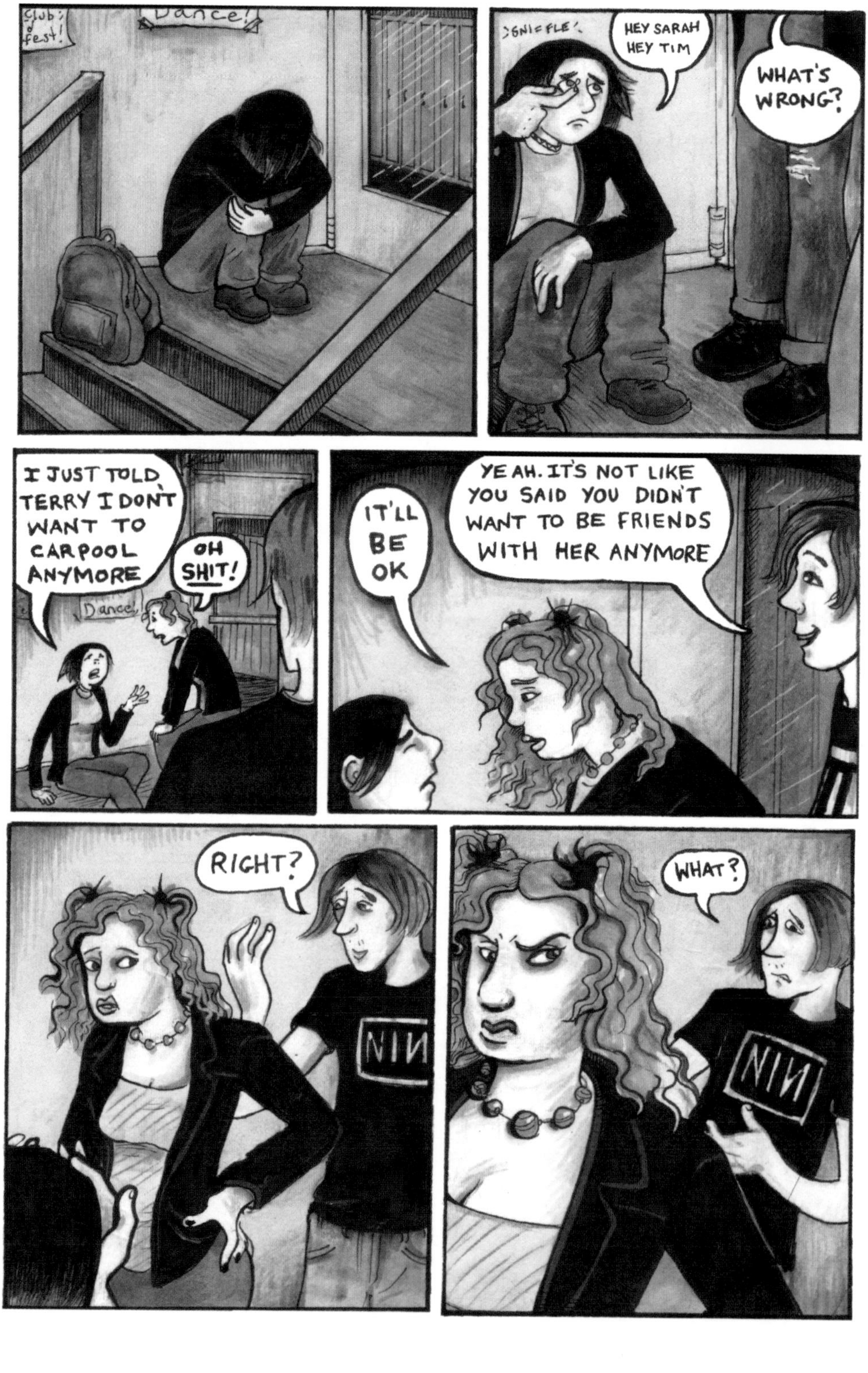
Club fest!
Dance!
>SNIFFLE<
HEY SARAH
HEY TIM
WHAT'S WRONG?
I JUST TOLD TERRY I DON'T WANT TO CARPOOL ANYMORE
OH SHIT!
Dance!
IT'LL BE OK
YEAH. IT'S NOT LIKE YOU SAID YOU DIDN'T WANT TO BE FRIENDS WITH HER ANYMORE
RIGHT?
NIN
WHAT?
NIN

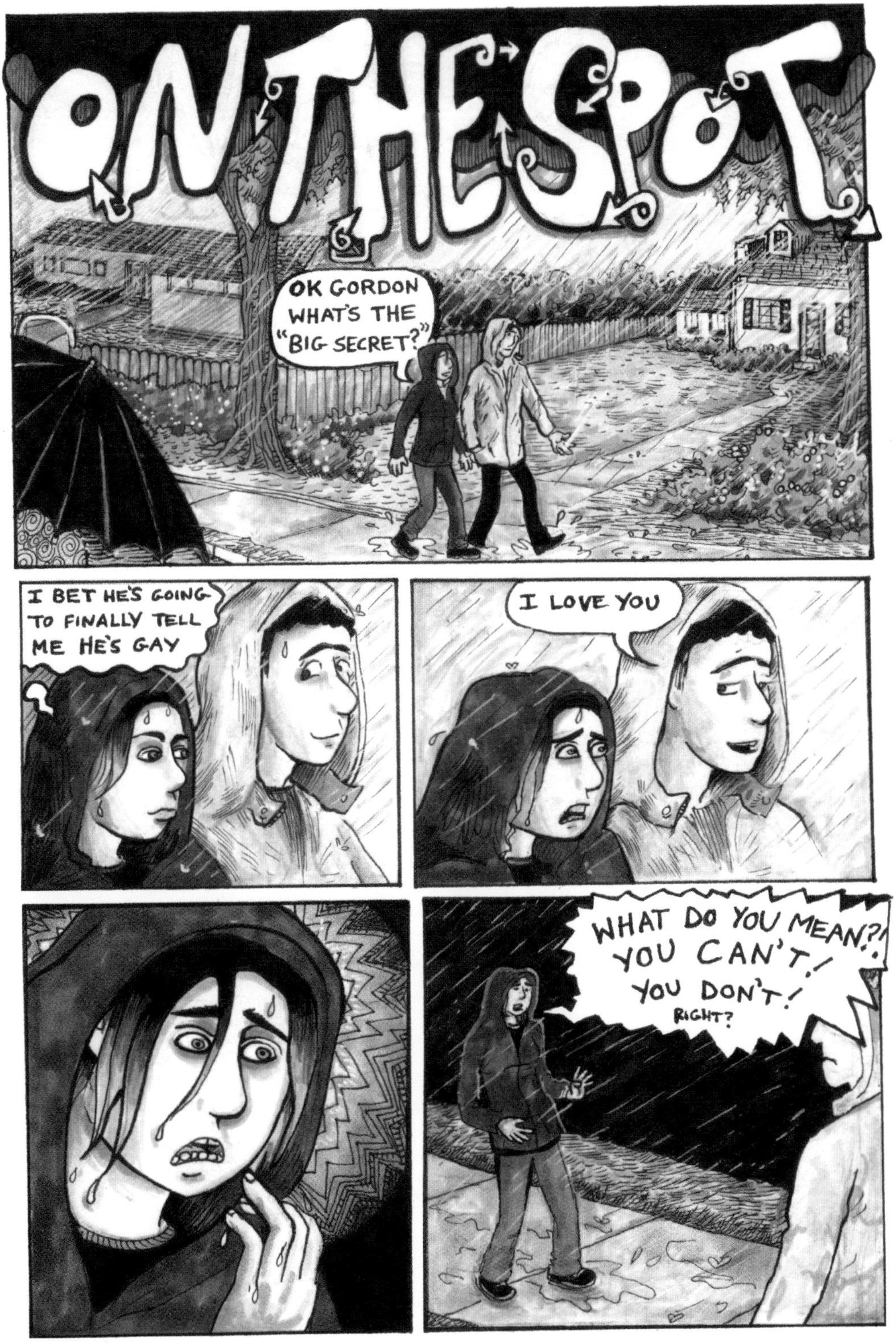
ON THE SPOT
OK GORDON WHAT'S THE "BIG SECRET?"
I BET HE'S GOING TO FINALLY TELL ME HE'S GAY
I LOVE YOU
WHAT DO YOU MEAN?! YOU CAN'T! YOU DON'T! RIGHT?

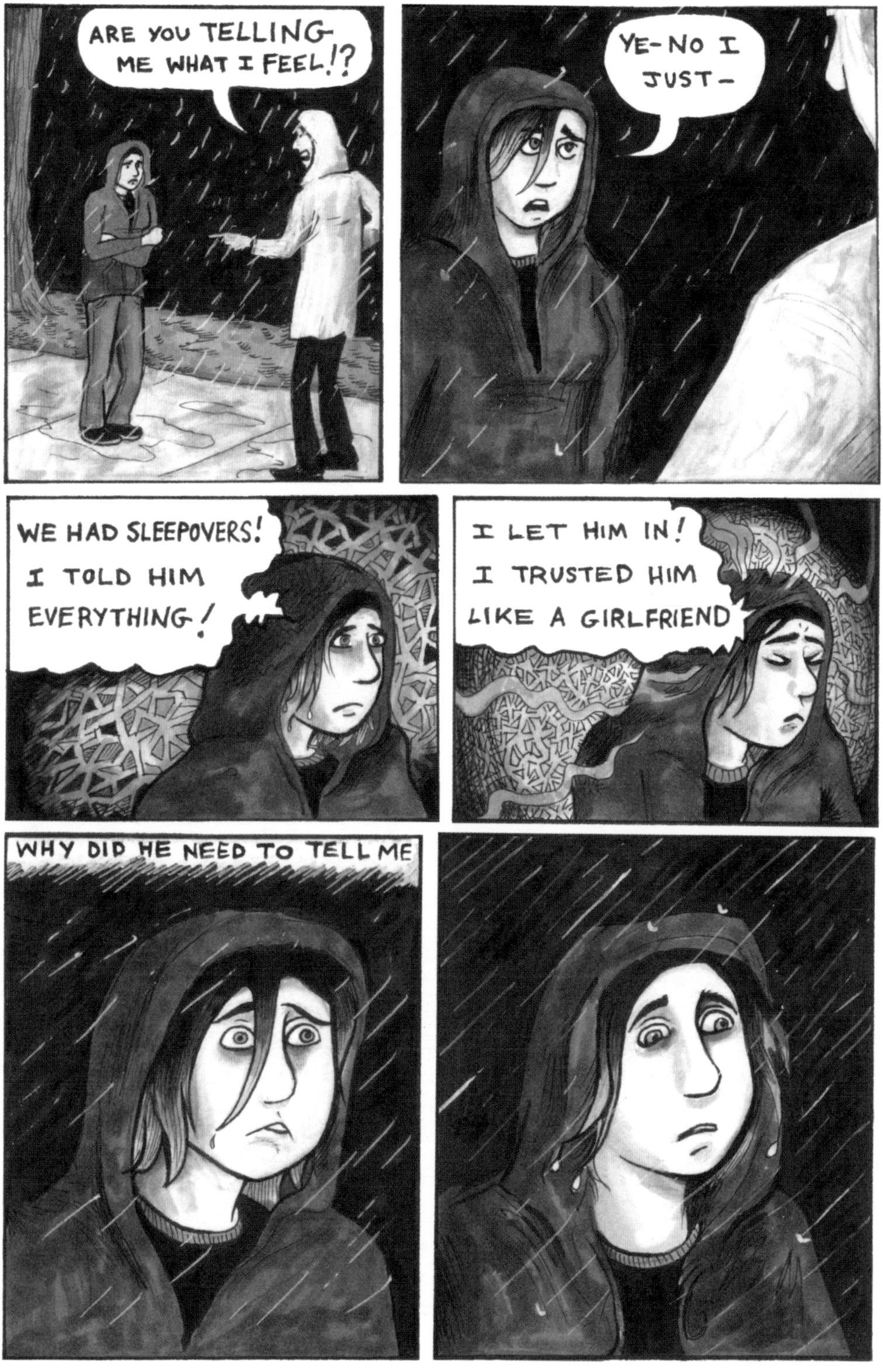
ARE YOU TELLING ME WHAT I FEEL!?
YE-NO I JUST-
WE HAD SLEEPOVERS! I TOLD HIM EVERYTHING!
I LET HIM IN! I TRUSTED HIM LIKE A GIRLFRIEND
WHY DID HE NEED TO TELL ME

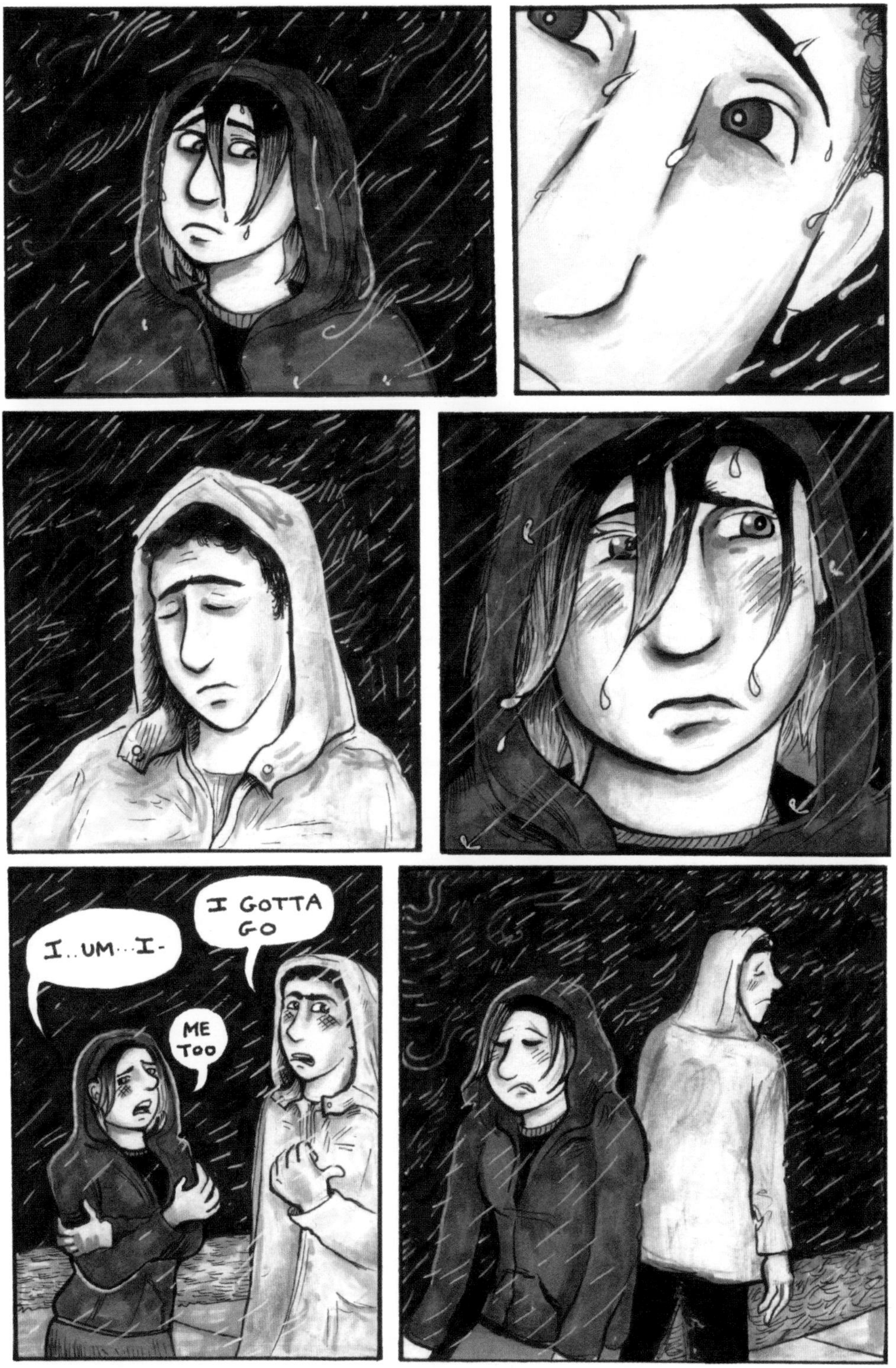
I GOTTA GO
I..UM..I-
ME TOO

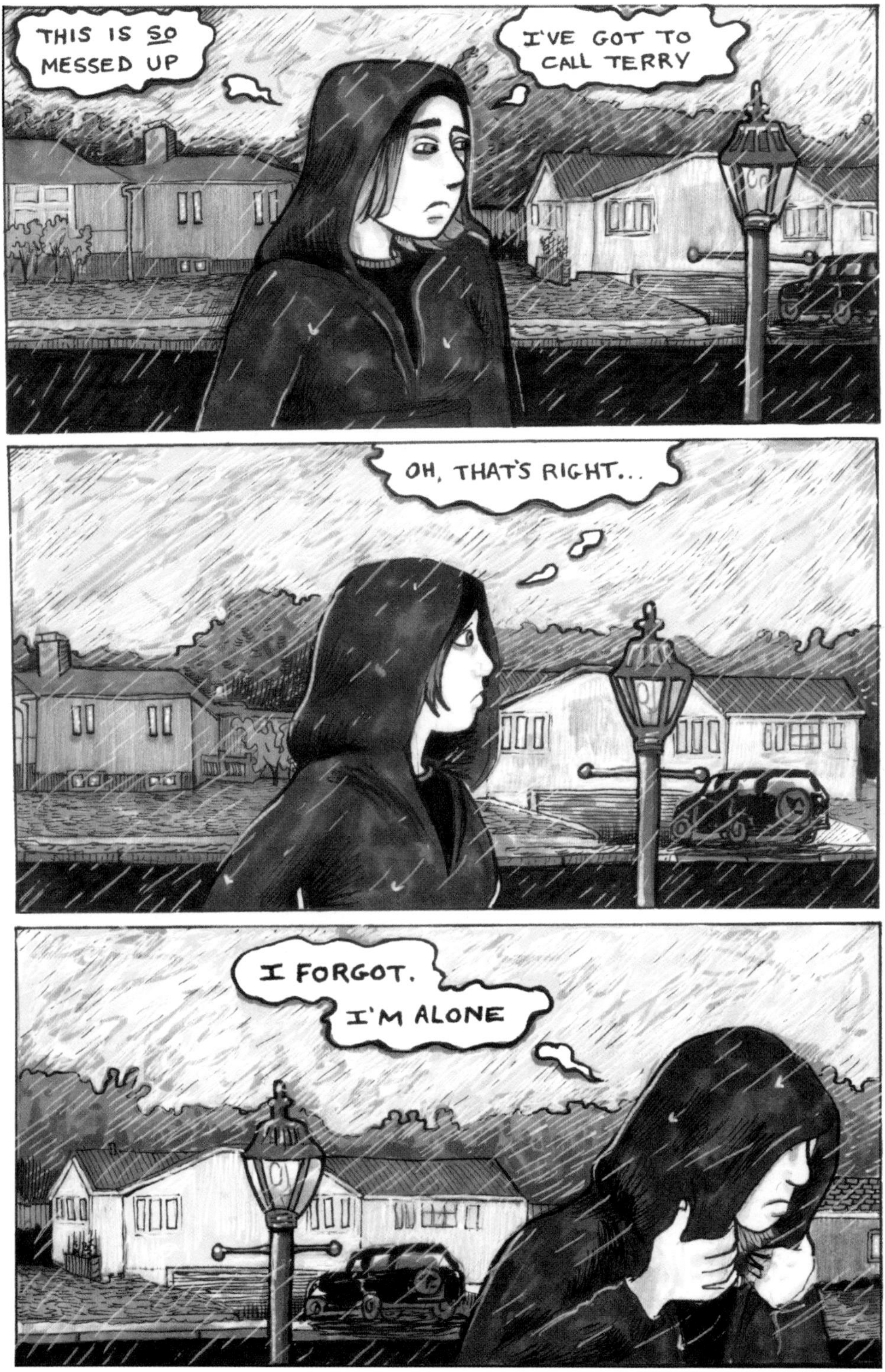
THIS IS SO MESSED UP
I'VE GOT TO CALL TERRY
OH, THAT'S RIGHT...
I FORGOT. I'M ALONE

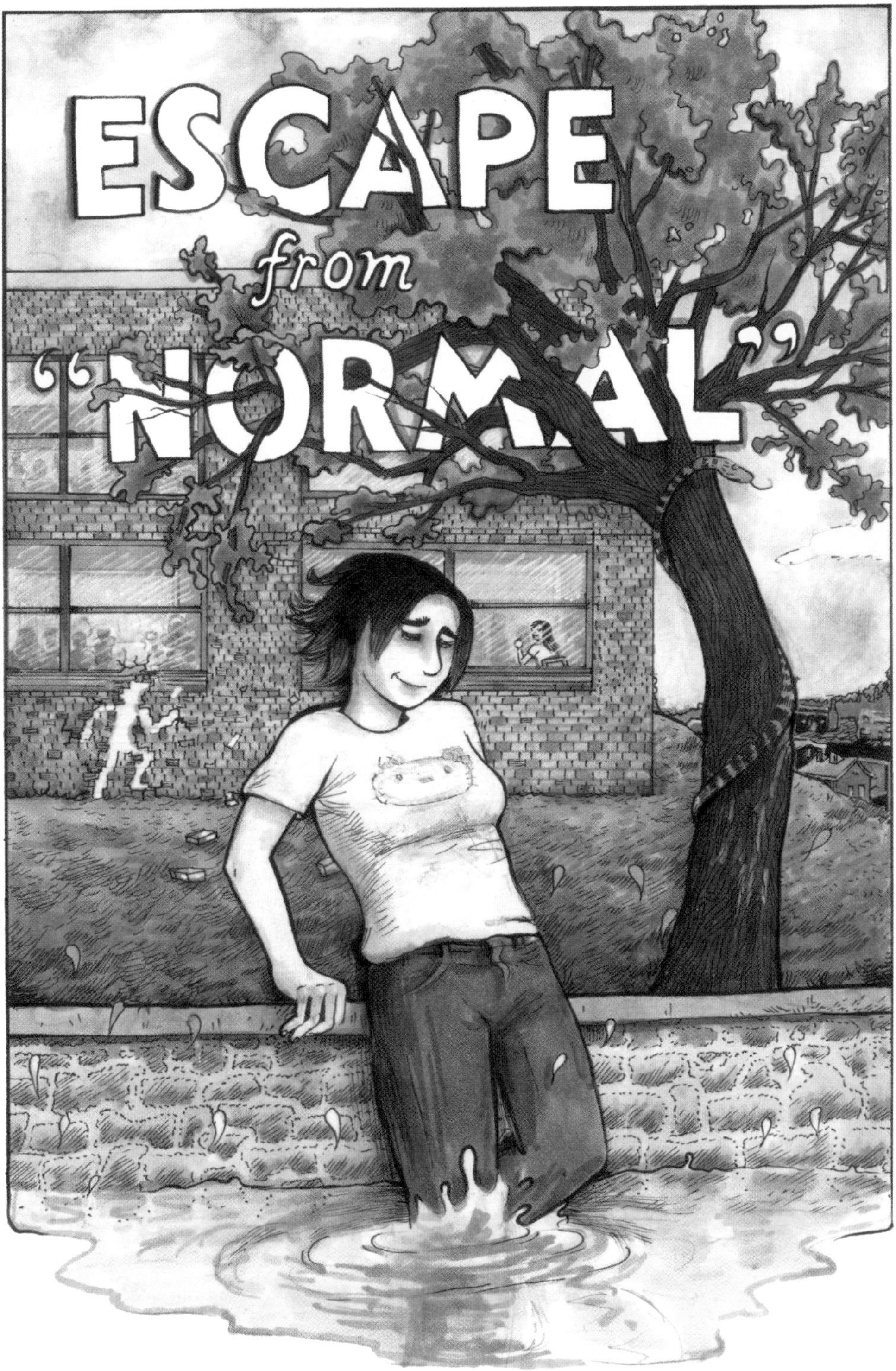
ESCAPE
from
"NORMAL"

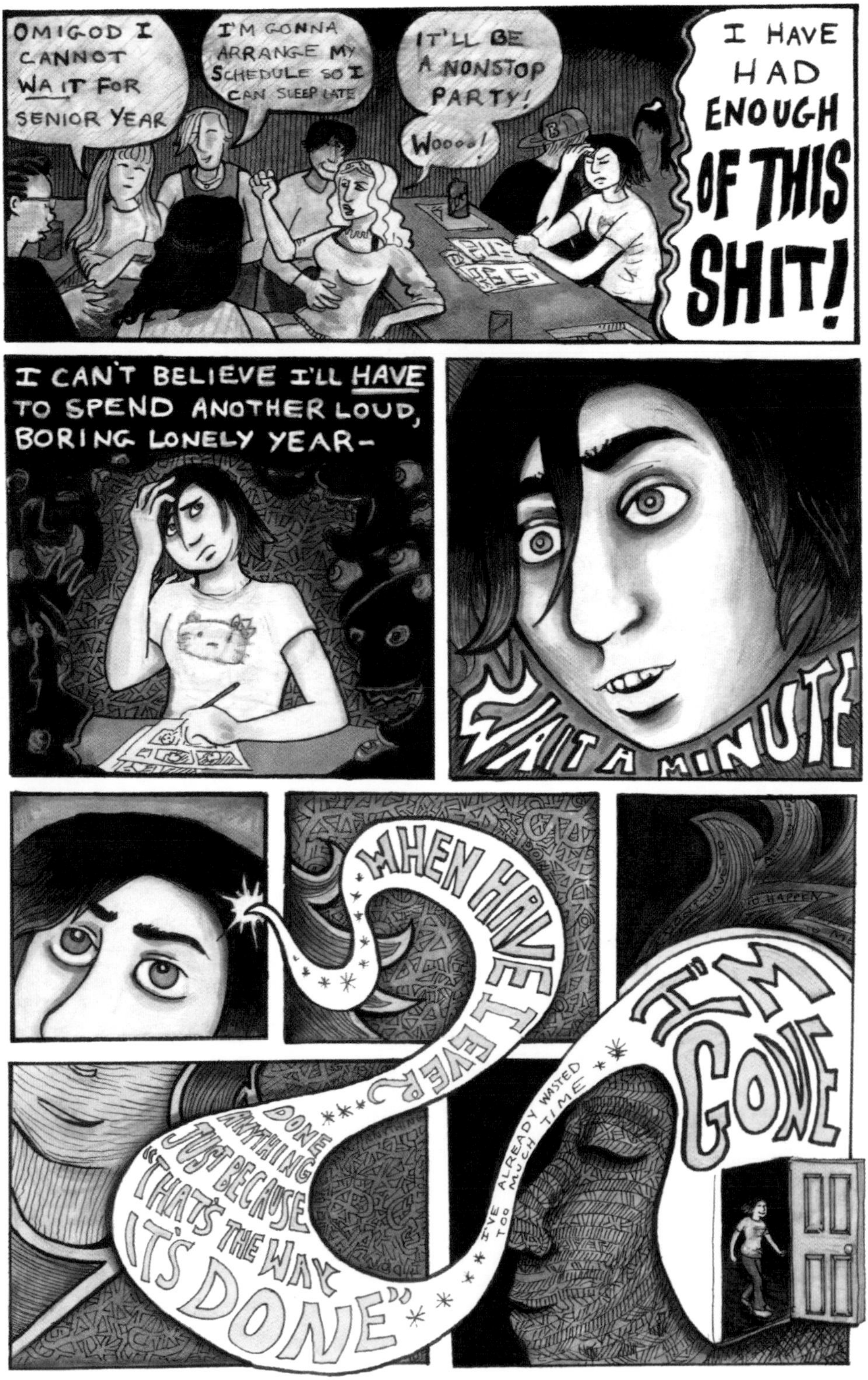
OMIGOD I CANNOT WAIT FOR SENIOR YEAR
I'M GONNA ARRANGE MY SCHEDULE SO I CAN SLEEP LATE
IT'LL BE A NONSTOP PARTY!
Woooo!
I HAVE HAD ENOUGH OF THIS SHIT!
I CAN'T BELIEVE I'LL HAVE TO SPEND ANOTHER LOUD, BORING LONELY YEAR-
WAIT A MINUTE
WHEN HAVE I EVER DONE ANYTHING JUST BECAUSE "THAT'S THE WAY IT'S DONE"
I'VE ALREADY WASTED TOO MUCH TIME
I'M GONE

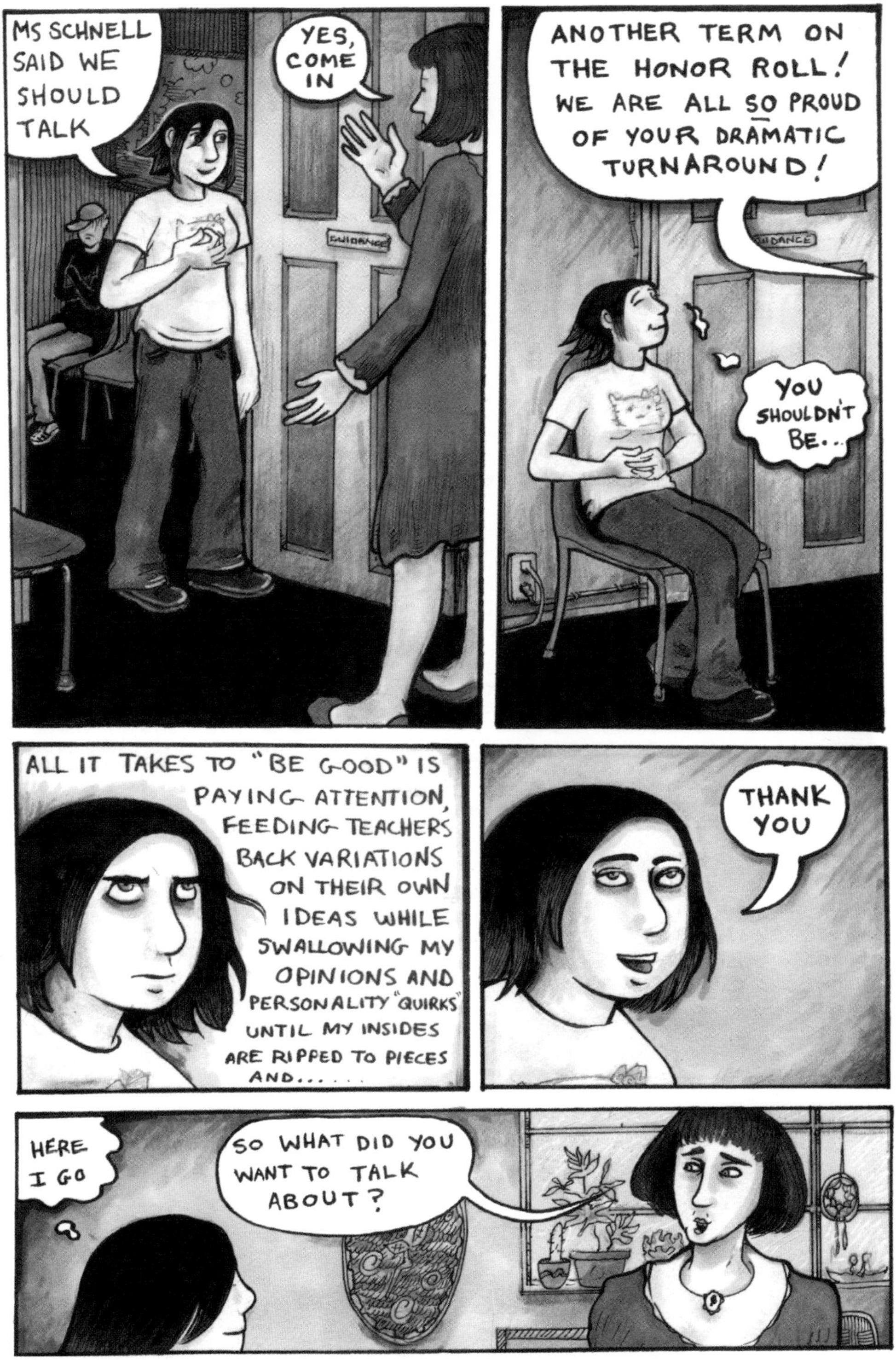
MS SCHNELL SAID WE SHOULD TALK
YES, COME IN
GUIDANCE
ANOTHER TERM ON THE HONOR ROLL! WE ARE ALL SO PROUD OF YOUR DRAMATIC TURNAROUND!
YOU SHOULDN'T BE..
ALL IT TAKES TO "BE GOOD" IS PAYING ATTENTION, FEEDING TEACHERS BACK VARIATIONS ON THEIR OWN IDEAS WHILE SWALLOWING MY OPINIONS AND PERSONALITY "QUIRKS" UNTIL MY INSIDES ARE RIPPED TO PIECES AND......
THANK YOU
HERE I GO
SO WHAT DID YOU WANT TO TALK ABOUT?

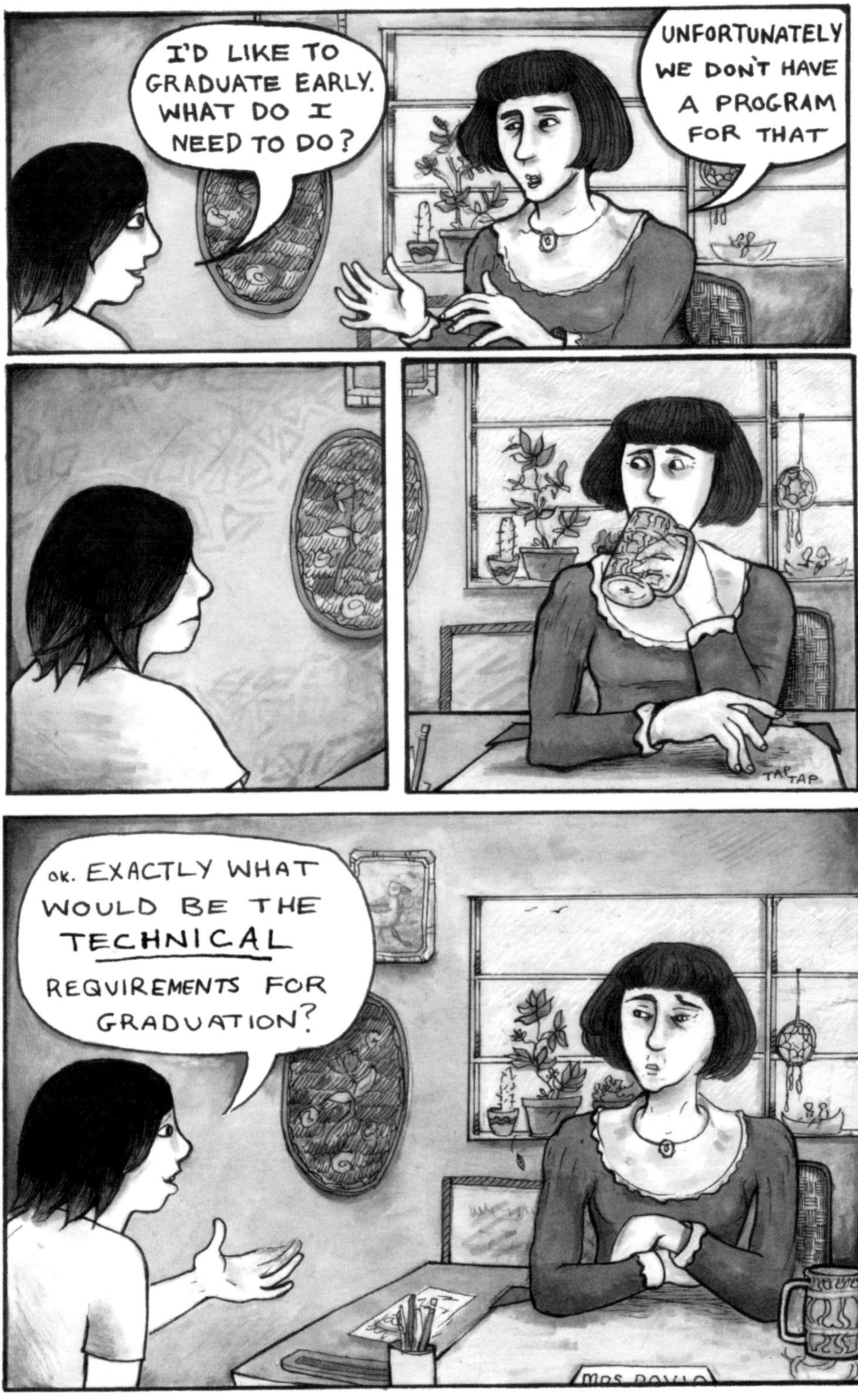
I'D LIKE TO GRADUATE EARLY. WHAT DO I NEED TO DO?
UNFORTUNATELY WE DON'T HAVE A PROGRAM FOR THAT
TAP TAP
OK. EXACTLY WHAT WOULD BE THE TECHNICAL REQUIREMENTS FOR GRADUATION?

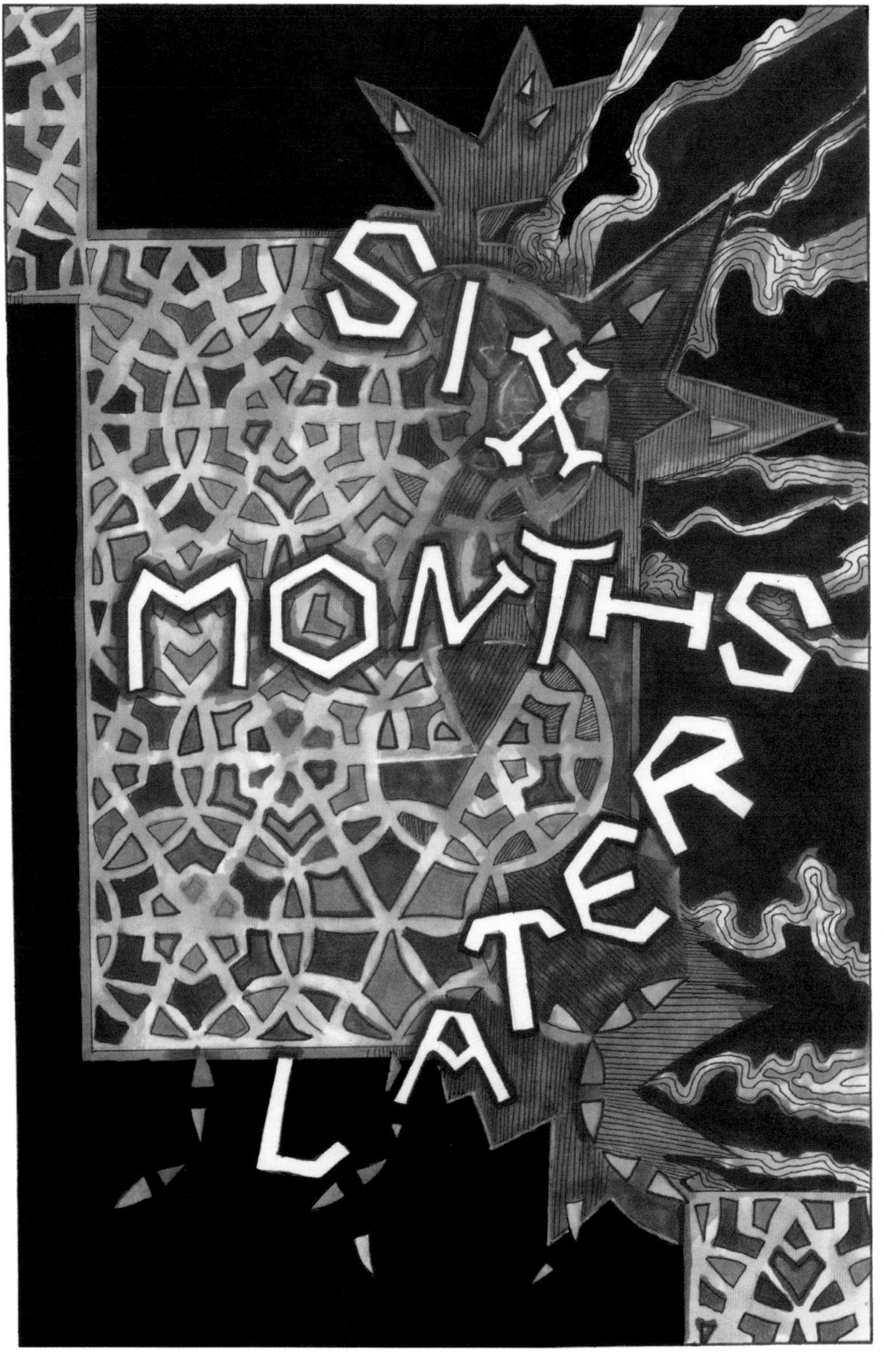
SIX MONTHS LATER

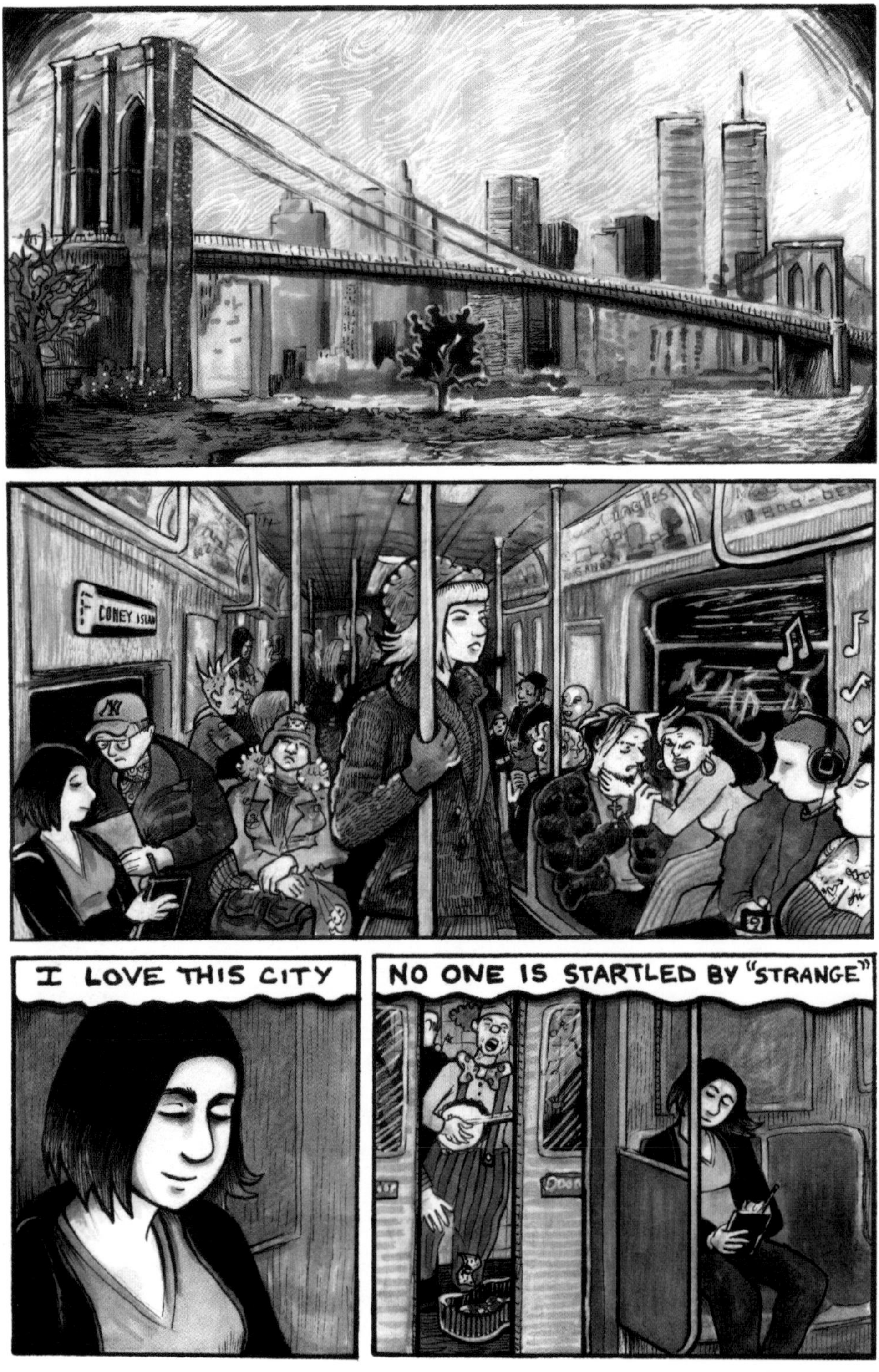
I LOVE THIS CITY
NO ONE IS STARTLED BY "STRANGE"

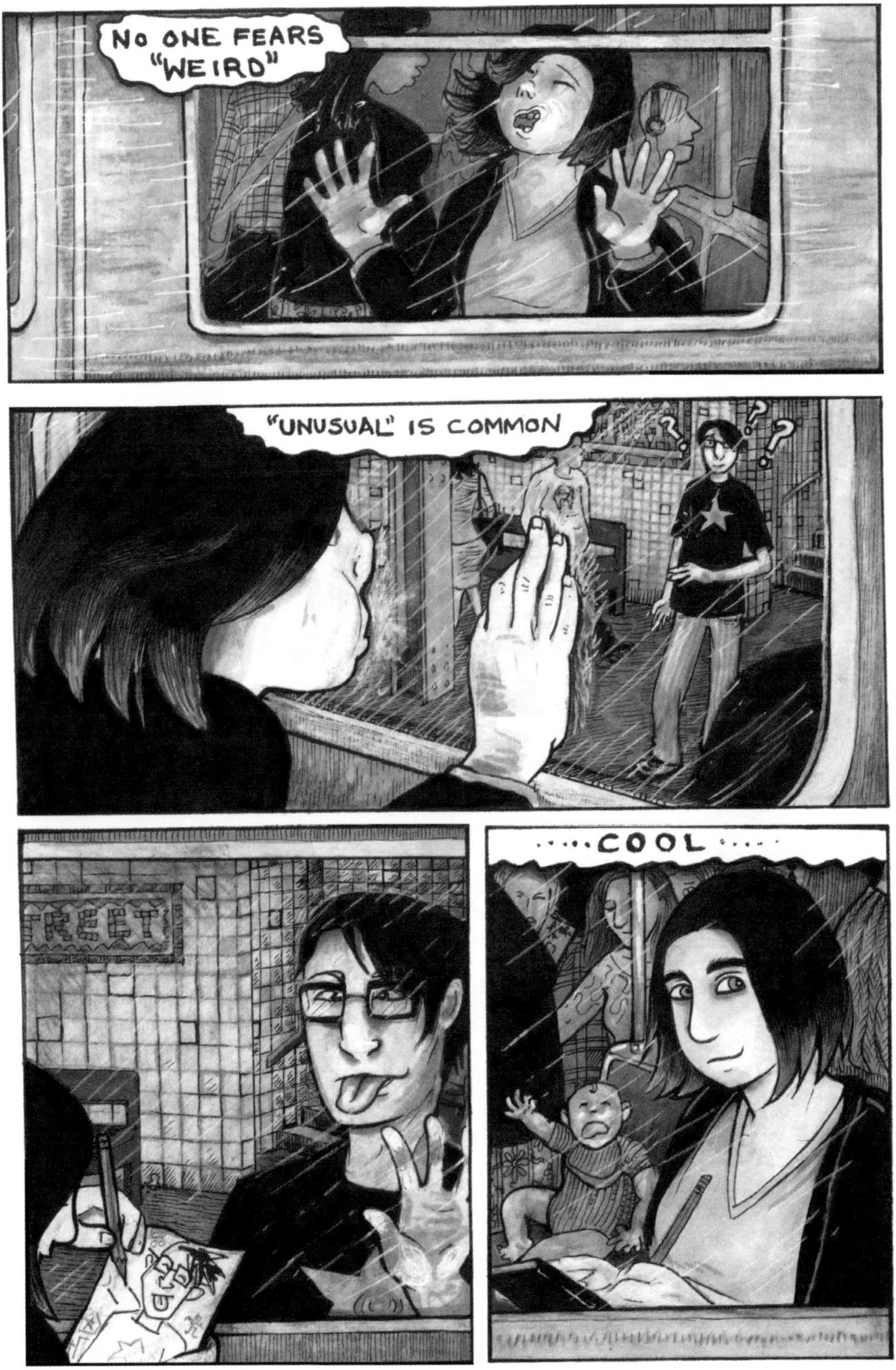
No ONE FEARS "WEIRD"
"UNUSUAL" IS COMMON
TREET
.....COOL.....

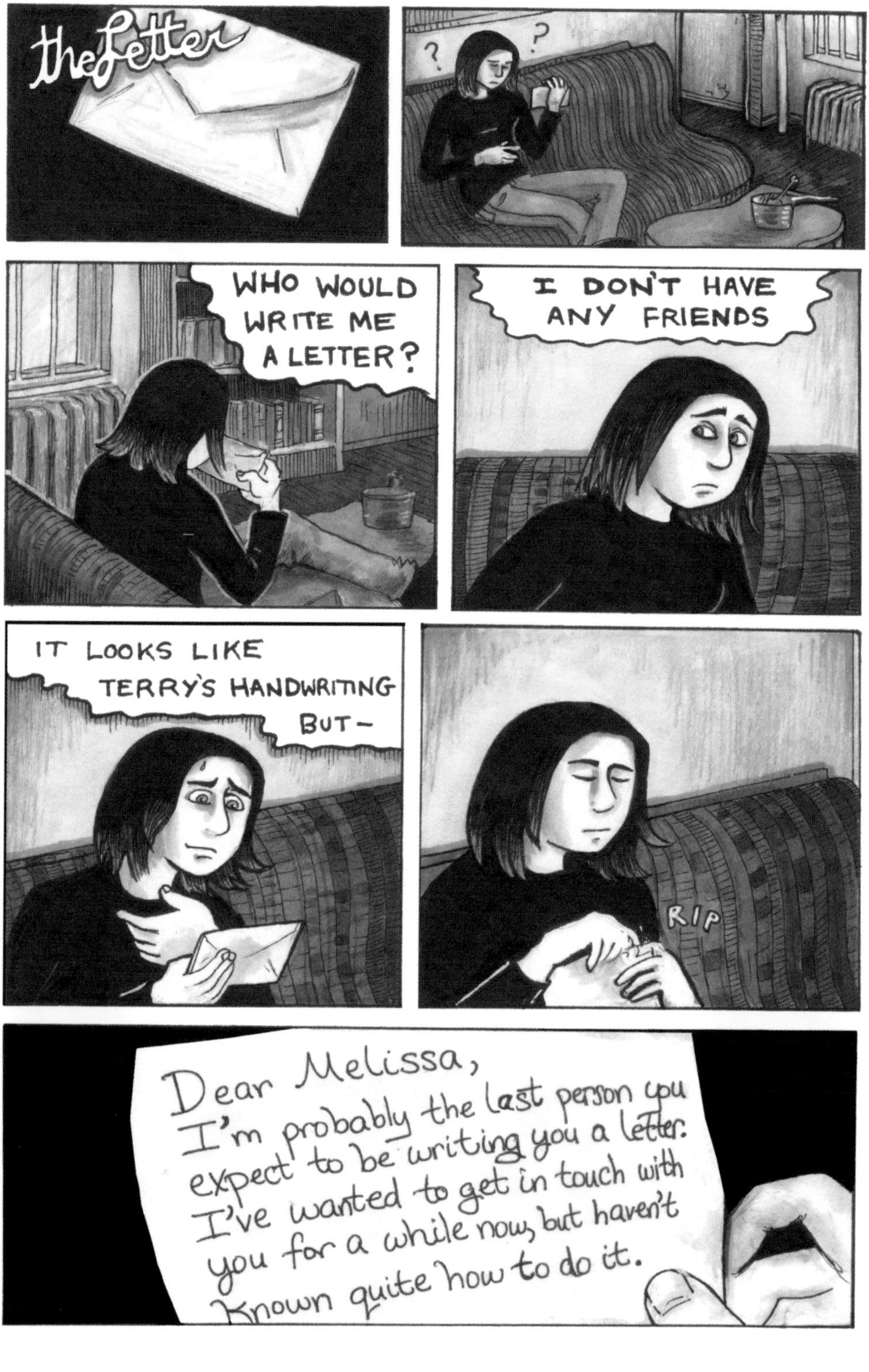
the Letter
?
?
WHO WOULD WRITE ME A LETTER?
I DON'T HAVE ANY FRIENDS
IT LOOKS LIKE TERRY'S HANDWRITING BUT—
RIP
Dear Melissa,
I'm probably the last person you expect to be writing you a letter. I've wanted to get in touch with you for a while now, but haven't known quite how to do it.

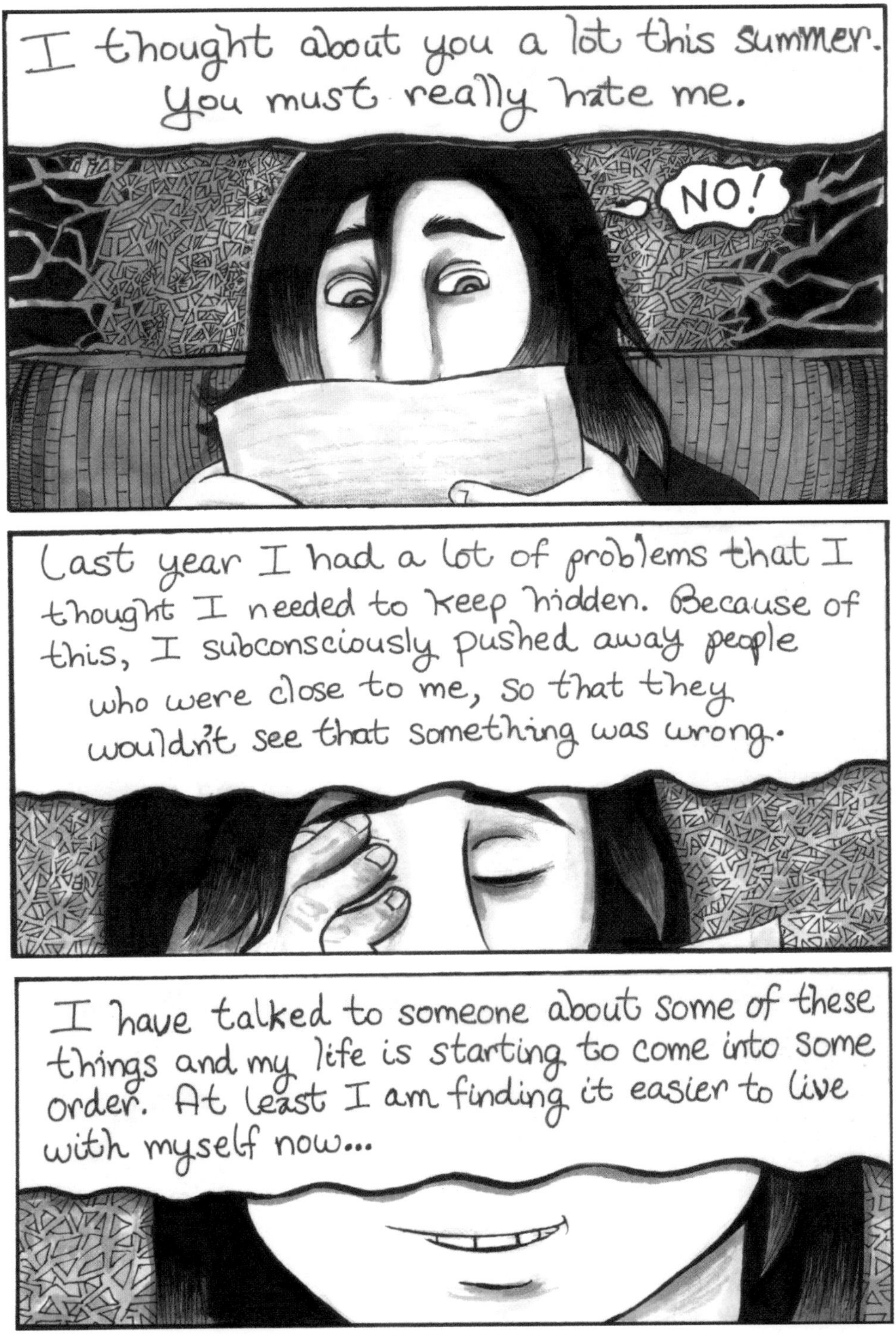
I thought about you a lot this summer. You must really hate me.
NO!
Last year I had a lot of problems that I thought I needed to keep hidden. Because of this, I subconsciously pushed away people who were close to me, so that they wouldn't see that something was wrong.
I have talked to someone about some of these things and my life is starting to come into some order. At least I am finding it easier to live with myself now...

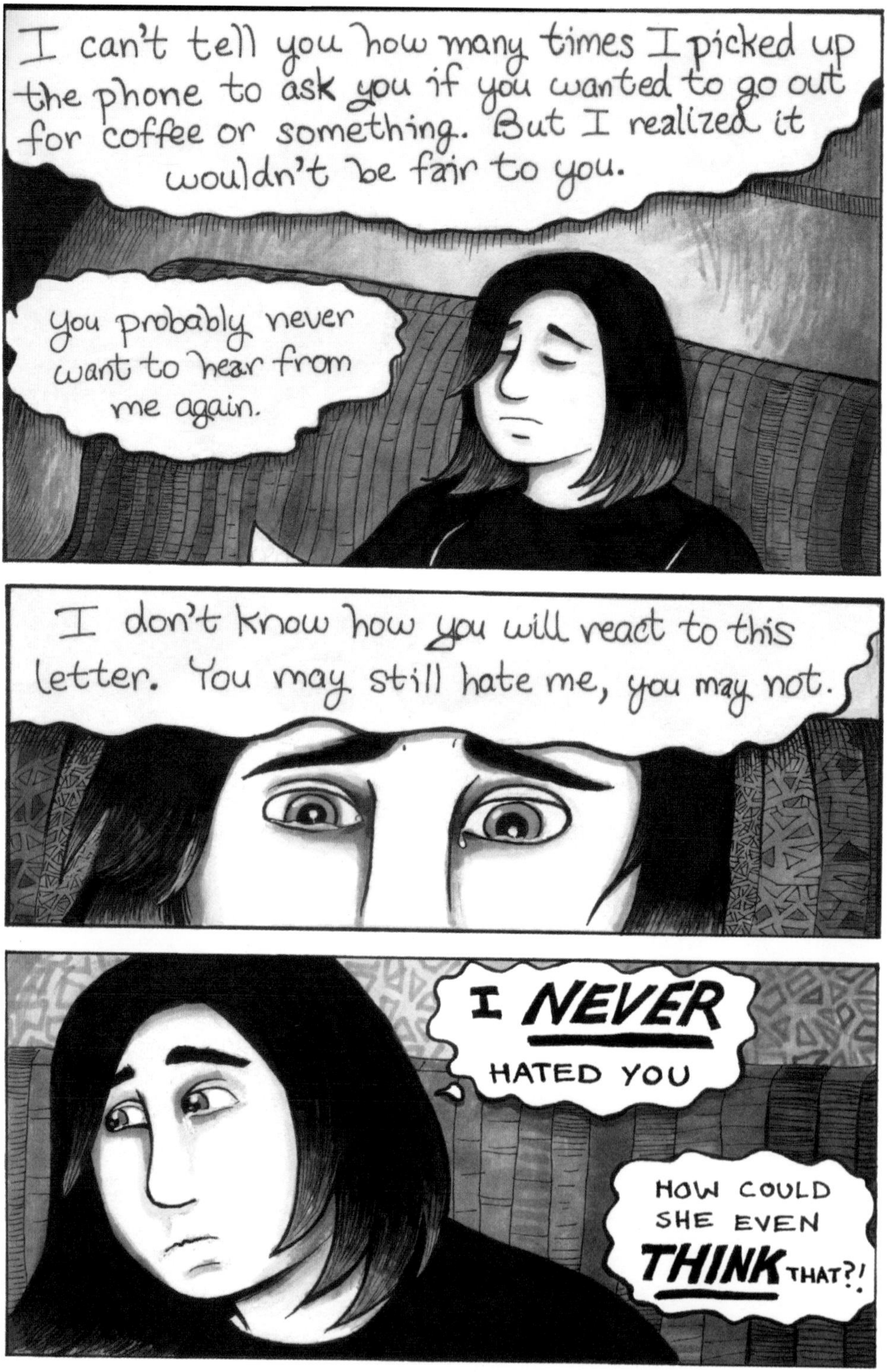
I can't tell you how many times I picked up the phone to ask you if you wanted to go out for coffee or something. But I realized it wouldn't be fair to you.
You probably never want to hear from me again.
I don't know how you will react to this letter. You may still hate me, you may not.
I NEVER HATED YOU
HOW COULD SHE EVEN THINK THAT?!

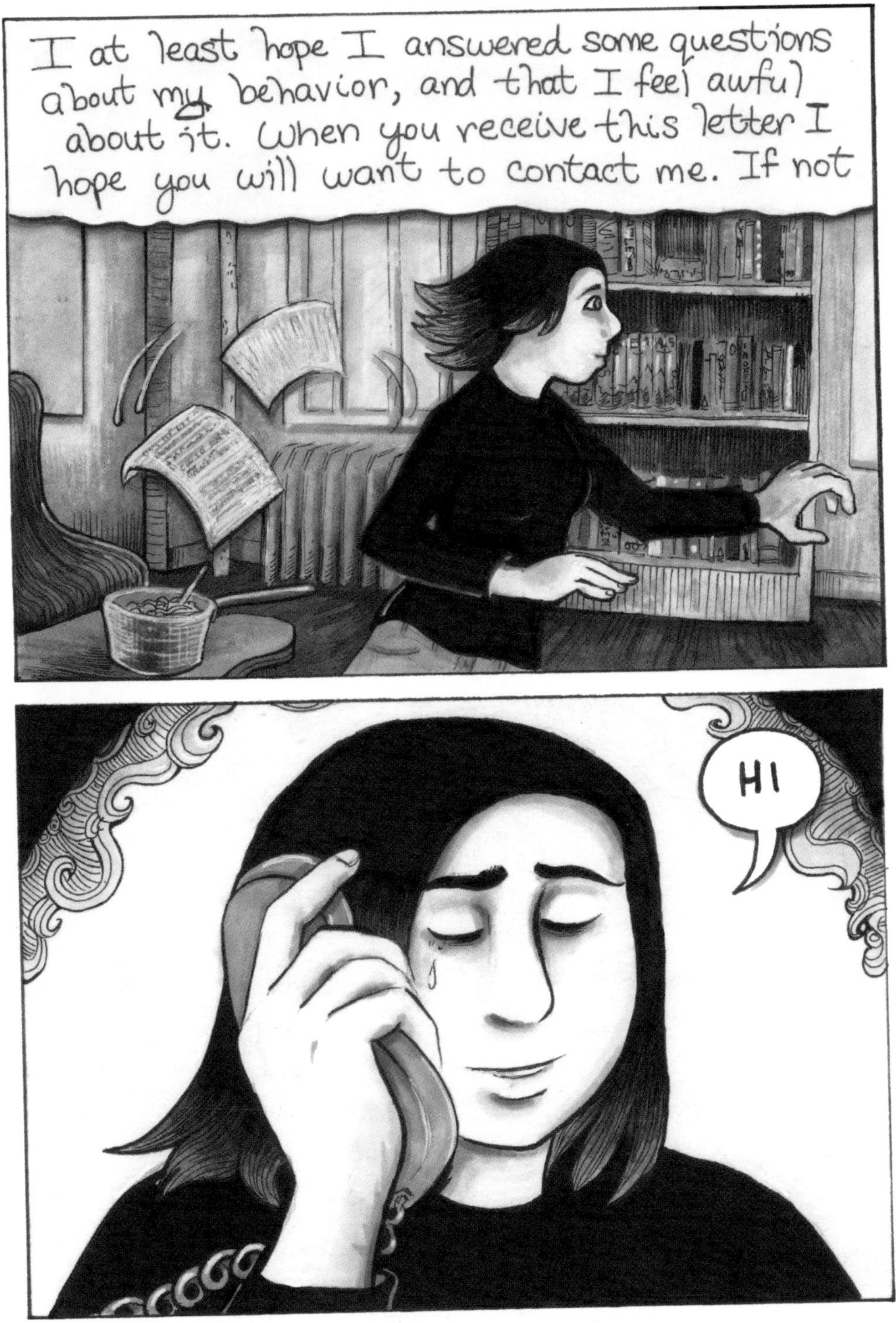
I at least hope I answered some questions about my behavior, and that I feel awful about it. When you receive this letter I hope you will want to contact me. If not
HI